Norfolk! Boston! Bermuda!

...three harbours that shaped a nation's future and Rob Ashton's violent destiny.

Rob Ashton was a hotheaded American skipper who gambled for the highest stakes a man can win—wealth, honor, and a passionate woman's lingering kiss. The year was 1775, a time to try men's souls with the smell of rebellion and blood. Fighting for a fortune in the sea trade, Rob Ashton braved the ruthless intrigue of traitors and Tories. He learned a desperate courage from hearts aflame with freedom. And before his ship touched port at three harbours, he also learned about love—the burning rapture of a mistress who was as wise as she was tempting!

THREE HARBOURS
F. van Wyck Mason

A BERKLEY MEDALLION BOOK
published by
BERKLEY PUBLISHING CORPORATION

TO MY MOTHER,
FINEST FLOWER OF A STURDY, SELF-RELIANT PEOPLE
AND TO
THE COLONIAL MERCHANTS OF AMERICA
WHO, BY THEIR STUBBORN COURAGE,
KINDLED AND NOURISHED THE FLAME OF LIBERTY

IT IS perhaps inevitable that some readers will wonder how closely I have adhered to the rigid pattern of history. To these I would say that the main facts, dates, and figures are as nearly correct as a painstaking and selective research can make them. The same also applies to such details as uniforms, military movements, legal proceedings, customs, currency and documents.

The writer of a novel which employs an historical setting is, I believe, to the careful historian somewhat as a landscape painter is to an architect. While a painter is at liberty to present and to emphasize those details of a scene which attract and interest him, an architect must present the most minute details of his plan. Therefore, in the selection of incidents used in this tale I have necessarily omitted or glossed over some historical events of great importance which unfortunately did not bear on the story.

My underlying purpose has been to tell how the early merchants of America's Eastern Coast lived, to show what they did and, on occasion, what they suffered. I have exaggerated their activities not at all. Every event reproduced has had its historical counterpart. Prices, rates of exchange, the nature of cargoes carried and the names of ships and their captains were selected from contemporary newspapers, journals, and broadsides.

The phraseology of Andrea's journal is based on that of Nicholas Cresswell, an Englishman who, fortunately for me, was traveling in the American Colonies at that time. When have Englishmen not traveled and recorded their experiences? To Cresswell's keen curiosity and analytical sense I owe many homely details which I trust will intrigue and amuse the reader.

In no place have I consciously played the partisan. It has been my earnest endeavor to show the Virginians, Scotch, English, New Englanders and Bermudians of that day as they were. All were selfish in a greater or a lesser degree, all were suspicious or contemptuous of anything unfamiliar and very outspoken about it.

The Ashton family is in its entirety imaginary. The only other fictional characters of importance are Andrea Grenville, Major Bouquet, Mr. Peacock, Edgar Leeming, Colonel Fortescue, Madelaine, and Katie Tryon. It goes without saying that the bulk of the minor characters are imaginary.

To Mr. Allen French of Concord, Massachusetts, author of that splendid volume, *The First Year of the American Revolution,* I owe my greatest debt of gratitude. In checking my description of the battle on Breed's Hill his advice was invaluable. To Professor Wilfred Brenton Kerr of the University of Buffalo goes my deep appreciation of his aid in verifying certain events in addition to those mentioned in his accurate and charmingly written "Bermuda and the American Revolution." What further data I needed on the Bermudian phase of this tale was made available through the kindness of Dr. Henry Wilkinson, Mr. C. H. V. Talbot, Assistant Colonial Secretary of Bermuda, and the Bermuda Public Library.

If it were not for the great good nature of my friend Mr. Jay Lewis of the Norfolk Ledger-Dispatch, I should have had a much harder time collecting material concerning the early days of that city. Thanks are also due the staff of the Sargeant Room in the Norfolk Public Library.

Concerning the Boston background, Mr. Robert H. Haynes, Assistant Librarian of the Library of Harvard University, and Dr. Clifford K. Shipton, Custodian of the Harvard University Archives, patiently answered my many queries. Professor Curtis Nettels of the University of Wisconsin ably advised my selection of source material. Mr. Theodore B. Pitman of Brookline, Massachusetts, furnished invaluable information concerning contemporary arms, and the uniforms of the British Army. Further help in this direction was afforded by the British War Office, the British Museum, and by Mr. Herbert Brook of the Yale University Press. Consequently, any factual errors should be charged to the author.

In conclusion I wish to acknowledge the aid of Mrs. Francis Payne Mason in supplying many of Captain Farish's New Englandisms, also valuable suggestions offered from time to time by my secretary, Miss Mary Louise Huntzbery.

Should a moralist insist on seeking a *raison d'être* for this tale, he may find it in the thesis that events, on occasion, can drive peaceful Americans to taking up arms in defense of their rights.

It means much to be reasonably free in the conduct of a business or of a profession. So thought the Colonial merchants during 1774-1775. They met a crisis and defeated it without the aid of a paternalistic regime. Should American merchants of the present generation be called to do likewise, let us hope they will meet the problem as courageously as did their forbears.

F. van Wyck Mason
CHURCH HILL HOUSE
SOMERSET, BERMUDA

Contents

Book One - Norfolk

PART I — WINTER: 1774

PART II — THE TIDEWATER: 1774

Book Two · Boston

PART I — THE MUSTERING: JUNE, 1775

PART II — BREED'S HILL

Book Three · Bermuda

PART I — THE DESDEMONA, SCHOONER

PART II — SOMERSET ISLAND

PART III — BOSTON

PART IV — PHILADELPHIA

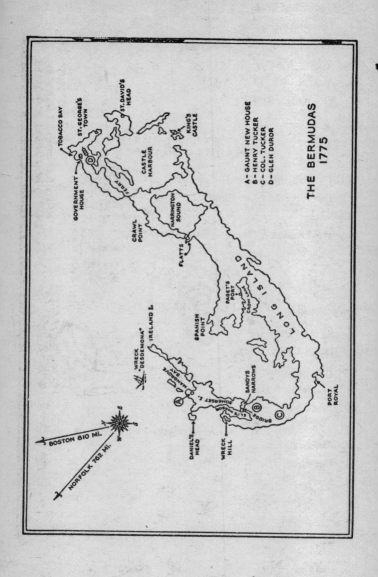

THE BERMUDAS
1775

A – GAUNT NEW HOUSE
B – HENRY TUCKER
C – COL. TUCKER
D – GLEN DUROR

ST. DAVID'S HEAD

TOBACCO BAY
ST. GEORGE'S TOWN

KING'S CASTLE

GOVERNMENT HOUSE

CASTLE HARBOUR

CRAWL POINT

HARRINGTON SOUND

FERRY

FLATTS

PAGET'S PORT

CROW LANE

LONG ISLAND

SPANISH POINT

WRECK "DESDEMONA"

IRELAND I.

MANGROVE BAY

SANDYS NARROWS

PORT ROYAL

DANIEL'S HEAD

WRECK HILL

BRIDGE

ELY'S HARBOR

SOMERSET I.

BOSTON 810 MI.

NORFOLK 762 MI.

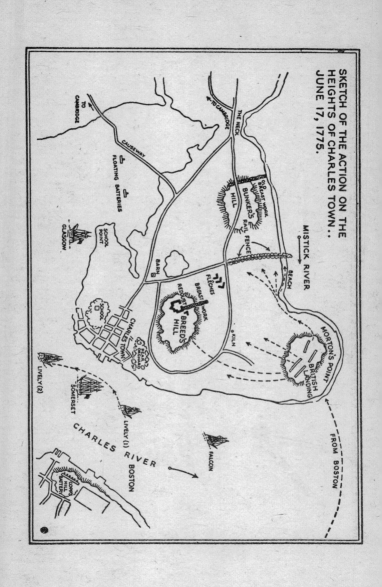

SKETCH OF THE ACTION ON THE
HEIGHTS OF CHARLES TOWN..
JUNE 17, 1775.

Book One

Norfolk

Part I

Winter: 1774

1 — PLUME'S CREEK

IT HAD just occurred to Rob Ashton that for a young fellow of twenty-seven he had recently bitten off a big mouthful. To get himself married and to start building his first ship within a few months of each other—even with the best of luck—was a large order. It seemed like tempting Providence. Still, his wife though barely seventeen was mighty level-headed, healthy, cheerful and he guessed Peggy loved him plenty. When it came to the new brig, his plans for her—Her? Quietly he chuckled. Sounded kind of polygamous having two female things on his hands at the same time. Maybe that explained why women and ships were so often antagonistic. The blood mounted in his normally high-colored cheeks. He surely hoped Peggy and the brig would get on. They should; both were designed from first-rate materials.

Stung by a biting west wind, he hunched farther over the tiller of his sailing skiff and, relieved of any obligation to make conversation, once more appraised a schooner building on Wilder & Son's stocks. Her tonnage would undoubtedly be greater than that of the brig whose keel he had watched being laid last week; greater say, by fifty tons. She might be bigger, but he couldn't see a sign of imagination, not a suggestion of sheer or of tumble home to this vessel's lines. He felt sure Peggy would agree with him. She could draw a neat sketch when she had the time.

The shipwrights had gone home, but smoke from a forge still climbed, mingling with low, steel-colored clouds. They suggested snow or sleet. He hoped the storm would not break soon; he hadn't seen his wife since six that morning and was in a hurry to get home. It was something to feel her smooth, warm arms go sliding up about his neck.

Momentarily he diverted his attention from the ship's hull, towering, nearly completed, above a forest of raw yellow shores and considered the man he had, an hour earlier, signed

3

on as master of his brigantine. The Yankee, huddled against the mast foot, was watching Norfolk's bluish-black outline recede. Rob Ashton was thinking the sea captain looked mighty like a shivery blue chipmunk with a blunt red nose. He would probably amuse Peggy no end. She hadn't met many Yankees so his way of talking should tickle her ready sense of humor.

Ranger of Norfolk. In big white block letters the name sprawled across another of those blunt, ungainly sterns Wilder had been building for nigh on twenty years. A smile plucked at the corners of Rob's wide mouth. Old John Brown would add this vessel to his fleet as unemotionally as a she-cat adds another litter of kittens to an already formidable tally. He would get no thrill out of it; he'd only cuss about the builder's charges.

He wished he knew when his own brig would stand so nearly complete. But she was going to be finished, if he had to trim every treenail himself. A mental picture of the brig as she would eventually look made him forget the grinding fatigue he was feeling. After a hard day's work at the small warehouse which easily accommodated Ashton & Co.'s depleted business, he had tramped all the way across town to Tom Newton's shipyard on Glebe Creek. There the chilled and apathetic movements of the slave carpenters had exasperated him into taking up an adz. With it he had trimmed three ribs while the snuffling black gang barked a pair.

Rob glanced at his hand. Though its palm was brown with calluses, the adz had raised a blister on the inside of his thumb.

"Choppin', I shouldn't wonder?" Came a faintly nasal interrogation from the sailing skiff's bow.

Rob nodded, smiled and drew his short-skirted coat tighter.

The skiff was rounding a reed-grown reach of the creek and the wind blew in stronger, more penetrating puffs. Ahead gleamed the warm yellow-red lights of Noatan, Robert Gilmorin's ambitious estate. Everyone along Water Street knew that molasses smuggled from the foreign West Indies had laid its foundations. They admired Gilmorin's cleverness.

Rob reckoned Peggy was going to have a home just as fine as Noatan some day. Then he grinned at his own cocksureness.

"Quite a sight," remarked the Yankee chafing big hands. Upstream was rising a great snarl of ducks scared from feeding in the lee of the shore. To a sibilant whistle of wings they raced by the skiff, breasts gleaming white and rust-colored necks stretched far out. Canvasbacks, by their long wedge-shaped heads. In a few weeks now Chesapeake Bay would crawl with waterfowl migrating northwards.

Game never had been more plentiful. Over at Williamsburg, the provincial capital, the burgesses had enacted a law forbidding owners to feed their slaves either canvasback or terrapin more than twice a week. Good thing Peggy was serving ham for dinner. Wouldn't do to put such poor man's fodder as wild duck before the new captain.

Why was Captain Farish still watching the ducks? What could he find so absorbing about a flight of canvasbacks? A queer customer; but then, most New Englanders were.

He hadn't wanted to sign on a Yankee master. It was running a big risk. But old Willoughby's rheumatics this time had tied him up into true lover's knots. He hadn't been able to run down a native master who would sign on at the rate he could afford to pay. That was the hell of it. Business had been booming ever since the Provincial non-importation agreements had broken down four years ago. He reckoned those bad floods they had had in France, Spain and Italy accounted for the high price of corn, wheat and salt pork. Now that the English had got reasonable to the point of repealing, partially at least, the obnoxious Townshend Acts, it was hard work finding bottoms fit to cross the Atlantic.

Farish he had first encountered on Boutetourt Street. He was swinging along brisk and trim as a gamecock. Though a scant five feet five, the little New Englander stood so straight he gave no impression of under size; middle-aged, he was bald as any capstan. What Rob chiefly liked in his prospective master was the shrewd gleam in his wintry blue eyes; it suggested that he not only saw, but observed what was going on. Stephen Farish had declared himself willing to sign on as master and supercargo at sixty Spanish milled dollars a month. Times were so good Norfolk captains were laughing at less than eighty. He didn't know much about Stephen Farish yet, but he did know how much twenty dollars meant right now. The Yankee's credentials were first rate and he had once owned his own ship and had papers to prove it. He was short all right, but on occasion an amazing big voice would come rolling out of his small frame.

Pity he was a Yankee—a damned shame. Everyone knew a

Bostonian would charge his mother for a drink even if he owned a lake. Rob knew first hand they weren't above dealing in goods stolen by slaves, indentured servants and other riff-raff. Another thing: Farish had been reluctant to tell how he had lost his own ship, but in the end he admitted a court of Revenue Commissioners had condemned him for landing a cargo of Cuban molasses at Ipswich one dark night. Farish was bitter, but philosophical.

"No use to take on about it," said he. "I'd not enough money to buy off the tidesmen—like a skipper of John Hancock's. One's a fool to run contraband without a mort o' palm grease aboard. Contraband, that's where the money is made, sir. Duty dodgers do a driving business these days running tea, Madeira wine, and raw sugar from the foreign Indies."

It appeared, in fact, that Farish had been only fresh out of jail before shipping as second mate in a Nova Scotian bringing salt fish to Norfolk for trans-shipment to Jamaica.

Rob, guiding his skiff around a weed-draped snag, again wondered what Peggy would make of the Yankee. Barely seventeen, she was proving a shrewd judge of character. Well, descended as she was from generations of tight-fisted Scots, she ought to be.

Flinging occasional flecks of spray over her bow, the skiff skimmed up the creek, weathering a series of miniature headlands formed by acres of reeds and wild rice. These, gone a sere yellow-brown, were sagging low over the water, as if cowed by an incessant lashing of winter winds.

Rob sat straighter. Any moment now they should sight the house—really an improved settler's cabin—he had bought. Tide-over, Peggy had christened it in a flash of unexpected humor. He always got a thrill at spying Peggy's kitchen smoke in the lee of a giant oak rising behind their home. Tide-over was, sure enough, nothing to be ashamed about; every young couple had to make a beginning. Most of the ten acres which went with the house fronted the creek; they ought to be worth something soon if Norfolk kept on growing at its present rate. His spirits warmed.

At first Peggy had been reluctant about moving so far out of Norfolk, but when she saw how rich the earth was and how well placed was Boush's Pasture grant, she said he had better buy. She was glad, too, he suspected, to be out of the range of her family. Only a few days back, in mimicking an acid old aunt to the life, she gave the show away.

"If you marry him, you'll regret it all your life, Margaret Fleming. The idyeh your buring yourself 'way out on Plume's Creek. And in such a miserable little cabin. Plenty of Negroes would turn up their noses at it. Besides, those Ashtons are a wild, unreliable lot. Take old St. John, Robert's own father. What did he do? Why, he ran off and married a bound maid! And an Irish wench at that!

"—Look at David. *There* is a mighty fine brother-in-law for you! A proud record he's made, gaming away the fortune his father left him to the last thin farthing! Too bad Rob wasn't left a tenth as much. Mark my words, Margaret, there is no trusting those Ashtons—even the best of them."

There were other pointers. For instance that night Mrs. Fleming's contemptuous tones came drifting out to the Flemings' veranda. He was sitting there thinking how lovely, how very lovely Peggy was.

"Andrew, as I have said before, and will always say, such a marriage is not to be considered! I won't have it! Peg shall not lower herself so. It would do all of us harm! You must admit his family—well, it has gone to pieces! Who are the Ashtons now? Nobodies!"

Suddenly, too somber eyed for her sixteen years, Peggy burst out, "That's not so! Oh, Rob, I'm *so* sorry! Mamma doesn't mean it. She doesn't know you."

To prove this, Margaret Fleming firmly, defiantly, stood with him before the altar of St. James's pretty ivy-hung chapel. That was three months ago, in November. It had been such a fine, warm day the loafers and pickaninnies hanging about the chapel door had not worn overcoats. Rob took this as a favorable sign.

They had a nice wedding after all. When Betsy Fleming realized Peggy really meant to have her own way—and she often did—she did her best. There was no point in supplying Norfolk's scandal cats with a banquet.

Only Peggy's parents, Rob's elder brother, David Mountford, and a very few of Peggy's closest friends were present at the ceremony.

Chilly and impassive as figures on the marble memorial plaques let into the chapel walls, Major Andrew Fleming and his wife watched the Reverend Dr. Love join their daughter to Robert Butler Ashton in holy matrimony.

7

At the wedding breakfast given in their mansion on Church Street Peggy's parents got a surprise. When, much earlier, Betsy Fleming showed her husband a list of people Rob had asked to have invited she sniffed.

"Big names, Andrew, big names; but they'll not put in an appearance. Wait and see if I'm not right."

Annoyingly correct as a rule, Mrs. Fleming was in error. Almost in a body, friends of Rob's father put in an appearance. Among them were famous sea captains, powerful merchants, rich bankers and ranking officers of the Provincial Army. An earl's son came, Captain MacCartney of H.M.S. *Mercury* who, though usually hoity-toity, got very drunk and fell downstairs in a most genteel manner. The sincerest compliment of all was paid by a party of those dour and grasping Scotch factors against whom St. John Ashton struggled all his life. John Bland, Fergus Sandys, Robert Gilmorin and Andrew Fleming's bitterest competitor in business, Neil Jameison, all drank their toasts—and much more. Major Fleming's wine was both excellent and free. Over from Williamsburg by private coach drove a dark and restless young Bermudian. He proved to be Mountford Ashton, a first cousin of the groom. Mrs. Fleming reckoned he had come more out of curiosity than anything else. Nevertheless he was there, representing the senior branch of the Ashton family. Before the breakfast guests were well jingled a touch of color had crept into Betsy Fleming's high boned and faintly yellowish cheeks. Rob, she commenced to address almost cordially.

"La, young sir, it seems your father's memory is warm held —for all his godlessness. You should have warned me so many of your family's friends would be coming."

"Why, Ma'am, I never reckoned so many would come," Rob replied simply. He was yearning for an end to all this fuss and pother. Why in time couldn't a couple of people get married without jumping through more hoops than a pair of trained dogs?

The wedding turnout bettered Rob's relations with the Flemings. He and Peggy were barely settled in Tide-over than Major Fleming rode out for a glass of negus. When Peggy went out of the room, he looked down his nose at Rob, cleared his throat, and suggested a post in the thriving business he conducted with Jamaica and the Leeward Islands.

"You could do worse than throw in with me, my boy," said he crisply. "Your brigantine is old, long overdue for the bottom. When the *Assistance* goes, you and Peggy will be out on a limb. Eh, what?"

He went on to offer, rent free, a house he owned just across the street from his own handsome brick residence; but with an unwise hint of patronage.

In declining, Rob was tactful beyond his twenty-seven years. He wanted neither the one nor the other. Politely he reminded Major Fleming that once, not so long ago, Ashton & Co.'s merchantmen had thrust their figureheads into the Caribbean's lazy, sun-lashed ports, into the slate-colored expanse of Boston Harbour and, on occasion, into the bleak and dreary port of Halifax. Ashton & Co., said he, was still in existence. He intended to keep it going, to make it grow. He had ambitious plans—sound, practical plans. His business would take care of Peggy and himself.

"He is being plagued stubborn and ungrateful," was Betsy Fleming's angry verdict. "It is unreasonable he should expect a daughter of ours to camp in that wretched, made-over settler's cabin. The idyeh her having only that worthless old Lom to help her!"

"Perhaps, Ma'am, it will prove a salutary experience," was the major's somewhat surprising suggestion. "All her life Mistress Peggy has been cosseted. I fancy she will miss the old comforts. Just wait, Ma'am, just wait. He will find it no easy time," the major continued comfortably. "Today political winds back and shift so fast the cleverest of us along the waterfront can't tell for sure how to trim sail. Young Ashton will overreach himself. That is my guess. Remember one thing, Ma'am. All the business he does is with Boston!"

"Boston? I don't understand you, Andrew. The trade always profited St. John Ashton."

"So it did," agreed her husband, lifting a decorous pinch from a small silver snuff locker on the mantelpiece. "But in the army I learned that 'always' is a treacherous word, Ma'am. In the 'Intelligence' today is more news from Boston. Two weeks ago a mob burnt more tea." His large, rather severe features tightened and his slash of a mouth grew thinner, more colorless. "That, mark you, comes to cap outrages on the *Dartmouth* and *Beaver*. John Brown tells me the Bostonians have defied Gage to suppress their own meetings. Fancy that."

9

"It sounds like downright sedition to me," Mrs. Fleming agreed dutifully. But her mind was on Peggy.

"Aye. Sedition it is. Parliament will not take it lying down. It's—why, damme, Ma'am, it's more—it's defiance!"

"Well, Captain, what do you make of Norfolk?" Rob inquired without removing eyes from a channel marker bobbing and revolving in the strong ebb tide.

Captain Farish wiped a drop from the end of his blue-red nose. "Well now, I presume Norfolk has its good points, like the Irishman said about the balky mule. But to my way o' thinking, it's a sight too flat and dampish 'round here. Ain't cold enough for honest February weather, either."

"If you enjoy having your ears frozen off, I reckon you're correct." Rob showed strong teeth in a good-humored grin. He was tacking towards a crab house perched crazily on pilings near the far shore. "Is game as plentiful up your way?" He jerked his head towards a snowy raft of wild swan. Taking lazy alarm the birds were commencing to paddle away. The rick was so vast it suggested a drifting floe. Over the dirty yellow water came their eerie trumpeting and the *ur-ouk!* of some Canada geese among them. Compared to the great white swans, the honkers seemed dwarfed.

"Can't say as we do," Farish admitted, squirting to leeward a deft parabola of tobacco juice. "Saw you studying that shipyard a piece back. Craft on the stocks ain't—?"

"No. She's building for John Brown. My brig's only just been stemmed in Tom Newton's yard."

"Um." Farish's brown features fell into deep lines; it was rather like watching an apple age before one's eyes. "Well, Mr. Ashton, I figger you'd do well to careen the *Assistance*. You don't mind my saying so? She's got some mighty spry leaks." He blinked utterly hairless lids. "Don't fancy navigating by sail and by pump handle. Not in winter time."

Despite a tight feeling about his heart, Rob shrugged. "She'll do as she is for a while yet. Because she'll have to. Besides, she's hardly worth patching up. Her papers say she was laid down in Bristol—back in 1737. Most likely half her bottom needs replanking."

Captain Stephen Farish chewed hard for a while, frowned at a half gourd bailer drifting about muddy water in the skiff's bottom. Under his coat of threadbare blue serge the mariner's shoulders rose.

"Well, I must say there's no call to dwell on her rottenness. If I fetch her to Boston, I can get her repaired cheap up there. I have friends. Your rice and tobacco will bring a tidy sum, shouldn't wonder. What with the troubles lately, vessels are beginning to steer clear o' Boston and land cargoes at Salem, Ipswich and Falmouth.

"Wish you would tell me why the Governor keeps a-crowding more customs cutters into Massachusetts Bay. It stumps me. The way the *Gaspée* got burnt ought to have showed those dumb-locks in Parliament how the wind blows over New England. But did it? No siree, it didn't! Every time a sea captain turns 'round he's got a new ordinance to fear, a new paper to make out, and a new tax to pay. You heard of their latest notion?"

Rob said he hadn't.

"Suppose a skipper ships a cargo for Spain, or Germany, or Sweden, on the way he has to touch at a British port, enter his cargo and pay duty! Means he has to sail 'way out of his course and lose a mort of money in wages and food. Now, what do you make of that?"

Rob considered, spoke equably. "In the end, Parliament generally does the fair thing. They repealed the Townshend Acts."

Farish shook his head in its round-brimmed hat of varnished black leather. "Only after we druv 'em to it with non-importation agreements." He went on. "Before we cleared Boston I heard tell the East India people have a smart oversupply of tea on their hands. Sam Adams said they aim to make us use it up."

"They'll have to lower the price," Rob said. "I can't see what's wrong with that."

The New Englander made no immediate reply. Later he asked, "Suppose I get you above middling price on your cargo? You'll let me patch the *Assistance?*"

Rob hesitated. To finance the building of his new brig would require strenuous efforts; at the same time, the ancient brigantine was his sole source of income.

"We'll see. In any case, you'll only do what's got to be done." He reckoned he had better throw out his bait right now. He looked Farish square in his slightly bulbous blue eyes. "I'll tell you something, Captain. If we get on and make money, you'll have the new brig."

11

To his surprise, the Yankee's expression did not change. "I'll put in my best licks, Mr. Ashton, and pare expenses all I can. Always have done my durndest for my owners—got my vessel that way."

A puff heeled the skiff over and Rob eased her into the wind a little.

"Well, here we are," said he cheerfully.

Farish, turning on his seat, could make out a small, white-painted dwelling on a wooded point. The owner's home lay dead ahead and looked tiny under the great oak back of it.

2 — TIDE-OVER

THE house was part frame, part log cabin, but the cabin part was clapboarded and framed in. Its walls and half its roof were overgrown with English ivy which still shone a dull green; but the surrounding shrubbery was brown and lifeless. As the skiff neared a rickety pier, white with a littering of oyster shells, Captain Farish decided that the best thing about Mr. Ashton's property was its location. From the cottage a body could make out three distinct reaches of the creek and, beyond them, the far off steeples of Norfolk. You could even make out a dim tangle of spars, wharves and warehouses.

A brown and white spaniel came bounding down to the water's edge. His excited yelps scared into flight a small flock of black ducks. Farish, watching their silhouettes against a sickly yellow sunset, felt warm springs of saliva rise at the back of his jaws. A big drake, smoking hot on the platter, would go just dandy. Crimanently! He'd swallowed enough salt food to pickle his stomach 'till Kingdom come.

Curious folks, these Southerners. Seemed decent and God-fearing enough, yet they didn't pull long faces about it. They enjoyed living, or appeared to. A few of them even had a real head for business. Yes, sir. In these parts a man could drink a decent skinful and not get called up in meeting. And if a pretty girl got minded to tack a few ribbons to her clothes, people didn't put her down as a fancy-Nancy or a French whore.

Stephen Farish wished he could make up his mind about

Mr. Ashton. This young feller wasn't a mite like chaps of his age in the Massachusetts Bay country. Seemed sensible enough, though to be building a ship at his age was maybe a shade overreaching. Still, if he knew where to trade, a man with a fast brig could make him a fortune these days. On the other hand, he was likelier to lose his pants buttons.

When young Mr. Ashton had first shown him the *Assistance* lying to Ashton & Co.'s wharf, he'd felt he was in luck. The brigantine's paint and bright work had been kept up, but what a turn he'd got when he saw her running gear! Land o' Goshen! It was frayed and gray as a wharf rat's whiskers. Some of her spars looked as if they'd come out of the Ark. Worse still, her bottom was foul; a regular marine hayfield. But it was good to sign on as master once more.

He hoped Solace hadn't guessed his humiliation at having to sail as second mate of a stinking Blue Nose schooner. He was hoping his luck had turned. Him and young Ashton had hit it off from the start. Maybe, in spite of hell, high water, or Parliament, they could build up a smart little coastwise trade. The new brig would go a long ways towards helping matters; especially if she carried a little contraband, say a few cases of French laces, Dutch gin or Spanish wines. Profits on such items sometimes ran sixty per cent—even higher if you knew where to land your stuff.

"Evening, sah!" hailed a thin voice. A Negro was shuffling, loose-kneed, down to the landing. He was very old. So old his eyes seemed veiled by a bluish film. A small gold ring hung from his right ear. The old man stood at the end of the pier, waiting for Rob to round the skiff up.

"Mighty cold, Mas'er Rob," he called, catching the painter Farish flung with a dexterous flip. "Reckon he fixin' to snow?"

"Feels like it, Lom. Everything ship-shape?"

"Yes, sah. Hi, you Toby!" He turned on the spaniel now rushing up and down the shore in a delirium of welcome. "Hush yo' fuss. Young Missis 'ginning wonder where you-all was."

"Captain Farish, this is Absalom," Rob explained, stepping ashore. "I shouldn't wonder but he's voyaged almost as far as you."

"Now do tell!"

"Lom was my father's cabin steward, then his body servant

13

when he went ashore." Rob's voice held an undertone of affection. "He taught Dave and me to sail."

"Howdy, Mr. Absalom." Farish extended a stubby, big-veined hand; Lom only stared on it in stupid surprise. He made no motion to take it.

Rob's wide mouth thinned a trifle, then he remembered. "Reckon we had better mosey up to the house. Lom will tie up the skiff."

"You go on up," the little mariner suggested. "I ain't bent stops on a spritsail since time out o' mind." After all, the Ashtons had been spliced only a few months. So early in the game a welcome-home kiss still meant a lot.

"All right. Lom, just you rake a mess of oysters before you come."

Rob's progress, hampered by Toby's welcoming leaps, commenced as a bone-weary walk, but the further he followed the path of crushed oyster shells, the more he felt his fatigue ebb. He chuckled. Peggy, he knew, had been watching his progress half the way up Plume's Creek, but he knew he would find her pretending to be very busy. She would be terribly surprised when he walked in.

Sure enough, when he opened the door, he saw his wife's small figure bent over the kitchen hearth.

"Supper ready?"

"Mercy! Rob, how you startled me!"

Heated by the fire, the alert oval of Peggy's face was glowing. His eyes lingered on her white linen blouse, blue bodice and full yellow skirt. She looked dainty, doll-like and she had tucked a pair of blue-dyed straw flowers into the dark hair above her ear. More color rushed into her face when she saw his solid figure nearly filling the door frame.

He saw that the rims of her large, dark-blue eyes were red from the smoke driven out of the fireplace. He must take a look at its flue the first chance he got.

"My poor darling!"

Hurrying over to her, he noticed a tiny, not unattractive, beading of perspiration on her upper lip.

"Where is your Yankee captain?" she queried. "Don't you dare tell me you left him in Norfolk! I am dying to see what he is like."

His face broke into a boyish, infectious grin. "Down at the landing. Coast's clear." He snatched her off her feet, dripping ladle and all, and, despite perfunctory kicks of protest, kissed her so thoroughly that when he put her down she dropped the ladle and, blushing, began retrieving a windfall of hairpins.

"Really, Rob, if you fail as a merchant you needn't worry. You would make a grand buccaneer! What *will* your captain be thinking?"

"The truth most likely," he chuckled. "Farish ain't much to look at, but he's smarter than an old he-'coon." He went over to wrinkle his nose over a big iron kettle. "What are you giving us for supper?"

"Why, ham, dear. You said ham, didn't you?"

"Reckon I did. What else? I'm fit to eat an ox and chase its owner."

Peggy held up a small reddened hand and commenced to enumerate on its fingers. Two or three burns were visible. "Well, Mr. Bear, you will have spoon bread, mashed turnips, yams and a mince pie Dolly Brush brought over today. That should hold even you. Oh yes, and there's some of that nasturtium pickle you fancy."

"Sounds elegant. Is—is there any Madeira left?"

She smiled wisely. "Yes. But ought we? Every day it grows dearer."

"We ought," Rob said quietly. "Remember, Captain Farish can make or break me this trip."

Peggy nodded acquiescence. "Good thing we didn't plan on canvasback."

"Lom get any?"

"A few. He only fetched in fifteen with the loading you left for him. He's showing his age. And powder's so scarce."

"He is slipping," Rob agreed seriously. "Anyone ought to knock over twenty birds with a shot."

"Mercy!" Brown hair flying, Peggy in a characteristic quick movement darted over to the fire and stirred the spoon bread. Rob watched her while peeling off the old brown coat he had worn to work.

"You located two extra hogsheads?"

"Yes, some of George Leavitt's best Aronoko. The tobacco will be delivered wharfside tomorrow."

"What did you pay?" Peggy asked quickly. Hints of her father's business face were in her suddenly alert expression.

He winked, tickled no end. "This deal was on the quiet. Fergus Sandys holds a mortgage on most of Leavitt's crop. You won't tell?"

"Never a word, Rob. How much?"

15

"Only five pounds a hogshead! And Leavitt grows the best leaf along the James. Know what Neil Jameison paid for some of Drewry's? Five pound fifteen! And his lot wasn't half so tender as mine. In Boston my Aronoko should fetch seven pounds ten—easy!"

"Seven pounds ten!" Her face lit all over. "Oh, Rob, aren't you the smartest thing? We'll be finishing our brig before we know it." Her arms had risen to encircle his neck when a faint crunching of oyster shells sent her hurrying back to the cast iron pot simmering fragrantly on an iron crane.

"Come in, Captain, come in! We don't put on much style just yet, but I hope you won't mind. Ma'am, may I present Captain Farish?" He felt right proud of Peggy and the friendly way she smiled even if Farish was just a Yankee sea captain.

The newcomer whipped off his leather hat and jerked a solemn bow. "Servant, Ma'am. A pleasure and a privilege."

He paused in the doorway, a small erect figure in canvas trousers, worn blue serge and pewter buttons. As soon as she got a good look at the bandy-legged little figure, Peggy knew what he reminded her of. David Ashton's champion gamecock, Hannibal, had the same self-confident stance, the same quick, bright eye and alert air. But the gamecock had no traces of tobacco at the corners of his beak. Peggy felt her cordiality wilt when she noticed a brown splash marking the captain's turkey-red waistcoat.

Captain Farish's wintry blue eyes began darting about like swallows trapped in a sailmaker's loft. Ham! The aroma was unmistakable. His weatherbeaten and rather harsh features contracted but then, out of politeness, he forced a grimace. At a glance he took in the lack of fancy trimmings, the scarcity of pots and pans, the fact that two of the sassers on the table were cracked. The tea cups didn't even match. Only a meager supply of garlanded onions and ears of corn dangled from the kitchen's bare, smoke-blackened roof beams. The young Ashtons must indeed be sailing close to the wind. But ham! Jumping Jehosaphat! His stomach squirmed at the very thought of salted meat. He began to cal'late a mite.

Meanwhile Rob was tilting some old Medford—bought for the occasion—into pewter sneak cups. "A tot of rum to shake off the damp, Captain?"

"Don't mind if I do. Well, Mr. Ashton, here's luck."

As they drank, Farish continued his covert appraisal. It

wasn't a bad idea to know how your owner was fixed. The candles weren't spermaceti—just common drips. They smelt a little like roast beef. Uneasily, he commenced to wonder whether young Mistress Ashton could cook—like Solace. He doubted it. Mrs. Ashton's hands and feet were too soft and small looking.

Once Rob had sought the woodshed and had begun to wash, he began cautiously. "This is mighty kindly of you, Ma'am, to invite me here. You've no notion how weary a seafaring man gets of preserved food. Salt horse is all right at sea, but fresh meat for shore, that's the ticket! I declare, Ma'am, after seeing them canvasbacks on the crick I'm all of a water to taste one."

Peggy's hand faltered in basting yams candied in molasses. She turned a distressed face. "Duck? You said you like canvasback?"

"Indeed, Ma'am, I have heard nothing but praise for the bird. Was I mistook, or didn't I see a mess of them hanging from the eaves?"

"Why, yes, they are canvasbacks and—and some mallards." Peggy was conducting frantic calculations. Could it be managed? The new captain must be pleased. Nay, more than pleased, charmed. How often had her father commented that the success of a voyage could be measured by a captain's good will? If Rob would pass the rum again, she judged she could manage. Now where in Heaven's name was Lom? He'd a positive gift for disappearing when it was least convenient. Just then, as if in answer, he shuffled in with an armload of wood.

"You plucked three of those royals you killed this afternoon, Lom?"

The filmed eyes widened until their whites became concentric circles. "Why no, Mis' Peggy, you didn't say—"

"Of course I told you. You weren't listening!"

Lom's lower lip began to protrude like a slice of bluish liver and stubbornly he shook his grizzled head. " 'Deed, Mis' Peggy, you is mistook. You 'lowed we was gwine have ham tonight. Ah didn't—"

Peggy stamped her foot. "Hush, Lom. Just you get to work on three of the fattest canvasbacks—hens, mind you—and be quick about it!"

"Yessum." Lom shuffled away, muttering, arms hanging loose from their shoulders; the picture of gloom. His voice drifted back. "Ducks agin. Always ducks. Ain' we ever goin' get no mo' hog meat?"

"I am so sorry, Captain. I hope you will forgive Lom's stupidity." Peggy had a pretty air of concern. "You won't mind waiting?"

"Nary a bit, Ma'am," cheerfully replied Stephen Farish.

Hopefully Lom thrust his head back into the kitchen. "Ma'am dem ducks is froze mighty hard."

"Which makes them easier to pick," Peggy replied. "Now hurry up and ask Mr. Rob to fetch in the Dutch oven."

Captain Farish sighed, settled comfortably into a chair and tilted. He wished it was a rocker. Missus Ashton was a girl of sense, it appeared. Another tot of the Medford would go well, but he didn't dare hint again. Watching the play of firelight on a frosty windowpane, he fell to wondering whether maybe he could smuggle aboard a half cask of powder without being seen. Gunpowder was fetching breath-taking prices around Boston.

Rob came in carrying a big tin reflector oven. What with the weather and the cold water, his face was red as fire. "Going to blow tomorrow. Wind's hauling southeast."

Once the tin oven was propped before the blaze Peggy smiled over her shoulder. "Any news from Boston?"

The news, Farish told her, was middling bad. More riots, arrogance and brutality from the garrison. More well-meant stupidity on the Governor's part. Worst of all was the way the customs officers kept on riling everyone by their vicious enforcements. A party of Tories had chopped down the Liberty Tree in front of Butcher's Hall. More tea had been burnt.

Peggy's wide, wing-like brows became merged. "Tea again? I vow, Captain, I never could understand all this fuss over tea. The tax isn't high—only three pence a pound. People could pay it without grumbling, I should think."

She's a smart piece, no cornstarch airs, Farish appraised. But maybe a mite too smart for her husband. When he realized she was not just making conversation, he asked casually enough, "You are not King's people here, Ma'am?"

"No," Rob replied quickly. "And we're not Whigs, either."

"That's a sensible way to look at things—as long as you can." Stooping, the New Englander patted the spaniel which had come to sniff at the heavy white metal buckles on his shoes. Farish was watching his words, Rob sensed. "I'll try to explain, Ma'am, and I can give you two answers. First off, this here tea tax gives the big mouths like Sam Adams, Dr. Joe Warren, Ruggles and Jimmy Otis—he's half cracked anyhow—something to caterwaul over. 'Taxation without representation,' says they. But that ain't the trouble." Farish pursed his lips to spit but remembered in time. "Three-quarters of the people in England ain't represented in Parliament no more than us."

"Then their talk is of no great moment?"

"Not yet, Ma'am. But the Stamp Act of '67 put the lawyers, printers and writers on the side of the big mouths, mostly. The real reason has to do with trade—it most always does. It's the East India Act."

Peggy put down her spoon, sank onto a stool from which she could give the turnips an occasional stir.

"East India Act? I fear I don't understand, Captain."

"Well, Ma'am, you see it's like this. Up in New England there's quite a passel of us making a living out of the carrying trade." Farish began speaking more quickly now, and his blue eyes became narrow with concentration. "In the old days us merchant masters freighted cargoes from our seacoast to England, the West Indies, and all over Europe." He raised a finger. "That let us seafaring folk earn our freightage and our lays—shares, you call 'em down here—and we made a living." He held up another blunt finger. "The merchant-shippers, the farmers, the fishermen, and the distillers all made a living, too." He lifted a third finger. "Most of us don't build our own vessels. We buy 'em. That keeps the shipwrights and chandlers busy. See how it goes? Nigh 30,000 of us earned a living that way. Maybe more. I don't know."

Farish paused to tuck his feet on the rungs of his chair; there was a strong draught beneath the door. It was blowing harder. He could hear the wind roaring among dead leaves on the giant oak.

"Well, Ma'am, once we got to the other side we used to come rolling straight home deep with British and foreign goods, and we earned our freight again. The importers would buy wholesale, job the merchandise and sell retail. You do it yourself, Mr. Ashton. Well, all this will stop if the Parliament don't repeal this here East India Act."

"Stop? Why?" Rob was frowning, deeply absorbed as he stood by the fireplace with his wavy brown hair brushing a string of onions.

"Why? Well now, Mr. Ashton, I'll tell you why." Farish's

voice grew hard and flecks of color commenced to show along his cheekbones. "That there Act gives the East India Company the *sole* right to import tea and some other goods direct and *in their own ships!* That is, they can import tea without going to pay duty in England first. Anybody else has to pay duty here and in England. By law, we ain't allowed to import Dutch or Russian tea—only English. Right now the East India people are selling tea dirt cheap—cheaper even than Hancock and the rest of the big wigs can smuggle it. It slips in slick as a string without knots. Won't take you long to figger how long an independent tea trader, paying a double tax and freightage, will stay in the business."

"Just a minute," Rob objected. "The East India people have to pay freight, too."

Farish snorted. "Not by a jugful. Didn't you hear what I said just now? The company owns its own vessels and mans them with brown Sepoys. Don't pay them poor fellers 'nough to keep a roach going, either."

"It doesn't seem right," Rob admitted.

"No more it is, Mr. Ashton. But, mind you, the trouble don't end there. The Company is opening its own stores and selling *di*-rect to the public. Now d'you see why we won't stand for this consarned Act? It leaves us seafaring people and the shipbuilders and the provincial merchants out in the cold. The Company can, and does, undercut their prices something scandalous. Once the American merchants are broke, the Company will histe prices higher n' a cat's back. I hear tell they already done it in India."

Rob thought hard; here was something that hadn't occurred to him before. Peggy, too, was looking pensive.

"It won't last, Captain," Rob said slowly.

"It has in India," Farish maintained emphatically. "Just you wait. In a few years a handful of big companies will own America lock, stock and barrel. The Hutchingses, Tom and Elisha, they're the old Governor's sons; Richard Clarke & Sons, and a few others."

The candles had lowered before the three sat down to dinner. Though Rob and Peggy started in as soon as the first canvasback had been carved, Farish bent his head, asked an inaudible blessing. During the meal conversation languished, but Toby, banished into the night, mourned and kept scratching at the door.

Peggy laughed while decanting the Madeira. "Not much

20

more of this for us, Captain. They say the duty's going up again."

At length Farish sighed, belching delicately behind his hand and made an effort at polite conversation. "Norfolk's a likely spot for a port—in peace times."

"Why only in peace times?" Rob asked, holding his Madeira to the light.

"British Navy. If there's trouble, I'll give Norfolk a wide berth."

"Well, there won't be trouble." Rob felt no urge to debate. What he wanted most was to digest his dinner in peace, look at Peggy, and listen to the sleet tap with tiny febrile fingers on the windows. Toby, admitted at last, lay before the fire, his light brown coat gleaming. He whined softly and his legs worked in pursuit of a dream rabbit. When Rob looked across at Peggy he felt the blood sing in his ears. She looked extra pretty like that with her dark hair a little rumpled and her color heightened by the fire.

"Now I mind me of a voyage to Dominica," Farish began and Rob sighed. God help them! The Yankee looked like one of those long-winded sea captains who could only be shut up with an axe handle. Drowsily, he again considered his wife. The bodice of her dress had lifted her breasts a little under the frills, making them seem riper than they really were. Suddenly he took to wondering how many petticoats she might be wearing. Anywhere from three to five. It was right good fun to make a guess—even more to check up.

"—But says I—and I'll always say—she oughtn't to have broke up so quick. Ribs was too light—away too light. Can't have speed and strength, too. But she was a dandy sailer," Farish's booming voice concluded.

They moved into a tiny sitting room which, with a bedroom, completed the whole downstairs of the cottage. Before a bright blaze of pine knots they reseated themselves. It obviated the expense of whale oil or candles. A saving girl, Peggy.

For some time everyone was too comfortable to talk, then Farish got up and narrowly examined the fireplace. It was new and so constructed that its base lay two feet above the plain pine floor.

"Never did see a hearth set high like that. Throws the heat fine," remarked Farish.

"They build them that way in the Bermuda Islands," Rob

explained not without pride. "My father came from an island called Somerset. Some of my family is still living there."

"I wish you would build one like this in the kitchen," Peggy smiled. "A high fireplace saves a woman's back more than you lazy men ever think."

The captain's eyes roved along the rough plaster walls and stopped at a framed sampler bearing the inscription, "Margaret Randolph Fleming. Her work. Finished 1771."

"That's tidy work, Ma'am."

Peggy flushed. She was beginning to like this brown-faced fellow.

The captain lifted the frame from its nail. Slowly he read aloud the cross-stitched lettering.

"Lord, what is Life? 'Tis like the Bow that glistens in the sky,
We love to see its Colours glow, but while we look they die."

"That's gospel truth, Ma'am." Bald head glistening in the firelight, he replaced the frame and passed on to inspect an engraving.

On the mantel shelf stood something which caught and held the New Englander's eye. It was a tiny ship's model done in ivory. The hull, he decided, was that of a sloop, or of a full-rigged ship. Very beautifully executed, it was carved, he judged, from a walrus tusk. Though the model's masts had been snapped off, tiny ivory cannons poked out of her ports and she rode her ebony stand with dignity. She reminded him of a beaten French privateer he'd seen lying off Fayal.

Rob suddenly asked, "Should we load more salt or more molasses?"

"Salt, I dare say. Most men can get along without rum, but dummed few without salt." Farish dislodged a bit of canvasback from his teeth with the nail of his little finger. "Suppose we ship fifty bushels of salt and leave a dozen barrels of molasses for the next trip? Ought to clear a tidy sum."

"Yes," Peggy said soberly, "you ought to. Mr. Ashton and I are counting on this trip—a lot."

Farish saw his chance. "In that case, hadn't you better get the *Assistance* shipshape 'fore I clear for Boston? There'd be small fun and less profit in trying to dodge a bulldog with the spars and rigging in her now."

Peggy's dark blue eyes flashed. "Run? But why on earth should you have to run from one of our own war ships?"

Captain Farish's bronzed features lost their comfortable look. "Why, Ma'am, when we was off Cape Henlopen last week the *Liverpool* frigate hove us to, and pressed seven out of our crew. We were left so short-handed a squall near dismasted us the next day."

Rob frowned. "Yes, I heard about that. Mr. Abyvon, our mayor, has protested."

"What happened?" Peggy demanded.

"Captain Sackville called him a damned, stinking, ungrateful provincial—had him hustled out of the ward room."

"Do we—er, refit before I clear?" Farish innocently inquired.

Rob stared into the flames a little before he said, "No, Captain. Any work that is done will have to be done in Boston. It—well, you said yourself—it will be done cheaper there."

No use admitting to a new master that after the cargo was paid for there wouldn't be enough left in Ashton & Co.'s till to buy the brigantine a second-hand trysail. The voyage to Boston, he reckoned, ought to net enough to finish the brig's hull and leave something for a few essential repairs to the *Assistance*.

His mind ran on. Next trip he would clear the brigantine for Charles Town in South Carolina, but make a run over to the Bermudas on the way. On Water Street he had heard the islanders were very short of produce. A return trip with salt should take care of the brig's spars, sails and other gear.

"For a fact, sir, I wish you'd heed what I've said." The captain's lowered voice was almost pleading. "Your vessel's pumps ain't fit to dry a canoe." He would have said more, only Rob's wooden expression warned him to press the point no longer. His arguments were getting him nowhere fast. Hanged if young Ashton wasn't proving as careless and easygoing as the rest of the Chesapeakers. Up 'til now he hadn't given the impression.

Embarrassed, Farish again studied the ivory model. He got up, skirted the sleeping spaniel and stood squinting up to it, brown hairless head cocked to one side.

"A cute bit of carving, Mr. Ashton."

To keep from falling asleep, Rob got up, too. "It is. But

the *Grand Turk* looks right now as if she'd finished hard action."

"The *Grand Turk,* eh?" The pine knots sputtered as if scolding at an uneven wind which was making them flare from time to time. "Where'd you get her?"

"She's the model of a privateer my grandfather took off Finisterre in the French war in 1756. The next year he rolled home in her from the Rio Plate; gunnel-deep with Papist silver and gold enough to fit out a pair of merchantmen. He went into the Brazilian trade."

"That a Turk at her figurehead?"

"Yes. The Grand Turk—some call him the Sultan."

"A tidy bit of carving," Farish repeated admiringly. "Land sakes, a body can even make out the little crescent in his headdress."

"Take it to the light." Charmingly impulsive, Peggy lifted down the model, put it between the little sea captain's horny hands. In the mariner's brown palm the ivory hull lay fragile and lovely, like the wreck of a yacht in the trough of a tan colored sea.

"Godfreys, but she's beautiful. Look at all them little cannons." He shot a glance at Rob. "How come she got raked so bad?"

Rob laughed. "Misplaced confidence on my mother's part. She let me play with it when I was little. Reckon I tried to find out how she was put together. I mean to get her repaired."

"You prize her a lot, I presume," Farish observed, stroking the little ship's smooth under side with the tip of his forefinger.

"Yes. And her name." Rob carefully selected a "yard of clay" from several in a rack beside the fireplace. From a sheep's bladder pouch he commenced to fill its bowl. The rite always made him feel like an old married man. "My father founded his fortune in a snow by the same name."

"*Grand Turk?*" Farish tested the name, rolled his eyes at the flame-reddened ceiling. "Don't it sound a mite heathenish for a Christian vessel? Hope you ain't thinking of calling your new—" His voice died. It was plain Robert Ashton was intending to christen his new ship just that.

Rob was fitting the model's ivory keel back into its ebony stand when the spaniel raised his head, listened a moment, growled. It was sleeting harder than ever and the wind roared in the oak's high branches. Toby growled again and trotted over to the kitchen door.

"What ails the critter?" Farish wanted to know. "It's the darkey, mebbe?"

Peggy shook her head. "No. Lom went to his cabin some time back."

A lull in the booming of the wind let the three of them catch a distant clatter of hoofs. On the frozen ground the horseshoes sounded staccato.

"Who will that be?" Farish asked, toasting legs incased in coarse gray stockings.

"Some Sons of Liberty," Peggy told him with a little laugh. "They'll be coming back from their muster at Thoroughgood's."

"How can you tell that, Ma'am?"

"Nobody else would be so drunk. Can't you hear them yelling?"

Farish could, by cupping his hand to his ear, catch a few wild whoops. The spaniel kept on growling. When Rob peered out of the kitchen door, he dashed through it and set up an excited barking.

"Oh hush your fuss, you old fool. They've gone on."

When the dog refused to be silenced, Rob gave his wife a level look and crossed to an earthenware jar with a lid. It said "ginger" in blue letters, but what Rob took out of it was a big old-fashioned horse pistol. After snapping open the frizzen to look at its priming, he said:

"Reckon I'll find out what's worrying him. Pour the captain a bit more Madeira, my dear."

Then he shut the door to the kitchen. Peggy liked the way he went to investigate. No fuss or feathers—just capable. They heard his shoes crunch off on the oystershell walk. The dog quieted.

Captain Farish arose eagerly. "Might Mr. Ashton be needing a hand?"

"I—why, I don't know," Peggy replied. "Out here on the edge of town a lot of queer people pass—vagrants, runaway slaves, you know, and such."

Farish listened, but Rob's footsteps were lost in the booming of the wind. He swung about, treating the young woman to a penetrating glance.

"You've something on your mind, Ma'am?"

She nodded, stepped closer. "Yes. The *Assistance* really is as bad as you make out? Please tell me the truth."

"I hate to say it, Ma'am, but she's a sight worse. She's so leaky I'll warrant some of her cargo will suffer."

"What needs most to be done?" Peggy demanded, looking steadily at him.

"Mr. Ashton at least ought to let me fix the pumps, and reeve some new running tackle. The fore course's canvas is so old it wouldn't hold even a spit of wind. Her main topmast's sprung, too. But I guess maybe it will last to Boston. What is really bad are them rotten planks in her stern—"

"Could they be replaced without careening?"

Farish hesitated; the firelight glanced off his bald head when he nodded. "I allow so. Being as she's still out of ballast."

"Well," Peggy spoke hurriedly, "you go ahead and get the pumps fixed. Replace the worst cordage and buy the sail you spoke of. Of course those rotten planks will have to come out."

Farish looked sharply at her. "Yes, Ma'am. But where will I find the money?"

To his surprise the girl's fingers closed on his wrist. Right now she was a determined looking piece. She was looking years older.

"I—I will bring it to you tomorrow morning. Have the carpentry done in the late afternoon and don't you dare use any new sails 'til you've passed the Rip-Raps. I want to surprise Mr. Ashton. You'll say nothing to anybody. Understand?"

"Nary a word, Ma'am." He grinned.

If young Mrs. Ashton intended to override her husband's decision that was her concern. Under normal circumstances the male in him would have opposed such an obvious compounding of a breach of connubial discipline. But the thought of Solace Farish and the children living next door to charity in Cambridge decided him. He was taking tall chances at best in navigating such a frail old ship. Was it his business where the supplies came from? He smiled at her back when she got up and opened the kitchen door. All at once he heard Ashton's voice.

"I can't take you in, Jemmy." He was talking low and quick. "You know I would if I could, but I can't. You know how things are these days. Everyone has got to be careful.

Look, here's a duck and a slab of cornbread. Go down past the spring in Shawl's hollow and you'll find a lean-to. I use it hunting. You ought to be able to make out there 'till you decide what to do."

"Thankee, sir, and Gawd bless yer. Thankee."

"Who is that?" demanded Peggy's clear, efficient voice.

"It's Jemmy Potter, the ostler at the Crossed Keys."

"Isn't that Felix Jarvis's ordinary near Thoroughgood's?"

"Yes, Mum," a voice whined. "I bin running Mr. Jarvis's stable. Yer remembers me, don't yer, Mum?"

"Why of course. What can have happened? Tell him to come in, Rob."

"He is not coming in," Rob spoke with finality. Peggy ought to mind her own business. Before a guest, too. He experienced a rising exasperation.

"And why not, pray?"

The way Mrs. Ashton drew herself up prompted Farish to follow her into the kitchen. He saw standing just outside the door a hatless, very bow-legged individual with flat round face and small anxious gray eyes. He could see him clearly in the light of a pine knot thrown onto the dying cook fire. The little man carried a reddish lump over one eye and blood, now dried, marked his grimy cheek. The apparition's breeches of coarse duroy, worsted waistcoat and lumpy woolen stockings all were rank with black swamp muck. He kept glancing fearfully over his shoulder.

"Thankee, Mr. Ashton. Thankee, Mum." Jemmy caught up the mallard drake Rob had given him and jerked a bow which set his queue, clubbed in an eelskin, to wagging like a preposterous tail. "I'm leaving straight orf. I wouldn't want for to get yer in trouble. Us King's people 'as got to—"

King's people? Farish's sparse eyebrows rose.

Casting a warning look at his wife, Rob snapped. "We're neither Tories nor Whigs, just Christians, I reckon."

She would not meet his eye, but insisted firmly, "But Rob, we *are* King's people! Come in and warm yourself."

"No!"

Peggy started to insist, but a sudden, unfamiliar paling of Rob's lips held her silent.

"Well, Mister, you look a mite ruffled. What's happened?" Farish inquired.

Jemmy Potter's uneven yellow teeth sank eagerly into the

27

wedge of cornbread and when he spoke, little crumbs tumbled through lips swollen as from a blow.

"The Sons of Liberty, blarst 'em all to 'ell, was 'olding muster over at Thoroughgood's place. This a'ternoon, it bein' me day orf, I goes over to Flora's meadow for to watch 'em." He sought Rob's eye. "I didn't do nothing but larf, sir. I swear to God I didn't! I couldn't 'elp it. Them militia was that comical wot with their defaulter's parade uniforms and their firelocks canting every which way." The way Jemmy straightened as he spoke showed Rob he had all of an ex-regular's contempt for militia. "So 'elp me, at a simple 'right wheel,' they fell orl over themselves like a calf on a picket rope."

Rob couldn't hide a grin. He, too, had watched the Independent Company of Princess Anne at their exercises. But Farish wasn't smiling.

Jemmy shot Peggy a glance from anxious, bloodshot eyes. "I just larfed a little. Surely there weren't nothink so orful in that, were there, Mum?"

"I wouldn't have thought so," Rob cut in shortly. "What did they do?"

"A big, loud-mouthed sergeant named Leeming leaped orf 'is 'orse and grabbed me by the scruff of me neck. 'Larf at the Sons of Liberty, will yer, ye bloody Tory? We'll teach you respeck'." Jemmy fumbled the crumbs from his mouth and blinked in the light from the kitchen. "You knows 'im?"

"Yes, I know Leeming. Get on with it," Rob said impatiently.

"I swore I didn't mean nothink, but 'e set up a yell for tar and feathers and all the militia stopped their drill. I remembered the stable I bin a-building with me wages and pension money, so I tries 'ard to explain. But it weren't no good. They'd 'ave tarred me but for Captain Brush—John Brush. You know 'im, sir? 'Im what owns the ware'ouse on Town Back Creek? 'E made 'em 'old on for a bit.

" 'Don't be fools,' says 'e. 'Jemmy's orl right and 'e didn't mean any 'arm.' But Sergeant Leeming says, says 'e, ' 'E'sa damned Englishman. 'E's orlways 'anging 'round on muster day'—which ain't true, sir.—'Wot 'im and others like 'im needs is to be torght a lesson.' " The bedraggled figure shifted the duck to his other hand and took another bite of cornbread. He was panting less now.

"They locks me in a room 'til their manoovers is done,

then they fetches Mr. Jarvis. 'See to it," says Mr. Phipp—'e's a leftenant in the Winston troop—'you don't employ no more traitors at the Crossed Keys or some fine day you'll wake up and find your inn ain't 'ere any more.' "

The little ostler standing in the now diminishing sleet looked so woebegone Peggy suddenly ran over to a small keg standing in the woodshed's corner and drew off a pewter mug of cider.

"Oh, you poor creature! Here, wash the crumbs out of your throat."

Jemmy Potter's muddied chin quivered. "Thankee, Mum, and Gawd bless yer kind 'eart! I were near forgetting people could be kind."

"Go on," Rob said, in a hurry to get the man on his way.

"Well, Captain Brush, 'e wouldn't let Sergeant Leeming's men tar and feather me, but they did ride me on a rail. In the end Leeming 'e lays the flat of 'is sabre across me back a few times and Leftenant Phipp says, 'Now get out of Princess Anne County and don't never come back. We'll not be so easy the next time.' "

Jemmy stared hopelessly at the three people in the kitchen. "Wot can I do? My last bob is tied up in the stable. Right now I ain't got a copper to me name. Where'll I go?" He shivered. "Gawd! Ye'd 'ave thought I was a fox the way them Liberty boys 'unted me to the edge of the woods, 'ooping and 'ollering. And now, I'll be going, sir, I wouldn't want for to bring trouble on yer. Ye've been mighty kind."

"Where are you heading?" Rob asked.

"For the Great Dismal Swamp, I guess."

"Don't you do it!" Peggy burst out. "They have no right to drive you from your property—your stable. Go talk to the sheriff. He will protect you. In the meantime, why don't you look for work at John Brown's warehouse? I'm sure he will help you."

John Brown, eh? Stephen Farish's eyes sought the kitchen's smoke grimed rafters.

"Thankee, Mum. I'll try 'im. I—" Jemmy's attempt to knuckle his forehead ended in a sudden start when on a pike beyond Brush's pasture hoofs again clattered. The fugitive bent low and, clutching the mallard, blundered off down the creek towards the distant lights of Norfolk.

Peggy lingered in the doorway, one hand clenched tight

against her breast. "Oh, the cowards! How dare they persecute an old soldier just for laughing! Sons of Liberty indeed!"

"Margaret! Be quiet!" Rob ordered sharply. "Come inside."

3 — THE SONS OF LIBERTY

CAPTAIN FARISH returned quickly to the sitting room and, idly at first, then in deepening interest, fingered what must be a set of plans for the new brig. The fact that Mr. Ashton had drawn plans for so small a vessel was in itself unusual. At Salem, Ipswich and Marblehead, where the best ships in America were built, a shipwright planned his vessel as he went along. He would mount stem and stern posts first, then lay the keel and commence framing out from amidships. Any inspirations would be more or less spontaneous and only then put into execution. What Farish beheld neatly rendered in India ink caused him to bend his hairless head in admiring concentration.

What with his specifications for pickled and boiled timbers, Mr. Ashton was aiming mighty high. Imagine calling for copper tree-nails below a merchantman's water line! Crimanently! What did Mr. Ashton think he was building? A yacht? A ship-of-the-line? Tapping hands softly behind back, Farish considered the way the brig's bow was to be sheered. Why in Tunket was he planning to step his mainmast so far forward? Involuntarily, he moved his head in disapproving jerks. Suddenly he recognized her. She was the *Grand Turk* drawn to a working scale!

One thing was certain sure. What with that tricky rake to her masts, Mr. Ashton's brig was either going to be speedier than a cat with its fur afire, or she'd be a miserable failure, a laughing stock wherever she went. If she did prove a success, though, her speed would pay for her in jig time. Um. Could be pierced for six guns. Maybe Mr. Ashton wasn't quite so easy-going as he put on.

Farish straightened hurriedly when the young couple reappeared, she with color high and he with jaw set at a stubborn angle.

"Hope you don't mind, but I've been taking a look—"

Farish broke off. Mrs. Ashton's eyes were growing very tense and round.

Horses, several of them, were advancing down the lane beside the meadow. When Peggy started up, her husband warned in a low voice:

"Stay where you are!" His eyes sought Farish's, asked a number of silent questions. Then because the riders seemed to have halted, he went to look out of a window. Turning, he said over his shoulder, "Nobody's been here, understand?"

He made out four riders whose horses were blowing and snuffling in the darkness. One of them swung off, looped the bridle over his arm and led his mount right up to the door. The beast shied back and the man cursed under his breath as Toby suddenly appeared and began a shrill series of yelps.

Rob watched a second horseman dismount, a big fellow with a sagging stomach. He wore a uniform of some sort. He began to stamp his feet and the others swung their arms as they sat in the saddle. The leader, wearing a triple-caped riding coat, rapped loudly on the door with his riding whip handle; the gesture irritated Rob no end. What right did he have, coming to pound on a man's door at nine of the night?

He felt little better on recognizing the leader as Matthew Phipp. A dark, sardonic fellow, he would much rather preach Rousseau's philosophies at the Spread Eagle, the worst rebels' hang-out in Norfolk, than 'tend to his law practice.

"Hi, Rob! Will you open up, please?"

"Who is it?"

"Lieutenant Phipp, Sergeant Leeming, an' two more Sons of Liberty, by God!" rasped the second dismounted man. "Open up or you'll get to hear from some more of us."

"Be quiet," Phipp ordered, "I will do the talking."

Quite deliberately Rob slid back oak bars fashioned by the original owner. They were plenty stout enough to keep out Indians.

"Evening, Matt. What can I do for you?"

The civility of the greeting surprised the leader into taking Rob's offered hand. "Evenin', Rob. Deuced cold night." He sounded embarrassed and hunched his shoulders nervously under the light gray riding cloak.

"Yes. Reckon sleet will be leaving off soon, though."

Lieutenant Phipp cleared his throat. "Sorry to disturb you. Seen anybody about just now?"

"Why, no," Rob replied easily. "Why?"

The two men on horseback put their heads together, muttering something Rob could not catch. The fellow called Leeming started to speak but Phipp cut him short with a peremptory gesture.

"We're hunting for a fellow, an Englishman, named Potter—Jemmy Potter. He is—was—ostler over to the Crossed Keys." Ill at ease, the lawyer pulled off his hat, studied its interior a moment. He brushed a' hand over his forehead. His breath, rising in small white puffs, became gilded by firelight beating through the open door. It revealed handsome intense eyes, a tangle of dark red hair and a wide red scar along his cheekbone.

Rob grinned. "I don't use the Crossed Keys much. What's he done?"

Swelling his chest until the tarnished brass buttons of an old blue militia uniform threatened to burst, the sergeant swaggered forward. Rob could see that the coat's scarlet facings and his waistcoat of the same color were peppered with food stains.

"He was spying on our muster! That's what he was! By Jesus!"

"Spying?" Rob laughed, incredulous. "Why, he's only a groom. Where do you get such crazy ideas?"

A pasty-faced, thin fellow in a dingy gray hunting shirt leaned forward in the saddle. Said he in a hoarse, passionate voice, "After we drove him out of Thoroughgood's we searched his room. There was British army papers in his ditty bag! He was corporal in the 5th Dragoons."

"But he's been discharged, hasn't he?" Rob pointed out. "He isn't in the army any more."

"Maybe. But that don't keep Potter from being a spy," the hunting shirt man insisted.

Sergeant Leeming's small pale eyes narrowed to either side of a colorful nose.

"Once a bloody-back, always a bloody-back, says us. We aim to find Potter, eh Bub?"

"Sure we do, Sergeant." The fourth rider who had just clumsily dismounted from a shaggy farm horse leaned a long-barreled squirrel rifle against the house and began methodically to rub his beast's thick legs. He wore an old Provincial militia uniform coat and a knitted scarf of blue wool over a leather waistcoat. "We'll stretch his neck if we catch him."

"You'll be fools then," Rob said. "Anyway, I haven't laid eyes on him."

"You're sure about that?" Phipp sounded very suspicious.

"Of course. Why shouldn't I be?"

"Sergeant Leeming was waiting on the road for us. He thought he heard your dog bark at someone, then your door stood open."

"By Jesus, there wasn't no 'thought' about it," Leeming growled. "I got eyes in my head, ain't I?"

Rob's diaphragm stiffened when he saw a coil of rope slung to the thin fellow's pommel. It wasn't thick rope, but it was plenty strong enough to hang a man. All four of the wind-bitten riders carried pistols.

"Well, I still haven't seen anybody. What my dog smelt was a 'coon. There's a mess of them living in those basswoods along the edge of the slue."

The sergeant uttered a derisive snort and, after blowing on purple-red hands, passed his reins to the man he had called Bub.

"So it was 'coon, was it? Wait till I find me a pine splinter. I bet a half jo I'll find blood spots on the ground."

Rob stepped into the doorway, filling it. He was getting pretty hot, but reckoned he had better hang onto his temper. "Shouldn't wonder but you would, seeing's my nigger killed some ducks this afternoon." He spoke confidently, but at the same time he was afraid cornbread crumbs and Potter's footprints might show on the new sleet.

"I'm going to take a look about," persisted the sergeant.

"Stay out of my house, you no 'count trash!" Peggy darted past her husband. "You heard what Mr. Ashton said? That will be enough from you." Tight-lipped, she turned on the lieutenant, now standing aside, uncertain, increasingly embarrassed. "What ails you, Matt Phipp? You ought to be ashamed, riding around at night like a madman! If you'd mind your practice more and leave politics alone, you might get somewhere." She had known him since, as children, they had attended Grief Randolph's "Genteel Academy of the Dance."

Collecting himself, Matt Phipp bowed. "Servant, Ma'am. I regret we have disturbed you and so long as Rob is sure no one was here, we'll be going. Mount up, boys."

"Hold on Lieutenant—" Leeming began, but Phipp cut him short.

"That will do!" he snapped. "You heard my order?"

"Have it your way this time, Lieutenant. But right now, I'm saying we'll soon be riding this way again. All the damned Norfolk merchants are Tories and English lovers."

The thin man suddenly stopped swinging his arms. He bent forward in his saddle and fixed a steady, accusing gaze on Rob. "Woe unto the oppressors of Israel! Search your soul, Robert Ashton! Dare you support the Babylonians and Jezebels ruling in Whitehall?"

Rob merely stared. He didn't know whether to laugh. Leeming, the berry-faced sergeant, took fresh courage and slapped his pistol butts.

"Let's get a light. What say, boys? Troops got a right to look for a spy anywheres. Says so in Roger Stevenson's 'Military Instructions'—Chapter Six."

"That may be so." Farish suddenly stepped out into an oblong of yellow light flooding the frozen ground. "Howsomever, you fellers are barking up the wrong tree."

"What the hell—?"

"Listen to me, young feller. I hail from Boston. I'm a member of the Committee of Fifty-One. Maybe you ain't heard? It was us started the Sons of Liberty!"

Even the horses cocked surprised ears at the small sea captain's big booming voice. The riders, visibly impressed, kept quiet, their chilled faces intent.

"End o' this week I'm sailing Mr. Ashton's vessel up to Boston. She's carrying supplies the Patriots need. Got anything to say to that?"

Phipp laughed quietly and settled his cloak against the west wind's bite. "I reckon not. You sound like a sure-enough Yankee and from what I hear, Tory sea captains 'round New England are scarce as brains in Parliament. Mount up, boys, and let's get going."

The lawyer had started to swing up onto his horse when, in a nearby tangle of myrtle and holly, sounded a sharp rustling.

"By Jesus, there he is!" Leeming swung to the sound, jerked out a pistol. "Told you he was somewhere around!"

"There's nobody there," insisted Rob sharply.

"Like hell there ain't!" Ignoring Phipp's urgent, "Don't be a fool!" the sergeant fired at a dim blur among the undergrowth.

Terrified yelping and a violent threshing was the immediate result.

"Toby!" A staccato *smack!* marked the impact of Rob's fist on Leeming's face. Arms flailing, the sergeant went staggering backwards off balance. He landed at his horse's feet. Snorting, it began rearing and backing away.

Rob sprang forward, but the man in the blue and red uniform made no effort to rise, only lay cursing under his breath. When Rob breathing hard, stepped back, Leeming raised himself on one elbow and began feeling his jaw. Dazedly, he spat some bloody spittle.

"Give me that pistol, you fool!" Matthew Phipp was roused to cold fury and when the other hesitated, he stooped and jerked a second and still loaded weapon from Leeming's belt.

The sergeant only stared at his assailant with a malevolent intensity. Lying there with sleet rime marking his shoulder, he reminded Rob of a moccasin whose back Lom had broken with a paddle. The same ugly glitter had shone in the reptile's eyes.

"Toby's all right," Peggy called, returned with the cowed and trembling spaniel in her arms. She stood straight and serious, but her heart was singing at the way Rob had stood up to Sergeant Leeming.

Furious, Phipp ordered his men to mount up. "I deeply regret this disgraceful affair, Ma'am. My apologies," said the lawyer once his men had moved off. Then he spurred his tall hunter and cantered after the other Sons of Liberty.

4 — THE HURRICANE GLASS

"I'LL call you around six," Ashton warned Stephen Farish. "The tide will be ebbing so it shouldn't take us long to reach town. Hope you won't find the loft too uncomfortable; it's all we've got for a guest room these days."

Rob peered up, anxious. It was turning colder. Maybe he'd better give Farish the goose down comforter off their bed; two slept warmer than one he had learned recently. "Reckon you will be warm enough? I can get another quilt."

"Won't need it. It's a sight snugger here than in most stern cabins." Over the wind's impatient rattling of the woodshed door Farish's voice sounded muffled. All of him save legs in well darned stockings had vanished through a trap door at the top of some ladder-steps built nearly a hundred years earlier.

Rob hesitated, "I want to thank you, Captain, for the word you put in a while back. I didn't want trouble."

"Don't mention it." The New Englander's homely brown face reappeared, framed in the square of the trap door. "Good night, sir, and thank your Missus for them canvasback ducks. They was elegant. I been telling my Solace since time out o' mind there ain't no use cooking a duck till it's brown and tough like a paring of the Devil's hoof."

A gust of wind shook the whole cottage and a leaf blown in under the door skittered across the kitchen floor. Rob's candle was equipped with a hurricane glass or it would have gone out. Down on Plume's Creek a flock of wind-tossed geese, lighting in, evoked a querulous welcome from those already bedded. Tonight their honking sounded eerie, restless. Perhaps Jemmy Potter had passed that way.

An unfamiliar sense of oppression descended on Rob. By God, these days a fellow had to sit up nights figuring out how to keep his business together and his backside out of jail. His father, St. John Ashton, had picked a good time to live; life in his day must have been simple and uncomplicated.

Rob drew a slow, deep breath. He wasn't used to excitement and violence, hated it in fact. But he had enjoyed slapping Leeming down.

He frowned. One thing was certain. He wouldn't stand for Peggy, new bride or no new bride, grabbing at the tiller of family politics whenever she disagreed with him. She had better learn that now as later. The more he thought on her stubbornness about asking Jemmy in, the more indignant he became. What would be Farish's opinion of an owner who couldn't even handle his own wife? He'd make her understand a thing or two before they blew down the hurricane glass.

He lingered in the kitchen, framing a series of severely polite and inflexible pronouncements then, shading the hurricane glass with one hand, he sought the living room. He found it in darkness save for the fire's lazy glow. He was pleased that Peggy hadn't yet gone into the bedroom; in there, she'd a way of distracting a man's serious thoughts.

He drew himself up. "Margaret, I want to—"

"Oh, darling." She came gliding towards him. "I thought you'd never finish with Farish. I've been wanting so to tell you how mighty proud I am! You were grand with that dreadful Leeming creature!"

"But Margaret!" Desperately Rob recommenced, floundered; his pronouncements escaped like mercury through his fingers. All he could think of was Peggy. She was standing before the fire but half turned aside. Her face wore an expression of radiant expectancy. He never had dreamed such a look could shape the features of Betsy Fleming's daughter. The throbbing coals had deepened the color of her slightly parted lips at the same time betraying spasmodic motions of her breast.

Shutting the plank door behind him, he put down the candle and cried in a thickening voice, "Peggy—I—I— Oh God, but you are lovely! So unbearably lovely!"

"To you always, I hope," she murmured. The dark blue eyes grew softly luminous. Slowly, she parted slim arms, let her head tilt back a little.

A delicious astonishment seized him; the laces of her bodice were hanging loose and the top of her frilly blouse was slipping low, lower, baring smooth shoulders. The fire's heat beating on his back passed through his body in a succession of impulses so hot they seemed to warm the palms of his hands pressed tight to her waist. He neither saw nor suspected her small smile over his shoulder.

A man, he frantically attempted to remember, should never allow his good sense to be carried away. Peggy had interfered when she had no call—oh hell! He might as well have tried reason against the sweeping force of a freshet. Moments such as these were unnerving, they were so unexpectedly paradoxical. Until a few weeks ago, he'd had no hint that such ardent flames could heat the cooly poised girl he had courted.

In her burst of passion she was astonishing. If that marble Madonna Neil Jameison's master had brought from Sicily had abandoned her pedestal to spin and whirl in a bacchanale, the act could not have been more surprising.

"Ah, Rob, my own man," came her tremulous heavy whisper. She smiled up at him and he could have sworn small fires smoldered in the depths of her eyes. Sometimes, off deer shooting with his brother David on the edges of Great Dismal he had noticed a similar lambency in the eyes of a hound lying beside a campfire.

When he bent her, passive, tremulous over one arm, the

loosened gathering string at the blouse's neck gave way, baring her arms to the elbows. He pressed his face, glowing as though scorched by an August sun, to the shallow valley between her high, immature breasts. Light as hovering butterflies her fingers brushed his wavy brown hair and undid the sober black bow clubbing it over the nape of his neck. This was all right, Rob had to remind himself. Weren't they decent married folks? He began to speak in a hoarse, urgent undertone.

"I love you, dear, and I'll have the Ashton fleet back again soon—and the great warehouse—everything—everything!"

Her laugh came softly tender. "Oh Rob, I'll be content, whatever you do. I do believe in your star—you will succeed, I feel it!"

Without warning she whirled away, deliciously disheveled, ineffectually clutching the fallen blouse and catching up the candle at the same time. At the door of the bedroom she paused, darting a mischievous look over her bare shoulder.

"How many petticoats?"

Grinning, Rob deliberated. "Three yesterday, five the day before. Four?"

"Right, Mr. Ashton," said Peggy and blew down the hurricane glass.

5 — CAPTURE

NEARING Alton's Corners, the second crossroads out of Norfolk on the King's Highway, Matthew Phipp drew rein, shiveringly certain that his riding cloak was much too thin for such weather. His three followers pulled up, too, forming a dark knot on the frozen road. He was dead tired and so plainly, was his mare. Perhaps that pious fool, Lemuel Heinz, had finally got enough of riding around in sleet and rain; there seemed no tiring him though he looked just skin and bone. Maybe that was how a man got, humped over a book binder's bench, seven 'til seven, six days a week and then reading the Scriptures half the night.

Matt Phipp cast Bub Jensen a meaning look before he said, "Well, I reckon there's no use looking any longer."

"There sure ain't," obediently agreed Bub. "Potter must ha' holed up in the marsh somewheres."

"And eating food them Ashtons give him." Badly swollen lips and jaw slurred Leeming's words. "Tell you, boys, that sort of thing has got to be stopped." Viciously the sergeant spat, smearing his cleft chin and his dull red waistcoat.

"If Ashton is proved Tory, he will be dealt with. We will tolerate no King's people in our jurisdiction," Phipp promised. He could cheerfully have wrung Leeming's neck right then. Ever since the Independent Company had been formed, he had despised the sergeant's loose mouth, wind-breaker ears and the white-headed pimples with which he was perpetually afflicted. "Take your pistols, Leeming, and don't ever go letting them off again without orders. Understand? Fool stunts like shooting at a dog make us look silly."

In sullen silence Leeming accepted his weapons. To hell with this snotty slob of a lawyer. Who did he think he was? Trying to play the officer and him without even a uniform coat.

After blowing on his hands Phipp continued in a brisk and businesslike tone. "On Saturday next, this troop will muster as usual at noon sharp in Billy Flora's meadow back of the Crossed Keys. From Thoroughgood's we will conduct an exercise march over to Portsmouth. Captain Brush aims to show them over there we won't stand seeing Virginia mortgaged to the Scotch and English bankers—not without a fight. Now you fellows better go home and get some rest."

"I'm not tired," Heinz hotly protested. In the gloom his weak, oddly intense eyes seemed like smudges in the pallor of his face. "No Son of Liberty should tarry by the wayside until the Viper of Oppression is driven from this fair province."

Leeming made a flatulent noise with his lips. "Stow the fancy talk, Deacon. Potter's got away and besides, my tail is plumb wore out."

"Oughtn't to be. You sure sit on her plenty when there's any work to be done," drawled Bub Jensen, shifting his rifle across the pommel. A solid figure in reversible leather breeches and an ill-fitting uniform coat, he sat a big raw-boned nag marked by collar galls on either side of its shaggy neck.

"Say—" Leeming began, but Phipp cut in hurriedly.

"You show a commendable zeal, Heinz, but your horse is played out. Oh, one more thing. From now on all ranks of the Independent Companies will wear either a red sash or a red cockade to muster. Order has just come down from Williamsburg."

Bub looked up, grinning. "You mean we can wear sashes 'round our bellies, Mr. Matt?"

"No. Over your right shoulder and knotted over the left hip. But I wouldn't worry, Bub, you'll still be giving the girls a treat."

Leeming sniggered. "Say, speakin' of the girls, who's for a little canter down Avon Street? A bark made port from Dominica yesterday; brought some Creole huzzies for French Annie's parlor. Luke Williams says they was pretty as speckled pups."

Balefully Phipp regarded his sergeant. "Haven't you enough bastards playing around Norfolk Borough already?"

"Jesus, no, Lieutenant. A poor man's pleasures ain't many, but havin' fun with a girl is somethin' he don't have to pay for—not if he knows his way about. Where was it you said we was to muster?"

"Thoroughgood's, I said. Men having sabers or swords or carbines will bring them. Every trooper will carry two pistols, six flints and a half pound of powder. Canteens and bullets will be served out."

Heinz straightened, blinking worriedly. "You said a half pound of powder, sir?"

"Yes. In a weatherproof horn or flask. What's wrong?"

"Dunno as I can scrape so much together. Powder nowadays is right scarce. The British Pharaoh's provost marshal has been sending his helots around to take up every speck."

"That's right," Bub volunteered, nodding his big head. "Some lobster-backs off the ships busted right into Mr. Granby's shop and confi—confica—took away all he had yesterday. Didn't pay for it neither, 'cept with a piece of paper."

Phipp shivered. He was chilled clean through and would probably come down with a cold. "Well then, bring as much as you can, Heinz. Dis-missed!" He tried to give the command a brisk and military ring, the way Captain Brush did. But it didn't sound quite right. When he got home he would have to practice some more.

"Good night, Lieutenant, sir." The book binder, drawing himself up, executed a wide gesture intended for a salute. His earnestness set up a twitching at Phipp's mouth corners. The poor damned fool must be thinking he was a soldier already!

Well, the sooner Heinz and the rest of the Independent Company learned their mistake, the better.

"Good night, Matt," Leeming called, further ruffling Phipp's temper. Damn the fellow! He was one of those exasperating lickspittles who, whenever he dared, presumed on boyhood acquaintance to call superiors by their given name.

"Bye, Bub," Leeming nodded, big teeth tearing a twist of tobacco. "I'll be keepin' one o' them Creoles warm 'case you show up."

Phipp gathered his reins. "Oh, for God's sake, Leeming, hush your mouth and go home! Come along, Bub."

The lawyer rode off at a walk, following the right fork of a road leading towards the Glebe Creek side of Norfolk.

Bub snuffled disconsolately into his scarf. He knew Mr. Matt was due at a meeting somewhere in town and he had been hoping the lawyer would maybe stand him to a tankard at the Spread Eagle. He hadn't the price himself and Ed Leeming never stood treat to nobody. Yup. A piece of cheese and some of Tom MacSherry's ale would slip down right easy.

Cripes! A northeaster like this went through a feller like salts through a goose. What was a Creole? An Indian of some sort, maybe? If that was so, Leeming must be lying; long hunters and the backwoods people let on Indian squaws weren't much good. Not much tits to a squaw, they said, and they stinked something fierce.

"Pull up!" Phipp warned in a sudden undertone. "Can you tell what's going on?"

Bub, rousing, saw that a pinpoint of light had appeared 'way off down the road. Steadily it bobbed up and down. He straightened in his saddle.

"It's soljers. I kin see red coats and muskit barrels flashin'." Bub was proud of his good eyes.

"Sure?"

"Yessiree! What do you reckon them Britishers are up to, Mr. Matt? At this time of night?"

"That is what we are going to find out," the lieutenant softly informed him.

As the light drew nearer, a faint and dismal creaking began to be heard.

"Hadn't we better ride off in the woods, Mr. Matt? Or maybe ride in town ahead of 'em? Might git ourselves in trouble."

"No. Stay still." Phipp spoke sharply. He was occupied in trying to estimate the strength of the detachment. They would be about eight or ten in number, he judged, and led by a tall sergeant carrying a box lantern. If a commissioned officer were in command, he wasn't to be seen, so, patting his mare's shivering withers, Phipp waited. The detail tramped nearer, marching at ease and carrying their muskets to suit themselves, all except a big private pushing a creaking, heavily loaded handbarrow.

From their white tunic facings and lace, the redcoats were marines, not regular infantry. Phipp now was able to distinguish curious low caps of scarlet. He had never seen any like them before. To the front of each brimless cap was fixed a visor-shaped pewter plate bearing a monogram. Big pewter buckles stamped with an anchor secured the intersection of white crossbelts. The marines were marching with bayonets fixed, forming a rough square about a prisoner who, despite the biting wind, wore only breeches and shirt.

Bub, staring ill-at-ease, kept hoping Mr. Matt would ride off, but he sure pitied that prisoner. He was a big, thick-limbed fellow and the wind was blowing his unbound hair all over his face. He clumped along with head hanging on breast. No wonder. About the captive's neck a length of fuzzy old rope had been knotted and his powerful-looking arms were lashed behind him. Every now and then one of the marines would lower his musket and give the bound man a little jab with his bayonet, not for any particular reason, but merely to see him wince. Through hair on the prisoner's left leg, bared where his white woolen stockings had fallen, two dark lines were meandering down into his shoe.

Suddenly aware of the two horsemen waiting in the lee of a bank, the sergeant ordered his detachment to halt. Silvered buttons on his cuff glistened as he saluted.

"Begging yer pardon, sir. Is it much further into Norfolk? The leftenant marched us out by a different road."

"No," Phipp told him. "Only about two miles. You are in command?"

"Yes, sir. The leftenant got cold and rode on into town."

"Two miles? Oh, Jesus!" panted the man at the handbarrow. " 'Ere, Beaky, you wheel this bloody back-breaker awhile. I've done my trick."

By spurring his mare further out onto the road, Phipp was able to see what the handbarrow contained. A keg of French

42

powder—"Charleville Premier Qualité" was stenciled in white on its end—three or four pistols, and maybe half a dozen rusty old muskets and Spanish fuzees.

"That's a fine animal, sir," the sergeant remarked as, setting his lantern on the ground, he began methodically to adjust a most unmilitary blue and white muffler about his neck. A private, standing to one side, furtively slipped a long-necked bottle from a back breeches pocket into his coat-tail; carefully he tested its cork with his thumb. Another of the marines was trying to cram a case of sailmaker's needles into his cartridge box.

"See you've been busy," was Phipp's dry comment.

"Aye, sir. An informer warned the provost marshal there was illegal arms concealed in Pitson's boat house. We dropped in after dark." He glanced at the barrow, then at the shivering prisoner. "Fancy. We found this here Aaron Weaver hiding in the sail loft, and him carrying three pound reward on his head."

"A deserter?"

"Yes. Jumped the *Liverpool* frigate five days back, he did, which he'll live to regret."

"Three pound for us," one of the marines amplified, "and, since it's second offense, three hundred with the cat for him."

Quick as a released spring, the prisoner spun half about, got free and ran over to raise a desperate, quivering face beside the mare's shoulder. "Save me, sir! For God's sake, save me! The cat—they—they'll cut me to ribbons with it this time. Oh God! God! I—I can't stand it again. They'll kill me!"

In Weaver's terror Matt Phipp recognized a frantic, animal-like quality. The back of his neck began to tingle. The man's panic was all the more dreadful because his was essentially a strong, kindly face suggestive of habitual self-control.

"Why did you desert?"

"I never enlisted," the prisoner gurgled. "They'd never the right to take me! I'm not a Britisher sir; I'm a free, law-abiding citizen of Massachusetts." A tear began to course uglily down the prisoner's swollen cheeks and his chin quivered pitifully. Snarling annoyance, his guards closed in. Weaver flinched closer to Matt Phipp's horse. "You're Provincial, too. For the love of God, do something! Save me! They'll flog me to death aboard the ship. Sackville's a devil! My family's starv—"

Weaver's voice choked off abruptly. A weasel-faced corporal had recaptured the halter end, gave it so vicious a yank he pulled the prisoner sprawling backward across the road's frozen ruts. At once the other guards joined in dealing the fallen wretch a series of kicks. Their black spatterdashes, or knee high gaiters, swung hard.

"Stow it, Pepperill," grunted the sergeant, picking up the lantern. "He'll get his aboard the *Liverpool*."

Another jerk of the halter heaved Weaver, half strangled, to his feet. He stood there, swaying, chin marked by a thread of blood. In an agony of terror, his eyes sought Phipp's, but the Virginian's expression remained blank.

Said he, "On occasion all of us meet with bad luck. A smart man makes the best of it."

Like light from a blown-out lamp hope vanished from the prisoner's eyes and his body resumed its slack, beaten attitude.

The sergeant coughed, husked and then spat. "Nah then, you mothers' mistakes. Form *threes!*"

While the rest of the scarlet-clad detail fell in, the marine whose turn it was at the handbarrow slipped out of his crossbelts and laid them on the load with his cartridge box and bayonet. Muttering he undid the silvered buttons of his tunic so far down that a hairy mat burst through the white facings.

"Come along, Mister Three Pound Reward." When the corporal holding the prisoner's lead rope gave it a tug, Weaver moved off, limping heavily.

Phipp nodded a silent farewell. Bub's blank-looking brown eyes clung fascinated to the stumbling prisoner.

The marine detachment, Phipp noticed, was moving at a faster pace. They seemed uneasy, too; kept looking off into the gloom and marched closed in together. Rhythmically their muddied black gaiters swung back and forth behind the sergeant's lantern. They seemed eager to reach the security of Norfolk.

"They act scared," Phipp told Bub. "Maybe they'll have reason to be."

When he and his companion had ridden a hundred yards down the road, Phipp said, "You turn back home, Bub. That crow bait you're aboard of is getting ready to quit."

"But Mr. Matt," Bub began, disappointment puckering his

red moon of a face, "I—I'm tolerably thirsty, and you said—"

"—You'll get a double ration of ale tomorrow. Do as I say and take that nag back slow. You had better not wait up for me."

Phipp, glancing over his shoulder, could yet see the British sergeant's lantern, but it was again just a yellow pinpoint down the King's Highway. Still shaken by that awful fear in Weaver's face, he turned his mount off the road. He reckoned if he could reach Norfolk inside of twenty minutes, something might be done.

The mare's hoofs rang crisply hollow as he spurred her across a frozen field littered with dead tobacco stalks, drooping suckers, and broken tobacco sticks. With the wind tearing at his hat, Phipp put his mount at a rail fence. His heart lifted in sudden doubt but, tired as she was, the mare sailed it like a frightened doe.

6 — GAMECOCKS AT THE SPREAD EAGLE

NEW and solidly built of brick, the Spread Eagle Ordinary loomed flush to a narrow brick sidewalk separating it from the mire and often pig-infested bog holes of Cumberland Street.

Tom MacSherry was inordinately proud of his tavern's leaded windows, of the blue and white eagle screaming on its signboard, of its pine-paneled taproom, and of a huge roasting spit in his kitchen. A fat old mongrel, running on a treadmill, turned it. The Spread Eagle's six comfortable beds could, and often did, accommodate as many as eighteen travelers. But MacSherry's greatest pride was what he called the "four-barreled" privy out back. It was brick, too, and had a flagstone walk leading to it clear across the backyard.

"No standing in line of a morning for my guests," he boasted, looking Ma Coverly, who ran the Harp and Crown at the corner of First and Mariner Streets, bang in the eye.

Lulled by dancing flames and the spicy odor of Madeira mulling on a little brass trivet, David Ashton mused on his favorite seat by the taproom's chimney corner. Only vaguely Rob Ashton's brother heard an occasional horse go clip-clopping over the frozen mud of Cumberland Street, the distant rattle of some watchman's staff as he dragged it along a picket fence, and the soft *slap-slap* of cards falling on the other side of the room.

Um. John Holt had printed in his paper that Boston was remaining rebellious. Parliament was threatening the town with a more stringent military occupation. Those Yankees surely seemed to believe in themselves.

When voices sounded outside the inn door, he sat up, surprisingly alert. Tom MacSherry heard them too, and hitched a leather apron more squarely over a belly which, during his progress to the door, juggled gently under a red and white striped waistcoat. The whist players—a quartet of Scots, David judged from their lack of conversation—turned, eyes following a half grown Negro boy who had come running out of the kitchen.

But David Ashton didn't look. Instead, he abstractedly watched the barmaid dab at her stringy yellow hair, smooth her apron and rearrange a set of dingy ruffles edging her bosom. He smiled faintly at the familiar routine. Katie wouldn't be a bad looking piece, ran the undercurrent of his thoughts, if she'd half take care of her appearance. The wench had been blessed with a luscious, almost Junoesque figure and her regular features bore an inexplicable suggestion of breeding. She had, moreover, a complexion most women would give their best earbobs to possess. But what attracted him most to Katie was the genuine warmth of her smile and certain changeable lights in her very wide-set gray-green eyes. Lucky their lashes were long and several shades darker than the girl's tawny mane.

Absently David speculated on the date upon which Katie might elect to replace that beer splashed blouse and her oft-spotted blue and white calico skirt. She was a sly piece, though. When she bent to mop the lead-topped bar, he could see her biting her lips to deepen their redness.

"Your corporal is late tonight. On duty, or has that sergeant of marines put his nose out of joint?"

"Oh, no sir," replied Katie demurely and breathed with ecstatic vigor upon the tumbler she was polishing. "Mr. Pepperill and me still keeps company. He's a great comfort, is Mr. Pepperill, and *that* open-handed you wouldn't believe it. He was ordered out tonight on duty," she added, "so I ain't expecting him 'til late."

She fixed a look, unconsciously wistful, on David Ashton's

six feet of stature as, garbed in an elegant bottle-green satin coat and white silk breeches, he lounged not ungracefully across the chimney corner bench. For a thousandth time she noticed how his right brow, set a bit higher than its companion, lent young Mr. Ashton a quizzical expression. It set girls a-sighing. And the way the dark brown hair grew into a point on his forehead. It wasn't powdered tonight, but was neatly clubbed at the nape of his neck with a broad, swallow-tailed grosgrain ribbon of Lincoln green. She pondered again what kind of weapon could have given his rather thick nose that slight swerve to the left. Once more she decided that it was attractive, rather than disfiguring.

"So your corporal is off a-serving of our Most Gracious Sovereign? Fixing to marry him, Katie?"

"Oh la, sir, Mr. Pepperill will do for a—a passing fancy, but when I tie up, I'm wanting someone better." The barmaid blushed and peered intently into a copper pint pot set among an uneven rank of vessels before her. "Some chap with a bit of quality to him."

"And it's quality you ought to have, my sweet. Such a complexion and figure would be wasted—thrown away, on a hang-dog enlisted man." He leaned forward, elbows on table and gray-blue eyes mocking. "Out of curiosity, Katie; just when did you last take a bath?"

"Oh la, sir, that was in October. River water's been colder'n Blixen ever since."

"Did you ever consider heating any?" David queried, tapping strong white teeth against the mouthpiece of a German porcelain pipe he favored.

"La, Mr. Ashton," protested the girl in frank surprise, "wouldn't that be getting above myself?"

"And why so, O fairest of Lord Bacchus's handmaidens?"

Katie giggled. "Oh la, Mr. Ashton, how you do run on! Why, Mrs. Rogers, the parson's wife, she takes an all-over once a month, but *she's* quality!"

"Even quality has its gradations," David murmured. "Soap and hot water seldom prove fatal to barmaids; my word on it."

Katie halted her mop cloth and stared, red lips parted uncertainly.

"I vow I've been intrigued by a certain smudge lodging behind your left ear," David continued in lazy amusement.

"Don't suppose you recall when it got there? It was the night Hannibal beat Mr. Love's silver hackle—a fortnight since—"

"Oh la, Mr. Ashton!" The barmaid's easy smile glistened. "That *were* a good bout. Mr. Pepperill, he won—"

"—Pray forget about the chicken fight, Katie. The subject of this discourse is hot water. You are, I believe, aware of how often I bathe?"

Katie ducked her yellow head and, giggling, returned to her tumblers. She knew, none better. Every other day she toted a tin bath and seven pails of scalding water to the young gentleman's semi-permanent quarters upstairs.

A deep sort, Mr. Ashton, she reflected. A girl couldn't ever tell what he was really thinking, or how much he meant of what he said; and he said the funniest things. The funniest thing of all about him was the way he kept his hands to himself. On occasion she had experienced a secret sense of grievance. Maybe she wasn't good enough for a young gentleman who had once been a rake-hell about London? Maybe that was it, but every other buck in town, young or old, would get his hand under her petticoats given half the chance. Not that she minded it a great deal. That was as much a part of her job as the squeal and half slap she gave in return.

Working for Mr. MacSherry wasn't bad, indeed not! It was a sight better than slaving for that old bitch, Ma Skillings, who would flog a girl on her bare bottom if she so much as spilled a grain of salt. And Mr. Skillings! The mere recollection of his clammy hands made her shudder.

Of course, there were things about working at the Spread Eagle she didn't really like, either. Some evenings Mr. MacSherry expected her to fetch a hot toddy up to a rich planter—and stay for a while. Of course, these gentlemen made her presents. Why, young Mr. Lovelace who owned Esmeralda 'way up the Elizabeth River even gave her a little gold locket. But she didn't like staying. Funny, Corporal Pepperill didn't mind her pleasuring with the planters. She even suspected him of dropping a hint now and then to some of his officers. Could a girl ever really understand a man?

Her thoughts raced on, keeping pace with her busy hands. When the day came and somebody who *was* somebody married her, she'd never so much as look at another man. Never. She didn't care about looking at men, anyway—indeed she didn't. In proof of which she found herself looking at Mr. David Mountford Ashton. Now why should an elegant gentleman like him be lonely? But lonely he was tonight and no mistake, in spite of that be-damned-to-you look in his lazy gray-blue eyes.

The spit dog which had been asleep under one of the tables sprang up barking as, on the threshold, appeared a widely grinning Negro in wide canvas breeches and red and white striped jersey. He loomed tall as a giant. Golden earrings and the six large brass buttons on his blue shell jacket gleamed when he entered, carrying a wooden clotheschest under each arm.

"Good evening, Plato," Ashton glanced up. "Mr. Leavitt in town?"

"Yessuh, Misto' Ashton. He right behin' me, suh. He near froze to deaf—"

"Heyo, Davey!"

"Heyo, George! Damn my blood, but I'm glad to see you!"

Into the taproom stepped a broad-shouldered gentleman nearing forty. He was beginning to put on fat, but his build yet suggested activity and alertness. Above the collar of his mulberry hued surtout Mr. George Leavitt's features, still lean of outline, shone a peculiar copper-red. High and prominent cheekbones, straight jet hair, and eyes of the same hue prompted the assumption that, a few generations ago some Leavitt had taken a squaw to share his cabin.

"Well, Davey. How's the bully boy tonight?" he called, limping the length of the taproom. Doc Gordon had never been able to extract the Frenchman's bullet from his knee joint. "Hell's fire! It's fit to freeze a man's heart out on the river—damned tide was running dead against us towards the last."

After shaking hands, he stamped over to the fire to toast legs encased in leggins of oiled deerskin. Sleet clung in silver beads to the planter's cocked hat, to the bright red cockade on it, and to the three short capes of his surtout.

"Katie! A brace of rumbullions! Fast as you can brew 'em!"

"Welcome. La, Mr. Leavitt, you are looking real elegant tonight." Katie came bouncing out from the bar and bobbed an awkward curtsy. Easy-going Mr. Leavitt was a favorite of hers and was, without question, the most generous of the James River planters who from time to time liked a drink "brought up late."

"How's my darling chick tonight?" Laughing, Leavitt flung

an arm about Katie's waist and, without effort, heaved her up to a seat on the bar. Her breathless giggles grew louder when, after fumbling in his pocket, Leavitt pulled out some money and began to grope beneath the grimy hems of her voluminous petticoats. "Dammit, wench, where *is* that garter?"

"Oh, sir, like me, it's just become undone." Laughing, she made to push him away.

"Then, ducky, it's lucky you have two legs."

"Oh-h, sir, please don't! Your hand's too cold!"

The card players and a couple of mahogany-faced sea captains, who had been witnessing Leavitt's arrival with more than casual interest, turned, grinning. Katie's long legs, even in holey white cotton stockings, were pleasingly rounded. Perched on the edge of the bar as she was, their whole length became visible ere a two shilling note found its traditional resting place.

"Oh, Mr. Leavitt, ain't you awful?" Katie wriggled down and, laughing, ran for the shelter of the bar.

"And now, my dear, don't forget those rumbullions. Ask the other gentlemen present what they fancy."

Brows puckered, Katie revolved the two shilling note between her fingers. "Please, Mr. Leavitt, what's this?"

"A spotless specimen of the newest currency, my dear. Virginia's best, and quoted at a par with sterling. It is, my chick, sound as the Bible, so don't go fretting." He dropped onto a seat beside Ashton and inquired in an undertone, "You reached the others?"

"Yes. That's Captain Rudder yonder on the left. The other is Peart. Matthew Phipp and the rest should all be here by ten. You've news for 'em?"

"News enough, Davey, news enough! Thank God, I've time to thaw out and to win a couple of pounds."

Two more slaves dressed like Plato came shuffling in, their skins gone slate gray with cold. One carried a portmanteau and the other lugged a bundle, shapeless because it was so swathed in blankets.

"Hey, you, Crambo! Take that stuff upstairs. You, Virgil, take Ginger into the kitchen to get warm."

David's crooked brow arose. "What have you got in there? The last remaining virgin along the Jeems?"

A low, wicked, delightful chuckle arose from Leavitt. "What Virgil carries, my boy, is the one and only gamecock along the Chesapeake who can whip the lights and livers out of Hannibal!"

"So?" David's dark face was losing its lonesome look. "I presume you have more of that pretty new currency?"

Briskly the plump planter rubbed his hands. "Aye, but I'm warning you, Davey, Ginger's a regular hellion. He killed Billy Rountree's Caesar last week and never got scratched himself. How's your bird?"

"Hannibal and I stand eager to oblige."

"There, Mr. Leavitt, I put enough Jamaica and Barbados in this to thaw you out from head to foot." Katie smiled, offering a huge, steaming rummer, bright with strips of orange and lemon peel and sprinkled with cloves and bits of cinnamon. "I warrant it'll warm your best friend, too."

"He can stand a bit of thawing," the planter agreed, black eyes a-glitter. "Well, Davey, here's a hot corner of hell for a certain Scotch factor!"

David noticed that one of the whist players, a small man whose face under an untidy scratch wig looked wizened and brown as a walnut, turned and looked hard at Leavitt over his shoulder.

"Fergus Sandys been threatening again?" he inquired.

The copper-skinned planter jerked a gloomy nod and his shadow mimicked him on the pine paneling behind. "Yes. I don't reckon that damned leech will be satisfied 'till he's picked me clean as the Campbells plucked Lucius Sykes. Maybe you didn't hear? On a week's notice they foreclosed on Portabello. Confounded Shylocks didn't leave Loosh so much as a nigger cabin to his name. Remember Dancey Vance below Westover? Well, last month the Scotch—rat 'em all—took his place away. Dancey was a hard worker and the smartest planter on the river, but two bad crops in a row gave the skinflints in Aberdeen their chance."

"What's happened to him?"

"Poor devil went out to Kentucky. The Indians scalped him and all his folks." Leavitt's black eyes, staring into the leaping flames, glittered not quite like a white man's.

"Take me. Fifteen years ago my father needed hard cash to buy a gang of field hands. He borrowed five hundred Spanish dollars from Fergus Sandys so today I am up to my ears in debt to Balfour & Bannard; his people in Glasgow. Right now I'm damned if I know whether I'll find even the interest."

"La, Mr. Leavitt, that's plain tootle, ain't it?" Katie burst out from behind the bar. "Why everybody knows you own a thousand acres of the primest tobacco land along the Jeems; and a big passel of niggers to work it."

"Quite so," Leavitt sighed. "That's the devil of it, ducky. It requires money, a lot of it, to run a plantation the size of Powhatan." He turned his head towards the landlord who had just entered, bringing with him an aura of cold air. "Tom, how much money—silver and gold coin, that is—do you take in these days?"

"Precious little," the innkeeper admitted. "Just provincial notes and bills of exchange on the Sugar Islands. South of Philadelphia hard money is getting right scarce." MacSherry, pursing fat lips, blew the foam from a tankard of ale and swallowed gravely. Said he, "But why do you go on buying through factors, Mr. Leavitt? Everyone knows they skin you planters something shameful."

"Because I can't buy supplies direct."

"Why not?"

"Because, as you've just said, there's very little gold or silver to be had in the Southern Colonies. The English merchants won't pay us planters in cash—only in credit against our tobacco. They advance us too much credit for our own good. Most English and some Scotch bankers charge no interest at all for the first two months and only five per cent after that. Credit, but no cash; that's their motto."

"But why won't they pay in cash?" David inquired curiously.

"Well, Davey, I reckon they figure us Virginians might want to trade abroad where we can buy cheaper. Hell's fire! It's for the same reason we ain't allowed to sell tobacco anywhere but in England!"

"It's a crying shame," MacSherry agreed solemnly.

"It's an outrage," David commented. "But a clever outrage."

Patches of bright red were appearing on Leavitt's cheekbones. "Think so? Well, wait 'til you hear of Fergus Sandys' latest trick. He has just written offering *not* to foreclose!"

"Trick? Not foreclose? Damme, George, I don't follow your reasoning."

"No, he won't foreclose—bless his withered old Scotch heart—not if I sell my whole crop to him alone!"

"Well, what's wrong with that?" David asked curiously. "Tobacco prices are up."

"Sandys won't foreclose on condition I sell him all my Aronoko at *twenty per cent* off the market price!" Leavitt explained bitterly.

"Twenty per cent!" David's jaw sagged. "You can't mean it, George! You're funning me."

"Wish to God I were," was the planter's gloomy rejoinder. "I reckon it's partly my fault; every Leavitt I've ever heard tell of would liefer ride to hounds than study accounts. Most of us planters would. But the factors are to blame a lot more." Leavitt drank a deep gulp of his drink. "The story goes like this: When a crop is in and cured, some canting Jack Presbyter with a meek smile and a nimble tongue comes sailing up from Norfolk.

"'Yon's a verra splendid crop!'" Cleverly Leavitt mimicked a Scot's nasal tones. "'Yer in luck, Mr. Leavitt, indeed ye are. Yon 'backy wull fetch top prices i' England—twelve poond' the hogshead, I'll be bound. Yer in luck, too, freight rates are doon so low they are touching bottom. Assurances? Mon alive! They're lower than the bottom o' the Atlantic. Noo, Mr. Leavitt, what merchandise can Balfour & Bannard pick up fer ye abroad? A spinnet for Mistress Kitty? A set o' the classics for young Master Jerry? They're selling them noo for on'y fifty poond'. Of course, ye'll be wanting new wardrobes for a' the family. And for you, Mr. Leavitt, how aboot a cabinet o' rare French wines? Or maybe yer fancying a new chaise? Mr. Brandon has ordered one—only £500—'"

Angrily, Leavitt finished his drink and ordered two more. "Four or five months later comes Chapter Two. I receive a letter like this:

'Norfolk
October 10, 1773.

Most Respected Sir:

Messrs. Balfour & Bannard deeply regret to inform you that due to an unfortunate and unexpected glut on the London tobacco Exchange, your crop brought £2,000 less than we most confidently expected. It is the more Unfortunate because, as a result of certain troubles with the Spanish King's ships, freight Rates have mounted ten per centum. North Atlantic Assurances are up twenty per centum.

We take great pleasure in Reporting our success in executing your valued Commissions abroad. The Goods have arrived safely and in good condition. Shipment is being made this day per sloop *Polly*.

> Your humble obedient servant,
> . Fergus Sandys.' "

Leavitt sighed, made a spreading motion of his hands denoting helplessness. "Again I fancy we planters are to blame. We never should accept goods at a dearer price than we ordered them at—and, mark you, they always *are* dearer!"

"Well, why do you?"

"Hang it all, Davey, it's deuced hard to face waiting four more months for needed supplies. The women folks won't hear of a further delay. But we upriver men are getting tired of such dodges." Leavitt's forefinger indicated the scarlet cockade on his hat. "See that? Well, we're all wearing one of these, or a blue and buff one—the Whig colors. We are in earnest in one point. We will not rest 'til Parliament curbs these blood-sucking factors, and outlaws inherited debts."

"I'll no' listen to mair o' this zany chitter-chatter!" The card player who had turned before sprang up. "What call ha'e you proud and lazy gentlemen to greet? 'Tis we Scots wurrk oor eyes oot; 'tis we deny oorsel'es every pleasure. 'Tis we risk oor lives on the sea."

David Ashton, deliberately turning, inquired with insulting politeness, "Who might you be?"

"Gordon MacLeod, chief bookkeeper to John Brown."

"Pray proceed." David was curious. What might the factors and their adherents be thinking? With a few notable exceptions they controlled the trade of Norfolk.

"If it were no' for we Scots," snapped the nut-faced man, "there wouldn' be tuppence worth o' trade done in a' Virginia. A fine pack you provincial planters make wi' yer lazy evil ways, yer gambling and yer wenching! 'Tis we must gamble if or no' some French or Spanish privateer doesna' seize oor ships and goods. Who keeps the currency in order? Who finds the monies to fight yer plaguy frontier wars?"

"Maybe your sort do find the money," David Ashton admitted coolly, "but who gets killed keeping the savages in order? Who goes into debt for the privilege?"

MacSherry came bustling forward, a fixed smile decorating ruddy features. "Come, come, gentlemen. No bickering, please. Have you heard, Mr. Leavitt? Tom Newton is betting five dollars to three on Mr. Ashton's bird."

"Let us hope such confidence will be rewarded," David laughed, aware now that, quietly enough, two gentlemen in dark green riding cloaks had come in.

"Tom Newton and Johnny Gilmorin," David murmured.

Giving Leavitt and Ashton all but imperceptible nods, they sought another table. Meanwhile, the Scotch bookkeeper paid his bill and stalked out, muttering.

"Your bird fit, George?" David queried.

"Fit as a fiddle. Plato kept hot bricks under his cage."

MacSherry, hugely delighted, bawled, "Porters!" so loud a trio of black boys came tumbling out of the kitchen with cornmeal mush all over their thick lips.

"Bun-nose, you slip over to the Indian Queen and let folks know Mr. Ashton's Hannibal is matched. Jerry, wipe your nose and pass the word over at the Harp and Crown. If any gentleman has a bird to match, tell him he's to fetch it along."

Half an hour later the low-ceilinged taproom reeked of tobacco smoke, wet wool, liquor fumes and pungent body odors. Already two pairs of stags—green birds never before pitted—had been matched and fought.

"Number two was a real fast fight," Captain Ben Rudder opined. He looked very spruce and well set up in a suit of new sea-going serge. "Kind of like a couple of privateer sloops in action."

Katie, hard put to fill so many mugs and tankards, was sweating like a June bride, as Tom Newton put it.

Small feathers drifted about, settling on men's coats and in their hair and soon bright blood specks began to stain the sanded floor of the inn's portable pit. When it came time for the main bout, smoke hung in a blue nimbus about a huge ship's lantern suspended from the rafters. The atmosphere would have been worse, but the door kept opening and shutting. The spit dog, banished to the backyard in the interests of fair play, mourned as a bitter sleet squall stung him.

Towards the end of the second bout Katie's marine corporal, blue-lipped and running at the nose, pushed his way into the ordinary and, stripping off his scarlet tunic, tied a green baize apron about his middle. Whistling cheerily, he set to work at Katie's side, very matter-of-fact.

"You're late tonight, Mr. Pepperill," she chided, slapping aside the hand with which he pinched her rear.

"We was ordered out without notice." He wiped his sharp little nose on his sleeve and gave her a sly, foxy look. "Took a bleedin' deserter, we did; means three quid split among eight."

"Then I can have the blue petticoat?"

He nodded half heartedly. "Ye'd do better with a ribbon for yer hair. Looks like a bloomin' last year's rat nest." Though perspiration had beaded Katie's features and was staining dark half moons under her bodice's arm holes, Pepperill cast her a lecherous look. "Gawd, ducky, yer a sight for sore eyes. When will MacSherry leave you go?"

"With this main on 'twon't be until late. You're tired, Mike. Why don't you go up to the loft? I'll wake you when I come in." She hoped he didn't notice her crossed fingers. Since five-thirty that morning she'd been on her feet, scrubbing the taproom floor, washing dishes, tidying up the bedchambers and tending bar when Mr. MacSherry was too busy.

The corporal nodded and went on washing tumblers. "All right. But for Gawd's sake, wash yer neck. You smell like a mink."

"Dirty Shirts was riding tonight," he volunteered. "Sergeant heard they mustered down to Thoroughgood's."

David Ashton, lace cuffs stripped back from forearms dark with hair was entirely serious for once. He used a piece of broken glass to scrape Hannibal's spurs to a carefully calculated point. The horny growths were thin now and keen; nearly as deadly as the steel gaffs favored in the West Indies.

MacSherry beamed, roared welcome; rum and Holland gin were going faster than ale now.

David, satisfied, tucked his bird under one arm and, after relighting his queer porcelain pipe, called, "Heyo, George! Reckon we're ready." The red bird pecked savagely at his wrist, then flicked his head, glaring defiance at the crowd from clear, sherry-colored eyes.

The fanciers crowded in. "Ain't the red quill an ornery little cuss?" "Look at them spurs." "And them eyes! Crooler nor old Satan's." "Some bird, Mr. Ashton; good luck to ye." "Who'll take two to one on the red quill?"

"Weights, gi'e us weights," called some renegade Scot. "I'll no' bet 'til we hear the weight."

Leavitt's bird, a wiry Dominique, weighed four pounds six ounces, giving him an advantage of three ounces. This caused some shifting of odds, but confidence never deserted David's dark, intense face.

"Rush it to him, General," he whispered while lifting Hannibal, restless and belligerent, off the scales. "Our war chest is getting mighty low."

The crowd had begun to shove and jostle good-naturedly for position.

Across the pit of yellow pine planks George Leavitt, stripped to his ruffled shirt, perspired profusely in trimming his rangy white Dominique. Lips compressed, the planter was deftly shortening his bird's longest wing feathers lest, when the cock tired, his pinions might foul the enemy's spurs. Watched by anxious backers, the Indian-like planter then trimmed his bird's ruff. This would make it hard for red-eyed Hannibal to find a hold. Leavitt's eyes shone beady now, very steady between narrowed lids; but his hands quivered just a little. Katie reckoned this bout must mean plenty to the master of Powhatan.

Serious, but still smiling, David elbowed a path to the pit and stepped into it. His pump heels made a soft grating sound on the sand. To see better, Katie and her corporal climbed onto the bar.

"Will you judge, Tom?" David asked MacSherry, then hastily added, "You agreeable, George?"

Leavitt, busy biting gently at Ginger's close-clipped comb, nodded his narrow blue-black head. The white cock struggled, glaring at the glossy red-brown bird between David's hands.

"Stand back gents! Don't crowd the pit!" The innkeeper bent, puffing a little, and used a spoon handle to divide the freshly sanded floor into halves, then he waved the owners to diagonally opposite corners of the pit. MacSherry looked first at Leavitt, then at David. "Finish fight, or best of three rounds?"

"Finish!" simultaneously agreed the owners.

"Now stand back, gents! Please stand back. These here birds can't fight if you don't give 'em room.

"Gentlemen, bill your cocks!" MacSherry called and in an instant silence fell. Briefly the two birds were held at arm's

57

length, just close enough to permit them to peck at each other. Between his hands David could feel Hannibal's muscles tightening, the bird's whole wiry body a-quiver. It was just as well; his shot at the Spread Eagle hadn't been paid in two weeks.

"On the line!" MacSherry ordered. Sinking onto their heels in their respective corners, the owners set their birds on the floor, but still restrained them.

"One—two—three. Go!"

Leavitt and Ashton stood up, hands flung wide apart, watching. At their feet a feathered tornado was sweeping the floor. Mouths open, the onlookers surged forward and began to yell.

Twice, thrice, the fighting cocks leaped into the air, fanning shortened wings in a furious effort to maintain equilibrium. Meanwhile, their legs worked in a series of lightning jabs driving the spurs forward. Only the trained eyes of veteran fanciers could follow such a rain of blows. Almost at once, however, the knowing began to offer odds as one gamecock or the other got in a telling blow.

"Three to five on the red! Three to five on Ashton!"

"Take you!"

"Ten shillings even money on the Dom!"

"Done!"

The first flurry did no real damage, left both warriors circling, necks outstretched, clipped ruffs flaring. Lazily, white feathers and red went drifting off among the damp and muddy feet of the onlookers.

David glanced up, caught George Leavitt's dark eyes. "Ten pounds more?"

"Damme, make it twenty! Ginger is stronger!"

"Done!"

Another two flurries slowed the cocks enough to make them pause and glare at each other. They held their wings half extended for better balance. A sudden shout made pewter mugs along the walls rattle. The Dominique had charged and, fighting a savage flurry, tumbled Hannibal onto his back. In a flash the white gamecock sprang up on his enemy, pecking and slashing like a demon in feathers.

Odds on Hannibal sagged. Exasperated curses began to rap out.

"Four tae three on yon white fowl!" croaked the Scot.

58

"Done!" snapped Tom Newton, biting his lip.

At length Hannibal, badly punished, broke loose and, shuffling, squared off again.

"Five pounds more?" David's nostrils were pinched looking when he shot his question at Leavitt.

The planter, squatting on his heels, merely jerked a nod.

In a murderous hurry to press his advantage, the Dominique charged in and, rising into the air, made a buzz saw of his spurs. Instead of rising to meet him, Hannibal this time ducked, passed cleanly under his adversary.

No sooner had the white, disconcerted, landed off balance, than the red bird pounced on his back and drove a spur into the upriver gamecock's neck. A resounding roar billowed about the taproom. Bright scarlet blood spurting from among his feathers, the Dominique floundered and made a valiant effort to stand. He ended by toppling crazily onto his side. Panting, punished by Hannibal's relentless spurs and beak, he tried to scrabble away, but the keel of his breast only sketched a pathetic groove through the scattered sand and feathers.

Leavitt, bending low, set up a staccato, *"Cuck! Cuck!"* like that of a hen.

"Finish 'im! Finish!" screeched the red quill's backers.

MacSherry dropped onto one knee. The way he was going, Hannibal might get fast into the other cock. If he did, the birds must be parted and Mr. Leavitt would be allowed to "handle" his bird.

A red feathered Nemesis, Hannibal began worrying the white chicken's eyes with his beak.

"Ten tae one on the red!" bawled the Scot, sweating at every pore. He only raised a laugh. Everyone could hear the breath rattling hollow in the white bird's throat. When the Dominique's head sank onto the sand, mugs hanging to the rafters rattled to the great yell David gave.

Tautly, Hannibal was strutting, one fiery eye fixed on the ungainly snarl of pinkish red feathers. At last the red bird threw back his head, beat his wings and emitted a strident crow. The crowd bellowed, pounded one another on the back, called each other to witness.

Still smiling, David lifted his bird. Gleefully he suffered a series of vicious pecks delivered when he began sponging off Hannibal's cuts with a mixture of rum and water. Just before

59

he picked up the bird, he took a small mouthful of rum and squirted a bit into the gamecock's bloodied beak.

After a hard fight Hannibal enjoyed his tot of grog as much as any prize fighter.

7 — COMMITTEE OF CORRESPONDENCE

IN THE still crowded taproom bets were being settled, not without dispute, when, together with certain other unobtrusive individuals, Matthew Phipp entered the ordinary. David immediately noticed that the lawyer's right side and shoulder were streaked with mud and sleet. He was limping a little, and his wry, impulsive mouth was drawn into a bloodless line resembling the scar along his cheek.

"Hello, Matt, take a header?"

"Yes. Damned near frozen, too," he added, holding chapped red hands to the flames.

"Come to my room then. I've a fire there."

Carrying Hannibal under one arm, David started for the stairs. Unbidden, George Leavitt went in advance, holding a candle above his head. Waiting impatiently on the landing, they found Captain John Brush, Tom Newton and Robert Taylor, a much younger man. They carried their hats and coats. No one spoke, but everybody looked sharply at everybody else as they shuffled down the bare boards of a long corridor which was beginning pungently to smell of riding clothes.

"Everybody here?" Leavitt inquired once the two merchant captains, Peart and Rudder, had stalked in, uneasy over the presence of so much quality. Nervously Rudder fingered a broad band of soft lead securing his queue. David Ashton surveyed the faces crowding this, the inn's biggest bedroom. His main impression was of eyes, brown, blue, gray, black— all ill-at-ease, all questioning. Three more were expected to appear, he told Leavitt.

A few minutes later a knock at the door preluded the arrival of the missing men. Of them, two were in their late fifties, plump with prosperity and soberly dressed. The third was dapper and dandy in a canary silk waistcoat, a stock of black silk and a tailored suit of fashionable bottle green. Despite the weather, this oldish gentleman's hair was neatly powdered and tied with a black silk ribbon nicked in its ends into swallow tails.

A low chorus of voices greeted him respectfully. "Good evening, Mr. Jameison." Then politely, but with more caution, "Evening, Major Fleming, and evening, Mr. Inglis."

"I'm surprised old Fleming came," Phipp muttered, his thin face looking sharp as a hatchet by the candle light. "Be careful what you say before him, David, even if he is your brother's in-law."

"I'm more surprised to find Neil Jameison here," David returned quickly.

"Your brother ought to be here."

"He wouldn't come."

"He'd better show up soon. When men like Jameison come around, it's time he followed."

"Jameison hasn't committed himself," David reminded.

Jameison, David knew, was one of Norfolk's shrewdest merchant princes. About sixty, there was no suggestion of age in his gray eyes which never swung quickly but appeared to stare unseeing at whatever attracted his attention. Though Jameison was much the richest man in town, there was a genuine simple friendliness in his manner, very different from the pseudo-democratic airs of Andrew Fleming. Phipp judged the Major hadn't been out of the army long enough to mix readily.

Robert Taylor winked at Ashton. "Where did you take that roll in the mud, Matt? Couldn't you wait to get the wench into a bed?"

At a sudden guffaw from the two sea captains Phipp flushed.

"Quiet please!" Captain Brush, the tallest man in the room, held up a hand and spoke sharply. "There's small point in advertising this—er—meeting. What's happened to you Phipp?"

Everyone gathered about, weather-colored faces brightened by a fire behind David and Leavitt. Phipp, tired out, rested an elbow on the mantelpiece while briefly describing the incident of Jemmy Potter and the Independent Company. He expurgated somewhat his account of the call at Robert Ashton's place, but the tragedy of Weaver he recounted in compelling detail.

"So they were jabbing this fellow with bayonets?" Samuel Inglis spoke quietly.

"Yes."

"—And you intended raising a posse to free this deserter?" demanded old Major Fleming in succinct accents. His gray eyes looked hard and bright as bayonet points.

Phipp jerked a nod. "Yes. It seemed the only decent thing to do. Only I hadn't ridden half a mile when I put my mare at a ditch. She slipped. Broke her neck. I walked the rest of the way."

A murmur circulated the low-ceilinged bedroom. Most of them knew Matt Phipp couldn't afford such a loss.

Gingerly the lawyer rubbed his bruised shoulder. "Wouldn't have minded losing her so much if there was anything to show for it."

David's dark face lit. "Maybe we can do something for Weaver even now. Any chance of getting the poor devil out of jail?"

Major Fleming, looking every inch of his six foot stature, caught his breath, but at the last minute bit off what he was going to say.

Phipp turned to Brush. "What is your opinion, Captain. Is there any use?"

Captain Brush, after a moment's hesitation, said he thought not. He was still wearing his gorget of gilt silver and his red and blue militia regimentals. Business was evidently none too prosperous over on Town Back Creek. Brush's coat was patched in several places and, though a full complement of brass buttons secured its lapels, they did not match. Brush, whom David scarcely knew at all, was at once a small merchant and the owner of a struggling plantation. Like most large men he was slow of speech and reaction. Right now his open, weatherbeaten features looked worried.

"I would not say there is any use."

"But how can we let a fellow Provincial—"

"Mr. Ashton, I assure you nothing can be done!" This time Brush spoke sharper. "By now, the military will have Weaver in irons and chained to the jail wall if they have not already rowed him out to his ship. Any attempt on the jail would be out-and-out illegal and might lead to bloodshed."

"That would not do!" Inglis agreed emphatically. He blinked over square lensed spectacles. "Private sensibilities not withstanding, we have no grounds nor any desire to interfere with His Majesty's military laws. We are all lawabiding subjects."

Leavitt threw more wood on the fire and Phipp and Captain Brush warmed their hands at the rekindled blaze. Young Gilmorin, Taylor, Newton and Jameison stood aside, sampling a steaming bowl of rumbullion. A network of tiny scarlet veins flung over Major Fleming's cheekbones showed up sharp in the candlelight. Gruffly he cleared his throat and spoke with an acid succinctness.

"Mr. Ashton, since you asked me to come here, I demand to know what this meeting intends. I might add that I don't like the flavor of the talk so far; I'm damned if I do."

Matt Phipp glanced about, collecting eyes like a hostess preparing to quit her dinner table. "Major Fleming is right, gentlemen. It is time we came to the point."

David counted fifteen persons present including himself. The average age of the assemblage would be about forty. Either Robert Taylor or Johnny Gilmorin would be the youngest while Neil Jameison was indisputably the oldest man in the room. Present were representatives of practically all Norfolk's major interests. Inglis, the banker; Jameison, Fleming and Taylor, factors and merchants; Benjamin Rudder, master of the sea-going *Swallow;* and Captain Peart whose fleet of small sloops combed the tidewater for freight of all kinds. Tom Newton, shipbuilder; George Leavitt and John Brush, planters; Tom Cailborne and William Davies, ship chandlers; John Holt, the printer; and Matt Phipp, the lawyer, albeit an unsuccessful one.

Without further preamble Phipp told the assemblage he had asked Mr. Ashton to summon them as representative of Norfolk's best brains. News of importance to them all had recently arrived from the North.

Neil Jameison gently closed the lid of his tortoise-shell snuff box. "Well, Mr. Phipp, what might this intelligence be?"

Phipp turned to the copper-skinned planter from up the James. "Mr. Leavitt, I reckon you had better read these gentlemen the letter you got from Williamsburg."

With a solemnity so unfamiliar as to be readily impressive, Leavitt produced a pair of spectacles. David knew very well George didn't need them, but he set them on his hawk's beak of a nose anyhow. While unfolding the letter, his bright black eyes considered the circle of faces which, because the room was so badly overcrowded, had begun to sweat.

"This is signed by Richard Henry Lee—"

Major Fleming snorted. "Oh, that piddling radical!"

"No one will interrupt, please," Inglis leveled a disapproving glance at the Major. He returned it with interest.

"Courier declared Mr. Lee is writing to the leading men in all towns and villages of the Colony, asking everyone who is not a stubborn Tory to join in forming what he calls 'Committees of Correspondence.' "

"What might that be?" demanded Captain Rudder, nervously biting a tar-stained thumb. He felt at a disadvantage, wished he had stayed aboard his ship.

"These committees are expected to report to a Central Committee how the folks in their neighborhood feel. They are also supposed to read and pass on news from the outside. And that sort of thing."

Leavitt's jet eyes lingered on Major Fleming's florid, grimly determined countenance as he continued.

"At the same time, committees from the other provinces will inform us of what goes on in their direction."

"Sounds like a right 'cute idea," opined Captain Peart. "We-all could learn which way prices are likely to go, mebbe."

Phipp said, "That's so, but we will also get political news—which is more important."

"Nothing can be more important than the maintenance of trade," pronounced Jameison in his clear voice. "Without commerce there will be no politics."

Leavitt scratched his head. "That's very likely so, Mr. Jameison, but no matter how you look at it, I reckon this idea keeps responsible people in all the colonies and provinces working together. That's right, ain't it, Captain Brush?"

"It is. I feel it is our only hope of impressing Parliament."

"The non-importation agreement back in '69 worked that way," Inglis pointed out, "and we got rid of the Stamp Tax. Pray proceed, Mr. Leavitt."

"Mr. Lee writes we had better hurry up and form a committee. He will forward all our findings up to Philadelphia and Boston."

Robert Taylor stiffened from an inspection of his very elegant watch. It had cost him near two hundred Spanish dollars. "What? Virginians repo't to a lot of no 'count Yankees!"

Captain Brush rapped his knuckles sharply on a mug littered table. "That's not the idea, Bob. Just you remember the Yankees probably don't admire us the least bit more than we fancy them. Fact is, we're all in the same boat." The militiaman drew himself up and to David all at once his plain, honest face looked somehow noble. "Gentlemen, before we go any further, do you think it's fit and proper we should form a committee like Mr. Lee asks? Let's have a show of hands."

All but three men—Neil Jameison, Captain Rudder, and Fleming—voted "Aye."

In short order they installed Lawyer Phipp as chairman. After Captain Brush declined because he already had his hands full with the Independent Company, William Davis, a middle-aged ship chandler, was chosen to be secretary. Samuel Inglis was elected president. Most of the men present agreed to serve the Norfolk Committee of Correspondence in one way or another.

David's self-assurance was suffering a rude shock. After all the writing and running around he'd done for Matt Phipp, he had reckoned he would be made at least a minor officer of the new committee. But his name wasn't even mentioned. Characteristically, he had overlooked the fact that he neither owned a business, nor followed a profession. To these solid citizens he was a vastly amusing and companionable fellow; a mere buck-about-town with a sharp sword and deadly pistols. A far cry, this, he mused in acid amusement, from the standards of worth at White's and Brooks's.

Inglis stood up, scratched under his wig with the mouthpiece of his cold pipe. "Gentlemen, I am about to call the roll. Anyone unwilling to support this here committee will please withdraw." He looked hopefully at Neil Jameison and at Peggy Ashton's father. If it included those two men, the Committee of Correspondence could command instant respect. Small fry always followed the lead of a big fish. The president started off with the names he was surest of and earned a succession of "Ayes." Then, without changing his voice, he called "Major Andrew Fleming?"

Every eye in the smoky little bedroom swung to the ex-officer's impassive face.

"Nay," he snapped in a metallic voice.

"Captain Benjamin Rudder?"

The sea captain's brown chin went up. "No, damme! the *Swallow*'s all I've got and the British Navy's too big. I don't aim to see my vessel get took and condemned!"

Inglis caught his breath. "Neil Jameison?"

The dapper little figure arose. He cocked his head somewhat to one side and, fingering the fine lace cascading down his shirt bosom, said, "Mr. President, it is against my experience to enter into an important decision hastily. I wish to make no exception in this case. In principle I am with the Committee, body and conscience, but for the moment I must —er—withhold my practical acquiescence."

"To hell with your conscience, Neil," grunted Tom Newton. The shipbuilder was grimly amused. "It's so full of mothholes you've made a fortune. Surely, Sam, you didn't expect to see our Scotch friend Mr. Jameison climb out on a limb 'til he knows how strong it is and how much fruit it bears?"

Phipp's serious expression became intensified as he asked, "What are your reasons, Major Fleming, for refusing to join?"

The old officer stood up straight. "Because I am an Englishman and dead set against trouble with my country. Even putting loyalty aside, I am aware that every year British arms open new markets to your goods and mine. Only the guns of British men-o'-war keep the French and Spaniards from driving our vessels off the seas. You might also remember that Parliament has closed the United Kingdom's markets to all tobacco, rice and naval stores *not* produced in His Majesty's American Colonies! Many times England has sent troops to protect these Colonies from the French and the Indians." The ex-officer's head snapped back, his jaw went out, and he looked Matt Phipp bang in the eye. "There are my reasons! And I say—confound you all for a pack of ungrateful rascals!"

Everyone looked worried, hot and ill-tempered as, catching up his hat, Major Fleming started for the door.

Matthew Phipp's courtroom voice rang out. "A moment, Major. Will you allow an ungrateful rascal his rebuttal?"

Major Fleming halted, about-faced and said, "Well?"

"I will admit, sir, that British arms *have* opened new markets; but aren't you forgetting that we Provincials have been forbidden to deal in many of said markets? For permission to trade with the rest, we've got to pay a lot of heavy taxes, and obey God knows how many fool regulations.

"As you have pointed out, sir, the Royal Navy does protect our merchantmen; but at the same time it brutally and illegally impresses men from our ships. Not once, but many times, this navy has in effect raided the American coast. It's crews have stolen cattle, sheep and wood as they pleased. It is this same navy which enforces asinine laws passed by the Ministry."

Phipp's dark eyes were blazing and his tangled dark red hair lent him an air of impassioned earnestness. "You have told us, Major, that England has fought to maintain our frontiers, to protect us. Do you know why? Because these Colonies offer a vast, an unlimited market in which England can dump her goods!"

Matt was really orating now, David felt, and when Matt really got going he came near matching the eloquence of a hard-drinking backwoods lawyer he had once heard address the House of Burgesses. He had never forgotten the magic of the fellow's voice. Nor his name, Patrick Henry—or was it Henry Patrick?

"But I ask you, gentlemen, are we allowed to offer our crops and products in an open market? No! Not even when foreigners stand eager to pay us high prices in hard money! Such trade is forbidden under penalty of confiscation of ship and cargo!"

Once the lawyer fell silent, John Brush began to clap softly. David, too, applauded. Then all the others joined in except Neil Jameison and Captain Rudder. The old merchant sat very still, arms folded across the starched ruffles of his shirt.

Major Fleming gave Phipp an angry look and opened the door, but paused with one hand on its brass knob.

"Sir, you suffer hallucinations. These Colonies can't survive a year by themselves. If you keep on with this silly treason, the British fleet will sweep your ships from the seas—but not mine!"

At the door Captain Rudder also halted. A handsome man, he presented at the moment a puzzled and unhappy figure in white thread stockings, brass buckled shoes and seagoing blue serge. His bright blue eyes sought Peart, his life-long friend.

"You comin', Joe?"

The river captain half rose, then sank back on his chair. "Mah people is a-stayin', Ben." He was quite right. His business was stayin'. The tidewater planters were Whigs—nearly all of them.

Uneasy silence endured while the departing men's tread waned along the corridor. Captain Peart was thinking there was a lot of sense in what Fleming had said about the Colonies not being able to stand off Parliament.

"Why aren't you pulling out, too?" Holt the printer asked of Jameison. No more ardent Whig lived in Norfolk than John Holt; certainly none less afraid to say his mind.

"Well, Mr. Holt, I've a mind to hear what else Mr. Richard Henry Lee thought worth putting on paper. Believe me, Mr. Phipp, despite my friend Holt's remarks, I do favor your ideas. There's no denying Virginia is a cow milked by British capital."

George Leavitt resettled his spectacles and briefly considered the letter. "Up in Massachusetts, he says, they expect trouble, sure 'nough. So far can't tell how this trouble will start, nor how bad it will be. But they do know the Ministry is a-raging over the tea they threw in Boston Harbour last December. He says, too, the East India people are petitioning the Throne to punish Boston and make the Yankees pay for the tea. He says Massachusetts is boiling mad, too, over the suppression of their charter and their rights under it. A fellow called Sam Adams, he says the Ministry ain't fixing to give in. Mr. Lee says folks 'round Boston are bringing in arms and powder."

"They're really fixing to fight?" exclaimed Taylor. "A pack of mealy-mouthed Yankees? Ah don't believe it!"

Leavitt ignored the interruption. "The Boston Committee asks us to study on how gunpowder is made. Very little is allowed to come in these days."

Phipp sneezed. Damn! He *was* going to catch cold. His voice wouldn't be fit for the speech he was expecting to give in Portsmouth.

Leavitt raised his voice. "Most of all, the Boston people want to know whether we'll agree to import no more goods from Great Britain."

"What about exports?" Thomas Newton's bushy brows climbed and, abstractedly, he explored a hairy ear with a bone hairpin from among his wig's side curls. "I'm agin non-exportation."

"So am I," Tom Claiborne said. "Last time we fixed old Townshend's clock pretty well by just refusing to import."

"He don't say anything about exports I can see."

Such a sharp dispute followed that Hannibal cackled and

thrust his head out of his wicker coop. He was hoping another chicken was being brought in. Jameison wanted to know whether the term "Great Britain" included Bermuda and the West Indies. When Leavitt said he supposed so, the sweat stood out further on Captain Brush's forehead. All the horses and cattle and salt pork from his little plantation went to Jamaica.

By a majority of two votes the Committee expressed itself in favor of a non-importation agreement of some sort.

Barring David Ashton and young Johnny Gilmorin, no one gave a thought to the glamorous possibilities of an armed clash with the Mother Country. A bright ideal had been lurking in Phipp's dark red head since he had read Monsieur Rousseau's "Rights of Man." All the rest of the gathering were occupied with more practical concerns.

Roosters on the edge of town were sounding second cockcrow and the church clock showed midnight when the meeting broke up.

There was an unfamiliar sobriety to the "good nights."

8 — NEIL JAMEISON CONSIDERS

WHILE following his link boy's lantern across a series of frozen puddles, Neil Jameison thought hard. When he reached his big brick house, he did not seek the connubial four-poster even though he knew it was comfortably warmed by his placidly snoring wife.

Instead, he routed out his body servant and ordered a cup of strong tea. After donning a banyan of bright yellow and placing his wig on its stand, he pulled on a mulberry-hued turban and settled himself in a chair before the fireplace. Sighing, he propped feet on the brazen head of the right fire dog. It was strange, but he found he could think better with his feet elevated.

Out in the street there was stillness. The wind had dropped so much a dog barking in the distance sounded as if he were next door. Behind the wainscoting some mice scurried, squeaked softly. Shutting his eyes, Jameison relaxed; became lost in troubled thought.

"Let's see. News of the Boston tea riot got to England last month, but most likely the Ministry won't act for another month or six weeks, and even then they won't do more than send the Yankees an ultimatum. That will take time, too." Because the chill of the room had begun to strike in, he pulled his dressing gown collar higher. "If I add six or seven weeks for a winter passage, I'll have at least three months." That, Neil Jameison judged, gave him enough time to bolster his business against the impending embargo. Yes. A handsome supply of goods could be imported before the axe of non-importation fell.

He went down to his office on the ground floor and, despite the raw chill, checked his liquid assets and cash on hand. Good thing he had the *Richmond* and the *Dinwiddie* in port. If he was lucky the *Agatha* might get back from Halifax in time to clear for England.

Next he considered a probable market for various commodities. In the event of trouble, arms, of course, and powder would bring the biggest returns. But munitions were risky cargoes; too risky. He didn't want any ships confiscated. If the trouble came to fighting, wine, surgical instruments and medicines would be worth their weight in gold. He would have to include fine cloth, silks, Irish linen, ticklenburg, glassware and all the tea Riggs & Conway could lay their hands on.

All at once his swift calculations faltered. Suppose there wasn't trouble? The Ministry had backed down before. Then he would find himself ruinously overstocked. Still, there had never before been anything to compare with the Boston Tea Riots.

He opened his penknife and cut a new point on his goose quill.

At the same moment, Sam Inglis, not two streets away, was melting wax to seal the heaviest order he had ever sent abroad. The Bostonians were right, sure enough, and he would back them against the East India Company—right up to the limit. But Inglis saw no reason why he couldn't be patriotic and still pick up a tidy bit of change. He began writing in a firm, precise script.

In his solid, unimaginative brick residence, Major Andrew Fleming sat bolt upright at a solid mahogany table. He, too, was driving his quill over sheet after sheet of foolscap. Once he had finished a list of orders to Messrs. Hornblow & Gilson

70

of Liverpool, Peggy's father treated himself to a nip of brandy against the cold. Lips compressed in a grim line, he then wrote another list addressed to John Murray, 4th Earl of Dunmore, and Royal Governor of Virginia. The list included not only names, but the date, hour, and the place of the Committee's meeting.

Conscience and business sense satisfied, Andrew Fleming went to bed.

9 — H. M. S. LIVERPOOL

ASHORE church clocks were debating the exact moment of ten o'clock. Out on the harbour H. M. S. *Liverpool* swung to her anchors, her lights aglow and the delicate tracery of her tall rigging showed jet against the sky. In her wardroom Captain Sackville and his officers, red-faced and jolly, were dining some of the town's undoubted loyalists; Major Fleming, John Brown, Dr. Alexander Gordon and Robert Gilmorin.

Through eight courses of soup, game, roasts, puddings, head-and-pluck, whipped sillabubs, cheeses, cake and a monstrous big suet and raisin pie they doggedly ate their way. At the same time the company sampled in succession sherry flip, claret, burgundy, Madeira, eggnog, brandy sling, and punch. Dr. Gordon, possessing what he conceived to be a fine baritone, felt moved to raise "Four and Twenty Fiddlers." The hosts picked up the lilting refrain and made the wardroom ring to a chorus more notable for energy than harmony.

The song echoed through the frigate's hull and drifted over Norfolk Harbour's glassy black waters. On deck chilled marines, pacing their posts, grinned to themselves. The wardroom must be 'aving a bloody fine beano! Seamen detailed to row Captain Sackville's barge listened and, deciding that the gentry were still distressingly sober, composed themselves for a nap. By now they knew the barge wouldn't be shoving off until the wee small hours. In their hammocks on the gun deck, marines, trying to sleep, cursed resentfully.

In the frigate's lock-up far forward, the song reached Aaron Weaver as little more than an elusive undertone. He blinked and shivered. Plague take them! Their caterwauling had roused him from that not unpleasant lethargy into which he had sunk at sundown. Now his brain again was stirring the bitter broth of Fact. It seemed ages since two marines had marched him forward from the wardroom; the court-martial had sat there. He blinked. He still could see the court ever so clear, sitting beyond a wide mess table. White wigs, gold epaulets, navy blue tunics and marine scarlet. All the faces glaring, staring at him like a row of images. No mercy in any of those eyes.

Three times a hundred lashes with the cat! The heavy irons on his wrists conveyed their bitter cold into his arteries.

Deep in his consciousness the singing stirred memories of a life so remote it seemed as if someone else must have lived it. "Four and Twenty Fiddlers!" Why, at Jenny Boardman's wedding last August, Serena and him had danced to that very tune. Even now he could remember every last thing about the party—hay fresh and fragrant in a loft overhead, the faint sweetish smell of fresh cow manure, a barn floor clean swept and scattered with cornmeal. And all the big fisher-lads stamping and swinging. Lordy, Lij' Trimble had sawed his fiddle fit to bust its strings, but he couldn't drown out sexton Tasker's tootling flute.

Three hundred lashes! Weaver's manacled hands joined themselves. They were big-knuckled and purpled by old gurry sores and fashioned to handle nine-foot oars. Well, he guessed he'd never again go salmon spearing along the Kennebec in the spring, nor feel his back tendons crackle under the drag of a well filled net. There would be no more net mending at night and on stormy days, and no more studying a yellow sunset and calculating where the blow would likely come from. It was hard to remember the taste of steamed clams and the sweet savor of a chicken lobster dripping with butter.

Three hundred lashes! If by a miracle he survived them, what use would he be to Serena and the children! The toothless and foul mouthed English sailors aboard vowed no man ever came through more than a hundred and amounted to sikkum afterwards.

What had he done? God Almighty knew he had not hurt nary a one of His creatures. Of course fish weren't creatures, just reptiles. All he had wanted was to get back to Falmouth in the province of Maine.

He was not afraid to die. He really wasn't. All his simple, hard-working life Aaron Weaver had feared a jealous God, just as the parson and the Bible said he should. He had paid his taxes and, back in '60, he'd served the Crown with the militia against Montcalm. A year ago he had been elected a deacon of the church because he kept the Commandments and only cursed when a seal got into the nets.

Who'd have smelt trouble when a frigate's topsails came lifting over the horizon? Him and the rest of the boys in the *Nancy Anne* had took her for what she was, a man-o'-war. They cal'lated the boat she put over wanted a mess of fresh haddock for the officers' mess. But straightaway he'd guessed something was caterwampus from the way a twerp of a midshipman swarmed over the *Nancy Anne*'s rail. It was easy for him; the little fishing snow was riding deep under a great haul of cod and halibut.

Even yet, Aaron couldn't rightly remember what came next because he'd been cracked on the head. But him and George Wenlock and Abner Taylor had all come to with a taste of stale blood in their mouths and the news that they had become ordinary seamen serving aboard H. M. S. *Liverpool,* 44 guns. When he tried to stand on his rights, a bosun's mate knocked out an eye tooth and split his lip.

In New York they caught him trying to jump ship into a bum boat. That first flogging didn't bear thinking about. 'Round Falmouth folks had always talked of his courage and strength, and he figgered he did have as much grit as most, but the twentieth swipe had jolted a scream out of him and he'd never rightly got ahold of himself since. Now he faced *three hundred lashes!*

A flogging was bad enough, but the degradation of being dragged across the deck like a common criminal, that was what he really minded. Very well he knew what to expect. Hardly a week went by but some unfortunate wretch had his sentence read to him at the foot of the mainmast. Aaron knew very well what happened after that. The bosun's mate would strip off the culprit's shirt and lash him, spread-eagled, to a hatch grating. The bosun would pipe all hands on deck. If any other men-o'-war were in harbour, details from their crew arrived to witness the punishment.

The first time he'd seen a flogging, strong as he was, he'd been among the three who fainted. It was hard to forget the hissing swish of the cords and the dull impact of their knotted ends on bare flesh. Worst of all was the way blood flew from the lash ends—it was like water from a wet towel. Before the business was done you could see specks of blood staining the deck and the white cross belts of the marines who, with fixed bayonets, stood about in a hollow square. Sometimes the flying gore even marked the bulwarks.

A soft singing noise commenced to sound in Aaron Weaver's ears. It seemed soothing and pleasant, very pleasant; kind of like the wordless lullabies Serena hummed to the children when they were small. Knees thumping softly, Aaron Weaver slipped from the wooden box on which he'd been sitting and, kneeling, raised a blank, blind face towards the musty deck beams above.

He prayed. "Our Father, which art in Heaven, I know I ain't much 'count, but I've tried to live right. I know You mean it all for the best, but it does seem a mite hard on Serena and the children. For myself, I don't ask anything, but please, Heavenly Father, keep an eye on Serena. She ain't so strong and her folks are all dead. And if You can, try to look the other way for awhile, because I don't want You to see. It's just that I guess I ain't nigh so strong as I thought. And—and—," if was an effort to get the next out, "please forgive the British captain and his officers and all those who have trespassed against me, as I do forgive now. Amen."

Aaron Weaver sat up, feeling infinitely more peaceful than he had since that day last September when the *Liverpool's* boat came a-pulling over the cold gray waters of the Grand Banks.

He still couldn't understand about that man on horseback, the one who had been on the road the night he got captured. The horseman had talked hard, but his eyes had been friendly. For awhile Weaver had thought he might get rescued. But he hadn't been. Maybe Virginians liked the English better than they did New Englanders.

High overhead he heard the ship's bell strike a series of double notes. Soon the sergeant of marines would be making his rounds. Though he gazed fixedly at the irons on his wrists, he was seeing a stretch of the Maine coast—barnacled granite rocks, yellow-brown weed rising and falling in cold, dark blue water. In the background grew pines, dark green and sturdy; a mighty bulwark against the wind. Yonder lay the little brown marsh back of his house. The gulls would scratch up clams on the flats there, then, carrying them aloft, would drop them to smash on stones above the beach. The ground was thick with broken shells; little Enoth had cut his foot there.

Heavy boot soles clumped in the dark corridor, a key ring jingled and the singing in the wardroom swelled very loud as a bulkhead door creaked back. A light partially dispelled the gloom of Weaver's cubicle. A square window had been let into the cell door. It was set with two thick iron bars. Between them appeared the sergeant's not unfriendly face. A lantern held below lit his chin, the tip of his nose and the pewter plate on his cap.

"They were over-'ard on yer, Weaver," said he. "Captain Sackville's orlways 'ard." Putting his mouth to the bars, he whispered, "If ye've any money, I'll try to find yer some opium pills. Yer don't feel the knots so bad."

"It's mighty friendly of you, Sergeant," Aaron said in his friendly nasal voice, "but I ain't got a penny. I'll make out, though. I'll make out somehow."

The white facings of his scarlet coat yellowed by the lantern light, the marine sergeant lingered. He seemed to be groping for something to say, but in the end he shrugged and went to look into some other cells. Snores and curses reassured him of their occupancy. He bent low under a bulkhead and stalked out.

"Make out"? the sergeant was thinking. Gawd's truth! That poor bloke of a Yankee didn't know it, but even if he lived, he'd never walk straight again. A cat, the way Captain Sackville ordered it laid on, would bare a man's back muscles before a hundred strokes.

Again that soothing music began to sound in Aaron Weaver's ears. He commenced to undo his belt. Fortunately it was long. During the afternoon he had noticed an eye bolt let into the deck beams. What it was for, he couldn't guess, but he knew it was there. His fetters hampered him so it took some time to locate the iron eye by sense of touch. When he found it he threaded the loose end of his belt through the buckle and made it fast. Good job the lock-up was situated in the bow. The upsweep of the deck gave more headroom here than in other parts of the ship.

Aaron Weaver climbed up on the biscuit box and slipped the leathern noose over his head. That sweet, ineffably peaceful humming noise grew louder, like a swarm of bees drawing near. He drew a deep breath, then expelled it before he kicked the box backwards and out of reach.

The humming noises swelled to a deafening crescendo.

10 — SAILING DAY

PEGGY ASHTON'S pen whispered across the ledger before her:

Norfolk
February 19th, 1774

Account, *Assistance*, brig'tine

Harbour Expenses
To:	Wharfage	£ 8- 0-0
	Lighterage	12- 2-0
	Labourers per Candless	11- 5-0
	Rum	4- 1-1
	Food for voyage to Boston	12- 7-6
	Pilotage two days @ 9s.	0-18-0

She paused, yawned, and picking up a horn-handled pen-knife resharpened her goose quill. Dust drifting about the draughty, rat-infested warehouse filled her eyes, made them heavy. A sad, monotonous chant raised by stevedores hoisting the brigantine's cargo inboard was beginning to grate on her nerves. Since six she had been driving this pen over what seemed like an endless succession of ledgers, invoices, manifests and bills of lading. Her fingers felt so stiff and wooden they might have belonged to someone else.

From time to time she turned to peer out of a window at her back. It was so veiled by cobwebs she could barely make out the *Assistance*'s weather-grayed spars against a cold blue sky. Sweating in the cold winter sunshine, Rob heaved harder than any of the sniffling slave stevedores. He drove them hard, though, because under this stiff west wind he knew the tide would ebb early and Farish was impatient to lose not a moment. She rested a little, watching the gray gulls wheel and mew above the brigantine's tops. Now and then they swooped very low. They were hopeful of a smashed cask or barrel.

The pimpled, half-grown youth Rob dignified with the title of shipping clerk turned a stupid, freckled face. "Was it one or two kegs o' molasses for Colt & Co., Ma'am?"

"Three. For pity's sake, three! And mind you don't let

those careless boogies drive a bale hook into the flour sacks. They go as part of Monks & Peabody's order."

A spring bell tinkled hysterically, then a swarthy man with an enormous wart on the side of his chin clumped in from the street. A quid bulged in one of his grimy cheeks.

"Howdy. Heerd tell you is lookin' for deck hands."

"That's so," Peggy admitted briskly. "And you can take off your hat in my presence."

The intruder stared, but complied. He seemed highly amused. "Wal, I got a pair o' niggers outside—likely sailors. Seein's it's you, Ma'am, I reckon you can sign 'em on for a dollar and half a day; apiece—and found."

A dollar and fifty cents! Peggy's diminutive figure stiffened on the stool to counteract the sinking in her heart. Right now Ashton & Co.'s cash balance stood at fifty dollars. Every other sou-markee was invested in the old brigantine lying out there with the flood tide making up under her keel. Peggy thought hard. She had been hoping to pick up a couple of hands at seventy-five cents apiece. That was five cents below the lowest current wage. In Norfolk it was reckoned an eleven-day trip to Boston in wintertime. But the *Assistance* was so old and slow she couldn't count on fetching Boston in under two weeks. Twice fourteen was twenty-eight, then there would be a week in port up there. Nimbly her fingers flew over a mental slate. Fifty-two dollars and a half! That left Rob not a fip to go and come on. It was clear she couldn't afford to pay even seventy-five cents. At sixty-five the bill would be forty-five and a half Spanish dollars.

Said Peggy, pushing the dusty hair from her eyes, "A dollar and a half! Mister, I never did hear of such nonsense!"

The intruder sniffed, shifted his chew and rolled a bleary eye. "Seein's it's you, Ma'am, I'll let you sign them niggers for a dollar a day an' found."

Peggy gave him a sweet smile. "I will sign them on at sixty cents."

The labor contractor's unshaven jaw sagged. "What's that?"

"You heard me. That's a good price," Peggy informed him staunchly. "Aren't many ships clearing this time of year, and you know it!"

"Where's yer vessel for?"

"Boston. She will be back here inside of a month. You might just as well get those hands out of your barracoon and earning money instead of eating their heads off."

77

Grubbing in his nose with a dirty forefinger, the contractor deliberated. "Eighty-five cents a day," he grunted. "And you can take it or leave it."

"Sixty," reiterated Peggy Ashton, slipping off her stool. She dusted hands no longer so soft and white as those of Peggy Fleming and, pointedly ignoring the contractor, went over to check some invoices. It was easy to act mean; she was feeling uncommon spiteful. Not twenty minutes ago Lucy Gilmorin and that hateful snip of a Sally McKinney had strolled by all decked out in white beaver hats tied with silk strings under the chin. They were the rage and they knew she knew it, even if she couldn't own one. She could have killed them both for their smug look of commiseration when they noticed her bent over a ledger with her skirt tucked up and the stripes of her old outer petticoat in plain sight. They hadn't come in; they had just minced along giggling, with their silly heads together.

But most of all, her heart ached to see Rob straining out there, helping to lash down the brigantine's deck load of barreled turpentine. A man of his position shouldn't be seen sweating about a wharf like a day laborer. But of course Rob had no choice—not these days. She wondered whether his cousins in the Bermudas—wherever they might be—ever worked like that?

From the tail of her eye she noticed Rob quit work to talk with a Mr. Aldrich. She recognized him as a tidesman from the Customs House.

She jumped at the contractor's sudden, "You win." Having surveyed the gleanings from his nose, he jerked a curt nod. "Take 'em then for sixty-five."

If he expected appreciation on Peggy's part, he was disappointed.

"I warrant you take advantage of my sex, sir," Peggy demurred. "Let me see these sailors."

The dealer thrust his battered head out of the door. "You, Ben, and Buff, come heah!"

An undersized Negro, so round-shouldered as to look hunchbacked, shambled in after wiping dull red mud from his naked feet. The office then darkened momentarily at the entrance of a huge slave. His skin gave off a grayish-blue tone rather than chocolate-brown, and there were some tribal scars on his cheeks. They were arranged in a crude chevron pattern. His front teeth had been filed into blunt points. He moved slowly because a stout chain joined two rings welded about his ankles. Both the Negroes clawed off red woolen stocking caps, then stood staring at the gritty planking beneath their feet.

"You can send that last man out," Peggy ordered sharply. "Mr. Ashton doesn't want any trouble-makers aboard."

"Buff ain't no trouble-maker, Ma'am once he's aboard ship. He's a fine deck hand."

"Nonsense! He's a blue nigger; you can't fool me. Once a mean nigger always a mean nigger." She pointed to the tip of a welt showing about the neckband of the big Negro's ragged shirt. "The idea your daring to offer me a nigger with whip marks still hot on his back! And this other one! Look at him. Why, he's not strong enough to pull a spoon from a pot!" The last objection was entirely perfunctory; there were big muscles in the shorter seaman's legs and arms.

Hesitantly the giant slave's tawny eyes climbed and fixed themselves on Peggy. He did it in a hopeless, miserable sort of way. She could tell he knew he wasn't going to be signed on and, because of that, he would get another taste of the contractor's rawhide whip.

He was wrong. Five minutes later Buff and Ben were contracted for as ordinary seamen at sixty-five cents a day—and found.

"Now, Ben, just you get out to the wharf and set to work." she flung at the hunchback. "Tell Mr. Ashton I hired you."

"Yassum, and de Lawd bless you. Hit's powerful slim rations in dat ol' barracoon."

The tall blue-black Negro's hands made ineffectual little motions. He was trying to say something but couldn't.

"Hush yo' nonsense, Buff." Peggy understood Negroes better than most. Blue niggers, she knew, were prouder than the brown ones. Whipping seldom made any impression on them. She picked up a key the contractor had left on the desk and tossed it to him. "You can unfasten that padlock. I reckon you have better sense than to try to run away."

"Oh! Yassum! Yassum. Buff work bestis he kin."

He bent. His thick fingers quivered so hard he could not turn the key right away. Still kneeling, he looked up and his tawny eyes gave her a look, immeasurably pitiful, yet somehow dignified.

"Give me that lock! You'd likely spoil it!" Peggy's tone was sharp. She felt ready to burst into tears. "Now, just you mosey out and go to work."

"Yessum." Fetter ends clanking, the giant backed out past a heap of bear and 'coonskins Peggy had wheedled away from a long hunter fresh in from the back counties.

Mercurially, her mood changed and, humming, she climbed back on the high stool. For those skins she had paid next to nothing. And to think of having signed on two strong hands at sixty-five cents a day! The saving would buy quite a lot of victuals! What with ducks and seafood so abundant, she and Rob ought to make out all right for the next five weeks.

She was sanding the Monks & Peabody invoice when Rob came in, perspiration gleaming on his cheeks, emphasizing some nearly invisible smallpox scars. More sweat ran in shiny little rivulets down to the base of his neck and stained his shirt. She smiled at a small smear of tar marking his forehead.

"My God! Haven't you finished?"

"Yes, Rob just this minute. It took time to reckon Hancock's order." She hesitated. "The coastwise tax on tobacco is a shilling a hundredweight, isn't it?"

"Told you so fifty times. Where's Hutchinson & Brother's manifest? Where is it? Come on, find it! The pilot is here."

A weedy individual wearing a checked shirt and baggy canvas trousers was swaggering up to the office door. As he reached for its latch string, he spat a quid onto the dirty snow. He wiped his mouth on the cuff of a fortunately brown woolen jacket and entered.

"Tide's set to turn. Ship ready?" he demanded, staring boldly at Peggy's ankles.

Luckily Rob didn't notice. "Yes. You can go aboard. The bosun will show you your quarters."

"Got my fee?" the pilot demanded suspiciously.

In silence Peggy counted out eighteen shillings.

The pilot, pursing tobacco-stained lips, frowned. "What's them things? Ain't you got sterling?"

Rob shook his head. "That's Virginia currency and it's at par with sterling, so you needn't be turning up that unwiped nose of yours."

Suddenly the pilot walked through the warehouse and continued on down the wharf towards a dilapidated angel forming the *Assistance*'s figurehead. Long since, one of the allegorical lady's out-stretched, beneficent hands had been carried away; only a splintered stump remained.

It suddenly dawned on Peggy that Rob was hopping mad about something. A small stab of fear pierced and deflated the exultation she had been feeling over the furs and the Buff and Ben deal. Rob, she reckoned, had found out about the repairs or the new sail.

She flushed down to her bodice when she remembered the calm way she had deceived her father. Bold as brass, she had presented a list of supplies Stephen Farish said he could not do without. Rob, she told her father, was too busy to come. Heartily ashamed of her father's greed, she had agreed to Fleming & Co.'s terms: payment in forty days and ten per cent interest for every day over. He could have lent the money fifty times over and never noticed it. Her legs went weak and wobbly when she reflected on how absurdly touchy Rob was about debt. Maybe David was to blame for that.

Rob pointed at the furs. "How did that trash get here?"

"A trapper came in from the upper Susquehannock. He needed money and I got them very cheap. I thought I'd send them along as my share."

"Don't be a fool. They have more bears in Massachusetts than they have in Pennsylvania."

He was mad, unmistakably.

"Maybe, Honey, but not so good as these," Peggy placated. "See how beautifully they're tanned; the fur won't come out. Pull it and see. I got all five for less than twenty dollars and six 'coons thrown in. It was too good to miss."

She was right, but it made Rob mad just the same. What with doing three men's work, he was tuckered out, and he'd jammed a splinter under his thumbnail.

"Where'd you find those last two hands?"

Raising a beaming if dusty countenance, she told him. But he was pulling on his coat, not looking in her direction.

"You didn't hire much," said Rob, digging at the splinter with his penknife. "One is a humpback and the other's or'nery. Why couldn't you find me a couple of decent men?"

She stared at him, round-eyed. He had never talked to her so before. "Why, I—I had to take what we could afford. W-Why, Rob, w-why don't you ask how much I p-paid for them?"

"Well?"

"I—I got them for s-sixty-five cents a day each."

"Oh, you did, eh? Well, I say they weren't worth it!"

Weren't worth it? Peggy's chin quivered and her eyes closed. And she'd saved him a lot of money.

By now, she was sure he had found out about the supplies. Otherwise, he would never have dared talk to her so. Somebody over to Fleming's must have told him.

Rob burst out unexpectedly, "Aldrich was here just now. He says the Royal Port Authority has voted to levy a coastwise salt tax!"

"But they can't, they have no right to!" In her relief Peggy almost shrilled.

"Of course they haven't, but still I can't clear without paying it. I've had to cancel the order for Jameison's hides. But the ship is cleared."

"Can't you protest?"

Rob's neck went red and began to swell as it did every time he got really mad. "Oh, don't be so stupid! What if I do put up a holler? Who is going to listen? The Crown's revenue officers and the Crown's admiralty courts work hand in glove. They can find a hundred ways to make trouble for me if they want to."

"Oh!" Dismay conquered relief. "How awful, Rob. How much is the tax?"

"A shilling a bushel."

"Why, Honey, that's near as much as we—you paid for the salt."

"Of course. I reckon Colonel McClanahan aims to get rich in jig time." His jaw shut with such a snap Peggy surmised he was figuring what must be left out of the new brig. "My God, I wouldn't wonder but the Yankees with their eternal yelping about 'arbitrary taxes' are right."

"Oh, I'm so sorry, Rob," she murmured.

Captain Farish appeared at the office door, his breath in a steaming halo about his face. The New Englander's manner was curt and on his brown features had materialized harsh, unfamiliar lines.

"We must cast off directly, sir. The manifests and bills of lading are ready, Ma'am?"

Peggy gave them to him then, after warming her hands at a dying fire of sea coal, slipped into a gray serge cloak. It was an old, old one and she hated it because it would not wear out.

"I notice you got the stern painted," Rob remarked, sealing

instructions to Messrs. Richard Clarke & Sons, his Boston agents.

"Found a pot lying about," Farish stated without batting an eye. "Cal'lated it might tighten up the seams some."

Rob and his wife stood alone at the end of the empty wharf, shivering in the raw February wind. They were watching the brigantine's slave crew warp her out into the Elizabeth's greenish-yellow current.

Farish and the pilot were standing by the wheel, the former bellowing, brazen-lunged, through a leather trumpet at hands casting off topsail clews. The pilot was busily whirling the wheel. The ebb, running now at top speed, rounded the *Assistance* up to a sheet anchor which had been rowed far out into the stream.

Buff, Peggy noticed with inward satisfaction, was pushing hard against his capstan bar, helping hoist the green old cable inboard.

Rob said nothing. He was too dog-tired. He was thinking that the brigantine wasn't much to look at. She looked terribly shabby and old. Farish had been dead right about the main topmast. It *was* sprung—no doubt of it. He hoped it would last to Boston.

Well, out there sailed every penny he and Peggy had. But, by God, they didn't owe a fig to anybody. The devil take Andrew Fleming and his patronage! Every bone in his body ached. What an idiot David had been to play the macaroni about London. The poor devil had only got burnt. A tenth of the sum he had gambled away could have made so much possible for Ashton & Co. Yet some folks said a younger son had been damned lucky to inherit the old *Assistance*. Maybe so. St. John Ashton hadn't been given half such a start in life what with old Sir Mountford more or less kicking him off the Bermudas. Vaguely, he wondered what the Bermudas might be like.

The *Assistance* was beginning to pick a course down the harbour. It was a ticklish job. The river was jammed with ships of half a dozen nationalities and rigs. Peggy gave his arm an ecstatic squeeze when a faded Union Jack was hoisted to the old brigantine's main gaff. She slid heavily by a great ungainly Dutch *hoecker,* or hooker, as contemptuous provincial seamen called her sort. Farish set the main topsail and broke out his jibs. A creaking of blocks and the thump of halyards thrown from belaying pins onto the deck floated ashore.

Well, for better or for worse, there she went. The words struck a chord of memory; he groped until he found Peggy's hand. They stood closer together.

As happened uncannily often, she expressed the words in his mind. "Well, Honey, for better or worse, there she goes."

"And she will come back," Rob muttered. "She must!"

While they stood there with the harbour gulls mewing above their heads, it occurred to him to seek an omen. As a boy he'd got into the habit. Sometimes his omen had been trivial; the direction in which his mother moved her hand, sometimes it was the number of times a dog barked.

The omen came, he reckoned, when the wind shifted and began blowing from a weatherbeaten black barque berthed at the next pier. His sense of depression deepened. The breeze was bringing a dreadful stench, reminiscent of a dirty privy. The barque had made port on the flood tide, but he had been too busy to notice what she was like. It required no imagination to translate the origin of that awful smell.

A Guineaman was discharging slaves at John Brown's wharf.

Part II

The Tidewater: 1774

1 — TALK IN A BEDROOM

DAVID ASHTON opened a tentative blue eye but shut it promptly stifling a small groan. God's teeth! His head throbbed like the clapper of Big Ben. Why in blazes had he thought it so clever to toss off a pot of alicante on top of a double basin of Johnny Gilmorin's kill-devil? The belated wisdom only made him feel worse.

A rustling, clicking sound at the far end of his room intrigued him into making a second effort to stand the light. Hannibal, his plumage copper-red in a beam of morning sunshine, was strutting vigorously up and down his wicker run just as brash as if the big gamecock from Wilmington hadn't given him a pretty argument before cashing in. David lay motionless; the morning air was sharp even for late March, and the embroidered night cap was comfortingly warm about his head. Damn! His mouth felt as if the whole British army had marched along his tongue in stocking feet.

At last he summoned enough energy to reach down from his four poster—he had won it from Tony Stewart at pharo—and thump on the floor with a pump heel. Hannibal cackled, regarded him from a suspicious sherry-red eye.

The walls doing a May dance about his head, David sank back into the secure and comforting depths of the feather bed. He surely hated the idea of parting with such a noble bed—it was just wide enough, just hard enough—but he reckoned he'd have to.

Captain Sackville of H. M. S. *Liverpool,* damn him for a snotty, sneering, blue-jowled devil, was too confounded lucky. Maybe some day he'd admit he couldn't win at pharo. It definitely wasn't his game. Bad luck, too, having Hannibal out of the running for the next three weeks. It would take easy that long for those slashes in his side to heal. Plague take all Carolina chickens; they bred 'em too big down there.

85

Alas, it was now inevitable that David Ashton, Esq., must go to work. He deliberated opening a *salle d'armes*. Why not? That was not a bad idea. Not at all! He had a good wrist and a steady hand with a dueling pistol if he hadn't been fighting the punch bowl too hard. The ladies, God bless 'em, entertained a definite weakness for masters-of-arms; the men an added courtesy.

Reaching up, he gingerly massaged temples throbbing like drums played by Negroes fresh from the Middle Passage. If their masters allowed it, new slaves liked to drum and dance all night before the crude image of a snake, or in front of an old black billy goat. You could hear the drumming of escaped slaves almost any moon-lit night if you stood on the edge of Great Dismal Swamp. It came as a sullen *mutter-mutter* from the depths of that vast fen.

David was becoming disappointed at the turn of political events. During the past month not one event promising excitement had taken place. The damned Bostonians hadn't rioted in weeks, and what few letters reached the Committee were sterile, tiresome reports, recommending this and deploring that. God's teeth, it looked as if Parliament actually didn't dare to monkey with those blue-nosed psalm-shouters up in Massachusetts.

Queer, how uncommon grave Neil Jameison and Sam Inglis had looked when they learned how dead set the level-headed people in Boston were against more of such lawlessness as had destroyed the tea. Old Dr. Gordon was going around showing a letter. It claimed the Massachusetts Provincial Government was talking about paying off the East India people and coming to terms with the Ministry. If they did that, everyone felt sure there would be no fighting.

He yawned and stretched until the tendons in his arms crackled. Plague take the Yankees anyhow!

In the street below, he heard jingling bells and the clopping hoofs of a pack train setting out for a trading journey among the new villages beyond the Blue Ridge Mountains. Maybe he would go out to the far West, too. Out to Ohio—to Illinois, even. Plenty of fighting there, all right.

He recognized the rattle of pots and pans, the yipping of the spit dog chasing Katie's cat around the stableyard and regular as clockwork, successive slams of the famous privy's doors.

For March this promised to be an uncommon fine day. Like

a golden cloudburst the sunlight beat through windows he had taken care to close on going to bed. No night air for Davey Ashton, drunk or sober.

A *salle d'armes?* He supposed there must be a big enough room over Andy Fleming's warehouse. Damn him for a pompous old skinflint and a goddam grasping Tory to boot! Fleming would probably ask a lot of rent, though anybody else in Norfolk would be glad to make things easier for an in-law.

His mind, in the mysterious way of that organism, sped back through time to London. Before his mental eyes reappeared Andrea Grenville. A year and more had passed, but so vivid was his recollection of her magnificent temerity, he could remember just how she looked. The Honorable Andrea Grenville, my Lord Cavendish once declared, was always ready for a fight, frolic, or a flirtation. Her light jauntiness in the face of terrific losses at whist was the talk of Whitehall and the dandified beaux of Almack's danced to her nod. Even "Jockey" Rockingham's rake-helly crew worshiped her after she won a midnight steeplechase against Sir Bertie Clough.

Andrea? Odd, he remembered her best as she had looked on the morning of the Wedderburns' hunt breakfast; her rather long face was shining and wetted by an early morning shower, a light scratch showed below her ear and a single bronze ringlet dangled over an eye of changeable gray-green. Odd thing. All told he and Andrea hadn't had a whole hour alone.

One night she looked at him after a disastrous session at loo. "David, I fear we are dark stars, we two. Just damned dark stars! No one sees our real light. Wager twenty guineas the cards will break me before they do you."

That had been one of the few bets he won in England. His fingers tightened at the mere recollection of December twelfth, 1772! In under an hour the business, ships, warehouses and stock, the home on Church Street, furniture, horses, coach, everything—went slipping over the green baize into Lord Camden's palsied, dead white fingers. The noble earl needed them no more than a cat needs three tails.

Andrea must be married by now, David reckoned, and breeding a new generation of hunting men for some hearty wastrel. His vague resentment at the idea was dispelled by a knock. Katie appeared, broadly smiling over a tray set with copper chocolate pot and crumpets.

"O fairest Hebe in all this southern realm, I give thee greetings." Waving a derisive brown hand, David hoisted himself up on his elbows. Then, groaning a little, he slipped long and wiry arms into a bed jacket of cerise silk. He pulled off the night cap and began vigorously to rumple his dark hair. Perceptibly his bloodshot eyes grew lusty with life.

"La, sir, you gentlemen made a big night of it. Cat ain't come down off the cupboard even yet, and Mr. MacSherry's that sick to his belly he says he's tasting hair!"

Expertly Katie slipped a bolster behind Mr. David's shoulders. Her eye lingered on the Valenciennes at his night shirt's opening and on the curly close mat of chestnut hair beneath. How sharp those uneven brows of his stood out against the pale bronze of his skin; they gave her a queer turn every time she looked at them.

She felt sorry for Mr. David. He must feel awful. Puffy half moons lurked under his eyes, but his speech was clear and his breath clean—not like Corporal Pepperill's when he woke after a drinking bout.

Mr. David must still be a little drunk, she realized, because in a half-hearted way he inserted a finger beneath the ruffle across her breast when she bent to place the tray across his legs. Still abstracted, he tied the napkin beneath his chin and began to butter a crumpet. Katie, meanwhile, commenced setting the room to rights. No quick task this morning.

All at once he drew a breath in exaggerated amazement. The wench looked uncommon pretty in her crisp white mob cap; beneath it curls, formerly dusty yellow, shone golden. She was wearing a frilled yellow apron and a short-gown of clean blue calico.

"God's teeth, Katie! Does my nose—er, do my eyes—deceive me? You—you bathed?"

"Ye-yes, sir. Last night."

"Well, damn my blood! We live in an age of miracles! And you've even washed your hair!"

A tide of scarlet flooded the barmaid's face and breast. "You was right, Mr. David. It felt kind of good. I—I'm fixing to wash every other week—all of me," she announced with a sort of desperate determination. "And—and I aim to better my education."

"Better your education?" That would be gilding a nonexistent lily. Poor Katie. She could neither read nor write.

She nodded, twisted a corner of her apron between embarrassed fingers.

"Don't do that!" he snapped with such force that crumpet crumbs flew wide over the coverlet. "Looks silly and it spoils your apron. Who is—er—undertaking your—er—formal education? That sergeant you've been taking up with?"

"Yes, Mr. Davey. He went to a school in England and he writes a lovely genteel hand. He's learned me the alphabet—most of it."

"Why now, that's simply splendid, Katie," he declared in genuine approval. "To date, your education seems to have been somewhat neglected. Why?"

She took her birch twig broom over to the fireplace and commenced to sweep a powdering of blown ashes into the hearth. "I never had no home—a home, I mean. Ma, she said my Papa was Squire Tryon."

"A squire?" David exclaimed, then cursed because he had spilled chocolate onto his bed jacket. "Which one?"

"Squire Hugh Tryon," Katie said without turning her head. "He, well, he wasn't exactly married to my Ma."

"Oh! Who was she?"

"I—I couldn't say for sure. Ma Shannahan 'lowed the Squire's wife sent her packing right after I was born. She put me out to live with her—Ma Shannahan, I mean. Squire got himself scalped in the Indian wars of '65. Anyways, the family moved away, but I stayed on with Ma Shannahan. She was drunk most of the time."

David, feeling somewhat recovered, approved the way Katie spoke. It was without a trace of self-pity. Her statements were shockingly matter-of-fact; she spoke as if such a rearing was what any illegitimate orphan must expect.

"Sometimes the old woman got the horrors real bad; she got to seeing what she called the wee people—little fellers with blue heads. She near killed me once, so when she got that way I used to run out and sleep in one of the nigger cabins. I—I reckon I would have starved but for the niggers. When I got to be twelve," Katie methodically retrieved a muddied stocking from the mantelpiece, "Ma Shannahan sold me, indentured me that is, to Mrs. Skillings. She got £50."

"And for how long?" David put down his cup of chocolate, regarded her with fresh interest.

" 'Til I'm twenty-one."

"And how old are you, my dear?"

Her gray-green eyes widened, wavered to the floor. Never before had Mr. David called her "my dear." Not like just now, anyways. A warm flush of pleasure swept over skin which felt strangely fresh and smooth.

"About nineteen, Mr. David, but I ain't exactly sure."

"Do I gather you have small affection for this Mrs. Skillings?"

Katie's eyes narrowed and a sullen twist deadened her wide mouth. "I hate her. She treated me something terrible. She beat me for nothing. No matter how early I kindled fires, it wasn't early enough. The water wasn't hot enough, not even when it was boiling, and she'd fetch me a box on the ear if I used a leaf of tea more than she reckoned was enough. I hate her—one of the children was always getting lost, but I couldn't help it; there was five of 'em."

"But what about the other servants? Did she treat them the same way?"

"Oh la, sir," she laughed. "There wasn't no other servants —not after old nigger Julia died. Just me."

"I wouldn't refer to black people as niggers," David corrected quietly. "Nice people seldom do."

"Thank you, sir."

"What about Mr. Skillings?"

Katie's wide-set eyes narrowed as, slipping Mr. David's stocking over her arm, she inspected it for holes and laid it aside. "Oh, he ain't much 'count. He didn't bother me much, not until I was—well—I guess I was fourteen."

The barmaid's voice dropped and she made a deliberate ceremony of measuring out a cup of cracked corn for the gamecock. "One day I was picking huckleberries in the back pasture. Mr. Skillings he comes up and says, 'Come with me, Katie. I got somethin' pretty to show you.' He took me over in the bushes awhile—when we came out I—wasn't the same. Mrs. Skillings was awful mad when she found out about it."

"But how did she find out?"

"Why, why, I reckon I was acting kind of scared—and— and my clothes— That was the first time she tied me when she beat me."

"God's teeth!" David's eyes flashed. "You mean to say she beat you on top of—of the other?"

"Sure she did, Mr. David; she called me bad names—a—a trollop, a lustful whore; that was only some of them. She promised I would end my days in prison."

"Did she whip you often?"

"Pretty near every week, even when I—I was sick. She's

90

a powerful woman, is Mrs. Skillings. I reckon she must find pleasure in giving a whipping; she used to flog the children something awful, too. I stood it as long as I could, Mr. David. Honest I did. I wanted to serve out my time—honest-like. Maybe I could have stood the whippings, but what with Mr. Skillings always fixing to get me out in the bushes, I had to get away. The nig—the black people helped me to get here."

A pretty picture, David mused, but far from unique. Under the best of conditions the lot of apprentices and bound servants was no bed of roses.

"Aren't you afraid they might find you?"

"Oh, I reckon not," Katie replied hurriedly. "The Skillingses live 'way back in the woods, back of Plymouth."

"Plymouth? Where's that?"

"It's on the Roanoke in North Carolina. The Skillingses don't see much of anybody from outside, excepting the minister."

An impulse of generosity prompted David, "Pass me my purse, Katie. It's likely behind the wash basin."

When she found it, he selected one of his last remaining sovereigns. There were only three. "My dear, I want you to buy a kerchief to put around that pretty, clean head of yours—get a green one; green and gold has *ton* nowadays. It is the mode, the last cry. And, by the bye, stick to your sergeant 'til he teaches you to read and write."

Katie became radiant, then sobered. "Mr. David?"

"Well?"

"I don't need a whole sovereign for a kerchief. You lost so terrible much at pharo last night."

David's eyes snapped. "Take it, you damned slut, and be quiet!" He couldn't bear sympathy over her failings.

Abashed and mystified, Katie obediently dropped the coin into the front of her dress and in silence continued to straighten the room. Lord, what could have made Mr. David get so mad? The ways of the quality were still beyond her. She had reckoned she was in for a box on the ear when she'd said that.

Equanimity restored, David presently inquired, "What's become of that weasel-faced corporal who used to hang around you?"

Katie tossed her head. "Oh, *him!* He was too dirty and ignorant. He couldn't even sign his name. I got rid of him."

Considering how often Katie and the corporal had shared the stable loft, David found the objections amusingly significant.

"Don't go too fast, my dear. Pepperill wasn't so bad as many. Gets drunk only twice a month, and he doesn't toss his money about—except on you. I'd venture the fellow's really in love with you."

"Oh, I reckon he is," Katie admitted carelessly, "but he stinks something fierce when he takes his clothes off, and he breaks when—"

"That will do, Katie," David checked hurriedly. "It's your affair of course. Have a care, though. I've noticed a right mean look on his phiz sometimes."

"Oh, I'll manage; the sergeant's over him, too." Katie spoke confidently. She hesitated in lifting the tray. "Mr. David?"

"Well?"

"Maybe you'd be right kind and advise me about something?"

Laughing, David threw back his head. Strong and regular teeth gleamed. "Gads my life! Can there be someone in this world who values my advice?"

"My sergeant's ship is for Boston next week. He lets on he will be lonely without me. Should I go?"

David, one brow raised, studied her face. "Does he want you to go—married?"

"Why—why no."

"Good! Then by all means go," came the surprising advice.

Her eyes flew open. "You mean I shouldn't marry the sergeant?"

"Exactly, my dear. Once he is married to you, the worthy fellow's chief interest in you will center on how well you wash his small clothes and how quiet you keep the mess of brats he'll get on you."

"Oh!" From under long lashes she gave him a slow look of dawning comprehension. Very quietly she slipped from the room.

Feeling the wisest of beings, David sighed. Unmarried, Katie might better herself, but then on the other hand she would probably get herself knocked up someday soon and then she'd be really bad off. It was a wonder she hadn't had a baby long since. Whatever she did, he would miss her soft slurring voice and her bursts of breathtaking frankness. A courageous creature, Katie, come to think of it. In Boston there would be more soldiers and the larger town would give more scope.

He stretched then, swinging his legs out of bed, stared at the flat purse on·the chair alongside. A good job Rob had invited him out for the night. Peggy liked him well enough, too. She loved hearing about London, about every detail of the routs, balls and masques he'd attended during his brief burst of glory. Her eyes would dance at such times, but Rob wouldn't say much.

He reckoned he had better make Peggy the compliment of a locket or something; then she would surely invite him to visit at Tide-over for a few days. Life wasn't altogether amusing out on Plume's Creek and the fare was Spartan these ·days. He wondered why Rob was getting so confounded worried about not hearing from his brigantine. Well, maybe he'd reason to look serious. Two months had passed since the *Assistance* had cleared·for Boston.

2 — JOHN BROWN CALLS

IT HAD got so warm that willows edging Plume's Creek had lost their furry sprouts and were beginning tentatively to leaf out. All the fields and the marshes were alive with migrating blackbirds, bluebirds, hawks and wild doves. Amid that same myrtle tangle in which Toby had nearly met his doom little warblers in gay mating plumage teetered and chirped.

Peggy sang too. On such a glorious spring evening who could help singing? From the kitchen door she saw how low slanting rays from the sunset were touching the gilded weathervane on St. James's spire. They drew from it brief flashes like sparks flying from beneath a smith's hammer.

"After all, Norfolk ain't so prodigious a town," she mused, vigorously stirring the gingerbread dough, "but it is the biggest and the most genteel in Virginia. You can't laugh at a town with six thousand people."

March and the beginning of April had been fine so far as to weather, but she would not willingly relive those weeks. Not knowing about the ship kept gnawing rat-like at her peace of mind.

The thud of Rob's axe busy behind the woodpile struck her ear as she glanced across a broad meadow lying behind the cottage. She hoped Lom wasn't going to waste time getting back from town. She had to have the sugar and bacon before she could get on with supper. La! It would be fine to see David and Johnny Gilmorin. Before long they would begin talking about deer shooting and that usually got Rob wound up. She had worried over him. For the last ten days he'd been sitting 'round with an odd tight expression about his mouth. She went into the yard and emptied a pan of scrapings, for the hens. There weren't many chickens, nor many scrapings, either.

"What shall we give them to drink?"

"Why ask? You know we have only hard cider," Rob retorted, looking at her with that forced smile she was coming to hate. He set down his axe and stretched his shoulders backwards. "What time are they due?"

"About seven," Peggy replied, dabbing her hot red face with a corner of her apron.

"Don't do that! It makes you look just like a cook."

Barely in time she bit off an angrier retort, only said, "Well, I am a cook, aren't I?"

"I'm sorry, dear, really." Slowly he rumpled his wavy brown hair with both hands. "Oh, Peggy, why don't that plagued ship make port? Here's all this fine weather and not a lick of work being done on the brig. I—I feel sick!"

"I know, Rob," she murmured, patting his arm. "Father used to say there's nothing worse for an active man than to have to do nothing." Only with difficulty could she make her voice sound confident. "You know, dear, if anything has gone very wrong, we must have had news of it before now. She will come in soon, maybe tomorrow."

"Tomorrow!" His tired brown eyes considered her gravely. "Haven't we been saying that every night for weeks? Where is she? What's happened? Oh God, if I'd only done what Farish wanted. I was a fool not to have her overhauled! At hindsight I'm a past master. How does our money hold out?"

Peggy winced; she had hoped to avoid the subject.

"Why, Rob, we will make out all right," said she cheerfully.

He refused to follow her lead, "Tell me, Peggy, how do we stand?"

"In hard money we have one shilling and sixpence," she

admitted simply. "But Honey, we'll make out just the same. We can always——"

"No! No matter what happens," Rob said quickly, "I won't borrow."

"But what is so awful about borrowing?" Peggy demanded with one eye on the fattest of the three remaining hens. 'You know very well most of the merchants in town borrow when they need extra capital."

"Yes, and so do the planters upriver! Just look at Vance, Leavitt and the rest!" A forced grin wiped ten years from his features. "Peg, don't fret. I—I'll get us through this somehow. Reckon I'll mosey down and take a look at the trot line. Breakfast may be waiting." All at once he swept her off her feet and squeezed her so tight to his sweaty chest she was breathless.

"La, Mister Bear," she smiled, vastly relieved. "Don't you dare to be so rough! You've burst me a stay string and they cost money."

He set her down. "If you don't stop looking so almighty cute, it will maybe be a rib next time."

Whistling for Toby, he swung off down the path to the landing and the reedy shore beyond. Down there black birds were darting in swift little swoops.

If only the future proved half so pleasant and tranquil as this evening sky. Well, the next few weeks would tell a lot. A year from now he'd either be established or penniless. It wouldn't be the latter, of course. Once the new brig got to sea and began earning money, he would lease a better warehouse; one with a private wharf. Later, he would send his ships—he thrilled to the plural—on the longer, more profitable run to the Mediterranean.

Rob caught up a stick and tossed it out onto the creek's yellow-gray surface. He startled a gray heron which had been prowling along the shore. The bird uttered a harsh croak and, springing into the air, went beating slowly off, faithfully reflected by the glassy stream. On the far side of the creek a bob-white whistled the mating call—three notes with rising inflection.

Sinking onto his heels, Rob retrieved the trot line's end from the stick to which it was tied. The line tugged at his fingers. Right away he knew he was in luck. A pair of big rock fish and a hardhead, long as his forearm, were hooked.

He fashioned a rude crook from the fork of a hazel bush,

then threaded his catch, gill and mouth, upon it. After kicking off his blunt-toed shoes, he dug half a dozen mannoe clams and rebaited the hooks. He started back to the house wishing to God it wasn't necessary to eat fish again. He'd give a lot to taste beef or pork once more. He reckoned Peggy would, too, though she never did complain.

Muddied and slimed with fish, he neared the cottage and saw a horse hitched to a post sunk for that purpose in the back yard. He lengthened his stride. David wasn't expected so early. Still, one never could tell when David would turn up for an appointment.

The moment he saw Peggy, he suspected that David hadn't arrived and that something was wrong. As soon as he laid eyes on John Brown's untidy wig and nutcracker features, he was sure of it. It was typical of the old man that he would ride all the way out from town rather than waste sixpence on a messenger.

"Weel, Mr. Ashton," his creaky old voice snapped. "Whaur might my tickings be? My Osnaburgs and the Russian ducks I ordered twa months ago? Are ye no' aware that spring is here? Pack trains for the back country are making up and more river schooners sail every day. The shopkeepers keep clamoring for hardware, china and tea! What wi' yer delay, I'm losing a fortune!"

Rob gave Peggy the fishes and summoned a smile he hoped was placating. "As I said yesterday, sir, your shipment's on the way. My vessel will be making port any hour."

John Brown's features, whisker framed and brown blotched by age, did not relax. He was coldly furious and no mistake about it.

"Aye, yon's what ye've been repeating the whole last fortnight! Every day I'm losing accounts. Aye, and yon Neil Jameison gains customers—*my* customers! For auld lang syne I was pleased tae do yer feyther's son a kindness, but mind ye, I'll no' wreck my business oot o' sentiment."

"The *Assistance* will reach Norfolk very soon, Mr. Brown," Peggy put in desperately. "I know it!"

"And do ye so?"

"Yes, we—we had word today. A fast sloop spoke her three days ago—off Cape May."

John Brown took a sparing pinch of snuff, gave her a sharp look. "What sloop?"

"Why—why—"

Rob flushed. Peggy was a fool to talk like that. The old skinflint knew every vessel in port.

"Why—why, I forget."

"Like enough," the old Scot snorted. "Weel, listen tae me, Rob Ashton. I must ha'e delivery o' my goods come three days, or not at all!"

"But Mr. Brown, I—"

"—Ye'll mayhap recall a delivery clause in oor contract? It may interest ye to lairn the *Gladys* made port today. In her is just what I need."

On bowed legs looking pipe-stem thin in breeches of patched doeskin, John Brown swung over to a nag nearly as ancient as himself. One foot in the stirrup, he warned over his shoulder, "Now, mind ye, ye must deliver my goods before sundown day after next, else I tear up the contract and ye can fiddle for yer merchandise—if it ever fetches Norfolk. I bid ye gude nicht, Madam. And you, sir, remember what I have said." He rode off down the lane, bumping on an old-fashioned French military saddle.

"Oh, Rob!" Peggy, panic in her eyes, rushed to her husband's side. John Brown's order formed the very backbone of the Boston venture.

He swallowed hard. The scope of the threatened calamity was too great to be appreciated all at once. He felt sweat breaking out on his forehead and palms; this was odd because his stomach felt cold as a barn during a January gale. If word got about he had lost John Brown's order, every tuppence ha'penny merchant around Norfolk town would feel privileged to cancel also.

God in Heaven, what *could* have happened to the *Assistance?* A storm? A plague aboard? Perhaps a revenue vessel had halted her at the entrance to Chesapeake Bay. Nowadays the King's officers seemed extra eager to conduct inexplicable, arbitrary inspections. Not a week earlier the *Swan*, out of Charles Town in South Carolina, had been held up three days, losing half her cargo of vegetables. What made the outrage more inexcusable was the fact that her papers all were in order. The patrol sloop's commander had detained her because the *Swan*'s captain spoke a little piece about his rights on the high seas. The Britisher swore he was going to teach at least some of the damned Provincials respect for the King's ships.

3 — THE TEST PAPER

BEYOND a wide meadow nearest the King's Highway rose a series of strident whoops, then someone made the woods resound with a lusty view-halloo.

"That," predicted Peggy, "will be Johnny Gilmorin, and David; probably tight as a new pair of shoes."

Over a rail fence into the meadow sailed a tall gray hunter. He landed smoothly and at a steady, surging gallop came across the field spurning high into the air some oyster shells spread for fertilizer. The rider frantically waved a buckled hat. Fifty yards in the first horseman's wake appeared a second. His yellow coat shone bright as a butterfly against the gray outline of woods just beginning to lose their severity. He, too, kept raising the view-halloo.

Peggy was right. He in the lead was indeed Johnny Gilmorin and the other David. Of course, they had been drinking. Rob frowned. They were idiots to ride so hard over soft ground; either of those hunters was likely to pull a tendon. Sudden resentment surged. What was the sense of galloping about the countryside half drunk and for no good reason?

Peggy misunderstood, gave his hand a little squeeze ere she urged in a tenderly fierce undertone, "Rob, don't worry about John Brown any more. Please don't! It makes me feel sick to see you look so poorly."

But still Rob stood there, muddied, smelling of fish, and frowning as the horsemen jumped a second fence.

"I am a sight. I'm going to tidy my hair," Peggy said and ran inside, leaving only Toby to study his master with perplexed liquid eyes.

As his guests pounded across the last field scaring the daylights out of a big cottontail feeding on new sprouted clover, Rob drew a deep breath and forced a hospitable smile. It wouldn't do to let them even suspect how critical things stood with him.

Peggy, reappearing magically fresh in prim white apron and cap, made her guests a graceful curtsy. At the same time she had trouble in downing a pang of humiliation. The others looked so smart in their top boots, doeskin breeches and skirted riding coats. There was lace on their shirt fronts and a gay and reckless light in their eyes. And there stood Rob with his hair untied and falling all over his face. His shirt was rank with river mud, and fish slime was on his hands clear up to their wrists. That, characteristically, neither of the guests noticed such trifles was lost on her.

Young Gilmorin's clear brown eyes lit as they fell on Peggy. Vaulting off, he flourished his brand new hat and swept the ground with it while making a leg in the manner prescribed by Mr. Grief Randolph. David's bow was more easy and graceful and he murmured something about "a pastoral goddess" while kissing her hand. Even Rob laughed at the way Peggy blushed. There was a lot of laughing and chatter before the hunters—Johnny's property—were cooled out and, minus saddles, were tethered to a well gnawed rail back of the kitchen.

With a flash of embarrassment Rob realized there wasn't a pint of corn on the place. When the animals cooled some more he said Lom would give them extra big piles of hay.

"Present, Ma'am, and with the most distinguished compliments of the new whip of the Norfolk Hounds!" Johnny was only twenty and couldn't help looking his admiration as he placed a flask of French brandy in Peggy's tiny hand.

The older brother flung a careless arm about the younger's shoulders. "Gads my life, Robbie, even if you are a bridegroom, you might come to town more often."

"What's the use? It makes me sick to see the business I'm forced to pass up."

"Aren't there other things beside the state of trade to talk about? I feel dashed put out you never drop in at my rooms." Automatically, but unconsciously, he multiplied his single chamber into a suite. Noticing Peggy absorbed with Johnny Gilmorin's small talk, he sobered, drew his brother aside. "By the bye, I now have means of learning news before most people."

"That's good," Rob said, but his mind was far away.

They went inside. Rob was proud of Peggy's perfect equanimity. If it had been Madeira at two shillings the bottle, she couldn't have poured the cider with more easy grace. She was saving Johnny's brandy for later.

"Your friend Captain Sackville was inquiring after you," Gilmorin remarked, wiping a spattering of mud from eager, good-natured features.

"Sackville? Why, Johnny, I don't reckon I know anybody by that name. Who is he?"

"Captain of the *Liverpool,* frigate. He wouldn't be pleased to think he'd made such a trifling impression. Remember the captain at that ball Papa gave last autumn?"

"Oh!" Peggy recalled him now—a lean, waspish man with brilliant glittering eyes and a mouth as thin and red as a sword cut. He'd given her quite a flutter, had Benedict Sackville, for all his Whitehall ways with the rest of the Norfolk girls. "What about him?"

"His ship has been ordered to Boston. There's sure 'nough going to be trouble there."

David came over, leaving Rob to splash water into a wooden bucket beside the kitchen door. "Well, sweet sister, and how do you fancy this bucolic existence?"

"Vastly, David," she maintained demurely. "The songs of the blackbirds and wrens sound sweeter than the meows of the gossip cats after Church. The cardinals and jays I find more faithful gallants than your bucks-about-town."

She gave Rob a fleeting, heartwarming smile. "Why not let David and John look over your plans for the brig?"

Young Gilmorin nodded eagerly. "Ah, the brig! Davey's been telling everyone she's of a wonderful new design."

In rising impatience Peggy glanced down the lane. Lom should have been back hours ago and here was supper almost ready and no sugar to candy the yams. She hoped Johnny Gilmorin's appetite was so good he wouldn't notice the humbleness of her rough and filling fare.

Just then the Negro clumped into sight around the outhouse. He must have borrowed a dug-out and paddled up the creek.

"Well, it's about time you got back," said she. "Now just get yourself washed and put on that old linen coat of Mr. Ashton's."

Despite John Brown's visit, the meal, lit by a single Phoebe lamp, proved unexpectedly cheerful. The cider, Peggy surmised, must be more potent than she had imagined.

When they went out into the sitting room, young Gilmorin bent eagerly above the brig's plans.

"That bow looks elegant. If it doesn't let her drive under, it will split the waves as neat as a knife." He jerked a nod at the model above the fireplace. "Your inspiration?"

Rob smiled. "Yes. But if you think it's easy to magnify her proportions to a working scale, try it!"

"I'd rather not," drawled the young elegant, offering a silver snuff box engraved with his own crest. Rob managed to take a pinch but his work-thickened fingers made only a clumsy imitation of Johnny's deft technique.

David for once sat quiet, sucking at his German pipe and studying his brother with a strangely thoughtful eye. When Peggy announced she must set some bread dough, he shook off his abstraction quickly enough. Gilmorin gave David an imperceptible look when the latter stood up as if to warm his backside at the fire.

"I say, Rob—" Johnny Gilmorin hesitated. He wasn't used to considering what he said before he said it. "Down on Water Street they say you are going to become one of Norfolk's big merchants some day—before very long, that is."

" 'Some day' can be a long time, Johnny," Rob countered. He was puzzled by Johnny's manner—and David's. Both of them acted as if they were expecting something to happen.

"Well, I suppose you've heard that more King's ships have been ordered to patrol duty on the Bay?"

Rob's fears for the brigantine returned with an overpowering rush. "Yes. But in spite of it, all importers have doubled their orders over last year."

Gilmorin gave him a look containing more than a little of old Robert Gilmorin's penetrating shrewdness.

"You know why these extra ships are ordered here?"

A small silence fell in which could be heard the rasping of Toby's teeth against an old ham bone. He must have crawled under the house, Rob thought, in spite of the boards Lom had put up to keep him out.

"I reckon so. Over to Moxham's store a peddler was saying the Yankees are all for reviving the old non-importation agreements. Is that it?"

"Yes. That's it. But this time the Yankees and we, too, aim to go further—a lot further," David broke in, his dark cheeks flushing with excitement. He dropped his voice. Obviously he didn't want Peggy to overhear. "I'm your brother, Rob, and Johnny's your friend. We came here to see that you make the right choice."

"I'm not fixing to make any choice at all." Rob stated quietly and went over to the fireplace. A stubborn set to his jaw, he looked at the *Grand Turk*'s ivory model.

"I'll admit I mayn't be the fellow to preach," David said with characteristic honesty, "but all the same, your danger is not—" To a quick warning from Johnny, he broke off short, swung to face the door. "They're coming?"

Young Gilmorin nodded.

For a third time hoof beats clattered in the lane and Rob's high color paled a little when Peggy called out, "Who is that?"

Quickly Gilmorin went to the kitchen door. "Don't worry, Peggy, it's only Matt Phipp and an officer from the Independent Company. They said they might stop by."

Peggy appeared, flour up to her elbows and dusted on brows and cheeks.

"Who is the other man, John?"

The dim rays of the Phoebe lamp emphasized Gilmorin's grimace. "A new officer. Nothing fancy, I reckon; they say he got around enough of the younger troopers to get himself elected an ensign."

Peggy was irritated. "La, Johnny, don't beat around the bush. Who is he?"

"Edgar Leeming."

"Leeming! He's not coming into this house!" Rob announced emphatically.

Instinct prompted Peggy to cross to her husband's side. "You had better let him in, Rob; in these times a man can't afford many enemies."

Rob was struck with a sudden suspicion. "This call is your doing?" he asked David.

The older brother inclined his head and went on fashioning a horse's head out of a bit of beeswax with which Peggy had been strengthening some thread. Conscious of Peggy's eyes hard and bright upon him, he began to talk rapidly.

"The Norfolk Committee has been ordered to find out and report to Williamsburg who the Tories are around here. You can see we would have to come some time? Johnny and I reckoned it might go easier if we were around when the Committeemen called."

From the start this had been an unlucky day, Rob reflected, and the sound of Leeming's arrogant voice ordering Lom to "walk the critter 'til it cooled off" suggested no redeeming ray of good fortune.

"Howdy, Matt, what can I do for you?" Rob was resolved to tread warily.

"Not a great deal," answered Phipp pleasantly. He looked

less bookish, more practical, in the Independent Company's blue and red uniform.

Leeming still wore his food-spotted sergeant's tunic, but now the bright crescent of a gorget swung high under a chin lumpy with old pimples. To his sloping shoulders an ensign's narrow gold epaulets were carelessly sewn. His manner was ingratiating, however, almost servile.

Rob was relieved when Peggy went out to draw some cider. He had learned he couldn't predict what she'd say or do when things got delicate.

Nervously rubbing his scarred cheek, Phipp said, "Let's come to the point. I suppose by now you realize, Rob, you must come in on our side or the other?"

Leeming, who had been gawping at the brig's plans, smiled slyly. "Templeton couldn't make up his mind, neither. Too bad his farm caught fire last night—it set fire to his house."

It became very still in the room. Rob asked, "You mean Hayward Templeton's house?"

"Yes, ain't it a shame? Templeton has lost everything."

"A coincidence, of course," Phipp cut in hurriedly. "The Committee does not countenance violence. In Maryland and further north, dozens of business houses are facing bankruptcy."

"Times are good," Rob said.

"Not for them. Their local Committees of Correspondence have blacklisted them for importing goods from England. No one dares do business with them—they'd get proscribed, too."

Phipp was talking now in dead earnest, almost pleading. His unruly red hair kept falling over his forehead.

"Won't you believe us, Rob? All the Colonies are terrified —not so much over the East India Act, but the idea back of it. We all know it means an end to our livelihoods, to our business freedom."

"Of all the nonsense—!"

"Your brother, Johnny here, and I have come in all friendliness. It doesn't pay to get mad."

"Me too," reminded Leeming, helping himself to a handful of hickory nuts.

David got up and began to walk back and forth. "Listen to me, Rob. Everyone knows you have—suppose we say 'loyalist tendencies'? Well, that's honorable. But loyalty carried too far can become a form of cowardice."

Rob felt badgered and unhappy. "It appears to me you're the one to be careful, Davey. Provincials have been tried for sedition and sentenced for saying no more than you have just now."

"I'll risk it," David rapped. "Oh, for God's sake, make sense, won't you?" He was worried over Leeming's smug silence. He knew damned well that that boot-licking bastard wasn't missing a syllable. This whole business would be retailed with variations to suit the ignorant and vicious "Dirty Shirts" inhabiting the upper creeks and stump lots. If that happened, anything was possible. They loved an excuse to do a little wholesome plundering.

Phipp said impressively, "We are trying to save your business, Rob. Listen." His voice swelled, booming in the smoky-smelling living room. "In a few weeks, or months at most, only two sorts of people will live in the American Colonies: Patriots and Tories! Leeming, pass me that Test Paper."

The night's stillness crept indoors. The crackling of hickory logs burning in the kitchen sounded like the noise of a distant skirmish. They could hear Mrs. Ashton treading out some sparks.

Leeming thrust a long sheet of paper into Rob's hand. Heart beginning to pound, he scanned a form printed on John Holt's press.

I ————, gent. residing in the Royal Borough of Norfolk in the Colony of Virginia, do herewith swear upon my honour:

1. To Maintain my Allegiance to my acknowledged Soverain, King George III.

2. To defend to the Death the Rights and Privileges granted by Royal Charter unto the Colony of Virginia.

3. To sustain the Struggles of any American Province or Colony to retain Rights and Privileges granted under similar Charters.

4. I will grant no Service, sell no Supplies, nor lend any comfort whatsoever to His Majesty's armed Forces now engaged in oppressing the American Colonies.

5. I will not Purchase, traffick, nor deal in any produce or Manufacture originating or imported from Great Britain or Ireland.

6. I will not sell, traffick, or consign any goods or Mer-

chandise coming into my possession for delivery to Great Britain or Ireland.

7. I will Arm myself and hold myself ready to march in the cause of Justice on one Hour's notice.

8. I do *solemnly* pledge myself to the Cause of Justice and to the support of American Liberty.

Signed this 15th day of April, 1774.

Carefully Rob read the Test Paper, not once, but twice—which was like him. At length he laid it upon the table beside the smoky little lamp. With a wry smile he said,

"The only thing lacking here is a declaration of independence."

Impatiently, David snapped his fingers. "A fig for independence! Who in blazes wants independence? Nobody but a few crackpots up in Boston like Sam Adams and James Otis. What we demand are only our rights as freeborn Englishmen. Surely you can't deny that?"

Rob fingered his chin. One could see how he would look ten years hence. He addressed no one, communed with himself aloud.

"I suppose you know Governor Dunmore has arrested three Test Paper signers? Right now they're on their way to trial in England, charged with treason. One of them was a merchant. You fellows don't seem to realize a man can lose his business if he signs a thing like this. And he would lose it legally."

"Legally? Nonsense!" Phipp snorted. "Since when is it legal to transport a provincial for trial in England? What possible chance would he have over there of facing a fair and impartial jury? In my opinion, Ashton, you'd better sign."

"Oh, don't force him," Leeming drawled, cracking a nut between grimy palms. "A half-hearted partisan is a heap worse than none."

"You'd better sign it, Rob," Johnny urged. "I—I beg you to. We've always been good friends, haven't we? And isn't Peggy my cousin? Listen—even Neil Jameison has signed. What do you think of that? It means he is on our side."

Neil Jameison? That gave Rob serious pause. Jameison was about as shrewd at politics as he was at business. Still a big

105

majority of the important merchants were for declaring for the King.

He leveled at Johnny Gilmorin a questioning glance. "Seems odd to hear you talking Whig with your father—"

Johnny flushed, but made light of the inference. "Papa is English born; besides he's uncommon stubborn." He chuckled. "The poor old boy has bought me a lieutenant's commission in the Royal Americans. He actually expects me to accept it."

"—And if you don't?"

Johnny's recklessly good-looking face screwed itself up as, spreading his hands, he shrugged. "Why, I reckon that means it's out for me—O-U-T—neck and crop." He saw his point and pounced upon it in boyish eagerness. "You see, Rob? I ain't afraid to take sides."

"But you have no business at stake." Rob went over to stand in front of the fire. His legs, heavy muscled and powerful looking in shiny blue serge breeches and white cotton stockings, were cast into silhouette before him. David undoubtedly meant for the best, but since when had David been right about anything? Johnny Gilmorin, with his gaming and racing and wenching was only eager for excitement—and hang the expense! The main thing worrying him was that Neil Jameison had thrown in with the Whigs. He cleared his throat and everyone in the room looked up expectantly.

"Gentlemen, I reckon I feel the way you do about losing our Charter rights: if it comes to that I'll fight. But right now I'm not so sure the English business men won't bring their Ministry to its senses. They stand to lose too much." He paused uneasily; then, in a lower voice said, "I don't think any of you can figure how hard I've been working to get back our family's old customers, to build up my father's commerce to where it was. I am sorry to disappoint you. Signing this paper is too much of a gamble. I can't risk all that."

In the background Leeming scratched his head and helped himself to another nut.

"What time is it?" Phipp demanded harshly. He was angry and disappointed at having ridden all this way for nothing.

"It's ten o'clock," Leeming said. "We might as well hightail back to town."

In the starlight the horses looked unnaturally tall. Their nervous trampling drew little ripples of echoes from Lom's cabin, from the creek shore and most of all from the clump of bass-woods across the meadow. Toby ran among their legs barking. Thompson's dog and Dickinson's fox hounds half a mile away responded with yelping enthusiasm.

Matthew Phipp looked disgusted as he swung up onto his horse. "You are making a serious error, Rob," he warned in his precise, carefully considered manner. "I hope you will find no reason to regret it."

Johnny Gilmorin laughed, kissed Peggy's fingers. "Well, there is still time to bring him into camp." Then he put his knee against the hunter's shoulder, swung up and settled into the saddle gently as a lark alighting on a fence post.

Leeming climbed aboard an angular mare and doffed his cocked hat to Peggy with an exaggerated politeness. She did not seem to notice.

She was smiling up at Phipp and wagging a ridiculously small forefinger, "Don't keep David at the Crossed Keys too late, will you? I will leave out the latchstring."

David turned in his saddle. "Don't fret. I'll be back early. Too big a night of it yesterday. Oh, damn my blood! Heyo, Rob, I clean forgot!" He produced a paper folded and sealed. Peggy's heart dropped like a plummet taking soundings, and she thought it would never come up when David added, "Major Fleming asked me to oblige him."

Thank fortune! Rob was too busy to look at it. He put the piece of foolscap into his pocket and reached up to shake Matt Phipp's hand.

"Good night, Matt. Don't think I'm not appreciating your riding out this way." He even offered his hand to Leeming.

The new ensign was in no hurry to take it. His gap teeth glinted as he said, "We're expectin' to have you in with us before long, Mr. Ashton. Yep. Shouldn't wonder if it came about sooner'n you think."

The four horsemen turned and the cottage lights faded on their backs as they trotted off between old rails fencing the lane.

4 — THE DEMAND NOTE

A STREAM of tobacco smoke was drifting out of the top of the kitchen door when they turned back to the cottage. Peggy went cold once Rob began fumbling in his coat pocket. He was, of course, looking for the note David had brought. Too well she guessed its contents: she understood her father's concept of sound business practice. Her stay strings seemed made of wire; an irresistible force drew them tighter, tighter. Once she had dreamed a huge bear chased her and she had run and run but couldn't cover any ground. Now she felt the same sense of panicky helplessness.

"Oh, God," she thought, "let me think of something! I must divert his attention! He'll be terribly mad." Even though she couldn't think of a thing to say, she stammered.

"Rob, I—I—"

"Well?" He paused just inside the kitchen, looking very grim and thoughtful. In frozen horror she watched his thumb-nail rip the paper wafer sealing Major Fleming's note. "What's the matter? Why do you look like that?"

"Oh, I—I don't know, Honey. I reckon I don't feel well."

"Better go to bed, then. There's no use waiting up for Davey. I'll be along in a minute."

The small snarling noise of ripping paper sounded like the crack of doom and, watching him in a wild panic, she backed up against the living room door, the tips of her fingers pressed to her lips. Oh, why must he find out? Now of all times!

Robert Ashton, Esq.,
Respeckted Sir:
Yr. Vessel being Overdue now by nearly a Month we feel justified in exacting paym't for marine supplies delivered per yr. order to Vessel Assistance, Feb. 17th last.

Demand herewith the sum £50-6-6 and accrued Interest, or Land or Merchandise to that value.
Yr. Humble ob't serv't,
Andrew Fleming.

At first Rob's expression hardly changed at all, then a nerve began to tick in his cheek. Next a big vein swelled on his temple and stood out like a blue cord under the skin. As he reread the demand note, his hands began to shake.

"He must be crazy!" he cried thickly. He wanted to think so, but he knew very well Andrew Fleming wasn't given to making that kind of an error. In a queer strained voice, far more alarming than any burst of temper, he asked, "Margaret, can you tell me what your father is talking about?"

She flushed scarlet. For the past two weeks she had been preparing explanations against this moment, but now she couldn't think of a single one.

She summoned her most appealing smile. "You must forgive me, Rob. I know I had no right, but—but—Captain Farish said—"

"Did Farish ask you to order these supplies?" He was towering over her, all blazing eyes.

"No," she admitted in a frightened voice. "I—I asked him."

"By what right did you mislead your precious skinflint of a father this way?" The day's accumulation of irritations and that persistent sense of impending disaster combined to stir him to a blind fury. Toby cringed, slunk into a far corner of the kitchen and peered fearfully from a corner of his eye.

Peggy went white and fell back a step. "Why, Rob, I—I only wanted to make sure—I was so afraid—" She felt her insides dissolving.

"You know how I feel about borrowing—especially from your family!" His voice was sharp and metallic as nails falling onto an iron plate.

"Oh, Rob, I know I hadn't any business to—and—and—" In an abandon of misery she started blindly towards him. She wanted to throw herself onto his chest, to plead for and to receive forgiveness. Instead, a white light broke before her eyeballs and the crack of his slap drew a frightened whimper from the spaniel.

She staggered into a corner and, in her terror, her knees gradually gave way until she had slumped onto the floor. He reached for a thong used to punish the dog, hesitated; then, giving her a look of supreme contempt, walked out into the dark.

Near dawn he got into bed and, turning his back, made a rigid pretense of sleeping.

5 — ASHTON & CO.

NEXT day he saw his father-in-law and ate crow. It came hard humbly to beg the major to grant him three further days of grace. But he did it and came home smarting as if he'd taken a licking. Great God! What had happened to the *Assistance*? He reckoned she was lost, but he wouldn't admit it to himself. He didn't dare.

During the next two and a half days only short, essential phrases broke the silence in the white-trimmed cottage on Plume's Creek. Rob, at once sharply impatient with himself, was yet determined in a desperate sort of way that Peggy must never again meddle in the policies of Ashton & Co.

He ploughed and planted a vegetable garden, mended the section of pasture fence David had broken in a bad jump, and spent half a day picking off some crows which had been raising the devil with his new-sprouted corn. He hung their stiff black corpses to saplings and watched them bob and sway in the warm spring wind.

Every time he noticed the faint red bruise on his wife's cheek it took a lot of resolution not to take her in his arms. Worst of all was his certainty that what she had done hadn't been done selfishly. Of course, he reminded himself at their silent breakfast the second day, one couldn't expect a woman to realize it was downright dishonest to sign her husband's name without asking him about it first. That was just what she had done. She had endorsed his signature to Farish's list of necessaries. He learned the details of the matter from crabbed old Benson, Fleming's chief clerk. Mrs. Ashton, said he, had 'lowed her husband was too busy to come over himself.

It was desperately hard going on like this, particularly with anxiety gnawing like a beaver at the roots of his self-confidence. But to allow further interference was like letting two pilots fight over the wheel of a ship in a narrow channel.

He spent the morning on the little landing stake, pretending to fish, but really thinking in weary, desperate circles, trying to figure a way out. If the brigantine didn't make port within the next six hours, he was done for. He knew what he must do. Tide-over cottage wasn't any great shakes, but the land

110

around it must soon become valuable, easy two hundred dollars an acre—maybe three. Norfolk was growing fast and buyers most always had a hankering for waterfront property.

A pair of wood ducks, gorgeous in their spring plumage, scaled by and, making a small splash, settled out on the creek. After a sharp look about they floated reassured on the glassy surface and rested from nest building among the oaks upstream.

Yes, he'd have to sell. He and Peggy had to have something to live on. Old Fleming would be tickled pink. He had tried for many years to get a piece of St. John Ashton's business hide, but he never had succeeded. All Norfolk knew the major made a habit of exacting full weight for every pound of flesh due him. The best thing he could do was to go in town and have a talk with Mr. Sydebottom, the town clerk. Sydebottom was friendly. He would most likely know where a sale could be arranged to the best advantage.

Peggy, following the little oystershell path down from the house to tell him dinner was ready, felt tears sting and rise under her eyelids when she saw him hunched at the end of the landing. To see him inactive was so unfamiliar as to be terrifying. She simply could not get used to seeing him loaf about the place taking a long time over the simplest job.

That slap had done things; something young and spontaneous seemed to have vanished from their scheme of things. Yet she was honest enough to admit that Rob had been perfectly justified. Most husbands, her father included, would have grabbed that strip of leather and given her the very devil of a hiding.

A honeybee rising from a clover bud circled about her head like a small baffling problem, then droned off. Oh, *what* had happened to the *Assistance?* Peggy paused above the landing, gazed down at the broad lazy creek and the faint bluish haze which, hanging over it, softened the outline of trees on the far shore. She, too, became gripped by an overwhelming premonition that the *Assistance* wasn't going to come back. Her conviction was so stark, so insistent, she almost cried out. But she didn't and went on down the bank instead to tell Rob dinner was ready.

They got through the meal somehow with old Lom shuffling about and looking like a chapter from the Book of Job. It was plain he was baffled and desperately unhappy over the way things stood.

Rob pushed his chair back from the table and looked at Peggy steadily. "I reckon I'll be going in town. Do you want to come?"

The frills of a neat lace cap fluttered to her quick nod. She could foresee how bad it was going to be for Rob in town. All the other warehouses would be busy with this sudden unseasonable activity. But not Ashton & Co.'s. Poor Rob.

"I would like to go, Rob. I would like very much to go."

He sensed her underlying meaning. "All right. We can stop in at the Spread Eagle. Perhaps they will have news of her there." It was bravely spoken, but she could see he knew very well there would be no news.

Very soberly Peggy came around the table then suddenly bent and kissed him on the forehead. He put his arms about her, pressed his head tight to her breast. Convulsively she held it there.

Gravely the two got ready for town. Rob brushed his shiny serge jacket and scraped the marsh muck off his shoes. Peggy got out her prettiest chintz pocket then took two quick stitches with a needle and thread to hold her Paisley shawl together—pins were too dear to risk.

"Why don't you wear a cockade of some kind?" she suggested. "Most everybody does these days. It looks monstrous smart."

"I would, except I can't make up my mind what color to wear."

Once the skiff was made fast to a clump of oyster-encrusted pilings at the foot of Frenchurch Street and Peggy stood primly smoothing her skirts on the wharf, Rob squared serge-clad shoulders and drew a slow breath. His old brigantine was not in the harbour anywhere.

"Isn't there someone you'd like to visit?" he suggested, rather than inquired. "I—there is a business matter I must attend to. We can meet later at the Spread Eagle. It's on Cumberland Street, corner of Cove."

Peggy raised a stricken face. "Oh, Rob, Honey, I—I'm so truly sorry. Let me speak to Papa. Please! I'm sure—"

"No!" said he shortly. "It would be no use. Your father has been waiting this chance for a long time."

"When shall I look for you? I think I will drop in on Lucy Gilmorin."

"In about an hour; but David is almost always at the Spread Eagle 'til sundown."

"Very well, dear, but—oh—I wish—*Mayn't* I go with you?"

When Rob shook his head, she drew the Paisley shawl higher on her shoulders and reset the China silk handkerchief she had tied under her chin. "We will weather this, Rob," she said firmly. "We will weather this—somehow." Her tiny erect figure started off up the street. Fortunately it was familiar to her; she couldn't see three feet ahead.

Once out of sight she paused. She needed to act quickly and she knew she would lose a lot of time if she stopped at Lucy's. Lucy Gilmorin was such a gabby-cat.

Her brother-in-law, she had heard, was fairly intimate with old Neil Jameison these days; and David, in his sporadic, unpredictable fashion, was devoted to her. Maybe he could, and would, talk Neil Jameison into lending a hand. Surely he wouldn't balk at a mere fifty pounds. What was fifty pounds to a rich man like him? She might contrive it to let Rob think the money came from David!

The idea of going straight to the Spread Eagle was terrifying. Nice women did not appear unattended at tavern doors —few even entered one with husband or brother. Suppose someone saw her go into Tom MacSherry's ordinary? Lest her courage fail, Peggy hurried along, almost ran, only mechanically noticing the passage of a line of two-wheeled ox carts. They freighted huge hogsheads of tobacco to the storehouses on the far side of Norfolk. The oxen, big cream-colored beasts from the West Indies, plodded by, snuffling, drooling, and setting their feet down in the dust with deliberation. A freighter's wain jolted by, its ungreased axles screeching like pigs in a slaughter house. No one seemed to pay any attention, though the hot April sunshine had tempted most shopkeepers to leave open their doors. Peggy hastened by a row of hawkers standing on the narrow brick sidewalk. A herd of half grown pickaninnies were playing prisoner's base in a vacant lot; there were not many such left in Norfolk.

For some reason the Spread Eagle seemed deserted, so, heaving a grateful sigh, Peggy timidly passed beneath the ordinary's blue and white sign. She peered through a half open door and relief grew at seeing no one in the place but a sturdy yellow-headed wench. She stood just inside the door and her eyes were screwed up in an effort to read an advertisement posted to the inn's notice board. Peggy delayed speaking, examined the young woman with a penetrating curiosity. This, she reckoned, must be a "handy-girl," one of those abandoned huzzies men joked and bragged about when they thought they weren't being overheard.

Peggy drew her shawl closer and, although it contained less than sixpence, took a firmer grip on her blue chintz pocket. But the yellow-haired barmaid was too occupied to notice her presence; she was scratching her head in puzzlement over a long word.

Peggy prolonged her inspection. What a perfectly awful way to make a living! Imagine pouring liquor for strange men and having to let them put hands under your petticoats whenever they'd a mind. She sniffed. It was like the sniff her mother gave when a house slave got pregnant of God knew what big black buck. A girl like this must be callous; stood to reason she hadn't any finer feelings. For all this tavern wench's looks would please even a fussy man, she was bad. One of God's lost lambs. Maybe she didn't have any soul? Black slaves and Indians didn't, so most people believed; or at best their souls were picayune affairs.

She felt irritated when she noticed the yellow-haired girl's clean calico dress, the spotless kerchief knotted around her shoulders, and a little gold locket hung about her neck. Nice looking maybe, but all of it had been paid for by sin—carnal sin. Just what carnal sin was Peggy didn't know for sure, but she reckoned it was something awful. What made Peggy maddest of all was to realize that women like this—whited sepulchers, the Reverend Dr. Love called them—could come and go as they pleased; they hadn't to explain to anyone. Fancy being free to talk to anyone whose looks you happened to like! There was something intriguing in such a license—especially at seventeen.

Handy-girls, Mrs. Fleming had always insisted, were responsible for half the trouble in the world—and rum for the other half. Tavern wenches were given to getting gentlemen in trouble, generally by claiming some nasty ash cat of theirs to be his offspring. Along with Peggy's indignation grew a fascination for the subject. It was yellow-headed doxies like this who kept married men staying in town late, got them to neglect their wives and homes. However, Peggy admitted it was the freedom of girls of this class which made, by comparison, the business of always being a lady such a dull occupation. Her aggravation grew with the reflection that men doubtless spoke their real minds to a tavern wench. To ladies like herself, they only said what they thought they ought to say. The wench's pink and yellow prettiness became irritating as a personal affront.

"Is Mr. David Ashton here?" she spoke quite sharply.

Katie, startled, raised wide-set eyes, then gaped. It was right seldom a real lady appeared at the Spread Eagle's oak and iron door. La! She was quality and no mistake. Tiny hands and feet, clean cut features and big dark blue eyes. This lady put her in mind of young Mr. Gilmorin's racing mare.

She smiled in friendly fashion. "Why, yes, ma'am. I reckon he is, but I ain't sure."

"Well then, move! Don't stand there like a bump on a log." Peggy felt desperately uneasy. Suppose someone saw her in conversation with this doxy? "Go find him! Tell him Mrs. Ashton wishes him to come at once."

"Mrs. Ashton!" The girl's wide-set eyes became enormous. Her face flamed, then turned white. "Did you say *Mrs. Ashton?*"

Peggy indulged in a very unladylike stamp. "Yes, you slut! How dare you keep me waiting like this!"

The girl inside the door all of a sudden broke into an inexplicable grin. "Oh, I reckon you must be Mrs. Rob Ashton?"

Peggy caught her breath. Why, this poor silly fool must have thought her David's wife. Merciful Heavens! She supposed David must have had to do with this common creature! She reckoned so. Men were like that. What else could have made the wench go so white? Intuition told her this yellow-headed girl was in love with David!

"Will you find Mr. Ashton?" she stormed.

"Oh, yes, Ma'am, yes, Ma'am." Starched petticoats rustling, Katie fled into the ordinary's interior so fast that a couple of somnolent teamsters lounging inside roused up. Her feet took the stairs two at a time and, breathless, she halted before David's door.

Cripes! How mad the lady downstairs had got. But she'd no leave to call a girl—all for nothing—a slut. It wasn't so. She wasn't a *slut!* Well, maybe she was at that; the lady downstairs was quality and ought to know; still, it wasn't nowways fair for Mrs. Ashton to speak so. Katie had been minded to call names back, like she did at the fancy women who yelled at her from waterfront dives like the Hawse Hole and the Bosun's Gaff.

When she rapped at Mr. David's door, her fingertips tingled a little as they always did.

"Come," his voice invited.

When she turned the knob, she saw Mr. David was in his shirt sleeves and his dark hair untied. It brushed his shoulders. He sat near the window bent over a desk with papers piled all around him. Two or three of the sheets had been rejected and lay on the floor defaced by big splattering black X's. That was shamefully prodigal, Katie thought. Such paper nowadays cost eight pence the sheet.

"Well, my fair Hebe, in what manner may I serve you?" he grinned rubbing his eyes with his knuckles.

"Someone's to see you downstairs," Katie began, then she burst out, "Mr. David, am—*am* I a slut? A real honest-to-God slut?"

David Ashton's sensitive dark face tightened, then relaxed. "No, my dear. Whatever you've had to do, or have wanted to do, you have never lost your self-respect. You are a pleasant, healthy and, I believe, an intelligent young animal; not a slut."

Katie felt the cold band about her heart loosen. Somehow Mr. David knew just how to make a girl feel better, surer of herself. Mr. David knew everything.

She added, "It's Mrs. Ashton downstairs. She's by herself."

"What!" The very idea of Peggy's approaching a public house sent him leaping for his coat. Pulling it on, he started for the door. "How long has she been here?"

"Why, why, about five minutes, I reckon. She was—"

"—And you let her wait! Damn my eyes, but you are a stupid slut!"

He brushed by her and, in plunging across the taproom, trod square on the spit dog; the animal fled yelping to the kitchen. At the door he looked for Peggy and saw her standing a few feet away. She, like everybody else in sight, was staring in the direction of the wharves and the tangle of spars showing above them.

A series of wild whoops and Indian yells were making nearby houses resound. Heads were thrust out of windows and people opened their doors.

It was some damned sailor on a spree, David decided, hurrying to Peggy's side.

"Yow! Yow! Wow!" A figure raced into sight, hatless, running as if all the Seven Devils were at his heels. Twice three times in midstride he bounded into the air like a boy on the last day of school. Horses standing at hitching posts turned mildly curious heads, then cocked their ears. Panting, round-eyed, Robert Ashton bore down on the Spread Eagle, oblivious to the frantic yipping of a playful mongrel running alongside.

"Peggy! he roared. "Peggy, darlin'!" He pounced upon his wife, lifted her small figure and spun her around twice before he kissed her with such a resounding smack that, as Mac-Sherry said, "You could of heard him clean over to Portsmouth."

Peggy stared. Terrified. Aghast. Of course he was drunk! The long strain had sent him off his head!

"Oh, Rob," she begged, struggling in his arms. "Do be calm. What is wrong, dear?"

David came hurrying up. "Easy on, old fellow. What's wrong?"

"Wrong? Nothing! Nothing is wrong in all the world! The *Assistance* is back!"

6 — TOLLING BELLS

"YES, siree! We made a plagued slow passage up—with that fished topmast. I dared not crack on much canvas." Farish, fingering a chin dark before its weekly shave, glanced out of the stern ports. "It took considerable hunting 'round to land the right buyer. Them furs for instance—but I made a forty instead of twenty-five per cent profit on them. Same with the turpentine and salt. Then I had to wait a week to find room at Will Gibson's yard. He give me far and away the lowest estimate for repairs, so 'twouldn't have been good business to go elsewhere."

"But I still don't see—" Rob objected.

"There was trouble with the laborers. They're that het up over new troops coming to Boston they couldn't keep their minds to their tasks." He added quickly, "I done the best I could, Mr. Ashton."

"And a damned fine best. Only it *was* a bit trying waiting for you."

Three days later Rob went aboard, found Farish on his quarterdeck running through a sheaf of papers.

"What would you say about a trip to Charles Town?"

"Massachusetts?"

"No. Charles Town, South Carolina. What do you think?"

"I'd say no, Mr. Ashton. Boston is the spot. Prices everywhere down East are higher nor a seventy-four's skysails. If you could contrive to dig up some gunpowder—even a few barrels." The sea captain dropped his voice, "Man alive, it's selling for two dollars the pound!"

"Why mention it?" Rob demanded, a trifle irritated. "I've told you there's not a smitch around Norfolk. Powder can't be bought for love nor money."

"Wal, now ain't that a pity?" Farish blinked. "Still, there ain't much wrong with tobacco and salt prices up there, either." Brows knitted, he selected a slip of paper. "Here's your invoice for a hundred bushels of salt. Bought it out of a Bermuda sloop an hour ago."

"How much?"

"Two and six a bushel."

"That's fine; that's sixpence under the market." He beamed on the New Englander. They were getting on better all the time. "What time tomorrow will you want to clear?"

Farish squinted over the rail at a planter's barge threshing grandly by. Its owner lolled in the shade of a canopy, watching its sweeps swung by four big blacks in red and yellow striped jerseys. They were bucking a strong tide. "Provided your Aronoko is stowed in time, 'round noon tomorrow."

"Good. Now about what should the hides fetch?"

"Good grade?"

"Prime."

"Well, I cal'late I might get two dollars apiece above last trip—say seven."

"Let's hope so," was Rob's meditative comment. "Your repair bill has cut down my operating capital."

"With any luck on this voyage, we likely will make up for the repair bill," Farish assured him. "Then I shouldn't wonder you can go ahead with your new craft even faster than you figured to start with." Stooping, he absently stroked the ship's cat, an enormous swaggering black tom which, so the boatswain boasted, had strewed the whole Atlantic coast with dusky kittens.

"You don't reckon on any delays this trip?"

"Shouldn't meet a one," Farish promised. "This ship's as trim now as Solace on Sunday. And the crew I've shipped this trip has gumption enough to discharge the cargo themselves."

Bending over a table set on the *Assistance*'s spotless decking, the leather-featured master ran through the manifest, then regarded the owner not without respect. "How come you figger the Bostonians might be short of cordage?"

"You said there is a dispute going on with the Crown over the sale of naval supplies up yonder; stands to reason the market isn't getting a normal supply."

"Just and right. Right and just." Farish's bald head nodded agreement. "The Admiralty has requisitioned half of what's to be had." He was feeling better these days, now that he'd a sound bottom under him again and spars aloft which didn't need nursing like they were dry reeds. If matters got no worse around Massachusetts Bay, like enough him and Ashton would work up a pretty piece of trade. When he went up to command Mr. Ashton's new brig, he'd get Hezekiah Coffin's oldest boy to master the *Assistance*.

By Godfrey's the new vessel sure promised to be a slick sailer. All morning he'd poked and nosed around Newton's shipyard, though he knew durned well he ought to be down to Aldrich's buying stock fish and seabiscuit. Yes. There was something mighty tidy about that there brig's lines. The graceful forward rush of her bow got him all het up inside, like a third glass of rum.

Only one thing went against him. As he had guessed, Mr. Ashton was set on calling his new vessel *Grand Turk II*. While he was watching that morning some carpenters had stepped her figurehead. Though it was a tidy bit of craftsmanship, he still held, and always would hold, that *Grand Turk* was no fit name for a Christian vessel.

Silence, beyond the lapping of wavelets along the brigantine's bilges and the sing-song of stevedore gangs discharging a Marblehead schooner over at Major Fleming's great long dock, ruled the sunlit quarter-deck. Master and owner were very busy checking bills of lading against the manifest.

Farish straightened first, rubbed his bare scalp and stifled a yawn.

"Wal, we ought to clear a pretty this voyage. But mind you, I mustn't lose a day—not with all them lemons and limes aboard. They're pretty near ripe already—some of 'em, and—"

He broke off. Somewhere ashore a deep-voiced bell had begun to toll. *Blong—blong—blong!* The tone of it was definitely funereal; long instants passed between each stroke of its muffled clapper.

"Reckon somebody must have just died," Rob remarked, and kept on driving his quill across the foolscap.

A nice cheerful place to work, this. The ship was pleasanter than the warehouse office with its draughts, dust and dirt. Farish had made a world of change in her. For instance, the decking in the stern cabin had been scraped and oiled. Clean white paint was on its paneling and trim and made it look bigger, though a ten by twelve cabin would never seem spacious under the best of conditions.

When a second bell joined the tolling, Rob looked up. A third joined in the lugubrious lament. "Hear that? Must be a big-wig who's dead."

"Yes. I guess likely."

An iron clangor, relentless, insistent, beat over the town's roofs and came rolling out over the harbour. A ray of light glancing off the water lit the faces of the two men as their eyes met. The black stevedores stopped their singing, their feet no longer stamped along the deck. All of them turned their heads towards town; listening. Rob started to write again, but more bells were clanging, swelling the funeral chorus until gulls perched on the lime-whitened roofs of warehouses took alarm and began taking off. Heavily they flapped out over the harbour. The pealing bells, Rob sensed, now were sounding more than just funereal; they were taking on an alarmed cadence.

"Maybe," Rob said suddenly, "we had better find out what's happened?"

The two went aloft and along the wharf through the warehouse and out towards Lawson Street.

The shipping clerk came running out to meet them. "Look —Mr. Ashton! Look over there! They're putting up the shutters on Neil Jameison's warehouse."

"Then it's him who must have died," Farish said.

Sharply Rob shook his head. "It couldn't be. I talked with him not two hours ago. Besides, see there?"

He pointed. At intervals down the street various freight sheds, warehouses, and stores were closing their shutters. People were congregating on street corners under the whale oil lamps rigged there.

"Maybe you had better shutter-up, too," came Farish's preoccupied warning. "When everybody else is expecting trouble, it don't do to tempt Providence."

As they secured the shutters the three of them could see a stream of employees hurrying out of Jameison's warehouse. Some, carrying their coats over their arms, began to run up the street towards the main part of town. Others paused, as if bewildered.

"Hi! Johnny, what's happened?" Rob hailed young Gilmorin, David's friend. Oddly enough, he was wearing a sword in midafternoon.

"This! This!" Excitedly he ran up, brandishing a single sheet of paper marked with a broad black mourning band. "The Marblehead schooner brought it this morning, but the news has just got out. It means fighting for sure! Everybody says so!" He started off, but Farish's hand shot out, gripping him by the elbow.

"You ain't said what's happened, son."

Johnny flushed angrily, then grinned. "Why, that's so. Here, read it!"

With the force of a blow, black headlines sprang to meet Rob's eye.

BLOCKADE OF BOSTON!

Port Ordered Closed to Trade From
June 1st, 1774. Gen'l Gage
Proclaims Rigid Blockade.

A shiver started under Rob's collar, coursed down his back and branched into many little icicles.

"Godfreys! It can't be so!" Farish exclaimed. "The Britishers wouldn't dast!"

"But it is so!" Johnny exulted. His lively brown eyes were snapping. "Read what it says! Read it! The ministers say Boston ain't to be the capital of Massachusetts any longer—it's Salem now."

He snatched back the paper and read aloud, " 'His Majesty's Customs House and Courts of Vice-Admiralty will be

121

transferred to Marblehead.' Do you know, Rob, not even a skiff will be allowed across Boston Harbour? Not 'til the Yankees pay damages to the East India Company and sue for the King's pardon!"

Farish's plain little figure seemed to gain stature. Said he gravely, "Wal, Mister, you can write this down on the tail of your shirt. Boston stands on her bounden rights. She won't sue. She'll rot first!"

7 — FORECLOSURE

MATTHEW PHIPP'S prediction speedily bore fruit—bitter fruit. News of the Boston Port Act spelled a doom to the old time carefree and friendly spirit of Norfolk port. On encountering certain neighbors townsfolk took to looking the other way, or fixed them with grimly hostile stares. The English and Scotch, few of whom had ever dreamed the Ministry would order so drastic a punishment, were frankly dismayed. Of necessity committed to the Government side, they steadfastly, even more obstinately manifested their loyalty.

By evening of the day the news arrived almost every store, warehouse or ship in town was known as Tory or Patriot property. Ship crews, weatherbeaten and bandy-legged, swaggered up Cumberland Street with cutlasses hung to their belts. They were spoiling for a fight. The taprooms of the Spread Eagle and of the Pied Bull became centers for small anxious tradesmen; planters smelling of manure began pouring in from outlying districts. Ma Coverly's Harp and Crown and the much older King's Arms more soberly catered to the wants of factors and their employees, to the Customs force and to other persons in the service of the Crown.

Lemuel Heinz, pale face twitching, scaled the Pied Bull's mugscarred table and laid searing Biblical curses upon the Pharaohs of Williamsburg and London.

The day following Norfolk's lament over Boston's punishment Robert Ashton and Stephen Farish deliberated over mugs of ale in a grimy ordinary. It lay across the street from John Brown's factory.

"Mr. Ashton, I presume you have made up your mind?" Farish wanted to know. "Today's 'Intelligencer' says the blockade of Boston will for certain begin June first. Today is the second of May. Now if Leavitt's tobacco shows up today, I'll have time and to spare in fetching Boston. Yes. I can get under the deadline sure fire. Everybody says ships already in port will be allowed to clear." Pursing thin lips, the New Englander blew the foam from his ale but paused, wooden noggin half raised to his mouth. "By the bye, can I for sure figger on the tobacco by tomorrow?"

Rob, leafing through some finger-marked bills of lading, paused. "I reckon so, but I wish to God I could be sure. Peart vowed up and down he'd bring it alongside today."

"Then you had better figger on my sailing tomorrow," Farish warned.

"You need ten days to Boston?"

"Nine anyhow. We're allowing a mort of time, but this time o' year I'm bound to meet fog off Cape Cod."

Rob, slowly revolving his noggin between calloused hands, merged straight brows. "Joe Peart's sober and reliable as any river captain sailing the Bay. Always has been. The tobacco should come alongside any hour. You've got no choice but to wait for it. Rest of the shipment wouldn't justify my risking the ship up there."

"Mr. Ashton, couldn't you mebbe locate some other tobacco?" the New Englander suggested, irritably fanning an eager halo of flies from his ale. "I don't hanker to cut matters too fine. But it's your vessel, not mine."

"No. Gilmorin and Brown and the rest of the factors have snapped up every leaf of Aronoko and Rappohonak in the market; whether it's stemmed or not. Besides, I bought Leavitt's at an extra fair price. If worse comes to worst, I can maybe track down a few hundred weight of Sweet Scented along the York River."

Farish shrugged and fanned himself with the turkey wing an untidy kitchen slave brought him; the afternoon was growing very hot. "Well, I pray the Aronoko turns up. With this heat, we are going to lose some of them melons. A few sacks went moldy last night."

Two days passed without a sign of George Leavitt's tobacco. Rob, cursing the extra expense, chartered a pinkey to cruise up the James with urgent orders for Peart to hurry.

Three more balmy spring days passed and notices began to appear on Tom MacSherry's bulletin board. A squadron had arrived in Massachusetts Bay to carry out the blockade and more rigidly to enforce His Majesty's customs regulations. Hundreds of British regulars had been ordered to return to Boston. Two battalions of red-coats were encamped upon the town Common. Bloody, often fatal brawls were the order of the day in the doomed town.

Anti-Ministry feeling grew in Norfolk. The Provincials felt unhappy about that quartering of British troops on fellow civilians. Somehow they had been expecting reasonable treatment from the King, if not from his Ministers.

When on Saturday, the seventh of May, Rob pointed his skiff down Plume's Creek in the direction of Norfolk, he was blind to the morning's soft blue sky, to the lazy clouds lifting above the green billows of foliage on the banks. He never noticed the softness of a breeze blowing off shore and bringing with it the perfume of marshes and backwaters now in full flower. For once he failed to enjoy the sweet reek of fresh ploughed land. He was too savagely impatient with George Leavitt. What could have come over him? Had the planter broken their agreement for the sake of a better price?

Had Peggy talked out of turn? She knew about the deal. And it wouldn't be unlike her father to try out-bidding; everyone fancied tobacco grown at Powhatan. It was hard to figure out the delay. Still, the copper-skinned planter's word had always been as good as his bond; maybe better.

Rob's eyes felt dull, his skin dry and old. All night long he had debated what he had better do.

He steered his skiff around a drifting snag, absently watched a number of muddied turtles go *plop-plopping* off into the tawny creek water.

When he reached the warehouse he found Farish pacing up and down. Watching him sat Captain Peart, lantern jaws working nervously on a quid. The river captain's checked shirt was open and a big brass belt buckle over his round belly flashed like an angry eye as he turned to face Rob.

"Howdy, Misto Ashton."

" 'Morning, Captain. Glad to see you here at last."

"Wal, you won't be fer long!" Farish predicted. That the Yankee was hopping mad Rob could tell with half an eye.

His initial sense of relief faded once he glanced down the wharf. On it stood no great wooden hogsheads; just the familiar litter of discarded spars, broken cases and odds and ends of lumber.

"Where's my tobacco?" he demanded sharply.

"Aye, sir, and well may you ask!" Farish sputtered. "There is no tobacco, and my crew eating their heads off for nigh on a week!"

"No tobacco!"

"Nary a bunch!" Rob's captain snorted. "Comes of trusting to a consarned river sailor."

"Hush yo' trap, you no 'count Yankee!" Peart jumped up, towered above the little New Englander's aggressive figure. "Misto Aston, Ah'm sho' sorry, but Ah couldn't help it."

"The hell you say!"

He drew nearer Rob, his long gaunt face hard. "The hell Ah say! Misto, d'you-all reckon a week up the river didn't cost me nothin'? All Ah got to show fer it is thirty hawgs Ah picked up at Jackson's landing."

Anxiety broke through Rob's self-control. "But good God, man, where is Mr. Leavitt's tobacco? He swore he'd ship me twenty hogsheads! I've got to have them. Did he ship by somebody else?"

Peart's spittle described a long parabola, splashed into the office's cold fireplace. He gnawed one end of a gray mustache fringed with yellow before he drawled,

"Mr. Ashton, Ah reckon we are both out o' luck—plenty!"

"What do you mean?"

"The factors hev took over Powhatan."

What!

"That's just what they've done." Like a solemn parrot in a ragged gray jacket Peart wagged his head. His gaze sought the distant, dropping-stained roof of Fergus Sandys's big brick warehouse. "Aye. The Scotchman foreclosed when Mr. Leavitt said he'd be damned if he'd assign Sandys the whole of his crop."

"By God, he wouldn't dare!"

"But he did," Peart insisted; biting off a fresh chew. "Some bailiffs and a sheriff rode over from Williamsburg and took possession three days ago. Folks say Leavitt will be stripped clean. But jist mark my words, gents; Sandys is sho' goin' to be sorry he sicked them bailiffs on Powhatan. Squire Leavitt's raising the countryside. Every planter along the Jeems is getting set fer a fight!"

"Set for a fight? Now do tell!" Bleak satisfaction lit Farish's wintry blue eyes as, clamping strong yellow teeth into a plug of nigger heel, he tore off a generous bite. "Well, now I've a notion some folks up to Boston will be glad to hear about this." He dusted off his hands and looked Rob in the eye. "Now, Mr. Ashton, what d'you cal'late to do? Can you find any other tobacco before it's too late to clear for Boston?"

"How about it, Peart?"

"Reckon *you* know the river warehouses have been cleaned out slicker'n a chicken pie at a cake-walk."

In Rob's head calculations formed and re-formed like troops at exercise. Half his lemons were mildewed now and many of the limes had gone bad; all the while harbour expenses were piling higher. For a little he stood staring out at the *Assistance* and her crew snoozing in the sunshine. Only Buff, the big slave, was working, splicing a hawser; his naked shoulders glistened with sweat.

"There is enough time," said he at length. "I reckon you'd better clear this afternoon tide for Wilmington in North Carolina. Sell the lemons and limes for whatever they bring but hold on to the cordage. Buy rice, as much as you can of it. If there is to be a blockade of Boston, I reckon the people there will begin storing food pretty soon. Leave space for twenty hogsheads of tobacco. I hear plenty of leaf is warehoused in Wilmington. With so many ships gone into the Atlantic trade, the owners can't move it north."

He went into the office and climbed up onto the high stool Peggy usually used. Talking all the while, he began to point a quill. Peart, pushing his peaked leather cap on the back of his head, went over to inspect the *Grand Turk*'s model. Rob had brought it in town to illustrate a point to Tom Newton.

"Soon as you make port get in touch with Huger & Buxton," Rob said to Farish. "Even if you get in at sundown. I don't need to tell you we have got to move fast." He nodded thoughtfully. "By the time you get back from Wilmington I will have found some more salt. Also, I will know better how things are going in Boston."

Farish, a grim set to his jaw, started for the wharf. He couldn't abide the idea of Solace up there all by herself. She was in Cambridge, five miles out of Boston and comparatively safe, but what with the British quartering troops everywhere, it wouldn't do to have a squad of lobster-backs messing about the house; not with Hester just going on fifteen.

Farish got the *Assistance* up to Boston with two days to spare. Since she was one of the last ships in under the deadline, her cargo cleared a handsome profit. It paid for the completion of the new brig's hull and made possible the copper treenails Rob had wanted so much. He didn't want any expensive leaks starting below the water line; wooden treenails, no matter how carefully seasoned, had a nasty trick of shrinking sometimes.

8 — RUNAWAY

TOM MACSHERRY was the first to perceive the drawing power of news items posted to a small hoarding beside the entrance to the Spread Eagle. These items were no more than bare headlines, but a discreet notice intimated that details might be read on another board within. Oddly enough the second bulletin board was situated at no great distance from the bar.

Soon tradesmen, travelers and politicians developed a habit of visiting the Spread Eagle for news fresh as the coach line and post riders could bring it. Nowadays Tom MacSherry's shiny red face seemed set in a perpetual smile. He even began to toy with visions of an elegant coffee room. It would rival the Diana Room of the Raleigh Tavern at Williamsburg.

One day it was said the province of Massachusetts had defied England. The next day the statement was denied. A report stated that a thousand British troops had been ordered from Halifax to Boston. Tom, to make the item more arresting, quietly raised the estimate to 2,500. Later it was proved that only a few hundred infantry had arrived, but earlier arguments had dried many a throat.

A few items admitted no doubt. It was undoubtedly true that independent companies were raising all over Virginia, Maryland and Pennsylvania. They were called "Independent" because, being privately raised, paid and equipped, they need brook no orders from the Royal Governor. Their recruits swore allegiance to the Crown, and only to the Crown. Parliament, the Governor and everybody else could go hang. They paid no attention to orders issued by commanders of the Provincial militia.

George Abyvon, Lord Mayor of Norfolk, denounced such units as illegal. He would permit no companies to be raised within the confines of the Royal Borough. He could do nothing, however, to prevent the small tradespeople, artisans and laborers from mustering just outside the town limits. This they did every holiday and even on Sunday. Grinning shamefacedly, they tried to drill carrying tobacco sticks as muskets.

David Ashton, promised the lieutenancy of a company in the process of raising, had purchased and was, with unaccustomed earnestness, undertaking the study of a handbook by one Roger Stevenson. Frowning, he scanned its title: "Military Instructions for Officers Detached in Full. Scheme for Forming Corps of Partisans, Illustrated with Twelve Plates of Maneuver Necessary in Carrying on the Petit Guerre."

On its flyleaf Matt Phipp, inspired by enthusiasm and good Jamaica rum, had written, *"Fas est ab hoste docere. Ovid."*

For Katie Tryon news items appearing on the Spread Eagle's notice board served a double purpose. They were also her primer. There was no one in the taproom so, slowly and painfully, she began spelling the words out loud.

"RUNAWAY

£ 10 reward. Mulatto boy. Sam, 16 to 17 years. A great Villain but a very good Barber.

John Bland."

Katie nodded to herself. She was beginning to read pretty good now—even long words like "re-ward" and "mu-lat-to." The sergeant said breaking up a word that way made it easier.

Mr. David had been right, of course. She had done like he advised when her sergeant of marines said something about getting spliced. The minute she said "no" to the idea, the big Englishman bought her a lovely picture of a place called Naples—a real steel engraving. She hung it over her bed where she could lie still and admire it. Even better; the sergeant now was spending near twice as much time with her over a greasy primer he'd bought her. She knew he was vastly tickled to feel that she thought enough of him to go along.

What a smart man Mr. David was! He'd been right about washing all over, too; nowadays the planters who wanted a drink late at night—with company—tucked five and ten shillings into her stockings. Before, she had felt lucky to get two

128

or three. Hidden in the lining of a little clothes chest she'd bought against the voyage to Boston was amassed a growing sum. Nine pounds so far, and most of it in silver! Paper didn't feel like real money, somehow, no matter what people said. Money of her own! She thrilled at the very thought of owning property. That very afternoon she intended buying a cloak. She wanted red, but it would have to be gray because Mr. David said gray went well with her eyes. She was pleasantly aghast at the thought of spending a whole pound all at once.

It was only ten of the morning and business hadn't begun to pick up yet, so, laboriously, she commenced to decipher the fact that a Mr. Thomas Shore was offering to an eager public "Keyser's famous Pills for Removing and Eradicating the most Confirm'd Veneral Disorders." She was pondering the exact nature of "Veneral Disorder" when she heard the door open. She turned and her welcoming smile became a grimace of terror. Her legs froze into stark rigidity.

There, framed in the door, towered Mrs. Skillings's forbidding figure! Her mealy-mouthed husband was there, too. Worse yet, Mr. Goodwilling, the assistant sheriff, stood behind them, his official halbert in one hand and an important looking piece of paper in the other.

Mrs. Skillings flung out a wiry arm, pointed. *"There* she is! The dishonest, ungrateful slut!"

Katie wanted to run, but fear held her motionless.

"The i-dee your running off from such a nice comfortable home! Come here, you outrageous cozening doxy!"

"Oh, no! No!"

Mrs. Skillings's abuse brought MacSherry tumbling out of his counting room with fingers inky and steel-rimmed spectacles shoved high on his forehead.

"Oh, Mr. Tom help me!"

"Here, here! What's all this?" Katie's gurgling cry of despair was an efficient spur. "What do you think you're doing to my girl?"

"Your girl, you outrageous, immoral publican!" shrilled the gaunt woman at the doorway. "I'll have the law on ye!" Mrs. Skillings's hard black eyes glittered with menace.

MacSherry was fond of Katie and fonder still of the trade she undeniably attracted. As yet he hadn't noticed the sheriff standing out on the sidewalk, red and uncomfortable looking.

"Law for what? What ails you to stand in front of a respectable ordinary, screeching like a scalded cat?"

"Scalded cat!" Mrs. Skillings snarled. Her nostrils were opening and shutting like the gills of a fish. Her sallow complexion actually assumed some color as she glared down a long reddish nose at the angry landlord. "Don't you misname me, you wrinkle-belly rumblegut of a innkeeper! I'm a lady, I am! I warrant it was you encouraged this poor misguided creature to desert her home and her obligations. Don't you dare deny it!"

MacSherry took off his glasses and prepared to shed also his self-restraint. "Desert what? You cock-eyed bag of bones!"

"Her's a runaway!" Mr. Skillings piped up. "Her's bound to us for two years, three months and five days more!"

"Katie!" Honest Tom MacSherry's outrage became deflated. He looked badly worried as in a paternal gesture he put a big red hand to the girl's shoulder. "Is this so? Tell me true. If it ain't, me and Mr. David will fight for you 'til the cows come home."

Katie choked, gave him a bewildered, tear-drowned look, then nodding, commenced to blubber.

"Leave be awhile, Ma'am," the innkeeper pushed aside Mrs. Skillings's grabbing hand. "There's a mistake somewheres. Katie's a good true girl."

Not until now did the sheriff rest his halbert against the door frame and step inside the inn. He unfolded the paper as he came.

"No, this here is a boney fide indenture contract, doo and properly executed. Mrs. Skillings has the right. And this here's a warrant of arrest issued by the sheriff of Roanoke County. I got to respect it. I reckon you will have to turn this Katie Tryon over to her folks. It's the law."

"It sure is." Skillings stepped from behind his wife. He was a lanky individual boasting stringy chin whiskers, a clay-tinted complexion and in either cheek sagging pouches caused by interminable tobacco chewing. He sucked air in between widely separated teeth and offered a limp, moist hand.

MacSherry ignored it, addressed himself to Mrs. Skillings. "Look here Ma'am, I like this girl. She's hard working and lately she's been learning the self-respect I reckon you didn't ever teach her. How much does she owe you?"

Katie's mistress folded bony, uncompromising arms above

a belly distended by frequent child bearing. "Above two years' time. We love her like a daughter, Luke and me. If you want to buy her off, it'll cost you a hundred pounds sterling."

"A hundred smoking devils!" MacSherry burst out. "Talk sense! I can buy a pair of big Irish girls for the half o' that."

"—But not Katie," Mr. Skillings's reedy voice put in. His mouth, very red for so pallid a countenance, loosened.

"She's just like one of our children to us," Mrs. Skillings announced.

"I—damme, I'll buy her contract! Give you twenty pound' Virginia currency," MacSherry offered; he couldn't stand the sight of great round tears sliding over Katie's fresh cheeks, one by one.

"No!" Mrs. Skillings's narrow jaw clicked shut. It sounded kind of like a sprung trap, MacSherry thought. "We might maybe do business at fifty pounds, but I won't take one farthing less."

"M-Mr. MacSherry," Katie gasped, clung convulsively to his arm. "P-please b-buy me! I—I got nine pound I c-can give you. I sa-sa—"

Mrs. Skillings whirled, beady eyes lighting. "Oh, you have? Nine pound! Well, now ain't that nice?"

"You'll take it?" Katie choked.

"You can be sure I will. I'd have you know, you greedy doxy, them nine pound is mine! Anything you earn while you're indentured to me is mine. You can't own property. You've no more rights than a nigger. Where is that money?"

"Oh-h, Mr. MacSherry, ain't there nothing we can do?" wailed the barmaid, burying her face in her hands.

The sheriff stepped forward; he didn't like the way things were going. "No. Tom's made a fair offer and it's been turned down. All you can do, Katie, is to pack your things and go along without no fuss."

Dumbly Katie disappeared wincing under the pressure of Mrs. Skillings's dirty fingernails on her ear. A pace or two in their wake Skillings shambled along, gaping at a series of broadsides advertising ship sailings. At the rows of gleaming glass on the bar he grinned and wet his lips.

"God damn it, Harry, this ain't right," MacSherry snarled, catching the sheriff by his arm. "I took her in starving, and look at her now. That girl's been happy here and she's doing right well by herself. Them folks is poor white louses."

131

"Reckon they be, Tom, but it ain't for me to interfere," the sheriff stated, wiping his forehead. "Law's law and I'm hired to make it respected and obeyed." He dropped his voice. "Just between you and me with the door shut, folks like them Skillingses oughtn't to be allowed servants. By Jesus, I'd hate to be that girl when they gets back to Carolina."

Presently the three came clumping back downstairs, Katie in her dirtiest, oldest dress and carrying clothes bundled into a shawl Johnny Gilmorin had given her for New Year's. The runaway's yellow hair had fallen in strings over her eyes, but she made no effort to push it back, or to meet the pitying glances of black servants gathered, round-eyed, at the kitchen door even when they called, "Goodbye, Mis Katie, de Lawd be wif you." The spit dog waddled forward, a puzzled expression on his undistinguished countenance. He looked anxious, too. Katie was forever sneaking him a tidbit.

Wearing the runaway's best scarf and carrying a pocket filled with gewgaws bestowed by the upriver gentry, Mrs. Skillings tramped triumphantly across the taproom, her run-over heels grating on the clean sand Katie had spread there.

For the first time in years Tom MacSherry could find nothing to say, could only squeeze Katie's hand hard when she shuffled by. She'd brought him a lot of business, she had, and she was such a pretty, cheerful wench, too. He felt so bad he broke a rule and poured himself two big drinks at the bar.

On the edge of town the Skillingses turned off the King's Highway and followed a track towards a scattering of mean cabins and shanties. They halted at last before a grimy little ordinary named with unconscious felicity. A huge rusty bear trap dangling from the inn's sign crystallized Katie's sense of helplessness. The Trap Inn, she read. She felt so sick and scared she wanted to throw up. Her eyes, she knew, were swollen and smarting; her nose was all red and dripping.

Once they all three stood in the Skillingses' sour-smelling bedroom, Mrs. Skillings turned with a dreadful smile and spoke in honeyed accents.

"Katie, I reckon yer needing to be learned to appreciate a good home when you got one. Come here, dearie, I'm a-going to put some color back in them purty cheeks of yourn."

Five, six cracking slaps snapped Katie's head back and

forth. Dazed, she reeled to one corner of the room, cowering there behind a fending elbow.

"How's that?"

"Well, well, praise the Lord! To think our prodigal daughter's been found." Skillings's thin voice quavered with anticipation. Having peeled off his threadbare coat, he was unbuttoning a shirt the bedraggled frill of which was stained with splotches of egg. Jesus God, but it was fine to see the wench again! She sure had grown into an eyeful! He had forgot how pretty she was; having filled out helped her looks. Yes sir, she'd make a hot armful when they got back to the hayloft. He bet she'd been learned any number of cute whore's tricks in Norfolk. Norfolk was a bang-up sailors' town; the best south of Phillydelphy. Everybody said so.

"There," panted Mrs. Skillings, "that maybe will bring you back down to earth, my high-flown fancy-Nancy. Now just you march your big backside over to that creek and cut me half a dozen switches—so big." She held up a big-knuckled, water-withered forefinger. "For every one that's too small you'll fetch me a extry, understand?"

"Yes."

Again an open hand made Katie's teeth rattle. "Call me Ma'am, you bastard slut!"

Half dazed, Katie stumbled out into the warm glory of the day. Wandering heavily across the yard she earned an appraising and approving glance from the Trap's proprietor, sprawling beside a hound dog on a bench against the inn's unpainted side. A lean blue shoat moved unwillingly out of her path and a few chickens cocked bright suspicious eyes at her swollen cheeks. Mumbling a frightened incoherent prayer, she hunted until she came across a clump of willows growing yellow along the bank. A wren sauced her from the depths of the thicket.

Hampered by blurring tears, she commenced selecting switches. This must just be the end of everything. She reckoned now she'd never get to learn to read and write good now; she'd never get to show Mr. David— Pepperill had been right, she'd never amount to more than a camp girl.

Pepperill! She was so startled at her deduction she cried out. It was him! He swore he'd pay her off when she took up with the sergeant and sent him packing. Cripes! What a silly fool she'd been ever to tell him about Roanoke County and the Skillingses. Pepperill had peached on her—of course he had! Why, the damned little piss ant! She'd—no, there was nothing she could do now.

She wondered what the sergeant would do when he found her gone. Probably nothing. Most English were sticklers for the law—'til they'd lived in the Colonies awhile. But Mr. David? He was smart and well educated, and he knew 'most everybody. Slowly a vague idea began to take shape. She had better make no trouble now. Her tousled head nodded several times.

Finally she found enough switches, terribly pliant and smooth, and slunk back to the house, tendons in the backs of her legs taut and her arms twitching.

The lumpy old bed had been pushed to one side and Skillings was taking some coats from a stout hook let into the room's greasy looking wall. Lips compressed beneath a faint mustache, Mrs. Skillings tested the switches, accepted them.

Said she, stripping off her jacket and rolling up her sleeves, "Just you peel off them petticoats."

Somehow Katie's bungling, trembling fingers undid the strings securing three of them and they fell with soft impacts onto the gritty floor. Her skin went hot, then got pebbly it felt so cold. The scrape of the falling cloth sent shivers up the insides of her legs. One white petticoat, clean save for a rust stain in its hem, remained.

The sight of it seemed to enrage Mrs. Skillings. "Will you look at our fancy lady? White underpinnings—and lawn! She must ha' rolled with half the town to earn such."

When Katie had undone her garters and her white cotton stockings had gone slipping into ugly wrinkles, she straightened and stood still.

"Hold out your hands, you huzzy!" Mrs. Skillings's harsh voice was sharp as a knife. "I'll learn you Christian humility. I'll learn you to keep your place!"

Skillings removed the strap from a ragged canvas blanket roll.

"Oh, no! Don't tie me! I—I won't run! Don't tie me!"

"Hold out your hands!"

Clumsily Skillings tied Katie's hands together, tight, then lifted them over the hook, forcing the victim to teeter on the tips of solid, square toed pumps. She squirmed when she felt Mrs. Skillings's rough fingers breaking the strings of her blouse. The cold air came rushing in over her breasts. She felt the ripped garment hauled up over her head, blinding her and ready to muffle outcries. Naked, she shivered; felt goose pimples prickling her shoulders.

"Oh—don't hurt me—" Panic seized her. "Don't—! I know you'll kill me!"

"Hush, you ungrateful piece. You're going to learn obedience and appreciation for the care me and Mr. Skillings gives you." Her switch hissed like an angry snake across the helpless girl's thigh. "Cheat me—?" *Swish-crack!* "Run off—will you?" *Swish-crack!*

Mrs. Skillings did a cruelly efficient job. Diabolical was the cunning with which she made the limber willows lick about the run-away's body. Katie began to moan, then screamed outright. The withes felt like red hot wires licking around the tenderest, most intimate regions of her body. In vain she danced, writhed and twisted first one way then the other.

"Mercy! For God's sake mercy!" she babbled sure that the woman meant to kill her.

Mrs. Skillings was sweating hard; her sour body odor invaded the room as, with unabated ferocity, she changed switches and relentlessly continued the attack. Katie's skin was criss-crossed and striated with dark red weals. The room was whirling, the floor sinking away; the white hot agony of the blows was beyond endurance. They felt like swipes of scalding water applied with a brush. Her strength went suddenly, her head sagged forward and her knees buckled. Shuddering, she hung from her strapped hands, dimly aware that trickles of blood were crawling slowly down the backs of her legs.

"Easy, does it, Ma," Skillings warned. "You'll have her unfit for travel." He didn't want her permanently marked—as it was, her backside would be livid for weeks. He was remembering the pale sheen of her buttocks.

"There! Now I reckon maybe you'll know your place."

Katie was semiconscious when Mrs. Skillings threw aside her switch and sank panting onto the bed. Great dark stains marked the woman's armpits and transparent threads of saliva had gathered at the corners of her mouth.

Said she recovering breath. "Don't stand there nekkid as an egg. Get into your clothes. Guess you ain't got no shame!"

Mr. Skillings hiked Katie's hands over the hook and pulled her torn blouse back into place. He even steadied her over to a chest of drawers, but he grabbed one of her breasts as he did it.

"One petticut will do for you, Miss. Tie up that bag, Luke, and hump your lazy bones. The schooner will be setting sail come another hour, and it's a right smart walk down to the dock."

Schooner? Sail? Katie's brain only dimly registered the words. She swayed trying to tie her jacket any which way. Her fingers were quivering so hard the strings slipped through them, but her bottom smarted and she was in no hurry to pull up a petticoat. Let old Mealy-Mouth stare all he pleased! He had seen her before.

Schooner! The word crawled into her consciousness. Katie grew panic-stricken. Once they got to sea, not even Mr. David could find her, help her. When she stopped to pick up her oldest yellow petticoat a fresh deluge of tears dripped from the tip of her slightly snub nose.

9 — "Fasting, Humiliation and Prayer"

During the misty, germinating heat of late May, inhabitants of the Chesapeake country lived from the arrival of one courier to the next. News relayed from the North lent many a struggling provincial journal a temporary success. The warmth eared up tall corn stalks, and tender leaves of tobacco widened magically. In the handsome brick capitol at Williamsburg events also burgeoned.

On May 24th the House of Burgesses considered the plight of Boston. The Massachusetts capital was facing a fate as tragic and final as that of any ruined city along the Mediterranean. Reports had it that not even a waterman would be allowed to row his boat of vegetables from one wharf to the next. British harbour guards, so the rumors went, would impound every small boat they could lay their hands on. Dusty post riders reported that starvation faced the Bostonians; food which could have reached them after a half mile's sail, would have to be carted thirty miles by land.

Promptly the Burgesses designated June 1st, 1774, as a day of fasting, humiliation and prayer. As promptly the Royal Governor ordered the House of Burgesses dissolved.

Defiant, Peyton Randolph, Lee, and some seventy others

reconvened in the Long Room of the Raleigh Tavern. It was comfortable, familiar, and just around the corner from the ivy draped capitol. There a defiant legislature listened to the eloquence of Patrick Henry and George Mason. Ignoring the disapproval of merchants, factors and sundry Crown employees, they there considered a circular letter penned by the despairing but undaunted Boston Committee of Correspondence. It was entitled, "A Resolution Taken on May 13th." Patrick Henry made a lot of one of its paragraphs:

—"If other Colonies come to a joint Resolution to stop all Importation from Great Britain, and Exportations to Great Britain and every Port of the West Indies, till the Act for blocking up this Harbour be repealed, the same will prove the Salvation of North America and her Liberties. Otherwise there is high Reason to fear Fraud, Power and most odious Oppression will rise triumphant over Right, Justice, Social Happiness and Freedom!"

Rob was aghast at the celerity with which the Burgesses voted to adopt an "Association recommending the Disuse of dutied Tea and all East Indian Commodities." Further, the lawmakers set August 1st as a date for the convening of a provincial assembly.

To commercial men only one thing was certain; trading was becoming a very hazardous occupation. As a result, the town's tobacco sheds, warehouses and lofts bulged with an influx of prohibited goods which could only be sold at auction, and on the orders of the Committee of Correspondence. English ships were ordered back to sea with cargoes unbroken. Virginian vessels laden with British produce were given the same treatment. Vessels hardly docked than their owners sent them ploughing back over the Atlantic, deep with Colonial produce. Exportation was not yet forbidden. The price of Negroes soared on a well-founded rumor that the new Virginia Assembly would pass laws against continuing African slave trade. Consequently, slave stevedores, carpenters and sailors earned their masters handsome wages, even two Virginia dollars a day.

Only in the matter of business were the Tidewater merchants as one. Jameison, Brush and Inglis traded earnestly and even coöperated with Gilmorin, Fleming and John Brown —and Robert Ashton.

The public temper, however, was growing less tolerant. It was no wonder. Every few days John Holt printed inflammatory and highly biased accounts of General Gage's threats to the blockaded Bostonians. Said Holt, because of swaggering redcoats even virtuous women were not safe from insult on the streets; riots between town and garrison were growing more frequent and bloody. Any ship, no matter what her registry, attempting to enter Boston was to be turned back. Ship captains reported prices in the beleaguered town as rising, though neighboring colonies sent fish, grain, and cattle, gratis. If any ship's papers were not absolutely in order, she was forthwith seized for condemnation proceedings administered by judges appointed and paid by the Crown.

Norfolk's taverns buzzed to an amazing bit of news. Captain Rudder, avowed Tory as he was, had had his ship seized by a British sloop of war! It came about because he failed to register a cargo for Cadiz at an English port! The poor devil was taking the loss of his *Swallow* mighty hard. No wonder. He was beggared.

During early September, when professional shots went out in dugouts to kill rail birds, spermaceti candles and whale oil lamps glowed late in the warehouses crowding Main and Knight Streets. In Major Fleming's office the Scotch and English factors gathered one night to discuss what course loyal-minded traders should adopt. It was high time, John Brown declared.

More and more the river planters were shaking off their old time lethargy and seeing to it that the flames of anti-factor resentment were fed. Loyalist merchants on their way to and from their business now were greeted with threats and curses. By a scared little nigger boy some patriot sent John Brown a box containing a cord tied like a hangman's noose. Two days later, Major Fleming awoke to find his front door spattered with tar and feathers. It disturbed the old soldier not a bit. But a sharp falling off of his business did. The Scots talked and the English listened and nothing came of it; despite complaints, business was still brisk enough.

By day and under starry summers skies, David Ashton, Matthew Phipp and young Johnny Gilmorin—now driven from under his father's roof—rode the countryside to Suffolk, to Cape Henry and clear down to the Carolina border. Earnestly they begged hard-handed farmers to spare each sheep or lamb they owned. Wool would be scarce, they pointed out, priceless ere long.

"Mutton prices are real high," complained the gaunt, nut-brown farmers inland.

"Maybe so. But when the embargo gets going," David said, "your wool will fetch you a smarter profit still. Here's something else to reckon on. It's said up North the British intend blockading our whole coast! If you will write to the Williamsburg Committee and ask for seed grain and instructions how to plant it, you'll get them."

As one, the share croppers and small planters wanted to know should they stop planting tobacco? Sure money only was made in tobacco; the dumbest God's body knew that.

"That's wrong!" Matthew Phipp argued in his sleek lawyer's voice. "Your tobacco is going to rot for lack of transportation. You can eat corn and rye and wheat, but did you every try to eat tobacco?"

Lemuel Heinz deserted his book bindery, spent his whole time riding, preaching against the Babylonians of St. James's in remote villages. With appropriate Biblical quotations, the lanky, fiery-eyed fellow distributed handbills prepared by the Committee, urged the inlanders to dig up the earthen floors of old stables and tobacco houses. They were to boil this earth in a manner fully set forth and fix the volatile salts. Thus might be distilled saltpetre, all-important ingredient of gunpowder.

The great landowners summoned their tenants and offered prizes to the woman, black or white, who spun the best cloth. Not even the heat of an unusually scorching Virginia August shriveled the passionate eloquence of Peyton Randolph, Patrick Henry and Richard Henry Lee addressing a Provincial Assembly sweltering, wigless and coatless, in Williamsburg.

Tremendous excitement attended the passage of a provincial non-importation act and the election of Virginian delegates to a great Continental Congress to be assembled in Philadelphia in October. All this was made easy because the Ministry, as if anxious to cap its previous follies, passed the Quebec Act. Its provisions were enough to set the most conservative Church of England member afire; and Virginia was solidly Episcopalian. The very idea of popish peasants in Quebec and Montreal enjoying equal religious rights! It wasn't to be tolerated. Next thing you knew the Pope, instead of King George, would be running the American Colonies! Most of all the Virginians seethed over Parliament's presumption in calmly assigning to the administration of the governor in Quebec all lands to the westward of the Province itself. Outrageous! Nobody knew how far west the land belonged to Virginia.

Matthew Phipp, in grim satisfaction, told all and sundry how the Boston Committee had forwarded "A Proclamation to Rebellious Hypocrites." It was signed by General Gage, the new governor. Surpassing Sam Adam's most sanguine hopes, the proclamation was contemptuous, as irritating to proud Southern agriculturists as to smug Northern mechanics.

With the approach of cold weather food was growing scarce in Boston, so John Holt's busy press declared; not only for townsfolk but for the British, unhappy and shivering in that gloomy, silent town. Travelers gave the devil his due, reported that General Gage had tried to alleviate the worst effects of the Quartering Act by attempting to build barracks for his troops. But the cantankerous Yankees, said the voyagers, would lift not a finger to help, no matter what the wages, and always the King's men-of-war patrolled Massachusetts Bay. Over two thousand mariners and half as many shipbuilders, chandlers and stevedores, said they, were roaming Boston's empty docks. By the dozen fine tall ships felt their rigging rot and heard rats scurry about their gaping holds.

During the early fall a stride was made of which almost everybody in Norfolk approved. The Virginia Provincial Assembly enacted a law forbidding any further importation of Negro slaves. Said the lawmakers in a special pamphlet:

"The African trade is injurious to this Colony, obstructs the Population of it by Freemen, prevents Manufacturers and other useful Immigrants from Europe from settling among us, and occasions an annual increase of the balance of Trade against this Colony."

Old John Brown frothed when he heard about it. He had lived in Virginia since '62 and no one could tell him slaves weren't a valuable commodity! Further, he would be damned and double-damned before any bob-tailed convention of backwoods lawyers could dictate what he could and couldn't import in his own vessels. Next day, sure enough, he cleared his brig *Fanny* for the slave markets in Habana.

Like a heavy liquid slowly heated, the emotions of the Tidewater people quickened. Nobody had left town, but some people said Major Fleming had mentioned withdrawing from such a hive of traitors.

It proved a beautiful fall and the yellowing tobacco stood wide and tender, but whether any of this crop would ever see the other side of the ocean no one dare prophesy. September 5th came and on that day assembled the long-anticipated Congress of the American Colonies. Everybody in Norfolk was all of a lather to know what Richard Henry Lee was telling the high-and-mighty Philadelphians. Was he standing up to the weathercock-minded New Yorkers and to the shrewd, sharp-faced Yankees? One of Patrick Henry's witticisms gave the whole town a laugh. He'd got right up in Congress and said he was for delaying complete non-importation 'til December because "we don't mean to hurt even our own rascals."

Daily came rumors that Congress had decided this and that; next day the rumors would be denied. But at last the Provincial Congress adjourned and everybody held his breath; Robert Ashton as long and as hard as anybody. What steps had been decided up there in Carpenters' Hall? Their findings would very likely ruin half the businessmen in town and make the eternal fortunes of the rest.

One dreary gray morning late in October, the word got about that the Colonies' answer to the King's Ministers and their oppressions was ready. People dropped everything and, hopeful, or just plain scared in most cases, ran to town pell-mell.

Tom MacSherry was first to nail a copy of "The Continental Association" to his bulletin board. Almost at once he regretted this haste. Both of the Spread Eagle's leaded front windows got smashed by a jostling, cursing crowd trying to get near enough to read the news.

Rob Ashton, one of the early comers, lost his hat and had his pocket picked of a sixpence. On the point of suffocation, he could only brace himself against the door jamb and try to shove his way clear.

"My spectacles!" wailed an old man. "Pray don't break them; they cost three pound'!" But nobody heeded him.

A swarm of ship's carpenters on the fringes of the crowd began yelling. "Read it, somebody! Hey there! Read it out!"

"Sure, read it!" panted a gangling farmer carrying a manure fork.

"Better read it, Mister," gasped a one-eyed seaman struggling at Rob's left. "Quick—we'll get mashed, else."

"No!" roared another voice. "Don't let no bloody Tory read it!"

"Tory? Who's a Tory? Where is he?" Luckily the jam was so great no one could move forward or back, but Rob felt a savage grip on his shoulder loosen the seam of his coat sleeve.

Just then a shout went up. "Hurrah! Here's Cap'n Brush. Come on, Committeeman, you read it!" "Sure, let old Slow-and-Steady read it!"

"It's as you wish, boys, but I can't fly over there."

A way was made for Brush. He drew near the door and the notice board alongside of it, outwardly jovial, though his wig was askew and half his coat buttons were torn off.

"All right, boys, if you'll leave me a rag to my back and keep still, I'll read it." In a hurried undertone he added to Rob, "Get into the inn—out back door—"

The Independent Company's captain braced powerful shoulders against the crowd and made room for Rob to push by him.

Somebody yelled, "Don't let that damned Tory go! Keep him 'til later!" But the big committeeman had put a hand to either side of the notice board and was shouting for silence.

John Brush read in a carrying, parade-ground voice. It filled the whole narrow street, resounded along the wood and brick fronts of houses and shops. As much as he could, he shortened long paragraphs and simplified phraseology. No word of protest arose against the document's reaffirmation of allegiance to the King.

" 'We do, for Ourselves and the Inhabitants of the several Colonies, whom we represent, firmly agree and Associate, under the sacred ties of Virtue, Honor and Love of our Country, demand a return to the Conditions prevailing before the year 1763.' "

The Congress, it appeared, insisted that Parliament repeal their duties on tea, wine, molasses, etc.; their Act extending the Admiralty Court's powers beyond their ancient limits; the Act under which a person charged with an offense in America might be transported to England for trial; the oppressive

142

Acts of 1774 respecting Boston town and Massachusetts Bay; and last, but not least, the obnoxious Quebec Act.

"Hooray!" bellowed Bub Jensen, looming large on the edge of the crowd. "Hooray for Cap'n Brush an' the Committee! That's tellin' them English bloodhounds a purty piece!"

"That's sho' nuff telling them," grunted the farmer with the manure fork, "but what Ah wants to know is—what is the Congress goin' ter *do?*"

"We'll do plenty!" "Stow yer gab!" "Go on, Cap'n. Read us the rest, Cap'n. What are we-all goin' to do?"

Brush turned, face red with exertion. "Quiet! Quiet please! How can I read if you won't keep quiet?"

"Aye, aye, sir. Pipe down, lads! Pipe down!"

A boatswain began shrilling on his pipe and the crowd rocked with laughter but presently grew still.

Bracing himself anew, Captain Brush read out that the Congress had adopted almost *in toto* the ideas of the Virginia Provincial Committee which had met in August. On December 1, 1774, a uniform non-importation agreement between all the colonies would go into effect. This would supersede local laws of the same nature.

A great billow of sound rolled down the street, scaring a hitched stallion into such a frenzy he ran away and smashed Mr. Lewis Hansford's new shay all to pieces.

Non-importation! More than one face went blank— thoughtful—then despairing.

Intelligence that no more slaves were to be imported aroused a more nearly unanimous yell. Even Major Fleming, listening from the shelter of a nearby doorway, nodded.

Brush turned to face the crowd. "The storekeepers and merchants among you had better listen to this. You are warned that when the embargo is applied, you must not raise prices above their normal level! We are all going to suffer, that's plain as a bull's parts, but the Committee isn't going to stand for anybody's taking advantage of the situation."

Again loud shouts rang down the street. "Bully for you Cap'n!" "That's the kind of talk we want to hear!" "Let's throw a crimp into them Scotch bloodsuckers. Go on!"

"The Congress says no one is to drink tea, whether it's dutied or smuggled." Brush caught his breath and mopped the sweat before going on. "Every patriotic citizen is invited to burn his tea in public."

It was the river captain, Peart, who put the question everybody in the dusty, hoarse crowd was asking himself. "So much for non-import but say, Cap'n, what does the Congress say about *exporting?*"

Bending, Brush squinted, then ran his fingers along a paragraph. "It says here we can go on exporting 'til next September 10th, 1775."

"Does this mean our West India trade, too?" Captain Rudder, unshaven and more than a little drunk, bellowed his question from the front of a shoemaker's shop. He had not been the same since the revenuers had seized his vessel.

Brush hesitated, then said, "I'm afraid it does."

Abruptly the crowd's jubilation evaporated. Why, eight-tenths of the live stock and nearly all the lumber and grain exported from Virginia went to feed slaves and otherwise to maintain the great plantations in Jamaica, Dominica and Barbados.

Congress had included the West Indies, Brush hurried to explain, because seventy and more members of Parliament owned plantations there. The sooner the M. P.'s purses felt the pinch, the sooner they would change their tune.

Sobered now, the throng listened to pleas for rigid economies, for the discouragement of "extravagance or dissipation," especially of all "Horse racing, gamecock fighting, exhibition of shews and other expensive Diversions and entertainments." Strict economy in mourning gear and garments was enjoined.

John Brush, fumbling for the buttons missing from his coat, was looking mighty grave. If he saw Major Fleming duck back, out of sight into the entrance of North & Sandys's shipping office, he gave no sign of it.

Matthew Phipp was climbing the steps of Barstow's stationery store.

"Now you know what we aim to do." Phipp's voice rang out inspiring as the shrilling of a fife. "In the name of Liberty will you enforce this decree?"

"Aye!" "To the last Tory dollar in town!" "Aye, I'm set to burn my tea right away."

"Where? I'll join you."

"In front of Gilmorin's store. Let's singe the old bugger's wig!"

Leeming pushed forward his lumpy face, all a-sweat. "That's the ticket! Come on, boys, now's the time to smoke out every Tory's rat nest in the town!"

"Drop such talk!" Brush's hand closed on the ensign's collar and his eyes blazed.

Rob listened to it all, bewildered, in the depths of the ordinary. Until now he hadn't realized how intense so many people were over the blockade of Boston. Why, it lay near a thousand miles north and was a Yankee town at that.

He heard Brush's resonant voice saying, "Violence will not be offered to anyone except as the last resort and then only on order of the Committee." Brush didn't want rioting. Fires got started that way, and fires were no respecters of political convictions. Besides, if Tories got hurt, the King's ships would soon be putting in an appearance. Against men-of-war Norfolk would be helpless as a mouse in a pickle jar.

10 — CARGO NORTHWARD

"HI, ROB!" David came clattering down from his room, fingers all inky and busy with the strings of his riding cape. "I was going out to look for you."

"For me? Why?"

His hand closed eagerly on Rob's powerful wrist. "If your brigantine is in port, I can make your eternal fortune."

A slow, amused grin spread over Rob's features; they were still brown with the summer's tanning.

"Yes? Want to send her to China?"

David impatiently shook his head. "No! No! Don't fun me. I'm serious, dead serious." He glanced about then added in an undertone. "This is just in from Boston."

There was an unfamiliar gleam of expectancy in his brother's eye Rob thought as he nodded his thanks. In search of better light, he led out through the tavern's kitchen, ducking under a whole battery of bright copper pots and pans. Halted in the backyard, he read:

A Schedule of Prices in Boston, September 20th, 1774

	Normal Price	Present Price
Salt	3/ the bu.	£1. 10/ the bu.
Linen Cloth	3/ the yd.	25/ .–27/ the yd.
Woolen Cloth	18/ the yd.	£4. 5/ the yd.
Rum	2/ the gal.	20/ the gal.
Loaf Sugar	1/ the lb.	10/ the lb.

Rob's lips pursed into a soundless whistle. If this was aboveboard, here *were* profits. Holy sailor! He reckoned he knew where to lay hands on nearly a hundred yards of stout Scotch cloth. Salt pork he further noted, was selling at thirteen shillings sixpence the hundred weight! Down here it sold for around five!

Narrowly regarded by his brother, he stood in the inn's sunny stable yard, thinking hard. A hen led a brood of downy yellow chicks over to the manure pile and began scratching in a fine exhibition of maternal energy. Only indistinctly he caught the hum of the crowd. It must be dispersing gradually down Cumberland Street.

Would he? It all depended how strong the trader was in him. A tense, half smile plucked at David's lips. Damned if Rob would ever learn to make up his mind in a hurry. The only time he moved fast was when a covey of partridges got up under his feet. He was deadly quick then.

Rob was thinking these were the sort of profits a merchant dreamed of all his life. That there must be a catch to this somewhere, was his next instinctive reaction. He wondered. How generally were these prices known? Suppose, for once, Davey was correct and no one else knew? If he could get the brigantine off inside the next two days, why, he'd have the price of the *Grand Turk*—completely commissioned.

Just the same, he hesitated. Beneath the surface of David's manner he sensed something, but couldn't lay fingers to it. What was it he wanted? Long ago he'd learned that David never did anything without expecting a return. Why this burst of friendliness after a noticeable lack of cordiality of late?

Rob couldn't blame his brother for it. His job as chief of couriers for the Norfolk Committee stamped him as an outstanding patriot—or rebel as old Robert Gilmorin persisted in terming the malcontents.

Moses in the bulrushes! A three hundred per cent profit was worth a risk! What about expenses? Staring vacantly at a coach horse which was drowsing with head thrust out of a stable window, he commenced to calculate. Crew wages were still high as a kite and so were harbour dues: on the other hand, Farish had learned that Salem merchants were granting free use of their wharves and warehouses to shippers carrying cargoes destined for Boston. Should he send the

Assistance up there? Why not? Old St. John always said a smart trader had to run occasional risks—or stay small.

He began to button his coat. "Come along, Davey," said he.

When investigation bore out David's assertion that the price list was a unique specimen, Rob set furiously to work. He also took unusual precautions. Next day, creaking wains, heavy laden wagons and huge two-wheeled oxcarts began backing up in rapid succession to Ashton & Co.'s loading platform. In short order, Neil Jameison stopped by quite casually. He learned no more than John Brown, sitting in the look-out atop his storehouse and trying through a telescope to read the names of consignees on sundry casks, boxes and barrels.

Peggy's pen, flying over the ledgers, never ceased its busy scratching. What was Rob up to? She felt spiteful because he'd volunteered nothing beyond a perfunctory remark about feeling inclined to venture a cargo up to Salem. Despite many eager hints he had remained deaf. What hurt her, and hurt her deeply, was the fact that Rob no longer discussed his plans; he had not since the night Matt Phipp brought out the Test Paper. It peeved her—she had a good business head and had proved it more than once. Paradoxically, Rob very readily would have admitted it.

For so late in October it was sticky, absurdly humid. When she passed the back of her hand over her forehead, she wasn't surprised to find it soaking, because perspiration went trickling down between her breasts every time she bent over. To her deep satisfaction they were maturing. Secretly she had always resented her slim, boy-like figure. In his slow, good-natured way Rob plagued her about it.

She stopped, erased an incorrect figure with a knife blade, then used a piece of stag's horn to burnish the rough spot. This unseasonable heat must be getting her. She had not felt any too chipper the last few days. In the morning she woke up feeling logey, heavy; to get breakfast was a terrible chore. She was deeply grateful that she had Lom to spare her the really heavy work.

Chin on hand, she rested, peering at the long rows of tobacco storehouses and the town's steeples sprouting behind them.

Why was it? Rob nowadays seemed to have little time for that delightful tomfoolery which once had formed part and parcel of their relationship. Why, he had not even remarked on the coral and gold Italian earrings she had put on. And she had selected them simply because he liked them. She reckoned both of them had been working too hard. But there was always so much to do! Momentarily she longed for the old lazy, luxurious life in the big house on Church Street. Guiltily she banished the picture. Rob, she felt, would be a winner in the long run. He was hard to understand and provokingly slow sometimes, but with her to prod him on, he—and she—would show Papa that she knew a good man when she saw one.

A trifle uncertainly she crossed to the water bucket and drank deep from a wooden noggin tied to its handle. Her stomach felt queasy. A touch of the megrims, no doubt.

In the late forenoon David appeared at the brigantine's gangway. Dark eyes intense, he drew Rob aside.

"Committee has ordered me to Boston. They want me to see what's really going on," he went on with a quick flash of strong white teeth. "Mind my going up on the *Assistance?*"

So there it was! Rob felt relieved. Davey hadn't had the price of a passage and had been too damned proud to admit it.

"Why should I?" He grinned, unbuttoning the top buttons of his breeches and resetting shirttails dislocated by exertion.

"You've done me a fair turn, Davey, a fine fair turn." With regard to himself, it wouldn't be a bad thing for people to know he was doing the Committee's Chief of Couriers a favor.

David clapped his brother between the shoulders. "Obliged, Rob. So long as we Ashtons stick together, we'll do; no matter how the Congress and Parliament get along." In the same breath he continued, "I would like to take Johnny Gilmorin along with me. If you have room?"

"Johnny?" Rob hesitated, but could find no valid objection. "Well, I suppose it can be arranged. Oh, one thing; if a man-o'-war stops my ship, there won't be any talking out of turn?"

David stiffened. "You really don't think I would?"

Rob shook his head. "It wasn't you I was thinking of. Johnny gets heated up mighty quick."

"I'll be responsible for him. Now, one last matter. It will be right expensive living among the Yankees. You don't mind if I venture a dozen barrels of molasses? It can go as deck load. I can pay my shot that way."

Rob wondered momentarily who would have advanced

David money to buy molasses. He presumed it might have been Neil Jameison, Tom Claiborne, or another of the Whig merchants. Though he'd a feeling of vague disquiet, he decided not to inquire. Davey was touchy about the queerest things.

"The tide turns at five this afternoon," was all he said. "You will have to get your molasses here by three—and bring cables to lash it. I haven't got a foot to spare."

His answer was, to Rob, surprising. "The molasses will be on your wharf by one o'clock."

"All right. Warn Johnny to send his sea chest over 'round four."

"And now a rumbullion—just to celebrate? On me."

"Can't. There's the salt pork yet to stow. God knows how Candless dares call that fool yellow boy he sent a boss stevedore. He can't even button his weskit straight. Now get along and kiss the girls goodbye—all of them." He grinned. "Norfolk will be having another day of fasting, humiliation and prayer when the word gets about."

"Oh, I'll be back before the little darlings have learned to miss me." David chuckled. "Only one is pregnant."

Impulsively he flung an arm about his young brother's solid shoulders. "I appreciate this passage, Rob, I vow I do. Believe me, the day isn't far off when you'll be glad to have done the Committee this favor."

"What do you aim to accomplish up there?"

"As I said, talk to certain folks, get a first hand impression of what's what in Boston. The Committee hears so damned many lies and rumors we don't know what to believe."

It was a beautiful evening. Rob thought it one of the finest he could ever recall. Though this October weather grew crisp with the falling of the sun, the atmosphere was yet not cold and damp. The sweet scent of marsh grass and the acrid smell of fallen leaves burnt in the town made an elusive, delicate perfume. Again from the end of the wharf he and Peggy, she all but worn out, watched the *Assistance* drop downstream, her patched and weathered canvas yellow-gold in the sunset.

"Ain't much breeze," Rob commented, "but the tide's making out good and strong."

So it was. It swept the brigantine past three great men-o'-war which, just that morning had dropped anchor off the gray old fortifications on Four Farthing Point. For better ventilation the nearest frigate had triced up her ports; as she swung to her anchors, the sunset successively glanced from the iron muzzles of her cannons.

The effect was so startling Peggy gasped, "Look! Rob! Don't those flashes look as if she were firing on Norfolk?"

Rob, groping for one of his omens, nodded, but said nothing. Prophetic? On the *Assistance*'s stern poop they could make out David in his gay yellow coat. He looked soberer than usual. Johnny Gilmorin in a dashing light blue cloak with a scarlet lining, however, acted excited enough for two. He might have been off to China instead of only to Boston.

"He's so young and gay," Peggy sighed, seating herself on a nearby bollard. "He's an incurable romantic. I fear Boston won't meet his expectations."

Both the voyagers took off their cocked hats and shouted something but a marine's drum, beating a call aboard the *Mars*, frigate, drowned out their farewell.

Three hundred per cent profit! Rob squared his shoulders in a characteristic, familiar gesture, and turned. He flung an arm about his wife's waist and kissed her gravely. "What say, Honey, shall we go by Tom Newton's and take a look? They are supposed to step the *Grand Turk*'s foremast today."

"Oh, Rob, I'm so awfully tired——" Peggy began, but there was such eager expectancy in his look she managed a damp smile. "All right, let's. We can sleep late and go over accounts tomorrow."

"That's a sweet angel! Wait 'til you see how much has been done!" Talking sixty to the minute about what he planned to do to his brig, Rob handled her down a landing stage beside the wharf and into the battered sailing skiff.

She faltered then sat down quite heavily, though in a boat she was generally easy enough.

"What's the matter, Honey? You're looking a bit peaked."

"It was awfully close in the office." She smiled ruefully at her ink marked fingers. "I will feel better as soon's we get out on the river. Oh, Rob! I am so anxious to see the brig. It's been a week since I've been over."

Rob sailed his skiff right up into the shadows of the brig's stern. So close Peggy could touch her rudder. His brig's stern, he judged, was the most graceful ever seen in Norfolk—a symphony of imagination, workmanship and design. Inordinate pride filled him when he pointed to a pair of carved sea horses and long tridents supporting the scroll on which her name was painted.

Above, there were more sea horses and an anchor, just as they appeared on the Frenchman's ivory model. If you compared it to the elaborate poop of a man-of-war, or an East Indiaman, the adornment wasn't so much, but it beat all hollow the looks of any other ship out of Norfolk.

Her name, *Grand Turk II of Norfolk,* was done in sturdy block letters black against the hull's white paint. Holt's paper had described her as "an elegant vessel, lovely as a modern Argo." Even the "Virginia Gazette" had run an article condemning the *Grand Turk*'s radical departure from accepted design. By the dozen, seafaring men invaded Newton's yard. They stared hard at her, debating whether she wouldn't be too tender in a stiff breeze. Some naval officers inspected her with almost disconcerting interest.

"Damned if I don't make a prize of her some day!" one of them grunted. "Like the looks of her."

She towered very tall on the ways. Peggy was thinking she had never seen a ship so clean-lined and high-sided. At the same instant a pang of jealousy commenced to burn within her. Did Rob care more for this wooden thing than for her? To watch him now it would be easy to believe so. His expression looked exalted. She knew now why sailors thought women unlucky aboardship. Ships took men away from their wives—to other women. Ships took men's lives, broke them, flattered them with illusions of mastery.

It was the first time she had looked at the brig from the water. From there she could appreciate how well Rob had done; she could admire the wonderfully graceful sweep from under her bilges, the subtle blending of lines towards the bow.

"You have done it!" She spoke in a strange, unfamiliar voice. "You have the model—magnified a thousand times. She'll bring us all the good things in life, won't she, Rob? When will she be finished?"

"Soon as I get money from the Salem shipment. Call it another two months, Honey."

"I'll be so very proud when she's launched; so proud of her —and of you," Peggy sighed. "None of the other merchants will have a—have a—a vessel to touch—" She was going to say more, but didn't. As she looked at the *Grand Turk,* the brig grew bigger and bigger, huge as a ship of the line! Her sides heaved as if she were breathing. Why, her single bare mast was reaching high into the heavens, higher than the steeple on St. James Church. All at once her stern rose up—up.

"Come on," Rob's far off voice was saying, "hop ashore. I want to see if Newton's built the mast step like I told him. Oh—!"

Peggy's small body quietly slumped off the seat into a puddle of muddy water on the skiff's bottom. Lazily her limbs relaxed and her head fell over sidewise against a box of fishing gear; her skirts began to blot up the bilge water. Panic-stricken, he jammed the skiff onto the sloping, chip-littered beach, then lifted her onto the stern locker.

"Peggy! Peggy!" he pleaded, but she didn't seem to be breathing. Appalled, he began yelling for help. The shipwrights had all gone home and the old sailor Newton kept on as watchman was very deaf.

By an heroic effort Rob pulled himself together. Forced himself to think. When a woman fell victim to the vapors, people eased her stay strings, splashed water on her face and chafed her wrists. But which in blazes did they do first? The stays seemed a complicated affair, so he rubbed her limp hands for all he was worth.

Still she lay colorless, her breast still as a stone. He whipped off his hat, filled it with dirty harbour water—there was nothing else—then slipped it gently onto her muddied upturned face. Like a punch between the eyes came the realization of how life might be without her. To his infinite relief her lips stirred, then, with terrifying slowness, her eyelids rolled back.

"Peggy, darling! What's wrong?"

She managed the ghost of a smile, spoke in the faintest imaginable voice. "Reckon we'll be havin'—baby sometime next spring. Must be twins—I feel so bad."

Part III

Salem: 1774

1 — MAJOR BOUQUET

HER yards whining comfortably against their parrels, the *Assistance,* brigantine, bowled under full canvas. She ploughed a white ruler mark down the Cheasapeake, stretching yellow-brown between low-lying streaks of shore. Great clouds of migrating ducks, geese and brant passing before the setting sun cast a shadow over the Bay. By tens of thousands they roared into flight, filling the air with the sound of wings, then broke up into disordered squadrons, whirling black as death against a salmon-tinted sky.

Valuing caution above haste, Captain Farish took it easy.

"We will weather the Capes after dark," he announced, scanning the topsails. "What with this wind we should easy see Chincoteague to looward by sunup. Maybe you don't know, Mr. Gilmorin? They have Spanish horses on that island. Fact. Been there for years. Swam ashore from a wreck, so they say, nigh on two hundred years ago."

"Like the Chesapeake dogs, I reckon," Johnny smiled. He was watching some deck hands relashing the deck cargo.

"Chesapeake dogs?"

"Yes, they got washed ashore from a ship and crossed themselves with otters."

"What they good for?" Farish inquired, interested.

"Retrievers."

"I don't believe a dog would cross with an otter," David objected. "When it comes to mixing breeds, animals have more sense than men."

The little New Englander's harsh countenance grew pensive.

"Maybe so, but they do say Sarah Goodhue's Persian she-cat—Goodhue brought her back from Turkey, or maybe it was Africa—got had by a thumping big he-'coon one night in Brattle's swamp. Folks say she tore up enough ground to

153

plant a New Hampshire farm, but she started a new breed o' cats. Fact."

By Gad, this was more like it, David thought. He had been getting uncommon fed up with Norfolk. Especially since poor Katie had dropped out of sight. He had missed her—her crude tact on mornings after, her cheerfulness, her flattering respect for his judgment. Her going had left quite a gap. When he got back he would really try to learn where she was.

Captain Farish had counted without the moon when he ordered the helm put over and set a course to nor'-nor'east. The brigantine was logging seven knots when, like a ghost of doom, a small frigate stood out from behind a headland. Her lanterns signaled, "Heave to, or take the consequences!" Farish astounded his passengers with the lividness of his language, but hauled his wind and waited for a boat put over by the man-of-war.

"Turner, take the wheel."

Farish dashed below. Godfreys! It would be just too much to get ordered back to Norfolk for having broken some piddling regulation. Everything, he guessed, was shipshape about the papers. He ran the crew over in his mind.

Wasn't one of them but talked genuine Virginian excepting, maybe, that young gentleman friend of Mr. David Ashton's. Isaac Frye, enjoying a free deck passage, was too poorly of some strange tropical disease to do more than shiver in the lee of the bulwarks. Mr. Rob Ashton *would* figger expenses to the last brass tack, then give a poor distressed mariner victuals and passage and not expect a finger's weight of work in return. Frye's accent might, at a stretch, have once been English; but he swore he had been born and bred in Province Town on Cape Cod. If the dod-gasted Britishers impressed Frye, they wouldn't be getting much.

A lantern in her bow, the warship's boat came swinging and bumping alongside. Ashton and Gilmorin kept so mighty calm they weren't convincing. They went over to sit on the molasses barrels, capes gathered in their laps. If Farish hadn't been so busy backing his topsails, he would have seen the muzzle of a pistol peeping out from beneath young Gilmorin's blue cloak.

"Ahoy there! Heave us a line."

When Farish's boatswain complied, a sailor in the boat caught it first try.

"Ship h-oars!" ordered an officer and half a dozen tall oars were flipped to the perpendicular. They spattered water on the rowers.

Farish, leaning over the rail, could make out a black-browed young lieutenant sitting in the stern, vastly self-assured and truculent. His single epaulet sparkled bright in the light of a second lantern on the boat's floor gratings.

"I cal'late you want a peek at my papers, sir?"

"Where are you bound?"

"For Salem, sir."

"Thought so from your course."

"Here's my log and other papers."

"The devil take your papers! Save them for some ratted customs officer's backside. Lower a ladder. You're to take Major Bouquet aboard."

The merchantman's crew, black and white, lined the rail, staring fearfully across at the frigate. She now lay hove-to, less than a quarter of a mile to windward. A quarter moon was silvering the man-of-war's royals and gallants, made the crest of the seas gleam like white silk.

Without affection, the provincial sailors viewed the jersied, barefooted seamen below, noted their blue shell jackets, their varnished, black-painted straw hats and the brass hilts of cutlasses lying on the floor beside them. A tough lot, David thought, but not half so husky as the *Assistance*'s mariners.

Farish, torn between anxiety and relief, called down, "Well, sir, I don't know as I have room aboard."

"Room!" snapped the naval officer. "Damn my eyes, you're bloody well going to make room! Rig a ladder in a hurry, you confounded farmers. How is Major Bouquet to climb up the side?" While the frigate's jolly boat swung and splashed under the brigantine's counter, the dark-browed lieutenant cursed everything mercantile and colonial.

The two Virginians stiffened among the shadows forward. Johnny Gilmorin would have got to his feet, but David gave him a warning look.

A few minutes later an officer, portly and purple-faced in his starched ruffles and regimentals, came wheezing up a rope ladder rigged for his benefit. David watched him teeter on the rail an instant like an outrageous Humpty Dumpty in scarlet then he lurched inboard. He would have hit the deck had not Mr. Turner, the mate, and two of the crew eased his fall.

"Gad's my life!" roared the new passenger. "Can't you boobies use your betters with more care?" He was rubbing the knee of white satin breeches stained from his near fall to the deck. He glowered at Farish. "If your men break my luggage, you'll rue it, you cod-faced clown."

Much as he'd a mind to speak his piece, Farish clamped down on his tongue. This wasn't his vessel.

Angrily, Major Bouquet set straight a silver-laced cocked hat. "What is your charge for a passage on this dung barge?"

"Three pounds." Farish spoke softly, but he was boiling to dot the Britisher. Big as he was, he cal'lated he could take him all right.

Breathing through his nose, the major directed bulbous, boiled-looking blue eyes upon the lieutenant who had scrambled aboard with catlike agility.

"That correct, Leftenant?"

The naval officer who was, with patent disinterestedness, thumbing through the manifest snorted. "Eh?"

"I say, is three pounds proper fare to Salem?"

By the lantern light David could see the lieutenant scratch his long blue-black jaw. "Cursed if I know, Major. This rascal talks like a Yankee so I'd give him half what he asks—be on the safe side. Look at the hangdog phiz on him. Yes, I'd pay the rogue one pound ten and dock him five shillings any time he shows cheek."

"Now that ain't fair," Farish began. "My owner said—"

"—Plague take your owner, fellow," the lieutenant said coldly. "He should feel uncommon honored to accommodate one of His Majesty's officers. What kind of cabin have you for Major Bouquet?"

At Farish's bleak expression David's heart had begun to thud as it had not since that fatal afternoon when the Ashton fortune had gone slipping off the card table. There was going to be trouble because there were only two very small cabins; vessels as old as the *Assistance* were seldom designed to carry passengers. The mate, a sallow faced Carolinian named Turner, was bunking with Captain Farish, while David and young Gilmorin were jamming themselves into the mate's hutch of a cabin.

Farish stood very straight, his brass buttons winking in the lantern light. "Wal, sir, there just ain't no more cabin space."

The lieutenant stiffened. "No space? Then as Gad's my life, you'll make some!"

"These gents hold the only spare cabin aboard, and they have paid for their passage—in full." Grimly, Farish indicated the two Virginians on the molasses barrels.

"Well, I'm paying, too," Bouquet bellowed. His fat figure wabbled to the motion and he kept one hand clamped onto a brace. "I say, Jenkinson, can't your fellows pitch these beastly Colonials out of a cabin?"

Before David could stop him Johnny arose, vastly dignified, and went stalking over the dew-wetted deck. "Sir, I find your manner—"

He got no further. David, having recognized a deadly silken quality in Johnny's voice, ran up alongside. "Be still!" He grabbed young Gilmorin's elbow so hard he winced.

Though it was hard work, David Ashton managed a really elegant bow. "We shall be delighted, Major, to oblige you. Vastly pleased."

Both Englishmen frowned, looked disconcerted. "Eh? What's this? What did that puppy start to say?"

"Nothing of any consequence."

Major Bouquet, however, was not to be mollified so easily and, heavy jaw outthrust, he came lumbering over the deck. He looked, thought David, in his scarlet coat and with his purplish-red cheeks and inflamed eyes, like a man of fire. "What was it—?"

Johnny was trembling in his fury. David could feel him. God's teeth! What would the crazy lad say next? Johnny fooled him for once.

Said he evenly, "I—why, I said I didn't like the manner—" he nodded at Farish—"his way of addressing a representative of His Majesty's Army."

The lieutenant in blue and white put down the manifest, stood glaring suspiciously. He seemed about to speak when Farish said:

"If you wish, sir, you can stow this gentleman's luggage in my cabin. It's larger than Mr. Ashton's. Me and Turner will bunk elsewhere." His none too lofty opinion of Mr. David Ashton's character was undergoing a revision—upwards.

Major Bouquet snuffled, turned aside. "I daresay it will do, once your lice and bedbugs have been put out of it. Inigo, mind you get my things stowed convenient, else I'll make your backside smoke." He fixed a fearsome glance on his slave, a furtive Negro youth with small gold loops in his ears. "Yes, and burn some sandalwood—that'll help rid us of the stink of these fish-eating psalm shouters."

Up from the frigate's boat her crew handed an imposing succession of sea chests, cases and hampers. Several of the last emitted pleasing gurgles, David noticed. The naval lieutenant cast about a final glance before setting foot to the rope ladder.

"Goodbye, Major. I regret we couldn't have found you better accommodations, but half a sty is better than none. Half a sty! Get it? Ho! Ho! Deuced clever, if I do say so."

"Eh? What was that?" In the rays of a reddish-yellow lantern the scarlet-clad figure blinked stupidly.

"I said 'Half a sty is better than none.' Witty, what? Have to notice it in my journal." Half over the rail he paused. "Well, old chap, expect to find you warming your sack over the ashes of Boston."

"Never doubt it, Jenkinson my boy," boomed Major Bouquet. "Never you doubt it, provided I survive the stinks of this hooker."

"Hooker!" Farish bristled. Fortunately the report of a recall gun fired aboard the frigate checked him. Call his vessel a hooker! With murder in his heart, Farish surveyed that scarlet expanse below the major's heavy gold epaulets. David felt moved to sardonic amusement. The fellow was so gross his fat legs were knock-kneed. What in blazes was coming over the Services? Everyone said they were becoming top-heavy with titled whore's sons, drunkards and fools. During the French wars there had been no such specimens about, so old St. John had said.

Lips mighty thin and colorless Farish turned to his mate, "Mr. Turner, move your dunnage and mine out of the after cabin."

Then he ordered the yards braced about. Rigging creaked, sails slatted and presently the *Assistance* resumed her course. The frigate's lanterns began to dim, to show lower over the sea.

Said Johnny Gilmorin, black eyes very hard and bright, "Captain Farish, by coming aboard at the last moment I fear I have discommoded you. I will sleep in the cargo."

Major Bouquet heard him and turned, mottled cheeks

blown out and pop eyes menacing. "It appears a certain puppy needs a lesson in deportment. When *I* required a cabin, you were blessed if you'd stir. But now, sirrah, you willingly surrender it to a pinch-penny Yankee."

Johnny Gilmorin swept such an elegant bow David was proud of him. With the frigate's boat well away, he no longer felt it necessary to interfere.

In wicked pointedness Johnny replied, "Indeed, I do not understand you. I have never objected to doing a gentleman a favor."

Sheer outrage momentarily held Bouquet silent, then he exploded. "Damme! You shall answer for this!"

Johnny made another leg. "I shall be delighted, my dear Major, to accommodate you at any time and at any place, but do I not take an undue advantage?"

The Englishman goggled, puzzled but unimpressed. " *'Advantage?'* God bless my soul! I am a dead shot! I'll have you know I've killed three men! What d'you mean—'advantage?' "

"Why, sir," in the semidarkness Johnny smiled wickedly, "surely my slight figure forms but a miserable target compared to the magnificent proportions of your bloated carcass."

The major stared as if unbelieving of his ears. His eyes bulged still more. At length he announced with a deadly clarity, "My seconds shall wait on you the instant we reach shore!"

Roaring for his servant, he waddled aft.

Farish, who had stood listening, beckoned David. "Mr. Ashton I presume you know how much the success of this here trip means to my owner—and your brother?"

"I reckon I do, Captain. Why?"

"Wal, I grant this Britisher would git a hen rabbit mad enough to chase a dog, but just warn your young friend to mind his P's and Q's, or I'll have to take a hand. If we're ever to fetch up in Salem, we've got our work cut out. Fact."

2 — THE ASSISTANCE, BRIGANTINE

A FOG which had descended with the imminence of dawn was growing steadily denser. In dim, silver-gray banderoles it drifted in and out of the rigging, gradually banking up in woolly strata which soon obscured even the lowest yards.

Tiny, crystal clear drops strung the shrouds and ratlines as the smothering mist eddied about the deck and among the braces.

From a chicken crate lashed into the longboat a rooster crowed. Immediately a furious reply arose from the depths of the *Assistance*. The rooster answered half heartedly, then, despite Hannibal's persistent insults, withdrew his head between his wings and moped.

Somewhere in the shimmering gray expanse a dog barked such a tiny bark it seemed to have been let in on the horizon by a pinhole. The starboard watch, in patched coats of oiled linen, sat huddled in the lee of the bulwarks, shivering and cursing the fog.

"Hear that bark?" Isaac Frye demanded excitedly, and his gaunt brass-colored face lit. "By gravy, we ain't so fur off the Cape! What with the lead showing sand bottom and twelve fathom, I'll eat my wig if we be so very fur off Province Town." Though he was shaken by a violent succession of tremors, he kept on smiling.

"Heah, Mista' Frye." Buff loomed up out of the foc'sle and offered a tin cup. "Doan' drink it all, jes' tickle yo' teefs wid dis grog. My, my! You sho' is gettin' dem shakes agin, pow'-ful bad."

The deck passenger shook his head. "I don't feel bad, not when I kin smell cranberry bogs, salt marshes and dryin' fish. You can smell them ever so clear."

The watch nodded, even though they knew he couldn't. The wind was blowing on-shore.

Gratefully he gulped a mouthful of black Demerara rum laced with water. "These shakes ain't all fever," Isaac Frye explained. "It's getting so near home. Yes, sir, many was the time I figgered I'd never hear yonder surf in my ears again."

He tilted his wasted head towards a faint and monotonous booming sound which had prompted Captain Farish abruptly to alter his course to the eastward. High in the fog a lost gull kept mewing plaintively. The rattling of an idle block sounded very loud.

"You fellers know? In Cuba the surf don't sound like that —not a bit. Cold water surf sounds all crisp and lively, ever notice?"

"That's so," agreed one of the men. "If you pour water from a cold spring, it don't sound nothing like pouring hot water out of a tea kettle."

"Dasso," agreed Buff and sank squatting on his hams; the

160

empty cup dangled from his forefinger. "Dey don't sound no-wise alike. Dey's mighty hard men, dem Spanishers. How come you got took, Mista' Frye?"

"I ain't never really figured it out," Frye stated, scratching the back of his neck. "My schooner was stopped by a Spanish cruiser off Sant' Jago."

"When was that?"

"Three—four years back. In '71, I guess."

"But there warn't no war then," the boatswain objected. "How could they?"

"I dunno, Mr. Holcomb, but they seized and condemned us just the same— Hi, Willie, you see anything yet?"

Out on the bowsprit the cabin boy was peering ahead into the shifting vapor. "No, sir, it's thicker'n a Blue Noser's head."

At the masthead another member of the crew was straining his eyes. Often a lookout high up could spy the spars of another vessel poking up out of a low fog.

"None of us ever did figger why the *Espiritu Santa Elena* fired. We was hove to. But they did, without warning. Killed Luke Waring and Willie Peabody straight off. Joe Lincoln and Fred Coffin died later on in the *calabozo*. Splinters."

The boatswain made a sucking noise in his teeth. "Didn't they hold no prize court?"

"Nary a t-trial," Frye chattered. His teeth began clicking like the castanets sailors brought back from the Captaincy-General of Guatemala.

The boatswain was feeling real sorry for Frye. God in Heaven, the whites of his eyes were yellow as lemon peel and everyone aboard had seen fetter scars, ridgy and all purple-blue from infection, ringing each of his wrists and ankles.

"They jest marched us from Cienfuegos dock to a *fortaleza* and bent on the *grillos*—them's irons. F-Forty pounds they weighed. And nigh on f-four years we lay and rotted among runaway n-niggers, murderers, crazy people and, now and again, a p-parcel of revolution-minded people. It was them got treated the w-worst. G-God, the way the Spanishers treated them dem-democratical prisoners would make a shark cry."

"What did they do?" a young sailor queried.

"Gave them the *cepo*."

"What's that?"

"They'd throw a running bowline 'bout your private

parts and h'ist you up to a ring in the ceiling. They let you hang 'til you'd talk or fall."

A young sailor laughed nervously. "Aw, go on! White men don't do such things. It's too ghastly. An Indian might, though, I expect."

Buff rolled his eyes. "Doan' you believe dey don't! Dem Spanishers and de Jamaica planters, dey got worser tricks den dat."

"What would they do to a woman?" the boatswain interrupted.

"Why, they'd hang her up by her tits, though they mostly pulled right off." Frye shivered. "I still can hear them females screeching—"

A silence descended. The gentle slap-slapping of reef points against canvas supplemented a hushing rush of the sea along the *Assistance*'s beam. Just abaft the foremast the black cook was getting breakfast over a fire kindled on a sand-filled box.

"You sure must have had a hard time."

"Aye. I must be tougher nor whalebone or they'd have pitched my carcass into that old lime pit back of the Morro months ago."

"Them Spanishers never told you why they took the ship? Nor what you were jailed for?"

"No. We never knew. No more than that rooster over there. Our captain swore up and down we hadn't a speck of contraband aboard—just flour and barrel staves. But such happens all the time. Plenty out-the-way jails in the Foreign Islands is crammed with British and Colonial mariners. Like me, they don't ever learn why they're there. Often as not, the commander of a garrison don't even know who he has in jail because the jailers draw so much a head for each prisoner.

"Take me, I'd be in Sant' Jago yet only a parcel of *insurrectos* brought in the yellow jack. Fever got going bad so they marched us across to Cienfuegos to another fort. As we were crossing the town my chain got snagged and I cussed. A fellow standing on the sidewalk spins about—he was the British Consul.

"'Why, God bless my soul,' he bursts out. 'Are you English?'

"'No sir,' says I, 'I'm from Massachusetts Bay Colony.'"
A chuckle went up from the circle.

" 'Well, that's the same thing,' says he. 'What are you doing here?'

"I told him I didn't know and he nods and goes on. A week later some *soldados* marched in and unlocks my irons.

" '*Vaya!* Get out of here,' says the captain of the guard. 'Don't let us find your dog's backside of a face in Cuba again.' "

With a limber little finger the boatswain dug wax from his ear. Shaking his head experimentally, he said, "Well, you've got to hand it to that consul."

"That's the funny part of it. When I went to thank him, he 'lowed he didn't know how it come about because his protest couldn't noways have got to Habana and back by that time." The deck passenger sniffled. Before he turned to stare into the fog off to port, he blew his nose between fingers so skinny they resembled a hawk's talons. His voice dropped. "I c'n hardly wait. Marthy will be a tol'able big girl by now, I guess. The other—" he hesitated.

"What about de other, Mista Frye?"

"I don't know. You see, it wasn't due for a month after I signed on the *Esther*."

"Slum! Slum gullion!" called the cook. Lustily he beat a ladle against a frying pan. "Come a-runnin', er Ah'll sho'ly spill it in de scuppers."

The young sailor called the stock reply of, "Aye and rot the wood away."

Everybody laughed as if they'd heard it for the first time.

Stephen Farish, stolidly pacing the poopdeck, was of two minds. By and large, this fog wasn't such a bad thing; it exempted his brigantine from molestation by roving patrol ships. Still, no skipper in his right mind enjoyed cruising blind near the treacherous shoals off Cape Cod. He cal'lated pretty soon he'd take in the courses, slow down and keep the lead going; it'd be a sin and a shame to have weathered the voyage so far and then come to grief.

Every time he thought how smart Mr. Robert Ashton was about this trip, a grin creased his leathery brown lips. By Godfreys, he had shipped only what was likely to bring highest prices. Tobacco, salt and cloth. Especially that woolen cloth. Yes, sir! Mr. Ashton was the sort of owner a skipper could cotton to. Shipped the right sort of merchandise to where it was wanted, and he didn't expect a master to turn in big profits when the cargo wasn't really saleable.

He peered forward. The fog seemed to be thinning a mite; yes, he could make out the consignee's name, Hovy & Son, daubed on the dark red molasses barrels lashed under the break of the forecastle. He listened intently and when he could catch no booming of breakers, he returned to his ruminations.

It came hard to swallow that dod-gasted major's sass, but it wouldn't be for always. Besides, he was might keen to reach Salem and learn what was afoot. Solace had written that Eben Phinney had got himself elected a Committeeman. He was, she said, making plenty of money while being patriotical. Mightn't be such a bad idee to talk with MacKintosh; having been Captain-General of the Liberty Tree, he ought still to be of some importance.

It ought not to take long to sell his cargo—he hoped not, anyhow. He was all of a lather to get back to Norfolk so's he could supervise the finishing licks on the *Grand Turk*. By gum, he would talk Mr. Ashton into setting extra-heavy deck beams—heavy enough anyways to handle the weight of a battery.

Nodding to himself, he mechanically checked the quartermaster's course with the compass. Yes, sir, he guessed he could, when the time got ripe, argue Mr. Ashton into piercing the *Grand Turk* and applying for a letter of marque's commission. Jericho! What a dandy handy privateer she'd make. The *Turk* should have the heels of any cruiser, French or British, he'd ever seen; provided of course the brig didn't turn out to be crank. Yes, sir. Him and Ashton could make a fortune gobbling up slow-sailing, big-bellied English merchantmen. Imagine Serena in a fine big house like Gardiner Green's on Pemberton Hill. There was a lot of cash in privateering. But he still didn't favor the new brig's name—too heathen sounding.

Below, David Ashton was repacking his sea chest. When he had done, he used a worm to draw the charges from his pistols. Next he wiped their flints and frizzens with a dry wool rag. Then he reloaded and reprimed the pans with fine Charleroi powder.

He could hear Major Bouquet's snores resounding in the next cabin. So Homeric was their volume, they fairly made

164

the bulkheads rattle. David didn't wonder. All last night that bloated swine had sat alone in his cabin guzzling port. Around midnight he fell off his chair and his black servant went in to heave the worthy major onto his bunk. He still lay on it with his wig lying on the deck and his black, close-cropped hair looking somehow obscene against the vivid pink of his scalp. An hour ago he'd been sick. The stench made David's nostrils wrinkle. Grateful to be free of this cramped, bug ruled cabin, David softly whistled "Petticoatee" and threw his last odds and ends into a pair of fine English saddlebags.

"*Cuck! Cuck!*" observed Hannibal, executing a belligerent shuffle in his wicker coop. He was spoiling for a fight and pecked viciously at David's hand when he offered some cracked corn.

"You'd better stop carrying on; that was only a barnyard rooster you heard. He wouldn't give you a bit of fun. Bide your time, my little warrior; in a few days we'll learn what Boston chickens can do, if the British ain't already et them. Reckon you could win me a horse and maybe an English saddle?"

From somewhere beyond the porthole came a noise. It sounded just like the slamming of a gigantic door. It was not a crisp sound, but a resounding *boom!* David, recognizing its origin, straightened quickly and banged his head so hard on the low lintel of the door he saw stars. Just the same, he plunged out into the passage. Then he paused and went back to get his pistols. He jammed them into his breeches top, then tossed a traveling cape over his shoulder and again started for the deck.

At the foot of the companionway he collided with Johnny Gilmorin. The young fellow, all eyes, was tense and shaking with excitement.

"You heard it? You heard that cannon? Means a man-of-war! What are we going to do?"

Snapped David, swaying in the narrow passage, "Nothing yet, but this is serious. Keep quiet, or I'll make you regret it!"

"Why—why, David!" Johnny stared.

A hard smile flitted over David's mouth. "You're too confounded impetuous, Johnny. Now listen. Go to Farish's cabin. If that British porker shows signs of coming to, keep him *quiet!* I'm going up to see what's going on."

The flush faded from Johnny's smooth cheeks. "Just as you say," he agreed and ran back down the white painted passage towards the stern. He wanted to make a good soldier.

At the head of the companion, David hesitated, peering aft, then to either side. Farish himself had taken the wheel, replacing the quartermaster. He stood, a dim, alert silhouette amid the drifting mist, craning his neck to starboard. His profile was outthrust and tense. A second booming report came rolling and skipping over the ocean like a flat stone flung by a boy. It sounded much nearer.

"It's two ships, sir," grunted the mate, cupping a hand to his ear. "That other couldn't have come up so quick."

Farish snatched a leather speaking trumpet. "Masthead! Ahoy!" he bawled. "Can you see anything?"

"No, suh! It's thick like wool up heah."

Farish made no comment, but shifted his course two points to port. Presently he said, "Charge the signal cannon, Mr. Turner. If she fires again, we had better answer."

Over David's dark features came a sudden rigidity. Quickly, he climbed half a dozen steps to the quarterdeck. The day, he noted, was growing lighter; despite a rising wind the fog was as thick as ever.

"What's up, Captain?" he demanded, crossing to the wheel.

"Can't tell which way that feller's headed," explained the master. "And I ain't keen to sound my bell because only a bulldog would be cruising hereabouts. No use letting on we're here 'til we have to."

"That's good sense," David agreed with such earnestness Farish gave him a sharp look.

"Even if they do send us a boat, we're in no danger. What's got your sweat up so?"

"Oh, it's hot below and I've been packing," David replied, keeping an eye on Turner. He was removing the cover of a small cannon—a "saker" the North Carolinian called it. Then he went to a nearby locker in search of a powder charge.

"It will be best to fire a gun," Farish seemed to be thinking aloud. "They may take us for another man-of-war and leave us be. If we ring a bell she'll know certain sure we are merchantmen. Wish to God the bulldog would fire again."

"Why?" David asked studying the fog.

"Because I hear breakers again. Means we can't be but two spits and a jump off Province Town. I don't dast carry a port helm much longer."

166

Everyone aboard the *Assistance* jumped when a third report crashed through the gloom. It sounded less than a quarter of a mile off the starboard bow.

"Too close, by Godfreys!" Farish set his jaw and ground the wheel down, heading the brigantine even more to port. Staring fixedly past the main shrouds, he yelled, "Light your match, Mr. Turner, and touch her off!" Her yards and canvas a-rattling, the ship fell off to leeward.

David stepped closer. "Captain, I reckon we'd better take a chance of getting run down."

"Eh?" The New Englander's head swung sharp to face him and hard lines went slanting down from the corners of his nose to his chin. "What's that you're saying?"

"Tell Turner not to fire."

"I am master of this ship! Hold your peace."

David drew himself up, looking extra tall in his long military-cut cape. "Farish! I say tell him not to fire!"

Farish's blue eyes became more wintry; he looked dangerous for all his small stature. "Stand aside. Touch her off, Turner. Quick!"

Everyone could hear the rhythmic rushing swash of a ship ploughing over the water—fast. From dreadfully near the screech of a block and tackle came knifing through the wall of fog.

"Drop that match!"

Turner spun about and gave a little startled yelp. He was looking down the muzzle of one of David's pistols.

"Drop it! Step back!" Like reports made by a drover's lash the words snapped from David's lips.

"Now by the Eternal—!" Farish exploded, but checked his rush when the pistol and the deadly eyes behind it swung in line with him.

No fool, he halted, then went back to the wheel.

The soft hiss of the mate's linstock glowing on the damp deck sounded very loud. The little signal gun gleamed dully, looked out of its port at the shifting murk.

"If everyone keeps still, we'll get out of this," David said.

All three men on the quarterdeck of the brigantine heard the creak and groan of cordage grow louder. They could catch the tramp of feet, voices. It would be a near thing.

"Deck ahoy" the lookout hailed, a frantic urgency in his tone. "Port your helm! Port! Port! *For God's sake!*"

David only glanced aloft, but Farish was on him. He

slapped the pistol clattering into the scuppers. In one quick bound the master then caught up the gunner's match and jammed it into the touch-hole of the signal gun. An orange flame spurted vertically and the little cannon surged back against its recoil ropes just as a member of the crew screamed, "Jesus! There's her bowsprit!"

Quick as a swooping hawk a tall ship materialized out of the smoky atmosphere, rushed straight at the brigantine. Spouting frantic curses, Farish spun his wheel away from that thrusting wooden finger. Wise members of the crew flung themselves flat.

David could only gape through the signal cannon's bitter smelling smoke in helpless dismay. That onrushing bowsprit, dolphin striker and diamond-shaped netting were almost overhead.

He heard the stranger's Officer of the Deck yell, "Starboard helm! Starboard!" But the great brown hull kept on, the sea boiling past her stem. A yellow streak punctuated by gun ports swept into sight; the muzzles of two bow chasers peered out of their ports like sinister eyes. The crews of both vessels were yelling and shouting. Turner helped Farish grind the wheel over as far as it would go. His hat had fallen off and his bald head glimmered in the ghostly light.

A grinding, rending crash, as of a tall pine falling in a forest, filled David's ears. The whole vessel lurched like a fish struck by a spear. Aloft ensued a furious snapping and crackling as overstrained cordage broke and writhed. Canvas ripped, snarling like a mad dog. Over, and still further over, heeled the brigantine's deck. Everything loose went tumbling. A yard crashed down amidships; smashed the long boat.

In a daze David glimpsed gilded scroll work, freshly scarred and gashed, rush by; also the name *Falcon*. A great wave spewed up between the colliding vessels. Spray flew yards high, drenching the lesser craft's deck. The grinding diminished as the merchantman staggered off to port. Farish, it turned out, had been able to change his course enough to avoid worse than a hard, glancing blow.

David told himself that if Farish hadn't taken time to fire the gun, he could have avoided a collision altogether.

An enraged voice began bellowing, "They fired on us, sir!"

"Then fire back! Sink the lousy dogs!"

That high, brown-painted side and its line of gaping gun ports were falling away fast now.

"Down for your lives! Down, everyone!" Farish flung himself flat to the deck. Turner followed his example.

David was too stunned by the swiftness of the catastrophe to grasp the little Yankee's meaning. Into his face sprang fountains of flame. A cannonball screamed by him, sucked the air from his lungs. Then followed a deafening roar. As he reeled back through a choking blast of smoke, he heard a devastating *crack!* near the foremast.

"Don't fire!" Farish's voice was hoarse and frantically he waved his hands. "For God's sake, don't fire again! We are unarmed!"

But again and yet again the *Falcon*'s guns slammed projectiles at the brigantine, smashed her gig and tore a great ragged hole through the fore course. From their shattered coop several hens flew right over the rail and landed in the water. Others raced crazily about the deck. One missile struck the bulwarks and showered the merchantman's deck with a murderous shower of splinters. The *thud-thud* of debris falling onto the deck kept the terrified crew cowering. Someone had set up a series of shrill screams—one strident, agonized cry on the tail of the last. The acute agony of them set David's teeth on edge.

"Heave to!" Astern lay the man-of-war, a big sloop. Seen in the fog and smoke she presented an infinitely menacing silhouette.

Farish scrambled to his feet once the foremast began to give out a strange grinding sound. Crackling, the spar swung in an eccentric semicircle, rocked until the overstrained stays gave way, then toppled over the port bow and raised a smother of spray. Snapped lines, blocks and halyards rained onto the deck; then, as suddenly as if she had run aground, the stricken merchantman lost way. To David's nose came the pungent odor of burning pine. Gasping, he noticed that the cook's fire had been spilled over the deck. Here and there the fallen forecourse was beginning to smolder.

No more firing took place; the *Assistance* was too obviously helpless. In the trough of the sea she rolled sullenly as a rain filled canoe.

Farish never gave David a glance. He picked up his hat, all dripping, from the water and stood shaking it. "Get up, Mr. Turner, they'll not shoot any more." His face was like granite as he helped the ashen-faced mate to his feet. "What ails you? Scairt?"

"Hell no! Swallered my chaw when the fo'mast went."

A boat put off from the man-of-war, then another filled with scarlet-coated marines. They came along in a hurry, pulling hard over a succession of oily rollers. The naval oarsmen lost the beat, got tangled up when a wave would get under the stern of their boat. It shot forward.

A grim, tough-looking lieutenant of marines was first to clamber over the shattered bulwark. He leveled an espantoon, a sort of short-hafted pike, and two of his sergeants presented blunderbusses.

"Who is master?"

"Me."

"Say 'sir' when you address me!"

"Very well, sir," Farish replied in a grating voice. "Maybe you'll explain why you fired into me? I'm a peaceful merchantman."

The marine lieutenant did not reply at once. Coolly he was estimating the brigantine's situation, the damage done her.

"What can you expect if you fire into one of His Majesty's ships?"

Farish wet his lips. "We only fired a signal gun, then you ran us down."

The Englishman was one of the cold, efficient sort who could hang onto his temper. "I believe signal guns are not customarily charged with shot. Or are they along this coast? Your fire smashed our hawse hole."

"What-what?" Turner stuttered, wiping a thread of blood from his cheek.

"I speak distinctly, I believe."

"But we'd no charge of metal, sir. That hole was caused by the collision. Maybe one of our anchor flukes did it."

The marine only shook his head, sharply motioned David, Farish and his mate to the port rail. Then he ordered the boarding party to round up the rest of the brigantine's company. Soon seamen, black and white, appeared under guard.

Farish said nothing, kept his eyes fixed on a stream of blood which, issuing from beneath the smoldering topsail, was sketching a bright and gruesome course among the fallen spars.

A violent scuffling and a roar of rage preceded the appearance of Major Bouquet. In stocking feet, breeches and rumpled shirt, he burst out of the companionway, brandishing a dress sword.

"What's this? What's this? Mutiny? Piracy?" Blinking short-sightedly, he gaped at the wreckage all about.

On recognizing the marine officer's uniform, he started waddling over to the poop ladder. "Well, sir, who locked me in my cabin? Had to break damn' door— I'll see someone hanged for this! I'll—"

Major Bouquet got no further because his foot encountered molasses flowing across the deck in a gold-brown tide. Uttering a startled oath, he executed two or three fantastic dance steps in his efforts to regain balance. They were all in vain, his feet slipped out from under him and on massive shoulders he coasted impressively across the deck until he came to rest among the wreckage of some barrels smashed by a fallen yard. A hen which had been perching on them fluttered off to perch on the forecastle.

The wigless, coatless major's expression was so ludicrous that the British seamen exploded into loud guffaws. Even the marine officer's mouth twitched momentarily.

"Gad's my life," the Englishman asked of his sergeant, "what's this? A new form of tip-cat?"

Wiping molasses from his hands, Major Bouquet scrambled to his knees and picked up his sword. It was sticky and dripping with the goozy stuff, but he shook it at the marines.

"Come down here, you damned sailor's pee poles, and I'll tip-cat you!"

The lieutenant's smile faded. "Who is he?"

"Major Ponsonby Bouquet of the 52nd Line Regiment," David told him. "Every inch of him."

"Gad, that barrel's sharp slatted!" Rubbing his stern, Bouquet turned to stare at the ruined casks. Suddenly the gross figure stooped and everyone could see a smear of blood dyeing his soiled white breeches. "Damn my eyes, what's this?" With his free hand Major Bouquet drew from among the broken staves a molasses-covered bayonet, then a pike head and a pair of pistols. Bouquet squinted at the bayonet, rubbed a section of it clean. "Fabrique de L. Aguiel, St. Malo," he read. "French weapons!"

The lieutenant's jaw clicked. "Smuggling foreign arms? Well, well! French arms. That alters matters. You are, I perceive, an extrapeaceful merchantman, Captain." The marine's sarcasm was deadly. "Sergeant, fetch a rope and secure these honest mariners."

"In the supply room, suh, they's a chest of irons," Turner

suggested. He had been captured by the French once and knew that irons, although heavier, didn't cut a man's skin so bad nor cut off his circulation. Only trouble with them was they were heavy and, at this time of year, cold.

Once H.M.S. *Falcon* had been repaired as well as might be, a work party came rowing over from her and helped the captive crew to clear away the wrecked foremast. Onto its stump they began lashing a spare mainyard. It would do well as a jury mast.

To David, slumped stony-faced on the quarterdeck, the ringing thumps of hatchets and hammers sounded like undertakers preparing a casket. The Boston Committee, he reckoned, was going to be sorely disappointed. It made him right sick to know that all the munitions money George Leavitt had collected upriver was going to go for nothing.

Farish, seated alongside, picked irritably at the rusty chain joining his manacles. He was in a terrible frozen rage. When they put the irons on him, he turned to David and growled, "I pray the Lord my God, your brother is granted a chance someday to take this out of your hide!"

"You overlook, I believe, our purpose in running this risk." David was at pains to explain. "You are still a member of the Boston Committee?"

"I am."

"Then you would have been very glad to see those ˙arms reach Boston?"

"That is so," came the grim reply. "I would have risked my life, and gladly, to bring 'em in."

"Then why act towards me as you do?"

"Mister, if you had told your brother what you intended, I'd have only respect for you. But it was the trick of a sneaking dog to take advantage of a trusting relative. Do you realize what you have done? You've smashed your brother's business. Ruined him!"

David shrugged. "I hadn't imagined anything like this could happen. Who would have?"

"You're a fool. Anything can happen at sea nowadays." Farish snorted, looked off through the thinning fog. "Well, you'll get your come-uppance soon enough. It's no piddling matter to damage one of His Majesty's ships. Her people will stick to their claim that we fired on her. See if they don't. They want prize money."

Turner raised a sallow, mournful face. "Smuggling weapons ain't no slight matter these days, neither. Thanks to you, Misto Ashton, we can all figger on a trial in England. If the cou't finds us, we'll likely get shipped out to the East Indies as slaves. It's happened befo'."

"Remember, gentlemen, we suffer in the sacred name of Liberty," said Johnny Gilmorin from his place at the end of the row. "Why look so hard on the dark side? We'll get out of this somehow."

Farish spat over the rail into the slate-colored water. He could cheerfully have murdered both his owner's brother and this young whippersnapper with his high-falutin' nonsense about "the sacred name o' Liberty." Liberty? Cat's backside! All anybody wanted was a fair chance to sail his ships and a chance to put by some hard cash against old age.

The marine lieutenant jerked the sharpened bullet with which he was writing at a corpse but recently uncovered. "Who was that?"

"Deck passenger, suh," Turner replied. "Name of Frye."

"First name?"

"I ain't sho,' suh,"

"It was Isaac," Farish grunted.

"Where from?"

Farish glanced off to port, saw that the fog had all but cleared away. Yonder above the shining dunes of the Cape shone a dark green line of scrub pines and, away off up the shore, was the blur of roofs and a couple of steeples.

"He hails from over there—Province Town."

"Pitch him over," the lieutenant directed and went on writing.

"I protest, sir!" Johnny cried. "This is inhuman. He is entitled to a Christian—"

"Rebels forfeit all rights," the lieutenant remarked without looking up from his writing. "Keep your damned mouth closed or you'll be taught how."

A sickish tremor wrung Johnny's belly when a brace of marines dragged Frye's corpse, all bloodied, over to the rail. A jagged pine splinter sprouted from his chest. In blood the dead man's calloused heels sketched parallel lines—lines which thinned.

"Grab his heels Mike," panted a corporal passing hands under the dead man's armpits. "Easy does it. Heave-ho!"

The body went tumbling awkwardly down to the water. It

raised a resounding splash. A knitted cap of blue wool the boatswain had lent Frye remained floating after the surging, pink-tinted bubbles had subsided.

The flood tide, Stephen Farish calculated, would be pretty strong right here. It was making in towards Province Town.

3 — INTO SALEM

H. M. S. *Falcon,* sloop of war, took her prize in tow. By consequence, the brigantine set up a sullen heave and toss which endured over to Chatham. The trip was a nightmare to the sixteen men who found themselves jammed indiscriminately into a forecastle designed for eight.

"Sociable and folksy," was Farish's dry comment.

The air grew so inexpressively foul that, inside of an hour, David's head set up an excruciating ache which would not leave him. The irons around his wrists made him smile. Well, well! St. John Ashton's eldest son now wore the fetters of a common felon.

"Yes. I'm a low dog; that damn' Yankee was right," he decided belatedly. "Poor Rob. Reckon he's hurt so bad he will never forgive me. The good old Ashton luck again! With all the Atlantic to cruise in, that ratted sloop had to smash into us."

He was worried over how his game chicken was making out. He missed Hannibal's bright, inquiring eye and the swaggering independence of him. Like as not, though Major Bouquet claimed to have an eye for a good gamecock, he would think it the very devil of a joke to have Hannibal served up in a stew.

The prisoners had to wait all day for their single ration of food and water, but Johnny Gilmorin's irrepressible cheerfulness went a long way towards helping people through the ordeal. He sang bawdy tavern ballads and quoted Sir John Suckling until Farish, inexpressibly shocked, begged him for God's sake to be still. Good humoredly, Johnny switched to riddles and guessing games. Then, declaring they all should deem it a privilege to suffer like this in the name of Liberty, he goaded Farish into an argument which lasted for hours.

The boatswain momentarily floored them both by drawling, "What's all this to-do about Liberty, Mr. Gilmorin? Once you've seen a Boston town meeting, ye'd know we wouldn't know what to do with Liberty if we got it. The British make some mistakes; we all do. But they been figgerin' out this Liberty business nigh on five hundred years, so they tell me, and so far they done it purty well. I wish you'd cast an eye over some of the plugs calling 'emselves Sons o' Liberty."

Around sundown the forecastle door was unlocked and, backed up by hard-faced marines in salt-stained cocked hats, a seaman handed down a couple of pails of water, half a dozen stale loaves and some stew made of salt pork boiled with callavans peas.

For some reason the prize was held for a week in Chatham on Cape Cod. On the last night there a breeze rose out of the northwest and developed into an icy gale which knifed through a thousand crevices. In vain the prisoners shivered, cursed their scanty coverings and begged the guards to fetch more.

Despite the forecastle's overcrowded condition, the irons on David's wrist grew cold as ice and started an aching chill climbing to his shoulders. When the rest of the prisoners had fallen asleep, he felt Johnny Gilmorin hitch over closer. Through chattering teeth he murmured.

"Reckon we must be off our c-course. Feels like Lab-Labrador. N-Never thought we-we'd come to this, d-did we?"

"No," was David's sober admission. "I reckon this is part of what happens if you lose."

"I d-don't mind," Johnny said. "Honest I d-don't. You know, Davey, at first I thought about this trip as—as a kind of g-gay adventure—like those of the old G-Greeks. But since I've seen things like our being forced to take Bouquet aboard, that broadside, poor Frye, and now this—well, I'm b-beginning to believe in this Liberty idea. It ain't just a slogan."

"I'm no saint," David said, "but I'm getting to feel like you when I remember some things I saw and heard in England. There was only one person"—he almost named Andrea Grenville, but didn't—"who seemed real."

"We'll get away," David went on after a pause. "Don't ever doubt it. I have been figuring on a way—"

Two more days dragged by and not once were the prisoners allowed on deck nor had they the use of any sanitary utensil. Under Farish's orders they utilized one corner of the forecastle as a latrine. They were largely successful in avoiding contamination, but the stench was fearful.

On an extra cold morning in early November they were aroused by an unaccustomed thudding of feet on deck and the noise of a cable roaring out of its hawse hole. When at last the forecastle's doors were unbattened, a slate-colored sky dotted with hurrying flocks of ducks and geese met their eyes.

The British marine sergeant pinched a bulbous red nose, observing, "Gawd, wot a charnel 'ouse stink! Form up, you gallows bait! Form up!"

Chains clattering, unwashed and unshaven, the prisoners crept out into the daylight. Mercilessly it revealed the torn and filthy condition of their clothes; their linen smelt rankest of all. It had not been changed for over ten days. All in all the people off the *Assistance* resembled nothing so much as a gang of seasoned convicts.

Farish, shivering, blew on his numbed hands and in sullen curiosity surveyed his vessel. He saw that the British had rigged their jury mast cleverly enough to stand the weight of two jibs and a small staysail. Ingenious, too, was the crazy web of guys and stays supporting the damaged main mast. He had to admit the Britishers were handy seamen. They hadn't repaired the smashed port bulwarks, though, and the ragged plank ends put him in mind of teeth in a blue shark's jaw. He felt relieved to see that the main hatch was still battened down so, near as he could tell, the cargo hadn't been touched yet. Maybe, if things didn't go too consarned bad before the Admiralty Court, he might save Mr. Ashton a little something. Even a mite would be welcome. 'Tarnal shame about the Scotch wool cloth. Godfreys. *He* hadn't shipped those plagued foreign arms, nor his owner, either.

David, too, was peering forward, interested to see whether the rest of the molasses barrels were still there. They were. The name Hovy & Co., daubed in white across their tops, stood out clearly. Deeply depressed, he shifted his attention to shipping lying at anchor in Salem Harbour. He counted over thirty merchantmen of all rigs and burdens. Though the town itself seemed austere and rather insignificant in size, its port was furiously active.

Some churches, a brick courthouse and a few imposing clapboard houses crowned a little hill overlooking the harbour. The white paint on them looked very crisp and fresh against the gray and brown background of the trees. One glance about gave David an idea of how badly Boston must be suffering. Every warehouse lining the ice-skimmed shore was crammed to overflowing with goods. From where he stood on the captured brigantine's deck, he could see being unloaded great cases of British calicoes, Irish linens, cutlery, French glassware, barrels of paint and wine and other commodities the colonists could not manufacture as yet.

Though the noisy little harbour terns had departed on their migration, quantities of gray gulls lingered, fattening on an unaccustomed harvest of drifting offal. Mewing and laughing by turns, they circled about the busy Customs cutters and above stout-sparred vessels from Liverpool, Bristol, and Glasgow.

It was so cold David could see the breath of deck hands and stevedores working on the overloaded docks. Everyone was wearing a jacket and many seamen sported red woolen stocking caps which, dangling down their backs, lent them a rakish air.

Everywhere small boats rowed about. Their waggling oars resembled the legs of water beetles crawling over the surface of a mill pond. Clustering, like shoats about a sow, a number of scows and lighters surrounded a tall barque from London. The *Assistance* was far from being the only prize in port. Farish's depression deepened as he counted four other craft flying colors at half-mast. There was the brig *Neptune* out of Sandwich; the brig *Countess of Argyll* of Charles Town, South Carolina; the schooner *Annabella* of Falmouth; the ship *Peggy* from Philadelphia.

Prize crews were drying sails in the pale yellow sunshine. These slatted stiffly in the cold offshore wind.

David was surprised to learn that Major Bouquet had remained aboard. He appeared while they were waiting for a barge to come alongside, his gross features as lumpy and purple as ever.

Sight of the scarecrow prisoners furnished him such vast amusement that he clapped hands to the 52nd regiment's buff-colored waistcoat and laughed until tears coursed down his blotchy cheeks.

"Congratulations, my rebel friends. It's a famous parade you make. Ho! Ho! Ho! Dear me! Can this be our sweet-scented Virginia gentleman?" He made an elaborate leg at

177

Johnny Gilmorin. "Alas, I fear we must postpone our little meeting. I venture in handling a pistol you would find those fetters somewhat of a handicap?" And again he went off into boisterous shouts of laughter.

It was a difficult thing to do, but David summoned a smile. "You consider yourself a sporting man, do you not, Major?"

The big figure in scarlet bit his laugh off short. "Sir, I don't advise you ever to doubt it!"

"Oh, I don't! I was sure you'd understand why, despite this misfortune, I wish to keep my gamecock, if nothing else."

One of the prize crew had appeared on deck carrying Hannibal, outraged and ruffled with the cold.

"That the bird?"

"Yes, Major. If you admire a grand little fighter, grant me this kindness."

Major Ponsonby Bouquet hesitated. The clear cold air coupled with the fact that, early the night before, he had reached the end of his port, inclined him to gracious condescension. He flicked an imaginary speck of dust from his gorget, beckoned the seaman.

"Put that fowl down, my man. My rebel friend, Mr. Ashton, wants him, to eat no doubt! Ho! Ho!" Vast shoulders aquake with mirth, Bouquet lumbered off towards the gangway but hesitated, turned, staring at David. "You amaze me —you show signs of courage. Too bad there ain't more like you in these beastly Colonies. Might hope to see some real fighting later on then. As Gad's my life, I'd give twenty pounds to find a regiment of rebels that would dare stand up to the 52nd!"

"I note your offer, Major," called Johnny Gilmorin, "but if you lead them, remember to march backside foremost. Then we'll recognize you straight away."

4 — PRIZE COURT

SNOW, light and feathery as winged seeds, was falling in the prison courtyard when, after securing the middle of their ankle chains to their beds with strips of rag, the prisoners started for the courthouse. A month's beard darkened their cheeks and they still stood in the clothes they had worn when they were captured. The stench of them was by now appalling. Only the *Assistance*'s officers and passengers had been permitted to shave once a week.

Lining the narrow, snow muffled street stood a band of youngsters; school books under arms, they sniffled in the cold. Briefly they surveyed this line of blue-lipped men tramping along between red-coated guards. The sight was becoming too common to hold their interest long. They started off coasting on the hills back of Salem. Their shrill and joyous whoops echoed and re-echoed among the severe and generally unpainted clapboard dwellings.

The party passed a detail of grenadiers from His Majesty's 5th regiment of the line. David watched them pass, shoes squeaking on the snow and white-gaitered legs swinging in unison. How big they looked bundled in gray great-coats. They had tucked their chins deep into high, upturned collars, but their hands looked red and stiff on the brass shod butts of the six-foot Tower muskets. A breeze, whipping the black bearskin coverings of their shakos, wrought fleeting designs, like wind on a laprobe of wolf skin.

"It is going to snow harder soon," Farish predicted. "When high gray clouds come a-pouring down from inland like that, there'll be a-plenty."

Halfway to Court the column swerved to avoid a fallen horse. As usual, a throng of idlers was offering voluble advice but not lifting a finger to help.

It was pleasantly warm in the courtroom. David looking about, realized this with a sense of surprise. After nearly a month in Salem jail, one forgot there were such things as soap, hot water, clean linen and beds. In grim amusement he stared at his hands. Could these grimy paws with black crescents of dirt under each broken nail be his? He looked sidewise at Johnny, then suddenly squirmed. God's teeth! Thanks to the heat, lice in his clothes were becoming active. As it warmed, Johnny's body began to exude the indescribably foul odors of flesh long unwashed. Johnny noticed it himself and looked so apologetic David grinned.

"Reckon I'm no rose myself."

On the bench sat three judges appointed to adjudicate the libel's validity. The grim, hawk-featured presiding justice looked mighty impressive in scarlet robes and a full-bottomed wig.

The Court Cryer called for order, began reading an order to hold court:

" 'By his Excellency Lieutenant-General Thomas Gage, Governor, Commander-in-chief and Vice-Admiral of this colony, to the Honorable Peter Oliver, Jonathan Sewall and Charles Paxton, judges of His Majesty's Court of Vice-Admiralty:

" 'Whereas Captain John Linzee, Commander of His Majesty's sloop of war called the *Falcon* by his humble petition to me exhibited setting forth that the said John Linzee in pursuance of his duty against His Majesty's enemies did on, or about, the 11th day of November last past, attack, seize and take a certain vessel called the *Assistance* belonging to one Robert Ashton, a subject of His Majesty residing in Norfolk in the Colony of Virginia, laden with divers goods and merchandizes and contraband arms, and hath brought said same ship and lading into this port of Salem in order of adjudication and condemnation. And by said petition hath prayed for a Court of Admiralty to be holden for trial of the same at His Majesty's Court of Vice-Admiralty held at the courthouse upon a libel exhibited by John Linzee, Commander of His Majesty's sloop of war the *Falcon*. The officers, mariners and marines belonging to the Same

Against

A certain vessel called the *Assistance*, the property of a British subject one Robert Ashton, and also against all and singular the cargo and lading on board. Her tackle, apparel and furniture kindsoever.

Officers attending: Wm. Woolen, Marshall
Ed. Winston, Register
John S. Petit, Cryer

Given under my hand and the Public seal of this colony this 18th day of December, 1774/5 in the 14th year of His Majesty's reign.' "

Once the cryer had done, some further spectators were admitted. Charles Paxton donned a pair of steel-rimmed spectacles. From behind their square lenses his cold gray eyes deliberately wandered over the double row of defendants.

Judge Oliver glanced at his colleagues, then cleared his throat. "You may read the Libel, Mr. Cryer."

" 'A libel filed by Captain John Linzee, November 16th, 1774, in behalf of his officers, mariners and marines of His Britannic Majesty's sloop of war, *Falcon*, against the *Assistance*, a brigantine rigged vessel of 220 tons burthen and registered in the port of Norfolk in the colony of Virginia. Said vessel is alleged to have been taken off the seacoast of this Colony in the act of transporting arms and weapons contrary to law and without having made due application of permission to transport same. It is further alleged said vessel, when summoned to heave to, did resist by firing a cannon into H. M. S. *Falcon*. Said *Assistance* hath been brought into the Counties of Suffolk and Essex, and for the trial of this captain, his passengers and crew, the Court of Vice-Admiralty for the Middle District of the Massachusetts Bay Colony is now held, this twentieth day of December, 1774.' "

There was a brief rustle of papers from the bench, then the chief judge began to speak in succinct accents.

"Pursuant to the laws of this colony I do now charge that the owner or owners of the vessel and cargo and contraband taken as aforesaid, or persons concerned shall appear and show cause (if they have any) why said vessel or any of them and their cargo and appurtenances should not be condemned."

Faggots burning in a big iron stove back of the bench made a noise like distant musketry while the Proctor for the libellants made his plea. David listened with eyes fixed on the Royal Arms rendered in oak. The carving was secured to the wall just above Judge Oliver's snowy wig.

As a speaker the Proctor for the appellants—or defendants—left much to be desired; his voice droned on and on like the rumble of a mill wheel. David's eyes wandered from the Royal Arms to the back of a marine standing nearby. Between his shoulderblades his scarlet tunic bore a greasy mark caused by pomatum from his queue.

Captain Linzee of the *Falcon* stated his version of the affair in blunt, nautical terms. The brigantine, he swore, had made desperate attempts to evade capture.

The lieutenant of marines, next being sworn, described his boarding of the brigantine. Firmly he maintained that the signal cannon, so-called, had been charged with ball.

"Was this ball ever found?" demanded Mr. Gray for the defendants.

The missile had not penetrated the *Falcon's* side, Captain Linzee asserted, but had nonetheless smashed several planks before rebounding into the sea.

"Were there other balls in evidence—on the deck?"

"No, but balls fitting said cannon were discovered in a nearby chest."

Fingering a long blue chin, Judge Paxton interrupted to observe it was odd that a peaceful merchantman bound for Massachusetts Bay should find it necessary to carry cannonballs. Was there any explanation?

There was, Mr. Gray promptly replied. Said ammunition had been left over from a time when the brigantine sailed in the Jamaica trade. That the judges patently disbelieved this was all too obvious, and the public resented their incredulity. Everyone knew that a master sailing for the Caribbean was a plain fool if he didn't take along at least one or two pieces of ordinance to overawe semi-piratical Spanish fishermen and traders.

Again and again Judge Oliver rapped for order, but people occupying back benches kept up their muttering. Public resentment came to a climax when Major Bouquet, waddling up to the stand, testified to seditious utterances made by the brigantine's officers and passengers. In his opinion they were, the lot of them, traitors down to the soles of their feet, and bent on succoring His Majesty's enemies.

During the noon recess the prisoners were herded into an unheated room adjoining the court. It was quite devoid of furniture. As soon as the door had slammed to, the youngest of the crew commenced to blubber.

"Ain't none of us ever goin' see Norfolk again! We'll get transported—every last one of us, see if we don't!" He clung to his despair even when some kindly citizens sent in a big pot of ale, bread and a steaming kettle of codfish chowder.

Johnny for the first time was looking worried and Farish's dried apple of a face was the picture of discouragement. As for David, he was utterly appalled at the hopeless ineptness of Mr. Gray's defense. Why, dammit, the meaching-mouthed fellow wasn't fit to hold a real lawyer's wig bag.

Only Buff, the giant negro, remained unperturbed. After all, the jail food was some better than he got in Candless's barracoon back in Norfolk, and he didn't have to work. He was used to leg irons and had showed the others how to weave rags about the gyves. That generally prevented chilblains when the winter wind came whistling through the jail's many paneless sections of window.

During the early afternoon Captain Stephen Farish and Turner, his mate, gave their testimony. Firmly they vowed they hadn't known of arms having been brought aboard. But the disclaimer only succeeded in intensifying the blank expression on Judge Oliver's austere countenance.

"Is it not true," demanded Mr. Alexander, Proctor for the Libellants, "that the officers, as well as the owner of a vessel, are expected to know the exact nature of a cargo carried by them? Is it not the law that *all* merchandise carried must appear upon the manifest? Is it not only a master's right, but also his duty, to refuse to sail with an improper cargo?"

Farish and Turner, Mr. Alexander implied, had been too lazy or too disloyal to investigate the cargo's true nature.

Turner got angry and his chains rattled loudly when he sprang up. "By God, suh, do you expect us to drain every molasses barrel?"

"Silence! The prisoner will not interrupt." Judge Oliver's gavel thumped heavily.

Mr. Alexander made an obsequious bow. "Your Honors, the facts are as I have represented them. These men were transporting a cargo of foreign arms destined to strike at the authority of our most gracious King." His voice rang in every corner of the bare and musty smelling courtroom. "On behalf of my clients I implore you to find their libel a true bill. I hold that the owner, Robert Ashton, the prisoners Stephen Farish, David Ashton, John Gilmorin and Andrew Turner have, beyond a doubt, been proved guilty of a treasonable conspiracy to smuggle arms into this Colony!"

"Your Honors!" David struggled to his feet. "May I speak?"

Judge Oliver's slash of a mouth thinned ominously, but he ended by nodding.

"While it is entirely true," David began in a low-pitched voice, "that Mr. Gilmorin and I planned to import illicit arms into this Colony, it is also true that I misrepresented the nature of this cargo, not only to the officers of the *Assistance*, but to her owner. The owner, gentlemen, is my brother."

183

Soldiers surrounding the prisoners glanced sidewise, looking at him from dully interested eyes.

"The prisoner may proceed," snapped the presiding judge.

"I beg of you, your Honors, to dismiss the other prisoners. They are indeed innocent of any illegal intent. The fault is John Gilmorin's and mine; but principally mine, because I collected the arms and arranged for their transportation."

David stood erect, a grimy unkempt figure outlined against the whitewashed wall. Everyone was looking at him now, especially a pretty girl in the second row. She reminded him a bit of Katie, but she wasn't as large and her gray eyes lacked the greenish tinge. The scratching of the court clerk's pen continued.

"Your Honors, I beg mercy for these men, if you may find none for me," David went on, gripped by an unfamiliar exhilaration. By George, he wasn't doing a bad job of this! The public was turning and whispering and that girl's gray eyes were fixed on him in hero worship. Yes, he reckoned he could square Rob before the court and give the crowd a scene to remember. Later he would escape.

Johnny was amazed. By God, he'd never heard Davey cut loose like this at a Committee meeting. He felt vaguely disturbed. What would he say next?

"Most of my fellow defendants have families. The owner of the slave members of this crew will suffer through no fault of his." Gripped by the swing of his peroration, David prolonged it. It was a glittering moment. Even the *Falcon*'s officers were looking at him in astonishment. "As a last inducement, may I state that my brother, Robert, is a most loyal subject of His Majesty?" David drove home his main point with triumphant emphasis. "That gentlemen, is why I did not inform him about the arms. He never would have allowed them aboard his vessel."

All in an instant there came a change in the temper of the weather-beaten, drably dressed spectators.

"A Tory ship?" "To hell with her and all her crew." "Let Ashton and Gilmorin go!" yelled a young sailmaker and was promptly ejected by two tall grenadiers.

"Name *me* master of a Tory ship!" Farish glared his contempt, muttering, "What rinktum are you up to now? Save yer own skin, would ye? Well, if you get loose, you'll be taken care of!"

Scarlet robes rippling like waves in a sunset, Judge Paxton

184

leaned forward. "Are we to understand, Mr. Ashton, that your brother is a Loyalist?"

David flushed, glanced unhappily about, struggled in the snare into which he had blundered. "Why—why—yes. He refused to sign what we call a Test Paper."

An ironic smile broke through the impassivity of Judge Sewall's granite features. "Indeed? Then it is more the pity he was not loyal enough to make sure of what his ship carried." Tallest of the judges, he leaned to the right, whispering with Judge Oliver. Their powdered heads lingered close together.

Bewildered, David sat down; his one consolation was the grateful regards of the crew. Johnny Gilmorin looked quite puzzled and bent his head.

"Why'd you say that? Rob's no Tory—if they ever hear of this in Norfolk, it won't—"

He broke off as the judges gathered their robes and retired to deliberate.

"Condemn the ship!" "Free Gilmorin!" "Free Ashton!" "Hurrah for the Continental Congress!" "Jail Farish!"

Tumult among the public benches grew so uproarious that grenadiers armed with blunderbusses went back to quiet it. David swallowed hard. Plague take it! Try as he would, he seemed only able to involve everyone more disastrously.

In Stephen Farish's opinion the deliberation of the judges appeared ominously brief. Within ten minutes the jurists entered, resumed their places. Judge Oliver peered the length of the now stuffily hot courtroom, then cast a glance out at the windows. A furious snow storm was raging. He cleared his throat and passed a sheet of paper down to the bailiff.

A stillness descended, impressive in its completeness. The bailiff had a bad cold but all could hear him read:

"Verdict of this Court. We do unanimously find the libel against the *Assistance* brigantine of Norfolk to be a true bill. She is hereby condemned, together with all her cargo, tackle, furniture and appurtenances kindsoever. Proceeds of the sale shall be divided as prize money among the officers, marines and mariners of the *Falcon,* man-of-war, according to the rules and regulations therefor prescribed. Because of extenuating circumstances, we hold Robert Ashton acquitted of treasonable intent and exempt from further prosecution. We do find Stephen Farish, captain of said vessel, Andrew Turner, mate, guilty of firing shot at a ship of the Royal

185

Navy. David Mountford Ashton and John Pingree Gilmorin, owners of the contraband materials of war, we find guilty of a conspiracy to violate the laws of this Province."

Other members of the crew were catching their breath; they were like men expecting to be doused with cold water. Two or three of them had shut their eyes and the youngest was clasping his hands in an agony of prayer.

"—We do hold the remainder of the crew of said vessel guiltless of wilfully transporting illicit arms; but, as a warning, their personal property aboard the vessel condemned is hereby forfeited. They are hereby discharged."

"Innocent—innocent!" The youngest sailor leaped up, dirty hands outspread. "Oh, thank you, my lords! Thank you!" He doubled up weeping. The boatswain sat still, staring straight ahead. Though slow to comprehend, the black seamen at last broke into incredulous, ivory-toothed smiles. All except Buff. Said he in an undertone, "What fo' you grinnin' at? How's us gwine keep wahm? How's us gwine git back to No'folk?"

"Stow it, you black dogs!" A beefy sergeant major in charge of the guard turned such a menacing face that the Negroes cowered.

"There will be no further demonstration." Judge Oliver's voice grated like a knife over a whetstone. "Remove the discharged prisoners."

When it was done and the clatter of chains had subsided, the bailiff blew his nose loud as a battle bugle and sang out:

"David Ashton, John Gilmorin, Stephen Farish and Andrew Turner, rise and hear the sentence of this court."

Hands tightly gripped before him, David obeyed; somehow the drama of the moment had completely evaporated. The irons on his legs felt extra heavy and he became overwhelmingly aware that he was very hungry and dirty.

The presiding judge faced, not the prisoners, but the spectators. Farish's deeply-lined face had gone bronze-yellow and his lower lip became pinioned between his teeth. If he got a long stretch, whatever would become of Solace? It was plenty shameful enough to think of her working as a goody in a dormitory at Harvard College. Her earnings were miserably small and the children, growing fast, needed so many things. Deep inside of him he prayed.

"Grant, O Lord, that I may not appear afraid in the face

of mine enemies. Lord, I didn't betray my owner. You know that. Move the heart of this Englishman to mercy. Amen."

"—As a warning to other disaffected, dishonest subjects of the Crown, and as an example of the fate awaiting such, this court herewith sentences David Mountford Ashton to ten years' penal servitude and to transportation from this province to a destination later to be decided. John Gilmorin, to five years' penal servitude and transportation. Stephen Farish—"

The mariner leaned forward a little, staring at that vivid splash of robes beneath the royal coat of arms. He cupped his hand to his ear as if he couldn't hear Judge Oliver's ringing words.

"—In view of the prisoner David Ashton's statement, we do hold you, Stephen Farish, not guilty of wilful conspiracy. But—" Blood rushed through Farish's arteries, —"we do find you guilty of a criminal negligence at a time when all loyal subjects of the Crown should be alert against treason and rebellion. We do, therefore, sentence you, Stephen Farish, to serve one year at hard labor in His Majesty's prison at Boston."

Farish sat down. He had really been expecting much worse from those pale-faced men on the bench. Still, three hundred and sixty-five days was a long time to be apart from Solace. He smiled faintly; perhaps, if matters didn't get caterwampus in Boston, Solace and the children would be allowed to come in to see him sometimes. What bothered him most was whether the home folks would believe he had mastered a Tory ship. He'd have starved first. Robert Ashton was as near neutral as a body could be. After all, the *Assistance* had been carrying badly needed supplies to Boston.

Turner was bound over to observe the maritime laws of the province for a period of two years. The sentence at first drew from him a husky croak of joy. But then he looked glum. Though free, he must report regularly to the court, and how could a mariner follow his calling if he had to give an account of himself before a magistrate every few weeks?

Judge Paxton commenced to collect documents scattered before him and Judge Sewall mechanically straightened the lace at his throat. Judge Oliver turned to the bailiff.

"The prisoners will be removed to His Majesty's prison in Boston, there to wait the further instructions of this court."

Ten years—if he lived—of chains, loathsome food and

dirt. David shivered. What a fool, what an utter stupid ass, he had been to meddle in politics! It would be 1784 before he was free again. Where would they transport him? To the West Indies? India? Canada? The realization slowly came to him how long a year was.

"Come on, you." A guard let his musket's butt drop on David's toes.

Part IV

Bristol: 1774 - 1775

1 — MESSRS. KENYON & GILMORIN

"PLAGUE take Bristol and its confounded dismal weather!" murmured the Honorable Andrea Grenville. She deemed Bristol the dreariest of seaports, even in summer.

"You desire Mr. Kenyon, Ma'am?" Kenyon & Gilmorin's senior clerk fluttered visibly. Seldom did so gracious a vision brighten the firm's offices.

"Please inform him that Lady Andrea is here," she said, tightening a scarf which secured a new white beaver hat.

"Yes, m'lady. He shall be informed directly of your arrival."

A coal fire crackled invitingly in the grate of this long, desk-barricaded room; to it she held out a slim foot protected against the muddy slush of the streets by a dainty golosh of gray leather trimmed with squirrel.

Though not unpleasurably affected by admiring stares from several pale-faced clerks, she was nonetheless irritated by the monotonous *scratch-scratching* of their pens. Andrea continued an aimless circuit of the accounting room.

How was she looking? Confoundedly like the witch of Endor, no doubt. Tony Du Bois never would learn when to let his guests go home. She peered warily into a small mirror the silvering of which was beginning to peel away. There looked out at her an undeniably attractive face, rather long, animated and humorous. A delicate, firm and aristocratic nose. Under it lurked an appealingly short upper lip. The mouth was wide and had a faintly reckless twist to it. Beneath the beaver hat shone a single curl of bronze; irritated, she noted it still revealed traces of powder. She studied her hazel eyes to see what color dominated. No golden glints today— just plain brown. Though not very large, they were set satisfactorily well apart. She frowned at telltale red veins crisscrossing near their corners.

189

Attracted by a dull thundering which made the floor quiver, she strolled over to a window and lingered there. A line of carts was entering a passage situated directly below the office. It permitted freight to be hauled into a courtyard and in turn made it possible for wains to roll up alongside of ships lying to either side of Kenyon & Gilmorin's T-shaped wharf. By raising her eyes, Lady Andrea could make out tens and dozens of similar warehouses, mostly unpainted and dingy. Beyond them rose a confused tangle of spars and rigging. In the smoke-dimmed sky a few untidy-looking gulls flapped aimlessly.

Bemoaning lost sleep, Andrea drew a deep breath and became intrigued with the idea of identifying as many as she could of such a multitude of odors. Nostrils crinkled, she listed: fish, tar, tobacco, turpentine, paint, and a strangely erotic odor of cured hides. Most provocative of all was a blend of spices: cloves, cinnamon, ginger and pepper.

Restless, she traversed to the street side of the office and stood looking out on a depressing vista of tiles, shingles and sullenly smoking chimney pots. There were dozens, hundreds of chimneys, each spewing out a tendril of yellow-black smoke which, climbing a few yards, dropped soot on the snow on the roofs.

Below, a dray was clattering over greasy-looking cobbles. The big horses pulling it leaned into their collars and set down their shaggy feet as if weary to death. The driver sat hunched all over with a battered three-cornered hat pulled low over his face. In the dray was a huge coil of hawser, a maul and a couple of barrels. On its tail board two small ragged boys perched like grimy sparrows. To either side of the street below, old, old houses leaned toward each other like a weary team of plough horses. The passing dray forced a woman with a market basket to flatten against a wall already stained by flying mud. Her shrill curses rose, but the driver never lifted his head.

"There can't be an uglier city in all the world," Lady Andrea decided, turning away from the dirty panes. She preferred windows looking out on the ships and the harbour. Her interest stirred; one of Kenyon & Gilmorin's vessels was casting off. Out on the wharf she recognized Mr. Kenyon's plump short-legged outline. Queer, considerable bustle and some hilarity usually attended a ship's departure, but today the knot of men remaining on the wharf stood close together, silently watching her high sides begin to slide slowly away.

"I say, my good fellow, where is that ship for? India? Italy?"

Mr. Wattles, the chief clerk, nearly upset his ink in his eagerness to be of service. "No, m'lady. The *Dauntless* is for Rhode Island."

"Rhode Island?" She gave the weary-seeming old man a dazzling smile. "That is a Turkish island in the Mediterranean, is it not?"

"God bless you no, m'lady." The chief clerk looked startled, then deeply apologetic. "There *is* an Island of Rhodes just where you say, m'lady, but this here one is just one of our American possessions."

"In the West Indies no doubt?"

"No, m'lady. Rhode Island is in North America, near Boston, if I may make so bold."

Poor little man, could he ever be bold? He looked so colorless, so thin, and his eyes were red, too—but not with Tony Du Bois's wines.

North America? Odd, in all her two years about London and the Court of St. James's she could recall having met but one American. She must have met many of them, of course, but only a certain Virginian remained as a definite personality. Yet he had dropped into her life and out of it again all in a fortnight. Why had he made so distinct an impression? Perhaps even in the early morning hours, when candles were guttering and the air grew stale about the gaming tables, there had been a vitality, a breath of freshness about him suggestive of sunny woods and windy meadows. As she stood there peering blankly out on the harbour's gray water, she especially recalled the way he sat a horse. She fancied she would always remember the ineffable grace with which he could clear a three-bar gate. It had been remarkable how instinctively they had taken to one another. Poor young American. He had bungled his campaign against the citadels of Smart Society.

"It's just as well he went when he did," she meditated. "Davey Ashton and I would never get on. Too confounded much alike." Still, she wondered.

"Does the tobacco I am smelling come from Norfolk?" she asked suddenly.

Mr. Wattles said, "Yes, m'lady, almost all of the firm's tobacco is grown in Virginia."

She turned, the better to view a row of wooden hogsheads barely visible through the door of a warehouse. Davey had once said Mr. Kenyon's partner in America was a neighbor of his. How vastly droll to imagine that some of the brown leaves stored below might have sprouted on Davey Ashton's own land! Despite his staggering card losses, he must still have plenty of property. The Duke of Cumberland vowed all Virginia planters were rich as Croesus.

Mr. Kenyon bustled in, chafing chilled hands. At the sight of his caller standing tall and composed before the window, his plump little figure bowed so profoundly a topknot of gray hair clinging to the glassy surface of his scalp became visible.

"A pleasure, Lady Andrea, and the richer for being unanticipated." Suddenly he glared about the counting room. "Why has Lady Andrea been kept waiting out here? She should have been shown into my private office. Wattles, come here!"

The old chief clerk slid down from his stool and, as he hurried forward, thrust his goose quill behind his ear, deepening an inky smudge already marking his yellowed wig.

"What in blazes d'you mean by keeping Lady Andrea waiting out here?"

Blinking, Mr. Wattles faltered back a half step. "Why, why, Mr. Kenyon, I didn't think there was a fire going in your office, sir."

"Have you no wits? Of course there's a fire." Kenyon knew perfectly well it was so tiny it threw little heat.

The old clerk cringed in such abject fear that Andrea felt sickened.

"Confound it, Wattles, I fear you have not sense enough to be a chief clerk!" growled Kenyon, blowing his nose. "On Friday you'll go back as a simple senior—very simple!"

Wattles's dull face worked. In appeal he held out a grimy hand covered with swollen blue veins. "Oh, oh, no! Please, sir, I beg you! I couldn't stand the disgrace. All my life I have worked for this. I do my best to give satisfaction, sir."

Andrea observed the avid gaze of the other clerks. They looked too brutally hopeful.

"Please, as a favor to me, let Wattles keep on as chief clerk," she begged. "I really preferred being out here."

"Eh?"

She trained on him her most devastating smile. "Yes, in truth. You know, Mr. Kenyon, how I hate being alone. It gives me the megrims. From in here I could see the ships."

She never forgot the old clerk's look of passionate gratitude when Mr. Kenyon, again loudly blowing his nose, grunted:

"Since Lady Andrea intercedes—but mind your step, Wattles. Now then, the rest of you stop your stupid gawking. D'you think I pay you ten and six to sit gaping like yokels at a coco shy? Be at your work, or you'll be on the street come Friday!"

To Andrea it was utterly astonishing that anybody so small and insignificant as Mr. Kenyon could inspire such abject terror. All for ten and six, too. Merciful heavens! It dawned on her that these poor creatures must *live* on such a sum! Exist, rather.

Flushed, she followed the merchant into a small office littered with a multitude of dusty ships' models, renderings of new vessels and queer samples of merchandise. The room smelt of mice. Sure enough, she spied two holes; one was in a far corner of the mop boarding; the other behind the leg of Kenyon's desk. Private signal flags framed behind glass hung on all the walls. A sketch on the desk intrigued her enough to pick it up.

"What a lovely ship!"

"She's a brig, Ma'am. Ships have three masts."

"Well, ship or brig, she is beautiful. Exquisite! There is poetry to her lines. *Grand Turk?* What an odd name. Is she yours?"

Kenyon smiled, shook his head. "No. She's building in Norfolk. My partner saw her, fancied her lines and bribed one of the shipwrights to copy her dimensions." He pursed his lips, "She's too pretty to be profitable, I fear. But if this *Grand Turk* proves fast, why—we'll build us one like her. Maybe two."

"But is that—well, is that done?"

Mr. Kenyon's smile was tolerant. "Of course. Gilmorin writes she is being built by a rival. He'd copy a vessel of ours quite as quickly. Pray seat yourself."

Kenyon handed her to an armchair smelling of mildew and dust. It faced a tiny open fire. After removing a sherry-colored surtout and hanging his beaver hat to a hook, the merchant placed a small lump of coal on the grate.

"Better, eh?" he suggested and, turning his back to the hearth, warmed his palms behind plump buttocks.

"It *is* cold in here. I vow I can see my breath."

"Heat dulls the wits, I find, Lady Andrea," he observed, looking down at the charming young woman frankly sprawled in the chair before him. Dashed handsome legs to her; long and with neat ankles. Suddenly he felt his years.

"Cards again, or the races?"

"Prodigious bad luck with both. Alas! No horse seems to go as fast as the money I wager on him," she replied, looking not at him but into the coals.

"I regret to hear it."

"Thank you. Fact is, Mr. Kenyon, I stand in desperate need of money."

Methodically, Mr. Kenyon produced a snuff box of tortoise shell from his coat tail, helped himself to a pinch.

"May I remind you, Ma'am, that Kenyon & Gilmorin have already forwarded their quarterly dividend?" He cocked his head at the ceiling. "On November 23rd, I believe."

"Yes, I know it all too well." The girl smiled wryly and one of the legs Mr. Kenyon was admiring commenced nervously to swing. "I—I, well, I must borrow against my next dividend."

Kenyon permitted himself the most delicate of shrugs, studied the lid of his snuff box. "That would be difficult, most difficult, Ma'am. Instead, why not sell some of your holdings in Lincolnshire?"

Andrea laughed and spread her hands. "That, dear Mr. Kenyon, went—months ago."

"Well, then, that shop your father left you in London?"

Andrea raised a palm before her lips and blew away some invisible object.

Kenyon's heavy brows merged. "Your house in London? Surely that's not gone?"

"Oh, no. Papa entailed it. But I have rented it for twenty years."

"How much a year?"

"A thousand guineas, but—"

Mr. Kenyon's disapproval was mixed with relief. "You've been had! It's worth two thousand at least. Still, with a thousand a year you can manage."

A grimace troubled Andrea's bright mouth. "The rent has been paid for twenty years in advance. That is why I let the house go so cheap."

Mr. Kenyon looked genuinely alarmed. "Gad's my life! Don't tell me you have lost that money, too?"

Gossamer scarf ends fluttered faintly to Andrea's nod. "Every farthing of it. It was a monstrous mistake to have taken up Macao with my kind of luck—and against George Germain. Plague take him!"

"But your father's plate? The tapestries?"

"The Jews have 'em, Mr. Kenyon. My luck has been infernally bad this autumn."

"Gad's my life! I can believe it." The little merchant groaned and mopped a forehead suddenly become wet. When he sneezed over his snuff, he couldn't take the least pleasure of it. To think of gambling away 20,000 guineas? Why, most merchants couldn't gross half that much in three years' trading!

"What of your jewels? Surely—"

Andrea raised a reddish-brown curl from her ear. A puncture was visible on the lobe, but no ornament. Her slim fingers, Kenyon noted, were stripped of rings.

"I vow, Mr. Kenyon, you are slow to understand. All I have left is this one smart gown and a chest of garments too out of mode for the high-priced Jews to consider."

"But your friends? You've dozens of them." Kenyon's shrewd, fat little face was puckered into such worried amazement that Andrea almost laughed. "You are of the nobility, Lady Andrea. Surely—"

"Of the 'tea and trade' nobility," she corrected. "Don't deceive yourself into thinking the old families will ever forget Papa made his fortune in trade." She bent forward, extending slender hands to the kindling blaze. "Yes, Mr. Kenyon, you'd have no task finding plenty of homely cats, whose families fought at Agincourt, vastly hopeful of beholding—" she raised a whimsical brow—"these shapely limbs garbed in sackcloth and ashes, and the less sackcloth the better."

Andrea Grenville arose with graceful deliberation and moved over to the window. It had begun to rain, she noticed, and here she was without the price of a chair.

"Now do you see, Mr. Kenyon, why I must have an advance against my next dividend?"

"All too well," came the deliberate reply.

The senior partner of Messrs. Kenyon and Gilmorin went over to his desk and picked up a newspaper. He sat down and thumbed through it until he came to an article. He didn't like what he had to say. There was something about Lady Andrea's frantic impracticality which fascinated, even while it horrified him.

"Have you read the news today?"

"I fear I read very little."

"Well, you had better read this."

"No. You read it—give me the tone of it."

"Very well," soberly agreed the little man, replacing the single folded-over sheet. "In brief, the American Colonies have embargoed our goods—"

"Embargoed?" Andrea murmured. "What a fascinating word! Sherry would love it. What does it mean?"

"It means, Lady Andrea, that the Colonists—rat 'em!—refuse to buy more of our goods."

"But why? What can Kenyon and Gilmorin have done?"

"I don't mean just this firm's goods, Ma'am. The embargo applies to all British goods."

"Of prodigious interest, no doubt, but what can this have to do with my unhappy affairs?"

"I fear, Lady Andrea, it will add to your long tally of woes."

"What do you mean?" She faced him, incredulous. Her hands clamped down hard on the back of a chair. "Are you trying to say you won't advance against my next quarter's dividend?"

Homely round face filled with concern, Kenyon rose from his desk, came forward. "It isn't that I will not, Lady Andrea, but simply that I cannot. You and, if I may say so, others more urgently in need of dividends are not likely to receive a farthing this coming year."

Like blows of a wooden club striking a block, the words thudded on Andrea's ears. A curious breathlessness gripped her. Never once had it occurred that this ultimate resource might fail. Wide-eyed, she tried to concentrate on what the plump little man before her was saying.

"Mark my words, Ma'am, before a year is out many a trading house will be struggling for life; many a firm will have closed its doors forever. You will see those wharves out there choked by idle ships. It will probably not interest you, but back in '69 and '70 we learned what an embargo can do. Those confounded non-importation agreements in America were only partial, and badly enforced, but they came near wrecking us. This time Kenyon & Gilmorin intend to be somewhat better prepared."

Mr. Kenyon's face grew flushed and he drew himself up, cock sparrow-like. "Before another month is out all our clerks save one or two will be let go. Unless those bloody idiots in Parliament—" wrath momentarily thickened the speaker's voice—"show some sense, we must take steps. No dividends! That's our answer to the fools in Parliament. It will be the same in Glasgow and Liverpool."

"But—but why this embargo?" Had she ever called it a pretty word?

For the first time a trace of contempt showed in Mr. Kenyon's manner. "I daresay you've been too occupied to hear that Parliament has ordered the port of Boston closed? Well, Ma'am, it has, after already goading the colonies— and our clients—into defiance of a sort. Possibly you noticed a vessel leaving my wharf just now?"

"Why, yes," Andrea was clutching at her chair arms. She felt hot and then cold. Broke! That's what she was. Stony broke!

"She is the last ship we intend clearing for America. If what Mr. Gilmorin in Virginia writes me is so, the *Dauntless* will very likely come sailing back with bulk unbroken." Though the speaker's voice sank, indignation lent it volume. "To speak plainly, Ma'am, unless this blockade of Boston is lifted very soon, our export trade to America will lie dead, dead as Cromwell! Before long the import trade will also die."

"But why is this—this stupid state of affairs possible?"

"The King's lick-spittle friends, men with an interest in the East India Company, and a few big planters in the West Indies wish to roll in gold. Mark my words, Ma'am, because of these greedy swine now in power, mariners are going to starve; all over England factories will fall silent; and we merchants will be ruined!"

Andrea stared at Mr. Kenyon from bewildered eyes. Amazing! America, a far off place no one hardly ever heard of, was causing all this trouble. Come to think of it she recalled a vague discussion of something happening in a wretched provincial town called Boston, or was it Quebec?

In any case, Rodney Vaughan had bet that Boston had not 16,000 population. He had won, too.

Deliberately she put out her tongue and wet her lip. "In other words, Mr. Kenyon, you can do nothing for me?"

"I have always done when I could, have I not?" he reminded.

"Yes. You always have done." With the jerky movements of an automaton she drew on a pair of red gloves.

"I protest, Lady Andrea, I wish I might aid you. Your father was a stout friend in the early days of this firm—bought shares when we needed a new ship. It was a sound investment, of course; still it helped us."

Crossing to a cabinet, he brought out a decanter of sherry and two glasses. "I will speak plainly, Lady Andrea. To weather this storm we merchants will have to tax our every resource. Even so, I am not at all sure we can keep above water after a year." Gloomily, he handed her a glass which she placed absently on the desk. "How much money have you?"

Andrea shrugged, emptied a lace pocket into her palm. Two new shillings clinked, lay white circles against her red gloves.

"Behold the extent of my present fortune. A princely sum, to say the least?"

She tossed the coins onto his desk, then moved again to a window. The ship Kenyon had mentioned had cleared the wharf and was standing down the harbour, flag whipping smartly in the breeze. She could see sailors in blue jersies with red handkerchiefs tied about their ears crawling out along the yards. Their bare feet must get very cold on such a day.

Suddenly she turned. "Mr. Kenyon, how much does a passage to America cost?"

He smiled tolerantly. "That depends to where. America is a big country—easy twenty times the size of England."

"La, Mr. Kenyon! Well then, to—to Virginia."

"Sixty pounds," he told her at once. "But you will be pressed to find decent accommodations at such a price."

"Sixty pounds! Is that all? Why, I—"

"You have sixty pounds, Lady Andrea?"

Her exultation faded. Of course she didn't have sixty pounds; she had exactly two shillings.

"A pity you didn't come to me a day earlier," Mr. Kenyon

remarked, sniffing his sherry. "I would gladly have granted you free passage on the *Dauntless*."

"Why then, 'tis all very easy! I'll await your next vessel."

Kenyon paused, sherry glass poised at his lips. He seemed to be looking far beyond the window on which his eyes were fixed. "I shall have no more ships sailing for America. Not for a very long time, I fear."

2 — THE JOURNAL OF ANDREA GRENVILLE

SINCE the candle could last but a few moments longer, Andrea spread the journal more firmly on her lap and quickened her writing.

> 74 Spens Street, Bristol
> Friday, January 27th, 1775

When I consider my mode of Life a month ago and of today, am fair thunderstruck that the same Andrea Grenville can be penning these lines. Today is my last in England, for how long, God alone knows! Come what may, am Resolv'd not to return until I may do with Honour & Proof that I am become other than an idle Waster.

Today had narrow Escape of Tony Du Bois. The sweet Idiot has ridden clear from Bath in search of me. But I desire neither Him nor his Money, much less his sour-fac'd Family. My cloathes, last relicks of my Flowery Years, have bro't altogether £15. Mr. Kenyon was moved to assist me with another £10.

Vow I never beheld anything droller than the Jew's expression when he chanc'd on a Mottoe, "To Roddy Vaughan, from one Ass to another," stitch'd across the Seat of my blue camlet Skirt. Fear the Hebrew does not understand our Whitehall wit, though he laughed prodigious Loud and granted me an extra 6d. I have purchas'd for my Venture six Petticoats, 2 Nighttrails, 6 pair cotton Hose, I pair lisle Hose, a Sacque, a striped callicoe short-gown & two Aprons. When I consider the Chemises Andrea is doom'd by Poverty to wear, I trust she shall not be cast up by the Sea. All for £3/5/2d. The 2d. was for a bag of Lavender, Andrea must smell Fragrant.

To the booking office this morning of the *Charming Nymph*. She is a sorry packet and is neither charming nor suggests any Nymph I ever heard of. The ag't is a gross fellow named Wm Cunningham. He fills me with Apprehension. Vow my limbs did tremble like Jocky Rockingham's after a 6th Bottle of Oporto. Fortitude, my dear. Other passengers seem common Folk in reduc'd Circumstances. Nevertheless, they are not yet reduc'd to indenturing their Services for a Passage. Mr. Kenyon is not so well informed as he believes; have secur'd Passage for £20 notwithstanding his Declarations I would have difficulty in finding one for £60. For £20 must consider myself Fortunate to share a cabin with 5 other Females of assorted Age and Station. Am not too discouraged. This Voyage cannot last long, and I am strong & healthy & Determin'd to mend my Fortunes.

Have wrote to Uncle Matthew in Bombay my Irrevocable Decision to try my Fortunes in America. Wonder if I shall chance on David Ashton in Virginia? Plague take the Rascal! His bold dark eyes haunt poor Andrea most inconsiderate.

Shall not sleep over much tonight. The *Charming Nymph* is posted to sail at 7. Would I could rid myself of Misgivings 'rous'd by Mr. Cunningham's eagerness to take up my Ticket as soon as I sign'd it. Trust he does not intend to Cheate me. Must trust to Providence.

Candlewick is about to Fall so must end this for today if I am to have light to find my Bed.

Post Scriptum: Against the Voyage have Bath'd & Wash'd the last of powder from my Hair, a chilly business & none too successful for want of sufficient hot Water. Chamberwench eyes my plain new Garments askants, fearful of no Tip, I mistrust. For one thing am grateful, I leave England near penniless, but with all debts completely cover'd up.

Saturday, January 28th, 1775

Ship *Charming Nymph* towards America.

Fine pleasant weather. Have been sailing down the Bristol Channel & pass'd two East Indiamen, prodigious big Ships carrying many little Sails set outside of the bigger ones. Mariners call them "stoomsels." To my mind the Indiamen vessels look very clumsy.

Sunday, January 29th, 1775

Today we touch'd Plymouth where I saw Transports taking on Soldiers & Supplies for service in America. Trouble there must be Greater than is generally Known in England. At least one Reg't. embark'd while I watch'd: the 64th of the line someone said.

Slept passing well last night. But meal of stockfish this Night was abominable & my quarters are Wretched. A year ago would not have believ'd it possible to exist in such a malodorous little Hole. Susan Blake, one of my cabin Mates, is queasy all the time; another poor Soul named Rebecca Williams is in little better Case. Teresa Conway is a spiteful red-haired Vixen and makes life wretched for us with her continual Complaints. Hourly do deliver Thanks to my Maker for proving myself such a fine Sailor. As remedy against squeamishness the Carpenter advises drinking a Quart of Sea water. Susan did so, felt much Remedied.

Cannot hazard how long this Passage to America will endure. Pray it will not be over-long. Mr. Barber, the mate, has a confounded bold way of looking at my limbs even in ugly cotton Hose. Were they cased in Silk I would fear the worst. Shall not don the Lisle pair all this Voyage.

Monday, January 30th, 1775

So tumultuous rough Today I can scarce contrive to move my Pencil. Am most apprehensive, but not yet queasy. (Thanks to the Almighty!)

Cannot see how I can endure further. They have crowded yet another wretched Female into the Hutch Mr. Cunningham calls a Cabin. She bears great white pustules on her Face. Made complaint to Capt'n Knox & got laugh'd at for my Pains. Something is strange about this Vessel. Crew too contemptuous of Passengers for my understanding.

Grow more uneasy every time I see Mr. Cunningham. He is a low fellow. He has taken to warm his Bed a silly young Wench of Fourteen. Two others of my fellow Passengers have done likewise with Capt'n Knox and Mr. Barber. No doubt they thus assure themselves greater Comfort, but am Resolv'd to hold out where I am. Poor Andrea has not repulsed the Advances of the Rakes of Almack's & Brown's to be seduc'd by an unwash'd Mariner.

Pass'd a French ship of the line Homeward bound from their West Indies. The biggest thing afloat I have ever seen. Her Stern was monstrous fascinating and quite cover'd up with gilded Carvings. Our Sailors vow they could carry her themselves, but I do doubt it. Counted four rows of big black Cannons. A fearsome Sight.

Tuesday, January 31st, 1775

On this last Day of January which has proved such an evil Month in the Fortunes of Andrea Grenville, she is compleately Undone. So are the other poor Wretches aboard. This Wm Cunningham is what the crew name a scaw-banker, a heartless Villain which, while enticing Unfortunates like Myself with offer of cheap Passage to America, has trick'd us into signing Articles of Indenture!

Having waited until we are far out to Sea, Capt'n Knox this Day summon'd all passengers able to be about to the foot of the Mast. Swearing horribly, he flung Orders at us as if we were a parcel of Blackamoors. When I, like a Silly Fool, confidently did challenge his Authority, he produc'd the Article I had sign'd while deeming it my Ticket. Have learn'd one thing: never again will Andrea sign a Paper without reading same from beginning to its End. But alas, the Harm is done. When I land, my Services will be bound over for three years to this cunning Cunningham. (Not a bad pun considering my situation.)

Am sure now my Determination to seek America without the Knowledge of Help of my Friends is compleate Folly. It seems the *Charming Nymph* is not for Norfolk at all, not even for the Virginia Colony. She is for a port called New York in a Colony of the same Name where there is a shortage of Servants. Heaven pity the Housewife who purchases poor Andrea's Services. She cannot even boil Water successful.

Wednesday, February 1st, 1775

Wm Cunningham is a loathsome Brute. Trapping me behind one of the Boats, he attempted to Embrace me, panting no end of glowing Promises. I bade him cease and when he did persist, I bit him so shrewdly on the Hand he cried out an Oath & vowed to be Reveng'd of it. Fear me he will be. Yesterday he did beat a serving Maid who named him for what he is, a monstrous great Villain with no more Heart than a Shark.

Am resolved on one thing. Will not allow myself sold like a Sow at a village Fair. I pray God to sustain me in this Hour which my own Folly and Improvidence has bro't upon me.

Will Fate decree that I shall chance on Davey Ashton? Mayhap New York and Norfolk are but a few hours' coaching apart. If so, mayhap he will aid me in finding Honourable Employment of some sort. As a Governess? My French is tolerable good, excepting always Irregular Verbs.

Susan is very sick, taken of a Flux which causes the poor Soul to rave. Have attended her all Night. The red-haired Vixen mov'd to gag her, but by most ungenteel threats I forced her to Desist.

Thursday, February 2nd, 1775

A fearful Tempest is blowing. Ship tosses like a chip. Everywhere people shriek & tear their Hair. The mariners bid us expect the worst.

Friday, February 3rd, 1775

Storm increases rather than abates. The pumps are kept going all the time.

Today passengers are forc'd willy-nilly to take their turn at the Pumps. Teresa swore she'd not lift a Finger but she changed her tune when the bosun black'd an eye for her & loos'd two teeth. Earn'd blisters on both my Hands from my turn at the Pump handles. Believe we cannot endure this storm much longer.

Sunday, February 5th, 1775

Was awoke from an uneasy Sleep by a nip of my Foot. I scream'd to behold a huge Rat nibbling most industrious on my Toe. Now they run all over the Ship which the sailors vow means we are doom'd to sink.

Towards Morning the vessel groan'd in all her Parts and a terrible crack sounded on Deck. They say the foremast has been carried off. In this Hour I thank God I leave no Parents or Husband to mourn me. Naught but a few wastrel Friends who if they ever think of it may drain a Bumper to the memory of poor Andrea Grenville.

We are all in God's hands.

Part V

Norfolk: 1775

1 — SPRING SCENE

IT had been one of the coldest winters even the oldsters of Norfolk could recall. The ice became so jammed up people could walk across the Chesapeake clear to the Maryland shore. There had never been finer skating on Plume's Creek; everybody agreed on that. But otherwise it was such a winter as none of the city's six thousand inhabitants wished to experience again.

The population, cooped indoors by bitter winds, fairly stewed in politics. Party lines became more sharply drawn. On December first a ship bringing imported goods had been turned back with her bulk unbroken for, once the embargo got under way, the Norfolk Committee kept fast sailing boats cruising off the mouth of the Elizabeth River. Every vessel which would stop was boarded and searched for embargoed goods.

It was to be expected, of course, that some British masters would not heave-to and show their papers; but the Committee found a way of dealing with them. On docking his vessel, a defiant master would find a sullen, threatening crowd of mechanics, sailors and Sons of Liberty waiting on his wharf. Since such gatherings were much too dangerous for the local authorities to cope with unaided, the City Council turned a deaf ear to complaints, recommended an appeal to Williamsburg.

The closest Norfolk came to a real clash was on the 12th of March, the day John Brown's brig *Fanny* made port from Jamaica carrying twenty shivering slaves. When word got about that John Brown intended defying the Committee, the other Tories for once lifted no finger to lend him aid. They, too, felt that the slave trade must go. It was a bitter scene when Samuel Inglis and Neil Jameison appeared on Brown's

205

wharf. Speaking for the Committee, they requested, then advised, the old merchant to re-ship his blacks.

John Brown invited them all to go see the Auld Clootie. He made no bones about having armed the tough English slavers and crews of his other ships. There were three in port just then. To a mob armed with clubs and stones, heavy pistols and brass-hilted cutlasses looked too dangerous so, muttering, they backed down.

"I ha'e the right to trade whaur and how I will!" John Brown exulted. "And I'll break this skipkinnit embargo tae a hundred pieces!" It did not help matters that he actually brandished a pistol under the nose of Major John Brush. He had been promoted the week before.

Next day an Independent Infantry Company was mustered and came tramping into Norfolk for the first time. People gathered, fearful, yet curious to see what would happen. There was going to be a fight if the expression on those faces beneath the long-barreled game rifles meant a thing. Children ran alongside the marchers, staring their admiration though uniforms were scarce and individualistic.

Again John Brown had the laugh. The imported slaves had been trans-shipped during the night and were well on their way towards the barracoon of a dealer up the Potomac.

On the day following John Brown's successful defiance, the Committee published broadsides reading:

To all Patriotick Citizens be it known that one John Brown, a merchant doing Business on the Foot of Main Street in Norfolk, is a TRAITOR to the Cause of American Liberty.

Any man who trafficks or Deals with said John Brown in any matter, kindsoever, will also be adjudged an ENEMY to our Liberties. Debtors are warned not to pay their Debts to said John Brown. All patriotickal intended Persons will shun this Rascal.

March 13, 1775   By the Norfolk Committee

Almost overnight the volume of John Brown's business began to diminish. Because no contractor dared lease the old Scot a crew of slave stevedores, he lost a shipment of flour. Many bales of cloth mildewed. Perishable foods spoiled for lack of hands to move it indoors. Though Jemmy Potter and Brown's six remaining clerks worked hard, they could accomplish next to nothing. Finally it got so bad that a pair of clerks could have handled the business. Other merchants looked virtuous—and profited. Days passed on which not a single customer entered the Scot's storehouse. His only visitors were Tories in as bad a case as himself. He hated getting back and forth from his home; loafers were always insulting and got downright threatening sometimes.

In the end the Committee won. John Brown, faced with ruin, ate humble pie; begged them to lift their boycott. Sam Inglis dressed the old man down in no uncertain terms. When the Committee slapped a five thousand dollar fine on him, Phipp said Brown's face looked like a chip from a granite rock.

The affair of the *Fanny* was not yet settled, however. Ensign Leeming and a gang of hand-picked bullies laid for Dan Mayhew, captain of the slaver, when next he made port. Reinforced by seamen bitter because they'd been out of work for weeks, Leeming's men grabbed him just as he was leaving the Harp and Crown. They tied a placard reading "Traitor" about Mayhew's thick neck, then frog-marched him over to Tom Newton's shipyard. Someone had remembered seeing shipwrights heat tar for the calking of Robert Ashton's brig.

There had been a snow storm the day before, which was unusual for April. It had come roaring in from the ocean to powder the housetops and streets as a final farewell from winter. The snow had already melted except for a few patches in sheltered places.

Rob, lingering to complete an odd job, watched the whole affair from the deck of his vessel. John Brown's captain had both eyes blacked and blood was trickling from a corner of his mouth; a stone had hit him so hard as to smash a couple of front teeth. He was the lone, pitiful focus of a yelling mob.

A sudden sense of outrage gripped Rob, though he had always been dead set against the slave traffic. In a practical sense slave labor was bad business. Still, it didn't make him feel any better to see a decent mariner like Dan Mayhew half stunned, yanked this way and that, with his wig gone and his seaman's serge spattered with horse droppings.

Mayhew, terrified, was fluttering like a bird in a snare. Rob could hear him gasping.

"Mercy! Don' harm me, lads! I never hurt ye, Billy. Oh-h Mr. Leeming! Make 'em shtop! Don'—don'!"

Captain Rudder, who had lost his vessel to the British, bawled to Leeming, "Take it easy, Ed! Let's give him a chance."

"Aye!" Peart pushed forward, grabbed the prisoner. "Lend a hand, Ben. Heave him up."

Indignant, solitary, and unobserved on his foredeck, Rob watched them hoist John Brown's captain onto an up-ended turpentine barrel. Mayhew crouched there, not daring to look one way or another.

"Bloody cowards!" Rob whispered when he saw the victim raise a fending arm and spit blood. He wanted to interfere, but there was the brig to consider. He himself was skating on mighty thin ice. He would have to sing low and mind his step at least until the *Grand Turk* was ready to go to sea.

"Down on your knees!" "Hang the damned Guineaman!" "Kneel, you Tory cutthroat!"

"Don' lads!" Mayhew gurgled. "I—do—you—wan'— Don' hurt me!"

"All right then." Rudder, more than a little drunk, brandished a brown fist under Mayhew's nose. "Beg forgiveness of A'mighty God and the coun'rymen ye've disgraced an' cheated by yer' damn' greed!"

Dan Mayhew's voice, in the monotone of terror, rang out in the cold April air, but because of his broken teeth it was hard to understand him. In the most abject terms he beseeched forgiveness, a chance to prove himself devoted to the liberties of America. His coat had ripped half down his back; his stock was gone now. Many little blood spots flecked his shirt and white canvas breeches. Crouched on his barrel, he presented a forlorn, terrified figure.

"Thanksh for mershy, gentlemen," Mayhew gasped in conclusion. "Didn' know I wash doing. Didn' mean anybody harm. Sh-swear I didn'. Won' ever shail 'nother ship for Brown!"

"Yer damned right ye won't," roared Leeming. "Nor will anyone else after we've done with you. Get aside, Rudder, this here's Committee business."

"Oh pleash!" the victim's voice climbed to a scream. "For the love of God don' hurt me more!"

They tumbled him from the barrel head and dragged him

whimpering over a litter of timber ends, chips and shavings to the tar kettle. He yelled in agony when a couple of roughs tilted two buckets of hot tar over him. Roar on roar of laughter arose when they saw Dan Mayhew, dripping and bedraggled like a huge fly fished out of an inkwell. They left him on a bale of oakum, groaning, sobbing hysterically.

Next the mob sought the Port Master's Office. Forcing their way in, its leaders demanded of a chalk-faced clerk the manifest for the *Fanny*'s cargo of slaves. When he produced it, Leeming growled:

"You may be a smart lawyer's pimp, but yer going to learn a new trick."

While the crowd looked on, laughing like all get out, he crammed the clerk's fingers into an ink pot and dragged them across the manifest. They barred it with four smudgy lines.

"You can consider this manifest canceled!" Peart growled. "Next time we come to cancel a manifest we'll maybe use red ink!"

Next day half the people employed by the Crown threw up their jobs. Trouble came of that raid on the Port Master's Office; it was His Majesty's property. Governor Dunmore flew into a towering passion and ordered H.M.S. *Liverpool* to lie off Town Back Creek with her guns run out. Truculent marines were set ashore to guard Crown property. People laughed because even though no cases were being tried, they patroled the courthouse grounds. Some time back the Committee had "suggested" that no more cases be tried before a Judiciary appointed by King George but paid for with Virginia taxes. Benches in the courtrooms gathered dust.

Everybody, even his worst enemies, admired Robert Ashton for one thing. Not once did he ever reproach his brother. He made no attempt to explain David's astounding duplicity, even to himself. When people offered sympathy or expressed indignation he only turned aside in silence. His wife, and possibly Matt Phipp, alone guessed the depth of his bitterness. It was unfortunate that his undemonstrative temperament made it impossible to break loose with a stream of relieving curses. Instead he strove to forget the fact of David's existence. No matter how he looked at the matter, the facts remained.

Mr. Abel Hovey, of Hovey & Sons, who had attended the

prize court sitting, took pains to forward a transcript of David Ashton's testimony. Rob read it, then used it to kindle a fire. What had happened to Farish troubled Rob deeply. He'd grown mighty fond of his dry, dependable little master, even if he was a Yankee.

A good while would have to elapse before he could forget that night he'd gone stumping over frozen roads out to Tide-over. Peggy, showing her pregnancy in more ways than one, staged a tearful scene and uttered bitter, unreasonable reproaches when he told her he must sell Tide-over. Only in that way would he be able to finish the brig. She knew it as well as he did.

"Oh, the devil take that wretched ship!" she wailed.

"Peggy!" Rob groaned. "Don't say that! For God's sake, don't!"

"I mean it! *I hate her!*"

It in nowise helped matters that, when Peggy on her own initiative, asked help of her father, the old man curtly quoted the cruel old saw about making a bed and lying on it. Major Fleming considered her husband an out-and-out rebel.

"A smart merchant like Robert would certainly know whether his vessel carried contraband, and you can't tell me otherwise!" he stormed, beating the back of a chair. "French arms, mark you, for use against the Crown! I can't forgive that! No, Margaret, you will have to choose between the loyalty every self-respecting English subject owes his King, and Robert Ashton. He may be, as you say, a sound apple from a rotten tree, but he is a rebel through and through! I daresay you are proud to have a condemned felon for your brother-in-law? Bad blood always shows—"

Peggy thought of her baby and fainted.

Mrs. Fleming bent above the limp figure and, for one of the few times in her life, flared up at her husband.

"You are a brute, Andrew Fleming, a heartless brute to treat her so! And with her in the family way! If she had married the Devil himself, she is still our daughter. Mine, anyway."

But Andrew Fleming only snorted. "I'd liefer have her married to the Devil, Ma'am, than to an enemy of my Sovereign!"

So saying, the old officer marched from the room, shoulders squared and chin up. He had looked like that seventeen years earlier while leading the battered 37th back into action before Minden town. There was no shaking him now, either.

"You must give Robert up. Promise you will," Betsy Fleming begged when her daughter revived. "Believe me, child, it *is* all for the best! I know it will be a sore grief for awhile, but there is your child—my grandchild, to consider. You know very well you have not money enough to bear it in decent fashion. You should not be doing even light housework.

"Think of your father. This bitterness is aging him. He takes it hard when old friends look the other way." Mrs. Fleming's voice blurred. "Why, can you believe it, we've not been bidden to the Brushes' once this year! Neil Jameison cut your father dead on the street the other day. Think of it! And they have played chess every week since we all came to Norfolk together back in '59."

Her hand crept about Peggy's shoulders. "Listen, child; a reed cannot withstand a hurricane. To bend with the tempest is only sensible. When this stupid trouble is done, we will send for Robert."

Peggy dried her eyes, thought a long while. "Oh, I don't know! I don't know! I can't make up my mind. Rob—well, I reckon he needs me these days."

This was no less than the truth. The loss of the brigantine and the consequent sale of Tide-over had etched harsh lines about Robert Ashton's mouth and had tucked a little V between his wide-set brown eyes.

The night he learned the prize court's verdict Rob looked up Tom Newton. They worked 'til dawn revising plans and estimates for the *Grand Turk*. By a ruthless elimination of non-essentials, by reducing spare gear and by refiguring the sailmaker's bill on the basis of lighter weight canvas, they cut the original estimate by a third.

The following day Rob roamed Norfolk and the adjacent countryside. It took him three days to locate the right buyer for Tide-over. He was one Llewellyn Jones, a wizened Welsh corn broker.

"Aye, I know what is brewing in the trade world," he cackled. "I am selling out. The politicians don't bother with a small farmer much."

Though the sale brought enough to complete the *Grand Turk*, there wasn't any money left. At least, not enough to rent them a room in even the meanest ordinary. When the blow fell in December it was Peggy who recalled a small store-room to the rear of Ashton & Co.'s office.

"There is a fireplace in it. I'm sure there is. It backs up against the flue in the office. There are some old sails in the loft. Why couldn't we hang them 'round the walls and nail a tarpaulin over the floor? We would be very snug in there. Besides it would be something new to live out over the water." Desperately, she had tried to make light of their impoverishment. "We would be by ourselves, then, dear—much better off than in some messy, noisy inn."

Rob had jumped at the suggestion and, just before they vacated Tide-over, spent a couple of days preparing their new quarters. As she had suggested, he hung old sails to insulate generous cracks in the store-room's walls. He secured them fairly well by nailing rows of laths across the duck. He even amused himself by arranging rows of weatherbeaten reef points in decorative patterns. Of their furniture they kept only the big double bed and such trifles as were not worth selling. Along with Toby, the spaniel, Peggy's wedding silver went back to the Flemings' for safe keeping. She made no offer to sell the plate—not that Rob would have permitted her to, but he would have been pleased if she had suggested it. Lom, by an arrangement with the new owner was allowed to continue on the property. Tearfully, he begged to be allowed to move into town, but Peggy was adamant.

"It's only for a little while," she smiled. "We will be out in the country again soon."

During February they made out somehow, though the necessity of cooking and sleeping and living all in the same room called for ingenuity and forbearance. Peggy was exasperated at the way the fireplace kept on smoking no matter what Rob did to the flue. Even a larger chimney pot made no difference.

At another time things might have gone more smoothly, but as the winter advanced Peggy's temper became increasingly unpredictable and exasperating. She would, for instance, stand up under the most trying hardships, then would dissolve into tears over some trivial thing like a drop of chocolate spilt on her tablecloth.

The constant crying of the gulls grated on her nerves. Their querulous mewing was the first thing she heard in the morning and, all day long, numbers of the big gray birds stalked about on the warehouse roof. On still days the acid, fishy odor of their droppings permeated the whole building.

She found their new quarters dangerously damp. At high tide the harbour water licked around the oyster-encrusted pilings on which the warehouse stood. At low ebb a bank of mud beneath the floor gave off dank exhalations. She blamed her series of colds on this more than on the thin slippers she insisted on wearing when her ankles swelled. Dismal, too, was the persistent drip, drip, drip, of snow melting and falling onto the water so close below.

In cold weather it required Spartan courage to use the office privy; it was just a plain board with a hole cut in it in a draughty shed built out over the water. Rob vowed it worked like the ventilating flue of an ice house; he always went out first and got the frost off the seat.

But what really kept Peggy's nerves quivering were the rats. The warehouse was overrun with them; fierce black creatures with wickedly sharp yellow teeth. The first time one ate a hole through the tarpaulin on the floor and crawled out, its naked tail all shiny with mud, Peggy shrieked so loudly people summoned the watch. She never got used to them, never was allowed to forget their furtive presence. Almost always a rustling and scrabbling went on behind the insulation of old canvas. On one very cold night a fat she-rat tried to get into their bed and, as Rob was killing it with a boot-jack, it squeaked dreadfully and gave birth to half a dozen hideous, hairless, squirming baby rats.

Rob seemed to live with but one thought—to rush the completion of his brig.

"As soon after she's launched as it's possible, we'll live aboard her," Rob said. "I am building her stern cabin extra big. You should be more comfortable there; for a few months more I reckon we'll not be taking chances about the baby. After that—" he forced a confident smile—"well, I will be back on my feet again."

2 — LAUNCHING DAY

THEY were going to launch the *Grand Turk* when the tide was high—around four o'clock. It seemed impossible it was so. Peggy felt she could not remember a time when the brig had not been a dominant factor in her married existence. Today the brig would be sent down the ways, would for the first time feel water under her. Lying comfortable and warm beside Rob, she tried to peer into the future. What would the *Grand Turk* bring them? Fortune? Happiness? Certainly they deserved well of her.

She turned a little awkwardly onto her side and by the growing light of day looked at her husband. She smiled wistfully. Asleep like this with his hair all damp and rumpled he looked so much younger. A good man, she told herself, and brave. She was proud of the way he had rallied from the double shock.

Rob was lying on his back, profile showing up sharp against the dingy canvas beyond. Regularly little puffs of vapor rose from his nostrils. Strange, she had never before noticed there were quite a few red hairs in the stubble on his chin. She could just see the little pock marks along the ridge of his cheekbones. What a funny short nose he had, and his ears— she wished they were living a hundred years earlier—their strong lobes seemed fashioned to support gold rings. He had lost a lot of weight since last fall, and a stubborn set to his chin was more pronounced than ever.

A bright sunrise was indicating that this, the Great Day, was going to be clear. Presently she slipped out of bed and, without waking him, went over to throw tinder and kindling on some hardwood coals in the fireplace. She worked the bellows hurriedly, for the cold draught was beating up under her flannel nightgown and the canvas felt harsh and greasy to her bare feet. Before popping back into bed, she broke a skim of ice in the water pail and filled the teakettle.

A holiday mood suddenly seized her. Life really wasn't so grim. Of a certainty all must go well with the Ashtons from now on. She did something that she had not done in months. Though hampered by her misshapen abdomen, she edged over until the ends of her eyelashes could tickle Rob's cheek.

Still immersed in slumber, he reached up and clumsily rubbed the spot. Then, emitting a comfortable little "woompf," he let his hand slip back beneath the coverlet. When she repeated the proceeding he at last stirred and, semi-conscious, lay looking at her through half raised lids.

A smile spread over his thin brown features like a ripple over a pond. "Hello, darling. How is the big day?"

"Bright and a bit cold, Rob, but I reckon I've enough sunshine in me to keep me warm."

"Going to change its name to Sunshine?"

Peggy blushed so she buried her face in her pillow. Her voice all muffled reached him. "Now you hush! I wasn't talking about—that."

Contrary to his usual practice Rob made no immediate effort to arise, but lay still, fingers locked behind his head, smiling, listening to the snap and crackle of the fire.

"Sunshine. Sunshine? Not a bad name, especially if it's a her. If it turns out to be a buck, we can always call him Sol; he'll be a son anyhow."

"Lord deliver us from early morning wit! Stop it, you big silly. Don't you know it's bad luck to name unborn babies? Now up with you, Mr. Lazybones. Get your things on and fetch me some more kindling."

"Yes, my lady. But today you stay abed and I will fix the breakfast."

"How lovely," Peggy sighed, sinking back on the pillows. "The butter is in the brown crock to your left. The eggs are in the left cupboard drawer."

Right after breakfast Rob began looking about for an omen. He believed it was at hand when someone began to rap loudly at the office door. The caller proved to be a lanky, big faced seafaring man wearing a shipmaster's coat and a ring in his left ear.

"Captain Trott, at your service, sir," he announced.

"Come in, Captain. What can I do for you?" Rob was conscious of being subjected to the intent inspection of two bloodshot gray eyes. There was an indefinable foreign air about this red-haired fellow. It might be his old-fashioned cut clothes and his footgear, square toed pumps sporting huge brass bruckes. Captain Trott came closer, narrowing his eyes.

"You Mr. Ashton?"

"Yes."

"Robert Ashton, son of St. John Ashton?"

"To the best of my belief," smiled Rob. "Take a seat, won't you?"

"I made 'e port yesterday in 'e *Active*," the caller volunteered, running an eye over the little office. "Notice her?"

"The Bermuda-built sloop that anchored in the afternoon?"

"Aye." Employing his cuff, Captain Trott wiped a drop from the end of his blunt nose. He began fumbling in his coat. "Should have knowed ye straight off; you're 'e spit and image o' Mr. Hereward." Captain Trott nodded a big battered-looking head several times. "But you're bigger."

After handing Rob a letter, the Bermudian captain swung over to the fireplace. He lingered there toasting badly bowed legs and gazing at the ivory model on the shelf.

Here sure enough was his omen! Tingling with suspense, Rob went over to the window and slipped his thumbnail under a seal of blue wax. Fingers quivering a little, he unfolded a letter.

February 6th, 1775
Gaunt New House, Summers Isles

Most Respkt'd Cousin Robert:

It has ocured to Me that there is Small proffitt in prolonging a Family quarrell which is none of our jeneraton's making. Your Papa I hear, is dead & so is mine. Hereward, my oldest Bro. is becom somewhat Soften'd with advancing yeres. Therfor, I ofer you the Olive Branch in high hopes that you are as Reddy to take it as I am to ofer it.

A Virginia ship tuched hear not long past and having had ocasion to dyne with her Mast'r, lerned he knue you well & that your Affairs do Prossper. I do asshure you, Cousin, I am vastly pleased to lern of your Suckcess & am mov'd to wonder why it would not be to our mutewel Adv'tage to Conduct a Commerce between these Ilands and the fare Colonie you enhabit.

Most ridicklous rumours circulate amongst us. To witt: ere long Comerce between England & the W. Indees will ceese with America. You can beleive we in Bermuda are grately exerciz'd, since we can not for six Months survive without vittels & those other necesitties of Life wich come from America. We are so feeble and few we Dare not speak out 'gainst the inikwities of Parliament, but thar are many sleber (Do you understand?) amongst us.

That gave Rob pause. Sleber? The twerp can't spell. What in the world? Then he saw how the word should be read and, conscious of Captain Trott's intent regard, returned his attention to the letter.

Here, dear Cousin, is what I purpose. Ship as heavy a cargoe of Vittels as you may, salt meat, pottatos, and flower in partikular. I will undertake to bring you such Prices as will make your Mouth water. Gainst this I have to ofer Salt & a comoddity I hear you are most desirus of prokuring—gunpowder.

Gunpowder? Rob whistled softly. Not entirely a fool, this cousin.

I scarce need warn you to be most seekret about this. The crying Need of vittels in these Ilands will soon become known in America. Then prices must fall, but I believe, most respeck'd Cousin, that this epissel is the first inteligence America has of the dire straights of these Ilands respeckting true feeling. Shoud you decide to make this Ventur pleas send word by Captain Trott.
A final warrning. You had Best ship no Sgnik sdneirf. Our Governor has an Eager ear for trechery.
Pray present my compl'ts to the Virtuous Female who is your Wife. Am sorely vex'd Mountford wrote such a breef acc't of your Wedding. I would it had been my Good Fortune to atend it.

Yr. Respt. aff. Cousin,
Peter Ashton

Captain Trott promised to return for an answer and went swaggering off up Main Street towards the Pied Bull. Rob, in his delight relented and told Peggy all about it.
She was wholly delighted and chuckled so hard over Peter Ashton's spelling that tears gathered in her eyes.
"Heavens! Haven't they any schools in Bermuda?"
"He's probably a good fisherman," Rob grinned, "and there's plenty of sense to his suggestion."

By God! This was like finding money in the bank. He began to figure on how early the brig might be put in commission.

Cedars, fevers, shipyards and whales; that meant the Bermudas. The identification promptly popped up out of his memory. He tried to recall one of his father's rare descriptions of the old home. It was on a harbour called Mangrove Bay and Gaunt New House was a long white structure sprawling in three storeys up a ridge overlooking the bay. It was constructed of coral stone and roofed with the same material. For the love of laughing Molly Butler, St. John Ashton had left it—and his family's favor.

Rob wondered, as he stood there fingering the letter, what the Bermudas were really like. Waterfront gossip wasn't any too flattering to the inhabitants. Most sailors called them a parcel of pirates, wreckers and sharp dealers. Old Mr. Gilmorin always maintained that a 'Mudian's word wasn't worth a thin damn unless you got him tied down and backed into a corner. Exaggerations of course. But where smoke arises? He reckoned he would move cautiously, find out more as soon as he could about this group of little-known islands lying some six hundred miles out to sea.

"It's a sign!" Peggy's voice recalled him. "Oh Rob, I'm sure it's a sign! Wasn't it fine of your cousin to write like this?"

"It was mighty handsome," Rob observed dryly. "You'll notice there's a little profit involved?"

"Oh, you Ashtons are all alike—merchants! Merchants! All of you except—" She had started to say "David" but turned away, instead, to smooth the coverlet.

The tide was expected to be at flood around four o'clock and as a further favorable omen it promised to be a good high one. In astonishing numbers the townsfolk turned out to witness the launching. Every pile of lumber, every point of vantage in Newton's shipyard, was black with onlookers. Small boys even dispossessed gulls from the roofs of nearby shops and warehouses. What with trade so stagnant and businesses failing every week, the occasion had a rare entertainment value.

Expert opinions regarding the new brig's probable speed and seaworthiness were at a sixpence the dozen. Rob's radical departure from accepted rules of ship construction heightened interest to record proportions. The "Virginia Gazette" announced shipwrights had come from as far away as Baltimore, Annapolis—even Philadelphia, to find out whether Rob Ashton and Tom Newton were crazy as bedbugs or not. The crowd definitely liked the *Grand Turk*'s subtle, eye-pleasing lines.

A solid, shiny-faced lieutenant of the Royal Navy tramped up to the astonished owner and offered his hand.

"Pray, Mr. Ashton, accept my hearty congratulations for whatever they are worth. That is as fine a designed vessel as I have ever seen built in a British yard. Her lines are sweet, vastly sweet!"

Rob suspected sarcasm, but the lieutenant was wholly enthusiastic; so much so that people began looking his way and putting their heads together.

"If you Virginians can turn out more vessels of this sort, we won't be put to the bother of capturing French ships so as to sail in something better than a floating barn."

The Britisher's admiration warmed Rob more than the black Demerera rum Tom Newton was passing around. "Thank you, lieutenant. I expect great things of her."

From his position beside the capstan, on the brass cap of which was engraved *"Grand Turk II, 1775,"* Rob's glance swept aft. It seemed odd to see the long yellow deck cleaned of chips, shavings and sawdust. She looked more like a live ship though her two masts stood supported by only a few stays. Topmasts and other top hamper would be rigged later. Several thoughtful individuals noted and commented on the fact that the black painted bulwarks were plenty solid enough to stand piercing for gun ports.

Rob was feeling much as he had on the night Margaret Fleming promised she would marry him. He felt a wild exultation, a glorious soaring of hopes. This brig was reality now— born of a sliver of ivory, his imagination, and Tom Newton's craftsmanship. By God, she *was* beautiful! Worth every hour of agony and sweat and disappointment.

The hollow thudding of mauls knocking out shores brought him back to earth. Down on the muddy ground the usual horseplay was going on. Craning his neck this way and that, Captain Peart strode around the throng at the water's edge.

"Hey! What you counting there?" people demanded.

But Peart only grinned. "One, two, three," he raised fingers.

When he reached ten, he ran up and under the bow and cupped his hands. He had to bellow over the crash made by falling props.

"Hi, Mr. Ashton! This shore is going to be one lucky ship!'

"Eh? What's that?" Rob wanted to hear of anything lucky.

"Never was a lucky ship launched 'thout a cuckold or two in the crowd and by gobs, you've got ten here!"

Far in the background stood Robert Gilmorin, his eyes hard and black as bits of coal. He was thinking of the copy he had sent to Kenyon in Bristol, but even if the *Grand Turk* proved good, he wouldn't be building a copy of her. Not this year. With Kenyon & Gilmorin business was deader than dead.

Everyone spoke of how terribly he had aged since Johnny ran away, but he carried his handsome silver head higher than ever. Folks were sorry for him; he'd had such hopes for young John—his only son.

Neil Jameison was there and so was Major John Brush and Tom MacSherry dressed to the nines in a plum-colored coat and canary yellow waistcoat. Even John Brown came, truculent and defiant. Overhead gulls wheeled in idle curiosity and a drunken sailor fell in the saw pit over which the brig's planking had been shaped.

"You may run up the flags," Rob told Tom Newton gravely. At a signal from the shipwright huge British Jacks climbed to the heads of both stumpy masts.

The brisk April wind, freshening momentarily, blew out their folds. Peggy, waiting on a small platform below the bow, nervously fingered a bottle of sherry gay with blue and white ribbons. Matthew Phipp stood beside her, good loyal Matt, and Lucy Gilmorin had forgotten old scores enough to come along. The wind tore at her cloak and whipped the dark brown curls about her forehead. Out on the river small whitecaps chased each other furiously down to the Chesapeake.

Peggy felt her cheeks grow hot. "Lucy, do I show very much?"

She knew she did, but Lucy fibbed loyally, "Heavens, no, dear! No one would even *dream!* Now, don't fail to break the bottle."

"I won't! I've been waiting almost a year for this."

Her small face radiant, Peggy listened to the hollow sound of the mauls, the shouts of Tom Newton, anxious lest something go wrong. He didn't like to see the wind blowing so hard. It might tip the brig over as, precariously balanced, she rushed for the water.

The figurehead wasn't a yard above Peggy's head. How fiercely the swarthy-featured Grand Turk stared ahead! He held a silvered scimitar in his right hand and clutched a jewel casket in his left. The gilding on the Grand Turk's turban shone bright as brass. Into what strange, faraway ports would those bold painted eyes peer? On what enemies would they frown?

"Wish my hair would curl like that in wet weather," Lucy laughed and reaching up, stroked the long black curls of the figure's spade-shaped beard.

Peggy's attention was drawn to the sight of Ben Rudder scrambling unsteadily up a ladder which the workmen were trying to remove. He had a big cloth-covered bundle under one arm and was so awkward one of the laborers had to give him a hand on deck.

"Drunk again!" a woman in the crowd said. "It's a crying shame he don't pull himself together. He was a fine master once."

"It's his wife I'm sorry fer."

A boisterous yell arose when Ben Rudder reappeared; he was crawling out along the bowsprit.

"Here ye are, boysh. How's thish fer a mascot?" He brandished a pair of the biggest elk antlers imaginable. Though he almost slipped off half a dozen times, Rudder nonetheless lashed them to the sprit. Delighted, the crowd bellowed obscene suggestions as to whose they were.

A foreman mopped his face as he stopped before the shipbuilder.

"All clear, Mr. Newton."

The shipbuilder jerked a nervous nod. He always got the fidgets 'til a new boat was safe in the water. "Tell them fools out there to clear out of my way! They'll get swamped."

Despite fierce gusts of wind, many little boats were rocking off the end of the ways. People in them were ready with nets and dippers to salvage the tallow with which the ways had been greased. Lots of it would go floating off downstream and tallow was expensive.

Peart, standing on the edge of the crowd, felt someone shove him. It was a girl.

"How soon is she going to be launched, Mister?" she asked, setting down her milk pail.

"Why, any minute. *Christ A'mighty!*" Peart burst out.

"Why, Mister, there's no call to curse at—at an empty milk pail," the girl stammered.

"An empty pail! By God! Look!"

Every seafaring man near enough to see pointed his index and little fingers at the pail; that might ward off the worst of the bad luck. Every sailor in the crowd knew something terrible would happen if a woman carrying an empty pail came to a launching, or chanced by on sailing day. It was 'most as bad as having a rabbit aboard.

"Clear out of here!" Peart ordered. "Quick!" And once the bewildered young woman had slunk away, he turned the pail upside-down.

Rob leaned over the bow and smiled down at his wife. He called in a loud clear voice, "Mrs. Ashton, pray give this ship her name." And his even teeth gleamed.

Peggy's heart lifted so high she thought she was going to faint. At last! She called in a high trembling voice, "I christen thee *Grand Turk!*" and swung the sherry bottle so hard a bit of flying glass cut her finger. She never noticed it.

Mauls whammed twice more. A tearing wind squall stirred up eddies of sawdust and stiffened the flags until they stood out flat as if they had been cut out of tin. The *Grand Turk* stirred then shuddered and began to inch away from Peggy. A deep rumbling sound filled the air; it sounded like a heavy wagon crossing a covered bridge.

Rob's hat blew off and he held hard to the pin rail at the foot of the foremast. Houses, ships building on adjacent stocks commenced to recede. He glimpsed Ben Rudder, still perched on the bowsprit and waving his arms crazily.

"Look out!" he yelled, but his voice was lost in an ear-torturing screech. The sound swelled until it seemed as if some Titan woman were suffering a birth pang. The brig slid faster, faster, down the long straight ways towards the gray-yellow harbour.

The stern took water, hurled spray yards high and the crowd yelled themselves raucous. Under the impact the *Grand Turk*'s stern shot up. Two great walls of water went rushing away then, while the men aboard held on for dear life, the brig lurched out on the stream. She rocked violently, but came to rest; on an even keel, thank God. Cables securing the *Grand Turk* to the pier at which she would be rigged checked her movement, rounded her up.

On shore everybody was laughing because Captain Rudder had tumbled into the icy water and, suddenly sobered, was threshing about like a drowning cow.

3 — JEMMY POTTER ENLISTS

ON the morning of April 16th, John Brown summoned his employees. He looked at each of them as if he had never seen them before. Never had the big brick warehouse seemed so vast, nor so silent. Distinctly he could hear water lapping at the pilings and gulls crying on the roof.

He gathered his men in a covered cart passage leading from Main Street past the Office and on into the warehouse itself. They stood, awkward and embarrassed, amid a flood of warm sunshine beating through tall double doors. Jemmy Potter guessed he knew what was up. This time it would be his turn. A month back the old man had sacked three young clerks. Then, a fortnight ago he had given three more employees their walking papers. The wharf master, the weigher and two stock clerks had followed.

Bad times! Cruel times, mused John Brown. It was a wicked shame to sack such capable employees. Unconsciously procrastinating the evil moment, he raised his eyes to watch a pair of sparrows make vigorous love on a rafter. Two blue pigeons also were watching. A bitter taste filled John Brown's mouth, invaded his stomach, his very soul. What in blazes was a man to do? he asked himself in a hopeless sort of rage. Here he was with a stock of the finest goods Europe produced and no customers. It wasn't fair. He had paid the Committee's absurd fine, but even so he hadn't transacted fifty pounds worth of business since.

"Men, I ha'e kept you on so long as I could, but I can no maire," he began. Though he had lived in Virginia a long time, the Scotch burr persisted in his accent.

The old man could keep them on all right, Jemmy Potter reflected. Old John Brown was richer than Croesus, but being a merchant and a Scot at that, he couldn't be expected to go in for charity.

The tough little man checked his restless parade. "You

223

ha'e been gude, honest and faithfu' servants, all of ye; 'tis sore grieved I am tae say what I must. Gordon MacLeod here has been wi' me thairty years, so him I'm keeping on. The rest of ye desairve better than this. Blame yon domned rebel Committee, not me!" He faltered. "Losh, it's a crying pity!"

Angrily he waved his short arms at the overcrowded warehouse, "Look! Will ye all look on yon goods? What's to become of them? Rat food and moth food, that's what they'll be! Old Clootie's curse on a' politicians!"

"It's not your fault, Mr. Brown," admitted a round-shouldered little clerk intently inspecting an inky forefinger. "But well, it's hard—very hard on us——"

"Don't blame me," repeated the old man. "So long as I might, I resisted the illegal laws passed by Randolph, Mason, Patrick Henry, and the rest o' the rebels." He spread his hands in a gesture of angry surrender. "But I can no longer. Blame the have-nots! Blame the poor whites o' the back country. Always they plot and plan to hamper men maire industrious than their lazy sel'es." John Brown paused. When he spoke again the passion had left his voice. "In one thing we can a' take pride. We are no turncoats. We had our convictions and we ha'e stuck to 'em!"

"That's small consolation, Mr. Brown, when the stuffed shirts in Parliament won't lift a finger to help us," growled the senior clerk.

"They will send help," John Brown promised. "This American trade is too valuable. The English mairchants and ship owners already are raising a great lament. Mark my wo-rds, lads, ships and troops will come! The English are slow, but they never-r let go."

The old Scot's gaze wandered, eyeing the familiar scene. At regular intervals the musty gloom within was pierced by dazzling shafts. These, groping among the velvety shadows, wrought false high lights by playing on the white pine boards of packing cases.

"What ye had best do is no' for me tae say. Like me, ye are branded as Tories. Potter, here, has already suffered for his loyalty. 'Twas because of it I ha'e kept him 'til the noo." John Brown looked them each one in the eyes, then said, "When this trouble is o'er and if I still ha'e a business, come back. Ye'll find yer positions waiting." He heaved a long sigh. "Noo, ye had best draw yer monies frae Gordon MacLeod. Gudebye, I—I'm sorry. 'Tis a' so unco' needless!" For a second time the old merchant's voice broke. When, hurriedly, he turned on his heel, they all saw that his hard, nut-like face was quivering.

Smaller, more wizened looking than ever, John Brown clumped away, dwarfed among his mounds of merchandise. He walked out on the dock beyond the storehouse and sank wearily onto a pile of mahogany logs. There he remained, staring on the idle ships at Robert Gilmorin's wharf.

Jemmy Potter was the last of the discharged employees to pull himself together and only abstractedly joined the pay line, a column which, a few months earlier, would have extended the length of the tobacco shed alongside.

Gordon MacLeod sat at the paymaster's desk, frowning behind his spectacles and every so often blowing his nose with vigor. To think he had lived to see John Brown's staff reduced to a single clerk!

"John Dow?"

"Here."

"Three pound, seven and four. And God keep ye."

"George Ainslee?"

"Here."

"Three pound, four and six—and may the Laird presairve ye."

The employees accepted their pay in bemused fashion. George Ainslee especially wore a stunned look. Well he might. Ten years in the service of John Brown had taught him to look to the future with confidence. There were six children at home and his wife was poorly.

"Jemmy Potter?"

"Here."

"Two pound, eight pence—and gude luck."

Soft as falling leaves two notes fluttered onto his palm. Then the copper coins. Jemmy glanced at them. Virginia notes. Virginia! The name stung him into an unreasoning fury. Virginia! A damned treacherous slut of a place! Three years ago Virginia had invited enterprise, had offered wealth, happiness and security—a fair exchange for honesty and hard work. The Province had stolen savings hard-earned in the French wars, shillings amassed at the expense of wounds, hunger and grinding fatigue. Virginia. To hell with the place, and to hell with the bleeding swine who lived in it!

His bowed legs carried him out into the sunlight. Thieves, bloody thieves, that's what the colonists were! For no reason, they had burnt his stable. And now came this. It wasn't right; it bloody well wasn't fair!

"Wot in 'ell 'ave I done?" He began thinking aloud as he and Ainslee tramped along the street. "I ain't arsked nothink of these bleeding Virginians but a chance to earn me living. I bin sober and respectable. I ain't robbed, cheated nor murdered nobody, 'as I?"

George Ainslee did not answer. He was not even listening, but Jemmy neither noticed nor cared. "I ain't stirring up no trouble. Orl I did was to larf at them sod-busters pretending they was cavalry. A man's got a right to larf, ain't 'e? Gawd's teeth, I'll make these bloody colonial buggers pay! See if I don't!"

Ainslee turned his long pale face. He was a loose-jointed fellow and his eyes were of a soft brown. Right now they looked like those of a dog, lost and trying to find his master in a hopeless sort of way.

"You? What can you do? What can any of us do?" Ainslee demanded bitterly. "All the loyal merchants are letting their help go. I suppose you heard Kenyon & Gilmorin sacked sixteen more men only yesterday? There are three of their ships tied in the harbour. Look for yourself."

Jemmy Potter's good-natured expression dissolved into a mask of scarlet ferocity; in his small, pale eyes shone a deadly gleam.

"Wot will I do? I'll make 'em pay for wot they've stole from me, and pay dear! I—I'll rejoin the army!"

"Join the army! Why, Jemmy, you wouldn't want to do that, not really?" Ainslee's look of incredulity deepened. "Times aren't bad enough for that."

"I wouldn't, wouldn't I?" In his rage Jemmy spat clear across the street. "Just see if I don't! And don't yer think I don't know it's a dorg's life in the Service. It is. But s'welp me it's worth getting catted by some whoreson of an officer to get my own back out of these God damned patriots!"

He pointed at the shops and taverns along the street and his voice assumed a rasping note. "'Ow'd you like to see orl this a-blazing and a-burning? 'Ow'd you like it? They've done yer dirt, too! Well, my lad, more than one side can light fires and beat up honest working men and steal an old soljer's savings! Just you wait and see!"

"Sh-h-h," Ainslee begged. "They'll hear you."

"To 'ell with 'em." Jemmy linked his arm through Ainslee's

and his wink was sly. "Yus, I learned some narsty little tricks from the old von Spröcke's Brunswickers. I'm going to pay these Virginia buggers back. But if I was you, George, I'd go back to England."

"Wish I could, but where'll I find passage money?"

"Carn't yer sell your 'ouse?"

"Who'll buy it? Who'd dare buy of a Tory? My wife, she tried to sell some silver spoons last week. Know what happened? The silversmith—it was Mendez—looked through a list.

" 'Are you Mrs. George Ainslee, living on Catherine Street?'

" 'Why yes,' Agnes says, 'I am.'

" 'Well, Ma'am, we are not interested in buying your silver,' says Max Mendez and invites Agnes out of the shop so quick as he could. Tell me, what *am* I going to do?"

"Yah! To-rees! To-rees! Get a rope!" A row of small heads popped into sight above a plank fence across the street. "To-rees! To-rees!" they chanted. Neither man paid any attention; they were too used to it.

After they separated at the corner of Fenchurch Road, Jemmy went to his little room above the Harp and Crown's stable and counted his money. He was pleasantly surprised; since coming to John Brown, he had saved twenty-five pounds. Um. The twenty-five pounds ought to buy him a sergeancy when he showed discharge papers from the 5th Dragoons. A corporal's rank in any case.

When Jemmy Potter started for a dingy structure quartering a lonely platoon of Royal Marines, he set his feet down hard as if to catch the ring of spurs.

It was a vivid disappointment to learn that practically no cavalry was included in the British Army establishment in America.

The recruiting sergeant, an infantryman, wryly inquired, "Tell me sommat. You have served before and know wot this bloody army is like—for why does yer want to take the King's shilling again?"

"To make me change out of the bloody rebels. They've reamed me twice, and now, by Jesus, my tail is sore."

The sergeant grinned and his powdered head inclined. He pushed forward a printed form.

"Sign 'ere. We've recrooted few enough real soldiers in this 'ere Gawd-forsaken country."

4 — PETITION

Not since the return of the *Assistance* almost a year ago, had Peggy seen Rob so entirely happy. It was almost as if their dark hours following the brigantine's loss had never been. Every morning he was up at dawn and over at the shipyard where the *Grand Turk* rose and fell with the tide.

Peggy took his food over to him until the day Mrs. Fleming paid "the Construction Camp," as Rob called their one room quarters, her one and only visit.

"No lady, my dear," declared Mrs. Fleming, clearly shocked, "is seen on the streets when she—er—sticks out."

Peggy smiled, pushing a damp curl from her forehead. She had been washing Rob's small clothes and some petticoats.

"I'm sorry, Mamma, but nowadays I can't afford to be a lady. Besides, it's rather fun going wherever I please." Mischief sparkled in the depths of dark blue eyes. "Besides, Mrs. Rudder came to call."

"Call? The wife of a common sea captain—and a drunken one at that?"

"Oh, she meant all right. I really felt sorry for her. She was trying to get the new brig for Ben. So many ships are tied up, she is near desperate."

"But surely, my dear, one hears of some ships sailing?"

"Only coastwise vessels trade, and vessels in the Bermuda and West Indies trade. The embargo don't affect them yet, not 'til next November."

"Why do you say Bermuda *and* the West Indies? Surely Bermuda is one of the islands, isn't it?"

Peggy unpinned her apron and stepped into a plain yellow skirt. She'd been washing in a shawl and petticoats.

"Rob says Bermuda ain't a West Indie, and it's really not an island, but a whole lot of little ones. The old charts call them the Summer Islands."

"You seem to know a lot about it, my dear."

"Rob's father came from there."

"What else, pray?"

"Years ago Bermuda belonged to the old Virginia Company, but now they are self-governing, like a little Rhode Island 'way out in the Atlantic."

Mrs. Fleming put out a feeler. "Has—have—well, Rob has heard from his relations in Bermuda?"

Peggy told her "yes" but refused to be drawn out. It had not been pleasant to watch Rob repent that revelation of what Peter Ashton had written. Very well she knew he hadn't yet got over her going to her father about the brigantine's supplies. He didn't wholly trust her. She wondered whether he ever would again.

She slipped an arm about her mother's thin waist. "Suppose we go outside?"

As they sat in the hot sunlight at the end of Rob's empty pier, Mrs. Fleming viewed with distress her daughter's swollen figure.

"Margaret, I can't abide you to live in this rude place. You are alone too much of the time."

"La, Mamma, it's not so bad as it seems, though sometimes I'd give my silver shoe buckles to eat breakfast in bed; to have clean clothes just appear like—that." She snapped her fingers.

Betsy Fleming spoke quickly. "You know you can, my dear."

Peggy slowly shook her small head. "We are going to live aboard the brig soon. It will be nicer there."

"What! Live on a ship—a girl in your condition?"

"Yes, Mamma, a girl in my condition. The *Grand Turk* won't be ready for sea for another month anyhow and then—" the half smile faded from her lips. "Well, I'll give you my answer. I love Rob, but I'll not have my baby suffer."

Mrs. Fleming smiled privately. She had not dared to hope for even a hint of surrender. The Major had become absolutely set on the idea of removing to Canada—to a place called Nova Scotia. "Nova Scarcity" some people called it. He was, in fact, making plans to leave in June if the situation got no better. Her slim hand, blue with its network of veins, crept into the chintz pocket hanging from her wrist. Her shrewd gray eyes sought her daughter as though feeling their way:

"My dear," said she softly, "I have with me a great chance to help your husband."

"Why, Mamma, what do you mean?"

"He will thank you some day; you see if he doesn't."

"What have you got there?" She was disturbed at the furtive way her mother gazed about.

The only persons in sight were two Negroes dismantling a windlass on the next pier. It was strange to see John Brown's warehouse boarded up and four of his ships lying to the wharf with sails unbent. Parchment rustled softly as Mrs. Fleming held out a scroll.

"You must read this carefully, Margaret. It is a petition to the Throne. All the leading loyal merchants in town have signed it. You can see their names—even Dr. Gordon's."

Peggy read slowly, carefully, the list of signatures. It was imposing.

"But what does this have to do with Rob? You know he favors neither one side nor the other."

"When the day of retribution comes," Mrs. Fleming began in a confident voice, "as surely it must come, the traitors and rebels who now are making our lives so miserable will be brought to book. They will see their estates confiscated; they will see their ringleaders hanged; they will feel the just and awful wrath of our King."

Peggy was impressed. "Well, I still don't see—"

"If Rob's name was to appear on this petition it would act as a—a sort of assurance."

Peggy's eyes traveled rapidly over the roll of parchment. It seemed entirely harmless—merely a reaffirmation of loyalty to His Majesty King George III and a respectful plea that something be done to ameliorate "the distressfull condition of his Most Loyal Subjeckts in His Colonie of Virginia."

No hen had ever loved a single chick more than Betsy Fleming adored her daughter; all on her account she had put the petition bee into Andrew Fleming's bonnet. Relieved to be up and doing again, the old importer interviewed Justice Vesey the very next day and persuaded him to draw the petition in legal form.

The ink was hardly dry than the major went riding off to Williamsburg. He found little trouble in persuading loyal planters and the Scots who were occupying foreclosed properties to sign. Her father, Peggy deduced, must have ridden hundreds of miles.

"I had better talk this over with Rob."

Mrs. Fleming shook her head, but smiled at the same time. "Oh, cat's foot! You know Robert can never make up his mind on politics. Besides, this petition doesn't commit him to anything. You can see that."

"It doesn't seem to."

"It doesn't commit him to *do* a thing, does it?"

"No, but I really daren't sign his name, Mamma. I daren't." "There is no call to, my dear. That is where you can be helpful to him. Sign it as Mrs. Robert Butler Ashton. You have the right to, you know. Here is the beauty of it. If things go wrong for the King's Friends, you can vow you signed it without Rob's knowledge—which is perfectly true. But when his Majesty sends troops, you can say Robert was busy, or away on his ship and told you to sign it for him."

Still Peggy hesitated, pondering a decision from every possible angle. In the end the persistent urgings of a woman even more determined than herself, made her waver—and in wavering, she surrendered. This wasn't a bit like what she'd done before, Peggy assured herself. She wasn't signing Rob's own name. It was for his good, too. She took the parchment into the office and, after repointing a quill, wrote in a firm hand, "Mrs. Robert B. Ashton." There was no smile on her face as she sanded the document.

"You always were a sensible girl, Margaret," her mother murmured. "Some day Rob will thank God for it on his bended knees." Fixedly she looked out over the Elizabeth flowing yellow because of the spring rains. "I can see English men-of-war lying out yonder—frigates, sloops and ships-of-the-line. Virginia's punishment will be terrible!"

A sigh escaped the straight-backed woman in tabby velvet. She fumbled again in her pocket and pressed two pounds Virginia currency into Peggy's hand.

"Here is a trifle for your mother's favorite daughter. Buy something pretty, dear, for yourself." She folded away the petition and straightened her bonnet of green drugget. "You will fetch back the cake plate when you have finished with it? Perhaps you can talk Rob into coming to us for dinner next Sunday."

SWEAT tickled and trickled down Rob's shoulderblades. Under his supervision Newton's slaves had been sending up the fore topmast. It had meant careful work, but now the spar was rigged to his satisfaction.

Peggy appeared at the edge of the dock, a basket on her arm. "Well, Captain, and how does the work go today?"

"Capital, Mrs. A., capital. How does my new topmast look?"

Peggy obediently raised her eyes and said, "Grand. Which is the topmast?"

"That pole up there." He grinned. "The yellow one."

"My, Rob, you've certainly got a lot done since yesterday."

She snuffed audibly as Rob handed her down onto the brig. She loved the clean odor of the tar with which the deck was being calked almost as much as the smell of wet paint drying on the taffrail.

Forward, a trio of sailmakers were intent over plans flattened on a trestle supported by two saw horses. One of them moved over and used a steel yard to measure a spar tilted against the bulwarks. The capstan's brass-mounted head was covered with a tarpaulin, but Rob pulled it off to show his wife the brig's name engraved on it in flowing script. After that he conducted her below decks and into a cabin wide as the stern's beam. It looked cozy because the ceiling was low.

"That will be your bunk, Peggy. You see? I've had it built extra wide. Mine is over here."

"What about Sunshine?" Peggy inquired, slipping an arm through his.

"I reckon we can fix him up a crib in the chart locker." Rob grinned. "You can pull out one of the drawers and make a real sailor's berth for him. He'll be snug as a bug in a rug there."

"Oh, this cabin is monstrous sweet, Rob. The paneling, especially." Her fingertips wandered along the smooth birch with which the cabin was trimmed. Shavings and sawdust still lingered underfoot, but the stern ports had been framed in. They were not as large as Peggy would have liked, but they were far bigger than those of most merchantmen.

Pridefully, he then conducted her to the mate's cabin. It was tiny, with two bunks built one above the other, and a pair of clothes lockers.

"Reckon you will have to hire your mates to measure," she laughed. "Men 'round Farish's size."

Rob's manner quieted. "Poor Farish! I wish to God he could sail her."

"What are you going to do for a captain?"

"I have a dozen to pick from. But I don't intend to keep one on very long. Can't afford it. I'm going to sail her myself —like Papa when he began."

"Sail her? But, Rob, you don't know anything about navigation."

"I am learning," he explained seriously. "You would be surprised to find how much a merchant can pick up from his captains."

Peggy's smile thinned. Here was something upon which she had not calculated; definitely not! She had no intention of having Rob away at sea half the time. As for going to sea herself, she wouldn't; nor should her baby. She sighed, felt suddenly fatigued. For only six months along the baby seemed enormous. Her center of gravity had altered; time and again she would find herself lurching off balance and would have to catch at something. Small women always did have big babies, Mrs. Rudder said. Rob, in a teasing moment, assured her she resembled nothing so much as a hard-boiled egg on stilts.

They went back up the companionway into the sunlight and he made her peer down into the fore and aft holds. She was astonished to see how roomy they were.

About the deck a scattering of broad-axes, pod-augers, and chisels blinked blue-white in the sunlight. The blacksmith had set up a portable forge at the foot of the mainmast and was hammering out items of hardware. On the stern men were mounting davits for the *Grand Turk*'s longboat. Those for her gig already had been stepped amidships on the starboard side.

Rob's tarry forefinger indicated two small boats painted white and lying bottom up on the beach.

"Luke Martin made them," he announced. "Luke makes the best boats in Virginia, and the best are none too good for the *Grand Turk*. Reckon we can move aboard in about ten days, then it's——" He broke off, startled at the sight of a tear sliding down Peggy's cheek. Quickly he led her aft in the lee of the cabin house. "Why, Honey, what's wrong—do you feel sick?"

"You do love this ship better than me!" she wailed. "I can see it in the way you talk. I—I hate this brig. I hope she never sails!"

Frightened and bewildered, Rob flung an arm about her shoulders. "Oh, Peggy! Don't say such things. You're over-tired. You shouldn't have come all this way in the heat."

"Don't say anything." She sobbed unrestrainedly awhile, then wiped away her tears. "I—I reckon I'm a goose. I—I'm sorry. I d-didn't mean it."

But the fact remained. She did hate the *Grand Turk;* was wildly jealous of her. Deep within her she knew Rob would love seafaring, would spend less and less time ashore with her and the child. It wasn't right.

6 — ARTICLES OF ASSOCIATION

Two days later as Rob was going home Matthew Phipp came up to him on the street. From the look of him, Rob knew this was no chance encounter.

Phipp indulged in no sociable preliminaries. Said he, "Rob, we must have a talk."

"About what?"

"Tell you later. Come with me."

"Can't it be later, after I've had my supper? I've had a hard day at the shipyard."

"Don't be a damned fool." Matt Phipp's eyes narrowed and he spoke with emphasis. "You'll come along with me now if you know what's good for you! There is no time to lose. Holt's gone home and we can talk there."

Arriving at the printing shop, Phipp led the way to a small office opening off the press room.

In rising concern, Rob searched his mind. What the devil was up?

Phipp indicated a chair. "Take a seat."

"What the devil is this about? You talk like the second act of a theater piece." Rob wasn't finding the situation pleasant. He was dog-tired and hungry. Peggy had said they were going to have baked ham from Smithfield for supper.

"Why did Peggy sign that petition?"

"Don't talk riddles, man." Rob began to get irritated. "What petition?"

"A loyalist petition to the King."

"Are you crazy, or am I?" Rob forgot his fatigue. In the back of his mind was a terrible premonition. "She has signed no petition."

There was incredulity in the lawyer's tone."Do you mean to sit there and tell me that your wife signed old Fleming's petition to the Throne without your knowing about it?"

"Peggy signed—!" Rob's naturally high color deepened. "Just a minute. Let me see it!"

"Here is a copy." Grimly the committeeman handed over a sheet of paper with the printer's ink still wet upon it.

Rob looked Phipp bang in the eye. "I had no idea my wife signed such a thing."

"I thought you didn't know," Matt sighed. He liked Rob, and Peggy he had loved a long time without ever saying anything. He had sense enough to know he was too poor ever to stand a chance with the Flemings. "You will have to act fast. Leeming and his crew of radicals are burning for action. They will interpret the Major's petition as an invitation for ships and Ministerial troops to come here."

"But that's insane! Nobody wants troops sent here."

Phipp nodded. "Of course they don't. Just the same, you are now in serious danger. Resentment against Tories gets stronger every day. Some of the news from Boston isn't pretty. They say the British soldiers up there are raising merry hell with the Whig inhabitants. Some women have been raped—whores probably—but the effect's the same. Then again, the patriots in Boston are going broke by the hundred."

Rob temporized. "Hold on a minute. Let me read this thing over." But he didn't read. He was thinking: The little fool, the damned, meddling little fool! She had kicked over the apple cart again!

"How did you hear of this petition?" he finally inquired.

Phipp flushed and looked at the floor. "Oh, that damned rutting hog Leeming has been laying with old Fleming's chambermaid. She saw the thing on the Major's desk and sold it to Leeming for two pounds." The tall lawyer took a turn down the office, kicking aside smudged proof sheets as he went. "It's as simple as that."

Rob rose from his chair, then sat down again heavily. "What do you think is going to happen about this?"

"We don't know for sure. Almost anything. With so many people hungry and out of work, it won't take a lot to get them excited. I expect the radicals will try to force the Committee to jail everybody who signed that petition. The signers will be blacklisted—that much is sure."

"Blacklisted!" Heavy as a lump of lead the word fell from Rob's lips. He recalled what had happened to John Brown. He got up, crossed to the window and stood frowning out on the sunset.

"This is bad."

"Yes, it's bad all right."

"What do you reckon I'd better do?"

"Stop being a damned political eunuch and do what I advised nearly a year ago," Phipp said sharply. "You can't dodge picking sides any longer."

"But how can I when, near as I can make out, neither one side nor the other is right? Why in hell can't people leave me alone? I don't give two damns who runs the Colony. All I want is to trade. I've got a right to trade, haven't I?"

Matthew Phipp, watch fob and seals bright in the sunset, strode across the room and stood in front of Rob.

"What you want isn't important any longer. No one can live a wholly private life these days. Whether we want it or not, we are becoming small parts of a new theory of government. You know what people are saying?"

"No. What?"

"They say your brig has been built for a ship-of-war. The radicals claim you intend to sell her to the British."

"Of all the damned nonsense!" Rob exploded, and the cords began to stand out on his neck.

"—Maybe so, but that's what people believe you intend doing."

"Phipp, what do you reckon I'd better do? I couldn't stand to lose my brig. I'd sooner lose my right hand!"

"If you aim to keep your ship and to do business in Norfolk, you will have to sign a copy of the Articles of Association as quick as you can. A pile of them is over there."

Rob's fingertips felt curiously numb. Odd, a man signed his name so many times without its meaning much. But now whether he did, or did not, make a few loops and lines with a quill might change the course of his whole life.

Phipp's manner was more friendly. "You are showing good

sense, Rob, and I'm glad. The only reason the Committee has left you alone so far is because we felt sure you were playing fair with both sides. I am truly delighted that you see the justice of our cause. Our liberties——"

Rob's laugh was rasping, devoid of mirth. "Let the liberties go. You know damned well such high-sounding talk is just a side issue. Fact is, a lot of Virginians want to get rid of the factors because they owe the factors money. Again, most of our homegrown merchants ain't clever or dishonest enough to compete with the Scotch. The people here are sore because Parliament and the East India people are trying to squeeze more revenues out of them without making a profitable return for them. Reckon they are 'most as greedy as the so-called patriots."

Phipp's friendly expression froze and the crooked scar on his cheek flamed. "That's a bitter tongue, you've got, Ashton. You had better not talk like this in public."

"I won't. But you know I'm speaking the truth. This whole mess makes me sick."

Phipp made an impatient gesture. "Talk all you please, but you will still have to make up your mind. Let me tell you something; if you don't sign the Association, your brig won't be allowed to sail! But if you come in with us I undertake to convince the rest of the Committee that you didn't know about Peggy's signing. I can, and will, play up that you lost your ship through carrying arms for patriots in Boston." A bleak smile twisted the lawyer's lips. "—Even though I know damned well you knew nothing about the munitions."

At last he'd been driven into a corner. There was nothing to do but to sign. Rob crossed to a nearby desk, dipped the pen on it, then hesitated, looking over his shoulder.

"If I sign this, you will guarantee everything will be all right?"

"Yes, everything will be all right. You have my word on it."

"You are sure you can handle Leeming?"

"I'll find him as soon as I can. He will have to listen to me; I'm his superior."

The pen's slow scratching filled the musty smelling office with sound.

Rob blew on the wet ink. "Now can I go on trading?"

Matthew Phipp cast him a glance of sympathy. "Why, certainly—if the British will let you."

7 — THE RADICALS

DUE to a complete absence of stars the texture of the night was a flat, impenetrable black. A warm westerly breeze was blowing strong enough to muffle minor sounds such as those made by a small boat being rowed along the shore.

"What's the time?" grunted one of two oarsmen.

"Must be close to three," came the laconic reply of a man in the stern sheets. He shifted the tiller to port. "You'll have to pull harder. Tide's ebbing and it sets in strong 'round Four Farthing Point."

"Yer sure you kin recognize her?" inquired the second rower over the steady *clunk-clunk, clunk-clunk* of oars against tholepins greased and swathed in rags.

"Can I find the crease of my own butt?" By looking really hard the speaker could just discern the outlines of a stone jug of turpentine and bag of shavings lying between his feet.

The dank, sour reek of mud flats grew steadily stronger. Off to starboard water rats splashed stealthily beneath the docks lining Town Back Creek.

"Way enough!" called the steersman softly. The others stopped rowing and let the current carry them past a West India schooner tied up to Anthony Lawson's pier. Out in the river the riding lights of several vessels blinked and winked. The ebb, running stronger every instant, was swinging ships to their anchors, causing sections of rigging momentarily to obscure their lights.

On shore a lonesome dog barked, then a cockerel tried to crow but achieved only a ludicrous sound resembling the singing of a boy with a breaking voice.

"Ain't we pretty near there?"

"Yes, we're in Glebe's Cove—"

Odors of fresh sawed pine and paint grew strong.

"Where you fixin' to board?"

"Fore chains."

"Then lay on yer oars; the tide will take us right alongside."

The rowers obeyed, held their dripping blades horizontal. All three men peered up into the sky.

"There she is!"

"Jesus! It's blacker'n a nigger's arse tonight. You sure?"

"Yep. C'n see her two masts."

They saw a faint light beating through some vessel's stern ports.

"Hells bells!" breathed the port rower. "Goddam watchman's up."

"Makes no difference; he's deef as a—" The leader who had sat in the stern broke off, desperately smothering a cough with both hands. His effort made the whole boat shake. "Careful! Fend her off with your hands, you damned lunkheads!"

When this was done the skiff was permitted to describe a slow arc until her bow pointed upstream and she lay right alongside. Foot by foot they edged the small boat forward against the tide. It gurgled under her bow. At last the forechain plates loomed overhead. A little distance forward, a jib boom jutted dark against the sky, but it was impossible to distinguish more than a dim blur of yards and topmasts.

"Wait here and fer Christ's sake keep quiet!" the leader whispered as, stooping, he unbuckled his shoes. He stripped off his stockings and when he felt the cold, wet skiff bottom on his soles, he cursed. To his belt he secured two lengths of codline, then gripped a couple of deadeyes and climbed up the side.

The rowboat, freed of his weight, bobbed a little. Faintly the codlines whispered over the vessel's rail.

The port oarsman asked softly, "Which one first?"

"Shavings. Ease it up on the seat."

They gave a warning tug to the first line then gave the bag a boost. Breathless they watched it rise with a scraping sound soft as the rustle of deer entering a thicket.

"Like a duck's foot in the mud," whispered the second oarsman with forced casualness.

"Easy does it. Don't let 'er bump."

The stone jug, wrapped in lengths of burlap, made slower progress out of sight. Once it had vanished the rowers sat motionless, holding onto the side and straining their ears. A mist was commencing to rise from the harbour; it was like wood smoke. The teeth of the port oarsman began to chatter.

"Scared?"

"Christ, no. C-Cold."

"Bet you've wet your pants."

"Go to hell."

Surprisingly soon the steersman reappeared and clambered, panting, over the rail.

"Let her go. Quick! Don't row!"

Amid deathly silence the skiff drifted off downstream. One of the rowers saw the steersman rub his chin.

"What's the matter? Hurt your jaw?"

"Yep. 'Bout a year ago," Edgar Leeming admitted. "Feels better now."

8 — THE CRUISE OF THE GRAND TURK

"ASHTON! Wake up! Hey, in there! Mr. Ashton!" Dimly voices penetrated Rob's profound slumber.

"Someone's out there," Peggy murmured sleepily. "Better see what they want."

Whoever was banging on the office door must be in a tearing hurry. The hammering of his blows shook the whole building.

"Mr. Ashton! Come quick!" More voices, hoarse with excitement joined in.

Rob flung a surtout over his nightgown and, without waiting to put on shoes, ran out through the dark office. He picked up a sliver in his foot, but barely noticed it.

The men outside were banging still more insistently. "Wake up, Mr. Ashton! Wake up!"

When he reached the front of the office, he was startled to see gables and roofs across Lawson Street in silhouette. They showed up sharp against a dull pink glow. Even as he fumbled at the lock the pink brightened to a throbbing orange-red. As he opened the door, he saw a lot of people running towards the harbour.

"What's wrong? House afire? Lumber yard?"

"Jesus, no!" panted Bub Jensen's deep voice. "You better come quick. It's your new ship!"

Because the *Grand Turk* was new and her timbers had been freshly painted, the fire took hold in awful haste, spewing volcanoes of sparks sky-high and strewing the harbour shores with hissing brands. When Newton, to save his wharf and yard, ordered the smoking cables chopped through, the flaming brig started going out with the tide, threatening destruction to whatever lay in her erratic course.

She made such a terrifying spectacle that Norfolk people in later days declared the *Grand Turk*'s burning was the greatest sight they had ever witnessed—barring none! As if propelled by a great bellows, sheets of flame beat out of the brig's ports, roared up from her hatches and licked prettily out of her hawse holes.

Her yards crashing down, one by one, the *Grand Turk* cruised over a surface dyed scarlet as a sea of molten lava. Warehouses, dwellings and ships reflected the infernal glare. White painted steeples far back from the water looked as if they had been done in rose tints. People staring in openmouthed awe could read each other's expressions by the flames.

"Ain't it awful?" they asked one another in hushed voices. But they were thrilled and enjoying the spectacle.

Soon the doomed vessel's freshly tarred rigging caught, sketched fiery patterns amid clouds of rosy smoke. Over a thunderous crackle of the brig's burning timbers, the explosion of turpentine barrels made the harbour resound.

"Sounds like a bleedin' skirmish," Sergeant Jemmy Potter grunted to his men as he turned them out. "This will rooin poor Mr. Ashton. Seems like he leaned too much on the Tory side."

Vessels anchored in the *Grand Turk*'s probable path slipped their cables and, hastily setting jibs and staysails, strove to get out of the way.

As the fire was reaching its climax a shift of wind swept sparks over the town and some fool commenced to ring a church bell. A panic followed as waves of hot, acrid smoke and glowing ashes came rolling up all the streets from Smith's Point clear over to Dun in the Mire.

Aboard H.M.S. *Liverpool* drums rattled an alarm. Captain Sackville appeared on his quarterdeck only half dressed. After he had done roaring orders, he smiled wickedly.

"It appears that the rebels are sending a fire ship against us!"

By fives and tens the frigate's battle lanterns began to glow like fireflies coming out on a warm summer's night. The ominous creak of tackles raising gun port covers filled the frigate, but went wholly unnoticed ashore. His voice deadly calm, Sackville ordered out a stern anchor. This accomplished, he commanded the frigate swung about until her whole starboard battery bore, not on the blazing wreck, but on Norfolk. Sparks were commencing to fall aboard the *Liverpool,* but they were not so bright as the glow of gunners' matches below. Half naked powder monkeys began to run about, splashing water on the larger sparks.

Steadily the wreck drifted closer. The heat was so intense the officers shielded their faces with their hands. When it appeared that the brig could not avoid fouling the man-of-war, Captain Sackville ordered axemen forward and aft, ready to hack through the anchor cables.

"When those axes fall, you may open fire on the town," he instructed his officers.

By pure chance an eddy swung the *Grand Turk* clear of the frigate and, spouting fire yards high, she veered off on a new tack. Her first and last cruise ended on a mud flat near the entrance to the harbour.

Until dawn the *Grand Turk* lay burning to the water's edge, sending up a dense, leisurely pillar of smoke and steam.

9 — SALVAGE

WITH Rob, Captain Matthew Phipp could find no point of approach; even less could the other Committeemen who, tweaked by conscience and appalled by the nearly disastrous consequences of the arson to Norfolk, hurried to assure him of their sympathy. Phipp, nervously rumpling his dark red hair, alone came near guessing the depth of Rob's sullen hopelessness.

When the fact that the victim had previously signed the Association became known, none was more noisily deprecating than Edgar Leeming. In fact, he felt so badly about it he went over to visit friends in Portsmouth. The Committee, however, offered more than verbal sympathy. Neil Jameison, Sam Inglis and the rest brought such pressure to bear on local tradesmen that they accepted cancellation of contracts for supplies yet undelivered to the *Grand Turk.*

With business as bad as it was, not a few grumbled, but the Committee of Safety, as the old Committee of Correspondence was now called, had become all-powerful.

Three days after the fire Neil Jameison, dapper in black

satin and carrying a gold headed walking stick, dropped in at Rob's silent office. He placed on his desk one hundred pounds Virginia Currency. It was a refund against supplies purchased but unused, he said.

"It is not a great deal, my boy, but it is more than your father had when he came here. He was a whole man. I was very fond of him."

Rob said, "Thank you," without change of expression. To hell with Jameison! The old man had known just when to turn his coat; Rob hated him for being so smart.

The spruce old gentleman looked about briskly, like a wren inspecting a new bird house. His eye, as everyone's did, lingered on the ivory model, undusted on the mantelpiece.

"You should be able to get some money for iron out of the wreck," Jameison commented. "A lot of hard tackle must have fallen onto her bottom; that's still whole, so it should be there."

"I'll never go near that goddam wreck!" Rob wanted to kick the smug old fool in his pants.

Major John Brush took the initiative and at his own expense dispatched laborers who salvaged a not inconsiderable supply of metal from among the *Grand Turk*'s gaunt charred timbers. Without coming near to the office, Brush ordered the several tons of iron unloaded on Rob's wharf. Left there it made an ugly, rusty mound.

The very day the salvage was delivered, Norfolk was thrown into a turmoil by rumors of a pitched battle having been fought between British regulars and a kind of troops called minute men. The struggle had taken place, so the mud-spattered courier declared, near some villages called Lexington and Concord, in Massachusetts. The villages were not far outside of Boston, he thought. More reports arrived, fantastic, contradictory and hopelessly biased; but one accepted fact emerged. Armed rebellion had begun!

Once her pot-house politicians had finished spouting, Norfolk settled down to arm and drill in deadly seriousness. Two more Independent Companies were formed in Norfolk County; one recruited in Norfolk itself. As a stop-gap uniform the companies adopted one of the best ever devised for troops destined to fight in North America. It was the long skirted, loose fitting hunting shirt of a neutral gray or light brown. Fringes at elbow and hem and on the edge of a hood that could be drawn over the head in bad weather, lent to the wearer a dashing air. The ones of buckskin were preferable to those of linen; they didn't get stiff when wet, nor near as cold.

A mustering of the Dirty Shirts, as the Tories dubbed them, was a colorful affair what with the fox tails, buck tails and 'coon tails in the hats of these lantern jawed, tobacco spitting gentry. Some wore the words "Liberty or Death" painted on their chests in white.

But the women, especially from Norfolk and the big plantations, hotly protested so ungallant a uniform. Smart blue, yellow or green regimentals, that was what they wanted for their sons and husbands. Some few men from back in the swamps turned up in war paint and wearing scalps to their belts. A scalping knife or a war hatchet was the usual supplement to the long-barreled rifle most of them had brought along.

They looked, and were, a hard lot, and independent as all get out when it came to obeying orders.

Everywhere appeared lists of those who had signed the Articles of Association—and of those who had not. The price of arms, powder and ordinary iron sky-rocketed.

People began addressing John Brush as "Colonel" now, and a couple of Virginians who had had European training in the military science came down from Williamsburg to advise. They didn't prove of much use, though. You couldn't make the Shirt Men see any sense in the Continental practice of firing blind volleys from firelocks held waist high. They always had, and they reckoned they always would, pick out one special target for their rifles.

The biggest problem, everyone knew, would be powder. Half a dozen saltpeter mills, so-called, had begun operations in the country between Richmond and North Carolina, but the product they turned out was poor, not comparable to French, Dutch or even to Spanish powder.

When final reports about the Concord fight came through, the war fever mounted. Crowds gathered every day before the Spread Eagle's notice board and the Governor began threatening to arrest John Holt for printing seditious news. No matter who said what, the fact remained that British regulars had been made to run by a parcel of Yankee militia, and if Yankees could do that, my God! what wouldn't Virginians do to the lobsterbacks?

The illegal Virginia legislature, convening at Williamsburg, authorized patriots, who were affluent enough to raise a company at their own expense, to "beat their drums." Thus into every hamlet and crossroads cantered recruiting officers, lavishing promises of glory and promotion on prospective recruits. For awhile the cream of the Provincial yeomanry fought for places in the ranks of the Virginia Army.

In desperation, the Tories held meetings and formed military units. They were astonished and encouraged at finding out how numerous and how powerful they were. They also passed resolutions and collected arms. They would not quit without a fight and returned taunt for taunt and threat for threat. Gordon MacLeod caught Edgar Leeming alone one night and beat the daylights out of him.

To all the excitement Rob remained impervious. Mostly he lingered in his office, glancing wistfully now and then at the ivory model. At times he still couldn't get it through his head that his brig was gone.

A few days after news of the Lexington fight, Neil Jameison strode in, the gold seals of his watch fob all a-jingle. Rob mechanically greeted him, shook hands and indicated a chair. Beaming, the older man removed his hat and took out a snuff box.

"Try a pinch?"

"Thanks. Don't use it, sir."

"Well, my boy," began Jameison closing the box lid with a small snap. "As we all know, you have had a spell of bad luck; too long a spell. Possibly the tide has turned. The iron out of the wreck should bring top prices. Know that?"

"Prices?" Rob's meaningless smile dissolved and he stood straighter. "Do you mean that iron prices are going up?"

"Just that, Mr. Ashton. Just that. A blind idiot can foretell it. You've got a lot of good iron here on your wharf." Neil Jameison gave him a sharp look. "Suppose I offer you a hundred pounds for it? What do you say?"

Rob blinked. "One hundred pounds? Why, Mr. Jameison, you can't mean that. It can't be worth that much."

Faculties dormant for over two weeks were slow to stir. But they commenced reluctantly to operate. If a close trader like Jameison stood ready to offer one hundred pounds for a pile of rusty scrap, then it was dead certain somebody else somewhere was prepared to pay still more. You would never catch a wise old bird like Neil Jameison risking serious money unless he had a market waiting. Who could this buyer be? Rob racked his brains, but couldn't guess. Jameison meantime got up and put on his hat. "Mr. Ashton, I find it a trifle chilly here. In deference to my rheumatism, let us proceed to the Spread Eagle, share a small bottle, and discuss this matter further."

Rob's interest was stirring sluggishly, like a frozen brook under a thawing sun. He stepped into the bedroom and was surprised to find a note from Peggy. She said she had gone uptown to visit her mother. Recently she had begun to go out quietly, as if fearful of rousing him from his despairing lethargy.

"One hundred pounds?" he reflected. "Must be worth twenty or thirty pounds more, at the least. Let's see now, who'd most likely be wanting iron? Of course, that Lexington fight has brought this about. Gunmakers must be crying for iron."

There was a small factory at Rappahannock in Virginia, and Robert Reid made muskets at Chestertown in Maryland, but by far the bulk of native arms were built by Pennsylvania Dutch living around York and Lancaster. Their volume of production was small, but William Henry, Deckhard and Peter Reigart and the rest turned out some sweet rifles. No man with any pretensions to gentility was without one of the long-barreled Pennsylvania rifles—for some reason people called them Kaintuck rifles—or a fowling piece made by Donner.

"Thank you, Mr. Jameison. Come to think of it, I could do with a mug of ale." He put on his cap.

To start over with he had a hundred pounds, about five hundred Spanish dollars that was, left from the *Grand Turk*'s building costs. Walking down Cove Street in the gay spring sunshine he towered above Neil Jameison's sparrow-like stature.

He was thinking, "If I can maybe scrape together another hundred pounds, I'd have enough, if I clip corners, to charter a ship and scrape together some sort of a cargo. After all being such a red-hot patriot, I'll probably get bottom prices and some credit maybe. About a ship I can't be choosy and there's the crew and port expenses still to be figured. I'll have to trade mighty sharp."

As he and Jameison passed, many people hailed him or came up expressing regrets over the brig's burning. But Tories, some of them old friends, looked the other way. One of them muttered "traitor" while stalking past.

The sun felt good on his back. Some chickens, scratching happily in the center of Main Street, appeared homelike and pleasing to the eye. When the smell of apple blossoms came drifting over from an orchard in Dr. Gordon's yard, Rob suddenly became aware of a remarkably lovely day.

He let Jameison stand him to three tankards of ale and at the same time worked his host's offer up to one hundred and twenty pounds cash, or one hundred and thirty credit. He began feeling better. It was something to get around Jameison. Few men did.

"I'm much obliged for the ale," he told the dapper little man in black. "And I will consider your offer with care. Suppose I let you know tonight?"

"I'll give you one hundred forty pounds for the iron. What do you say?"

But Rob shook his head, smiled and went out.

Since most gunsmiths hailed from Pennsylvania, he sounded Tom MacSherry for news of such strangers.

"There's half a dozen, Mr. Rob," the innkeeper admitted. "I have a pair of slab-sided Dutchmen staying here, and I'm that full up I had to send a couple more over to the Pied Bull. Hey you, Jack Rabbit! Is there any Dutchmen over to Ma Coverly's?"

The Negro's teeth gleamed. "Yassuh, three ob dem in de half crown room on de secon' flo'."

During the afternoon Rob pursued visiting Pennsylvanians and in the end came upon Phillip Wolfheimer and Joel Faree guzzling beer at the Pied Bull. Might they be interested in the purchase of old iron?

The Pennsylvanians kept their fat, shiny faces as wooden as ever, but Wolfheimer couldn't mask a little gleam in his china blue eyes. We-ell, they not especially interested were, but they the iron might look over, *ja?* In broad-brimmed brown hats and curious round coats of the same color, they waddled after Rob down to the wharf.

Voicing a conventional disparagement of the quality and condition of the scrap, they made a bid. It was absurdly low.

Rob told them so. Said he wasn't going to waste more time if they were only funning. He knew Johan Miller was at—

Joel Faree threw up pudgy hands with a fervent, *"Behüt mich Gott!"* when Wolfheimer without warning offered one hundred and sixty pounds in hard money. He offered to pay in Portuguese escudos. *Gold!* Rob felt like throwing both arms around the gunsmith's fat little body. Gold would buy a lot more per unit than Viriginia paper—no matter how sound the bankers claimed their Provincial currency to be.

Phillip Wolfheimer took no chances. All within an hour he not only sent a cart and a gang of niggers, but produced a small stack of broad yellow pieces.

Sitting before the fire that night, Rob chuckled to think how he had done old Jameison in the eye. The whole transaction had been smartly planned and executed. He started to tell Peggy about it, but she seemed too wholly lost in thought.

10 — THE OLD HOME

PEGGY could not recall ever having seen her father look as he did that afternoon. No wonder. When she entered the serene, sweetly familiar old residence on Church Street she found the house slaves, very glum of expression, taking down pictures. It was like a blow in the face to find that the familiar lace curtains had disappeared. A Turkey red stair carpet which once had muffled the fall of her girlish feet also was gone. Its removal left a broad pale band in the center of each tread.

Clad in a dark blue banyan or dressing gown, Major Fleming was wearing a sword. Peggy recognized the weapon immediately. It had been presented to him on a marshy plain before the town of Minden by the Duke of Brunswick himself. Her father, she noticed, was standing so straight that the beginnings of a round stomach had disappeared.

"Come into the library, Margaret," he directed in exactly the same wooden tone he had used when she had been naughty and he was expecting to spank her.

"Oh, Papa, must we?" All the way up Church Street she had been feeling desperately tired. It was amazing how fast the child in her was growing. Twice within ten days she had been forced to let out her calimanco dresses. Her ankles had swelled from the walk up town and she had never, she thought, felt lower in mind and spirit in all her eighteen years.

"Pray seat yourself." The words were a command rather than an invitation.

Round-eyed and trembling, she chose a comfortable old leather armchair in which she had curled on many a rainy afternoon. She was grateful that, so far, the library had not been disarranged. Rows of calfskin bindings, neat gilt titles remained in military alignment. From above, a plaster bust of Themistocles gazed down with blank pupils, just as it always had. As if to complete the illusion Toby raced in and, barking in a delirium of joy, bounded up into her lap. Once there, he quieted quickly, looked happily up into his mistress's flushed features.

"Margaret," her father began. "It is deucedly unpleasant, but we must face facts. You are married to a rebel. In my family such a situation cannot endure."

"But Papa, Rob isn't really a rebel!"

"He is! He signed the Association," Major Fleming contradicted; but, instead of meeting her eye, he surveyed an engraving of King George III hanging above his work desk.

"Furthermore, your brother-in-law is not only a notorious traitor, but is now a convicted felon." She heard his voice as if he were talking from upstairs. "I repeat, Margaret, it is impossible for me to consider a rebel as my son-in-law."

"Oh, please don't say such things! Rob only signed the Association to save his ship—our future! Can't you understand?"

"I can see only that he signed it," was the old officer's implacable retort.

"But, Papa, there is still time for people to come to their senses, isn't there?"

"I can't see how," Major Fleming said, marching back and forth over the Turkey red carpet. "That disgraceful affair at Lexington has settled things. Gad's my life! His Majesty's troops ambushed, murdered by a pack of Yankee farmers— It—it's incredible!"

As she patted Toby, Peggy's gaze sought that corner on which Mimi, her little papillon dog, had once made a "mistake." Though faint, the stain was still in evidence. Tears started to her eyes. Mimi. How many ages had passed since she played with that foolish little pet? What had happened to the secure old life of Norfolk? What had become of a society in which everybody liked 'most everyone else? Had there ever been such wonderful things as tilting matches and courts of love? Had neighbors ever held turkey shoots and ridden to hounds? How long since anyone had given a fancy dress ball or a whist drive? Tears, commencing to roll down her cheeks, exasperated the grim old man.

"Stop that infernal sniffling! You are eighteen now and a grown woman. You can, and must, make up your mind—as I have made up mine."

"You—you're leaving?" Dutifully Peggy wiped her eyes on the ruching of her sleeve. As usual she had forgotten her handkerchief.

"Yes. I have sold my schooners to a New York firm; Livingston & Co. What they will find to do with them God only knows, but that is their lookout."

She became frightened. To think of Papa's having sold those schooners! Why, they had been his special pride—"Fastest craft in the Barbados run, by Gad!"

"But, Papa, you *can't* leave Norfolk! Not really. Why—why, it's your home, the only home I know. You've lived here almost twenty years. All your friends—"

"—My friends have most of them become traitors and rebels, unfit associates for a loyal Englishman," he interrupted. "I wish I could hate them, but damme, I can't! That is why we are leaving." He ceased his uneasy parade and stood over her as she sat slumped in the big chair. "In two days everything I own will be aboard the *Betsy*."

"W-where are you going?"

Andrew Fleming sighed, shrugged slightly, said without enthusiasm, "I hear there are good trading possibilities in a place called Nova Scotia. At any rate, land there is very cheap. We are going to go there."

"Oh, Papa, you can't!" Peggy's tone became at once imploring and angry. Toby jumped down and cocked a puzzled brown and white head to one side. "It would break Mother's heart and mine, too."

"The duty of a wife and child is to comply with the wishes of the head of the family," he announced, frowning at a crash betraying some slave's awkwardness. "Either you appear aboard the *Betsy* before ten o'clock on Friday, or—" he gulped, but kept on, "your fate ceases to be of concern to me. That is all. Goodbye, my dear. I pray God He will show you your duty."

Firmly he bent and, putting an arm about her, brushed cold lips across her forehead. The bristles on his chin scratched just as they always had. She cried in real earnest.

All that night she lay very still beside Rob, staring at a pattern of moonlight which, reflected from the harbour's water, wavered and shimmered on the ceiling. Even when the bright patch had completed a slow progress across the dingy canvas overhead she had not stopped thinking.

11 — RETREAT

LATE Thursday afternoon the whole town saw Major Fleming appear in Norfolk for the last time. The Major's wig had never been more carefully powdered, for he had donned the regimentals of the 37th Infantry of the Line. His tunic of glaring scarlet boasted bright yellow facings and lace of white with two red and one yellow stripe at shoulders, cuffs and collar. The revers of the uniform delighted the eye no less than the golden buttons securing them. Wholly immaculate shone the ex-officer's white breeches and gaiters. Eyes held straight ahead, ignoring the hoots and catcalls of swarming guttersnipes, Andrew Fleming marched the length of Church Street.

His sword hilt, Lemuel Heinz declared, sparkled bright as the gold cross on St. James's Church. As he jumped to salute, Sergeant Jemmy Potter thought he had never seen a stock tied at a more correct military angle. The gaping townsfolk commented on a crescent shaped gorget slung over the major's throat. Patiently burnished, it winked blue-white, dazzling as any diamond.

Many confirmed Whigs removed their hats as he passed and even the outspoken patriots looked both impressed and depressed. Not one of them could say Andrew Fleming had been anything other than upright, industrious and honest.

John Holt, wiping inky hands on his apron, turned to Inglis. "If more men like Fleming take to leaving Norfolk, God alone knows where we will end up."

They both bowed to the stiff figure in scarlet, but Fleming swung on down towards the waterfront, eyes fixed on space.

Following the major at a respectful distance two great drays creaked and rumbled along. In the first, Fleming's black slaves squatted among their absurd bundles. The bucks were grinning, but looking scared just the same. The women were moaning and their pickaninnies blubbered right out loud.

A stillness settled on Cumberland Street when down its dusty ruts Robert Gilmorin's red and yellow coach appeared. Though its curtains were drawn as if it were headed for a funeral, people knew Mrs. Fleming must be inside. Fleming's own coach, Tom MacSherry was saying, had been sold to a Spanish Jew who was making pots of money in the cloth trade.

Rob was not in town at the time. He had heard of a little schooner belonging to one Christian Southeby, a patriot trader ruined by the embargo; he had been in the cloth trade with Glasgow. Rob sailed over to Portsmouth to look at her. The schooner, as Rob had fully expected, was small and damp and her sails were very, very old, but she did have a wide stern cabin and there was plenty of room in her holds.

He didn't cotton to the *Desdemona* at all, at all; with such an awful stink in her bilges, she must be leaky. That her bottom was foul he could see from where he stood on Southeby's tumbledown dock. Discouraged, he went below and jabbed his clasp knife into her ribs, knees and sheathing. He struck sound wood every time. That made him feel better, because he had to have a ship; even a bull-nosed old bitch like this. The schooner's rigging was a sight to frighten the Dutch, but she could be chartered for six months dirt cheap. Seventy-five dollars a month. A pitiable rate, but Southeby was a sick man; so sick that the toothless old mulatto with whom he lived 'lowed she reckoned he'd never live to see the snow fly again.

When the *Desdemona*'s registry papers were produced, Rob found further cause for hesitation. Holy sailor! He hadn't guessed she could be so old! She had been built in Glasgow back in 1739!

When he got home he took a long drink of applejack from a jug he kept at the bottom of a tall clock in the office. To further encourage himself, he reread Peter Ashton's letter. What with the crying need for powder and the price rising every day, he had better reach Bermuda as fast as he could.

What bothered him most was what he should do about Peggy. Should he take her along? He didn't like the idea, but what else was there to do? He had kind of hoped that some of her old friends would offer to help. But they hadn't. Quickly enough he figured out the reason. Peggy had signed the petition and he the Association.

He began to reckon on his fingers. "Let's see. If Peggy has figured it right, the baby ain't due 'til late in June. But Doc Gordon seems damned sure nothing will happen until the second week in July. What's today? May third. Nine weeks before the fireworks go off."

Rob took another sip of the applejack. He felt better. Only nine more weeks, then Peggy could look and maybe act like herself again. Weren't babies made in a damned silly way? Funny that the Lord, who was so clever about so many other things, hadn't figured out a better method—'most anybody could. Nicer if babies came in pretty blue eggs—like a robin's. You could hatch it out with a whale oil lamp and have your wife to yourself in the meantime. He shrugged, returned to his calculations.

This time of the year a trip to the Bermudas oughtn't to require more than two weeks. Yes, it was perfectly possible to make the round trip and get back in plenty of time. Then, by Hector, he'd have money. Peggy would get the best of care.

12 — THE BETSY SAILS

AT SIX Rob arose very quietly and started for the door without making a move to awaken his wife, but she roused enough to push the hair out of her eyes and ask where he was going.

"Upriver a way. Better get some more sleep."

Normally his answer would have satisfied her, but she had a headache and felt piqued because he wasn't more specific. "What are you going to do?"

"Oh, a bit of trading," he replied, folding his neck cloth.

"With Jameison?"

"No. A man upstream—you don't know him."

"No, I suppose not." She got up and, bending awkwardly, shuffled into her slippers.

It was not a wise move. For the first time Rob experienced a sense of repulsion. How badly she looked with her features sallow and that ungainly body beneath its cambric nightrail. It was hard to love a woman who was jamming her hair any which way under a mob cap which could have been cleaner. Hurriedly he pulled on his coat and, crossing over to the dresser, unlocked the drawer in which he kept his money.

"You don't trust me any more, do you, Rob?" Peggy's voice was small and weary.

"Trust you? Why, of course I do. Whatever gave you such an idea?"

She shook her head slowly. "You don't trust me."

"Well, then, I don't! And you must have sense enough to know why. You had no business to go signing that petition without talking to me first. You know what happened because of it."

Had he been looking at her, he would have seen the slight trembling which seized her, the rush of hot color to her face.

"I reckon you meant it for the best," he assured her, as he had so often needed to remind himself. "Nowadays it's hard to know what to say and what not to. If I don't tell you anything, you won't be tempted to make decisions." He turned and, with forced tenderness, put an arm about her. He added, "I reckon you understand?"

"I understand," she answered dully and turned away out of his embrace.

"I'm right sorry," Rob said lamely, "but this venture is my last hope. I just daren't take another chance. Goodbye, Honey."

She only nodded absently when he paused at the door and blew her a kiss from his fingertips.

Once in the street, he moved briskly. A farmer named Jeff Arnold, Phipp had said, had an oversupply of salt pork from his winter slaughtering. He would sell cheap—only $3.25 the hundredweight. By buying a lot, he ought to get that meat for $3.10, maybe less.

"He doesn't trust me," Peggy repeated softly. "He won't ever talk business with me again. From now on I'll be just a confounded brood mare and pantry mouse—"

When Peggy finished her work, eight o'clock was clanging from the belfry of St. James's. In two hours her father and mother would sail—out of her life, if she did nothing. She did not consciously reach a decision, but she found herself lifting clothes out of the bureau. She hated the way the bureau teetered on the uneven floor every time she pulled out a drawer. In the small horsehide covered trunk which had held her trousseau, she commenced to pack her belongings.

A numbness possessed her, froze her emotions. Sometimes for long minutes she sat looking at a perfectly familiar garment. She resolutely refused to think when it came to packing some clothes she had made for the baby. Her hands seemed to move without volition. M. F. She saw the initials done in bright square headed brass nails on the end of her trunk. Margaret Fleming? Another person.

Absently she pulled on a dark green dress, then a short cape which would hide her condition as well as might be.

Mercy! It was nine o'clock already. Glancing out of the window, she saw the tide was rising. It had climbed high up on the oyster decked pilings of John Brown's wharf. Brown's dock was deserted save for a bare-legged nigger boy catching rock fish. It was dismal to see gulls walking about on the wharf itself. In the lee of a clump of pilings some oats were sprouting between the rough, splintery planks.

It was a glorious day, warm and mellow with spring. She moved more rapidly in gathering up her bonnet and stitching her shawl into place.

Hurrying to the door, she peered up Lawson Street. Merciful Heavens! Nobody was in sight save a couple of idle sailors lagging pennies in the shade of a big sycamore.

"Please!" she called. "Will one of you find me a cart right away? I must get to Fleming's wharf—please, it's very important."

"Why, yes, Ma'am. Straight away." One of the players knuckled his forelock civilly and, coat tails a-swing, trotted off in the direction of town.

"Try O'Hara's stable!" she called after him. She knew there would be a delay so she went back and sat down behind the same high desk at which she had used so happily to cast up accounts. The roof, warmed by now, began to give off the familiar smell of gull droppings and the tide was *lick-licking* under the floor.

A cart, drawn by a pair of scrawny horses, creaked into sight, then another, piled high with dusty flour bags. To her surprise they halted in the street before the warehouse.

"This Ashton & Co.?" the driver demanded, wrapping reins about the whip stock.

"Why, yes. But Mr. Ashton isn't expecting any flour—"

Deliberately the driver wiped his face on the sleeve of a

checked shirt. "Reckon Mr. Ashton forgot to tell ye, Ma'am. He bought a hundred sacks yesterday afternoon. Here's the receipted bill."

"Yes, I reckon Mr. Ashton forgot to tell me."

"Where'll I stack 'em?"

Peggy got up and opened the store-room door. Damp air beat in her face. "In the right hand corner. It's drier there. Mind you put some boards and poles under the bags. We— Mr. Ashton don't want the damp to get at it."

"Yessum. Hey, you Willy," he called to a Negro asleep on the load. "Back up them hosses."

It was a big load and every time the men dropped a flour sack small white cloudlets went whirling across the warehouse floor. Soon it looked as if it had snowed. Footprints began to register themselves. Once, in passing the door, the Negro ripped a bag on a splinter, losing half its contents.

"Careful!" Peggy snapped. "That sack will be deducted."

Flour dust was settling thick on her green dress and shawl and had powdered loose ends of her hair.

All at once she remembered the cart she had sent for. Shading her eyes, she squinted first down the street, then up at the church steeple. Heavenly days! A quarter to ten! A two-wheeled cart was turning into the end of Lawson Street. It came crawling leisurely in her direction.

"Please, Ma'am, will you sign the receipt?" demanded the miller's man.

Lips compressed, Peggy took the wrinkled slip, firmly crossed out "100" and wrote "99 sacks flour."

"Bring over another bag this afternoon," she warned. "Hear?"

She promised her carter, a blear-eyed rascal with scarcely a tooth to his head, five shillings if he got her to Fleming's dock by ten.

"I'll do me best, Mum," he promised through a fog of gin fumes. He nodded and handed her up onto the driver's seat.

Never had Norfolk's streets seemed so full of mud holes and, of course, on this particular day and hour a farmer had decided to herd his cattle across Market Square.

"Hurry! Oh, do hurry!" Peggy's small rigid figure seemed to be trying to push the cart forward.

"Ned's doing the best 'e can, Ma'am," the driver snuffled. " 'E ain't no bleedin' race 'orse."

In a futile effort to ignore the cart's dreadful swayings and lurchings, Peggy strained her eyes down the street. At the far end of it some tall masts were beginning to show in detail.

Two or three times people called to her from the sidewalk, but she paid no attention. She was too busy pressing hands to her stomach. Why, oh why, hadn't she thought to let the trunk go hang and go on by herself? Why hadn't she had enough sense to send a nigger boy running down to the *Betsy* long since? Even a slow runner could have done it, easily. Of course, it was that flour, that confounded flour.

"Oh damn!" Under the rattling of the cart she indulged in profanity such as slaves used when a wagon got mired. It did her good.

Half way down Duke Street she vented a sibilant gasp and in her desperation clung to the board seat. Clearly out of hailing distance, the *Betsy* was falling downstream! Already her jibs and her fore topsail had been set. The canvas shone yellow-white against the green slopes across Smith's Creek.

She said dully, "Never mind. Drive me back to the warehouse."

When Rob got home everything was in its accustomed place and Peggy was soberly preparing supper. Though a dozen kind friends had for his benefit described her ride across town, he never mentioned it; nor did he tell her a word of his day's activities.

13 — KATHERINE TRYON

KATIE TRYON thought Norfolk had not changed a great deal during the past year. Her eyes encountered the same brick houses, the same narrow streets, the same swarms of grubby children shrieking over their games. It was so good to smell the scent of cured tobacco again she felt like crying.

At the sight of masts and rigging sticking up above the houses her heart lifted. Two new houses had gone up on Colonel Anthony Walke's property. One of them looked as if it might be an ordinary, it was so big. Purple shadows deepened in the street. Those pigeons rollicking about the church steeples soon would be going to roost.

To keep her face in shadow, she pulled further forward a shawl knotted under her chin. It was a good thing dust lay so thick and cool on the street because her feet burned and her legs ached all the way to her thighs. For fear she would try to run off, Ma Skillings hadn't allowed her shoes 'cepting in the dead of winter, but she'd fooled her all the same. Katie's sunburned lips parted in a grin every time she thought of it. At night when the Skillingses were snoring, she'd get up and soak her feet in the brine they used to pickle salt pork with. It toughened them. Mr. David had once said English prize fighters did that to harden their hands. She guessed the advice was good. She hadn't had any trouble in getting out of the backwoods and down to the main road to the north.

Her luggage didn't hamper her much. In the ragged shawl bundle she carried over one arm was only a clean blouse and petticoat against the hour she would apply for work, a comb and a necklace made of beads of some kind. An Indian gave it to her when she fed him at the back door. Ma Skillings, of course, was out. The Indian claimed it would bring her good luck.

Well, it *had* been lucky, Katie figured. Why, she had only tramped the King's Road half a day when a long train of wagons came rolling up. She learned it was freighting salt pork, ham and bacon up North. When the boss freighter, a big, loose jointed man with squinting eyes and a perpetually bulging cheek, noticed her standing beside the road with her yellow hair glaring in the sun and her good-natured features glistening from the water of a spring she had been drinking at, he pulled up.

"Want a ride?" he invited. "Road gets stony along a piece —it's hard on bare feet."

He looked jolly and had a concertina on the seat beside him, so Katie nodded and for three days rode with the train. The trip was grand fun. It was so good to hear jokes cracked, to smell beer and eat tasty victuals again. She was honest enough, the first night, to admit it was good, too, having a real man again—even if he did smell of the horses a little. Pa Skillings was such a weakling and his breath stunk to high Heaven. Besides, how else could she pay for her fare and food? Katie's exuberant vitality, so long repressed, bubbled.

Said the boss driver, hugely pleased with her company, "By crackey, I wisht I hadn't my ol' woman back in New Berne—you shore melt down a man's vitals."

258

For safety's sake he made her ride under the wagon cover until they were clear of Roanoke County. But then she came out and sat beside him while he sang song after song—some ribald, some tender, and a new political tune somebody had written about the Congress's letting South Carolina rice through the embargo. The tobacco planters were plenty mad. His hearty voice chanted:

> " 'We as have no clothes, no grog, no tea
> To cheer our drooping sperrits,
> And snug in clover smugglers see
> Who have not half our merits.
>
> Isn't it a pretty story
> One smells it in a trice
> If I send baccy I'm a Tory
> But Charles-Town may send rice.' "

She'd got a bad scare when, on the second day, a pair of sheriffs came riding up with her description. She had barely time to fall back off the seat when they began asking the boss driver if he'd seen her. He had lied fluently, had carried conviction.

"Reckon you better not take a chance," the boss driver told her when, on the morning of the next day, his train prepared to swing inland. "What with the Province being so upset, they's a heap of runaways on the roads. If they cotch you again, you'll get quite a spell in the Bridewell and a smart flogging. I hear the magistrates are clamping down."

Her travel with the train made Katie feel fine, happy as a catbird on a pump handle. Rest and plenty of good food had wrought wonders. The last night she had gone in swimming and had scrubbed and scrubbed, and washed her hair, too. Afterwards she lay naked on the soft grass beside the river, stretching arms and legs unencumbered by clothes. It was wonderful. Hers wasn't a bad body she thought; it was soft, yet firm, and her thighs were not too wide. It was just as well she was so well built.

"Well, Honeybee, here's where you git off. Whoa!" The boss checked his team and, one by one, the other fifteen wagons stopped. "Sure ye won't keep on to Philly?"

"No thank you, Mr. Green."

"Well, good luck to ye, Honeybee, and God bless ye. Yer

259

a game lass!" The driver gave her a loud kiss, then a smack on the bottom. Playing a doleful tune on his concertina, he clucked to his horses. The wagons rumbled on under an arch of shifting dust.

Katie remained standing at the crossroads waving until the last swaying canvas cover crawled out of sight around a clump of pines. Then she looked up at a weatherbeaten finger-board. It read Norfolk—16 mi.

Yes, it was fine to be back! She felt it was almost like coming home. The idea of seeing Mr. David Ashton right soon made her almost forget the ache of her feet. Craftily, Katie walked bent over. She had always held herself straight in Norfolk, and was taller than most girls. Crimanently! but she was thirsty.

Despite falling twilight, she at last began to notice changes. So many shops had "To Let" signs on them and there was an uncommon lot of idle men about the streets. These ogled certain alluring curves revealed by her scant calico dress. She knew her breasts were riding to her stride; she could see their nipples outlined by the light cotton. They drew admiring glances. Before she reached the Market her blue challis skirt had been plucked a dozen times.

Long since, Katie had reckoned she must go slow about showing herself at the Spread Eagle. That would likely be the first place the Skillingses would warn the sheriffs to look. Bare feet slapping gently on the hard dry earth, she circled to the inn's rear and slipped into the stable. Pretty soon Tom MacSherry would come out to make sure the horses had enough hay and bedding. He always did that himself.

Heart pounding, she peered up at Mr. David's windows. A warming flood of joyousness banished her fatigue. They were lighted! Straw on the stable floor felt fine on her swollen feet so, after setting down her bundle, she went over to see if Maggie still stood in the second stall. Sight of the beast's furry white rump did her heart good.

"You old darling! I'm *that* pleased to see you!" She felt so happy she slipped an arm about the mare's shaggy neck and hugged it hard. There was a strange horse in George's stall.

Kitchen odors made her so hungry she filled a bucket from the well and though the water was faintly brackish—like all Norfolk water—she drank her fill. After that she soaked her feet until they felt nice and cool. Sitting there, she looked about. Mr. MacSherry must be prospering. The "Four-barreled" privy boasted a coat of fresh green paint and a new carriage shed was building beyond the stable.

She had dried her feet and was finishing the last of her bread, ham and cheese when a door opened and heels rang in the cobbled yard. Suppose this wasn't MacSherry? Heart thumping, she darted into the harness room; she remembered it had a second door. But she had no sooner reached it than she recognized the landlord's shuffling step and the little sucking noises he made through his teeth after supper.

He carried a cruize lamp in his hand and he nearly dropped it onto a pile of hay when Katie called, "Mr. MacSherry. Please, sir, I—I've come back."

"What? Who? Why, Katie girl!" He put the lamp down and, taking her in his big fat arms, kissed her hard on her cheek. "Well, God bless my soul! I'm some tickled to see you." He pinched her bottom. "Um. Seems a bit thin." He backed her off to arms' length, running his eyes over the gold-yellow hair braided and coiled about her head, at her wide features and honest gray-green eyes. "You look fine, my dear. Ah, it's often I've wondered, but I've never worried over you."

"Never worried, Mr. Tom?"

"No, my girl. You've something to you that will carry you on so long as the breath stays in your body."

Katie didn't understand, but she didn't care. It was oh! so nice to hear those cheerful Negro voices in the kitchen and a sudden gale of talk every time the taproom door was opened. She gripped her bundle.

"Mr. MacSherry?"

"Yes, my dear?"

"I can have my job back, can't I?"

"Surest thing you—" MacSherry began, then broke off frowning. "That is—Katie, you know I'd give anything to tell you 'yes.' But yesterday and the day before bailiffs from the sheriff's office have been over. They were looking for you and there's a twenty-five dollar reward up."

"Oh-h!" Katie's sunburnt features crumpled. "Why can't they let me be?"

"I don't know," MacSherry said, savagely forking hay into Maggie's manger.

"But can't you take me on—later? I—I'll hide a week somewheres."

"I—I wouldn't dare. They'd fine me cruel if I was caught harboring a runaway, deliberate like. There, there, girl, don't cry. I'll have to think of what can be done."

"Oh, thank you!" She gave his hand a grateful little squeeze then brightened. "Why don't you ask Mr. David what to do? He's clever. He knows a way to manage 'most everything."

MacSherry put down the hay fork. "Mr. Ashton ain't here nowadays. He—he's in Boston. The British threw him in jail for helping the patriots up there, so they say."

"In jail!" Katie was horror-stricken. Mr. David in jail! Why, it was just as if Mr. Tom said they had put the King in jail. "Why—why—that's impossible!"

"But it's true just the same."

A horse stabled down the line turned, whinnying softly, its eyes dully afire in the lamp light.

"Then I hate the British!" Katie burst out. "I'd like to kill them all."

MacSherry laughed and wiped his hands on his leather apron. "Ain't that a pretty large order?"

"I don't care. I would. Every one of them! The idear their putting Mr. David in prison!"

MacSherry nodded, but he was only thinking how pretty Katie looked with her cheeks flaming like that.

Sitting on sacks of oats and watching the furtive sallies of many mice, the two of them talked of what had happened. All the time Tom MacSherry kept pondering. He considered one plan after another, but discarded each one as quickly as it took shape. All at once he snapped his fingers so loud the spit dog came a-running.

"By gobs, Katie! Maybe I got a answer."

"Mr. Tom, what is it?" On her oat sack Katie straightened, eyes wide and anxious.

Tom lost his trend of thought for, as the girl sat up, the cruize lamp he had set on the floor revealed the unmistakable fact that Katie was wearing only two petticoats below the waist—nothing more.

"W-what was I saying? Oh, yes. Maybe you'd better leave Virginia and start again somewheres else? Tomorrow I guess maybe I can scare you up some identification papers." For over a year now the clerk of the court had owed Tom Mac-Sherry five pounds. He might as well collect it this way. He never would otherwise. "You can stay on the top floor tonight—nobody'll look there." He lived there by himself.

God, but Katie looked a flavorsome piece! He'd forgotten just how golden pretty she was. And to think he had felt only kind of fatherly at first. Oh well—it was only for one night.

"I can fix you up, and I never did give you your last month's wages; didn't want that old hen buzzard to grab 'em."

Katie, interpreting aright MacSherry's heightening color, rearranged her skirt. "Leave Virginia? Why, Mr. Tom, where else could I go?"

"Listen." MacSherry wiped his face and seated himself on a corner of the bran bin. His fat bottom ran over the edge, drooping comfortably. "Listen; you remember Mr. David had a brother?"

"Oh yes, sir. Mr. Bob, wasn't it?"

"That's near enough. Well, anyhow, tomorrow afternoon he's sailing for the Bermudas. He's a good man, right kind to people in trouble. Maybe, if I talked with him, he might take you along. In the Bermudas, wherever it is, you could make something of yourself."

"The Bermudas? Are they British?"

"They say so. They're some islands away out to sea."

To his surprise she burst into tears and clung to him. "Oh, Mr. Tom, I—I'm afeard to leave Norfolk. Norfolk's so fine. I love Norfolk."

"Well enough to spend a year in the work house?"

"Oh—no! No!"

"What can you do, besides 'tend bar?"

"I snitched a prayer book at church, Mr. Tom, and I have learned myself to read tolerable fair. I can write a genteel hand, too."

MacSherry said he would talk to Robert Ashton that very night, then by the back stairs he sent Katie to the top floor.

Because folks said Mrs. Ashton was going on the chartered schooner, Tom MacSherry calculated she would be right glad of another female's company—especially with her as big as a beer keg. At the same time, he decided he wouldn't tell Ashton about Katie's having been his barmaid, not unless he was asked a direct question. Chances were Mr. Rob would never in the world recognize the girl. During Mr. David's stay he had never been anything more than a casual patron.

Mr. David! As he went stumping down towards the harbour, MacSherry sighed. It was too bad about him. *There*

263

was a real Virginia buck! Always ready for a fight, a frolic or a footrace. He would, of course, tell Mr. Rob enough of Katie's story to win his sympathy for her. Once they got to sea, the girl would have to stand or fall on her own wit.

Mr. Rob Ashton fairly jumped at MacSherry's suggestion that another woman aboard would help matters all around.

"Who is this Katherine Tryon? What's her background?"

"She has been a bound maid, but she is good plain stuff. My word on that, Mr. Ashton! Her mistress abused her, beat hell out of her all the time so she is running away and I'm helping her. Wouldn't do it if I didn't think it was the right thing."

"I see. Well, I'll take your word on the rights of the matter, MacSherry. Has she any money? I'm right hard up."

"Here is two pounds against her passage. And it would be handsome of you to let her come for that."

"She is to wash Mrs. Ashton's clothes, serve meals and make up the bunks in our cabin," Rob quickly reminded.

"You'll find her willing enough to do anything to help."

"All right," Rob spoke succinctly. "Bring her down to the *Desdemona* tonight."

"Tonight?" MacSherry wavered. "Oh! I don't know about bringing her tonight."

"Yes. I'm taking a chance on this, of course. It's got to be tonight—or not at all."

"What time?"

"Around three o'clock."

"Three o'clock then." MacSherry brightened. He was afraid Ashton had meant before midnight. There would be plenty of time this way.

"I will find a hiding place in the cargo. Warn her she must stay below decks 'til we drop the pilot."

"Aye. And she will do it, too."

"She'd better. Not even the crew must know she's aboard." Rob began to chuckle and his chuckles deepened into laughter. "By God, MacSherry, I can't wait to see Mrs. A.'s face when she finds she has a personal maid aboard!"

14 — VALE VIRGINIA

A STRONG westerly wind blew down Chesapeake Bay and, filling the *Desdemona*'s sails, drove her past the pine-crowned dunes of Cape Charles. Rob stood beside Captain Ben Rudder in somber silence watching the outline of Norfolk blur, then sink slowly into the Bay. Aloft, reef points tapped smartly against straining canvas. The yellow-green water murmured increasingly loud along the schooner's sides as swells, beating in from the sea, charged under the bow.

The tide, Rob noticed, was just turning. Slowly it swung about a red painted channel buoy until, like an index finger, the spar pointed out to sea.

An omen?

Book Two

Boston

Part I

The Mustering: June, 1775

1 — THE WARS OF HANNIBAL

To BUFF, anxiously trimming Hannibal, it seemed on this mid-June evening as if the whole world had taken on a scarlet tinge, None of the other matches in Boston had attracted half such a multitude of officers. Though he couldn't read insignia, Buff reckoned about every rank in the British Army was represented.

He felt very alone and powerful small potatoes what with all these redcoats rubbing his elbows. Golly! He never had figured there could be so much gold lace, so many silk shirts and red noses in all the world. The different regimental facings—blue, buff, bright yellow, orange, and purple. Whoo-e-e! This was like moseying about in the belly of a rainbow. And Law's mercy, the perfume! And the wig powder! Sweating, hardly daring to raise his eyes, the blue Negro worked over the gamecock as carefully as he could.

He wondered how Hannibal liked this ruckus. Not much, he reckoned. The red quill was actin' mighty nervous. All this red about most likely caused it. For luck, Buff spat on the stumps of the bird's natural spur. Using a little scroll saw he had just sawed them off. He sure didn't like the idea of fighting Hannibal with steel gaffs on and he was only doing it because Mr. David told him he must. Mr. David must know best, but wrinkles cut across the chevron-shaped cicatrices on Buff's cheeks as he inspected the terrible little swords he must lash to Hannibal's legs. Slender, two inches long and double-edged, the gaffs were in addition needle-pointed and sharp as razors.

If anything happened no one could blame it on Buff. No suh. He had begged Mr. David, "Please, suh, Ah take mah chances, but doan' fight Hannibal wid none ob dem cutleries. Dey t'row him off balance, sho' nuff. He ain' used to dem."

David Ashton had hesitated, biting his lip, but when he

looked across his noisome cell and saw Johnny sitting limply by the window and looking out, so mighty sad, at some green islands dotting the empty harbour, he held to his decision. The black shadow of a bar falling on Johnny's face emphasized his waxen pallor. A few hours earlier Corporal Shaun Mahoney had settled all doubts.

"Mr. Ashton," he whispered when he brought the food at evening. "It's ordered to Halifax I am; the transport sails in two days. If I'm to help yez, I've got to finger me money tomorrey night."

Thanks to Hannibal's savage ring craft and the Negro's selection of birds calculated to bring real backing to a bout, the bribery fund had grown steadily throughout the late winter and spring. Right now there wasn't a more famous fighting chicken in North America than Hannibal. Always an excited roar went up when the wiry red gamecock was lifted from a basket brought on Buff's arm.

All in all, the wars of Hannibal had gone well and a bag of bills and silver hidden in the chimney of David's cell was growing.

One raw March night Major Bouquet chanced in on a fight with a port bottle under his arm and several more under his belt.

"As Gad's my life! I know that fowl and you—you black rascal! You were on the *Assistance!*"

"Yassuh, yassuh." Buff thought the bumping of his heart would choke him. "But Ah done got 'quitted, Misto Major, suh."

"Indeed? Well, damn your eyes, *I've* not acquitted you!"

"No suh, no suh, ob cou'se not, suh."

"You want matches for this bird, eh what? Well, I'll find them until that precious rebel's bird gets finished. Where do you live?"

Buff told him down on Fish Alley.

"Well, my fine black simian, understand this! That cock must meet any bird I find for him, or I will warn the provost and he will return you to Virginia for the runaway rascal you are."

After that Buff, scared half to death, had to do as Bouquet ordered. Once a week at the least, and generally twice, Hannibal fought in various inns and ordinaries and once over in Castle William before the officers of the 64th regiment. Beating another red hackle, he earned David a hundred dollars that night.

There were times when Buff felt tempted. Often he found in his great, blunt-fingered paws enough to buy freedom, but he didn't know what steps to take and he didn't dast try to find out. Yankee niggers were a treacherous, back-biting lot. Right smart, too—most likely they'd get his money somehow, then turn him over to a sheriff.

So always he gave Mr. David all of Hannibal's winnings excepting enough to pay for food and lodging. He hung onto a few shillings in case he got took with a misery and needed a mess of snake oil or something. He'd his eye on a monstrous big knife, too. You could take the parts off a flea with it, it was so sharp.

No suh, he didn't fancy this business of fighting Hannibal with gaffs. He wasn't so sure just how they ought to be rigged. From the corner of his eye he watched the rival handler, a weasel-faced, gold-toothed sergeant of marines. The prompt way the Englishman set to work showed he hadn't any doubts. Buff figured he must have served down in the West Indies where such contraptions were used all the time.

Making a pretense of waxing the linen binding threads they'd given him, he watched the marine stop a few drops of blood by chalking his bird's spur stump. Next the Englishman placed a square of very thin leather over the stump, then eased the ringed end of his gaff over it. Thus the artificial spur base came to rest snugly over the natural stump.

This accomplished, the marine bent his powdered head, sighting along the leg of his chicken, a huge silver gray bird just from Jamaica and bringing an imposing record of victories. Lips pursed, the sergeant made minor adjustments in alignment. What these might be Buff couldn't tell—and it worried him plenty that he couldn't.

Buff worked hard to align the steel spurs. He reckoned they ought to set pretty near like natural ones. But Hannibal didn't like it and kept pecking Buff's fingers when, using the linen threads, he tied the leather wraps around his legs. Were they too tight? He reckoned so. He overheard one of the resplendent officers saying if the ties were too tight a chicken's leg got numb. He loosened them, hoping it wasn't too much. Golly, how he'd like to carve up that purple-faced major man. He was doin' Hannibal dirty—that was what. Cutleries!

"Hurry up, you butter-fingered baboon!" Bouquet began

roaring at him. "You can't keep these gentlemen waiting all night." The big major had stripped off his tunic and when he strode about with his buff waistcoat undone you could see the fat wobbling on his chest and belly in great rolls. His face was scarlet as any mid-summer sunset, making his large pop eyes look blacker than ever.

"Yassuh, direc'ly, suh," Buff mumbled; eying the gray chicken with apprehension. Laws! If only they wasn't so much smoke! It made his eyes smart something fierce. He was one scared nigger and he felt awful bad. Just suppose Hannibal got hurted or lost the fight? Mr. David had to have the money.

This, he could tell, was going to be *the* fight of Hannibal's life—since he'd been handling Mr. David's bird, anyways. Yes siree, that gray chicken had a mighty fierce look about him, and he'd easy be heavier by four ounces.

All at once the roaring drone of voices slackened and died, abruptly leaving someone almost shouting, "—and her father gave him a kick on the bum and— Oh!" All the officers, stood to rigid attention, but Buff was too busy to notice until somebody drove an elbow into his short ribs.

"Stand up, you confounded idiot. General Burgoyne is coming."

The black bounced erect and stood, goggle-eyed. Everybody knew General John Burgoyne was one of the rankinest Britishers in Boston. In a civilian's suit of mulberry satin and a lace jabot which cascaded down his ample chest in a snowy froth the general entered briskly, but with dignity. His large, well spaced eyes were at once penetrating and good-humored. Yes, suh, the gen'ral sure was a handsome gent. Funny thing —the general and Mr. Johnny Gilmorin looked somehow alike.

General Burgoyne approached through the smoke haze. He was nodding in acknowledgment of salutes. It was so still you could hear the black silk bow of his wig tie rustling. The Major-General ran his eye casually over officers perspiring freely on this hot June evening.

"Pray proceed, gentlemen. I find it demned close in here."

The captains and lieutenants looked relieved. Gentleman Johnny was said to disapprove of gambling and certain other traditional army vices, but—well—

Buff felt powerful shaky when those damp red faces above

272

the scarlet coats came crowding closer. Laws! The snapping of snuff boxes sounded like dry kindling thrown on a hot fire.

"Li'l bird," Buff muttered, "dey's just de two of us 'gin all dese heah redcoats. But doan' you git skeered an' doan' you try no tricks 'til you gits used to dem cutleries dat damn' Major man say you got weah. Jest you look sharp, li'l bird, 'til you cotches on dat gray chicken how he fight."

Crowding about, the gentlemen in white wigs and glistening buttons asked a hundred questions, most of them foolish. Wind, beating up from the stable below, stirred tan bark in the pit, raised eddies of dust on the hayloft floor.

One thing was wrong. Buff looked about unhappily until a wolfish appearing lieutenant-colonel wearing a pale blue waistcoat and the numeral 18 on his belt buckle came up.

"What is it, my man? Something wrong?"

Buff ducked his head. "Yassuh. Hit's mighty dark in dat pit. Hammibal needs mo' light. He ain' no owl!"

"No owl? Haw! Gad, that's rich!" The hard-faced colonel beat his thigh. "Hear that, Stevens? No owl!" Presently he stopped laughing and ordered two more bull's eye lanterns brought. "Going to see that you get a fair show. Wouldn't, otherwise."

From the way the officer in the blue waistcoat stared at Major Bouquet, Buff reckoned he didn't think much of him.

A referee was appointed and promptly called the handlers into the ring. Bets flew like hailstones among officers crowding four deep. The size of the wagers terrified Buff. Why, these men were betting his own purchase price on a couple of chickens most of them had never seen before.

"Come, come!" General Burgoyne called from where he stood with slender white hands crossed on the top of an ivory-headed walking stick.

No suh. Hannibal didn't cotton to them gaffs. He kicked suddenly, slashing Buff's forefinger enough to make it bleed. Buff, with naïve commonsense, gave the money from David Ashton's "battle fund" to the lieutenant-colonel for placement. For all his forbidding looks, the Englishman seemed pleased. He waited 'til the chickens were weighed and when the gray bird's advantage showed up, he placed Buff's bets at good odds.

Across the ring the marine, peeled to his under shirt, was grinning. "Nah then, Boogey, don't frown. You orter smile. Tonight you'll be eating chicken soup."

Buff cackled nervously. "No *suh!* Hit's 'at barnyard rooster you got gwine get he toes browned in a oven."

The officers came crowding still closer, sweating; several of them, Major Bouquet especially, were a bit unsteady on their legs. Their breaths were rank with brandy and wine.

"Beak your birds!" called the umpire.

Hannibal, battle lights glowing red in his eyes, was quick enough to nail the gray chicken by its comb. He gave it such a yank the enemy bird emitted an outraged squawk.

"Dey's ten pounds ob Misto David's money on you, li'l bird," Buff breathed as he stepped back into his corner. "Win dis heah fight an' Ah reckon you won't have to fight no mo'."

It was an epic battle. Long afterwards among forests of the dreary, muddy entrenchments at Yorktown, British officers recalled that cock fight in Waller's hayloft.

Rumor had not lied concerning the gray cock's ability. Moon, as his handler called him, was fast; fast as greased lightning. Buff uttered a little moan when, during the third flurry, his trained eye caught sight of the Jamaican bird's gaff disappearing into Hannibal's side. It was so quick he couldn't tell how much Hannibal was hurt. Not much, he reckoned, because the Virginia gamecock never faltered and rallied furiously.

The battle went on evenly enough until one of Hannibal's gaff's got hung up in Moon's wing feathers and they had to be untangled. From the onlookers rose a continual hoarse clamor that routed the neighborhood out of bed.

Gradually the fight wore on towards a climax. Buff expected it would come in that flurry when Hannibal, instead of rising to meet his antagonist in the air, would duck under and then, turning, spring onto the back of his disconcerted enemy. Usually the fight ended then and there. Buff sensed the maneuver coming and so did the officers who had watched Hannibal fight before.

"There goes your three quid, Bouquet," called a captain of dragoons.

General Burgoyne narrowed his eyes, braced his plump body; in their excitement his subordinates crowded him.

"Gad," he muttered, "they are a deuced well matched pair!"

Once again the cocks squared away, necks outstretched, bloodied hackles flaring. The silver bird started his charge and Hannibal ducked. In the last split second Moon saw what his enemy was up to, swerved aside and raked Hannibal as the astounded red bird flashed by.

From that point on Hannibal forgot strategy and stood up to the bigger gray cock, matched muscle for muscle and heart for heart. Half an hour passed and still the gamecocks wearily, doggedly circled, swooped and slashed. They fought until they were so tired they could no longer hold their wings at the horizontal. The gray bird lost an eye but there was an ominously thick trickle of blood soaking Hannibal's side, and the back of his head was bleeding so hard it drenched the feathers on his ruff.

Beaks parted with fatigue, panting wildly, the chickens battled on, inspiring the officers to such an uproar that horses stabled below took fright and began whinneying and kicking at their stalls. Wigs slipped awry, perspiration coursed in streams down the faces of onlookers and quite a large red feather settled in General Burgoyne's wig, another on his shoulder. Bouquet, half strangled, tore the stock from beneath his triple chins and roared:

"Damme! I wager five pound more on the gray."

"Done! And be damned to you!" rasped the lieutenant-colonel standing grimly behind Buff.

"Brave little gladiators," sighed General Burgoyne, ever ready with an apt phrase.

A deep groan went up when finally Hannibal tottered helplessly over onto his side, his yellow beak blood-streaked and his sides working like those of a bellows. Though the gray bird punished him cruelly, Hannibal lay still, glaring defiance.

"Count!" snapped the officer in the blue waistcoat and the umpire counted slowly up to ten.

"One count for the gray! Handle your birds," he directed.

Buff snatched up Hannibal, squirted a little brandy from his mouth into the chicken's beak as the umpire began counting up to twenty-five. Next, frantically, he began to rub his legs. Were those spur lashings too tight? Buff wanted to cry because he didn't know.

"Go git him, Hammibal. You jes' cain't let us all—" he almost said "stay in jail," but remembered in time.

"Twenty-three, twenty-four, twenty-five! Breast the birds," panted the umpire. "For God's sake, give me a drink, somebody."

Bouquet raucously protested. "Damme no. They must be breasted at once!"

Hannibal must be hurt bad, Buff reckoned. When he set him down the chicken toppled over on his side as if his legs wouldn't work. Again the gray bird hammered him with a punishing beak.

"Count!" Buff begged.

The umpire nodded.

"Seven—eight—nine—ten! Two counts for the gray."

"Please, Misto Major, cain't Ah have time loosen dem lashin's jes' a little?"

"No!" Bouquet snapped. "Count, umpire."

"Swine!" someone said in a clear voice.

"The rules are in Major Bouquet's favor," rasped the lieutenant-colonel.

Bouquet, his eyes popping more than ever, turned to Buff. "Nigger, this time your chicken had better show fight or you will have lost."

"Yassuh, yassuh." In his excitement Buff began talking in a strange guttural language. He implored Ogune, Mambani and Kleh to lend strength to the blood-bathed bird between his hands.

"Breast your birds!"

Buff squatted on his hams, holding Hannibal towards a line drawn by the umpire's toe across the tan bark. The chevrons on his cheeks glistened as if oiled. Pointed teeth gleaming, he leaped back, yelled something like, "Sakaar!"

Hannibal this time remained on his feet and when the gray, also badly winded, came lumbering in, the red gamecock unexpectedly sprang into the air. Moon ducked and tried to dash out from under but first one then the other needle-pointed gaff struck home.

A tremendous, breathless shout made the dusty beams tremble as the gray bird wheeled violently to the left and tumbled over and over. For awhile Moon's wings beat in a senseless, spasmodic flutter. Hannibal turned to deal a coup de grâce, but was too weak. He slipped forward on his breastbone, lay panting and watching the slowing antics of the Jamaican gamecock.

"I believe, Major Bouquet, you owe me fifty pounds?" drawled the wolfish lieutenant-colonel. "Your bird has been hit in the brain."

This was so. The gray cock had rolled over on his back and though his legs still worked feebly, the marine made no effort to pick him up.

"Fight goes to the red chicken," announced the umpire, "and now—if Major Bouquet does not object—will one of you chaps give me a drink? My throat is about gone."

Buff's pockets bumped his legs as he walked; now and then gave off a faint clinking noise. Golly! He was fit to sink what with all them gold and silver coins! Carrying Hannibal under his coat and next to his skin, the blue Negro stepped out of the stable and went shambling off to his quarters in Fish Alley. His face was wreathed in an immense grin, but in his free hand he carried a short iron bar.

Glory hallelujah! Buff felt moved to break into a long paean of victory. He wanted to tell all the world what a great fighter Hannibal was and what a 'cute handler Buff was. Back in Africa when the warriors came back from a raid they had used to make up victory songs. He could barely recall their endless, monotonous chants. A thought sobered him. Hannibal needed fixing up. He had been stung mighty bad.

Once back in his quarters he lifted the gamecock out from his shirt. There were bloodstains on the faded blue cotton, but he felt encouraged to hear an indignant *cuck! cuck!* Buff lit his candle with a spill from the fire, supplemented it with two more.

Mr. David sure would be glad to hear his bird's eyes were all right. Narrowing his own, Buff parted the sodden feathers. Yassuh! That sure was a mean-looking hole. Whole question was, how deep was it? He sponged the bird's head and neck then, using scissors, snipped away feathers near the wound.

When Buff had finished massaging Hannibal's legs, the red quill looked a bit happier and accepted a second ration of brandy with obvious eagerness. Then he put the bird into his wicker cage and covered it with clothes.

"Now, Misto Hammibal, you will have to 'scuse me for awhile. Ah— Ah got 'po'tant 'rangements 'tend to."

Buff emptied his pockets and counted the coins as high as he could count. He was not sure how much Hannibal had won, but it was fifty pounds easy. Mr. David had only asked for forty.

2 — THE RIVER

A SMALL canvas bag of coins, dropped into Corporal Shaun Mahoney's hands, wrought the miracle.

"Heah's half," Buff told him. "Misto David give you de res' when he ready. An' doan you try no tricks, soljer!" Buff scowled. "Er Ah'll cut yo' ha'ht out." In the dim light, he looked really ferocious.

"Faith, then, 'tis meself will be careful."

At two o'clock the corporal came walking down the cell block. His heavy tread echoed hollowly amid the damp silence.

"A fine evening it is," said he, peering through a little barred window let into the wooden door of Cell No. 12. Quickly entering, he set down his lantern. "Hold out yer feet, sorr."

Heart pounding, David obeyed.

Corporal Mahoney made deft selection of keys. The gyves fell away.

"Now you, sor-r." Mahoney crossed to Johnny Gilmorin and the orange facings of his uniform were briefly bright in the candle light. Two keys clicked and another set of gyves lay, useless metal serpents, on the bug-infested straw. Mahoney might be doing nothing more dramatic than unlocking a woodshed door. It was lucky he was calm, David thought. Johnny was shaking like a colt the first time it smells a bear.

"Plaze to come wid me. Niver a noise now," pleaded the Irishman. He wheeled sharp about when David caught at his arm.

"What about Farish? We're not going to leave him behind."

"It's waiting in the alley he is," whispered the corporal.

Keys on Mahoney's big ring clinked a little as in single file the three men trooped along one faintly reverberating, stone-walled passage after another. Then down two stone stairs, gritty with dirt. Running rats. Doors and bars, bars and doors. A sour unclean reek of dirty human bodies. Prisoners snoring, muttering in uneasy slumber. Loose straw sticking from under doors.

At length the red-coated figure stepped into a store-room. Down from pegs he lifted two officers' cocked hats, one edged with tarnished silver and the other with gold. Next he pulled a pair of gray military cloaks out of a refuse barrel. Admirably they served to conceal the tatters and rags in which both prisoners now stood.

For the first time since he could remember David felt an urge to weep. The let-down was too great. The nightmare was over—or promised to be. The unbearable monotony, the dirt, the hunger, the lice, the gnawing fear of that moment when he and Johnny would be dragged away for transportation to God knew where.

"Follow me," Mahoney directed softly, then caught up a small bundle. "Ye will plaze walk straight like officers. If any guards stop us, say yer out o' the 47th. It's thim pants-rabbits o' the 6th have guard tonight. Talk English-like and curse to beat the divil. They'll lave yez be."

"Got that, Johnny?" David asked. "We're from the 47th."

"Yes," Johnny said and, briefly, his teeth stopped chattering. His hand sought David's and gave it a small ecstatic squeeze.

"Seems we're off to the wars again. I can almost feel epaulets and spurs."

"Stow the gab!" snarled Mahoney, turning a flat, red-brown face. "Here's yer cully."

Waiting in the jail yard among shadows cast by a pile of coffins crouched Farish. He was wearing a marine's cocked hat and cloak. The mariner did not even nod but fell in behind Mahoney's white cross belts and pointed light infantry cap. Little brass chains laced across its back jingled to his stride.

They made their way through an open gate and out into a street which was very black except for distant whale oil lamps. Before David realized it, the Irishman was following a path leading towards the water's edge.

"Now if the blessed Saints are kind, we will find our boat and be off."

"Our boat?" That Corporal Mahoney intended to go along was a complete surprise.

"Faith, yes—there'll be the divil to pay around that jail tomorrow."

Hidden among some high weeds and half under a deserted dock lay a rowboat. Once it was launched Mahoney prepared to take up the oars.

Farish stripped off his cloak and spoke for the first time.

"I'll take them oars. I can row quiet and I know the harbour currents."

"Fine. 'Tis the divil's own pull over to Lechmere's Point." Mahoney shrugged, settling comfortably onto the bow seat. "Now, we'll be waiting 'til the three o'clock patrol rows by."

They waited and sure enough the church bells had scarcely finished their drowsy tolling than a barge came pulling along the shore. It was manned by six rowers in addition to a pair of officers seated in her stern. David could see their gorgets shine in the light of a lantern set on the boat bottom.

It was wise that they had waited. The night was so dangerously fine one could see trees on the other side of the Charles. Millions of stars cast a perceptible sheen over the river. Frogs along the Boston shore grumped and grunted.

Fortunately, just as the fugitives pushed off, a small, steady breeze began to blow up the Bay from the direction of Boston. The corporal, no fool apparently, had paid attention to details. The rowboat's tholepins were cleverly muffled. More important still, the skiff was equipped with a little leg-of-mutton sail.

"I figger our worst time will come off Barton's Point." Once they were clear of the Boston shore, Farish peered eagerly about, was relieved to glimpse the patrol barge light away off up the shore.

"Thim Britishers have a man-o'-war anchored in the river mouth," Mahoney warned.

Farish turned, gaunt and hollow-eyed, to the Irishman who was laying out some parcels on the bottom gratings. "What about other patrols?"

"It's not sure I am, but ye'll maybe find wan off Little Cove and wan more near Fox Hill Island."

"Sailing or rowing?"

"All rowing, so they told me."

Farish grunted his satisfaction. "Lend a hand then. We'll make sail. If this breeze holds, we can out-run them."

Never, David thought, had he smelt a sweeter wind. His legs felt unfamiliar without the customary twenty pound weight to them. Absently he reached down and felt his ankle. He had no difficulty whatever in locating calloused ridges raised by his gyves. Small wonder. From December until June they had been there.

Johnny was all excitement. He kept saying to David in eager undertones, "Isn't it amazing? We are actually free!

Think of it! We can go where we like, eat what we like, drink what we like! By God, I'm going to eat for a week!"

"On what?" David inquired, watching the jet water slip by more rapidly now that the skiff's triangular sail was filling.

Johnny threw back his head in the old careless gesture. "The fat of the land, my lad. America is rich; there will be plenty of food. Soldiers get fed."

"Faith and not always," corrected the corporal. "Nor on the fat o' the land."

"I wonder what color Yankee regimentals are?"

"Avast!" warned Farish. "Quiet, and keep low!"

Following the direction of his look, they could make out the loom of a big ship, a man-of-war, swinging to her cables off a cluster of lights on the far shore. David guessed they must be in Charles Town. In the half light she looked so big David thought she must be a frigate, but Mahoney whispered that she was only a sloop—the *Lively*.

Astern Boston showed as a long, dark silhouette, punctuated here and there by lights. Farish steered with an oar; a stocky, forbidding figure who would not relax even when Mahoney from a haversack pulled out a bottle, a loaf of bread, some cheese and a piece of cold boiled beef.

"'Tis no banquet, bhoys," said he, "but 'twill give our bellies something to work on. 'Tis a long walk we face oncet we reach the Cambridge shore."

"What's in the bottle?" Farish suddenly demanded. "I got no coat under this cloak."

"Sure and it's rum distilled by some av the best churchmen in Medford. Yer welcome to a dram." It was evident that Corporal Mahoney, late of the 35th line regiment, was well pleased with life. He chuckled. "Faith, 'tis good St. Barnabas has been to my ould mother's darlint this night!"

"How did you get to Boston?" Johnny queried with his mouth full.

Interrupting himself only for reference to the rum bottle, Shaun Mahoney described how, to escape semi-starvation in Tyrone County, he had taken the King's shilling.

"It fair gagged me, it did, to wear regimentals sporting orange lapels," he sighed, "but I done it. Thinks I, Shaun, me fine bhoy, there's room for ye in America and none in Ireland. Why not let the ould German in Whitehall pay yer fare to the promised land?"

He had served only in Boston, Mahoney stated, and all the while had been awaiting a safe chance to desert. Other Irishmen were hoping for a similar opportunity. Och! What a grand life this was! Now he had one hundred pounds, a shoe-leather discharge from King George's Army and all of North America to roam over.

Johnny, comfortably sprawled on the bottom with long legs outstretched, asked suddenly, "I say, Davey, what about Buff?"

"Provided nothing goes wrong, he will bring Hannibal to Cambridge tomorrow."

Hannibal! He felt such a terrific sense of gratitude he wanted to buy that bronze plumed warrior a cage of solid gold. Never again would he pit Hannibal except for the fun of it and with muffs on. Life without a tussle would be barren for Hannibal, meaningless.

The skiff was slipping along quite rapidly, making only a faint gurgle under her stern. They glimpsed a patrol boat away off to port. She was poking around among the mud flats and pilings off Fox Hill.

David, his imagination warmed by the rum, locked grimy fingers behind his head and tried to grasp realities. It appeared this really wasn't just another dream!

"Well, Mahoney, what are you going to do next?"

The Irishman reflected, scratching his close-cropped head. "First off, I'm for chucking these rigimentals and bad 'cess to their orange facings!" He sighed gustily. "Next, I'm going to buy me the two prettiest doxies I kin find and the three av us will go to bed for wan whole week."

"Shame on you!" Farish snapped. "How can ye deliberately plan to lust like that?"

"Och, when it's over, I'll do me penance and lave a tidy soovenir in the poor box. A man's a man ye know, Captain; and me, I'm one o' the full blooded bhoys."

"And then?" Johnny was fascinated.

"Next I'll buy me a wee bit av farming land wid some big trees to it."

"—And then?"

"Then, savin' the captain's presence, I'll be going back to that bed again. Afther which I will join Gineral Ward's army. If there's any fighting going on this year, 'tis the fond hope o' Shaun Mahoney he will be mixed into it."

"That," Johnny chuckled, "sounds like a mighty comprehensive program, eh, Davey?"

"Yes. We've a strategist aboard, seems like. Our friend, the corporal, has a better idea of what he is about than most of the fine gentlemen serving His Majesty in Boston."

Johnny said presently, "Where do you reckon we can get measured for uniforms?"

"I don't know. Maybe we'd better join the army first. What do you aim to do, Captain?"

Farish, without removing his wintry eyes from the shore ahead, said quietly, "I guess likely you forget my wife is in Cambridge. You got me put in jail; now it 'pears you've got me out. That much credit I'll grant you, Mr. Ashton. But I've not been able to give my family a penny in six months. They've gone without many a meal o' vittels on account of your claptrap notions of fair dealing. Can't say as I'm thankful to you, Mr. Ashton."

"Why damn you!" Johnny flared, snatching at the heavy bailing scoop. "Of all the ornery, ungrateful——"

David caught his wrist. "Easy on! Captain Farish is right—absolutely right." He fumbled in the pockets of a coat gone so ragged it was out at elbows and had a fringe of loose threads dangling from its skirts. "Forty pounds, I believe, would cover most of your lost wages?"

"Near enough," the New Englander muttered, eyes still fixed on the nearing shore. "Why waste time talking about it?"

"Because I should like to make a settlement."

"Hot air is what they fill balloons with," was the New Englander's comment.

David passed over a small roll of bills.

Farish accepted the money calmly, counted, then pocketed it. "I cal'late that'll mend matters at home," said he.

Shaun Mahoney flapped an enormous paw in protest, then began to laugh. "Faith and to think I only charged a hundred pounds to get the three av yez out av chokey. Who'd have thought yer old blackamoor could lie so well? He swore 'twas ivry sou yez had."

"You might at least said 'thank you,' and damn you for a cold blooded fish!" Johnny glowered at Farish. He could not understand the little man.

"There's no call for you to get red in the face and foam up," returned Farish. He was devoting his attention to steering up a small reedy creek. A bittern, startled at fishing, went *gra-awk!* and flopped awkwardly away over a marshy plain to starboard.

The skiff had rounded the first bend with its mast barely clearing the wide flung limbs of a great oak when David, who had been sousing his head over the side, held up a dripping hand.

"Voices!" he whispered. "Not far off"

"The divil!" Mahoney's lax manner vanished and hurriedly he whipped off his pointed leather cap. The monogram G. R. flashed faintly, like ice seen at night, when he flung it into the water. The heavy brass plate on its front sank it quickly. The deserter's cartouche box of white leather followed, but not his bayonet. He could account for that because the garrison troops were forever selling them to the townsfolk.

Johnny stared into the blackness ahead but could see only willows growing on the crest of the bank. Both shores looked soft and reedy.

Farish snapped in a hoarse whisper, "Lower sail! Sooner we get ashore the better. What do you make it out to be, Mahoney? A British patrol?"

"Maybe. There was throops—sent—last—week to look about over—here." Mahoney's reply was punctuated by his struggles to get out of uniform. Emerging, he grinned wryly.

" 'Twould be a foolish thing to risk me neck getting yez free only to find it stretched before I kin enjoy me money."

Starlight showed the deserter's squat figure; dark hair stood out in patches all over his body. Astern, the Irishman's breeches, tunic and crossbelts were floating soggily out towards the Charles. He began pulling on a checkered shirt.

The voices seemed to have faded, but David, busy furling the sail, wondered if a dark pattern of willows ahead was stirring with more than the wind. Farish, meantime, was sculling with powerful strokes towards the port bank. When the skiff's keel grated over some pebbles, Johnny wrenched free the tiller handle. It made a handy club. A wicked, anticipatory grin froze on his features.

"Bear a hand!" panted the sea captain. "Tide's part out." By heaving on the oars they edged the boat shorewards a few feet more, but then it stuck fast. Mahoney's bayonet gave a little *wee-e-ep!* when he slid it out of its scabbard. David could find no better weapon than the heavy wooden bailing scoop. He swung his feet over the gunwale and found himself standing ankle-deep in muck.

"Come back!" he softly warned Johnny who was already a dozen steps in the lead. "Better all keep together."

"That's the ticket," Mahoney whispered, his bayonet cold gray by the starlight.

Johnny beckoned. "Come back, nothing! You come. Ain't it grand to be free again? And able to fight in the cause of Liberty?"

"Hush! Less fine talk," Farish warned. "More plain sense."

They were half way up a crumbling bank when the sea captain flinched back. Above him a dark figure in a three-cornered hat blotted out a segment of the Milky Way. Another head and shoulders popped into sight. It was bisected by a long barrel held at the diagonal. Still another.

A voice called, "Halt! Halt where you are, or we shoot!"

Mahoney dropped his bayonet and held up empty hands. "Go easy on thim trigger fingers, bhoys," he begged, "or ye'll be losing Gineral Ward four av the smartest recroots he'll enlist in a dog's age."

"He talks Irish," snapped a deep voice from the depths of an alder thicket. "Careful, it's likely a patrol from the 18th. They are rank with bog-trotters! I'm going down and see. Blow them to bits if they make a move."

"Shall we rush them?" Johnny breathed. "He talks like a Britisher."

"No, you fool! For God's sake stand steady. We haven't a chance."

David looked hard up the bank. That three-cornered hat seemed ominously like a British officer's. He felt sick, his bowels all puckered, at the thought of recapture.

Bushes threshed and up above someone coughed. A sibilant droning of mosquitoes impinged on David's ears. Though he felt a bite on his neck and another on his chin, he didn't dare make a move.

All at once Farish heaved a little sigh. He could tell that the man coming down the bank wasn't in uniform.

"Praise Mary!" Mahoney murmured. " 'Tis ten years I'm aged."

Farish called in flat nasal tones, "Any of you know Captain MacKintosh of Butcher's Hall? He was captain-general of the Liberty Tree."

"Yes. Who are you?"

"Stephen Farish. One of the Committee of Fifty One 'til the British jailed me."

"That's as may be," the unknown grunted and, having reached the water's edge, drew near.

He had a cocked pistol in each hand. David made out a severe, intelligent face beneath the cocked hat. The other was wearing only a waistcoat over a shirt ripped open because of the night's humidity. With manifest suspicion he stepped up to each in turn, then called to his men.

"They don't look like British soldiers, but they may be spies. Keep them covered and we'll search them up on level ground."

David could have laughed from sheer joy when he found himself standing with the others on a meadow eaten hard and flat by sheep. Ringing them in were a dozen roughly dressed men holding flintlocks at varying degrees of readiness.

These, then were some of the doughty rebels all America was talking about! They didn't look so formidable, David decided. Why, most of them didn't even have cartridge boxes; carried their powder in cowhorns slung over their shoulders.

Johnny felt dismally let down. No two were dressed alike and they ranged in age from a thin young boy in a coat much too big for him to an ancient who couldn't have been a day under seventy. The hell of a looking army!

The leader nodded approvingly at a man who had been locking Mahoney's bayonet to the muzzle of the Tower musket he carried and doing it as if he knew how. He turned to the prisoners.

"Who are you, and what are you doing here?"

Johnny drew himself up. "My name is Gilmorin, sir. My friend Mr. Ashton and I have come to dedicate our swords to the sacred cause of Liberty."

"My arse!" grunted the man with the bayonet. "Durned if I like the look of 'em, Cap. Do you? They don't talk New England."

"Of course not. We are Virginians, both of us," David explained. "Since Captain Farish is a New Englander, you had really better listen to him."

"All right. Go ahead, you."

"Don't know's I blame you for suspicionin' us, but I cal'late I can explain," Farish began. "We have just come across the Charles. This Irishman is deserting. Helped us escape from the Stone Jail."

"My land! You ain't really excaped prisoners?" When the boy shuffled closer, starlight glinted on a clumsy old fowling piece. The barrel of it was nearly as tall as he.

"Sure enough," Johnny replied in a friendly sort of way. "Ever felt fetter scars?"

"*I* have," the old man's reedy voice broke in. "Durned French held me and Billy Forrester in Quee-bec Castle two hull years. Lemme feel." Stooping, he closed his fingers over Johnny's ankle and slid them up and down two or three times.

"He ent lying, Cap. The ridges and smooth skin is there all right. Prison stink's on him, too."

3 — CAMBRIDGE

AT DAWN Captain Stephen Farish set off for Cambridge along the river road. Because he hated these men who had, he cal'lated, lost him his ship, he went without a word of farewell. He walked rapidly and gradually a smile began to hover over his leathery features. Wouldn't Solace be surprised—especially when he showed her the forty pounds? He hoped the children would still be in school. The bedroom door was pretty thin and there was a squeak in one bed post—or used to be.

Where would he find MacKintosh? He'd picked up considerable about the redcoat army—even behind the bars. The right people ought to know how poorly the King's troops were feeding, how some of the Irish recruits were trying to pick up enough spunk to change sides. Yes, and the Committee of Safety ought to know that Gage and Graves, the Admiral commanding, were at swords' points over Gage's holding on to command of nearly all the marines. Consequently, Graves wouldn't help Gage a mite more than he couldn't get out of.

Massachusetts privateers ought to be set cruising as soon as possible; they were needed to cut off supplies reaching General Gage from England and Canada. The Britishers would starve them. Who should he talk to? He guessed likely MacKintosh would know.

By sun-up David, Johnny Gilmorin and Shaun Mahoney, too, set foot on their way to Cambridge. But they followed the upper road inland from the Charles. They were feeling like new men, thanks to the hospitality of some Massachusetts troops detailed to the defense of a crude earthwork unimaginatively christened Fort Number Three. To Johnny's disappointment, the commander had packed them off before it was light enough to see much of what was going on. David, however, laughed when he heard picks and shovels going by lantern light.

"There's the Yankees for you! Even work at night, like a dose of castor oil."

Johnny grinned back. His lank hair clubbed with a length of cotton string was a ludicrous sight. "Reckon if they keep it up, they'll throw a few cramps into General Gage. Wonder where Mahoney's got to?"

"Nearest grog shop, I expect. It's three to one he'll be stony broke tonight."

Stomachs comforted by a bowl of stew and mugs of sassafras tea laced with rum, they swung energetically along the dusty country road. It was a glorious morning, dewey and fresh as only June can be. Thrushes and robins piped from every thicket and hedgerow. In wide, boulder-littered fields to either side larks whistled and, high in the dark blue sky, a red-shouldered hawk swung as if suspended by an invisible thread.

Soon they began to meet parties of sun-burned men under arms. The majority seemed to be farmers marching in any sort of order and wearing the oddest imaginable miscellany of homespun. They were traveling in both directions; some to Cambridge and others out to Fort Number Three which, David learned, had been constructed to thwart a British attempt on Cambridge. Colonel Gridley had said it could command a small bottleneck barely joining Charles Town Point with the shore.

Any kind of weather this morning would have seemed glorious, David exulted. Oh it was fine! Fine to be free, to walk again with no hampering tug at his ankles. What a heavenly privilege it was merely to be clean. Belying legends of Yankee parsimony, some men from Colonel Reed's regiment had passed over shirts and fresh breeches. David's were a little small. Especially welcome to David was a gift of some white worsted stockings. Curiously enough, it was going without stockings he resented most. With eleven dollars of Haninibal's winnings still in his pocket David had offered to pay, but the brawny farmers stared him into an ashamed silence. To show they held no hard feelings, their lieutenant invited him to join in the company's morning prayers.

In Virginia, he reckoned, he had never heard such earnest praying.

In almost every field or clearing men lay rolled up in coverlets or slept with their feet towards campfires which had long since smoldered out. Unshaven cooks and their helpers were sleepily collecting the blackened ends of faggots. Johnny remarked on how much the charred faggot ends looked like rings around a white bull's-eye of ashes.

"Hi, there! You come to help whip the bloody-backs?" called a fat man comfortably perched on a stump. His gun, with a coat dangling from its muzzle, stood propped against another.

"Reckon so," David smiled.

Not the least conscious of his unconventional attitude, the stranger began tucking his shirt into his pants. "Wal, when you git near Inman's, steer clear o' them New Hampshire fellers. You wouldn't believe how mean they be. Why, they'd boil down a mouse for its tallow. You'd do well to join up in my company. We're out o' Gerrish's regiment. Colonel Sam Gerrish's regiment. You can say Link Rowe sent you. Tell you what I'll do. If you sign up, I'll split my bonus money with ye and we'll all get drunk!"

All along the line they kept meeting men who urged them to join this regiment or that. No recognizable officers directed this great swarming of humans. Uniforms, tents or flags were nowhere in evidence. Only rarely did some unit on the march preserve even a semblance of organization. Twice they came across companies engaged at drill. The travelers sat on a stone wall for awhile watching one of them maneuver to the wheezed commands of a big pompous-acting fellow. He was wearing a sort of scarf knotted over the shoulder of a snuff colored coat. The scarf was made of red cheesecloth.

Johnny groaned softly. "Ever see anything like it? My God, and to think old Fleming called our company exercises the vague wanderings of a pack of clumsy cowherds! Compared to those lads, I reckon we drill like guardsmen."

David nodded absently. "Maybe, but look at their faces. Ain't one squad laughing or fooling."

By easy stages the two Virginians drew nearer to Cambridge. More frequently now they noticed fence rails missing. Here and there straying cattle wandered about the countryside. This untrammeled impression of New England etched itself sharply into David's mind. The grass and shrubbery were such a glowing green. Most of all he admired the elms which everywhere shot leafy branches skywards to descend in fountains of greenery.

The farmhouses amused Johnny no end. There would be a white trimmed clapboard house, then a smaller addition backed up to it, and then another still smaller, and finally a woodshed at the end, like segments on a telescope. And so neat! Even the backhouses were tidy behind lattices grown over by morning glories. Rose trellises built around others of them inspired ribald comment. Picket fences, now robbed of some of their palings for the benefit of campfires, showed careful construction.

Around nine o'clock they overtook a four-wheeled oxcart creaking along towards Cambridge at a snail's pace.

"My Lord," Johnny chuckled. "Even if this army can't drill, it sure can eat like hell! Will you look at all that food!"

Backed up against a low wall built of flour sacks two calves bawled and blatted over the tailboard. Further forward some potato barrels supported a number of swaying, creaking wicker crates full of plump hens.

The oxen looked dusty and tired and lifted their knobby legs with reluctance.

"'Morning," David greeted. "Looks as if you'd come a long way?"

"Yep. Have."

"From whereabouts?"

"Ipswich."

"Reckon you'll make a good lot of money?"

"Nope."

"Why not? There's a lot of troops about."

"Gift, Mister, to the Massashusetts army from the seelectmen of Ipswich."

"Haw!" Deftly plying a goad, the drover directed his great brown and white beasts over to a trough fed by a spring bubbling above the road.

Once they had helped the lanky native of Ipswich to ease the yokes of his span, they took a drink before they trudged on. It was growing hot.

David gave Johnny a quizzical look. "Gift, eh? Ever heard of the Yankees being so mean they steal from their own mothers?"

Young Gilmorin's pallid and sensitive features were beginning to show traces of sunburn. He grimaced.

"Reckon I have. Let's get on to Cambridge. I'm feeling right peckish again." He cut a switch and swinging it like a sabre, decapitated a series of buttercups. "I'm for the regulars, Davey. They see most of the action. Reckon they will be wearing blue regimentals—like our old provincial companies."

Through yellow dust raised by ever thickening traffic they tramped on towards a pair of church steeples and a cluster of shining roofs. They passed a milestone reading "Cambridge ½ mi." For all the activities of the military, inhabitants of the countryside acted surprisingly matter-of-fact. A smith was swinging his hammer over an axle glowing crimson on his anvil. A woman came out with a basket and began to hang up her washing as if this were any piping day of peace. But the number of men's ruffled shirts and small clothes she put to drying dispelled the illusion. Johnny, plucking a couple of daisies to tuck into the ragged buttonhole of his coat, deduced she must be an army laundress.

Not far from the outermost houses of the village the road was barred by a long, high, yellow-brown earthwork. Through a grove of maples it stretched far off to left and right. Men with picks and shovels were swarming all over the entrenchment. They were like ants. Another fortification was being thrown up on a hill a few hundred feet to the right. The first defense, a couple of freckled boys said, was called the Cambridge Lines and the second, Butler's Hill Redoubt.

A sudden doubt gave David pause. "Suppose the Yankees won't let us into Cambridge? What the hell of a joke if we came all this way for nothing."

To their complete surprise no sentries, not even a single officer, were on duty at that point where the Charles Town road passed through the earthworks. Unchallenged, the Virginians sauntered past willow fascines holding back the raw earth. On them a few fat white hens happily scratched for worms. On the far side of the works a quartet of militiamen in shirt sleeves had stood their guns against a wheelbarrow and were cooking a belated breakfast. The savory smell of frying bacon started miniature springs flowing in David's mouth and Johnny's expression was so wistful as to catch the eye of a red-faced fellow. He raised his arm, beckoned.

"If you're hungry, friends, set right down. I'm the corporal. We've et so durned much we're like to bust our pants buttons."

David smiled. "Then why go on?"

The corporal wiped his mouth on the back of a brown hand. "Got to eat these vittels to keep 'em from sp'iling. Go hungry tomorrow most likely, though. Ain't no reg'lar rationing done yet."

Another man in a flat Quaker hat and full-skirted brown coat belched comfortably before inquiring, "Where you boys hail from?"

Johnny told him, adding, "We reckoned we'd come up and see what kind of a war you are fighting."

"Virginia, eh?" The eyes of these solemn, long-faced militiamen swung sharply as if the visitors might be expected suddenly to change color, like chameleons.

"Virginia's a long ways off, ain't it?" one queried. "To the south'ard somewhere?"

"That's right. We've had a lot of talk down our way, but not much action."

"Say, you should of been 'round these parts on the nineteenth of Aprile," drawled a hawk-nosed fellow, dipping his fingers in the frying pan and using the grease to shine the barrel of an old, old firelock.

"It's a very handsome piece," David, hunger satisfied, felt an obligation to be agreeable. "French gun?"

"Yes, sir. Saint Malo muskit. My Pa, he captured her up to Louisburg." Lovingly he fondled the stock. "At the Concord bridge fight I knocked three redcoats ass-over-teakettle with her. She may be old, but I vum she's good for a few more Britishers."

"You all from Massachusetts?" Johnny inquired, seating himself on a pile of timbers.

"Us? Hell no! Only him." The corporal pointed to the man with the Saint Malo musket. "We hail from a real Province— Connecticut."

"Connecticut men would steal the pennies off a dead nigger's eyes," amiably remarked the Massachusetts man. He got to his feet. "Wal, see you fellers later."

"Say, Silas, see if you kin locate some salt somewheres; ain't any left in town."

The corporal declared the regiment they must sure enough join was Israel Putnam's. There was a real fighter for you!

"Old Put ain't but fifty-seven, and he's a real officer. Proved it when he took *Diana* and burnt her right under old Grove's nose. He's no snotty-nosed lawyer dressed up in a pretty uniform. He fit in the French wars, too; like a stack of black cats, so they say."

"Don't doubt it, but what's wrong with the Massachusetts people?"

The Connecticut corporal spat, looked David bang in the eye and declared solemnly, "Mister, up in this Province folks are so danged mean they would boil down a mouse for its taller."

David choked on a bit of fried mush, but managed to avoid Johnny's twinkling eye and keep a straight face as the corporal continued.

"Now you appear to be likely fellers, but you're strangers 'round here. Well, so are we Connecticuters. Stands to reason you'd be more at home with us. Don't it?"

"Maybe."

"Well, just you keep on into the village. There's a college there, but I forgit its name. We've got us a headquarters detailed in one of the buildings. Hollis Hall. Ask for Knowlton, Cap'n Tom Knowlton. You'll ketch him there if he ain't already left for Inman's. Rest of our boys are there. Can you remember?"

The corporal was eager to enlist two such able-looking recruits, even if they were Southerners and probably Church of England.

"Captain Knowlton at Hollis Hall. Right. I reckon we can remember. Thank you." David held out his hand. "There's a lot of sense in what you just said."

4 — CAPTAIN KNOWLTON

ON the outskirts of the village—Cambridge only sheltered some sixteen hundred souls—the prospective recruits became involved in throngs of villagers, farmers, soldiers, commissioners, sutlers, children, carts and dogs.

It was a pretty, tidy village built about a square. David

liked the way the churches thrust their slender white steeples through the vivid green branches into the June sky.

Johnny, with something like awe in his voice, remarked, "My God, Davey, I never guessed there were half so many people in America. Where do you reckon they came from?"

"Mostly Massachusetts," David hazarded. He paused, watching a squad of men awkwardly setting up a marquee. "Notice something queer?"

"Quite a few things. Which especially?"

"No horses around. Haven't seen a single cavalry troop yet."

"Why, that's so. At home easy half the boys would be a-horseback."

The village square presented a focal point for numerous supply carts which came rolling in, gray with dust and drawn by horses so thirsty they whickered and fought to get at the common watering trough. Their drivers, hot and impatient, cursed and snarled and sometimes used whips on each other. Everybody dropped what he was doing to laugh at two details of militia. Because their officers couldn't remember the right orders they'd got all tangled up.

Something must be in the wind, David deduced. Every little while levies in from the back country marched by on their way to camp along the Concord road. They weren't prepossessing; just a lot of sunburned men walking along under gun barrels of every length and pattern. Powder flasks slatted on their hips; blankets and quilts were rolled about their shoulders. They tramped by behind fifes shrilling "The White Cockade." One company got a big laugh because they followed the martial strains of a fiddle and a flute.

"How'd you like riding to hounds on that?" Johnny demanded, flattening to let pass an aide bumping along on a heavy-footed farmer's horse.

"Damned if these Yankees ain't mighty poor looking," David admitted. "Haven't noticed but three people wearing broadcloth in the last half hour. They're mostly big men, though."

He commenced making a mental map of the village. In four directions long, maple-shaded streets diverged from a central square; where they led there seemed no way of telling. All of them were lined with brick or clapboard houses of sturdy and often handsome proportions. Usually a picket fence guarded the residences from the street. Diamond paned and leaded windows were the rule. Framing the manure-speckled square were the village's few shops and a single tavern, the Blue Anchor.

All the streets, David saw, were much broader than Norfolk's and, though unsurfaced, were edged by curbs of rough hewn gray granite. Tethered to hitching posts commonplace riding horses stamped and switched at flies. There wasn't a blooded nag in the lot. Flower beds decorated nearly all the front yards and a few houses boasted little lilac plants, recent importations from China.

Johnny's eager eyes missed little. "The Yankees sure must waste a heap of time shining up. Why, I reckon you could shave in most of those door knockers."

To almost every wall were affixed regimental enlistment posters offering recruits extravagant pay, opportunity for travel and advancement. They paused to read one: "The Soldiers of this Company will surely return laden with fine Cloaths, Money and laurels." Another declared:

> To Patriotick-minded young Men
> Able in Body and Spirit Desiring
> to Serve in the Reg't Raising under
> Coln. Frye.

The ENCOURAGEMENT at this time, to Enlist is truly Liberal and Generous, namely, a bounty of TWELVE dollars, an annual and fully sufficient supply of good and handsome Cloathing, a daily allowance of a large and ample ration of Provisions, together with Sixty dollars a year in GOLD and SILVER money on account of pay, the whole of which the soldier may lay up for himself and friends, as all articles proper for his Subsistence and comfort are provided by Law, without any expense to him.

Those who may favour this recruiting party with their attendance as above, will have an opportunity of hearing and seeing in a more partickular manner, the great advantages which these brave men will have, who shall embrace this opportunity of spending a few happy years in viewing the different parts of this beautiful continent, in the honourable and truly respecktable character of a soldier, after which, he may, if he pleases, return home to his friends, with his pockets full of money and his head covered with Laurels.

"Ain't that the college?" Johnny asked over a rattle of drums.

"Yes, I reckon so."

"You know what it's called? The Connecticut man didn't say."

"My God, Johnny, you ought to know. It's Harvard College. Harvard is the biggest college in America. It has been standing over a hundred and thirty years."

"How do you know?"

"Fellow in jail told me so. Used to go here."

"William and Mary is older," Johnny maintained. "And eleganter, too."

"Maybe." David shrugged. He felt very tired after the long inactivity. His feet hurt like blazes and he was wishing he could find a brook to cool them in. He looked up the road. "Good God above! That building must be big as the Capitol at Williamsburg."

Fatigue momentarily forgotten, they halted before a long, well-proportioned red brick building. Its shutters, windows and trim all were painted white. Winged wooden staircases ascended to a white double door and above the roof shone a small gilded cupola with a bell in it. Opposite stood a building as big but without a cupola.

A carpenter emerged from a doorway and came shuffling over a lawn of dusty, discouraged looking grass.

"Are either of these Hollis Hall?"

"No. One with the belfry is called Harvard Hall; t'other is Massachusetts. Hollis is the third building to yer left. Better hurry. Rate these goddam chicken thieves they call militia are wrecking them, won't be but a few bricks left star.ding come another week. There now. Just look!" A bearded soldier went tramping by, lugging an armload of fence pickets. "Them is from in front of President Langdon's house."

On passing between Massachusetts and Harvard Hall, they found themselves facing a rough quadrangle. Under some trees a battalion of militia stood undergoing the inspection of a fat little officer. He was stamping along, using a gold-headed walking stick to indicate this man's shoes and that man's musket. Like many short men he made up for his lacking inches with a loud voice.

"God help me, how's a man to make soldiers out of such a crew of dim-witted mothers' mistakes?"

Drawled a voice from the ranks, "Naow, don't you take on so, Ebenezer. You'll be a-coming down with the strangary."

The officer went scarlet, glared, wavered, but passed on bellowing. "Not one of you has cleaned his piece properly. You, Johnson, just look at those shoestrings! They will break and you'll have shoes dropping off inside the first half mile of march!"

"Wal, Colonel, I gone barefoot for years. I'm used to it."

"You, Pierce, where's your bayonet?"

"Gee, Colonel Bridge, I must have lost it."

Heads craned about and a snicker rippled down the uneven ranks.

"Sure," somebody called, "up in Tyler's haymow. Bet that Beamish girl could find it."

Colonel Bridge brandished his stick. "Silence!" he roared. "I demand more respect! Of all the disgraceful, insubordinate hang-dog rascals I have ever been condemned to inspect, you are the worst!" His rotund figure straightened and his canary yellow waistcoat puffed itself out. "Captains, forward!"

Four men wearing sashes of various colors shambled around from the rear; apparently the last evolutions had left them stranded on the wrong side of the battalion. Only one officer carried a real sword, the second wore an old fashioned navy cutlass and the last two were shouldering espantoons.

After Colonel Bridge was done berating them in a big, angry voice, they saluted after a fashion and went back to where their companies scratched and spat under the elms. The colonel promptly disappeared in a bee line for the Blue Anchor.

Aided by raucous promptings from the ranks, the captains gave some commands and drilling recommenced, but whenever a private felt thirsty he would fall out of ranks and go over to get a hatful of water from the college pump. It was a wonder, David thought, the pump hadn't gone dry; a long line of men was waiting to use it.

"Hey!" he hailed a workman leisurely repairing one of many broken windows. "Which is Hollis Hall?"

The glazier set down his putty knife. "Hi, Mr. Coffin!" He beckoned a hearty, red-haired young fellow trudging by. He carried a pick axe over his shoulder. "Show these gents where you used to chamber, will you?"

The red-haired youth nodded, though he sharply eyed David's greasy coat.

"Come along. Have you just come in?"

"Yes. From quite a distance."

"Didn't bring along any powder, did you? We are getting plagued short."

"I tried to," came the dry reply. "But the British got it first."

"Is that a fact?" the youth demanded in precise English. Johnny could see he was too polite to exhibit undue curiosity. "Well, if you want to fight, you are just about in time. They tell us a big battle must be fought soon. I resigned from college two weeks ago to enlist. Prescott's regiment."

"Resigned from Harvard?"

Young Coffin's healthy brown features relaxed. "Yes. I am —or was, rather—a junior sophister here, class of '76. But for me no Bachelor's degree. I prefer swords to Sully and drums to Demosthenes. *Tam Marte, quam Minerva.*" He passed a grimy wrist over his forehead, pushed back a battered cocked hat. "Perhaps *tibi seris, tibi metis* is more apt? Like most of our fellow islanders my father is, most unfortunately for me, a damned, uncompromising loyalist."

Johnny grinned. "Mine is, too. Did he disinherit you?"

"Down to the uttermost root and branch, Mr.—?"

"John Gilmorin of Norfolk, Virginia, sir. And at your service."

"The pleasure is mine, sir. I am Nathaniel Tristram Coffin of Nantucket Island and a confounded bad bargain if you care to believe the proctors of Harvard College. I fear they were deuced glad to read my resignation." He made a wide gesture. "Verily, 'man proposes, God disposes.' I resigned to escape those cloistered walls and lo! the Fates lead me back into the Yard."

Johnny having presented David the three continued on past quantities of rough militiamen sitting in entryways cleaning muskets, washing shirts and mending gear. Others just whittled or dozed on the sunlit grass. The grounds were most unsightly because of uncollected rubbish and the ashes of cook fires built on the lawns.

"Where are all the students?"

Young Coffin laughed. "Dismissed early this year lest this licentious soldiery corrupt their tender morals, no doubt.

Further, I fear there are too many Tories amongst the students to suit the pious folk hereabouts."

The news came as a shock to David. "Then Harvard is a Tory stronghold?"

"Hardly that," young Coffin amended, fanning himself with his hat. "Better than half the students are patriot—*a capite ad calcem*. Yonder noble ivy-shrouded structure is Hollis Hall. Its privies stink. For whom are you looking?"

"A Captain Knowlton."

The red-haired youth set down his pick, wiped shiny features and considered gravely. "Seems to me I have heard of a Knowlton in the Salem Company which is quartered in Stoughton Hall yonder. Another, a friend of mine, is a sergeant of the Deerfield levy. Might your acquaintance be either one of these?"

"Hardly," said David. "Our Knowlton is from Connecticut and has quarters in Hollis Hall."

Nathaniel Coffin's manner grew serious and his tone changed. "My word! You actually are not thinking of signing up with a Connecticut Regiment?"

"Actually, I am," David said. "My friend here wishes to join the regulars."

"*Non est.* There are no regulars in the New England Army, except regular feeders. We have a surfeit of them."

"What's wrong with the Connecticut men? Seems to me they drill better than any of the other troops." He of course knew nothing about it, but thought it a good guess.

Young Mr. Coffin considered a large blister on the palm of one hand, poked it gingerly and winced. "That may be true; but, my friends, I fear you have yet to learn that the inhabitants of said Province are parsimonious to the point of drying out the bodies of little mice for the sake of the fat to be derived therefrom."

"I am getting so I surely would like to watch it done," David drawled, deeply amused. "We raise powerful big mice down in Virginia and they say we're kind of spendthrift, too."

"Wouldn't you like to talk to Colonel Prescott first?" the ex-scholar pleaded. "He is a fine officer. One of the best. I am proceeding direct to his office."

"Thank you, but I think we have made up our minds."

Coffin laughed. "Then if your will is truly like Caesar's and 'constant as the Northern Star,' I bid you *vale, vale, et si semper, inde semper!* Good luck to you both," he added more seriously. Heaving his pick up to a sweat-marked shoulder, he trudged on.

"Well, I'm damned!" Johnny for once was completely non-plussed. "Hear how easy he reeled off that Latin? He must be a real scholar."

"And a real man for all that. Those blisters were big as half-jo pieces."

The minute David Ashton saw the entrance to Hollis Hall he felt his judgment had not been far off. The usual litter of rags, papers and broken equipment was not lying about and the entry stoop was so clean a man could sit on it in white breeches. Many of this big brick building's windows were mended with paper and from them a colorful array of quilts and blankets was airing. A good sign. No other unit was doing this.

A serious-appearing young fellow in gray homespun was on guard and when David started up the steps he smartly lowered his musket, holding it crosswise to bar the entrance. Deliberately he scanned the two men from untrimmed hair to their shoes.

"Your business?"

"We want to enlist," David explained. "Where do we go?"

"You aren't asking commissions?"

"Whatever made you imagine that?"

"I believe I know educated men when I see them."

"You sound like an educated man yourself."

"I will be sometime, I hope," returned the bespectacled young man with the gun. "At present I am only a college tutor."

"Here?"

"God forbid!" The militiaman in the gray tweed hesitated, then resumed cautiously, "Have you heard of Yale College? At New Haven?"

"I'm afraid not."

"You will sometime, and so will this nest of Tories." The soldier's contemptuous nod included the whole Harvard Yard.

"Where are the troops—the ones who live here?"

"They should be down beside the river, drilling."

Johnny broke in. "Do any of them wear uniforms?"

"No. As I said, if you gentlemen are looking for commissions, you had better seek them elsewhere. Otherwise—" he raised his musket to the perpendicular—"you can come in.

300

You will find Captain Knowlton in the second room to the left; this floor."

David and Johnny stepped out of the warm sunshine into a narrow hall smelling of wet wood, soap, and birch bark smoke. To the right a badly scuffed staircase led upwards. Gray painted plaster walls were generously initialed by the knives of many generations of students but most of them had been painted over. "Hurray for old Put!" however, stood out freshly white.

David hesitated, deliberating what he should say to the Connecticut captain. Johnny beckoned him over to the foot of the freshly washed staircase. Tacked to the wall was a fly-blown placard.

LAWS OF HARVARD COLLEGE

Extracts Therefrom

Chapter IV

II   No Scholars belonging to the College, shall wear any Gold or Silver Lace, Cord or Edging, upon their Hats, Jackets, or any other Parts of their Cloathing, nor any Gold nor Silver Brocades in the College, or Town of Cambridge; and whosoever shall offend against this law, shall be fined not exceeding twenty shillings.

III   If any Scholar shall go beyond the College Yard, or Fences without Coat, Cloak or Gown, Hat or other Covering, allowed by the Authority of the College, (unless in his lawful Diversions) he shall be fined not exceeding six pence; and if any shall presume to put on indecent Apparel, he shall be punished according to the Nature & Degree of the Offence by the President or one of the Tutors; but if he wears Women's Apparel, he shall be Liable to public Admonition, Degradation, Rustication or Expulsion.

VI   If any Scholar shall be guilty of Drunkenness, he shall be fined one shilling & six pence, or he shall make a public Confession or be degraded, according to the Aggravation of the Offence. And if any Scholar persist in a Course of Intemperance, he shall be rusticated or expelled.

VIII   If Any Scholar shall profanely swear or curse, or

take God's Name in vain, be guilty of singing obscene Songs, or of Lewd and filthy conversation, he shall be fined from one shilling & six pence to three shillings.

XIV   None belonging to the College except the President, Professors & Tutors, shall by Threats or Blows compel a Freshman or any Undergraduate to any Duty or Service.

XVI   No Undergraduate shall keep a Gun, Pistol or any Gun-powder in the College, without Leave of the President—nor shall he go a gunning, fishing, or boating over deep Waters, without Leave from the President, or one of the Tutors or Professors under the Penalty of one shilling for either of the Offences aforesaid—and if any Scholar shall fire a Gun, or Pistol, within the College Walls, Yard or near the College, he shall be fined not exceeding two shillings and six pence, or be admonished, degraded or rusticated according to the Aggravation of the Offence.

XXVI   When any Damage (except by the inevitable Providence of God) shall be found done to any Chamber or Study inhabited, the Person or Persons to whom said Chamber or Study belongs shall make good the same—and when any Damage is done to any other parts of the College, or to any of the Appurtenances, such as Fences, Pumps, Clock, etc., shall be charged in their quarter Bills.

"Why, they ain't even allowed gold or silver braid! What kind of students come here? Can't be gentlemen." Then Johnny added, "Or maybe they're just poverty poor. Can't shoot, can't fish, can't get drunk. What in God's name can they do? Why, when I was at William and Mary we used to keep the punch bowl and a pharo game going for weeks at a stretch."

David couldn't help saying, "That is very likely so, but how does your Latin compare to that fellow's?" College was a sore point with him. St. John Ashton declared he would waste no money on college courses and had stuck to it. Probably he was right, David reflected. The devil a bit he would have learned—from books.

Further down the passage a deep, rather harsh voice was dictating.

"To: General Artemas Ward. From: Captain Thomas

Knowlton of General Putnam's Connecticut regiment. Most respected sir: We are in desperate need of powder, few of our men possessing more than a gill measure and a half. Why in blazes don't we get what we ask for? We really need it and I have wrote three times already."

A smooth voice interrupted. "That is hardly correct military phraseology, Captain. What you ought to say——"

"You dress it up, Bellinger, but, hang it, that's what I mean. Make those robbers in the commissary realize we have got to get more powder. It is plain murder to send our boys into action with what we now have. The British carry sixty rounds a man into battle, and we don't average ten. That's all! Write it out now." The speaker must have noticed David's shadow, for he called out sharply, "Who's out there?"

David Ashton walked into a bare little office equipped with three tables and a bed. Two men were sleeping on it. A pair of secretaries drove their quills over sheaves of paper.

"Captain Knowlton?"

"Here. What can I do for you?" The speaker was a tall, brown-featured man with a face like that of a Seneca Indian. Though he had on a soft leather shirt instead of ruffles and had clubbed his own hair without powder, he was strongly reminiscent of George Leavitt.

George Leavitt! David felt a twinge of homesickness. Where the devil was George these days? Fighting no game-cocks, he reckoned. Poor George.

"Speak up," Knowlton invited. "What do you want to sell? We need cartridge boxes if you've got any."

"We haven't any, Captain. Last I saw were down in Norfolk."

The Connecticut captain sat straighter and his two secretaries looked up, blinking behind their spectacles.

"Eh? Where are you from?"

David told him.

"So you want to enlist, eh? Well, I suppose you can." Then, suspicious all in an instant, he asked, "What rank would you want?"

Johnny started to say "sergeant" but David checked him. In the Stone Jail he had plenty of time to revise his scale of values.

"Suppose, Captain, we talk about that after our first battle? Maybe you can decide better. We neither of us know much about soldiering——"

A flush sprang to Johnny's sensitive features. "Why, how can you say that? You drilled with the Company over a year —and I for six months. Don't you call that soldiering?"

"Opinions differ," Knowlton smiled. "Some folks around here would say so; old Put wouldn't." He seemed pleased, though, and looked at David narrowly. "Can you shoot?"

A slow grin slid over David's dark features. It was a blessing to speak with confidence. "Mr. Gilmorin here has won the Norfolk County turkey shoot three years running."

"That's good—capital! What about yourself, Mr.—?"

"Ashton. David Ashton, sir. Well, I can 'most always hit a Spanish dollar at fifty yards."

"Eh?" Knowlton's satisfaction vanished.

"—With a rifle, of course," David hastened to amplify.

"Couldn't be done with a smooth bore."

"It couldn't—except by accident, sir."

"Down in Virginia," Johnny put in, "we mostly use rifles."

"I hear they are very precise. We have none around here, worse luck. Bellinger." Briskly he faced a round-shouldered man laboring behind a knife-scarred desk. "Enroll these men in my company. You have brought no weapons of your own, I take it?"

"No, sir," Johnny said. "We only got out of Boston jail last night."

Thomas Knowlton's thin lips formed no smile and he spoke sharply, "You were in prison? Why?"

When the Connecticut captain learned, he offered his hand with gravity. "We are honored, gentlemen, to number you in this company. It has not yet been the privilege of any of us to suffer so much in the sacred cause of Liberty."

A gleam danced in Johnny's eye and he nudged David. There wasn't a grain of nonsense about Captain Knowlton, yet he spoke of "the sacred cause of Liberty." By God, this was the kind of a man to fight under!

Over the soft snoring of one of the sleepers a secretary said, "One of them could have that Tower musket we drew out of the Ticonderoga supplies. And Josh Garner's got to go home. Remember?"

"Go home. Why?" Knowlton asked.

"Josh's Pa died last week. His Ma needs him on the farm, but he promised he would leave his gun behind."

"What make is it?"

"Spanish. But Josh says it's a fair piece." He addressed David. "You will be issued flints and ball and as much powder as we can beg or steal. Better look your gun over careful. Some of them ain't in first class shape."

"Here is a copy of the rules and regulations for this company." From a small stack Captain Knowlton selected two sheets of paper and passed them over to the Virginians. "Learn them by heart. Now, our Province pays privates £2 a month. You will each be issued a coat and a blanket—if and when we get any. You will have to buy your own camp kettle and anything else you may be needing."

"What do you use for money?" Johnny was tactless enough to inquire.

One of the clerks snickered.

"Why—er—Connecticut script," Knowlton said, dark features painfully flushed. "It's all we've got. But we will guarantee you plenty to eat."

5 — FATE OF A GLADIATOR

WHEN, after a meal of succotash, salt pork, and apple pie, the Virginians still found themselves in solitary possession of a squad room on the top floor of Hollis Hall, David sat up. Johnny, however, remained sprawled in comfort upon bright yellow wheat straw which, scattered knee deep, served as bedding. He yawned when David came over and said,

"Here is five dollars, Massachusetts. You'd better buy us some kerchiefs and shirts—extra pair of stockings for me, and a comb."

"Where are you going?"

"Take a look around for Buff. Ought to be out here by this time."

To find Hannibal's handler was surprisingly easy. The Negro was too tall and his blue-black complexion too unusual. A woman, marketing, said she had seen him loitering beside the bridge that led across the Charles River towards Boston. This bridge, David found, was heavily defended. To command it three cannons had been emplaced and, on a bend downstream, a mound of raw brown earth marked the existence of Fort Number Two. Further downstream another redoubt was being thrown up.

In a little field not far from the guard tent—one of the few in Cambridge—he found the Negro snoozing at the foot of a big oak. Hat over eyes and mouth open, Buff snored though flies explored and drank at his eye corners. A chip basket, carefully covered, lay in the tall grass beside him.

"Wake up, you no 'count rascal," David called. "Wake up, Buff!" He felt mighty uncomfortable at owing so much to the big, simple creature now scrambling to his feet.

"Yassuh, Misto David. Yeh! Yeh! Yeh! Bin lookin' all over dis measly li'l town fo' you, suh."

"Thank you. Was it difficult getting out of Boston?"

"Oh, no suh. Ah jes' let on Ah was goin' out buying hens fo' Gen'ral Burgoyme. He powerful pernickity 'bout his vittels, 'at gentleman. My! My! Lots Yankees 'round, ain't hit?"

"Seems to be quite a few, Buff."

Buff drew closer and spoke in a stage whisper audible at least twenty yards. "Misto David?"

"Well, Buff?"

"Heerd tell de British is fixin' to cross de ribber an' burn Charles Town!"

David whistled softly. "The devil you say! Where did you pick that up?"

"At de chicken fight las' night."

Under the stab of Conscience David forgot all about Charles Town. He was astounded to realize he had hardly given Hannibal a thought since the night before. "Hannibal is all right?"

Sable doubt clouded Buff's features. "Well now, Misto David, Ah cain't rightly say. 'At gray bird he give Hammibal couple right mean licks."

"He—he's alive?"

"Oh, yassuh. He plenty cussed dis mawnin'."

"Thank God! He isn't going to fight any more. He has done enough for me—for us all."

"Ah— Ah ain't kept nawthin'," Buff stammered. "Only jus' a l'il fo' eatments an'—"

David, for the first and last time in his life, clapped a Negro on the shoulder and shook his hand. "To anything you have kept back you are welcome. Soon's I can, I'm going to buy you and give you your freedom. I will never forget what you have done. Nor will Mr. Johnny."

"Free? Me?" Buff blinked. "Laws, suh, Ah wooden know

306

how ack. Couldn't Ah b'long to you, suh? You's de quality."

"If that's the way you want it, we'll see. Hannibal in there?"

Taking the basket, David moved further away from the dusty road, to the shade of a big chestnut. When he lifted the cover his heart swelled. The red gamecock was lying on his side, beak resting on the bottom of the basket. A single ruby drop glistened on its point. The bird's feathers of burnished bronze were barely stirring.

"How—how did this happen?" David demanded through a sudden blur of tears.

" 'Twas dem new fangled cutleries dat major man 'sisted on, sur," Buff muttered, awed to see tears slipping down a white man's cheeks. "Ah done told you Ah was 'feared ob dem. Wahn't mah fault, suh, 'deed hit wahn't."

"No. Of course not. It was my fault—all my fault. You just did as you were told. You find out who insisted on steel spurs?"

Buff, in the acme of distress, raised a crumpled shred of a felt hat and scratched the fuzz on his skull. "Mebbe you-all doan' remember, suh, but dey wuz a English officer on de ol' 'Sistance? Hit wuz him."

"Bouquet, by God!" David's eyes lost their whites. They looked black as smutty fingerprints in his thin face. His whole body set up a gentle trembling.

"Yassuh. He 'low he fit our way an' los', so he say 'Fight mah way, Black Boy, er Ah turns you ovah to de Sheriff man.' "

David said nothing, only slid the cover farther off the basket. When the warm sunlight struck the gamecock, a breeze beating down the glassy river lightly ruffled his feathers. He stirred a little. Half a hundred fights were mirroring themselves in David's memory. Battles at Belle Meade, Bizarre, Powhatan, Truxton, and big mains in Baltimore and Wilmington, North Carolina. Never once had Hannibal so much as flinched. Game clean through! Big, small, tough and tender, he'd licked them all. And now he was dying. There could be no doubt about it. The rose of his lacerated comb was fading to a dim pinkish-gray.

"*Cuck! Cuck!*" David called softly. "Remember me, little warrior?"

One sherry-red eye raised a translucent film shielding it from the light. Hannibal lifted his head the merest fraction of an inch then, wearily, it sank again. The ruby drop dripped from his beak and smeared the wickerwork.

6 — MADELAINE

ELI HASKINS, corporal of the 4th squad in Captain Knowlton's company, had the bluest nose and the reddest cheeks David had ever seen. He was jolly and plump and surprisingly efficient. Quite the reverse was Johnny Gilmorin's corporal, Hiram Edgell, a lean and bitter Methodist circuit rider. Johnny figured his corporal was fighting the Church of England just as hard as he was fighting the Ministerial troops; maybe more so.

Billy Colgate, youngest of the 4th squad, immediately attached himself to the good-humored Virginian. Perhaps it was the cadences of David's rich drawling voice which attracted him; Billy loved music, was already known as the spriest fiddler in Greenwich County. Barely seventeen, he had deserted an apothecary's shop in Stanford to carry his grandfather's four bore ducking gun after General Putnam's thumping drums.

"I'm sorry," Captain Knowlton had said, "but we can't enlist your black friend."

"Friend?" David had stiffened. "What do you mean, sir? He's just a nigger—a *damned* good one!"

"We don't allow swearing in the orderly room." Knowlton's black brows met over his beak of a nose. Like a majority of company commanders in a more than generally religious army, he discouraged profanity at all times. "About enlisting Negroes—the Congress has not yet adopted a policy. Of course, if he wants to hang around and make himself useful, he is welcome to his food and keep." Just the trace of a smile tugged at the corner of the Connecticut captain's mouth.

Two o'clock of the afternoon of Thursday, June 15th, found David stripped to the waist and perspiring heavily over a bullet mould. He reckoned Johnny was lucky. Johnny had been detailed to visit the armorer of a Massachusetts company with an armful of disabled muskets. He was also to get a worn-out pan cover spring replaced on the Spanish fuzee left behind by the Connecticut man whose mother needed him.

On such a warm day it was hot work melting down pewter mugs and ladles, leaden saltcellars, ink wells, and porringers. One and all they were chucked into an iron melting pot. David worked the bellows hard and the metal bubbled like silver soup. When it was hot enough, the alloy was run into a series of hand moulds. Belying sectionalism, patriotic residents of Weston had that day presented the Connecticut men with a pillowcase full of precious odds and ends. One tiny porringer drew a wry smile to David's lips. It was engraved, "G. D. B. to H. B. B.—1732."

When the lead had solidified, Haskins pried open the moulds and dropped the hot castings, hissing, into a pail of water.

"Why do we run all this buckshot?" David queried, blowing a drop of sweat from the tip of his nose. "I should think musket balls would be what's needed."

Haskins shifted his quid and spat into the fire. "Wal, when we was fighting the French and Injuns outside of Quee-bec, we most gen'rally used to drop six buckshot in under a musket ball. They fans out effective-like."

"My God," David grunted. "I should think so!"

"Yep. Sometimes you kin kill three men with one shot—especially Injuns without no clothes. They fights that way, most of 'em—Mohawks and Senecas in partiklar. Hey, Edgell! Where you find them rain spouts? Thought there warn't one left to this whole blamed college."

The Methodist had appeared in the doorway, dust-covered, panting, and lugging several lengths of twisted lead pipe. For once a grin was creasing the circuit rider's flat brown countenance.

"Verily, a judgment is come to pass! Brother, these here ain't rain spouts. They are organ pipes out of the Episcopal church of Cambridge! Praise ye the Lord for granting us Church of England lead to knock off Episcopal devils!"

Chuckling, the Reverend Edgell dropped a number of blue-gray tubes onto the floor; the resulting thump made the windows rattle. David, working hard at the bellows, noted

309

how carefully the Reverend Edgell laid aside his organ pipes.

When it came their turn to be melted down, Edgell collected all the resulting bullets and with his own hands used huge iron shears to clip off the sprew, or neck, by which hot lead was run into the mould. Humming a lugubrious hymn, the circuit rider finally smoothed down the resultant rough areas with a little file. Said he to Billy Colgate,

"When you load, son, remember to ram the ball home with the sprew facing up. Your ball will fly straighter then."

David winked at Haskins and the corporal said, "Reverend, there's a puncheon of water in the hall. I allow we could all stand a little drink. It's hotter than Tophet in here."

The instant Edgell's lanky figure, funereal in dusty black coat and breeches, had disappeared, David sprang up and seized the Episcopal bullets. For these he substituted the meltings of some pewter wine jugs and a woman's comfit box.

Haskins looked up under shaggy brows. "You are Church of England, I take it?"

David nodded, plumped the bag of bullets into a corner. "Reckon it's only fair and fitting for a churchman to fire his own style of bullet?"

"Fair enough. I'm Baptist."

After the 4th squad's evening meal of roast fowl, potâtoes and suet pudding David sent Buff skirmishing for blankets. If Buff proved as adept at pilfering as most of his race, he and Johnny should sleep warm, though they hardly needed coverings in such fine summer weather.

Dusk was more than a presentiment and an afterglow tinted purple the roofs of Cambridge; in fields and orchards surrounding the village, fires glowed brighter and the odors of wood smoke and cooking food hung heavy in the air.

David was passing a lovely little brick church—Holden Chapel—when Johnny dashed up in ecstasy.

"Davey! Davey! What do you think? Over by the Common there's a uniformed company!"

"The devil you say!" David was Virginian enough to be stirred. "What colors?"

"—I talked to their Lieutenant and if Captain Knowlton will let us go, he has promised to make you a sergeant and me a corporal next week! He has some enlistments expiring.

310

He said he could most likely get us commissions inside a month!"

"Some people are born damned fools and never outgrow it," David addressed the chapel's entrance. "Bet you've just been getting measured for regimentals."

From his pocket Johnny pulled two shreds of cloth. His light blue eyes were sparkling. "The uniform's bright blue like this, turned up with scarlet like this. Brass buttons and gold lace on the officers' hats. They're right trig."

"—And from where might this peacock company come?"

"Connecticut!" Johnny cried. "From Wethersfield! We could still be under old Put."

"What do you mean—'old Put'? I believe, sir, you speak of your commanding general?"

"Well, his own men call him that, don't they?" He went on without pausing. "There's a dandy tailor over on Brattle Street. He only asked five dollars earnest money on my tunic and he took all the measurements. Said he could convert it to an officer's uniform easy enough."

"—In other words, we still have no shirts, no stockings, no cooking kettle?"

Johnny's fine features grew dark with embarrassment. "Why—why, Davey, I'm right sorry 'bout that. I'll give it back out of my first pay."

"All right." David felt disinclined to quarrel; it was so fine to be free once more. "I'll get those things tomorrow. Know something? Wish to God we had our Independent Company up here. Damned if I can see how General Ward makes out without cavalry of any sort."

"Neither do I," agreed Johnny. "Say, Davey, you told Tom Knowlton what Buff said about the British and Charles Town?"

"Yes. But he didn't take much stock in it. Said rumors like that are a penny a hundred."

Johnny slapped his friend between the shoulders. "You got enough to buy us a couple of drinks? I'm drier than a charity sermon."

"Reckon so."

"Then why don't we go out and celebrate? Man alive! Last night at this time we were in jail! Just louse and flea pastures."

David nodded. A drink would go right well. All day he had been feeling mighty low over Hannibal. He reckoned he would never own another chicken like him.

The Blue Anchor was so jammed one had literally to fight one's way into that same taproom in which Lord Percy had, not so long ago, rested on his way to Lexington.

Eyes smarting, half suffocated by billows of rank tobacco smoke and heat, David tried to elbow a path towards the rear of the room. But he could not. Hemmed in by eager listeners, a politician was making a speech from the top of a billiard table. Both Southerners immediately paused. Like most Virginians, they dearly loved oratory for its own sake, fairly reveled in a telling stream of invective. David realized at once that this was no parliamentary address. The big-featured orator up there was in deadly earnest; his face glistened with effort.

"He's a member of the Committee of Safety," someone replied to Johnny's query.

"—And I say again, each one of you is doubly armed! The minions of Parliament have their weapons, but you not only have firelocks, but the Lord God fighting on your side. Lord North's hirelings march only for base silver and gold, but you go forward for our freedom and for our very lives!" The Committeeman waved his arms. "Shall we become paupers? Shall we fall slaves to the East India Company, like the miserable Sepoys of India? Never! Shall we permit the King's godless and debauched ministers to fatten forever on the fruits of our toil?"

"Never!" A shout went up, momentarily stilling all other noises in the tavern.

The speaker jabbed a tobacco-yellowed forefinger at one upturned face after another. "You! You and you! Will you lay your necks beneath the proud heel of General Gage? Aye, and the necks of your children?"

"No!"

"Of course not! That is why you have come here under arms! That is why more patriots will march and keep on marching until the tyrants are driven into the sea and destroyed as were proud Pharaoh's chariots!"

"Hurrah! That's telling 'em, Esek!"

"We have petitioned, humbly, decently, to the Throne," the orator resumed in a lower voice. "To what effect? I ask you—to what effect? Jeers! Abuse! The ruin of our shipping, the theft of all New England's trade."

He fell briefly silent.

"Fellow Americans, I declare before God Almighty, we

must fight for our very existence—all of us!" Haloed by smoke, the Committeeman glared down from his vantage point. "I tell you the British *must* be kept in Boston! If they march out and beat us, the bloody-backs will ravage and burn all the country, just like Injuns. They will shoot down our people in cold blood. You remember Concord? Lexington?"

A deafening clamor was his answer.

"Well, we licked them there and, with God's help, we can lick them again!"

The crowd was still yelling when the speaker climbed down and, after nodding to a few acquaintances, disappeared into the street. They heard him begin a fresh harangue on the far side of the square.

David threw back his head, sniffling loudly. By God, it was good to smell tavern smells. How often in jail he'd have pledged his very soul for a brandy sling, a gin swizzle, or even a glass of plain rye whiskey. Militiamen of all ranks were, in a general and heterogeneous democracy, standing each other to drinks.

"You said you had money?" Johnny prompted.

"Yes. But we will spend just a half crown."

"Call me a spy, will yez? By gobs, I'll smack that snout av yours 'round so far 'twill mate yer ear!"

When a tumult in a far corner grew louder. David slapped his side. "Sounds like our wild Irishman. Come on!"

They found Shaun Mahoney in a bad spot. Three hulking Yankees were ringing him around. Others stood ready.

Said one, "Let's search the damned Harp. He's a spy, I tell you!"

Mahoney's flat red face was tense, but he wasn't the least bit frightened. His longer upper lip slid back in a wicked smile.

"Stand back, ye bottle-nosed herring chokers! 'Tis me will take yez on wan at a time and ram them lies back down yer throats!"

With other plans in mind, David pushed forward. Smiling, he said quietly, "Gentlemen, you make a mistake."

"Och!" Mahoney sprang towards him, hand outstretched. " 'Tis Mr. Ashton himself, an' Mr. Gilmorin."

"And who might you be?" A black-bearded sergeant who wore his hair cropped unstylishly short turned, frowning.

Though he felt plenty riled by the sergeant's truculent tone, David was at pains to remain affable.

313

"I, my friend, am one of three prisoners—all good patriots —whom Mahoney here freed from Boston jail last night. In celebration of that feat, suppose you gentlemen join me in a drink?"

The calm persuasiveness of David's manner seemed to make acceptance of the invitation imperative. Soon the three Massachusetts soldiers were raising a popular new song entitled "Yankee Doodle."

At the end of it David moved over to a table. "After nearly half a year in prison, I fear I have near forgot the feel of cards. Even so, could I interest you gentlemen in a friendly little game? Whist perhaps?"

"Don't know it."

"Loo?"

"Never heard of it."

"Well then, it must be pharo. I take it for granted you gentlemen know pharo?"

"Cards," the black-bearded sergeant announced, "are the Devil's handmaidens." He stalked off.

At the end of an hour only David and Mahoney remained in the game.

At last the Irishman growled, "Wurrah! Wurrah!" and flung down his cards. "Faith, I just can't beat yez. 'Tis a wizard ye' are, Mr. Ashton, and thirty pound it's cost me mither's handsomest son to find it out."

"In that case, Mahoney, perhaps you had better hang onto the other seventy pounds? And now, my friends, let us drink deep from anything but the Pierian spring!"

David realized he was feeling pretty high. Under normal conditions he could have handled twice as much brandy as he already had aboard. Why, he would never even have felt it; but his long abstinence had fooled him.

Johnny, too, must have been feeling his cups, for he strayed away immediately they quitted the Blue Anchor.

Everywhere flew rumors. The British were sending three great armies to America. One was to be composed exclusively of Russians. If John Hancock, Sam Adams and the other leading makers of the Association were caught they would be sorry. General Gage had sworn to hang them on the spot. A great battle had been fought in New York, someone declared.

"That's a bloody lie," retorted another man. "I was there that day. There wasn't any battle."

Sniffed at by stray dogs, drunken militiamen lay snoozing in shop doorways. Others squatted on the granite curbs gambling in rings of light cast by lanterns set on the ground. Mahoney muttered something about "pressing a petticoat" and became lost in the throng of sunburned men in shirt sleeves and manure-smelling breeches.

David took a swig from a bottle of brandy he'd bought and, standing still, laughed right out until passersby gaped at him. Gad! He was feeling more like his old self than he had in months! Who-e-ee! He took another pull of brandy, shivering as the liquid grated on his throat. Yah—yah—e-e-e-o! He gave the view halloo, then checked himself with an effort.

Pretty tavern—good, that pharo. Mahoney—no gambler. Now he'd won back—money to buy decent gear. Could you buy a commission in this crazy Provincial army? Ha! Ha! Mahoney would have to cut down on his program. He'd probably leave out buying the farm.

God's teeth, but he was feeling fine—simply elegant! What a glorious warm night—stirred a fellow's vitals. No stink of stale straw. No delirious singing from some cell down the corridor. He stopped again and laughed over the way he had taken Mahoney. What else had that crazy Irishman intended doing? Oh, yes! Go to bed for a week. Typical Irish brag. Not even Sampson could. Good brandy. Find a wench? Why not? Six months, by Gad, without so much as a kiss! His breath came quicker.

Eagerly he bore down on a group of New Hampshire men beckoning from the glow of a hut cleverly constructed of sods and canvas.

"I'm going to challenge Gage—call him out," he announced. "He's no gen'leman. I'll lick him, that's what!"

"Hurray!" cried the New Hampshire men. "Come in, pardner. That talks like good likker."

"Sure is. Brandy. Have some?" He plunked himself on a food locker and, with alcoholic frankness, spoke of his trouble.

"Comin' in from drill I noticed a gal lookin' at us," volunteered a gap-toothed youth with a squint.

"You did? Where?"

"Out on the west edge of town—on the road to Concord. She was peeking out the blinds this afternoon lookin' kind of longing like at the boys. Maybe I'm wrong; she didn't say anything. Lives in a little brown stone house."

"Pretty?"

"Yep—kind of. Big brown eyes."

"Brown eyes are beau'ful," David announced. "I love brown eyes."

As if following a line of thought, David then said, "Gen'leman, le's drink to Virginia, God bless her!"

"Sure. Who's Virginia?" asked the gap-toothed boy. Everybody laughed and laughed. Then they began laughing all over again; when the brandy bottle had completed its circuit of the squad it was much lighter.

All at once David remembered Katie. By God, he sure wished he had Katie handy tonight. Katie Tryon. What a bloody fool he'd been never to take her, and she honing to slide in bed with him. Would have, any time, if he had even so much as crooked a finger. What the devil had become of her after her owners took her away? Funny, he could remember how once the sun had struck her yellow hair when she was opening his window.

He got up, giving the squad an owlishly grave "Good night." Further out on the Concord road he took another good nip. After the noise of Cambridge it was pleasant to be out here on the edge of the village. Only the crickets and the smell of new hay—a whippoorwill somewhere.

Gad, he certainly was hanging on a beauty! But when he swayed a bit, he straightened up. Gen'lemen didn't stagger. He wasn't drunk, not really. Just feeling fine, fine as silk. Breathing a little harder than was necessary, he set off down a dusty road, tripping now and then over bits of debris. A lot of people must have passed this way. He came across a small dead dog lying on the roadside; apparently it had been run over. Damn. The road was swaying just enough to make him concentrate. Must be getting late. In the distance campfires were burning down to sleepy blurs of crimson.

After another pull David decided on his course. It was very simple. If he saw a light at the brown house, he would go up and knock. If there wasn't any, he was going back to Chamber 34, Hollis Hall. He reckoned he wasn't really drunk or he could not have remembered that number.

When at last he saw the house, a small square affair hiding under two tall walnut trees, he was aware of his body as no body at all—just one terrible, burning hunger. He used his fingers to comb his dark hair. Must look nice. Mechanically he fumbled for nonexistent lace at his wrists, then reset the plain black stock about his throat. In rapid succession he gulped deep breaths of the night air. He would say very politely, "Excuse me, Madam, I wonder if I might have—" Have what? What would a man be asking for at ten of the night? Milk? Tea? Food?

Damn! No light. Standing at the end of a short walk leading up from the road, he vacillated. No light. Wouldn't that beat the Dutch? After six months, no light! No girl.

He was about to take another drink when he noticed a faint gleam penetrating a shutter to the left of the front door. Allowing himself no time to reconsider, he crammed the bottle into his pocket, marched right up to the door and knocked. No answer. He knocked again, harder.

His heart hammered louder than echoes resounding faintly inside. No one appeared. He waited, counting twenty slowly. Rapped again. "Always rap three times," the wags of Norfolk used to say. Suppose an angry farmer answered the door? He started away. No, damn it, he wasn't going! He was anyhow going to talk to that gal with the brown eyes. Maybe he could talk her into it. Impulses tightened his wrists. A step? Yes. A line of light wavering under the door. Silence. He had poised his knuckles to knock again when he heard a woman's voice.

"Who—who is there?"

"David Trelawney, Ma'am, of Williamsburg, Virginia," he announced with portentous gravity. David Trelawney for years had been his *nom d'amour*.

A chain rattled before the door opened just a crack and the light of a single candle revealed a not unattractive young woman in a neat brown dress with a white kerchief pinned crosswise over her breast. The New Hampshire boy was right; she had brown eyes. Big ones. This girl was so very small she reminded him of Rob's wife, Peggy.

"What—what do you require, sir?"

Milk? Tea? Food— Hell! All he could do was gape, smiling all the time. Her complexion delighted him; it was golden-buff like a bee's wing.

"Why—why, I was wondering—" He stood there, almost filling the door frame. Slightly parted lips gave his mouth an eager boyish expression. His eyes, still sunken, were master-

317

ful, yet at the same time appealing and avid of kindness. She was so demure and genteel looking David was sure he'd made a bad mistake until he noticed just a trace of paint on her lips.

"What do you think I want?"

The girl in brown looked at him slowly and candle light beating upward revealed a pulsing throat, the outline of strong high breasts, and a short and passionate upper lip. She caught her breath and her shoulders sagged.

"Pray come in, Mr. Trelawney," she invited with a forlorn attempt at jauntiness. "After all, I have been trying to get up my courage to say this all day. Somehow, to you it seems not so—so strange."

At any other time this would have given David pause, but long starved months and French brandy— He bowed formally and entered, closing the door behind him.

Once she had replaced the chain, she peered at him wide-eyed and fear crept into her expression. "Oh, sir. Have you never—am I so dreadful?"

He recalled the London manner. "My dear, I vow you—you are exquisite, a positive goddess!"

Dark lashes etched against her cheeks, she stood quite still, lips moist, a-tremble. He was so handsome, yet so hard about the eyes and mouth. But the way his dark hair tumbled over his forehead! His uneven brows both fascinated and frightened her.

He clasped her so fiercely she cried out softly, "Oh, sir, please!"

He remembered amenities. "I—I have with me some cognac," he told her in a voice unfamiliar to himself. "Would you care to try a little?"

"I would rather have some food," the girl murmured. "But let that pass."

For the first time he noticed faint blue shadows beneath her eyes, but just now they only made her the more intriguing; they were like faint reflections of her smooth, wing-like brows.

"Where shall we find some glasses, my dear?"

"My name is Madelaine," the young woman told him nervously. She began to pump water from a pump built over the sink. The candle light was poor but it revealed neat ankles and small feet. Madelaine turned, resting both hands on the edge of the sink behind her. So perfect was the circle of white around her pupils they reminded David of owl's eyes when she said in a barely audible tone, "You—have money? A little money?"

"Is that enough?" Hurriedly he placed three gold sovereigns on a checkered cloth on the kitchen table. The drip of the pump tinkled into a basin set below it.

She nodded, then drew a deep breath like a swimmer wading into cold water. "You are very generous—darling. Tell me, do you really like me?"

For a moment he did not move—did not dare. Still he could not believe after so many tortured, barren hours that an end had come to them. And in such a delightful way. Miracle of miracles! This girl, all warm and soft, was going to be his in a very few moments. All his. He could do with her as he pleased. He could feel the blood surging up into his head as he tilted brandy into two glasses. Hers he diluted with water. His hand was shaking so the bottle neck jingled against the rim of the tumbler.

"Here—drink it. It is good."

The liquor brought color rushing into Madelaine's cheeks and when he beckoned her to come and sit on his lap, she did so.

"Oh, my dear, I'm so glad it was you. You are kind— not beastly," Madelaine sighed, but her hand quivered in smoothing his cheek.

Great warm currents eddied about his brain. Again and again he crushed her mouth in voracious kisses. "Darling!" The softness of her arms and scented firmness at the base of her throat. Lower. In his eagerness to undo a pin securing the kerchief concealing her bare breasts, he tore it.

They lay on the bed, lax, exhausted. A great greenish-white star looking in an open window sketched a dim high light on the girl's forehead, ever so faintly outlined the contours of a small breast. It was a warm night.

"Look," said he presently, "do you see that greenish star?"

Drowsily her head moved against his shoulder. "Yes. It is very lovely."

"I'd like to take it out of the sky, darling," he murmured, "and tuck it into your hair."

"I'd always wear your green star, David."

He drew her closer. "I know, but suppose we leave it up in the sky where we both can look at it? It will still be our own private star."

"Always," she breathed.

Presently she said, "I didn't catch your whole name. Please don't be angry. I was so worried. What is it?"

"Ashton," said he before he could think.

"David Ashton? That's a nice sounding name, I think."

"Why did you speak of food a while back?"

"Because, dear, I haven't had much to eat—not for nearly two days," came the simple reply. "I am a Tory and a Tory's widow. None of my God-fearing neighbors will sell me anything."

"A widow?"

"Yes. My world ended two months ago. At Lexington. My husband was killed in the retreat." She raised slim naked arms and, locking fingers under her head, talked to the great greenish star. "That is why—I must find money to get away —to England."

David murmured, "I have more gold—a lot more of it. Enough, I think. I need you, Madelaine—dear God—I do— kiss me."

7 — BENEDICTION

THE 4th squad of Captain Knowlton's company was busy making as many cartridges as it could from a miserably insufficient issue of powder. When each man drew only a gill of the coarse black stuff, David cocked his eyebrow.

"Is that all? God's teeth! Down in Virginia a man takes more than this to a turkey shoot!"

"Wish to God we was going turkey shooting," Haskins grunted. "How's that Tower musket you drew?"

A few choice blasphemies expressed David's contempt of all smooth bore muskets in general and of this specimen in particular.

"How in blazes do the British expect a man to hit anything with no rear sight?" he fumed. "Damn' thing weighs fifteen pounds and won't shoot straight beyond sixty yards. You can't hit the broad side of a barn with this damned thing."

Curious, Billy Colgate came over. "What you doing with that wire?"

"Rigging a rear sight of sorts," snapped the Virginian, twisting some strands of copper wire into a loop just forward

of the lock. "It's mighty poor, but it's better than nothing."
He sighed down the cumbersome brown barrel. What
wouldn't he give to lay hands on the long-barreled Deckhard he had left in Tom MacSherry's care? Up to two hundred yards he could give these serious-talking Yankees a
shooting lesson.

Johnny from the next room called, "Hi! Any cartridge
paper in there? We're fresh out."

Around five of the afternoon an orderly, running streams
of sweat from under his wig, came clumping up into the
North Entry of Hollis Hall and inquired for the commanding
officer. Alert in an instant, Knowlton came out, thin-lipped
mouth still full of bread and honey.

"What is it?"

"General Ward says you should fall in your men on the
parade ground right away," the orderly puffed. "No fifes or
drums. Bring along any axes or spades you've got." With that
the messenger spun on his heel and went clumping off. He
walked on the sides of his boots as if his feet hurt.

"That's a newfangled way of delivering marching orders,"
Captain Knowlton complained. "Bellinger!" He licked his
fingers free of honey and went behind his desk. "The company will fall in within fifteen minutes. Every man will carry
at least five flints and as much powder and ball as he can lay
hold of. Lieutenant Bisley will take command of this detachment. I'm riding over to Inman's farm."

"Hey! What about food, Cap'n?" called Billy Colgate from
the stairs.

"Let the men bring whatever is handy," Knowlton advised. "They may get fed—but more likely they won't."

Drums rattled in all directions. Voices shouted. The Harvard Yard began to fume with activity. Out on the edge of
town conch shells carried as bugles by the Salem company,
began to moan. They made an eerie sound.

"Say, Cap'n, where are we goin' to?" presently demanded
Bellinger. Tucking a pen above his ear, he handed over a
page of instructions written in a flowing hand. It was as neat
as copperplate.

" 'We?' You're not going," Knowlton said shortly, buckling
on his sword.

Bellinger's permanently rounded shoulders bent and when

he straightened, he had in his hand a huge bell-mouthed blunderbuss such as boarding parties of men-of-war carried.

Said he, squinting over the square lenses of his spectacles, "Listen to me, Tom Knowlton; them Britishers' damned stamp tax ruined my stationery business and last month they broke my press to bits. If you think I'm not going along, you're plumb addled!"

The captain started to get mad, but being a good officer, laughed instead. "Very well, get your tail shot off, then!"

"Where we heading?" Bellinger persisted, cramming into his pockets a supply of cartridges.

"Your guess is as good as mine, Joe. This may be only one of those practice marches General Putnam is always hollering for."

An interval of more or less orderly haste ensued. It was punctuated by the frantic curses of soldiers searching their bedding straw for items of equipment.

Some found it strange that the company's newest recruit, though penniless and with only a swollen jaw and a missing tooth to show for a night's fun, should turn up so completely outfitted. Knowlton merely smiled. He felt small concern regarding Shaun Mahoney's ability to look out for himself. In the regulars soldiers got that way.

Already the parade ground swarmed with militiamen attempting to locate their units. Fanning themselves with wide farmer's hats and sober black tricorners, the Provincial army stood mustered in long lines, subdivided into companies and regiments. Bits of straw sticking to their clothes gave a lot of them a ludicrous, bucolic appearance. Not a few had caught chaff in their hair.

Self-important junior officers walked about, scarlet-faced, bellowing through cupped hands. "Shake a foot, you dunderheads!" "Gerrish's regiment this way!" "Whitcomb's men here!" "Prescott's men fall in here!"

Under a big maple stood old General Artemas Ward; he was too sick to sit a horse. Nervously he tapped the ground with an ivory-headed walking stick. Now and then he would bend over and trace a design on the earth to illustrate some point to one of his staff.

Three-deep, hot and excited officers clustered about the Commander-in-Chief. Dumpy little Colonel Bridge, blowing out his fat cheeks; General Putnam, hearty, big-faced and bellicose; Colonel Samuel Gerrish dressed to the nines in a snowy white tie wig, mulberry suit and an elegant French walking sword; Joseph Frye, newly appointed, but not yet commissioned Major-General. He looked somber and uneasy with this unfamiliar responsibility. Of more soldierly appearance was Colonel Gridley, hatchet-faced and standing very straight, as befitted a veteran of the Indian wars. He had just been designated commandant of "the regiment of the train"—of artillery.

Longest of all General Ward's head remained close to the white wig of Colonel William Prescott, a bold-appearing man with dark eyes and swarthy complexion. David almost laughed aloud when he first saw the Massachusetts Army's principal colonel. Of all things to wear on a march, Prescott had elected to don a bright blue and tan banyan—a sort of dressing gown! Around this he had fastened a belt very tight and had jammed under it a long French dueling rapier; even in its scabbard the weapon looked scarcely thicker than a tooth pick.

There were other colonels; David Brewer, Paul Sargent, Jonathan Ward were standing under the maple in a big hayfield northwest of the village—lately the troops had taken to parading around it. The sunset dappled their solemn expressions. All the staff was in civilian clothes except General Ward. No doubt he had felt it his duty, as Commander-in-Chief, to put on a militia uniform of faded blue.

Johnny bent forward from his place in the adjoining squad. "Hey, David! There they are! That's where we ought to be!"

"Wal, burn my pants! Ain't that pretty!" "Bet the redcoats runs a mile when they sees you!"

Raucous uproar followed the progress of the Wethersfield company towards their post. The Connecticut men, despite sheepish expressions, looked quite impressive and encouragingly martial in their cocked hats, blue and red uniforms and carefully pipeclayed gaiters and crossbelts. Wonder of wonders, they had even been equipped with cartouche boxes and bayonets!

Johnny scowled, "Ain't this just my luck? Going to war looking like a confounded rag-picker!"

A great majority of the Provincial troops were in homespun: gray, brown and neutral. Many favored three-cornered hats. The evening being sultry, they wore their coats knotted about their waists. Hardly any type of firearm manufactured within the past hundred years was not represented in the ranks, but, as far as David could see, there was not a single rifle in sight!

An hour passed and still the Provincials waited about in the dusk. Finally, the last stragglers showed up.

"Must be at least three thousand of us," Billy Colgate cried, white-eyed.

Mahoney ran a practiced eye over the muster. "Sonny, if there is here wan man over a thousan' I'll kiss yer butt before the whole brigade." Turning solemn, the Irishman tilted his flat, rather comical face in Corporal Haskin's direction. "Faith 'tis wings ye'd best be fitting to yer feet. God help these poor bhoys whin they faces up wid regulars. *Wurrah!* If he wasn't down to his last sixpence, Shaun Mahoney would niver be finding himself here!"

A drum, then another, commenced beating the long roll, exacting silence. When they had done, General Ward, leaning heavily on his stick and looking very haggard, limped out to face an army gathered in a great half moon.

He spoke briefly, succinctly, like a soldier. He reminded them of the heavy part they and their fathers had taken in long and victorious wars against the Frenchmen and the savages. The British, he told them, must be kept penned in Boston! There, General Gage's troops could do little harm. But once they got into the open country, the eighth plague of Egypt would be as nothing. He was, on the orders of the Committee of Safety, sending them on a mission of vital importance. No man was to flinch in his duty; it was not in the English tradition to shirk. They were to march at once.

No oratory, no fire-eating, David noted. Just a plain statement of fact.

The Commander-in-Chief turned heavily to a straight, handsome old man in a black surplice.

"Dr. Langdon, will you lead us in prayer?"

The snowy-haired president of Harvard stepped forward. Removing his scholar's cap, he knelt and clasped his hands before him. Slowly he raised tight-shut eyes to the evening sky. Hats whispered off by the hundred as militiamen followed suit, saving only those adhering to some denomination which forbade kneeling.

Mahoney fumbled until he found a rosary. That was no proper priest there, he reflected, but he might as well draw a ration of salvation with the rest. As Dr. Samuel Langdon commenced to pray, beads began to slip through the deserter's calloused fingers.

"O Heavenly Father," the old man's deep and reverent voice rang far out over the crowded field, "grant to these, Thy unworthy servants, Thy blessing. Grant to them strength each man to do his part. Comfort those which are in fear, O Lord, and support them in their hour of trial.

"Make the light of Thy Countenance to shine upon their arms, O Lord, and grant wisdom to their leaders. I do humbly beseech Thee to grant eternal salvation to any of Thy servants who may be called in judgment before Thy Awful Throne. Forgive them their many trespasses against Thy law, O Lord, and sustain Thy servants as they enter into the Valley of the Shadow of Death. For the sake of our Lord Jesus Christ, Amen."

For some instants the army, the staff beneath the maple and the townsfolk hemming them in, remained kneeling. Then, to a great rattle and clanking of accoutrements, they followed Dr. Langdon's example and got to their feet.

8 — NIGHT MARCH

"ATTEN-SHUN! Shoulder firelocks!" bawled Lieutenant Bisley, trying to imitate Tom Knowlton's way of giving orders.

When hands slapped stocks in a quick succession of miniature reports, Johnny felt a tingle race the length of his spine. He had never stood straighter, had never shouldered a musket more smartly. His high-strung features were tense. At last! Here at last was the first thin taste of a soldier's career. It was somehow poetic, he felt, to begin as a simple private. Next week a corporal's rank; within a month a sergeancy; then, having won his spurs on the battlefield, surely a cornet's or an ensign's commission! Later would come a position on the staff. He would climb up and up, like Grand Uncle Arthur who died, a Lieutenant-General, in Seringapatam. But he wished to blazes he was wearing a certain red and blue uniform already cut out at the tailor's.

"Forward—march!"

The Connecticut detachment picked up the cadence of drums massed back of the staff. To "The Pioneer's March" they followed Colonel Prescott's fine Massachusetts regiment out of the field. The march was towards the Charles Town road, towards the British in Boston! Johnny's heart sailed like a buck clearing a windfall.

Colonel Prescott's horse got frightened and broke wind with a shattering blast. A great roar of belly laughter rang in the ranks.

"I hear Billy Prescott's brought him along a bugler," Haskins hollered, and Lieutenant Bisley glared at him.

Now that the troops were in columns David had further opportunity to appreciate the extraordinary disorganization of the Provincial forces, the disparity in their numbers. In some companies marched as few as twenty or thirty men; others mustered nearly a hundred, approximately the strength of other regiments. Nowhere could he see any flags or any insignia for the officers, beyond hastily improvised brassards. A few veterans wore a blanket rolled about their shoulders and the same experienced men carried a majority of the water bottles.

The 4th squad became but a minor ripple in a black river of men streaming northeast out of Cambridge along the inland road. The sullen rumble of wagon wheels grew loud in their ears.

"Left right, left right!" Corporal Haskins, slogging along bent-shouldered, wondered where they'd be a night hence. It was queer to be up so late. It must be almost nine. Usually him and Dorcas would be sound asleep and snoring by this time. Jerusha! How Dorcas had took on when he marched away across the north field to the highroad. He missed her, too. Weren't any decent cooks in this army.

Before the troops were well clear of the village, continual halts and delays began. At such times the men would light pipes and sit by the roadside, speculating on what was likely to happen. The veterans lay down full length. Mahoney, too. Little Billy Colgate was yawning, but tried to hide it. Several men kept wanting to move their bowels.

Now and then a horseman went clumping back towards the village.

" 'Tis lucky we are 'tis a dark night," remarked Mahoney, puffing on a short clay pipe. "A blindman could see the dust we're raising clear across Amurica."

"Where's the captain?" the Reverend Edgell called.

"Gone ahead to talk with old Put," Haskins told him. "I allow we'll pick up the rest of our boys down the road a piece."

A rider came clattering up the road, bawling, "Out of my way! Out of my way! Important business!"

"That'll be Gerrish," somebody said. "The old rumble-gut's been drinking again. Bet he makes tracks if things get hot."

The farther the column marched, the slower became its progress. Towards ten o'clock all the infantry was ordered off the road and, after an interminable delay, a train of farm carts, loaded to the top with picks, shovels and spades, bumped by. Nowhere were any lanterns lit.

Though the sun had long since vanished it remained surprisingly hot, and tempers grew shorter as the slow miles unreeled. Always men kept passing up and down the column asking for this company or that regiment. It was seldom they got a right answer.

David, lying on the dew-wetted grass, became aware of an unforgettable obbligato in the tramp of feet, unnaturally lowered voices, the creak of leather gear and the occasional clank of musket barrels bumping. Fireflies danced over almost every clump of shrubbery.

From various fields along the route waiting units fell in, steadily augmenting the column's length. By the time the van of the army had passed a bridge over Willet's Creek, the river of men flowed as far back as one could see.

David decided it was typical of Knowlton and Israel Putnam that, when Mr. Inman's farm buildings hove in sight, the remainder of the Connecticut men were waiting just where they should be and ready to march. Unlike some units, they did not indulge in loud talk.

The nearer the Provincials drew to Charles Town Neck, the fewer grew the trees. Above and below the road the terrain was now composed of well-grazed pastures which soon resolved into a series of long smooth ridges.

"Golly!" Billy Colgate, who had started ahead to try to find a spring, stopped suddenly, gaping at a distant row of lights. They were small as fireflies. But they stayed put. "Look at that! Why, Boston's big as all get out!"

"—And full of Britishers, Bub."

"I ain't afeared of 'em," he called in his thin voice. But the boy wondered what he might do if a big grenadier came rushing at him with a bayonet.

From the crest of a low hill more men began to make out the lights of Boston blinking far away, across the Charles.

"No lights. No pipes," Knowlton kept warning.

It was good to have him back, David felt, and for future reference studied the Connecticut captain's bearing, his methods.

The axles of an overloaded cart began to give, creaking loudly. "Stop that wagon! You men take out the shovels!"

For the Connecticut regiment this accident proved a passport. Because they carried picks and shovels, they were passed up along the shadowy lines of men who cursed with envy.

"Them Connetycut horse thieves is going ahead to dig us a backhouse," drawled a nasal voice from the dark.

"No, we ain't," Haskins promptly retorted. "You twerps ain't got the decency to use one!"

A guffaw was quickly checked by Colonel Prescott's growl of, "Next man opens his mouth I'll break his jaw! How far back is Colonel Frye's regiment?"

No one knew.

The starlight was just strong enough on Charles Town Neck to let the Provincials glimpse wet boulders and seaweed littering beaches to either side. After all, the Neck was less than forty feet wide, so the army had to slow up and jam together to cross it dry shod. As the van passed on over and found room again in a wide field lying behind the loom of Bunker's Hill, some killdeers whistled. Charles Town, David learned, was built on the point of a spoon-shaped peninsula, dominated by two grassy treeless hills.*

At the foot of Bunker's Hill, General Israel Putnam and Colonels Prescott and Gridley were engaged in heated argument. Now and then one of them would refer to a map by

---

*Due to an error on the part of certain British Army cartographers, notably Montresor, Page, and de Bernière, Breed's Hill, lower and much nearer to Boston, was mismarked "Bunker's Hill." The real Bunker's Hill stood to the rear of Breed's Hill and was the scene of no fighting at all. Thus, the Battle of Bunker's Hill should properly be known as the Battle of Breed's Hill.—Author.

the light of a carefully hooded dark lantern. They were in deadly earnest. When he wasn't beating the palm of his left hand with his fist, Putnam, the Connecticut general, kept pointing towards Charles Town and Boston.

"Plague take a fort on Bunker's Hill!" he was rasping. "From Breed's Hill we can fire straight into Boston and singe Gage's wig. From Bunker's the range is too great, eh, Gridley?"

The engineer nodded reluctantly. "But there are no flanks to be covered and—"

Putnam's roundish face glowed a deep red. "To hell with the flanks! Gage will be too worried getting out of our range. Look!" He sank onto his heels and began jabbing at a map with the ferrule of his scabbard. "A battery on Breed's will drive the British ships out of the Mystic, out of the Charles, out of Boston Harbour—clear down to the Castle!"

Vehemently, Colonel Frye shook his head. "Nonsense! All you will accomplish is to sting Gage into action. A redoubt on Bunker's Hill would keep him where we want him—in Boston, and it wouldn't alarm him!"

"Where I want Gage," Putnam rasped, "is charging up to our muskets! There's been too confounded much shilly-shallying. Eh?"

Colonel Bridge had shoved forward a paper. "Those are the Committee of Safety's orders. Read them again, General." He was tired and the skin was gray around his mouth. "It says, 'A strong redoubt is to be raised on Bunker's Hill.' See? There it is. *Bunker's* Hill! 'With cannon planted to annoy the enemy coming out of Charles Town—'"

All at once Prescott, run out of the same mould as Israel Putnam, stooped over. His black eyes were hard and bright as he whispered into the Connecticut general's ear. Gridley fidgeted, stared anxiously out over the Mystic. The killdeers had fallen silent and only the grunting of bullfrogs in a mill pond off to the right broke the stillness. Uneasily, the troops on the beach and on the Neck waited.

Putnam got up, a hard grin on his mouth. "Gentlemen, we will obey the Committee's orders. We *will* fortify Bunker's Hill—after we have taken possession of Breed's Hill! Colonel Prescott will attend to it."

"You're a pig-headed old fool!" snarled Frye. "You'll get us all massacred."

"Silence! You'll answer for that later!"

"So will you!" Bridge cut in. "Look! A child can see how easy it is to get out-flanked on Breed's. I know! I have been there!"

Part II

Breed's Hill

1 — THE REDOUBT

"QUIET, for your lives!" A whispered warning passed from mouth to mouth down the column. "Men-of-war out there. They'll shoot the hell out of us if they take alarm." Last murmurs of conversation died away.

After their six-mile march along a road dusty even at night, the men were thirsty and dog-tired. They climbed Bunker's Hill in a long ragged line, sweating under picks, shovels and lugging timbers of which gun platforms would later be built.

Mahoney frowned, looked back on the Neck and the column writhing up from Fort Number Three on the mainland. "Sure and won't there be ould Satan to pay if we have to skeddadle back over this bottleneck two jumps ahead av a baynet?"

Marching in loose order, Knowlton's Company toiled over the side of Bunker's Hill and followed Prescott and Gridley down a long slope across a series of pastures separated by low fences built of glacial stones. In them cow droppings lay thick and the stones and the grass were so soaking with dew that the men were glad to get back onto a road even if it was only a cart track used at haying time. Passing under an occasional willow tree, the track led straight towards the lights of Boston.

The leading regiment proceeded in straggling fashion in two lines, each one following a rut. They passed some trees, then deserted the track once more and descended into a humid and mosquito-ridden little valley. An explanation for the pests was soon forthcoming for, in turning right, the column crossed a marshy field. The *suck-sucking* of muck sounded loud, somehow obscene. In it more than one shoe was lost. Over to the left, a few trees were dotting a long slope which rose gently towards the summit of a hill similar to, but smaller than Bunker's. None grew near the summit.

"Wait here and keep quiet!"

The Connecticut men dropped their implements, rested their muskets beside a rail fence and began to dig the marsh slime out of their footgear. After that they were only too glad to stretch out and stare up at the stars.

"Say, can anybody see a man-o'-war?" It was Bellinger, the company clerk. Though his blunderbuss was much heavier than most of the firearms, he had kept up very well considering his thin, badly bowed legs.

"There's one," Billy Colgate replied in a quivering whisper. "A great big sucker!"

"Where?" demanded a dozen voices. Several of them sounded nervous.

"If you'll sight right down this little valley, you can just make her out layin' off a point."

"Ye've good eyes, Bub," Haskins croaked. "I can't see a blessed thing."

So the enemy lay with shotted guns but half a mile away! The realization stung David's scalp. Removing his black, three-cornered hat, he rolled over on his stomach. He took care not to break powder charges, neatly rolled in newspaper, that were in his coat pockets. For a long time he studied the line of beach and water, shining the dullest imaginable silver under the stars, but could make out nothing except a series of stone fences. Then all at once he saw a tall-masted man-of-war, a brig.

Suddenly she seemed to dissolve in the gloom, to vanish completely. David tried a trick taught him long ago by an old Shawnee. He dropped his eyelids briefly then suddenly reopened them. The brig was even more clearly to be seen than before; even the sails furled on her yards, the streak along her side, and the black squares of gun ports interrupting it.

God's teeth, but he felt tired! He wondered how Johnny's martial spirit was bearing up. He reached down to rub the fetter scars on his ankles; they had begun to ache. This was hard going for men ill-fed and underexercised for six months. Damn! How handy the *Assistance*'s cargo would come in right now. When he remembered that he carried but eighteen rounds of munition he licked his lips slowly, thoughtfully.

Presently a man with a dark lantern came slipping and

sliding down from the summit of Breed's Hill. It was Colonel Prescott; the men immediately recognized him by his stature and straight carriage.

"Captain Knowlton?" he hailed in a cautious undertone.

"Here, sir!"

"Take your men and their tools to the top of Breed's Hill. Report to Colonel Gridley." And he hurried along the column.

The men began to sit up and look about.

"I don't feel so good," one of the Connecticut men announced suddenly. "I got a complaint in my bowels. Maybe I'd better go back?"

"I allow what you've got, Lem Barker, is the running complaint." Corporal Haskins spoke in a fierce undertone. "Just you bide where you are!"

Unhurriedly, Captain Knowlton knotted a white handkerchief about his arm. "You can see this. Come along." He picked up a spade and started slowly to breast the slope of Breed's Hill.

The 4th squad and the rest of the platoon scrambled after him with the long wet grass licking like little tongues. It soaked right through shoes and stockings. Gasping, they gathered at last on the hilltop and felt a faint breeze off the harbour fan their faces.

"See this line?" Old Colonel Gridley was showing Lieutenant Bisley and Captain Knowlton a white cord stretched over the earth in a straight line. "This marks the east wall of a redoubt. Dig down about four feet and throw the dirt towards Boston. Hurry! It will be dawn before we know it."

Other troops—Massachusetts men—came up carrying picks, mattocks and shovels—a lot of them. Under their captain's command the men awkwardly stacked arms.

Captain Knowlton pulled off his coat, spat on broad hands and drove his spade deep into the ground, saying. "Some of you fellows are dod-gasted clumsy with a firelock, but you ought to be Jim-dandies with a shovel. Remember one thing —if sunrise catches us above ground, we'll be nothing but a lot of dead heroes."

Dirt flew in a dark spray. Knowlton had been entirely right. With these tools the Connecticut farmers felt right at home.

Johnny paused, tore his shirt open and, gulping for air, grinned. "My God, you'd think there was gold down there!"

With an elbow David diverted an acid trickle of sweat from

his eyes. "Pity you haven't got your uniform along. You could break it in right quick."

"Hush up," warned the Reverend Edgell, "and dig."

On David's hands, softened even beyond their usual tenderness, blisters formed and broke, leaving raw patches. Though his body had become one great ache, he kept on swinging a pick. Damned if a Virginian should slack up before a pack of psalm-shouting Connecticut Yankees!

The raw earth smelt comforting, was heaping higher about the little redoubt. Every now and then some militiaman's spade would strike a rock and draw sparks. Prescott and Gridley strode about encouraging, scolding. They were everywhere.

Every half hour Captain Knowlton would lift a hand and call softly, "Catch your wind a while boys." He never seemed to get excited or tired. And he never swore.

For awhile the men would lie flat, chewing grass stems and listening to the long-drawn calls of sentries posted only twelve hundred yards away over in Boston. On men-of-war nearer but still swinging unalarmed to their anchors, the watch called, "All's well."

They were wrong. All was far from well. They'd damned soon find out, the grimy Provincials whispered. Johnny fell to wondering what was going on in the rear of the Provincial Army.

Distinctly the *plop!* of fish jumping in the river reached the diggers.

Towards dawn the dew fell so heavily Mahoney picked up his coat and wrapped it about the action of his firelock.

Said he, "Bhoys, this dew would drown the divil av a big tomcat. When the time comes, ye'd best dry yer flints and reprime entirely."

Long since, he had selected the most favorable route for his retreat. Definitely, he intended to be one of those few who would get away in time.

Farther back along the peninsula fresh groups of militia were blundering about, seeking their posts. David could catch the impatient undertones of their officers. To his right some Massachusetts men were certainly making the dirt fly.

"Time," Knowlton called. He got up and chose a pickaxe this time. Drive and swing. Drive and swing. Would Matt Phipp or John Brush or the other Norfolk patriots be willing to work like so many niggers in a ditch? Probably they would. They were in earnest, too. He would give a lot to see George Leavitt's face if he could happen by right now and find his boon companion naked to the waist and sweating like a pig.

Over in Boston a rooster crowed. Then another and another, sleepily. Not like Hannibal's fierce call. Poor Hannibal!

Somebody remarked, "It's going to get light any minute." As if to bear him out robins commenced to chirp among some apple trees at the foot of a slope to the left.

"Why don't somebody come up and spell us?" Bellinger demanded wearily.

"Yes. Why don't they?" Haskins said. "Why the hell should we do all the work for the army?"

Billy Colgate sank trembling onto a pile of dirt. "What chances for some food?"

"The hell wid food—'tis watter I want," Mahoney panted. "Ain't there no watter near?"

Captain Knowlton said to Johnny, "Gilmorin, suppose you scout around, see if you can locate a spring." The young Virginian was patently exhausted but he was so very game the captain felt sorry for him.

"Yes, sir," Johnny smiled and, after saluting, went trotting off down the slope.

A dim milky quality was invading the darkness. The sky lightened perceptibly. Then up from the river floated a noise so thin and shrill as to sound ludicrous.

"Peep! Peep! Peep!"

"Bosun's pipe," Mahoney commented. "The lobster-backs will have seen us at last. Now watch what happens."

Oars rattled and a small boat put out from the man-of-war's stern. She was carrying a sheet anchor with which to swing the brig about. The militia stayed their tools, peered anxiously at the two-master lying so ghostly to the eastward of the Charles Town shore. Down there voices bellowed, gun tackles creaked and whined and gun-carriage wheels rumbled across the decks.

Bom-m-m! A cannon shattered the pre-dawn stillness to atoms. Its report reverberated about Boston Harbour like a stroke on a titanic kettledrum. The startled Provincials were still catching their breaths when the man-of-war's whole starboard side seemed to explode into a blinding sheet of yellow flame. In minutest detail her spars, shrouds, and masts revealed themselves. Lower on the hill sounded a terrific crackle of branches. It was followed by a succession of heavy thuds.

The Provincials for the most part flung themselves flat or, in frantic haste, sought the half-finished redoubt. A few, kneeling began to pray wildly. One man clutched his head, sobbing that he was killed.

David felt his intestines writhe like angleworms in a can and into his mouth welled a sour, bitter-tasting fluid. But he wouldn't duck, not while one Yankee stayed on his feet. *Bom-m-m!* Another whistling screech.

"Come back here, you bloody coward! Come back here!" From the top of the hill somebody was yelling, but the deserter kept on running.

"Oh Christ—save me," whimpered Billy Colgate, hiding a twitching face in his arms.

"Dig, boys." Knowlton came stalking along, his face harsh and rigid as the ceremonial mask of an Iroquois sachem. "A cannon's bark is a hundred times worse than its bite. See what Colonel Prescott thinks of them? He's an old soldier, too."

The militiamen looked up. There, walking quietly on the yielding earth of the parapet was the Massachusetts colonel! He was pointing down the slope at something and when a third broadside boomed he calmly stooped, picked up a pebble and chucked it in the direction of the enemy.

"Get busy, boys," he called. "These iron musketeers whine, but they don't sting! Captain Trevett, I believe the parapet should be higher here."

Again a thuttering roar ended in a thud below, but higher on the hillside. David felt his throat close. So that was how cannonballs sounded when they came your way! Another ship started firing. They couldn't see her, but the ruddy flare of her guns threw the shoulder of Breed's Hill into relief.

The milky-gray quality of the sky was turning pink, so the militiamen made their shovels fly. The men-o'-war Mahoney identified as the *Lively*, 20 guns; the *Symmetry*, 20 guns; and a huge ship-of-the-line, the *Somerset*, 68 guns. They maintained a noisy but almost ineffectual bombardment.

Colonel Prescott and a couple of aides remained atop the parapet watching dawn extend the scope of vision. The Massachusetts colonel seemed worried about something to the left of the redoubt. Presently an aide came running down to Captain Knowlton.

Knowlton nodded several times and before the aide had climbed up a half completed gun platform to rejoin Colonel Prescott, he called:

"Get your guns and clothes, boys. We're going to be moved."

This order the 4th squad promptly obeyed. A breathing spell would come very welcome indeed. They were aching in every muscle and trembling with fatigue. When the captain led them straggling out of the redoubt and down the back of Breed's Hill, they had an opportunity to look about. David could see all three, no, there were four men-of-war! The fourth ship, a sloop, had been hidden by the buildings of Charles Town. She was lying off a little point. The ship looked so familiar he wanted to ask Johnny about it. Johnny, however, hadn't returned from hunting a spring.

David asked, "Anybody know the name of that ship?"

Mahoney spoke up. "Sure, 'tis the *Falcon*. She's fresh in from pathroll dooty."

The *Falcon*! Rubbing his forehead with a hairy wrist, David stared at her. She had brought him bad luck—plenty of it last winter. Was her presence an evil omen? He was worried. Omens! He remembered Rob. Rob was a great one for omens. He wondered how Rob would like being here? Probably all right. Rob was all-fired slow, but when he got started the grass didn't grow where he hit.

Well, for better or for worse, there in the river swung the *Falcon*, dark blue with a yellow stripe along her side and yellow topsides. In the dawn's light her furled white canvas looked bluish on the yards. Great puffs of woolly white smoke spurted regularly out of her side and often her cannon blew great hollow rings like those a smoker shapes for admiring children. On the hillside below the redoubt a series of dark brown geysers erupted, betraying the hopeless inaccuracy of her broadside.

The Connecticut men kept on down the hill, trampling daisies and buttercups and wild strawberries underfoot. Generally they carried coats and shirts over one arm and lugged powder horns and firelocks over the other. Hats were jammed on at every angle. Often stripped to the waist and streaked with earth, the Connecticut men made an odd appearance, but they had learned one thing. Colonel Prescott had been right. Cannon made an awful fuss, but did such precious little damage that no one flinched except Billy Colgate when a round shot came rolling up the hillside, ploughing up the flowering hay grass until it lost momentum.

The Connecticut regiment having reached a little meadow halfway between Breed's and Bunker's, Captain Knowlton indicated a stone wall and called out, "We are to wait here for orders. Don't stray off. Rest as much as you can. If any man has food, let him share it."

He came over to David who was trying, without much success, to bandage his blistered hands. "You've done fine, Ashton; especially when those fool cannons began. Where has your friend got to? I sent him to hunt water over an hour ago."

David sprang up, looking very tall. "Sir, I do not know where he is." His jaw took an aggressive angle. "I trust you are not implying that a friend of mine would run away?"

The captain smiled, shook his head in a tired gesture. "I imply nothing, Ashton. I merely asked."

Singly and in little bunches, the men sought a long gray wall and, resting their weapons against the smooth stones it was made of, flung themselves flat. They were damp with perspiration and terribly thirsty. A little food appeared from various haversacks and was divided with meticulous care. Bees hummed by on their way to work.

Around eight of the morning the war ships ceased firing. Their bombardment had not caused any real damage. In Prescott's little redoubt—it was hardly fifty yards on a side —the ringing thump of hammers and a hurried rasping of saws told of cannon emplacements nearing completion.

"Hurray!" someone cried excitedly. "By Crikey! Look, boys! We got cannons, too!"

Skirting the base of Bunker's Hill, progressed a short column of cannon dragged by oxen and horses. Men trotted over from adjoining fields and clustered about, staring at the harnesses of the gun teams. They were wonderful contrivances devised from odd straps, traces, and many lengths of faded and often frayed rope. No two sets were even remotely similar. The sunburned militiamen looked with some awe upon the dully shining iron tubes, but laughed at the home-made carriages upon which they were mounted. They had been built of new, unpainted oak and hand forged iron, and the clumsy wheels of farm carts had been attached to them.

A man with an axe cut in his leg limped by. "The British are coming over," he yelled.

"How d'you know?"

"On the hill you can hear drums going to beat the band over in Boston."

Johnny hammering at a gun platform up in the redoubt, heard them, too. Unable to learn where his company had gone, he reckoned he had better stay where he was. There were too many militiamen wandering aimlessly about already. Besides, he liked it up here. You could see all of Charles Town, and along the Charles River almost to Cambridge. As for Boston, the town showed up ever so clear. He counted five, six, seven steeples. One of them had a crowing cock for a weathervane. He thought it an odd design for such a nest of Puritans.

Colonel Prescott's bearing inspired him. In time he hoped he would get to be like Prescott. The Yankee colonel was so calm, all seeing, and so smart at making the best of things. It was a damned pity Colonel Prescott wasn't wearing regimentals and a real sword instead of that silly French rapier. He'd have looked grand as any picture. Every now and again the commanding officer would steal a glance over the shoulder of his banyan. He kept looking towards Bunker's Hill; obviously it was for reinforcements. A few stragglers were advancing over the grass with long-barreled guns slanting over their shoulders, but not a regiment, not even a single company!

" 'Tain't no use, Billy," called someone in a clear voice. "Those damned old women on the Committee have sent us here to die alone. We've been betrayed!"

Said Colonel Gridley, looking very frail and all of his sixty-eight years after the long night's activity, "You and Putnam were wrong, dead wrong, Prescott, in not fortifying Bunker's first. I still say you won't be able to hold this hill ten minutes against Gage's regulars."

In the fresh morning sunlight the New Englander's strong features contracted. "Nevertheless, I will hold it, Gridley. I will never retreat, so help me, God!"

But Prescott by now must have known that the engineer

339

was right. He should never have let hot-headed old Ike Putnam talk him into taking up this position. Safely out of range British troops could slip around his flanks on both sides. To check such a move he ordered some militia to occupy Charles Town which had been all but deserted for weeks.

"If you intend staying here," Gridley was saying heavily, "you had better build a breastwork to cover this slope. So long as you can hold it, the British won't be able to enfold your redoubt."

Work on a breastwork began immediately. As the sun climbed higher, men began to shed their shirts and to put on floppy felt hats. Calls for water grew louder, more persistent. There was no water. Just a little rum. No food, either. Nor did any reinforcements appear for the three hundred men in the redoubt.

Never, Johnny was thinking as he lay on the ground before the finished parapet, could he recall a more perfect early summer day. The sky was a bright blue and clear save for a few lazily drifting cloudlets. The smell of fresh-cut hay was pleasantly strong in the air.

A shadow fell over his shoulder and someone remarked, *"Ante tubam trepidat?"*

For once Johnny's Latin served and he grinned back. "Like the devil, I tremble. Got over that hours ago. How are you, Coffin?"

"Weary with well-doing," the Nantucketer declared. "Been running messages for Prescott till I'm fit to drop. But now—" he tossed a folded coat onto the ground and took up a position on the ground beside Johnny—"I am here. *Dulce et decorem est pro patria mori.* My father, I fear, would scarcely agree that the tag bears on the situation. Have a bite?" From a piece of greasy paper he produced a hunk of cold mutton.

"You bet. Reckon I could eat fried skunk right now."

The ex-junior sophister queried, "Are the redcoats really coming out? Everybody swears old Gage has cold feet."

"He's coming out. Why, he's got to, or be called a coward! What do you reckon will most likely happen?" Johnny asked, cutting off a gobbet of meat. "Think they'll try to drive us out?"

"I guess so." Nathaniel Coffin picked up the Spanish fuzee Johnny had been issued and a comical grin spread over his heated features. "Ye gods and little fishes! From what museum did you resurrect this relic?"

Hampered by a full mouth, Johnny mumbled, "She ain't so bad as she looks. Her lock's tight and the bore is small." He threw back his head in a characteristic gesture. "Lay you two to one I can knock off a Britisher at longer range than you."

The ex-junior sophister of Harvard College promptly produced a shilling, then hesitated. "I'd take you, but it wouldn't be fair. My firelock is almost brand new. Deacon Burret out at Concord built her for me. Kept it in my room and got rusticated two months last year. *Contra* Chapter Four, Section XVI."

Johnny handled the piece with interest. Good solid workmanship all right, but not a patch on a Kaintuck.

"Nevertheless, my friend, the bet still stands," he chuckled. Hesitating, he added, *"Sutor, ne superam cupidus."*

Nat Coffin laughed so hard everyone looked at him. "Your advice about a cobbler sticking to his last is good. Your last may be guns, but it isn't Latin. *Sutor, ne supra cupidam!"*

"Three deep bows—and still two shillings to one!"

"What's that?"

All in a moment the digging noises had stopped. Carpenters working on the gun platforms scrambled up onto the parapet. The buzz of voices swelled and swelled and swelled until men behind Breed's Hill came running to see what was the matter.

"Look there, by the North Battery! The British are going to cross! My God, will you look at all them boats?"

Johnny felt his last doubts disappear. Definitely, there would be a battle. On a long wharf bodies of troops were moving like red checkers in an intricate play. Big barges propelled by leglike oars began to crawl away from various piers and jetties, out over the Charles.

"By God, they dassent tackle Charles Town!" "They're heading for the Neck!" The breath of Panic blew over the redoubt. Colonel Prescott, sensing it, shouted.

"Stay here! They may not! They have sent no ships up the Mystic."

Breathless, the men on Breed's Hill watched hundreds of red figures climbing down into more, and still more, boats. Bells in Boston were striking a single note each. The sun beat down hotter than ever.

2 — THE RAIL FENCE

WHEN he became certain that those long lines of barges ferrying the British army were going to put in at Morton's Point, Colonel William Prescott was at once relieved and alarmed. So General Gage wasn't going to try to seize the Neck? Good! He was throwing away his one chance for a cheap victory. But so many regulars! Prescott hadn't figured Gage would deign to send more than a regiment or two to dislodge a pack of rebels.

To General Joseph Warren, who had just come up carrying, not a sword, but a musket, he called, "You are senior, sir. Will you assume command?"

But the Boston ex-doctor shook his head. Hard running had left him gasping. "Thank you, no, Colonel. I'm here as a volunteer—no more. Wouldn't think of supplanting an officer who has accomplished so much." But he was worried all the same. Pretty soon he asked, "What do you propose doing about that interval to our left?"

Though the breastwork Colonel Gridley had suggested was nearing completion, a wide gap still existed between the end of it and the shore of the Mystic River. That it presented a dangerous flaw in the Provincial line of defense everyone could see. It was all of a hundred yards long.

Colonel Prescott, mopping his shiny features with a kerchief, countered with another question. "Did you notice any reinforcements on the way to us?"

"No, but old Put is killing a horse trying to scare up some."

From their point of vantage on the parapet, the two officers watched the first British units disembark, leisurely, on a point perhaps a quarter of a mile distant. They made an ever widening red area on the green turf out there. Far to the rear wailed the conch shell bugles of some straggling militia company.

"Don't know what I can do about that interval," said Prescott as if to himself. "I haven't any reserve, except some Connecticut men under Captain Knowlton."

"How many of them are there?" Warren wanted to know.

"Only about two hundred."

"They can't hope to hold a fence two hundred yards long. Not against British regulars."

"Of course not." Prescott's tone was bitter and he directed a baleful look at Bunker's Hill. Upon its safe height a dark swarm of men milled uselessly. "If only those careful old maids over there would send me some reinforcements! Hell's bells! I'm going to send my reserve to build up that stone wall, anyhow!"

Thus, around two o'clock of the afternoon, a runner came panting up to Captain Knowlton, comfortably smoking his pipe in the shade of a small pear tree.

"Urgent orders! The Colonel says take your men over behind the rail fence yonder. Build it higher."

Knowlton tapped the dottle from his pipe. "For some time I have been thinking that would be advisable," said he dryly.

"Reinforcements are—on way," wheezed the messenger turning away.

"Reinforcements, hell!" called a red-haired fellow lying on his belly in the deep gress. "Ward has forgotten all about us buggers."

Ten minutes later Knowlton's tired command set to work. It lent them energy to know that the British were actually landing in force farther down the peninsula. Soon they would be coming this way. The fence, as they found it, was no higher than a man's knees. It consisted of stones and two wooden rails which raised it waist high.

Crisp, calm and as resourceful as ever, Knowlton detailed half of his force to fetch rails from a fence marking the rear side of the pasture. The others were directed to gather up armloads of fresh-cut hay. This they stuffed between the intersections between the rails.

"Hey, Cap, where in hell do you want these?" From behind, a squad had appeared. It was handling two six-pound cannons.

"Arrah! An' thim should be a help," Mahoney sighed.

Once his men had pulled aside enough rocks to form rude embrasures, Captain Knowlton ordered the cannon trained to cover a broad meadow stretching away before his position.

"Say, that's fine," said Lieutenant Bisley. "Now, where's the shot?"

"Shot? Oh, my God!" The leader, red-faced, turned and fiercely cursed two of his men. "What you carryin' round in place o' brains? You dunderheads hev clean forgot it!"

The artillerymen looked angry, rather than ashamed. "Go stick yerself, Callender! How wuz we to know we wuz suppose to bring it? You didn't tell us so. Nor nobody else!"

"It would also be helpful if you'd brought some powder," Knowlton pointed out, "not to mention spongers and rammers."

The officer in charge cursed and hurried off to the rear. They never saw him again.

The gunner sergeant exposed gapped yellow teeth in an apologetic grin. "Shucks, Mister, don't be too hard on us. We ain't ever handled these contraptions before."

"Where are the regular gunners?"

"Made tracks, damn 'em! Along with Colonel Bridge, Lieutenant-Colonel Brickett of Prescott's own regiment went, too! They got pains in their bellies quicker'n greased lightning once the British started to row over."

David's hands began bleeding once more and soon his nails split from dislodging and replacing the smooth glacial stones of which the fence was built. Billy Colgate and Bellinger were in no better way. All three of them were on the extreme left of line. From where they stood they could see the beach and the slimy green stones on it.

Advancing along the shore of the Mystic some Provincial troops came slogging along. It turned out to be Jonathan Stark's New Hampshire regiment. Some more Connecticut men were with him. They arrived surprisingly fresh.

"Took your own blessed time getting here," Captain Knowlton observed. He had been up and on the move some thirty hours now.

Stark cast him a contemptuous glance. "You can kiss my arse. It's time you Connecticut nitwits learned that one fresh man in a battle can lick five tired ones!"

A succession of messengers came sprinting down Breed's Hill, urging the defenders of the rail fence to make haste. They said a second flotilla was crossing from Boston. Colonel Stark, fresh and keenly observant, saw how fast the tide was falling. He deduced that a considerable width of beach would be passable between the end of the rail fence and the river. By merely following the beach, a British column might sweep by and turn the Provincial position, because most of the militiamen couldn't see under the river bank. Therefore, he ordered his stocky mountaineers down onto the damp sand. From boulders all green and white with slimy growth and barnacles they commenced constructing a crude breastwork.

A rythmic beating of drums drew David's attention. Then many fifes began to shrill "Britons Strike Home." They were real drummers off there. Their flams precisely together—a rattle-tat-tat-tat! a rattle tat-tat-tat! The Provincials raised heads in broad-brimmed straws and felts and tricornes, but they couldn't see anything because of the slope of ground down to the beach.

No ammunition arrived for the two field pieces.

Colonel Stark climbed up on one of the cannons, clapped his hands for attention. "You boys better form teams of three. When the first man shoots, the one next behind him will step forward and fire." He raised his voice over an insistent dull thunder raised by the fleet's broadsides. "Remember, we have very few rounds a man so every shot has got to tell! Now look alive all of you and pick out their officers. You can tell 'em by their pretty uniforms and they don't wear crossbelts. They'll have silver half moons hung over their throats and will carry swords or spears. Got that? Shoot at their officers and *aim low!*"

Everyone was listening, squinting up at Colonel Stark's chunky figure up there on the gun carriage.

"Best place to hit the rest is where their white belts cross. If any man fires afore I give the word, I'll kick his pants up to his shoulders." He said it as if he meant it. "Now take your positions and remember why we're here. If the British get past us, we may as well go home and fit handcuffs on ourselves."

David, troubled by Johnny's continued absence, made up a team with Mahoney and Bellinger.

"I'm probably the best shot, so I'll take Number One," he told them, hoping his voice sounded natural. "Mahoney, suppose you take second position. Bellinger, your blunderbuss ought to do some mean work at close range."

"If ye've niver fired wan av thim Tower muskets," Mahoney warned, "ye'd best close yer eyes forninst yez pull the trigger. Some av thim Brown Besses squirts fire from the pan."

On Morton's Point the martial shrilling of fifes grew more strident. Up on Breed's Hill breathless silence reigned. The defenders evidently were watching something.

"My God," croaked Haskins. "Look at that!"

345

In stately array two scarlet streams began trickling away from the great red pool collected on the grayish sand of Morton's Point. One division started climbing very slowly towards the redoubt on Breed's Hill. The other moved off trampling the beach grass and gray-white sand along the bank of the Mystic. They came straight towards the breastwork of boulders the New Hampshire men had just raised, and at the rail fence.

It was an awesome, breath-taking spectacle, a terrifying exhibition of power. In the distance British weapons gave off brief, thin, pale sparkles of light. The scarlet of their tunics as yet obscured the white of their breeches and gaiters. Formed in column, company after company swung into sight, officers marching stiff and proud alongside. The drummer boys looked like midgets. Nobody who saw it ever forgot the spectacle of old England's troops on parade.

A veteran of the Louisburg expedition said to the Colgate boy, "If you hold spare musket balls between the knuckles of your left hand, you can save time reloading. They won't fall out, either."

For a space the 4th squad was given time to watch the British left wing deploying at the base of Breed's Hill. They were having trouble in their advance. Time and again the ruler-straight ranks were forced to break up in order to scale a pasture fence. The British pulled down the rails whenever they could, but often they had to scramble over and re-form on the far side.

"By God, they're slow as kids on the way to school," grunted a bald old man two places down from David.

"Ye'd move slow, too," Mahoney grunted. "What wid thim packs and heavy coats, ivry mother's son is carryin' a hundred pounds or better, or I'm a nigger."

The other enemy column which advanced along the beach found the going much easier. The British came steadily on behind their drums the hollow beat of which was reverberating between the two hills. Larks flew up out of the grass before them, sped low towards the rail fence, then, seeing more men there, circled terror-stricken into the blazing sky.

Gradually, Mahoney became able to identify various units.

" 'Tis the light companies on the beach. We'll tangle wid 'em, too," he predicted.

"How d'you know they're light infantry? Look all the same to me," Edgell said.

"Do yez see thim big brass plates on their caps? See the shorter skirts to their coats? Thim wid the light blue lapels is the Welch Fusiliers. Behind thim and turned up in dark blue is the King's Own. Third in column looks like the 10th, or maybe 'tis the 38th. They're both in yellow facings. 'Way over yonder goes me own ould rigiment." The deserter looked a little scared, David thought, when he saw those orange revers.

"What are those big fellows farther back with the high black hats?" Bellinger inquired in a small, dry voice. He had taken off his spectacles quite awhile back but the red mark on his nose lingered.

" 'Tis the grenadiers," the Irishman replied. "From each British regiment is picked wan company av light infantry and wan av grenadiers. Big men goes to the grenadiers, small men to the light infantry."

"We'll pick them," piped Billy Colgate, but his thin, heavily freckled face was far whiter than his shirt.

"Steady now, boys. Get down low!" Trying to look stern and unimpressed, Provincial officers began walking up and down behind the rail fence and behind the boulders on the beach below.

Still no ammunition had arrived for the cannon standing so black and threatening—and useless.

The staccato *slam-slamming* of drums grew very loud. Now David could see the cockades and lace work on some of the officers' black, three-cornered hats. Being without packs, they strode easily along and their bared swords flashed. More details quickly became visible. As Stark had promised, colonels, majors and captains were easily distinguishable because of their massive epaulets and the gold and silver braid on their hats.

"Take your finger off that trigger!" Knowlton snapped at the Reverend Edgell, and kicked him on the rear when he did not instantly obey. "There's nothing to be afraid of; nothing!"

A gorgeous officer moved over to a big patch of greenish-white grass that rose to his knees. He shouted a command. The light infantry column halted. Like some movement of a precise machine, steel rippled and a metallic rattle marked the fixing of bayonets.

"To hell with them!" Colonel Stark bellowed down the line.

"If you hold your fire, boys, the bloody-backs will never get close enough to use those cheese knives!"

Like spilt water widening on a floor, tension spread behind the rail fence. The earth-marked militiamen pulled off their hats and, swallowing hard, sank low behind the tumbled stones of their fence. Many men knelt, or crouched over like a valet peeking in a key hole.

At a trot grenadier companies in tall bearskin shakoes began to deploy over the hay stubble some eighty yards away from the rail fence. Everyone could see the buttoned-back tails of their coats a-swing, and brass-tipped bayonet scabbards wagging like the tails of so many dogs. In that big meadow there didn't seem to be quite so many of them. But there were still plenty.

The big grenadiers formed a long triple line, shoulder brushing shoulder, their white-gaitered legs swinging in time to the thumping drums. They halted and the brass plates on the fronts of their hats flashed in the eyes of the Provincials, bright as the mirror of a mischievous child. Out in front of them marched white-wigged officers gleaming with gold and silver. These also halted and, turning, supervised last minute preparations.

David was only dimly aware of the fleet still thundering away at the redoubt.

Bellinger's nervousness caused him a series of spasmodic yawns. His voice sounded small and lonely when he giggled. "Promised my boys I'd fetch back one lobster-back apiece. Guess there's more'n enough out there to go 'round."

Down on the beach the British light companies had not halted. Their advance continued. It was breath-taking, unforgettable, seemingly inexorable. Still in column they resembled a long scarlet tide sweeping up along the beach. White wigs, glittering epaulets, flashing musket barrels. Stiff as posts, the officers marched many feet in advance of their men. Faces set, scarlet with heat and exertion. Closer. The swishing of their feet over the sand was clearly to be heard now.

Behind the fence the Provincials locked their teeth, tried not to look as scared as they felt and for the last time tested set-screws securing their flints. David mechanically snapped back his pan cover to make sure the priming had not sifted out. Then, like the other Number One men, he jerked out his ramrod and stuck the yard of steel handy in the ground by his knee. The men about him were shifting so as to bring their muskets to bear on the beach. The grenadiers were still lingering as if to see how the light companies would fare.

So steady, so mechanical was the British advance, David's heart began leaping like a speared fish. How little the drummer boys looked! They didn't act the least bit scared, only swung their brass mounted sticks with a flourish. Suddenly deep voices shouted out there on the meadow and the grenadiers came on again, kicking up the cut hay as they advanced. The drum beats grew deafening, sounded right on top of the fence.

In David's squad, farthest to the left along the rail fence, there was a hurried shifting of musket barrels back to the front. Let Stark's men on the beach look out for themselves! The carpet of cut hay separating the grenadiers from the rail fence was growing narrower.

From behind came Captain Knowlton's sharp, "Take sight!"

David rested the Tower musket on the top rail and through his improvised rear sight watched square red faces, all bright with sweat, take shape. The officer nearest him was a big hairy fellow. He was loudly cursing the heat.

The wood of David's musket felt very hot to his cheek when he settled its butt more firmly into his shoulder, but the skin on his shoulders felt cold as if it had been rubbed with ice. Swallowing hard, he swung his front sight until he saw, as if balanced upon it, the gorget of a very tall major. As in a dream he watched the Englishman's face draw nearer. He had a big livid scar across his chin. A curl of his wig had fetched loose from its pins and was bobbing to his every stride. All the rest of the world became obliterated by that figure in scarlet with light blue cuffs, light blue lapels and a white waistcoat. The gorget grew simply enormous.

Why in hell didn't Stark give the command? The damned British were right on top of them! *Why didn't he?* A Virginia rifle company would have fired minutes ago. Closer! Closer! The dancing half moon of gilt silver and a lace jabot under it looked to be hovering right above him.

Jonathan Stark's voice suddenly roared out. "Pick the officers! Aim crossbelts. Ready—Fire!"

Banging reports slapped at David's cheeks like invisible hands, but he held steady on the gorget and, by tightening his whole hand, squeezed the trigger. The clumsy Tower musket kicked him like a curried horse with a ticklish belly and a swirl of rank, rotten-smelling powder smoke beat back in his face. He couldn't help a series of hard, racking coughs. A swirling hurricane of flame and smoke spurted from between the fence rails. All in an instant a gray-white miasma eclipsed nearly the whole of that glittering parade in the meadow.

"Fer the love av Mary! Get out av me way!" Mahoney was grabbing at his arm, hauling him back. At once the Irishman poked his firelock through the hay covered rails.

David remembered his ramrod and had bent forward to grab it when a rift appeared in the wall of smoke. The hatless head and hunched shoulders of an officer showed up. He was clutching his cheeks and dazedly swaying back and forth, his sword a-dangle from a knot fastening it to his wrist. Out there the lines of muskets were wavering and bayonets were swaying like steel reeds under a gale of death. More heads materialized in the murk, some streaming blood, some yelling.

Terrible, animal-like noises arose beyond the curtain of smoke. Then a puff of wind from off the Mystic brushed aside the fumes. David felt his heart heave and he gasped as if a foot had been driven into the pit of his stomach. Not over sixty feet off lay a long squirming windrow of bodies dressed in scarlet and white.

A colonel stood alone, statue-still, with sword still raised. In his paralyzed astonishment he seemed not to notice a big sergeant rolling over and over on the ground at his feet. The N.C.O. was spilling yards of grayish-red entrails onto the new hay. A corporal in his death agonies snapped blindly at the turf, like a dog in a fit.

To the left of David's position a light infantry man was stumbling around in crazy circles.

"Oh, Christ! Christ!" he screamed and kept his hands pressed tight to his forehead. Nonetheless, a fine spray of blood was squirting out between his fingers. He tripped over a pile of corpses, then staggered on until he tumbled over the edge of the bank and fell down onto the beach, among the corpses littering it. Other wounded were blindly trying to burrow among the bodies. From behind the rails a musket roared and David distinctly saw the colonel's body jolt under the savage impact of ball and buckshot. Again a pall of drifting smoke descended.

The *click! clock!* of Provincial firearms being hurriedly

cocked sounded on all sides. There was need of haste. Eyes a-blaze, cheering, a second line of grenadiers was charging, hurdling their fallen comrades. David saw dark blue lapels out there this time—some white—a very few light blue. Here and there a survivor of the first wave staggered up, gray-faced, to join them. God! Too clearly he was remembering the way those deadly black holes had appeared in the tall major's gorget.

Bayonets, murderously a-twinkle, shone amid the dust and smoke. Again the rail fence spouted fire. Before the smoke shut down David, trying to tilt a powder charge into his gun, beheld the further effects of the Provincial fire.

No less effectively than before, the second volley had knocked the heavy companies backwards off their feet, had torn murderous gaps in their array. Howls, screams and curses became mixed in a fearful cacophony. As with trembling hands he poised a handful of buckshot over his musket muzzle, David watched a tough-looking grenadier's bearskin fly off. A small package fell out of it. He wondered what it contained.

Despite widening intervals in their ranks, the English bent their bodies as if walking into a stiff gale, kept on. Raising a hoarse cheer the Number Three men of the Provincial musket teams sprang forward. Foolishly, futilely swinging his hat, Bellinger was trying to fan away the blinding smoke. David, repriming in a frenzy of haste, watched the round-shouldered clerk rise, blunderbuss leveled, avidly awaiting a target to materialize. Down on the beach the slamming of reports was continual.

"Come on! Oh damn you for bloody cowards! *Come on!*" A red-coated major, wig canted over one ear, became visible in the meadow. With the side of his sword he was hammering at some privates who, hatless, were reeling back, coughing, and black with burnt powder grains.

Bellinger, sighting deliberately, dropped that major in his tracks. "That one's for Eddie," he cackled.

It was somehow appalling for David to watch the British third line come up, carrying with it broken remnants of the first and second ranks. Again a murderous volley smashed full into hot faces a-twitch with desperation.

Off to the right the grenadiers were faring no better. David, running forward to take Bellinger's place, glimpsed a slim lieutenant—a mere lad—running along the wavering line. He grabbed reeling men by the shoulders, shoved them forward, all the while yelling in a thin high voice.

"That shot's mine," someone said.

"In God's name, don't kill him!" Edgell cried. "He is too young—"

The young lieutenant broke his sword across the shoulders of a corporal. Then mad with fury when the soldiers kept on falling back, he turned and charged at the fence with the stump of his sword. Half a dozen privates started after the boy. A fourth volley mowed down all the survivors who had kept on.

There were no more redcoats and crossbelts to shoot at. The few British left on their feet were running or staggering back over the meadow. Of all the officers who had participated in this attack, David could see only two and these were still pleading with their men to come back.

The cloying, musty-sweet smell of blood and the nauseous stench of torn entrails hung heavy in the lifeless air. Some forty feet away a drummer boy lay crumpled, his small face a pulp. In a scarlet cataract his blood was draining across the smudged head of his drum. Agonized shrieks from the pile of men on the meadow made an inferno of sound.

The young lieutenant whom David had noticed suddenly came crawling out from behind a tangled pile of bodies. On his gray and shining face was a look of awful astonishment at what had happened to him.

A wounded sergeant flopped up on one elbow, cried, "Mr. Bruere, go back! They will kill you! Go back!"

"Water! Water!" New gorget swinging, the young lieutenant came crawling on hands and knees over the grass and the daisies were not whiter than his teeth, bared in agony.

"Stop, Mr. Bruere! That's the wrong way!" yelled the sergeant and tried to wave his arm in warning, but the pinkish and jagged end of a bone was sticking out just above his elbow, and his forearm dangled dreadfully limp.

"Don't shoot," gurgled the wounded boy. "Water! Kind friends, Oh, for the love of God! Water!"

Twenty feet short of the fence the young officer slowed, stopped his crawling. Then, like a frightened cat, he humped his back. He began to vomit such incredible torrents of blood it seemed as if he must be pumping from an inexhaustible reservoir. The flying gore splashed back from the ground, spattered his face, his white waistcoat. All at once he crumpled onto his side and lay still.

There was still continued firing up on Breed's Hill, but the enemy was retreating from it, too. The slope towards Boston and the harbour was carpeted with red and white bodies. All the way to Morton's Point the dull green of the ground was dotted with running figures in red and white. Without exception officers were cursing, beating at their men, trying to slow down the retreat.

Mahoney licked his lips. "Holy Mother av God! This *can't* be so! Why, thim regulars is running! *Arrah,* may they niver come back!"

David reckoned that at least a third of the attacking force had fallen. That the enemy officers had suffered out of proportion was attested by the number of bodies in gold epaulets and golden buttons. Stark's orders had been followed. One fantastic phenomenon drew everyone's attention. Quite a few muskets flying from stricken hands had plunged bayonet-first into the ground; they remained butt upwards, wavering among the dead like hideous weeds. Caps, packs, cartouche boxes, equipment of all sorts littered the meadow.

Billy Colgate's freckles stood out very brown on his pallid forehead. He was vomiting over the trail of one of the useless cannons. The Reverend Edgell knelt, feverishly begging the Lord to forgive him for having taken so many lives—even Church of England lives.

David Ashton was gradually recovering from his first sense of horror. He wanted a drink of liquor the worst way.

3 — CHARLES TOWN

IMMEDIATELY after the repulse of the British the wind died away entirely. Wounded men felt the sun grow scorching hot, howled and screamed for water. Only the sullen, futile bombardment of the redoubt by their ships and by a battery somewhere over in Boston marked any British activity.

Buff, shuffling loose-jointed and watchful over the Neck, kept a sharp lookout across a tidal millpond to his right. Yonder, some men—he didn't know which side they were fighting on—were poling two big barges into shallow water among some reeds. Each had a cannon mounted behind by a sort of wooden shield. Who-e-e! If them things started shooting, this Neck would be no place for a certain nigger. He looked up and watched a great lot of men swarming around the top of Bunker's Hill. Laws! They didn't seem to know where they were heading, no-how. Bluish heat haze, he realized, was obscuring the far end of this point of land.

A bony-faced farmer came shuffling to the rear. He was biting his lip and his face was a queer yellow-bronze color. Buff's eyes grew white. Blood dripped slowly from the farmer's shattered forearm. Eagerly, the dust closed over each drop, as if to hide it.

"Please suh, whe'h at is Cap'n Kno'len's people?" He repeated the query he had been asking all the way out from Cambridge.

"He Connecticut?"

"Yas, *suh!* He Connecticut!"

"Wal, you might come acrost him over there on our right —towards Charles Town. They say 'tis Massachusetts in the fort."

His information could not have been more erroneous, but Buff had no way of knowing it. The sight of that wounded arm was evoking unfamiliar, long dormant impulses. Buff's clumsy-looking fingers crept up to rub the chevrons of scars on his cheeks. He had no idea he came from a fighting tribe in Senegal, but he did know he was different from his lazy, good-natured, brown-black companions in slavery in lots of ways. "Stupid Bushmen," he called them. It was queer, but he really enjoyed a fight—a taste which had earned him shackles and many a session at Candless's whipping post. That, and the stigma of being "a bad nigger."

His conical-shaped head settled lower between his shoulders, but his step lightened. "Keep yo' eyes skinned, boy," he muttered. " 'At's a pow'ful lot o' shootin' up yander."

Along the cart track he was following came another wounded militiaman. He was profanely protesting to not less than eight chalk-faced Provincials.

"Git back to the fight, you consarned yellow-bellies! Git away from me. I don't need help half so much as the boys up to the fort." He halted and, leaning on his weapon—an old duck gun with an enormously long barrel—glared appealingly about. "Won't any of you dad-burned heroes go back?"

"Shucks," boomed a gloomy-visaged fellow in undirtied

nankeens, "we ain't going to allow a suffering comrade die on the road to safety."

"Won't one of you go back?" The wounded man's face was bitter, twitching.

"Whut for? Anyhow the British have run. They're whipped."

"They'll come back—damn yer ugly eyes! They're British regulars!"

Despite greasy duroy breeches and a very dirty red and white striped jersey, Buff made an impressive figure when he came padding up on bare feet. His smooth blue-black skin was glossy with sweat and the great muscles of his chest and arms stood out like sculptured bronze. Though his features revealed nothing, he was thinking, developing a crafty scheme.

"Please, suh. Ah heered whut you jes' said. Ah sho' would admire to go an' fight, but Ah ain't got me no gun."

The wounded militiaman jerked his head at the old fowling piece. "If you'll fight, nigger, she's yours. Here are some bullets and you'd better take along my powder horn."

"Thank you, suh! Thank you, kindly." Buff ducked his head several times.

Once he had unstrung his cowhorn of powder, the wounded man glared at the skulkers in bitter contempt. "Go on home and tell your Mas to put your diapers back on." He spat in their direction then said, "Good luck, boy, and give 'em hell!" He nodded to Buff and resumed his slow retreat.

Buff hadn't the vaguest notion about how to load a gun, but he climbed over the hot stones of a fence and took up a trot. He was heading for the gray-white roofs of Charles Town and the tree tops poking up between them.

Presently he overtook a man tramping in the same direction. This one was wearing the blue shell jacket and white canvas breeches of a mariner. When Buff asked him about loading, the seaman stared, then squirted tobacco all over a clump of fireweed before he said,

"Sure, I'll teach anybody who'll go ahead." He demonstrated with his own weapon, as they walked along. "First off, make sure there ain't no sparks left in the bar'l from your last shot. You'll get a couple of fingers blowed off, else. Then pour in so much powder." He raised a cow's-horn powder flask and tilted out a half palm full of coarse black grains. "Next comes the wadding. Got any?"

"No suh, Ah doan' reckon so."

"Well, here's some paper." He fished out a lot of ragged pages torn from some book and gave them to Buff. "Crumple it up and ram it home. Keeps the powder from running out, understand?"

Buff listened hard, ducking his head beneath a big floppy hat he had "found." They were nearly across the first meadow now with uncut hay whipping about their shins.

"Take five or six buckshot—"

"Whut dat, suh?"

"Six little lead balls like these. After them goes a musket ball. Ram in another piece of paper and tamp it down hard; keep the balls from rolling out. Now, let's see you do it."

In the shade of a little grove behind Charles Town they paused. Buff tried to remember the instructions, but it was hard work. To make matters more awkward, the duck gun's barrel was long, and five or six times the little man whose name, it appeared, was Metcalfe, had to prompt him.

"Je-*sus!*" he exploded. "Can't you remember *nothing?* I never did see such a dumb nigger! Look here, we better set down by that fence while I show you how to prime."

Eyes very round, Buff watched Metcalfe's methodical movements. After transferring shot and spare flints to his breeches, the mariner stripped off his serge shell jacket and hid it in the hollow part of an apple tree. Buff was powerful glad to sit down. Yes, suh. His feets sho' was tired, but they didn't hurt so much as before he threw away them shoes he'd hooked out of a supply wagon.

"Now watch close." The mariner's broad thumb pushed forward a section of the lock. "This here thing's called the frizzen. The flint strikes against it when it falls, and throws sparks into the pan which touch off the priming load. See this here little hole? Well, the fire squirts along it inside of the breech. It touches off that load of powder you dropped down the bar'l. See?"

"Yas, suh. Ah reckon so," Buff said. Surprisingly enough, he really had grasped the idea. Sparks into pan, fire into barrel. Powder explodes, bullets fly out. It really wasn't so hard.

Metcalfe reached up, pulled a green apple off a limb, inspected it, threw it away and got to his feet.

"What's your name?"

"Buff, suh."

"Well, come along, Buff. I guess the redcoats will have pulled themselves together by now. Maybe we can find us a bagnet or two down in Charles Town. They come in handy sometimes."

"Is 'at whe'h Cap'n Kno'len's folks is?"

"I dunno," Metcalfe grunted. He clumbed over another fence and started towards the outlying houses of deserted Charles Town.

Lots of militiamen were clustered about a big well, drinking eagerly. Their leaders were vainly trying to get them away. "Shake a leg! The British are coming back!"

Hopeful all the while of catching a glimpse of Mr. David or of Mr. Johnny, Buff followed Metcalfe down a street lined with empty houses. They looked very forlorn with their doors standing open and their windows mostly smashed. Men who had been sitting in the shade of the porches were reluctantly rising and moving off towards the northeast edge of the village. It was nearest to Morton's Point.

The big Negro attracted no end of curious stares with his scarred cheeks and pointed teeth. In a red and white striped jersey and carrying a six-foot ducking gun, he made quite a picture. When he saw how cannon balls had knocked in the roof of a big school house, his broad nostrils began opening faster. From a gaping hole threads of blue smoke were spiraling slowly into the cloudless sky.

Pretty soon they reached an orchard and found many Provincials gathered among the trees. They were all staring anxiously across at Boston and at a line of boats rowing over. They were filled with red uniforms. Reserves.

Metcalfe stopped, pointed past a schooner building on some stocks at a long wharf across the water. Lying to it was a big, full-rigged ship. Her topmasts were down and her yards bare of canvas. Her water line was foul with weed.

"Look at the poor old girl," Metcalfe growled with a savage oath. "I own her. God-damned Britishers wouldn't give me clearance last day before the Port Act began. That's why I am here."

Men skirmishing slowly out from Charles Town were just in time to see a second assault on the redoubt take shape. Once its reserve had been landed, the British command lumped together the decimated units which had already attacked.

As, bent well over, the Provincials advanced through a young pear orchard, they began to hear the groans of wounded British laid out on the beach in the broiling sun.

Some Provincials evidently had been in the orchard from the beginning of the battle. One of them called, "Say, friends, could you spare me a mite of powder?"

Another skirmisher lifted his head from the heart of a willow thicket. He and the three other men with him had been quite invisible. "Where are our reinforcements?"

Metcalfe told him, "There ain't reinforcements. That yellow twerp Gerrish won't move off Bunker's, come hell or high water! He's warning everybody to stay on the other side of the Neck."

"If that's so, then I guess we had better be going back pretty soon," drawled a powder-marked man. "What you doing here, black boy?"

Buff grinned. "Well, suh, Ah aims to collect me one ob dem pretty red coats with lots of gold onto it." But what Buff really yearned for was enough human ears to string a necklace with. Even if it was a little necklace. He could recall back home a round hut with a thatched roof—a headman showing someone a whole ramrod jammed with dried ears. He had been a great warrior.

The British drums were *slam-slamming* again, but not so evenly, and the squeaking of their fifes held hysterical overtones.

"Where would we be the most use?" Metcalfe asked of the crowd.

"Right here," said a man in a decent gray coat. "Since during the first attack we stung the British flank a lot, it stands to reason Gage will order Charles Town bombarded. We figure he will likely send troops to drive us out of here— or try to. It's my guess we will see plenty of action before long."

Buff was surprised to find how calm he felt. Who-e-e! In a little while he'd maybe be killing someone. All through the pear orchard sounded the thin slithering of steel slipping over steel; many ramrods were being driven home.

Buff felt his stomach tighten and his nostrils stiffen. He looked about and pretty soon he found what looked like a fine vantage point behind a stone well. The coping faced a rather wet cow pasture over which a British force coming to clear Charles Town must advance. Metcalfe came up to him.

"This is a dandy spot. Why, it ain't forty yards to the

nearest of them dead Britishers," he grunted. "Remember to hold low."

Down on Morton's Point the British Army was taking its own sweet time. The commander was forming two wings arranged in the familiar three line pattern. Even at this distance the waiting Provincials, chewing hay grass and luxuriating in the shade, could see shakoes and hats missing. Here and there the uncovered wig on an officer glistened like snow in the fierce afternoon sunlight.

Metcalfe said suddenly, "We were smart to clear out of Charles Town, the way we did."

Buff couldn't grasp what he meant though H.M.S. *Somerset* was slowly swinging with the tide. Gradually her port battery of thirty-four guns came to bear on the shingle and clapboard houses of the village.

"In about five—" A broadside from the *Somerset* drowned out Metcalfe's remarks.

A chorus of infernal voices screeched overhead and, a split second later, came such noises as a giant might make in chopping kindling. *Bom-m-m!* Over in Boston the "Admiral's Battery" on Copp's Hill joined in showering destruction on Charles Town.

A shell shrieked by. Buff cowered. Convulsively, he clasped both hands over his head.

Metcalfe laughed. "Take it easy, nigger. They ain't coming this way—yet."

Heart-stilling crashes sounded among the houses. Buff, shaking like a frightened colt, watched bricks fly from a chimney and fall into the street. Some of the bricks smashed windows clear across the road, scaring hell out of some militiamen. Under a steady rain of cannon balls, boards, shingles, shutters scaled up into the sky. A whole series of terrific smashing crackles reached the orchard.

Why, Buff wondered, had he ever been such a no-sense fool as to come looking for this sort of a death? Peeking around the well top, through the rough trunks of the fruit trees, he could see Provincials sprinting out of the village at a dead run. Every time a shot landed near they'd give such a funny little jump that Metcalfe and the rest of the fifty or sixty men lying hidden and safe in the orchard began to laugh.

All at once a long trail of yellow-white smoke arched itself across the deep blue sky and landed in a shipyard. Another band of smoke sprang from Copp's Hill and, crossing the first arc, sketched a gigantic, curving X. For the first time, Metcalfe noticed that the heights, roofs and docks in Boston yonder were black with onlookers. They had a perfect view of everything that was happening.

Buff's eyes bulged to see that unhealthy yellowish-green smoke begin to settle. A half finished ship took fire. In widely separated parts of the village, flames began to raise banderoles of smoke above the glassy river.

"Them must be red-hot cannon balls," Metcalfe averred, pointing to a pillar of sickly yellow smoke climbing from yet another house.

Said the man in decent gray, "What they've just now pitched into my home—" he nodded at a big, white painted house—"is a shell filled with burning sulphur. Artillerymen call it a carcass." He took out a neat metal flask and quietly reprimed his gun. "I am going to kill someone for that."

Within ten minutes Charles Town was blazing in a dozen places, then the breeze sprang up and began to blow a great blue-black pall of smoke over the Charles River and into the faces of the naval gunners. Immediately their aim got bad and some cannon balls began smashing through the young pear trees. But they hurt no one. Soon the bombardment ceased and only the fierce crackle and roar of the flames consuming Charles Town beat against Buff's eardrums.

Metcalfe emitted a startled grunt. "Look alive, boys. Here they come!"

For the second time the British Army moved off, still bent beneath heavy packs and under fixed bayonets.

"Any room here?" Singed, wild-eyed sharpshooters came panting up from Charles Town. "Bloody pigs burnt us out."

"Sure," Metcalfe, a natural leader, raised his voice. "Over behind that woodpile, shouldn't wonder. Let everybody lie low and stay hidden 'til I give the word. They can't see you in that long grass, either."

Battalion on battalion, regiment on regiment, the British, 3,400 of them, were on the move, swinging over a succession of fields, and climbing fences. Metcalfe's party on the flank could see how very slow the advance was. With livelier interest they also watched the maneuvers of a body of marines. Because of their black leggings and white lapels they were easily recognizable. In column they came tramping along the beach; obviously detailed to drive the last Provincials out of the village.

"Boys, you had better close in a mite," Metcalfe called. "There are a lot of redcoats headed this way."

And there were, nearly 200 in number. Buff, too terrified now even to run, beheld coming towards them two whole companies of marines in low caps with silvered ornaments and white facings to their scarlet tunics. That they had taken part in the first attack could be told at a glance. Some of the men wore bloodied rags tied about head or limbs. Not a few were limping. When they came closer, the Provincials in the orchard could read a sort of stunned expression on many of the sweat-bright faces.

A middle-aged, hatless officer carrying an espantoon was directing the advance. Only one other officer, a lieutenant, was to be seen. Sergeants and corporals were acting as captains and lieutenants. Many of the white breeches out there were marked with blood streaks.

A few impatient Provincials popped heads from behind the woodpile, stared mesmerized at the brilliant array moving forward across the cow pasture. The Royal Marines were now so close Metcalfe could make out an anchor and some oak leaves on their cap badges.

The officer saw the lurking skirmishers and yelled something. With a precise one-two-three the red and white ranks came to a halt. Like corn under a reaper, brown-mounted musket barrels swept down until the marines, holding their weapons waist high, were pointing in the general direction of the woodpile. Buff held his breath, cowered flatter than flat and felt his pants grow damp.

"Fire!"

The British volley struck only one of the Provincials. But he, a dark, unshaven fellow, was struck in the belly and began to scream, shrilly, horribly, like a hurt horse. Whirling, rotten-smelling smoke shut out all sight of the enemy.

"Get ready, boys!" Metcalfe called out. "Aim for their belt buckles."

About sixty militiamen rose up out of the tall hay grass, some standing right up, others sighting from one knee. They took steady aim, waited for the smoke to thin out. Buff put up his duck gun and squared his shoulder against its butt. Dim figures coughed and wavered around in the gloom. The marines' second rank was slipping through the first, in a hurry to fire.

The man in gray yelled, "One—two—"

At that range the militiamen could not miss. Buff, too rattled to pull his own trigger, watched the knees of a whole row of redcoats buckle, saw their arms fly up and queer caps of scarlet cloth go spinning through air. Muskets fell every which way. The hatless officer hadn't been hit. Buff whipped up the duck gun and fired at him.

The recoil made his teeth rattle and the comb of the stock cut his thick lips. What was it a man did first to reload? As he fumbled for his powder horn, Buff peered to learn whether he had killed his man.

He had missed. The officer was running down the wavering ranks, but his wig was gone and he had lost an epaulet.

Out of the pear orchard came another slamming volley, not so heavy as the first, but it hastened a slow backward motion of the shattered lines on the pasture. Now great gaps had opened in the marine formation. Men were rolling over and writhing among the tussocks and dry cow turds out there.

"Come on, marines, for God's sake! Don't run!" The only surviving officer ran back waving his little halbert. "Come back!" But the retrograde movement was gaining momentum. "Thompson! Harker! Stop those men!" he yelled. "Oh God! Why am I condemned to lead such wretched cowards!"

In a passion the hatless lieutenant reached up and tore off his remaining epaulet.

"There, damn you! I'm no officer of yours! Don't call yourselves marines! You act like damned frog-eating pimps!"

Violently he hurled the lump of silver lace to the earth and stamped on it. A few marines turned and started slowly back, jaws set, eyes ablaze.

Followed by less than a dozen men the lieutenant charged for the pear grove. In his rage and shame the Englishman was weeping. The tears traced clean paths down his powder-blackened cheeks.

"That's better. Now—" He got no farther. The man in decent gray had raised a handsome fowling piece and fired. The heavy bullet's impact knocked the lieutenant right off his feet. His halbert flew shimmering through the air.

More Provincials, smoked out of the village, came up, but the marine detachment was in full retreat, trailed by staggering, limping wounded.

Metcalfe saw the British of General Pigot's wing still on the slope of Breed's Hill exchanging volleys with the redoubt. They were falling back a second time, however.

Buff was trying to tamp home a charge when someone who swore he came from Colonel Prescott himself ran up and told the men in the orchard to fall back. More troops had been seen embarking in Boston. This time it was certain they meant to strike Charles Town in force.

He advised, "You had better retreat along the road that runs across the back of Breed's Hill. There is a barn over there. You might make a stand in it."

Buff caught at his arm. "Misto, whea's de Connecticuters? Ah's jes' *got* to find Misto David."

"Clear around on the other side of this point," the messenger called over his shoulder.

With the other men from Charles Town, Buff retreated. He had started to skirt the rear of Breed's Hill when a terrible old man with two big horse pistols in his belt pointed to the redoubt.

"Go up there! No back talk!"

4 — "STRIKE BRITONS HOME!"

To DAVID, Lord Howe's second attack on the rail fence seemed but the stupid repetition of an initial error. Somehow, the unflinching discipline of those regulars in the face of certain destruction was more appalling than admirable. Good thing he felt numbed to ghastly sights and piteous sounds. In some places the grenadiers had fallen in easily discernible lines. They lay huddled like game arranged after a drive.

From everywhere arose anxious, urgent cries for powder. Captain Knowlton went striding across a gap between the end of the breastwork above and the rail fence. Some stragglers had built three crude *flêches* of rails there. He asked the sunburnt militiamen if they had any to spare.

"Jesus, no, Mister. We got less'n two rounds apiece."

Knowlton hurried back and said, "Ashton! Get up to the redoubt—find whether they have any powder to spare. Even a horn or two would help. If there's none there, wait. Somebody might think to send some forward."

As he climbed Breed's Hill, David was surprised to note

that the afternoon was well advanced. Shadows were lengthening, deepening.

He found Buff hovering outside the sallyport.

"Misto David!" If Buff had had a tail he would be wagging it, thought the Virginian.

"What the devil you doing here, boy? Haven't you got good sense?"

"Oh, Misto David, is you all right? You doan' look so brash."

"I reckon I don't." David's eyes were hollow and red rimmed. His throat felt as if someone had gone over it with sandpaper. The one drink of water he'd swallowed came from a brackish pool and tasted as if it had lain overnight in an old boot. .

"If you have the sense God gave a goat, Buff, you'll chase yourself as fast as you can."

"No, suh, dat don't lissen right to me, suh. Ah reckons Ah stays."

"Well, come along, then."

"Yassuh. Ah's stayin' wid you, suh."

Colonel Prescott in his dirtied banyan was directing men to hatchet open some cartridges brought for the cannons. In very sparing fashion coarse black powder was being rationed into eagerly outstretched hats, horns and flasks. The meager portions gave David no answer to Knowlton's hope.

As soon as they had drawn their two or three rounds apiece, the powder-blackened Provincials scrambled back into the breastwork or sat on its parapet, watching swarms of redcoats land to the windward of Charles Town. Others were reinforcing the mangled regiments on Morton's Point. Prescott's head halted its slow motion to the right. He beckoned an aide.

"Howe has finally got his artillery where it will be of use. Soon he will be able to rake our breastwork. Tell the men in it to come up here."

David was debating whether he should go back and report to Knowlton that there was slim chance of any powder being sent when Johnny Gilmorin saw him.

"Davey!" He rushed forward, barely recognizable. David couldn't help laughing. Johnny's shirt was torn half off; his long, light brown hair was unclubbed and flying wild. One naked shoulder was black and blue from the recoil of his musket. A far cry, this, from the Johnny who doted on gay cockades and wigs of the latest *ton*. His face was so coated with burnt powder grains that the whites of his eyes showed up even brighter than Buff's.

"Hi, Johnny! Did I say something about the Yankees being scared to fight?"

Cried Johnny, a fine clear flame in his eyes, "They can fight! Damned if they flinched, even when some Britishers got right up to the parapet." He lowered his voice, licked his lips in puzzled fashion. "But, hang it all, Davey, they don't seem to take any pleasure in fighting. They're so—so damn' *serious* about it!"

He broke off. David was staring at a courier who had just appeared. He was wearing a very lumpy-looking hunting shirt. While he was talking to Colonel Prescott, its tie string came undone. Underneath the shirt, he was wearing a blue uniform turned up with red.

David, tired to the point of faintness, grinned. "My boy, doesn't that look like one of your Wethersfield peacocks?"

Johnny looked thunderstruck. He called, "Say, what's the idea covering up your regimentals like that? You ought to be ashamed!"

The Connecticut man looked sulky, blinked in the dusty sunlight of the redoubt. "Go ahead and laugh, but we don't aim to get joshed all day over some no-'count uniforms."

Johnny gaped, incredulous, shocked as he had not been by anything that had gone before. High God in His Heaven! This yokel was actually ashamed to let his regimentals be seen! It was the last straw. All day he had been looking for war as it ought to be; a bright gallant war. "Pray shoot first, gentlemen of France!" *"Mais non, tirez les premiers, Messieurs les Anglais!"* That sort of thing.

In the right kind of war men didn't writhe about trying to cram entrails back into their bellies with dusty fingers, soldiers didn't whimper with fear like little puppy dogs, officers didn't shovel dirt until their hands were raw and slippery. Soldiers never ran away, or pretended to get taken sick so they could go to the rear—like Colonel Bridge and Lieutenant-Colonel Brickett.

Suddenly Johnny felt a thousand years old, very tired and, now that those distant drums were tapping for the third time, just a little scared. That was wrong, too. Long since, the British should have admitted that they were beaten.

David, having read a measure of his disillusion, put a

hand to Johnny's damp shoulder. "One more repulse, Johnny, and even those damned brave bastards down there will have had enough. Then we can go back to quarters and get stink-o!"

"Come on up." Nat Coffin turned a profile gilded by sweat and sun. "Here's a couple of good loopholes. Find any powder? I have only three shots left."

Other voices, croaking with thirst, called, "Powder! Where in hell is some powder?" "Damned Committee's sent no powder all day!" "We've been betrayed—I told you so!"

"This time they mean business," an officer in muddied breeches said.

The British array was not so colorful. At last they had shed their heavy packs and a lot of them had removed smotheringly hot uniform coats. Not a few infantrymen had stripped to the waist, slinging over naked shoulders the crossbelts which supported their cartouche boxes and bayonets. With their tall bearskins and powdered hair the effect was grotesque.

The officers, however, had disdained to remove either coat or shirt, but their finery was sadly stained and their white leggings had taken on a pinkish hue from the bloodied grass stems which had brushed them. David, resting his musket across the berm of the earthwork, noted how motionless patches of white and scarlet dotted the slope from the crest of Breed's Hill all the way to Morton's Point.

Colonel Prescott, his blue banyan ripped and smeared, hurriedly rearranged the defenders. Along the redoubt's south wall he placed those men who were coming up from the abandoned breastwork. Headed by General Warren, the few remaining Provincial officers began checking powder flasks. Many were quite empty and the rest so sparsely filled the officers' expressions grew strained.

"Any men having bayonets had better fix them," Warren called.

"I got a war hatchet," proclaimed a man in a buckskin shirt. "That's better'n a baynit any time!"

When the British in their long lines again started climbing that series of stone walls which had gone so far to exhaust them in their previous efforts, no drums were beating. Grenadiers and light infantry were all mixed up with the regular line companies. David saw tall shakoes stand out like dark stumps in a red and white field. The short-skirted light in-

ntry coats looked frivolous among the longer ones of
gular length.

The enemy climbed faster, much faster than before. Na-
aniel Coffin's usual half mocking smile was absent as,
arefully, he tucked three bullets between the knuckles of his
ft hand, crammed six paper wads into the top of his
reeches.

David glanced sidewise. Johnny's face was pale and the
o delicate line of his chin quivered. The strain was getting
im. Farther over, Buff's head made a shiny black smudge
gainst the raw oak of a gun carriage. Tense as a hound's
ie big Negro's head was outthrust and his yellowish eyes
arrowed.

"Will you look at 'em come?" somebody muttered.

The British raised a cheer and kept on without waiting to
eform every time they crossed a fence; previously they had
lways realigned their ranks. The officers, though they must
ave realized their especial peril, were again well out in
ront.

A recruit just up from the rear leveled his gun barrel at a
ery fat officer waddling along. He was using his sword as
cane when he came to a tough spot.

"Put up that gun!" Colonel Prescott roared. The recruit
as too scared or too slow to obey, so the colonel jumped up
n the berm and himself kicked up the barrel. "Make every
hot count," he warned, jaw muscles twitching. "Let them
et real close this time. Close enough to see the color of
heir eyes."

Down by the rail fence, Shaun Mahoney, having used the
ast of his powder, dropped his musket and ran like hell. He
ntended to get over the Neck in time.

Unhampered by packs, the English scaled the daisy and
nustard flower-dotted slope almost rapidly and, at sixty yards'
ange, commenced firing very coolly. After each volley they
vould advance ten yards and fire again. The bloodied corpses
mong the flowering hay grass might not have been there.

The British fire intensified, for the first time became ef-
ective. Men were being hit. The Provincials crouched lower,
hielding their eyes from dirt sent flying by bullets. Thou-
ands of giant bees hummed over David's head and now and
hen a ricocheting bullet raised an eerie whine.

Colonel Prescott's ridiculously thin rapier wavered in the hot air. "Get set, boys. The officers first!" By the dozen, long barrels slipped over the top of the parapet.

David, peering over the tumbled earth, picked out an officer, a gross, fat-shouldered fellow with a big belly wabbling beneath a buff waistcoat. By God! That was Bouquet! The major's heavy features were shining as if lacquered and since he wore a soggy red bandage about his left arm, he must have been this way at least once before.

"Fire!"

The weird assortment of firearms in the redoubt roared and like dominoes the first rank of the British began spinning and tumbling about. But the other lines came on. A few scattered shots roared in an effort to check them. David thought of Hannibal, and took a careful bead on Major Bouquet's chest. This was the last of his powder.

In a hot rage he squeezed the trigger and must have pulled too hard. His ball merely tore some gold bullion from Bouquet's shoulder. The major roared and shook his sword at the redoubt. David had to hand it to that Englishman, the way he kept on coming!

Johnny not recognizing him, instead picked off a captain 'way down on the right. He winked at Coffin, said, "Pay me!"

"Forward, lads—got them!" Bouquet was struggling across a ditch below the parapet. He was dreadfully out of breath, but still could make himself heard. "Forward! Forward!"

The British, encouraged to be so much nearer their goal than they had ever been, set up a fierce yammering. A dozen half-naked grenadiers broke into a run; bayonets swinging, they poured into the ditch below. When more soldiers came, they began boosting each other up.

Meanwhile the Provincial fire had gone out like an old candle. The attackers, too, stopped shooting for fear of hurting their own men. To climb up onto the parapet the English were forced to use both hands. To do it some of them, unwisely, laid their muskets on the berm of the redoubt. David and some others snatched these up and began smashing at the powdered heads which came clambering up.

"Oh God, isn't there *any* more powder?" Johnny began yelling crazily. "Powder! Give me powder!"

Nat Coffin, stooping, caught up a stone. He heaved it with all his might and, catching a disheveled Englishman on the side of the head, dropped him cold.

When the other men saw that, they too dropped their useless muskets and commenced throwing stones. In astonishment the British wavered. The frontiersman sent his war hatchet spinning through the air. It split in half the face of a beefy sergeant swaying with leveled bayonet on top of the parapet. Right above David a figure scrambled into sight! Major Bouquet!

He seemed tall as the Colossus of Rhodes when he brandished his sword and roared, "Surrender, you rebels!"

"We are not rebels!" Colonel Prescott shouted.

Raising his rapier, he started forward, but Buff, crouched by a cannon's trail, heard Bouquet's voice and glimpsed him against the sky. In a flash he whipped up the duck gun and fired.

A full load of ball and buckshot struck Major Ponsonby Bouquet under his raised right arm. It ripped his scarlet coat into tatters, front and back.

"Dere's cutleries fer you!" snarled the Negro, then dropped his gun and joined a mob of fugitives fighting to get out of the sallyport.

A dying British officer falling into the redoubt dropped his sword almost at Johnny's feet. A sword! He snatched eagerly at it. This was more like it. Ha! The grip, though slippery with its late owner's sweat, felt fine in his hand— reassuring. Shouting, he turned with some others to dispute the British advance.

By tens and twenties attackers swept over the parapet and jumped down behind leveled bayonets. Dust rose in blinding eddies, figures disappeared, reappeared—red, homespun, white. Thumping sounds. Curses. Johnny parried a bayonet's point and drove his blade in hard. It pierced through the fellow's throat. Why, this was easy!

"Forward! Forward!" he screamed. The captured blade shivered, but he beat aside another bayonet and slashed back. Missed this time.

An eddy of Royal Marines swept up from the right, driving a few Provincials before them. Leaping backward, the Yankees were swinging desperately with their clubbed muskets.

"Nah then, ye bleedin' rebel!" Johnny saw a towering sergeant gather himself behind his musket, and fell back a step to win elbow room. His heel struck an abandoned pickaxe and he lurched backward off balance. All the world resolved into a long brown face set with blazing blue eyes, snaggle teeth and writhing lips. A shooting star of steel materialized between him and it.

"Don't!" Johnny screamed and, using his left hand, tried to deflect the down-rushing bayonet, but the point caught on his palm, punched clean through it. Drove onwards. Johnny felt his arm slammed tight against his chest. He suffered an excruciating, unbelievable pang, then distinctly felt the grating of steel against one of his ribs. The big sergeant had all his weight behind his bayonet so, quite easily, he pinned Johnny Gilmorin to the dusty trampled ground.

Magically the tumult faded. Johnny caught a fleeting glimpse of a white-pillared mansion and of a paddock nearer at hand. Some mares and their foals stood in it, switching flies beneath a summer sun. He heard a tender, beloved voice murmur, "You must go to sleep now, Johnny. You are tired and it is very late."

Nothing more.

David, fighting alongside Colonel Prescott, was much too busy to see what had happened elsewhere. Supported by a handful of men, Prescott was trying to delay the enemy until Provincials without bayonets could escape through the sally-port. Surprisingly enough, the more he whirled his Brown Bess by its barrel, the more strength David felt welling back into his body. There was, he discovered, a fierce and unsuspected satisfaction in this business of killing people.

He made such an iron windmill of his musket that the British began to give way before him. At once some Provincials rallied and were starting forward, but a light infantry-man slipped in behind David and jabbed his bayonet deep into the Virginian's right shoulder. Reeling under the shock, David dropped his musket and when the Englishman struggled to free his bayonet, he was pulled over backwards. A snarl of panting grenadiers closed in and a whole constellation of steel stars hovered above him. But a harsh voice rasped.

"Leave the wounded be, you bloody idiots! Get after the live ones, or they'll be back."

Sprawled across a litter of abandoned entrenching tools and firearms, David lay spouting blood over the floor of the redoubt. Confusedly, his half-closed eyes registered the passage of many shouting men, but the picture made no impression on his brain. An icy lump came into being in his stomach, began to expand. He must be bleeding a lot—should do something about it. Couldn't. Too tired.

A gay, mocking face looked into his—Andrea Grenville's—of all people. Was that Katie's rich, throaty laughter sounding so close? Were Madelaine's cool fingertips brushing his forehead?

It wasn't so bad just to lie still, comforted by the sun's warmth. Odd, the redoubt, the sky, everything, had begun slowly to revolve. The world spun faster. Faster.

A hand grabbed his good arm and tugged him over onto his back. A tired voice directed:

"Tie a rag over that hole in his shoulder. We must take some prisoners to show for this hellish day's work."

Book Three

Bermuda

Part I

The Desdemona, Schooner

1 — BEN

THE sun would rise in a few minutes, Rob Ashton thought. He turned to the quartermaster who at his elbow stood ready to heave the *Desdemona*'s log ship and asked, "Sure the peg is in tight?" He indicated a small ivory stick protruding from the frame of a wooden equilateral triangle. It was thrust into a hole drilled above a leaden weight attached to one corner of the log ship. The whole affair was slung at the end of a triangular bridle with leaders secured to the peg and to the triangle's two other corners.

"Yessir."

Captain Rudder inquired, "Glass ready, Mr. Ashton?"

Rob nodded, held up a small hour glass. It required exactly twenty-eight seconds to empty.

Rudder called, "Heave the log ship!"

As the quartermaster dropped the device over the stern, Rudder straightened, intently watching the stay line whip overboard. A wooden reel held between his hands spun so furiously it chattered on its axle. Rudder kept his attention riveted upon it. The instant a small strip of blue cloth lashed to the log line flickered over the rail, he yelled, "Turn!"

Rob flipped over the hour glass. Though he concentrated on the thread of falling sand, he knew that the log line, anchored at its far end by the log ship, was shooting out, for the *Desdemona* was ploughing quite briskly over the waves. One—two—three marks slid over the stern.

When the last grain of sand fell Rob yelled, "Stop!"

Instantly Captain Rudder checked his reel and, in so doing pulled out the bone peg fitted into the base of the log ship. Its resistance diminished, the contrivance immediately flattened out and skipped merrily over waves in the schooner's wake.

Captain Rudder said, "Read off."

When they had done reeling in the stiff, cold log line, it was learned that seven knots had been unreeled during the twenty-eight seconds.

For her, the *Desdemona* was moving right along.

"Thank you, sir," Rudder said to Rob and went over to chalk the reading down on a slate. Another would be taken at the end of an hour, and so on. Averaged, the readings would give the ship's approximate rate of speed for the twenty-four hours.

Presently Captain Rudder went below to write up his log book.

Yes, the *Desdemona* was proving a better sailor than Rob had been expecting. Seven knots. Not bad speed for such an old relic. The wind was fair, blowing fresh and not cold. If it held, he reckoned they ought to raise the Bermudas inside of ten days—nine maybe. The last of North America had been seen at twilight. He had been feeling better ever since.

Approaching the binnacle, he addressed the quartermaster. Though it wasn't immediately apparent, George Wincapaw was a sharp-faced mulatto with pale gray eyes. Large brown freckles gave the impression of being beneath his skin instead of on its surface. Two small golden rings set one above the other in the rim of his right ear glittered in the sunrise.

"Your course?"

"Nor'east by east."

"Say 'sir' when you address me."

"Yes sir. 'Sir' it is, sir."

The quartermaster blinked. Damned if he fancied the situation. Ben Rudder was supposed to be captain, wasn't he? Yet why did the owner take it on himself to check courses? The hell with the owner! George Wincapaw could steer a course truer than any ten average helmsmen.

Satisfied, Rob crossed to the break of the poop and stood there, yielding to the schooner's easy motion. The ginger-colored slave who had claimed to be a cook was bringing to the galley door a smudged brass kettle and a bag of ship's bread. These he handed to a big shiny black deckhand who carried them off to the foredeck. Just short of the forecastle the rest of his watch were gathered. The shiny-looking deckhand began ladling stew into wooden bowls which his companions held out. Apparently they didn't like the look of it and said so with many angry looks at the galley.

"If this boogie Rudder's signed is a cook," Rob reflected, "then I'm a monkey's uncle."

The supper served last night in the stern cabin had been scorched, completely barren of seasoning and altogether unpalatable.

Trailed by his footprints outlined in dew, Rob returned to the stern. He lingered there, studying the schooner's hissing, bubbling wake. It slashed a straight white trail across the ocean's gray-blue bosom. Following a prolongation of it, he saw, far astern and just rising above the horizon, the faintest imaginable white speck of a sail. It was, he reckoned, a coaster on her way to some northern port.

He wondered what was keeping Rudder below. In the matter of officers the *Desdemona* would, for the outward voyage at least, be deplorably short-handed. The after guard consisted of Rudder and himself. He had signed on Rudder because he had to. The master had been so long out of a ship he was damned glad to sign on at a minimum wage. He had fallen all over himself to get his name on the papers. It was further understood he was to complete and to correct Rob's faulty knowledge of navigation.

Unwisely, the cook clumped out to see how the crew was taking to his fare. He soon learned. Under a deluge of hearty curses, he whipped back into his galley so fast that the tail of a gray worsted cap curled about his neck like that of a pet monkey.

Something would have to be done in that direction. The fellow's dirty apron and smeared jersey were so ragged that his swart skin looked through at the shoulder; it was scarcely appetizing. Besides, as St. John Ashton had sworn, and proved more than once, a couple of well-fed hands got more done than three poorly found ones.

Where the devil had Captain Rudder taken himself? Rob wasn't worried. He was sure Rudder would straighten out all right, now that he had a vessel again. He'd been a good man, had Ben, one of the best before a British prize court sustained H.M.S. *Liverpool*'s outrageous libel.

Besides, he had sworn to let no liquor pass his lips while at sea. Poor Rudder! When he had brought his dunnage aboard two days earlier, his big tattooed hands were shaking something awful, but there had been no liquor on his breath. Still absently considering that distant sail, Rob wondered how far too much liquor might eat into a man's fiber. Even if he laid off liquor for good, could a drunk ever again be the man he had been before he began hitting the bottle?

Softly the wind beat against Rob's face and the sun, lifting clear of the horizon, gilded the schooner's mildewed mainsail. The topsails, stretched out of shape long ago, slatted as, comfortably, the *Desdemona* heeled over under a puff.

He was wondering what his cousin Peter Ashton might look like when he heard steps on the companion and Rudder appeared, his nose ludicrously bright in the sunlight. Cheerily he touched the brim of his cap.

"Well, Mr. Ashton, I'm damned if we ain't got a stowaway!"

Holy Sailor! Rob was hanged if he hadn't forgotten Katherine Tryon's existence.

"Really?" He smiled. "Fetch her up on deck and let's see what's what."

"Yes, sir." Rudder's figure, long and lanky in blue and white, started off, then paused. "What was that you said about fetching a 'her,' Mr. Ashton?"

"I said fetch her on deck. Don't worry. I know the wench is aboard."

"You *knew?*"

"Yes, I'm helping—" He stiffened.

Rudder's loose grin faded and he spoke seriously. "You've misread your signals, then, sir. The stowaway ain't a her—it's a him."

"What!"

"Yes, sir. A no-'count shrimp of a nigger. He was hiding in the forehold 'mongst the sacked onions."

"The devil you say! Where is he?"

"Forrad, sir. Hey, Qumana! Fetch that 'coon aft."

Rob's instinctive annoyance evaporated when it came over him that, far from being a calamity, it was a blessing to have a stowaway aboard. A vessel of one hundred and fifty tons called for more than a crew of six. Five and the cook was all the crew he'd been able to afford. An extra deckhand would be just about as welcome as a quart of whiskey at a barn raising.

"Please suh, please, doan' hu't me!" A scared voice preceded the approach of a small bow-legged Negro. "Ah will wu'k real ha'hd. Fo' Gawd Ah will!"

Fluttering in the grasp of a barrel-chested slave seaman,

the stowaway looked for all the world like a dingy black cockerel dragged from a coop. His shoulders were so stooped as to appear hunchbacked. When he was led closer, Rob received the impression of having seen him before somewhere.

Emitting a gurgle of terror, the stowaway flung himself onto the deck.

"Please—please, Massa, doan' hu't me! Las' week ol' compoun' boss done whupped me turrible bad!" In a frenzy of haste the runaway slave tugged up his jersey and when he turned around Rob felt his stomach go queasy. The stowaway's back was a criss-crossed pattern of half-healed scars. Some of the scabs had cracked across and tiny drops of blood were seeping through them. In the strong sunlight they looked like little rubies.

"Stop that damn' whimpering," Rob ordered. "Who are you?"

"Doan' you 'member me, Misto Ashton? Yo' Mistis done sign me on de ol' 'Sistance las' yea'h. Mah name is Ben."

Recollection came. Peggy had signed on this hunchback and another, a giant—a bad nigger. He had twitted her about them.

The stowaway began pulling together his shirt. "No suh, Ah didn' winter so pert, an' Misto Candless he say take it out of mah hide. Laws, Misto Ashton! Ah sho do wish you'd kep' me on de way you kep' on Buff. Ah been poorly, but Ah kin wu'k plenty ha'd on good eatments. Yessuh, Ah kin."

That Ben was in bad shape was easy to see. The slave's skin showed slate-gray instead of a healthy brown-black. His eyes seemed watery, but maybe that was due to fright.

"I reckon you wouldn't be much use at pulling and hauling," Rob commented. "You do anything else?"

"Well, suh, Ah was cook on a brig down to Trinidad two voyages. Folks 'lowed Ah didn' do so bad. Ef Ah could only——"

Rudder interrupting, pointed out, "Old Candless will make plenty of trouble for us, Mr. Ashton, when we get back. He gets mighty tough about runaway niggers."

Rob said, "To hell with Candless; never did treat his people half decent. We can worry about him later. See if the quartermaster can't find a decent rig in the slop chest. Then have Ben hosed down. You better pitch those rags overboard. They're crawling."

Rob spoke sharply. He hated vermin so much he'd devoted two whole days to burning sulphur and to thoroughly scrubbing the *Desdemona*. He couldn't stand the thought of Peggy living with rats and other vermin.

Rob turned quietly aside. "Better keep an eye on that sail," he suggested. "Begins to look at if she might be on our heels."

"The devil! What can she want of us?" Nervously, Captain Rudder licked loose lips and shoved a three-cornered hat on the back of his head in order to level a spyglass.

"She's brig-rigged," he presently announced, "and coming up with a bone in her teeth. Hope to God she ain't some damned nosey British revenue cutter."

"Our papers are all right."

"Maybe so, sir, but that makes no never mind to a bulldog when he's hungry for prize money. If he's so minded, he'll find an excuse to whip us into New York in no time."

Rob would not let himself worry, so he went below. The words of a popular London ditty reached him, charged with a haunting sweetness. Halfway down the companionway, he paused, trying to recall when last he had heard Peggy sing:

> "On Richmond Hill there lives a lass
> More bright than May day morn,
> Whose charms no other maids surpass,
> O Rose without a thorn."

His heart gave a glad surge. Their relations had been indefinably, secretively at odds for such a long time. An opportune moment, this, to spring his surprise. Peggy, he reckoned, would be mighty comforted and pleased to learn a woman had been brought aboard especially to attend her wants.

Instead of following a short passage into the main cabin, he turned right at the foot of the companion stair and a moment later stood before a door leading into the main hold. Here Tom MacSherry's protégée should be hiding.

Ever since the schooner had begun to rock and the sea to gurgle beyond the sheathing, Katie Tryon's sense of joyful relief had augmented steadily. It was grand to be so surely beyond reach of the Skillingses! Mr. Tom had been right. In Norfolk she would have been forever anxious, always peering fearfully over her shoulder. Everything would be simply perfect if only Mr. David had been the owner of this boat instead of his brother; not that Mr. Rob wasn't being almighty kind, she hurriedly reproached herself. She felt so grateful she intended working for him and Mrs. Ashton when they got to Bermuda as long as he wanted—for nothing. She hoped Mrs. Ashton had got over the grouch she'd had that day at the Spread Eagle. If she hadn't, she allowed she could bear it; the worst Mrs. Ashton could say or do wouldn't be a patch on Ma Skillings's efforts.

People like Mr. MacSherry and the Ashton brothers made a girl realize men weren't always the selfish brutes she used to think.

Whatever lay ahead, Katie was feeling mighty rested and encouraged. My, but it had been cozy lying in the dark, sleeping the clock 'round. Sacked corn and some flour bags didn't make a bad bed and the familiar smell of grain and cabbages lent a comforting sense of hominess. It was a surprise to her she hadn't felt seasick. She surely had expected to be.

By sense of touch Katie braided her hair, winding it upwards about her head into a golden crown. She had finished when the *cluck!* of a door lock not far away threw her into an inexplicable panic. Suppose this wasn't Mr. Rob? Suppose Tom MacSherry had played a trick and was selling her to some Boston or New York whoremaster? Come to think of it, there was no way of knowing he hadn't; such a dodge wasn't uncommon in Norfolk. Her terror grew when she recalled not even having read the name of this ship! Mr. MacSherry just led her out on a wharf and had pointed to a hatch yawning black behind a heap of freight.

"Get down in there. Keep quiet!" was all he had whispered.

She almost cried out once the door creaked open and a shadowy figure materialized. She went clammy all over with dread.

"Katherine Tryon?" the apparition called and her fears went out like a turned-down lamp. The voice was reminiscent of Mr. David's; a little deeper, but still very like.

"I'm here, sir."

"Good. You all right?"

"Oh—oh, y-yes, sir."

"Come along then. We'll go see Mrs. Ashton."

Peggy was still singing:

"This lass so neat, with smiles so sweet
Has won my right good will.
I'd crowns resign to call her mine,
Sweet lass of Richmond Hill."

She felt it was fine to be free of Norfolk, away from the town's sorrows, hatreds and disappointments. At eighteen she was still young enough to respond to the adventurous challenge of this voyage. Precious few young women of Norfolk, she prided herself, would even dream of going to sea in the family way, and seven months along. Yet she wasn't afraid, really she wasn't.

Though her bunk seemed narrow, she had put her own sheets and pillow on it, and the cabin wasn't proving as uncomfortable as she had feared. But something would have to be done about the cooking! That scorched and greasy mess Qumana had plunked down on the cabin table was enough to make her stomach writhe. Once the schooner got farther out to sea, she would talk to Rob. No use bothering him with trifles while he was keeping a weather eye out for the King's ships.

A crisp breeze beating in the wide stern ports playfully fluttered a blue ribbon she was stitching to a bonnet for the baby. She had decided to spend the day on deck. However monotonous it was in the cabin, upstairs—no, "aloft" was the right word—there was always something to look at. When Rob and Captain Rudder took sights and figured the schooner's position, she would listen hard. She had determined also to learn navigation so Rob might consult her in hiring future captains. Rudder, indeed!

She had become conscious of a guilty feeling. The baby's layette was scandalously small and so many of Rob's stockings needed darning. Well, during the voyage she would have time and to spare for knitting and stitching.

From her trunk she selected a fresh apron, a pretty flounced affair. Suddenly it struck her afresh that Rob was really a good husband, a fine, upright man with no small amount of courage. Certainly it must come hard to be sweet and considerate at a time when so many men turned away from an ungainly and querulous wife to play with other women. Never in her life had she been madder than when Charlie Vyner took a mistress because Lottie got pregnant, lost her looks and swelled up like a pan of dried apples set to soak.

Was she becoming very unattractive? A critical glance in a tarnished looking-glass screwed to the woodwork above her bunk reassured her. Her small pointed face looked rosy with health. Her eyes were clear and of a pretty shade of dark blue—if she did say it herself. Except for her figure, she was looking better than she had in a long time. Last night the schooner's easy motion and an obbligato of softly groaning timbers had lulled her into a profound and restful slumber. It was an unutterable relief to know the die of Fortune had been cast. Now she was very glad she had not reached her father's ship in time. She would never again let her impulses run away with her.

Recognizing Rob's springily solid footstep on the companion ladder, she hurried over to sit in an armchair he had brought aboard and clamped to the floor for her. Sitting down, her sticking-outness wasn't so apparent. She felt a sudden urgent need of his putting his arms about her; the way he used to at Tide-over. If Rob would only do that, she knew they could forget the awful winter and, erasing memories of distrust and constraint, start all over.

With skilled, swift fingers she dabbed her hair into place, smoothed the ruffles of her apron. Surely he must sense her mood, her craving for tenderness. Eagerly she faced the door. Her heart sank. Oh confound it! A second set of steps was advancing. She wished she could get to really like Captain Rudder—but she couldn't. He was so messy, and smelt so of chewing tobacco. His clothes gave off the odor of stale sweat.

"I beg to report a fine morning, Mrs. A." Rob greeted, swinging through the white-painted door frame. With his cheeks so windburned he looked handsomer than ever. Her heart skipped a beat when she saw how attractively a breeze had rumpled his hair. "I hope you began the voyage with a lucky dream?"

"I slept excellently well, Mr. A.," she retorted with mock gravity, "and I feel simply elegant. Dearest, do you know, I've a premonition this voyage is going to be grand fun?"

"Of course it will," he laughed and, bending swiftly, kissed her on the forehead. "I've a surprise aboard for you."

"A surprise?" Peggy was amazed to hear herself utter a school-girl's giggle. "What?"

"A stewardess, my dear. A nice young woman to make your bed, wash your clothes and to wait on you."

"Oh, you darling!" She held up her arms, but he had turned to the door and was beckoning someone outside.

"This is Katherine Tryon," said he smiling. "I hope she will prove satisfactory."

As Katie bent to enter the schooner's main cabin—a large one which ran across the vessel's whole beam—sunlight, glancing up from a wave, momentarily lit her face. To the last detail it revealed the friendly, honest good nature of it. Little flashes of light caught her yellow hair.

"Her!" Peggy stiffened violently on her chair. Her mouth sagged open and she leaned forward, eyes narrowed. Then, to Rob's overwhelming amazement, color flared into her small features. She half arose, but had to sink heavily back as the ship heaved.

"Get her out of my cabin! Send that shameless wench out of here!" The command was strident with outrage.

It was Rob's turn to stare. "But, Peggy, whatever—why, that's no way to talk! You don't even know this girl. How can you—"

"You! *You!* Be quiet!" Peggy's voice rose in a quivering crescendo. Angry tears glittered in her eyes. To think she'd been fooling herself. This was Charlie and Lottie Vyner all over again! How *dared* Rob take along this soiled tavern wench? Her fingers became pale claws on the chair arms.

"So I don't know Spread Eagle Katie? Bah! You insult my intelligence, you pitiable fool! I might have forgiven your picking anyone else." Her voice trembled with rage. "But you had to bring aboard the most shameless tavern wench in Norfolk. Your jailbird brother's ex-mistress! How dare you try to palm her off as a stewardess! For *my* sake you brought her along! Ha—ha—ha!" Her laugh was ghastly. "For *my* sake!"

Katie stood wretched, trembling. Her chin quivered. That awful stunned look on Mr. Rob's face was more than she could bear. She plucked up courage.

"Please, Mrs. Ashton, Ma'am, what you've been saying ain't so! I swear to God it ain't! Until today Mr. Ashton never did lay eyes on me. And," she added in the sullen undertone she used with Ma Skillings, "I never got in bed with Mr. David, neither."

"Then he was the only man in town you didn't," Peggy

stormed, her eyes round and deadly. "Get out! You—you damned huzzy! How dare you pollute a decent woman's cabin with your—your lewdness?" She snatched the word from a tirade with which her mother lashed indiscreet kitchen slaves. "Get out of here! Get out! Get out, both of you! Don't come near me, either of you! Oh—oh, if only I were—"

From a table at her elbow she snatched up a treatise on navigation and flung it—hard. The book hit Rob in the face and rocked his head back, but otherwise he remained motionless, eyes fixed on his wife.

"Katherine, go up on deck," he ordered without turning his head.

Katie went, drowned in a sea of bitter sorrow. Of course this solution to her problem had been too good to be true. All her beautiful, confident plans had vanished as completely as a soap bubble pierced by the straw of a teasing boy.

Long and patiently Rob argued, persuaded, but the longer he talked, the more surely a fragile and irreplaceable something died within him. From this hour things could never again be quite as they had been during the golden days at Tide-over.

Peggy retired into the hard impermeable shell of injured pride. Desperate doubts arose. Could she have misjudged Rob? Even if this were so, it was not in her to admit it—at least not quickly. After all, there was reason to suspect that this was the story of the Vyners all over again; she blew hard on that coal of suspicion.

The wretched scene persisted until Captain Rudder, quite unaware, came clumping down the companion. Halfway below he sang out, "Mr. Ashton?"

"Well?"

"That there brig is overhauling us. I don't like the look of things."

2 — The Fair Wind

Rob found Captain Rudder with a spyglass clamped to his eye. In trying to steady it he stood with his whiskey-bloated belly looped over the scarred and green painted taffrail. In an anxious knot the crew was gathered amidships. They were all staring back at the white sails and gray hull of a vessel storming up under the fresh westerly breeze. Every now and then the mulatto quartermaster would sneak a look over his shoulder. He looked mighty scared.

Rob asked, "Learned her nationality?" He felt weak, sickened by that session below.

"Not yet, sir," Rudder grunted, voice half lost in the hissing of the wake. "She ain't showing colors."

"Pirate?"

The other shook his head twice. "Ain't likely. Too far north. Besides, she looks clean. Saw a captured buccaneer down to St. Augustine once, reg'lar floating hog pen."

Katie, bare legs crossed under her, was crouched, forlorn, on a corner of the deck. Clutched in her lap rested the pitiful bundle she had brought aboard. She looked as if she expected to be ordered off the schooner within the next five minutes. Alone of those on deck she did not watch the pursuing vessel.

"Carrying guns?"

"Yes, Mr. Ashton. They've three, anyhow, to a broadside. Maybe five."

"Reckon she might be French?"

"She foots along so fast you may be right. But I didn't hear of no trouble with the French before we sailed, did you, sir?"

No, Rob said, he hadn't.

The ship astern was coming up hand-over-fist. No doubt of it. Since it wouldn't get dark for hours, it was obvious the schooner had no choice but to stay on her course and hope for the best. She stood about as much chance of outrunning the stranger as a cart horse might of outdistancing a steeplechaser.

Rob crossed over to Katie and in a strained voice snapped, "Why didn't you say you used to work at the Spread Eagle?"

"Why, I reckoned Mr. MacSherry had told you all about me," the girl replied so readily he guessed she must be speaking the truth.

"Well, he didn't. The harm's done. Neither of us is to blame. You had better make up a bunk in the main hold. I'll see you are given bedding. You will be comfortable there."

"Oh yes, sir." Katie lifted a tear-stained, woebegone face. "Oh please, Mr. Ashton, ain't—isn't there *something* I could do? Just setting 'round, I would feel awful bad."

"I don't know." He didn't want Peggy roused by sight of Katherine Tryon. An inspiration came. "Can you cook?"

Katie's broad face lit with a wide white smile. "Oh, yes, sir! I cooked all the time for Missis Skillings."

Rob nodded gloomily. He wished he could get his mind off that vessel astern, forget the quarrel with Peggy. But he could do neither one thing nor the other.

"Very well. There is a cot rigged in the back of the galley. You can move in as soon as I chase that food waster out of it."

Things were simplifying themselves. The cook would, willy-nilly, become an ordinary seaman; Ben would act as table steward and perform the tasks he had originally intended for Katie. Peggy would be pleased to have near her a man she had once befriended. Recently he had noticed she wasn't wholly forgetful of her kind acts.

By ten of the morning the mysterious brig was sailing less than a quarter of a mile astern and somewhat to windward. Watching her speed over the gray-blue rollers, Rob suffered reminiscent twinges. A pretty sailor, by God! He speculated on whether the *Grand Turk* might have outfooted her. He reckoned she would have. She should have sailed as fast as greased lightning. The stranger's bow was well designed, better than that of ninety-nine out of a hundred vessels, but it held coarsening traces of bluffness while his *Grand Turk*— The hell with it! He would never know.

The strange brig's master had set courses, tops, gallants and royals, and had braced them right, too. Not a square yard of canvas but was taut, straining with wind. Rob, through Rudder's telescope, noted that though many men were crowding her deck, they had not yet triced up her gunport covers. On the stranger's stern stood a knot of men. Two of them could be seen working over the main gaff halyards.

Rudder's big-knuckled hands tightened on the rail as he said, "They're going to show colors!"

A sharp tingling started just above Rob's buttocks. It felt as if he had sat on a wasp. Crimanently! How fast that brig sailed! A continuous smother of foam was spurting from under her bowsprit. She was overhauling the schooner so easily it seemed as if the *Desdemona* were anchored.

A cry broke from the crew as a small black package commenced to climb towards the stranger's main gaff. In an agony of suspense Rob's breath hovered in his lungs. When the brig forged abeam—just where her broadside would be the most effective—the man at the signal halyards gave them a hard jerk.

A resounding yell arose from amidships on the schooner. Into the breeze had sprung a Union Jack. Its red, white and blue showed bright against the cloudless June sky.

Swearing a blue streak in his relief, Rudder mopped his face with a faded bandanna. "Wish to Jesus I hadn't sworn off liquor. I could do with one damn big drink!"

Despite the breeze, trickles of sweat were creeping from under Rob's arms; they tickled his ribs. Suddenly he whipped off his hat and led the crew in three loud cheers.

Rudder lumbered over and began fumbling through the flag locker. When he bent on and hoisted the schooner's own Jack, the stranger's Negro crew and white officers raised a hoarse, answering yell. Already the brig was rushing ahead amid a lacy welt of spray.

"Well named, I'd say," Rudder observed, worrying off a huge chew from a twist of nigger-heel.

Executed in dark red on the gray brig's stern four words showed up sharp: *Speedwell, Port Royal, Bermuda.*

The second day out of Norfolk proved fair and, better still, a strong westerly breeze drove the schooner along at a comfortable pace.

"At this rate we ought to be raising the Bermudas in eight days," Rudder confidently predicted. "See if we don't."

"Ever put into the Bermudas before?" Rob queried. "St. George's, Port Royal, or Eli's Harbour?"

"Can't say as I have touched there, sir. They're out o' the way, them islands, kind of. But I've heard tell a master has to look lively once he's made his landfall. There's plenty of reefs offshore and Job Waller 'llows the Navy charts ain't worth the paper they're drawed on."

It was lucky, Rob realized, that his schooner was making such a quick passage. Some few onions were sprouting and the cabbages had begun to smell a little.

The situation in the stern cabin was not much improved. Peggy had adopted a cold, martyr-like attitude; was only formally polite at mealtimes. It was characteristic that, recognizing the hired captain's value, she would make a special effort to exempt him from her general displeasure. The effort was not so great as she had anticipated because Captain Ben Rudder was looking better. His eyes were clear, steadier, and much of the puffiness about his mouth had vanished. The white matter was disappearing from his eye corners.

Once Rob found him lingering above the forehold.

Said he dolefully, "Wish that there molasses didn't smell so much like rum."

Ben proved willing, but the stowaway was far from strong. When he cleared the table that night, the new steward's hands trembled and his breath stank.

Peggy could have murdered Captain Rudder for filling a rank clay pipe and lighting it from a whale-oil lantern swinging in lazy arcs above the table.

Drawled he, quite unconscious of offense, "If this here wind holds forty-eight hours more, we'll come near making a record passage. Even if that *Speedwell* was freighting victuals, prices will still be kite high, and we will be next in. Yessiree, you ought to clear a tidy sum, Mr. Ashton. On the voyage back you oughter do better still. All over the Tidewater they's an almighty holler for salt rising. If 'tain't for salt, they're beggin' for gunpowder. You heard? Committee of Safety has sent to France to bring over any powder can be bought." Rudder chuckled, blew a blue spiral at the cabin lamp. "Independent Companies ain't got but ten rounds a man. That's the hell of a fix for men who whack off salutes like they do."

Rob, bending above Colonel von Müller's "Treatise on Fortifications and Gunnery," nodded.

"Captain, what do Bermudians look like?" Peggy inquired, glancing up from the work basket in her lap. The lamp swinging in its gimbals was tiring her eyes. "Do they look very different from us?"

"Aye, Ma'am," Rudder replied humorlessly. "Ones I've seen 'round Norfolk and Philadelphy runs smaller, sicklier and ornerier than us. Reckon it's because they eat bad food and not enough of it—get the sour belly young. I've met a heap of 'em and let me tell you something, Ma'am.—If it takes a Jew to do a Yankee in the eye, why it takes a Bermudian to do a Jew! You got to watch a 'Mudian day and night. They're the most awful liars in Creation. A sensible body wouldn't trust them with a red-hot penny."

Peggy, smiling, bent her head to bite the thread of her sewing. "Don't you reckon they think the same of us?"

Rudder yawned to choke off a thundering belch. "Mebbe so, Ma'am, but it wouldn't be true. Must be slim fun living a lifetime on them little fly specks of islands."

"How far away are they?"

"Six hundred miles more or less due east o' Charles Town, South Carolina, Ma'am. Heard tell they divided themselves up into tribes like the savages and fight among themselves something fierce—only they use the Law 'stead of war hatchets. Set a lot on family fights, too. 'Pears to me like they hate everybody but themselves."

Now and then using a broad forefinger to dislodge bits of salt pork from between his teeth, the Captain talked on and on. As no one else, he made Peggy see rich, pestilence-ridden towns drowsing in the Antilles and in Spanish America. He drew for her vultures sunning themselves on roofs of red tile. He made her scent the perfumes of wild, steaming jungles in which, the Indians muttered, great cities full of gold lay forgotten.

Rob, resting his forehead on his hands, tried to go on reading but just the same he listened with one ear. Along Water Street Captain Rudder was famed for an ability to top the stiffest yarns to nothing.

Tattooed hands comfortably clasped over his belly, Rudder lolled in his chair, spoke of moon blindness, of terrible hurricanes, of landing on desolate islands to hunt wild pigs and cattle.

Peggy smiled and the lamp light deepened the color of her lower lip. "Pigs on a desolate island?"

"Aye, Ma'am. 'Twas the custom of captains exploring in the olden days to maroon a pair of swine on lonesome islands. Reckon they figured someone, themselves maybe, might need 'em powerful urgent some day. The Dons left some on the Bermudas."

Next day the wind was blowing not quite so fresh, but the weather was fair and seas kept boiling out from under the *Desdemona*'s clumsy stern. Captain Rudder assured Rob the schooner was well out in the Gulf Stream. In proof, he pointed to the water. It had turned a bright, vital blue and, continually, the schooner sheared through vast meadows of Gulf weed meandering over the ocean in bright yellow streamers.

Katie, on her way to draw water from the scuttlebutt, saw a flying fish leap out of a swell. She uttered a delighted squeal and set down her bucket.

"Oh my God, now ain't *that* something to see? Why, it's so pretty and little and light." It filled her heart with the same inexplicable delight as the sight of hummingbirds sipping from a honeysuckle vine behind Ma Skilling's corn crib.

Despite the prickings of conscience, she lingered whenever she could at the rail. Never would she tire of watching those pretty blue and white fish skip away from the *Desdemona*'s course. A wonderful, clean, salt-scented world was this life at sea. There was no pain, no filth, no ugliness to it; but it was growing hotter each day.

Every morning the sun beat down until the crew stripped themselves to the waist and men not on watch took to dozing in the shade of the bulwarks.

If one looked, one saw how abundant life was in the Stream. Quantities of porpoises—"dolphins," the quartermaster called them—played about the ship for hours on end. Mr. Rob seemed pleased, Katie mused, because Captain Rudder swore nothing was luckier than for dolphins to play along a vessel's course. It meant the schooner would sail a real fast passage. But if a shark took to following in her wake—!

Twice the schooner almost ran down turtles asleep on the surface. Barnacle-encrusted shells lazily awash, the great creatures floated until the *Desdemona* was almost upon them. But at last they would raise startled heads, then dive with their flippers clumsily kicking at the water. Katie could see them go scaling down, down until they became lost in the dark blue deeps. The Gulf Stream wasn't a bit like the Chesapeake's turgid yellow-green tide. Katie wished she could cut a ribbon from it. It would look elegant tied around her yellow hair.

Pity Mrs. Ashton kept on acting so mean. She was just cutting off her nose to spite her face. The poor tiny little thing sure was swollen all out of shape with her baby. There were a lot of things Katie itched to do for her. Why, she could comb out Mrs. Ashton's hair and dress it pretty-like; she could help her in and out of her clothes and wash her things. Best of all, she could bring her breakfast down to her bunk. Mrs. Ashton, she was certain, couldn't cotton much to smelly little Ben and his juicy nose. That nigger sure had a bad cold. He kept sniffling and rubbing at his eyes all the time. When he had come to fetch the food at breakfast time, he had talked kind of silly, but not fresh.

A shadow darkened her shoulder and, turning, she found George Wincapaw standing behind her, smiling. The mulatto had come up so quietly she was startled and annoyed.

"Well, Pussyfoot," she demanded, "what do you want?"

"Splitting kindling is hot work, Miss. I might do it for you."

Katie was ashamed of her irritation. The nigger was only trying to be friendly and today sure was going to be a scorcher. "Why, that would be mighty kind of you."

The quartermaster's pale gray eye flitted over her figure. Her thin pink cotton dress made it easy to see how she was put together. Sensing his not disrespectful inspection, she wished she had on the shoes Tom MacSherry had bought her. But the feel of the sunwarmed planks was good and she liked the sensation of digging her big toenails into tar softening between the deck seams.

"You like the sea, Miss?" Wincapaw ventured.

Katie threw back her head and her bright hair rippled. "Oh, I love it! The ocean is so clean, so big, so beautiful! There mightn't be a speck of land on all the earth."

"No," the quartermaster agreed quickly, "there mightn't. Maybe it would be better if there was only water."

"You been to Bermuda?"

The quartermaster's battered straw hat jerked forward. "Three times. Only a year ago, last time. Laid over in St. George's a whole month so I know them islands pretty well."

"What's it like in Port Royal?" Katie mentioned the only place she had heard of.

"It's all right. But me, I like St. George's."

"Is Bermuda a nice place?"

The quartermaster's gaze wandered to the foretop. "It is for white folks, I reckon. Tell you all about it when my trick's done. Will you be finished cleaning up 'round nine?"

Katie wavered. George Wincapaw was colored, or part colored anyhow, so he wouldn't dare go getting ideas. Besides, she felt lonesome and there was nobody else she could talk to. She ended by nodding.

The two rings in his ear clinked as he swung away on silent feet and a long sheath knife swayed over his thin buttocks.

"Mis' Katie?"

In the shade of the port bulwarks Ben was lying on an old sail.

"What is it?"

"Please come heah, jes' a minute?" The steward's voice sounded thin, reedy.

Bare feet softly slapping, Katie crossed the deck to him and inquired kindly, "What's the matter, boy? Is your cold worse?"

"Ah—Ah reckons so." Ben sighed, rubbed red-rimmed eyes. "Ask Misto' Ashton can he git someone—wait on table tonight."

Katie, squatting down, looked hard at him. "Where do you feel bad?"

The little Negro smothered a moan. "Ah dunno, Mis' Katie, but Ah jus' now got sick over de side."

"Shucks, Boy, that's the seasickness!"

"No, Mis' Katie, ain't dat. Ah been to sea. Feel lak de ol' Debbil drivin' red-hot nails thoo mah haid."

"You got a headache?"

The Negro's lips, gone a faint lavender, moved slowly. "Hit's wusser dat, Missy. Hit's a turrible misery."

Because Ben had begun to pant, Katie bent still lower over him. "What makes you breathe so quick like?"

"Doan' know, deed Ah doan'. Oh, Laws! Laws!" He pressed skinny hands to his stomach. "Hu'ts turrible. Effen Ah tries lift mah haid ever' thin' goes 'round and 'round and 'round."

Katie got suddenly to her feet. "I don't know what's ailing you, but you sure ain't fit to wait on table. I'll tell Mr. Ashton."

Ben summoned a faint smile. "Thankee kindly—Mis' Katie?"

"Yes?"

"Please doan' git mad, but—Ah—Ah is jes' perishin' for a drap water."

"Why, sure 'nough." Casting the prostrate Negro a look of compassion, Katie went forward and drew a dipperful from the scuttlebutt.

The slave drank eagerly, but immediately spewed it over his chest and the sail. Katie replaced the dipper on its nail beside the water cask.

Captain Rudder appeared at the head of the poop ladder. "What ails that nigger? Why ain't he working?"

She told him.

"I'll look at him. Mr. Ashton is asleep."

Katie didn't wonder at that. Since early morning Mr. Rob had been working with his chronometer, sextant and charts, laboriously plotting and re-plotting the schooner's position.

"Bet that damn' 'coon's got a touch of the sailor's vapors," Rudder grunted. He strode across a deck divided by the rigging's shadows into a black and white crazy-quilt pattern. "What ails you, boy? Too much good food all to once?"

Captain Benjamin Rudder was at bottom a kindly man. Not one of those hard-a-weather captains who found pleasure in hammering the delirious daylights out of a crew.

Ben raised his head, grinned weakly. "Finish no Sunday fried ain' better?"

"What's that?"

Ben nodded his melon-shaped head. "No. Gib pasture twenty blue—will next— Ah runs lightnin' not was."

Rudder looked sharply at Katie. "Why didn't you tell me he was out of his head?"

The girl looked at him, round-eyed. "Why, Captain, he was talking all right just now."

Rudder, coming closer, noticed a heavy dewing of perspiration on the gray-black features. Bending, he looked narrowly at the Negro's eyes. They were running big tears.

"My God!"

Katie saw Captain Rudder's face grow old and faded looking like a print left too long in strong sunlight. He fell back half a dozen steps, fumbling for a bandanna. He clapped it over his nose—tight.

"Fetch Mr. Ashton!"

The crew was dozing. All except Qumana who had rolled over onto his side and lay looking white-eyed at Ben.

There was a quality in Captain Rudder's voice which sent Katie bounding up the poop ladder for the first time since that awful scene. At the foot of the companionway she began calling, "Mr. Ashton! Oh, Mr. Ashton!"

Mrs. Ashton's voice answered, rasping, contemptuous. "Go away! He's tired out! Haven't you had enough fun today?"

Katie paid her no heed. "Mr. Ashton, please come on deck! Please!"

"Eh?" Bed springs creaked. "What's wrong?"

"Captain Rudder needs you—bad!"

By the time Rob appeared on deck, damp with sleep and rubbing his eyes in the bright light, the watch stood grouped in a brown-black cluster at the foot of the mainmast. All of them were staring at the steward who sprawled, twisting slowly, on the gray canvas topsail. Ben kept moaning and muttering. Now and then his toes would buckle over in slow flections and successively their broad pinkish-purple nails would catch the sunlight.

Rudder, his face gone a bilious gray, had retreated to the foot of the poop ladder. In a greasy blue serge coat and wide, tobacco-stained canvas trousers, he stood pressing a blue bandanna tight to his mouth. An eelskin into which his queue was tucked had been pulled too close to his head. Now it stuck out as if rigid with horror.

Rob, recognizing a distinctive putrid odor, caught his breath. He went forward to kneel at Ben's side. Katie stood wide-eyed but very quiet near the door of her galley. Wincapaw was craning his neck from his post at the helm and farther away, the deckhands were muttering fearfully.

Rudder cried out, "Don't touch him!"

Over his shoulder Rob said gravely, "I've had measles and the other—too. I can't catch anything."

Producing his father's thick old watch, he closed his fingers over the Negro's wrist. The skin on it felt dry, noticeably hot. Unseeing, the stowaway struggled to a half sitting position. He snuffled, then whimpered:

"Been Bill man will lak feel goin' not angel. When Black Goat ain't whut fo' is."

"Take it easy, Ben—lie back."

Rob locked his teeth, tried to forget the steward's fetid breath in concentrating on his pulse count. It was away

395

over normal. Um. When he examined the little nigger's neck, scalp and arms, he found several small swellings.

Suddenly Ben screamed and doubled, working his thin legs in a series of futile jerks.

When Rob straightened, his face was as wet as if he had dipped it into a basin of water.

"He's sick all right. A hard case of measles most likely," Rob said extra loud. At the same time he winked at Rudder. "Maybe we had better keep him away from the crew."

Swallowing hard, the captain kept fascinated eyes on the gray-faced Negro and when he spoke his voice quivered like a taut cable. "I'll sure keep him away! Overboard he goes, that's what!"

Rob straightened his shoulders. "Don't be a fool! It's only the measles!" Silently he damned Rudder for a dirty yellow-belly! If he kept on like this, he would scare the crew into spasms.

Rudder kept on backing away, his heels loud on the sunlit deck. "You can't fool me! Listen to me, you niggers. He ain't got measles! *It's the pox!* Your only chance is to pitch him over!"

Rob's neck commenced to get red and to swell. "Shut up! I'll tend him. I have had pox."

"But *we* ain't!" gasped one of the crew.

"Oh my Gawd! My Gawd!" Rudder was almost shouting. "Smallpox, and it's too late to turn back!"

Rob's fist landed on the end of the master's pulpy nose. When he doubled up under the blow, Rob let him have another, a beauty, right in the belly. Everyone heard the three distinct thumps caused by Rudder's shoulders, head and heels in succession striking the deck. Blowing on his knuckles, Rob turned to face the crew. They were in frantic fear.

"T'row him over! Please, Misto' Ashton, T'row dat hoodoo feller over! Dey's a chanct fo' us. Ben ent bruk out yet."

Rob jerked a pair of belaying pins from the mainmast pinrail. "Get back you fools!" Then he muttered to Katie, "Fetch the pistol under my pillow."

He commenced talking against time. Rob could always recall what followed. Creating a pattern of checkered and striped jerseys and ragged pants, the crew started aft. When the schooner rolled, their bodies all canted in the same direction, like so many parallel pendulums. Against the white deck the slaves looked mighty big and black.

While delivering a harangue covering panic, discipline and the ways of contagious diseases, Rob found himself noticing absurd and trivial details. One deckhand had a cataract whitening an eye; another lacked a big toe. He didn't dare think about the quartermaster. If Wincapaw was sneaking up from behind, he was sure enough done for. He listened hard, but could hear only the creaking of the main sheet blocks. No footfalls? Maybe Wincapaw, too, was immune.

Where had Katie gone? She hadn't let out a peep when he spoke to her, had only skinned up the poop ladder like the devil was after her. Maybe she had gone to hide.

Forcing a fierce expression, he glared into one after another of those shiny sable faces. The Negroes looked more like monkeys than ever right now. Dangerous monkeys.

He heard his own voice saying, "How'd you all like it if you were sick and I said, 'Pitch that Mohgreb, that Qumana overboard'? You wouldn't like it."

"But us ain't sick," grumbled the bullet-headed slave called Mohgreb. "We ain't got de pox. But we sho cotch him iffen dat Ben lib aboard. Please, Misto Ashton, wunt take a jiffy gib dat Ben boy de heave-o."

What could have become of Katie?

"Get back. Hear? One more yelp out of any of you and you'll feel your backs smoke!"

Qumana and a hand called Jason shuffled closer, arms hanging loose from their shoulders. Eyeballs white, other men began to follow them. The slave with the cataract eased a belaying pin out of its rack. From the tail of his eye Rob watched him step over Rudder's body. Blood, dripping from the captain's nose, was sketching an erratic course across the planking.

Where in the blue blazes was Katie?

Rob began talking faster, louder. "Don't be fools! If you boys mutiny, you'll get hanged. Hear? Every damned one of you. If you're going to catch it, you're going to catch it. You've all been plenty exposed. Murdering Ben won't help you any."

Never in his life had he been so glad to hear anything as a quick patter of footsteps behind him.

Katie shoved the big pistol into his hand, but he noticed it had lost its flint. He hoped the niggers were too excited to notice. Straight off they stopped where they were and fell back; without raising the weapon he started forward.

"There's an old tarpaulin on top the cargo in the forehold. You, Mohgreb! Jason! Fetch it!" A further inspiration came. "Squeegee, and you, Bullhead! Rig a tent over the main hatch. Hump yourselves!"

"Yassuh! Yassuh!" Habit won and the crew scattered in a frenzy of obedience. Rob felt more comfortable with the sick man berthed amidships. The crew would stay forward unless ordered aft and they'd all walk wide rings around the tent.

On the deck Rudder stirred, snuffled in his swollen nose, blew little scarlet spots onto the sun bleached decking.

"Get water from the scuttle," Rob instructed Katie. "Throw some into his face."

By sundown everything that could be done had been done. Sulphur and gunpowder were smoldering in the forecastle and both of Ben's blankets had been heaved overboard.

"Didn't know you had the pox," Rob wearily remarked to Katie. "Your pits don't show."

"Why, sir, I've never had it, not as I know of."

"What!" He gave her a steady look. "My sincere compliments. There is more nerve in your little finger than Rudder has in his whole yellow-bellied carcass!"

Katie flushed and her wide smile glistened. It was, he thought, a very clean, fresh, genuine sort of smile. "You've been awful good to me, you and Mr. David."

"Don't mention my brother!" The words came staccato.

In overwhelming astonishment Katie gasped. "But Mr. David was—"

"Be quiet!"

"Yes, sir." Coloring, Katie hurried off to her galley.

Before supper Captain Rudder shambled up to Rob, his nose a shapeless purple-red lump. He was very apologetic and hangdog.

"Must have went off my head," he explained, eyes on the deck. "I—I'm mighty sorry, Mr. Ashton. Don't know how I came to talk like I did."

Rob's lips thinned. "Talk? Hell! You acted like a God-damned coward!"

"I know it, sir, and I'm right sorry and ashamed. Honest I am."

Rob curbed his disgust. "You've got call to be. Well, the matter's over. Can I count on you from now on?"

Rudder's eagerness was almost pitiful. "Oh yes, sir! I won't give you no more trouble. Before God, I won't! I got myself in hand now."

"See that you keep yourself so," came the grim warning. "Five days from now we are going to find our hands full, I reckon."

When he thought of how Ben had handled the cabin's dishes and food cups, little icebergs started floating about in his stomach.

"We got the nigger isolated in time," he assured himself for the dozenth time, but, as an extra precaution, he ordered Katie to wash all the tableware in vinegar.

Aware of a change in the ship's easy rhythm, he paused at the head of the companionway. A glance at the yellowish-gray mainsail told him that the wind was fading out. The sea, however, was still running pretty brisk and all the sails were full. But now and then the topsails shuddered and their reef points *tap-tap-tapped* lazily against the canvas.

"Oh, Lawse! Lawse! Lawse!" Ben gurgled from a mattress lashed across the main hatch. "Oh Lawse! Lawse!" His cry kept on coming until its repetition grew maddening.

4 — PEST SHIP

NEXT morning a breathless calm was ironing out the sea. The Atlantic was like a limitless mesa of hot and oily water. It stirred only vaguely under the impulse of rollers lifted somewhere below the horizon. As the sun climbed, it gave off rays of fierce, penetrating heat. Scorching sunbeams beat through the schooner's sides, through her decks, raised more blisters on her faded paint work.

From the spars the *Desdemona*'s sails hung limp as washing on a clothesline. Crated chickens stowed in the long boat, along with a lot of huge and malodorous terrapins, parted their beaks and panted. Every soul aboard was sweating like a stevedore.

The water was of such deep blue it looked like paint. As the day wore on, heat reflected off the water struck viciously up under the crew's straw hats. By the afternoon, little ridges of tar caulking the deck planks commenced to soften and creep away.

When Rudder set the crew to sluicing the deck, it was so

hot that water evaporated almost as soon as a man's mop had finished its stroke. Under a canvas awning Ben moaned and whimpered louder than ever. Everyone knew that a rash was beginning to stand out on his skin.

The chalk mark Rob had drawn around the hatch was a needless precaution for all save Katie. Rob often noticed her contemplating with compressed lips the tortured wretch.

Once she begged, "Please, Mr. Ashton, can't I just put a cold cloth on Ben's face? He must be frying to death in this heat."

"No. He'll just have to take his chances. We're doing all that reasonably can be done."

Despite the breathless heat and the persistent calm, the crew seemed quiet. Maybe it was because Rudder kept them busy reeving new gear and found other odd jobs. The captain seemed, indeed, to have pulled himself together.

Only Peggy lingered in the grip of that terror which had swept the ship like a noxious squall. She insisted that the cabin door be kept tight locked and a blanket hung to either side of it.

On June 8th, her fifth day out of Norfolk, the *Desdemona* remained a lone, motionless and microscopic interruption on a vast continent of burning water. Today her iron work had grown much too hot to be handled without wetting.

The next day brought no relief. The crew took to muttering in corners again because huge whitish pustules were erupting all over Ben's face, neck and arms. Under Rob's fingertips the pea-sized lumps felt hard as shot. No room for doubt now. All along he had been hoping against hope that Ben might be down with nothing more than a very severe attack of measles. Sometimes the disease hit colored people as hard as this.

The stowaway's features swelled and puffed up into a grotesque caricature of a face. His chin, nose and ears grew huge, spongy looking. Whatever he swallowed was vomited right up again and he was delirious nearly all of the time. Often Rob had to call Wincapaw to help hold him down. It was incredible what amazing strength Ben's skinny frame could generate for a brief period. Suppose a human gorilla like Qumana came down?

At night when an uncanny stillness ruled the sea and the heat was less blasting, the patient, because his eyelids were swollen tight shut, often struggled up, shrieking of blindness.

At such times his wails echoed and re-echoed through the schooner, rousing the crew from uneasy slumber on the fore-deck. Even after sundown, the forecastle was too smothering to be tolerated and in this torrid atmosphere the few insects surviving fumigation multiplied by the hundreds of thousands.

"Oh, make him stop!" Peggy pressed moist palms tight over her ears. "Can't you make that damned nigger stop it?"

"He can't help it, Honey. I know it's awful—but I can't do anything. We've no laudanum aboard."

Peggy would lie panting, feeling perspiration course down her neck and between her swollen breasts. In the morning Rob saw purplish crescents her fingernails had dug into her palms.

Catching the pox was not Peggy's only fear. By now she was sure she was right, and Dr. Gordon was wrong. Her baby *would* come within the month. When she thought of giving birth in this smelly, hideous little cabin, she sobbed under her breath and chewed the pillow case.

It was hell lying alone, feeling her forebodings grow deep-er hour by hour, but she would not allow Katie to cross the threshold. To make matters worse, Sunshine was proving a very lively baby. In its struggles the infant sometimes kicked the air right out of her lungs. She reckoned it must be a boy to act so mean. Could she ever have been slim, neat and graceful? Had there ever been a time when, light as a dande-lion seed, she had whirled through the quadrille, had thrilled to the sprightly pace of a pavanne?

Amid blistering afternoon heat she pulled up the sweaty folds of her nightgown and listlessly waved a palmetto leaf over her naked body. Her gaze wandered through the stern ports, but she was finding the sea hideous. She hated its glaring, metallic copper-blue and the horizon, all crazed and wavering with heat.

For the first time in her eighteen years Peggy began to speculate about death. If one died, what happened? Did one go whirling off through the dark alone—all alone? Very likely she would catch the pox! Suppose her baby started coming? She found the prospect too awful, too terrifying to dwell on. Her chin quivered and she looked wildly about. Once when a tiny girl she'd got lost in the woods back of Sally Gil-morin's. Then she had felt just like this.

Death? Breath staggered in her throat. That meant no baby, no more parties, no more wild gallops across the

Virginia countryside, no more silly jokes and pretty dresses. Successive waves of apprehension beat against her imagination like the billows of a maddening sea. Sniffling, she arose and sought her mirror. A dark red rash was breaking out on her forehead! Horror chilled the skin on her forearms into goose pimples. Though the cabin swam about her, she rallied, clutching the back of her armchair. Eyes wide and staring, she examined her neck. Oh God! It, too, was speckled! She put out her tongue. It was gray and mottled with furry patches. Lightnings played in her brain. By a supreme effort she unlocked the door before her knees gave way entirely.

"Rob!" she shrieked. "Rob! Help! Help!"

He rushed below three steps at a time. When he wrenched aside blankets hung across the door, he found his wife crouched against her own little trunk. She was shaking, face buried in hands.

"I've c-caught it! I'm g-going to d-die! Oh, save me, Rob! Save me! Save me!"

When first he saw her, he felt hairs rise on the back of his neck. But then he looked more carefully, and tenderly picked up his wife's small damp figure.

"Darling, darling! Don't take on so. Please don't. All you've got is a heat rash—a common heat rash. It's nothing to fear."

She clung to him, torn by spasmodic sobs. "Oh, it's not! I know b-better. You're trying to f-fool me."

He shook her ever so gently. "Peggy, I'm not. I swear to God, I'm not. It can't be the pox—yet. Even if you had it, a rash wouldn't show for three days more."

"Oh, I don't want to d-die." Her arms were almost strangling in their pressure.

"You're not going to, darling. It's a heat rash, only a heat rash. Nothing more."

She pressed her head, oily with neglect, against his cheek. "Oh, Rob, take me home! I was so safe, so happy there! Why did you ever take me away?"

Having no answer to that, he kept quiet, but went on trying to soothe her.

The schooner's only other cabin was a tiny affair flanking that occupied by Mr. Ashton and his wife. In it Captain Rudder bit off a fresh chew and, using the back of his hand, pushed from his eyes a loop of grizzled hair. Then he opened the *Desdemona*'s logbook and wrote.

June 9, 1775

Position: 71° 6m long. 31° 12m Lat.
Distance logged this Day: None.
Weather: Clear and hot.
Wind: None.

Remarks: Flat calm for fourth Day. Have never beheld Sea so unnatural still. Sick Man much worser. Today great white pustules broke out on Face and Shulders. Crew very uneasy, but through God's Mercy Pox has not Spread. Mohgreb, Bullhead extra sullen. Will bear watching.

A drop of sweat fell from Rudder's chin and exploded into small drops, blurring the fresh ink. Cursing, he used a pen-knife laboriously to scrape away the spots. In the old days he'd always been proud of the neat way he kept his log. After burnishing the rough places with his thumbnail, he resumed his slow and painful writing.

Vegetables in cargoe spoiling Fast. If God does not send us a Breeze soon, we shall lose the Half of them.

After tucking the goose quill behind his ear, Rudder blew on the page 'til it was dry. Then methodically he closed the logbook, locked it in his sea chest.

In spitting through the porthole, he noticed the sunset sky. It suggested nothing so much as an inverted brass bowl. Licking lips cracked by sunburn, he bent over a chart unrolled across his bunk and plotted his course for the next twenty-four hours.

Oh goddam it! That bloody nigger was raising his holler again. Captain Rudder suddenly dropped his parallel rulers and lunged over to his sea chest. After spitting out his chew, he fished out a wicker covered demijohn and poured out half a cupful of red-brown Jamaica rum. It tasted good, by God! Mighty good. Fine as silk. It was just what a man needed un-der a strain like this. No more today, though. This would have to be all. He tilted up the cup, straining for the last drop. That burning sensation in his belly made him feel right good, better than he had in a hell of a while. But he must take care not to look too cheery; Mr. Ashton had been keeping a weather eye on him.

He glanced at his chronometer ticking placidly in its rack. It was after seven and he was overdue for his trick at the helm.

Katie sat on the hard little bunk built across one end of the galley. She was deeply worried. Tomorrow, Wincapaw predicted, the ship's company would know for sure if anybody had taken the pox. Cramps in the belly or a splitting headache were ominous signs. Nausea, the mulatto had warned, was even more to be feared. He had insisted she wear a charm, a string of thirty-nine blue beads, to ward off the disease. Gladly she added it to her own necklace of Job's tears—those smooth brown seeds which had kept her well for so long.

Sweat began to bead her upper lip when, after stripping to the waist, she commenced an inspection of her neck, back and armpits. In her bit of looking glass she saw some heat rash, but what really worried her was the cramps which were beginning to tug and stab at the base of her stomach. She was praying almighty hard the cause was a natural one. It had come early by three days if she'd counted right. She wasn't sure, though. A sudden recurrence of the dull pain made her catch her breath. Frightened, she sank teeth into her under lip.

Oh God. Was this it? She hoped she'd die before she got to look like poor Ben out there. Everyone was betting he would be dead before sun-up. His body was all lumpy, kind of like a toad's back, but covered with great white blisters. Blebs were showing up thick as swarming bees.

She had always been proud of her vigorous body. Imagine its getting rotted away! The eldest Skillings girl had been real pretty 'til she caught it; afterwards she used to cry at the sight of all those ugly holes over her nose and cheeks. Imagine lying on a stinking piece of sailcloth, gasping, vomiting.

Her hand stole up to rub the blue bead necklace as, slowly, she repeated "Abracadabra" eleven times. Wincapaw said eleven was the right number. Captain Rudder, she knew, had taken to wearing about his neck a bag of sulphur mixed with camphor. Jason went about holding an orange to his big flat nose, even when he went aloft. Yesterday Qumana had borrowed a needle and, using gunpowder and water for ink, had tattooed a queer design on his left thigh. It looked like a four leaf clover with a straw sticking out from between each leaf. When he finished, he had grinned like the devil.

Another cramp! Oh damn! Had she caught it? Just when she was learning to spell pretty good. If only a wind, a howling gale, would rise up and blow the pestilence away. But there were no signs of the calm's ending.

Nervously pulling up her waist, she went out. Tar which had melted during the day stuck to her toes. Even though the sun had set an hour ago the deck was still hot as Medrach's furnace and the stink of spoiling cabbages was enough to make a skunk jealous.

Too bad the poor lady below had to take on so about her being along, especially when there wasn't any call. Having a baby any time was no fun—but on a pest ship! Katie rested her elbows on the scarred bulwarks and wondered why no man had ever got her in the family way.

"Reckon it must be the Lord's way of looking out for me," she concluded.

On the morning of June 11th, the eighth day out of Norfolk, two deckhands came down with smallpox. They were Jason and a nondescript black known as Squeegee. A riot broke out when their plight was discovered and Rob was forced to use an oaken pump handle in quelling it.

In a dangerous state of despair, the balance of the crew took possession of the foredeck and defied authority. Pistols in hand, Rob then seated himself on the fore hatch patiently waiting for Thirst to reinforce him. Around noon the mutineers, parched for a drink, gave up. Before he let them at the scuttlebutt he kicked each one on the shins until he screamed. Then he invented tasks to occupy their minds.

On his way aft Rob stopped at the galley. Said he to Katie, "Get your things together. You'll bunk below."

"But—Mrs. Ashton?"

"Do as I say." His cheekbones stood out and his eyes were framed in brownish rings. "She is not well, so you will pay no attention to anything she says."

"I'd liefer stay up here. I ain't scared, Mr. Ashton. Honest, I ain't."

She didn't look scared and that was a fact. But, years ago,

Rob had learned you never could tell what crazy notions a scared nigger might take.

"Do as I say," he repeated pointing towards the poop deck. "But you can go on deck to cook meals. Find Captain Rudder and send him to me."

When Katie banged her knuckles on Rudder's door, the captain's voice penetrated its panels. It was blurred in an all-too-familiar fashion.

"Tell 'at God-damn' owner—go fry his butt. Ain't comin' out! Tell him 'f he wan's me so all-fired bad—come and git me." An oily *click-cluck!* struck through the stillness. "Hear 'at? 'A's a blunderbuss!"

"He's drunker than ten hoot owls," Katie told herself and wrung her hands out of pity for Mr. Rob. It was the merry hell of a time for the skipper to get polluted!

There was nothing to do but tell what happened. She was infinitely relieved when Mr. Rob swore feelingly but decided not to risk the contents of the blunderbuss.

Said he, "That soak is just scared and drunk enough to let fly for general results."

Well, now he had his answer to those speculations concerning drunkenness.

Around noon, Mohgreb came down. He had doubled over under a tearing pain in his abdomen. As, shrieking, he vanished into the forecastle, a sense of impending doom settled more heavily over the *Desdemona*. The three blacks remaining healthy, Bullhead, Qumana and the man with the cataract, again congregated in the bows. This time they brought along some capstan bars. Squatting on their hams, they eyed each other.

"Dey's a hoodoo 'boa'd dis ship," Qumana announced, looking on the burnished glare of the sea. "Dass whut. Us jes' gwine nacherally die less'n we git away. Ain' dat, so, Bullhead?"

The Negro addressed scowled, blew a small shower of sweat from his broad nose.

"Dasso. Reckon a Kraken got us by de keel."

The one-eyed deckhand goggled and quickly spat onto the deck to ward off ill luck. "Uh Kraken? What dat?"

Qumana shivered. "Yeh, what dat?"

Bullhead rolled yellowish eyes. "Kraken ol' monstrous Thing. He big lak a hill wid arms long like a white pine. He got big hooks fo' fingers an' he sink 'em into keel of a ship

406

—lak dis. He jes' hang on an' hang on—de ship cain't move nowheres—she jes, stay put—lak dis. At night de Kraken he breaves destruction ovah de side an' de folks on board dey sickens and dies—like us."

"Oh Lawse," moaned Qumana, rocking his body sidewise. "Oh Lawse! We's sho' 'nuff goners."

"Whut come next, Bullhaid?" the one-eyed man asked.

"De Kraken he keep dat ship right in one place 'til all de crew sta'ves daid. Den he pulls dat ship down under de water an' he eat de dead people. Krakens doan' relish fresh meat."

The one-eyed man glared savagely about. "Ain' no ol' Kraken gwine eat me! No suh! Ah—ah'll—"

"You what?" demanded Bullhead with a lugubrious look.

"Ah dunno—but—"

Suddenly Qumana raised a great hand. "Hush yo' mouf, boy, an' lissen. Ah got me a idee—"

An evil smile began to curve his liver-colored lips.

All afternoon the mutineers defied authority. Rob deemed it unnecessary to coerce them—yet. They were out of the way, muttering and mumbling up forward. Damn that cowardly swine Rudder! Damn the Committee of Safety, damn Parliament for starting the whole bloody business!

With his shoulders he blotted a trickle of sweat from his eyes. The air felt stagnant, lifeless, and so hot it seared his nasal passages when he drew a breath. Almost constantly he sipped from a bucket of water he had lugged aft. In the throbbing sunlight the skins of the deckhands resembled freshly oiled ebony. It was sure hell having to care for so many sick men. There was so little he and Wincapaw could do.

Next morning Squeegee died as quietly and unnoticeably as he had lived, but Jason lay in the forecastle groaning amid an indescribably foul stench.

Mohgreb had vanished.

None of the crew knew what had become of him, or so they said. Whether Mohgreb had jumped overboard during the night or whether the others had thrown him over there was no telling.

Rob didn't like the way Qumana was acting. Damned nigger needed a whipping, that was what. But he was too tired to administer it. Having had but an hour's sleep on deck, he was dog-weary.

Time dragged under the sun's ceaseless hammering. Rudder kept to his cabin, alternately roaring lewd chanteys, and subsiding into sodden, snoring slumber. When he awoke, he began swilling rum again. Sometimes he howled such horrible threats through his door that Rob ordered Katie to sit for long hours with a pistol cocked and ready.

As for Peggy, she acknowledged the girl's presence only because it was inescapable. Otherwise she lay on her bunk, bitter and silent, or crouched in her armchair, red-eyed and panting in the murderous heat. Her hair had grown lank and greasy and the heat rash was spreading, banishing the fresh pinkness from her complexion.

She had heard of disease breaking out on ships—on the *Betsy* one time. Her father's account of it had sounded exciting, but rather awful, too. This was different, though she herself was safe. No pestilence could creep in through a locked and barred door. Of course not. She wanted to question Katie about it to make sure, but she couldn't bring herself to speak.

What of the stern ports? Horrors! She lurched over, closed them, and she and Katie sat smothering until Rob came down and made her open them again.

When Rudder finished his rum, he stopped roaring and falling about, and slept till sundown. At nightfall he appeared on deck, clean dressed but shaking as with an ague. Little patches of white matter showed at the corners of his bloodshot eyes. He had tried to shave but had nicked himself so badly he had given up the attempt.

Rob said evenly, "You dirty dog! I ought to kill you."

Rudder shivered. "Yes, sir. That's just what I am—a dog. A low ornery houn' dog. I—I just couldn't help it. I—I was so terrible skeered." His look wavered to the motionless wheel. "Reckon we might raise a wind tomorrow? Glass is down two degrees."

Rob only glowered. "You got any more rum?"

"Oh no! So help me God, I ain't."

"I ought to knock your damn teeth out! Where did you ever find the gall to call yourself a blue-water captain!"

Rudder actually joined tattooed hands in entreaty. "Oh please, Mr. Ashton, please don't look at me like that. I can't bear it. Please don't! I'll never touch another drop, God strike me dead if I do!"

Dazed by fatigue, Rob snapped. "I'll shoot you if you do.

408

Now, damn you, you can go on watch. Keep the well niggers forward, no matter what happens. Tell Wincapaw to clean up Ben's and Jason's beds. See he does it."

Rob was still feeling sick over the way a long, blue-gray shark came cruising up the minute he dumped Squeegee's corpse overboard. Recently the monster had adopted a position off the schooner's motionless stern.

Rudder tugged at Rob's sleeve and his boozy breath stank with his nearness. "Please, Mr. Ashton, for God's sake say you forgive me!"

"Oh, all right. But remember what I said. If you drink again, I'll shoot you like a dog."

Rob sought the companion, clumping down into the sour smelling air below. The reek of rotten vegetables and the smallpox stenches were getting him more than cries and loathsome sights. First off he found and confiscated Rudder's blunderbuss—also a big sheath knife.

In the stern cabin he found Peggy lounging, more slatternly than ever in a food-spotted nightrail and rumpled mob cap. To his surprise, she showed a measure of animation.

"I've just remembered something," she said.

"What?"

"Inoculation!"

"What's that?"

"Why, every time the pox broke loose in Norfolk, Dr. Gordon went 'round inoculating folks. He gave people light cases. He inoculated Papa when the pox broke out three years ago."

"Yes." Rob yawned, but asked patiently enough, "But how is it done?"

"I know," Peggy said in her old, self-sufficient manner. "You thread a needle, run it through a blister on somebody who has the pox but who is getting better—like Ben."

Rob was aghast. "Have you gone crazy?"

"No! Inoculation is my only chance. It's safe. They used to have regular boarders come to Dr. Aspinwall's for it."

"But, Ma'am," Katie unwisely put in, "you oughtn't to take any—what-you-call-it, from a nigger."

"Hold your tongue!" Peggy blazed at her. Then to Rob, "I want it done tonight, done right now. A light case would save the baby—and me. If I get a really bad pox, we will both die."

Through a mist of fatigue Rob said, "But, Honey, you may not catch it at all."

"I will!" Her voice grew clear, hard. "I know I will!"

"I won't stand for such nonsense."

"You will! You'll do as I say!"

"No. You had better take your chance."

"I know! You want to kill me!" Peggy's shiny, heated features began twitching. "You want me to die! That's what you want! You want to get rid of me. Then you can lie in bed with that yellow haired trollop any time you please." She worked herself to such a pitch her words tore at Rob's eardrums like steel claws.

He was just too tired to argue. God. Hadn't he battled steadily the last thirty-six, or was it the last forty-eight hours? Maybe she was right. Peggy was so often right—or so determined. Maybe she ought to be inoculated. But with matter from a nigger? What further argument could he find? Through a daze of weariness he groped for logical objections.

She knew what should be done, she sobbed, and he didn't. In the old days—two years back—Dr. Alexander Gordon had been one of Major Fleming's closest friends. He had told her how inoculating was done.

Having won her way, Peggy became less hysterical. "Now, just do as I say."

"Yes—yes—yes!" He rubbed eyes which felt as if they had been dropped into hot sand and then put back in place. Of Katie standing miserably silent in a corner he inquired dully, "You want to be inoculated?"

She shook her yellow head. "I—I'd be scared to, Mr. Ashton. I'd liefer take my chances." She was feeling brave now that the true nature of her cramps had become evident.

It required all Rob's resolution to pass the threaded needle Peggy gave him through a bleb on Ben's forearm. He hoped he was doing it right; his hurricane lantern wasn't any too bright.

Ben felt much better, he declared. His fever was about gone but he felt weak like a hen rabbit.

In the forecastle Jason yelled in his delirium. Wincapaw slept and Rudder tramped mechanically across the stern. Back and forth. Back and forth. There was no use holding the wheel. Forward, the three mutinous deckhands remained huddled together. Rob beat aside the deadening waves of fatigue long enough to pass one of his pistols to Rudder.

"Take this. Watch Bullhead."

"Aye—that I will, sir." The skipper almost snatched in his eagerness to take it.

On re-entering the oven-like heat in the stern cabin, a revulsion seized Rob. Hoarsely he begged, "Peggy, for God's sake, listen to me. You mustn't risk this. You can't know for sure if—"

Her head went back to the old stubborn angle he had learned to dread.

"I do! I *will* have an inoculation!" Suddenly she smashed a tumbler on the floor. It shattered like an exploding shell and, stooping, she grabbed up a long and dusty splinter of glass.

"Don't!"

Before he could stop her, she dragged the jagged shard across her left arm. Against the pallor of her skin a thin scarlet arc appeared, widened.

"There!" She slashed again, and a third time. Deeper still. Bloody tears gathered, started to slide over the contour of her arm.

Katie, round-eyed among the shadows, winced when Peggy Ashton snatched the needle and its dangling, polluted thread from Rob's fingers.

"For God's sake—"

"Be quiet. I know what I'm doing!" Peggy clamped her teeth on her lips, pressed the matter-clotted thread into the deepest scratch and drew it back and forth. Rob watched her, shaking. Was she right? Probably. Most inoculated people got light doses, they said. It was sure that if Peggy got the disease full strength, neither she nor the baby could hope to survive.

He mumbled to Katie. "Stay awake. If anything happens, call me."

Then he collapsed on the stern locker as if he'd been hit on the head with a club. He was asleep long before Peggy could tie a rag about her blood-streaked arm.

5 — In the Horse Latitudes

Though a hand was tugging at his naked shoulder, Rob awoke reluctantly.

"Come on deck! Quick! Quick!" Katie, flushed and breathless, was bending above him and dawn was beating through the stern ports.

He got on his feet in an instant. "What's happened?"

"They—they've gone!"

"Who's gone?"

Katie screwed up her face, her gray-green eyes filled and she began to whimper. "It's—it's all my fault, M-Mr. Ashton. I—I reckon I fell asleep. Just waked up a minute ago. I reckon you had better lick me—good."

"Who's gone? Damn it, girl, don't stand there sniveling! Who's gone? Speak up!"

But Katie only hid her face in her hands and burst into terrified wails.

Rob cursed briefly, then clattered up the companion and looked about. Save for Ben in his little tent, the deck was completely deserted.

"Rudder! Captain Rudder!"

It was only five-thirty but already he could feel the sun's heat on the nape of his neck. Ben's voice was weak and thin as the mew of a new kitten, but in the breathless silence of ship and sea Rob heard him say,

"He gone, Misto Rob. He gone."

Aghast, Rob wheeled. The longboat was gone! Its davits were empty and the falls trailed slack over the side. Due to the pinch of poverty, it was the schooner's only small boat. Rushing to the taffrail, Rob strained his eyes on the western horizon. After a bit they located a tiny black pin point. From a rack beside the binnacle, he snatched up the spyglass and climbed to the main crosstrees.

From them he was able to see what was going on in the *Desdemona*'s dirty white longboat. Rudder and three blacks were pulling slowly, sullenly. Heaped in the bow were several sacks of provisions; a hogshead of water counterbalanced them in the stern. What made him maddest of all was that the deserters had stolen the crate of chickens, which, of course, meant no more fresh eggs for Peggy.

Too depressed for articulate expression, he lingered in the rigging, staring on the vast emptiness of the sea. Off to the southwest a lonesome little white cloud had begun to creep above the horizon. Vacantly he watched the cloudlet rise, sketch a replica of itself in the motionless sea.

Rudder had taken along charts and navigation instruments so it was a good thing he had his own set. St. John Ashton's old reliables. It came to him that if Wincapaw was aboard the longboat, he must have been lying on its bottom. Right away, Rob went below.

Shoes clumping loud, he searched the deck and was cheered to discover the quartermaster sound asleep on the galley bunk. All through the epidemic the mulatto had worked hard without complaining much, so he let him go on sleeping. Most likely Rudder had figured it was a risk to trust a hand so loyal to his owner.

After taking a drink at the scuttlebutt, he went to look in on Jason. When he thrust his head into the forecastle, the sick man made no reply to his greeting.

Jason lay hideously dead on his blood-soaked blanket.

Around noon a gentle creaking drew Rob's attention. Looking up, he felt astounded, almost awed, at the simple sight of the fore boom swinging slowly over to port. By God! Though the sails sagged, the air was losing its breathless quality. The sea was still flat as any dinner table, but it had lost is burnished look.

By two o'clock more clouds lifted over the southeastern horizon and brought with them a very gentle southerly breeze. Once more the *Desdemona* began to creep towards Bermuda along the 33° latitude. Towards sundown the wind freshened, then held steady, but against the risk of a sudden squall, Rob deemed it wise to reef in. In a stiff breeze two men and a girl wouldn't be able to do much.

Faint optimism returned to the remnant of the *Desdemona*'s crew. It was fine to have the maddening calm and the silence and heat over with—for a while anyway. Then, too, Ben was growing steadily better. His suppurating pustules were nearly dry and scales were commencing to form over the empty blebs. By degrees Rob and the others cleaned up a ghastly mess in the forecastle and fumigated it again with

413

sulphur and gunpowder. By hard work they restored the schooner to a degree of order.

Rob's main concern was whether his newly acquired knowledge of navigation would prove adequate. It was a pity the Bermudas made such a tiny fleck on the chart. Even a minor error would send the *Desdemona* cruising far out into the Atlantic. If he didn't raise the Bermudas within a week, Rob decided, he would come about.

He reckoned even a poor navigator could hit the coast of North America somewhere.

6 — THE NINETY-FIRST PSALM

To ventilate the cargo and so save what vegetables had not already sprouted or spoiled, Rob next day moved Ben to a bunk in the forecastle and took off the main hatch cover. When he saw how green the onion and potato sacks were with shoots, his heart sank. Further inspection revealed that the fresh vegetables had spoiled—nearly all of them, but his wheat, flour and certain other items remained undamaged.

The wind freshened enough to keep the canvas taut and send the schooner along at a steady five knots. George Wincapaw found it pleasant to teach Katie, sunburned and lithe as any Amazon, how to steer a straight course.

Thanks to a reasonable amount of sleep on the night after Rudder deserted, Rob was feeling more like himself again. He would feel still better when he could get more than three hours' rest at a stretch. As it was, he had to relieve the mulatto and Katie at the wheel.

On the morning of the second day after her self-inoculation, Peggy woke up to find her arm red and swollen.

"It's quite sore," she told Rob, "so I think I'll stay in my bunk." She smiled up at him from the shadows. "Don't worry, dear; such soreness is to be expected. It's only the inoculation taking. I am going to be all right."

"Of course you are." But when he stopped and kissed her forehead, he was alarmed to feel how hot it was.

All day long the arm swelled and swelled. By afternoon it had turned a dark plum color and the patient's eyes were bright with fever. Not for a moment would Peggy admit she was worried, but that night she called Rob down from his supper.

"Rob, please—would you mind reading to me?"

"Gladly. From what?"

"From the Bible. I—I haven't said my prayers in a week. I miss the help they lend me."

Fumbling in his sea bag, the first thing he struck was the cold surface of the *Grand Turk*'s model. At the contact he winced. Why had he ever brought it along? Right now he wouldn't admit even to himself that he might, far in the future, try to lay down another *Grand Turk*.

Trying to make his voice confident and cheering, he read for a while from Numbers concerning other people who had wandered far in search of security. With her fearfully swollen arm propped up on a pillow, Peggy listened intently. The pain, she admitted when he insisted on an answer, was shooting in fiery stabs clear up to her shoulder. Greedily she drank every drop of water he offered.

"That's better," she said. "Now read me something from the Psalms. They sound so soothing—something like music."

His calloused fingers leafed at random through the Book until he recalled a certain passage. Voice lowered, he began to read from the 91st Psalm.

"He that dwelleth in the secret place of the most High shall abide under the shadow of the Almighty.

I will say of the Lord, He is my refuge and my fortress; my God; in him will I trust.

Surely he shall deliver thee from the snare of the fowler, and from the noisome pestilence.

He shall cover thee with his feathers and under his wings shalt thou trust; his truth shall be thy shield and buckler.

Thou shalt not be afraid for the terror by night; nor for the arrow that flieth by day;

Nor for the pestilence that walketh in darkness; nor for the destruction that wasteth at noonday.

A thousand shall fall at thy side, and ten thousand at thy right hand; but *it shall not come nigh thee!*"

"Did you hear that, Peggy? 'It shall not come nigh thee.' "
Her hand, very thin and pale, groped out from the bunk

415

covers. Beneath the single sheet her body looked enormous. "That is very comforting. Please read it again."

When he had obeyed, she repeated very slowly the line, " 'But it shall not come nigh thee.' " Peggy sighed. "Good night, dear. I think I can sleep now."

The sea whispering under the stern sounded very restful.

"Rob! Rob! Wake up—oh, Rob! I need you."

He roused on the transom, turned up a lantern swinging in gimbals from the cabin beam, came stumbling over. "What is it?"

"I—I'm burning up! My arm, it—it hurts so I can't stand it."

He bent over then recoiled despite himself. Her face was flushed and a bright scarlet stain was dyeing her neck on the left side. It was not a rash. About the scratches she had made, the flesh was ballooning up, feverish, poisoned looking.

"Oh, Rob, Rob! My arm is killing me— Help! I'm burning up. I'm on fire— I'm so—so afraid—"

In an effort to reduce the fearful swelling of her arm he wrung out cloths in cold water but when he touched her ever so gently, she screamed outright.

"Cut it off!" she moaned. "Please cut it off. I can't stand this any longer!"

If only a doctor were aboard! Distracted, Rob shook his head. A fool could tell that the arm ought to come off, but for him to attempt such an operation would be tantamount to murder.

He gave her a drink and, heart in mouth, said, "I'm going aloft just a second to tell Wincapaw he must stand my trick. I'll be right back, Honey, and I won't leave you 'til you feel better."

He ran on deck, nearer to panic than ever in his life, but sight of the mainsail silvered by moonlight and the familiar black tracery of rigging across the deck sobered him.

Wincapaw stood, a lean and wiry figure, lightly gripping the wheel. "You are early, Cap'n. It ain't but eleven."

"Where is Katie?"

"Asleep, sir," the mulatto said with a curious look. "Is something wrong, sir?"

"Yes."

"Mrs. Ashton hasn't come down, sir?"

"No. She has a mortification in her arm—a very bad one. Tell Katie to come below."

When the quartermaster nodded, moonlight glanced off the two little rings in his ear.

"Ay, ay, sir. I—I'm mighty sorry, sir."

"If I only knew what to do."

"Tried turnin' her shoes upside down under her bunk, sir?"

"That's for nightmares."

"Maybe a bit of bleeding, sir?"

Bleeding! By God, that was it. He gave Wincapaw a grateful look and turned to face the sea. He drew several deep breaths.

When he got below he found Peggy tossing in a wild delirium. Heavily her ungainly figure writhed and twisted on the sheet. By the whale-oil lantern the infected arm looked black and had become swollen to gigantic proportions all the way to the shoulder. Her skin had gone dry and shiny and was like hot iron to his touch. The delirium gripped her with greater violence and she sat up, babbled incoherently of skating, of a party dress of blue lutestring, of her mother.

Presently a stupor claimed the patient and she sank into a lethargy so deep Rob had no difficulty in stripping back the sleeve on her good arm. When Katie appeared, anxious, but blessedly silent, he told her to fetch a basin.

"Reckon the only thing is to try bleeding," he spoke as if to himself. "Mind you hold that basin steady."

When he had drawn off a pint and a half of blood, Peggy seemed to grow quieter, so he tied up the awkward incision. For hours he sat, motionless, watching the purplish features of his wife.

Pearly streaks of light had commenced to erase stars of the lesser magnitudes when Margaret Fleming Ashton abruptly abandoned her labored struggles to draw breath.

7 — INTERLUDE

LATER that morning the wind freshened until a sea made up and white-headed rollers began churning along the schooner's beam.

Rob remained below, his mental functions in a state of

semiparalysis. All he knew was that his wife and their child both had died. Would the baby have been a boy? No matter, it was dead. How strange to think that never again would Peggy's small, earnest face look at him across the top of the big ledger she had kept so well. His look wandered dully over to her workbasket. Lying in it was a single stocking of brown spun yarn—one of his. Like a miniature harpoon she had thrust her needle deep into an incompleted darn.

A needle. He shivered. He'd never behold another without reliving the horrors just past. Well, after nearly two years he was once more facing the world alone. It would feel strange to think in the singular and with no automatic considerations. It occurred to him how essentially solitary a human creature was. He came alone out of Eternity. He suffered doubts, raptures and pain only in his own terms. In dying he departed to explore the Valley of the Shadow—alone.

A vague resentment stirred him when he recalled how eagerly Peggy had hung on the words of the 91st Psalm. Surely Peggy had lived as one of the Godly whom the Lord had undertaken to protect? She had ministered to the poor and to the sick, she had attended church regularly, and she had done her best to be a constant, helpful wife. Surely, her wilfulness couldn't be construed as a deadly sin? Why hadn't the Lord's shield and buckler turned aside "the pestilence that walketh in darkness"? A groan escaped him.

What use was it to go on struggling? To hell with Ashton & Company! To hell with everything. A swarm of bees seemed to be hiving in his head and his diaphragm was contracting like green rawhide set in the sun. Never had his eyes been drier.

He called Katie to the head of the companion. Said he, "Tell Wincapaw to bring the schooner into the wind. I want him down here, but you had better stay on deck."

He didn't want the woman Peggy had hated so to handle her body.

He told the quartermaster what he wanted and when Wincapaw returned he brought with him a brand new hammock and a big granite rock from the ballast.

The mulatto felt desperately uneasy. If only Cap'n Ashton would bust out with some real loud groans and yells. Right now the owner was looking like one of those weird people he had seen down in the French Sugar Islands. "Zombies" the natives called them.

"Lend a hand. We must—we must arrange—the—my wife's body."

The words fell heavily, like stones. They worked in a silence marred by the slopping of the sea and soft groanings of the *Desdemona*'s fabric. Because the schooner was lying in the wind, her booms creaked and various sheet tackles set up an awful racket.

Rob and his quartermaster lashed the body into the hammock of white canvas with the granite at its feet. They did a neat job.

Though he had scarcely seen Mrs. Ashton, the mulatto's pale eyes filled with tears when, in a halting monotone, the owner read the burial service. He read it as if the words were devoid of meaning.

Mechanically Rob closed the prayer book and stood, unmindful of time, above the muffled figure on the transom. At last he stooped and, for the last time, gathered Peggy into his arms. He was thinking such a small body would find this vast ocean very lonely. In a moment more no power on earth could ever bring Peggy back to him.

When, bracing his shoulders, he swung the body's feet out through the stern port, the canvas shroud in scraping its sill made a small harsh noise. He held to the dragging weight an eternal second, pressed it tight to his chest. Then, face going gray, he freed the burden and stepped back. A patch of bright yellow Gulf weed drifted across bubbles hissing under the stern.

8 — HARBOUR LIGHTS

SEVERAL nights after the death of Peggy Ashton, George Wincapaw stood at the wheel, watching stars break out by the hundreds of thousands. The moon, he knew, would be rising very late. He yawned. Christ, but he was tired! So was everybody aboard. For a green officer, Captain Ashton seemed to be doing fine with his navigation. His calculations showed the *Desdemona* to be sailing just about where she should. If the new navigator hadn't been making errors all along the line, Wincapaw figured they should raise Wreck Hill around daylight.

The mulatto looked down at the galley in which Miss

Katie was asleep. God in the foothills! How he wanted her! Every time he thought about her yellow hair and the way her breasts rode under the calico dresses she wore, he felt his breath stagger. Yes, by God, he'd give his left ear to crawl in bed with her. What made him mad was, except for that damned lick of the tar brush in him, it wasn't an impossibility. He wasn't bad looking, he knew, for his African blood hadn't darkened him much—plenty of Spaniards were darker—but it had kinked his hair a bit and had tinted his fingernails purple instead of pink at their bases. To Miss Katie he was all nigger, though. He could sense that.

If the wind slacked off some, he maybe could tie the wheel and slip down to the galley. But he had better wait a little.

What a mess, what a bloody mess the voyage had been! It was queer about Miss Katie's not taking the pox. Captain Ashton couldn't understand it, either. He reckoned someone must have inoculated her so long ago she had forgotten all about it. Damned good thing the sickness hadn't hit her. Under the wind and sun her skin had turned a deep gold-brown, the color of buckwheat honey. The tip of Wincapaw's tongue crept out and moistened hard, salt flecked lips.

Would she likely scream? If she did, he guessed there would sure be hell and repeat aboard. Somebody might get killed. Captain Ashton didn't get mad very easy, but Wincapaw quite distinctly recalled the way he had cooled Captain Rudder.

The hell with Ashton! By Jesus, he was going to give that yellow haired gal a play. There was always a good chance she wouldn't holler. Some white gals had a hankering for yellows even if they didn't dare admit it.

The quartermaster bent to pick up a stop lying at the foot of the binnacle, but checked himself in mid-motion. Had a very faint sparkle of light shone ahead? He glanced at the compass. Northeast-by-east, by Jesus. It was right on the course! He looked again and this time saw the light for sure before the *Desdemona* lost it by nosing down the back of a long swell.

Wincapaw craned his sinewy neck. Was that a ship under way, or a light on shore? At the end of five minutes he saw another light wink into existence.

As loud as he could, he yelled, "Land-ho!" down the companionway.

Almost immediately Rob came on deck carrying a couple of charts under his arm.

He flattened a chart under the binnacle light and checked the course. "That must be the Bermudas. Couldn't be anything else."

"Can you make out any land yet, sir?"

"Not yet. But I can see more lights, a whole cluster of them."

"Those will be the lights of Eli's Harbour, sir," was the quartermaster's confident prediction. "We sighted that first last time I was here."

"You are sure those lights couldn't mean anything else?"

Wincapaw studied the swinging compass card, shook his head. "Not with us sailing this course, sir."

"Then you have come in this way before?"

"Yes, sir. I remember it well. We can come in right close, by keeping Daniel's Head to port and Wreck Hill to starboard. There's a reg'lar channel."

"Yes. I see it marked. I reckon we had better come in through West Blue Cut?"

The quartermaster threw back his head but reflected only an instant. "Yes, sir. Coming in from the south you pick up Eli's Harbour lights on a nor'east-by-east course."

"Good. Hold on the harbour lights for awhile. We won't go in very close 'til it's light."

"Aye, aye, sir, but we won't be in dangerous waters for a good while yet. North of here would be risky."

Katie awoke and, all excited, followed Mr. Rob right out onto the jib boom. Her promised land! She felt feverishly impatient to see what these islands might be like.

When he returned, Wincapaw called out, "We're all right, sir. What we see is vessels laying in the harbour. If you skin your eyes, you can just make out Wreck Hill 'way off to port." With one hand he shaded the binnacle light and they all stared into the darkness.

The wind was dropping fast. They knew it because the steady hush-hushing of water under the bows came back clear, and much slower. At last Rob made out the hill, a dim, triangular mound of black rising boldly from the water. Then a long, low-lying island. Reddish yellow lights shone at irregular intervals along the shore but the cluster marking Eli's Harbour was unmistakable for what it was. No other similar concentration was to be seen elsewhere.

"How could you tell so soon those were anchored ships?" Rob queried, interestedly.

"Why, sir, they're live."

"Live?" Katie asked.

"See them two lights off to port? They lie low to the water and they don't stay still. If you'll watch the space between 'em, you'll notice."

"Why is that?"

"It's because vessels swing to their anchors." Wincapaw's spirits were rising with the thought that his hoodooed voyage was near an end. "Well sir, you hit Eli's Harbour square on the nose. Prettiest navigatin' ever *I* see."

"Good luck more than good management," Rob nodded and watched the harbour lights grow brighter. Around fifteen lanterns were ricocheting their rays over the water. He turned his head and called. "Katie, take the wheel and hold her as she is. Come along, Wincapaw, we'll strike the foresail. Reckon we had better not go in much farther."

"We're all right, sir. We can go——"

The quartermaster's further words were jolted out of his mouth for, without warning, the *Desdemona* suddenly bucked like a spurred stallion and her bow shot high into the air. Her whole hull shuddered and her masts tottered. Then, as she settled back on an even keel, from below arose a dull grinding and rasping. In Rob's ears sounded the successive, terrifying crashes of objects falling about below. As quickly as it had begun, the tumult subsided except for a sibilant hissing sound. The schooner resumed her smooth and silent progress.

"Christ!" Wincapaw picked himself up from the deck as Rob let go the brace he had grabbed. "There just *can't* be a reef 'way out here! We're on the course and there's the lights of Eli's Harbour."

"He'p! Misto Ashton! He'p!" Ben's voice, shaky with fright, floated aft.

But Rob never heard him. He was listening to that ominous hissing, rushing noise. When he ran to the companionway, air, blasting from the schooner's depths, beat in his face.

"You're the hell of a fine quartermaster!" he snarled at Wincapaw. "I'll skin you alive for this! You've punched a hole in her bottom."

Desperately Wincapaw shook his head as he grabbed the

wheel. "Can't make it out, sir. 'Fore God, we're on the right course! I can't figure—"

"Shut up! Where's the nearest shallow water?"

"To port—should be," Wincapaw gasped, sawing hard on the wheel. "Can't—"

"Steer for it! We're going down."

The *Desdemona* was filling very rapidly. Rob realized it as he sprang for an axe he kept handy against emergencies. His one idea was to hit another reef, but going as slow as possible. If the schooner didn't strike too hard, he might stand a chance then of getting her off later. Lodged on a reef, she couldn't go down right away. He rained blows at the fore halyards until the gaff crumpled like the wing of a duck shot in mid-air. In a wild flutter of flapping canvas the foresail tumbled down and its gaff raised a shower of water in hitting the sea.

Searching his soul for curses, Rob dashed aft, stood ready to drop the mainsail in the same brutally effective manner, as quickly as another reef revealed itself. There seemed to be none near.

"Look! My God, *look!*" As he stared ahead the quartermaster's eyes became concentric rings of white. "See that?"

"See what?"

"The harbour lights. They're going out!"

Cold to his fingertips, Rob watched the yellow-red gleams blink into extinction. Inside of a minute not one of the treacherous lights remained. Save for occasional, widely scattered spots of illumination, the whole low-lying shore line now lay shrouded in gloom.

"Wreckers—" Wincapaw choked. "The real harbour must lie somewhere to starboard—" He felt better. It really wasn't his fault the schooner had broke her back on the coral.

Katie came feeling her way aft, showing a bruise on her chin. A trickle of blood dripped from a corner of her mouth. Though she looked frightened, she only asked quietly:

"Are—are we fixing to drown, Mister Ashton?"

"I don't reckon so; it's not rough, and there must be more reefs around."

"He'p!" Ben wailed from the forecastle. "Won' somebody please come?"

Rob patted Katie's shoulder. It was the first time he had ever laid a finger on her. "Grab hold of that empty keg by the flag locker. Stay where you are and keep quiet!"

Then he went forward along the ominously slanting deck and returned, lugging Ben, mattress and all.

"Gawd bless you, suh! Ah sho was gettin' mighty skeered."

"Shut up!" Rob fought down a powerful urge to drop the wretched little slave overboard. But for this God-damned Ben, the *Desdemona* would have had a different sort of voyage.

Emitting many gurgles and queer thumping noises, the schooner definitely began to go down by the head. Soon her bowsprit was just clear of the surface, but the increased force of the swells argued the presence of shallower water. Suddenly Rob heard a sullen booming of surf breaking off to port, but by the dim starlight he couldn't see where it came from.

"There they are! To port!" Wincapaw whirled over the wheel.

"Hang on," Rob yelled at Katie and slashed through the main halyards.

When the schooner struck for a second time, her bottom made the same dull grinding noise. Long rollers lifted her, jacked her high onto a pan of coral. The impact was not too hard, Rob hoped. A second big sea roared up, heaved the wreck higher, then piled over her bulwarks like a line of enemy boarders. With an angry swirl the Atlantic began cascading down the forecastle companionway. Incredibly soon the whole foredeck was under water. The sea became littered with flotsam. Twice more the *Desdemona* was lifted farther onto the reef then, with stern fairly high, she came to rest.

Rob heard himself saying, "If the wind doesn't make up, we ought to be safe for awhile."

He was amazed to discover that, somehow, Catastrophe had lost the power of hurting him. Perhaps it was because he had given up thinking in terms of the future. When he waded forward, he learned that the deck was submerged as far aft as the main hatch. Warm, lazy-sounding rollers were eddying about the fore shrouds. They bellied out the half submerged jibs until, one by one, they split or were carried away under the strain.

By the light of a moon beginning to rise over the islands, he and Wincapaw cut away and salvaged the sails. As a consequence the *thump-thumping* of the spars against the bulwarks lessened.

When Katie saw that her galley still was above water, she kindled a fire and cooked a meal. To her chagrin, Mr. Rob would not even taste it.

9 — SALVAGE

BEN, sleeping on the poop deck, awoke in the early morning with the distinctive thud of oars against thole pins in his ears. He managed to rouse Katie, sleeping a few yards away.

Pulling over the flattening sea were three big whale boats. They carried no lights. Katie looked just long enough to make sure there were three, then fled below.

"Wreckers!" she gasped. "They're rowing out!"

Rob reached for Rudder's blunderbuss, but ended by leaving it where it was. Said he with a weary grin, "To the devil with it. All we need is daylight."

Wincapaw was up and looking very uneasy. Katie guessed he was scared stiff the wreckers were coming out to make a clean job of it. Survivors had an awkward way of disputing salvage charges.

The moon, combined with the first rays of dawn, gave enough illumination to let Rob make out three white painted whale boats expertly skirting a line of reefs. The foremost had six men at her oars and at least as many passengers. These sat crouched on the bottom.

Rob stood statue-still, unclubbed hair falling in a light brown mane over the shoulders of a blue woolen jersey. Almost dispassionately he watched the leading whale boat's bow shoot upward, watched her oars scramble in the anticline of a wave. Up! Up! Over the white-crested apex. Then the center of gravity would shift and the boat would lurch downwards, squirting water far out from beneath her bottom.

Two boats hung back in the gloom, but the other came pulling along in the lee of the reefs. The man at the steering oar had a not pleasing aspect. The leader, a burly fellow in a bright green shirt, got to his feet and, swaying, shouted:

"Vha-ant help?"

Rob waited awhile before calling back, "What the hell would you think?"

Rocking in the whale boat's stern, the Bermudian yelled, "Take you ashore! Five pound' a head!"

From his vantage point on the stern Rob shouted, "you *are* a slimy swine!"

Several of the whale boat's passengers turned flat leathery faces and scowled. A couple of them shifted blunderbusses to handier positions. They looked a wild, reckless lot in a miscellany of straw, felt and leather hats. Quite a few were obvious mulattoes.

"You got my price!" the leader shouted. "And you got no small boat!"

"Go to hell!"

"Vell, call it three pound' apiece. That's werry reasonable," the spokesman offered, as the steerer, a brutal fellow lacking his front teeth, sheered the boat away a little.

Rob took pleasure in the moment. "Your Ma must be mighty proud of you, Mister. Your Pa, too, if you know who he is."

From another of the predatory whale boats arose a hail. "Say, Bill, she's from Virginia."

Men in the leader's boat took council.

Katie heard one of the rowers say, " 'E hell with that, Bill! She got food aboard. Luk at all 'e cabbages in 'e watter."

The leader's boat came pulling over nearer, a black pattern seen against the background of gray. The dawn, brightening suddenly, showed her oar tips stirring water turned a deep emerald.

The man called Bill stood up on the stern locker to see as much as he could of the wreck.

"Ve are sorry for you," said he. "Too bad you should lose your ship dis vhey."

Seesawing over the waves, the other boats pulled closer. Their crews for the most part wore checkered shirts and wide, very dirty canvas breeches. Quite a few of them carried little gold rings in their ear lobes and at least a dozen wore brass hilted naval cutlasses strapped over their hips. Contrary to the mode prevailing in America and England, several of the Bermudians wore beards. Although no pistols were in evidence, Rob was very certain that enough lay under the thwarts to blow the *Desdemona*'s company into Eternity.

The man in the green silk shirt grunted something which sent his boat nosing through a bright patch of Gulf weed in the direction of the wreck. When she lay but ten feet off the beam, he looked up at Rob. There was no trifling in his manner and his gap teeth showed in a taut grin.

"You going to do business vith us?"

Rob affected sulkiness. "Sure. How else are we going to get ashore?"

"Vhut can you pay?" demanded the Bermudian. "Ve dun't vant to be hard on anyvon."

"Come aboard, Captain. We'll talk it over."

The Islanders brought their big whale boat up under the lee of the wreck as deftly as a jolly boat. But she was indeed a whale boat, Rob noted. Rusted harpoons rested in racks, hatchets, a lug sail, water beakers and bailing scoops all were to be seen. There were in addition four tubs for line, but these at the moment were empty.

The leader grabbed a dangling halyard and, light as a gull settling on a piling, swung himself up onto the *Desdemona*'s rail. There he paused, legs planted squarely apart, and looked things over. He was missing nothing.

The boarder's tongue crept out through gapped teeth to wet heavy lips. "From vhere did you clear?"

Rob told him, then added, "And what might your name be?"

"That is as may be, my friend," the other said. "Suppose ve talk terms? Ve have rowed a long vhey out to help you."

"That was most considerate of you, sir." Rob, striding towards the hard-bitten stranger, became possessed of an evil humor.

The Bermudian hooked thumbs in a broad leather belt. "Vell, how much can you pay?" He was brown as mahogany and he'd a big parrot-like nose jutting out from beneath the brim of a battered and rusty black cocked hat.

"I might pay ten shillings a head."

"Not enough," Bill objected, jumping down on the deck. He tried to look into the main hatch, but there wasn't enough light yet to see much.

"Say fifteen shillings?"

"Maybe. How many aboard, Captain?"

"Four. A deckhand, the young woman over there, the quartermaster and myself."

"Only four?" A measure of the Bermudian's alert jauntiness departed. "Vhere's 'e rest?"

"Why?"

"For Jesus Christ's sake, you couldn't come all 'e wheh from America vith a crew this size!"

"The others jumped ship," Rob explained curtly. "Suppose

427

you come aft, Captain. I'll need help in moving one of my deckhands."

The islander's stubbly jaw closed with a little click. "Help? Vhut's 'e matter vith him?"

"Don't rightly know," Rob drawled. "Maybe you can tell."

It wasn't reassuring to see the other whale boats, each manned by twelve men, come bobbing alongside. The occupants looked just as whiskery and weatherbeaten as the first lot. Resting on their oars, they craned necks to see over the bulwarks or grabbed at bits of flotsam. A few watched the blue-green water surge over and then retreat across the *Desdemona*'s submerged bow. As Wincapaw had predicted, the visitors were for the most part small and lean; nearly all had bad teeth. The second boat's helmsman lacked an eye and three fingers of his left hand.

"Here he is," Rob said, throwing back the rough canopy they had rigged over the convalescent. "Can't imagine what ails him."

When he saw Ben goggling fearfully up at him, the Bermudian's expression became such a comic blend of horror and disappointed greed, that Katie and Wincapaw, grinning expectantly from behind the wheel, laughed themselves wet-eyed.

The patient was certainly no vision of beauty. All his face, shoulders and the upper part of his body were encrusted with flaking scabs. He resembled some ungainly and loathsome reptile.

"Oh, my God, it's 'e pox!" screamed the Bermudian and, wheeling, ran back down the deck so fast he lost his cocked hat but never stopped to pick it up.

"She's a pest ship!" Green shirt billowing with haste, he vaulted over the rail and landed in the whaler on all fours, shouting, "Shove off, you club-footed baboons! Pull, for God's sake, pull!"

"Jesus! They are rotten with 'e pox!" "Pest ship!" "Pox!" Cursing a blue streak, the islanders shortened oars, levered their tips against the *Desdemona*'s side. In their hurry the rowers jabbed and banged each other with their sweep handles. Spray flew yards high.

If he hadn't been so nearly incapable of feeling, Rob would have laughed himself sick at their furious disappointment and at the comical way the wreckers went skittering off among the reefs. As it was, he only kicked the leader's greasy cocked hat over the side. It floated away over water which, between spurs in the reef, took on a pale green. A trio of little fishes, bright blue and streaked with glaring yellow, rose to nose about it.

After breakfast Rob shed his clothes, hung a case knife on a lanyard about his neck and, swimming easily, made a careful inspection of the wreck. Provided no sudden storm arose, they were in small danger, he decided. On the other hand there could be no hope of salvaging the *Desdemona*. The seas had shoved her so far up onto a plateau of coral she could only be gotten off at prohibitive expense.

A series of dives revealed that the schooner's bow was badly stove in. Through warm and amazingly transparent water he made out a discouraging mess of broken ribs and twisted, splintered sheathing. The poor old girl was done for, all right; and to blazes with her!

Long lazy strokes carried him off among reefs creaming lazily in the sunlight. His only interest now was the weird and unearthly beauty of the sea floor. A good swimmer, he dove and at leisure explored several emerald-hued little caves. Never, anywhere, had he beheld so many strange and exquisite sights. Wishing he might remain in this serene new world forever, he resented having to surface for air.

In a series of miniature canyons he discovered purplish sea fans, slender trees, and skull-like shapes fashioned of growing coral. But what delighted him most were the many varieties of sea anemones; their delicate designs and tints were too many to be numbered. Here and there the corals had united themselves into graceful arches, into temples and palaces tenanted by schools of fish so bright they might have been dabs of color from Neptune's paint box. Many of them came nosing up, flatteringly unafraid. Silver, blue, scarlet, pale yellow, Prussian blue and striped like zebras. Some species changed color a dozen times a minute.

Wincapaw watched the skipper for a while then, lithe as an eel, swam off on an expedition of his own. As soon as he left, Katie went down the foredeck to the water and slipped out of her clothes. It was sheer luxury to feel warm water licking at her legs and to wash all over just as Mr. David had told her. The water felt like caressing hands on her breasts and sleek white thighs.

She couldn't swim, but she intended to learn. My, it was

beautiful out here! You could see right down to the ocean's bottom. Why, you could even see a shadow of the bare main boom cast on the sand. Oh, the sea and the flowers, the pretty little fishes! She paddled happily about and her hair floating out was no less yellow than a raft of weed collecting in an eddy under the wreck's stern.

Of what would happen to her from now on, Katie hadn't the vaguest notion. Mr. Rob would get them ashore somehow, but after that—well—she must leave him. No fool, she knew she couldn't help but remind him of his wife.

Aware that Mr. Rob and the quartermaster were exploring the reef's farthest edge, she stretched her nude length on the deck where Ben couldn't see her. The sun warmed her right down to her bones like it had that day when she was coming back to Norfolk, with the freighter's train. Maybe the Injuns weren't so crazy? It would be simply elegant to go naked most of the time. Imagine having no clothes to mend, to wash.

Lying in the sun, Katie realized that during the voyage she had lost the last of her winter pallor and, with the ample fare aboard, she had put on weight. Somehow it just didn't seem possible that, just over a month ago, she had been slaving for that old bitch Mrs. Skillings, and now she was lying naked on the deck of a schooner wrecked off a strange island. A month hence where would she be? Lack of an answer troubled her not at all.

At length she rolled over and propped her chin on her hands. Carefully she studied the island. It lay a mile or more distant and looked very rocky. The coast line of it was slate gray and low lying except for two places where it rose to a considerable height. On top of a small hill a length of blank gray wall suggested the presence of fortifications, but at this distance she couldn't tell for sure.

Though dark green trees masked the rest of the shore, there was not a palm anywhere she could see. Resentment piqued her sunny mood. Imagine being in the tropics and seeing no palms! Here and there the long glaring white roof of a house shone among the tree tops. At various points lazy smoke columns crawled into the sky, but on the whole the island looked sparsely populated.

Above the land a long, woolly white cloud was hovering so fixedly it seemed to be anchored there by a series of invisible cables. The sky grew bluer and still more blue.

To Katie's delight a school of tiny fishes, scarlet as blood, swam dauntlessly over the bulwarks and darted over to the submerged forecastle door. The minute visitors hovered there until some pieces of wreckage knocked together and they scattered in colorful panic. Katie reckoned she had never seen anything move so quick—unless it was a gamecock's legs.

Many cabbages had floated through the open forehatch to the surface and now drifted about, bobbing up and down like the heads of a swimming regiment. It became time to think about getting dinner so she arose and stood smiling at the damp replica her body had left on the deck.

10 — QUARANTINE

AFTER his swim Rob ate such a hearty dinner he fell asleep propped against the binnacle. He was still harried by bad dreams. Almost always they took the same pattern. He would lift Peggy, wrapped in canvas, and carry her to the stern. When he braced to drop her body over, she would stir. The canvas would part and Peggy's face peered out, fresh, radiant and indescribably luminous; just as it had looked beneath her wedding veil.

"Rob, why do you do this to me?" she would ask piteously.

"Because you are so wilful," he could hear himself reply.

All in an instant her face would lose its light; it would crumple, grow swollen, discolored and hideous.

He slept heavily, snoring softly in his throat. Katie, careful not to disturb him, went over to watch Wincapaw tend Ben who was nearly over the contagious stage now, or so the quartermaster said.

Around three of the afternoon a breeze sprang up. It blew from the island and brought an elusive fragrance the like of which Katie had never smelled. She lifted her short nose and sniffed eagerly.

Wincapaw roused her from her abstraction by saying suddenly, "Boat's heading this way."

He took up Rob's spyglass and, after studying the distant craft, invited, "Here, take a look."

What Katie saw was a boat differing sharply from those which had appeared at dawn. Long and low in the water, she was painted white and boasted gunwales of bright blue. At her oars were six blacks wearing bright yellow shirts. A seventh Negro stood behind and above a canopy rigged over the stern. He was steering with a brass-bound tiller. She could distinguish two men under the yellow canopy. One of them was dressed all in white, but the other wore a red coat and blue breeches. In the bow of the barge crouched three white men with muskets lying across their laps. What chiefly attracted Katie's attention was the Union Jack fluttering from a short jack staff.

"She does look like a government barge," Rob agreed when they awakened him. After watching the leisurely, well-measured rhythm of her oars awhile, he went below and scraped the light brown fuzz from his cheeks. Also he dug out a decent suit and put on fresh linen.

When he got back on deck, the barge was drifting perhaps fifty yards abeam of the wreck. Upon command the grinning black rowers flipped their dripping sweeps to the vertical in ragged imitation of a man-of-war's crew.

Katie noticed that the white-clad man was decidedly plump and wore a bright blue bandanna knotted about his head beneath a broad-brimmed straw hat. He was young, thirty perhaps. In one pudgy hand he carried a palm leaf fan.

"Ahoy! What ship is that?" He spoke without bothering to bend forward.

Ashton told him.

"Heard you have plague aboard. That right?"

"Yes, we've had smallpox."

"Any new cases?"

"No. Not in a week."

"That's good." The young man in the straw hat seemed relieved. "Put us alongside," he yelled at the black coxswain.

"Yassuh!" He bent forward. "Pull sta-bohd, back po't! Easy—now—easy all!"

One of the nondescript white men put down his musket, grabbed a boathook. Again the oars were flipped up as, very deftly, the barge was brought under the *Desdemona*'s counter.

Puffing, the man in white scrambled over the rail. At his heels came a gaunt individual wearing a scarlet uniform coat sizes too large for him.

The minute Rob laid eyes on the foremost caller, he felt an instinctive attraction. He was so very jolly looking with his bright blue eyes, the humorous expression of his wide mouth and the healthy pink complexion of a baby.

Arriving on the poop, he jerked a bow. "Servant, sir."

Rob returned the bow and declared himself delighted.

"You seem to have received an ill welcome from Bermuda. My sympathy, sir." There was dignity in the way the plump young man offered his hand.

Rob warned, "We've smallpox aboard, remember?"

"Had it. So has Dr. Chamberlain. By the bye, I am deputy customs collector for this parish," he announced. "My name is Ashton—Peter Ashton."

In no single particular did he resemble the man Rob's imagination had pictured.

"You'll excuse my not wearing a wig?" he apologized. "It's just too blasted hot."

Rob shook his cousin's plump but surprisingly firm hand. "This is a pleasure, Cousin Peter."

"Cousin? Gad's my life! You can't be Robert Ashton?"

"I'm what's left of him."

"Why, my dear fellow, I'm charmed, delighted. Welcome! Welcome! Chamberlain! This is my cousin—the one I was speaking of." An instant later his manner changed. He looked acutely unhappy. "How did this happen?"

"A runaway slave brought the disease aboard in Norfolk."

When Peter Ashton shook his head, his shadow mimicked him on the deck. "I don't mean that. How did you come to get piled up like this?"

Rob explained the manner in which his quartermaster had been deceived into taking false lights for those of Eli's Harbour, into mistaking the loom of Daniel's Head for Wreck Hill.

"False lights!" Peter Ashton's fingers snapped loud as a pistol's report. The doctor, looking uneasy, watched his companion face the shore. "Just where did you see those lights?"

"Where that long beach is—the one with all the white sand on it."

"You could swear the lights were there?"

"No. But if you'll show some lanterns there after dark, I could be sure."

"No need. No need!" Then, to Rob's vast astonishment, his cousin burst into peal after peal of laughter. Even the doctor's sallow features screwed themselves into a grin. "Oh my God!" Peter hugged himself until his eyes watered. "It's superb! It's capital!" He went off again into such great roars of laughter that the men in the boat alongside caught the contagion and began to laugh, even though they hadn't the least idea of what was up.

Peter clapped his cousin on the back again and again. "Oh my God! If you only knew how funny this is—"

"I could enjoy a laugh right now," Rob smiled. "Suppose you tell me what is so funny about all this?"

"Tell you later. Oh, my God, this *is* priceless! Congratulate you. Fact."

Rob stared, suspicious. Then he thought he grasped the point of Peter's amusement. "If you imagine I'm about to collect insurance money, you're wrong."

"No insurance? All the better! Ho! Ho! Ho! Oh, my God, wait 'til Henry Tucker hears! He'll laugh, too, eh, Chamberlain?" Stomach a-quiver beneath the gold buttons on his waistcoat, Peter drove his elbow into the doctor's ribs. "No insurance? Hear that? Oh my God, this is perfect!"

Dr. Chamberlain's amusement, however, had disappeared. "I am sorry, sir; even if you are Mr. Ashton's cousin, I shall have to order you and your people into quarantine. No choice. Have to, you understand?"

"Of course."

Peter said, "Go ahead, Chamberlain, I'll take a look about."

"I take it you have had the pox?" the doctor asked.

"Yes. Years ago."

"You were lucky."

Lugging under one arm a portfolio of badly scuffed leather, the doctor seated himself upon the signal locker and produced a portable leaden inkwell. Screwing up his eyes in the bright sunlight, he cut a precise new point to a pen then, in careful script, noted the date of the outbreak of the disease, the names of the victims and the dates of their deaths.

He then examined Ben and pronounced him safely convalescent. Next he called Wincapaw but, on noting pocks scarring his cheekbones, dismissed him. When Dr. Chamberlain came to consider Katie, worried wrinkles appeared on his brow. She could see he was baffled by her failure to take the disease when she showed no signs of ever having been inoculated.

"Blessed if I know what to think," muttered the physician, turning away. "Must have had a very light case as a child. Again, there is yet time for her to come down with it. Another ten days will tell the story."

"Ten days!" Peter exploded. "Come, come now! Charlie, you can't keep my cousin in quarantine all that time."

A sudden obsequiousness on the part of Dr. Chamberlain was not lost upon Rob.

"But, Mr. Ashton, I really must put this ship under quarantine," protested he uneasily. "People would talk."

"That's so. No quarantine, no fee, eh?" Peter chuckled. "Smart about his fees is Charlie Chamberlain. Isn't every day he gets a pest ship to fuss over." From his sleeve Rob's cousin pulled an immense handkerchief. He used it vigorously on his face and on the palms of his hands. "Gad, it's a regular scorcher today! Haven't a spot of something wet aboard, have you?"

"There's a hamper of Fayal wine below. Suppose we sample it?"

Peter beamed. "Why not? May as well feel comfortable while figuring what's to be done."

Soon Katie was filling three glasses.

"Well, here's to your shipwreck!" Peter winked and chuckled so hard he spilt his wine.

"—And to the quarantine!" grinned Dr. Chamberlain, sniffing at his glass.

"Well, Cousin," Peter demanded, "what's your idea of a toast?"

"Here's to the present! Devil take the future!"

Gravely all three touched glasses and drank, then Peter shuffled over to the flag locker. Sighing, he plunked himself down, let the sea breeze beat up the legs of loose linen trousers.

Wincapaw went forward and tried to talk with the barge crew, but they eyed him distrustfully and shoved off when he leaned over the bulwarks.

"Now about the quarantine—" Peter turned to the doctor who, having undone his waistcoat, was removing his dingy red coat. Uninvited, he helped himself to a second glass.

"Provided you are reasonable, whatever you say is fine with me, Mr. Ashton."

Rubbing his pink chin, Peter considered. "Suppose, Cousin Rob, we reckon the girl's exposure from the date of the original outbreak? Say, Charlie, what is the usual quarantine for the pox?"

"Eighteen days, I think, but it may be twenty."

"Eighteen, eh?" The Bermudian's eye wandered up to the

435

main top. "First case was on the 6th. Um. That would call for only three more days in quarantine. Right?" His blue eyes flickered over to Chamberlain.

The physician smacked his lips. "That's right," said he. It had been a long time since he had tasted wine as good as this.

Peter accepted a second glass. "We can do one of two things, Cousin Robert. I can either send a boat to carry you to our regular quarantine station on Marshall's Island, or you can stay aboard. At this time of year you ought to be safe enough. If the glass starts to fall, I will come out and take you off in plenty of time." He grinned. "You've your choice, but I might tell you our quarantine station is no palace. What do you want to do?"

Rob's gaze wandered from Katie over to Wincapaw. He reckoned he could handle that situation all right.

"I reckon we will stay aboard, then. There ought to be some unspoiled grain in the main hold."

"Really?" Peter lowered his voice to an urgent undertone. "Well, I wouldn't tell a soul. This vessel is a total loss. Understand?"

"But she isn't, quite," Rob insisted.

Peter, good humor unruffled, winked elaborately. "I know a little about the cost of salvage operations around here and I'd say she is a *total* loss." He hesitated, savoring a sip of the deep yellow Fayal. "When you calculate your loss, write the figures in pencil. There is the rate of exchange to be figured," he added quickly. "I'll be glad to help you with that. Need food? Water? Anything?"

Rob shook his head.

"No? Then, as deputy customs officer, I'll post a guard on the beach. That will stop loose talk. After three days you can move in at Gaunt New House."

"I wouldn't want to crowd you."

"You won't." Peter was fairly bubbling in his eagerness to be helpful. "Plenty of room, Mountford and Hereward are away, so there is only Aunt Lydia, Susan and myself in the house. We rattle around something awful."

"Susan?" It was odd, Rob realized that he had never had a comp.ete description of his first cousin's family. He supposed the row over his father's marriage accounted for it.

"Susan is my sister, aged nine, and an imp from hell," Peter explained.

How odd, the same blood flowed in this big, pink-faced

436

stranger and himself. Was Hereward as plump? His recollection of Mountford at the wedding was of a thin, dark-complexioned youth.

Warmed by a third glass of Fayal, Dr. Chamberlain waxed more friendly, left medicine and instructions for Ben. When he slipped into his scarlet coat, Rob saw that its braid was torn and several buttons were represented by dangling threads.

"Don't you worry, Mr. Ashton. I will see about the quarantine. I aim to be helpful." He pumped Rob's hand. "You —er—might mention that to Henry Tucker when you see him."

"I will remember," Rob promised.

Peter started off towards his boat, surprisingly light on his feet despite his bulk. Suddenly he halted, snapping vexed fingers.

"What a damned mannerless oaf I am! I trust you left the charming Mrs. Ashton well? Mountford wrote of her as a veritable queen of beauty, a winsome—"

Rob's expression checked the flow of compliments.

"She—she was aboard?" Peter stammered, turning scarlet.

"She was the last one to die."

"Good God! How awful!" Peter hurried back and flung an arm about his cousin's shoulder. "And I never suspected. Can you forgive me?"

"How could you have known?" Rob reminded. "I didn't tell you. Somehow I—I couldn't."

"Poor Robert," Peter said and with a peremptory gesture dammed a flood of condolences from Dr. Chamberlain.

Giving his cousin a small reassuring hug, he turned away for a second time. "It may be, Cousin Robert, that you have come to the right place to—er—recover from your loss. Bermuda is interesting these days, one might say."

11 — GEORGE WINCAPAW

TOMORROW morning the quarantine would be lifted. George Wincapaw was considering this prospect with no enthusiasm. He knew what to expect ashore. At best, he'd be sent to some hutch in the slave quarters, even though he had been born free.

Life aboard the *Desdemona* hadn't been bad at all. Both Captain Ashton and Miss Katie had trusted him, had treated him almost like a white man. They never had adopted a snotty manner when he came around—most white people did, though. They treated him the same way they would a dog that was too valuable just to be kicked about. All his life it had made him sore. Couldn't he read and write? Didn't he know more about ships and navigation than many a so-called master mariner?

Colored people wouldn't have to do with him, even if he had wanted it—and he didn't. Of course real black wenches were flattered at being noticed by a man so nearly white, but they never would love him the way they did a big shiny buck. Only a quarter colored; but for all the heed any white girl paid, he might have been blacker than the ace of spades! Only once had he got to a white girl, but she wasn't right in her head so it hadn't been much fun. Besides, he had missed getting strung up by a matter of half an hour. That dim-wit girl stuck in his mind though. Her skin was so damn' smooth.

Sitting on the wreck's canting deck and comfortably propped against her mainmast, Wincapaw took another slug from a brandy bottle he had swiped when Captain Ashton had left the liquor locker unfastened. The spirits made him feel at once better—and worse.

Looking up the deck, he saw Katie sitting on the flag locker beside the captain reading aloud from a chart. Her voice sounded mighty soft and sweet.

" 'The Horse Latitudes are so named by masters plying the American Coast because of violent gales met in the 30° latitudes to 35° North. Many horses carried to the West Indies die because of injury and are flung overboard. During the months of April, May and June, whales are taken off—' "

Every now and then the captain would stop and correct her.

What would happen when they got ashore? The skipper must be pretty near broke. The cargo salvage wouldn't amount to much. His own future wasn't bright at all, at all. What with trade dead or dying all along the American coast, he'd find trouble landing a decent berth. White Bermudians who didn't follow the sea were precious few. They bred slaves to get as many sound seamen as they could. Normally there was a shortage of deckhands on the islands. This was so because nowadays the islanders were building and manning so many sloops and snows each year.

Captain Ashton sure had taken a fancy to that *Speedwell* brig. Earlier that day, he had asked Dr. Chamberlain who owned her.

"Some damned English-lover down to St. George's," the doctor had told him over a second bottle of port. "He clears her at this end, though, to get by paying duty. The Governor—damn him—don't get much change out of us West Enders. Nor anywhere else, for that matter. They say his salary is supposed to be £400, Bermuda—that's £265 sterling, but he ain't touched a penny in a year. We got that damned Englishman right where we want him."

Wincapaw sneaked another gulp of the brandy. Smooth stuff! But not so smooth as the skin of Katie's neck. He slid his sheath knife free of its scabbard and commenced trimming his nails. It was a damned handy knife, extra well balanced.

Over the sibilant rush and retreat of seas across the sunken bow he heard Captain Ashton say "good night." When he had gone, Katie stood up, stretched lazily, then lingered with face lifted to the sky. In that moment the quartermaster decided to take her even if it cost him his neck. He slipped off his shoes and, silent as a shadow, sought the poopdeck.

"Katie!"

"La! How you startled me." Katie whirled, made out the quartermaster's bony face and the two gold rings in his ear. He was standing right at her shoulder and his nostrils were opening and shutting like the gills of a stranded hornpout.

"Katie, Honey, I'm just crazy 'bout you. I'm burning up." He held out his arms.

"Why, you damn' fresh nigger!" Her hand caught him a smack across his mouth; a hard resounding slap which sent fiery pinpoints shooting across his eyeballs.

It was a mistake. In a flash he pinned her in such a grip she couldn't move. Then he jerked out his knife and shoved it against her. With that point digging into the underside of her left breast, she didn't dare move a muscle. One shove on that knife handle and she'd be dead.

"You squawk, I'll kill you."

Wincapaw began thinking fast. Katie had been using Captain Rudder's old cabin. There was no key to its door because

439

Rudder had lost it or taken it away with him in the longboat. If she didn't show up soon, the skipper might come up looking for her.

The soft pressure of Katie's stomach against his thickened his voice. "In a minute I'm going to your cabin. Hear? You follow right after." His teeth glistened and she could feel the furious hammering of his heart. "Try to get by, or raise a holler and I'll slip in and kill the skipper. He can't move near so quick as me."

Katie stood stock still. She was more scared than she had ever been in her life. Wincapaw wasn't fooling and you never could tell what a nigger might do when he got this way.

She nodded mechanically. "All right. I'll follow you, but don't you dast hurt Mr. Rob!"

Hard as the jaws of a pair of pincers, Wincapaw's fingers closed over Katie's wrists. "You make one little noise— I—I'll cut your heart out!" Slipping his knife back in its sheath, the mulatto turned and disappeared down the cabin companion-way.

First testing her bruised forearm, then the little bloody spot his knife point had caused on her breast, Katie remained rigid. If she just waited there, Wincapaw sure enough would come back and kill her. What to do? She didn't want any truck with a nigger. As a rule, she could think pretty fast. But not now. She never had looked a potential murderer in the face before. The nigger was liquored up, too, she realized dully. That made things extra bad.

This was what she got for having been so decent with Wincapaw. She had been a bloody fool. In sickened helplessness her gaze swept the deck and she saw light from Mr. Rob's cabin reflected in the water astern.

Then her eye lit on one of the empty kegs most skippers kept ready to heave to anyone who fell overboard. She was relieved to find the keg not so heavy as she had been expecting. Lugging it in both arms, she moved forward along the slanting deck.

She even didn't wait to take off her dress; she just waded out along the sunken foredeck until the water rose to her knees, to her thighs. Twisting one hand in a loop of rope secured to the keg, she commenced awkwardly to paddle. Good thing the tide was making, not falling.

It was a very long way to shore.

Part II

Somerset Island

1 — COLONEL FORTESCUE

KATIE TRYON felt pretty thoroughly exhausted by the time sand rose under her feet, but she didn't dare leave the water just yet for, away off to the left, glowed the quarantine guard's watch fire. Looking backwards she could see lights were moving about on the wreck. Mr. Rob and Wincapaw must be hunting her.

While clinging to the keg, she tried to learn what the shore in front of her might be like. There were no lights she could see and right here the island rose sharp from the water except where a series of little sand beaches made in. Choosing a course between various breakers, she headed for the nearest of these.

Tired but decidedly pleased with her solution of the problem, Katie tottered up a beach of soft fine sand and sank onto a patch of grass. She stayed quiet, listening to the slow rushing of the sea up the shore and to the nearer *pat-pat-pat* of water dripping from her clothes. Maybe she wasn't such a complete numbskull as Mrs. Skillings always said she was. Here she'd freed Mr. Rob of any further responsibility for her and at the same time had left Wincapaw to whistle for his fun. She felt a little sick, though, when she remembered the sting of his knife point.

She lay panting awhile, gathering fresh strength and wondering what she had better do. First thing was to get warm. Though her fingers trembled with exhaustion, she stripped off her dress and petticoats. She wrung them out hard as she could, then draped them on a limb to dry. They'd still be damp by morning, but this warm onshore breeze should start the drying process.

With hair slatting soggily between her shoulderblades, Katie ran mother-naked up and down the beach five or six times, fast as she could. That got her circulation started and her skin dried rapidly. At last, gasping and almost hot, she dropped down in the lee of an overhanging rock. It was a surprise to find how much heat the stone had retained. Why, in this little hollow the air felt right warm and the grass very soft. Since there seemed small use in lying awake worrying over what might happen, she went to sleep.

"Hup—ho! Pull—ho! Pull debbil! Pull baker! Hup—ho!" The chant finally penetrated Katie's unconsciousness. She lifted her head and as promptly cowered. Less than fifty yards offshore a green painted gig, narrow and low in the water, was threshing by under the propulsion of six very long sweeps. The oarsmen, giant blacks all, were naked to the waist and made their nine-foot sweeps bend at every stroke. The colored coxswain's body jerked to each stroke. So did the head of a sallow white man sitting beside him. It was fascinating to watch all those oars enter and leave the water in such perfect unison. Spray sparkled high as the craft shot by.

When the boat had flashed out of sight around a ledge, she noticed another gig also skirting the shore, but farther out. It was painted red and black. Then a third boat, a blue one, came pulling along as if in hot pursuit. Why all this tearing hurry? Katie wondered until, creeping to the corner of the ledge, she saw a big ship standing inshore. What she had seen, she deduced, were rival pilot boats racing for the fee.

A cardinal whistled cheerily from a nearby bush and Katie would have felt finer than silk had her vigorous young body not clamored so insistently for food. On taking an inventory of her condition, she discovered that the corals had inflicted only minor scratches—none of them on her feet, thank fortune! She braided her hair, plaiting it as neatly as possible. Her clothes, as she had expected, were still damp, but she reckoned they would dry on her in short order.

Barefooted, but otherwise decently attired, Katie seated herself on a log and tried to think up a tale that would hold water under any conditions. It wouldn't do to get taken up for a vagrant. If she did, she would get questioned and get put in jail for a runaway bound girl. She was still pondering the problem when a Negro fisherman came rowing by and began to pull wicker fish traps off the shore.

With his ragged straw hat and fine physique he made quite a sight, especially when quantities of bright colored fishes tumbled all flopping and squirming out of his trap. When he noticed her, he grinned and waved in such friendly style that she waved back, but she didn't dare ask any questions. She waited until the fisherman rowed on, then scrambled up a sandy bank towards some trees.

It wasn't an easy climb because prickly pears and Spanish bayonets grew so thickly. Each time one of the latter plant's sharp points stung her legs it hurt so she relieved herself with a round English oath. It was some time before she recognized the sound of wheels creaking somewhere off to her right. Turning in that direction, she came before long upon a narrow, rutted road winding along beneath the boughs of tall cedars.

Aboard the *Desdemona* she had, among her reading lessons, seen Mr. Rob's chart of the island. Therefore, she knew that the Bermudas were an archipelago arranged roughly in the shape of a fish hook and consisting of some two hundred islands of varying size. Somerset Island, she knew, lay at the West, or barb, end of the group and St. George's at the East, or eye, end. Since Mr. Rob's family was settled on Somerset, it seemed only logical to seek work in the direction of St. George's. After all, the colonial capital lay only eighteen miles away; hardly more than a good day's walk.

Accordingly, Katie struck off to her right down the road. The soil was so red and rich-looking it interested her. What did the islanders grow? Cotton? Tobacco? Rice? The surface of the road right here was sandy, but often soft limestone shone through. It had been ground and scarred by wagon wheels.

The rough highway commenced to climb and, now and then little box-like houses built of limestone blocks could be seen. They seemed poor little affairs centering an orbit of pigs, chickens and children. Occasional travelers eyed her curiously, murmured "good day" and stumped on. They were ill-dressed and suspicious looking.

A stone church topped by a remarkably graceful stone spire next appeared on the left. "St. James's Church" was inscribed on its notice board. Nearby some stone gate posts bore the name Church Hill but she could not see the house itself. Occasionally she passed a tethered wild-looking cow or a scrawny pig feeding in a microscopic pasture.

Resting in the shade of a tree, she watched the slow approach of an oxcart. A straw-hatted Negro walked alongside the span of stunted white oxen. It made Katie mad to see how, in wanton cruelty, he kept goading the near ox. In the cart several oily-looking barrels gurgled. Since the Negro looked surly, Katie decided she had best postpone inquiry as to her whereabouts.

To her sharp disappointment, nowhere did she see a brook or stream. Having swallowed plenty of sea water during her paddle ashore, she was beginning really to suffer from thirst. With each passing moment the sun grew hotter, hammered more unmercifully on her bare yellow head. She wished she had a handkerchief to tie over it. Wincapaw had warned against taking chances with the Bermuda sun, especially if you were blonde. If it got any hotter she decided to make a kerchief from a strip of her petticoat.

She passed two more houses, one of them quite a large affair boasting extensive slave quarters and a big low barn stretching off behind it. In the blue-black shade of a large shed some Negroes were washing a carriage with bright blue wheels and a yellow body. A low wall of gray stone was engraved with the very English name Willow Bank. The name Haydon's appeared in faded letters just a little farther on.

Alarmed by such evidences of denser inhabitation, Katie lengthened her stride. The sooner she left Somerset Island unnoticed, the better would be her chances of erasing the past.

The road climbed a hill, then swung right, skirting the base of the tallest hill she had yet encountered. Her feet had begun to hurt in earnest and she wondered how far it was to the bridge connecting Somerset Island with Long Island. Her mouth felt dry as parchment. At the next house she felt she must take a chance and beg a drink.

Not yet lost to curiosities, she gaped at a remarkable tree growing beside the road. It grew straight as any bean pole and, beyond an absurd topknot of leaves sprouting at its very tip, it boasted no foliage at all. The bark was rough patterned, like the belly of an alligator. Clustering like bats under the eaves, hung perhaps a dozen yellowish fruits. They looked like golden pears, kind of. Were they good to eat? Katie wished Wincapaw had told her. She was still craning her neck at the pawpaws when she blundered upon a solid figure halted at the entrance to a driveway. Twin pillars displayed the name Eli's.

The stranger held the reins of a saddle horse looped over his elbow. He had been digging to dislodge a stone from his mount's near front hoof when Katie materialized suddenly around a clump of bushes. Startled, the animal snorted and reared.

Perforce, the man released the hoof, crying, "Steady! Confound you, steady!"

"Oh, I'm sorry!" Katie gasped when the animal's curvetings knocked off the stranger's hat. "I'll get it."

"Eh?" He turned so angrily to face the road that she flinched back from the hat. "Damme, why don't you look where you are going?"

He was not young, Katie saw; he must be tapping sixty, anyhow. Beneath a carefully curled white wig, strong, almost severe features glowed scarlet as any love apple.

"I'm so sorry!" she gasped, gray-green eyes flying wide open.

She started to hurry away, but he bellowed, "Stop there!" in such a terrifying loud voice she obeyed. She halted, not daring to turn around.

"Come back here, Buttercup. I won't eat you." When still she hesitated, the stranger rasped, "Damn it, girl, do as I say!"

Katie Tryon turned and forced a smile. Sunburnt, hot and dusty in her faded calico dress, she reckoned she looked wild as any colt fresh in from pasture. Most of all she hated having this grim gentleman see her bare feet. The queer part of it was that this Englishman—from the way he talked she had no doubt he was one—seemed friendly.

"Buttercup, I wish to talk." After retrieving the smart-looking buckled hat from the rutted and ill-tended driveway, the Englishman led his mount a little distance along it, away from the main road. Once the mare stood quietly, he commenced to flick dust from lace spurting out of the blue cuffs of his yellow velvet coat.

His boots, Katie noticed, were expensive, English sewn; and so was his saddle. Tom MacSherry always said you could judge a man very well by the state of his leather goods and by the way he considered his horse.

"A regular stunner!" he observed coolly surveying Katie from heel to poll. "Fancy, old Jerry never mentioned you."

"No, sir," Katie agreed for want of any other observation.

"One of the Harvey girls?"

"Oh, no, sir."

"Jennings?"

"No, sir."

"Damme! Then you *must* be a Tucker. In Somerset, can't toss a pebble any direction and not raise lumps on a Tucker."

Though the Englishman spoke as if he'd eat a body up, there was a sort of twinkle in his gray-blue eyes. From the way his coat was turned back and frogged in military fashion, she reckoned the stranger sometime must have been an officer. But when she noticed that his belt was fitted with a hook to hang a sword on, she reckoned he was still with the army. Nowadays civilian gentlemen had about abandoned the old practice of carrying walking swords. A tingle of amusement seized her. He was so confounded sure of himself. But she wasn't sure of a single thing. Still smiling, she shook her head, gazed at him from beneath her brows.

"No, sir, I'm not a Tucker, either."

"Not a Tucker?" He seemed inclined to take the denial as a personal affront. "Not really?"

"Yes, sir, really."

"Well, then I'm damned! Who are you?"

Katie floundered, then characteristically took refuge in the truth.

"Katherine Tryon? Not a bad name, Tryon, not a bad name. Still I'm hanged if Jerry has mentioned any Tryons in Somerset."

"No, sir."

After he had beat the last traces of dust from his hat against the knee of blue whipcord breeches, the gentleman began to fan himself with it.

"Hot? What? Hanged if I understand how old Jerry's eagle eye for a neat-turned ankle missed like this."

Katie was feeling surer of herself. She understood his pattern. She'd seen plenty like him in Norfolk; retired army officers with a bark ten times worse than their bite. Graying, they'd their half pay and lived comfortably. Most of them had army records long enough to furnish conversation for the rest of their lives. They almost always were neat like this broad-shouldered, chunkily built gentleman. La! That was real French lace on his shirtfront.

"Your friend Mr. Jerry has never seen me, Mr. ——"

"Name is Fortescue, Colonel Hugh Fortescue." From his

pocket he produced an apple, fed it to his sturdy-looking mare. "Newcomer?"

"Yes, sir," she said hurriedly.

He regarded her more critically. "You ain't English. Don't talk Bermudian, either. What are you?"

"I—I come from Maryland."

"Maryland? Eh, where in the world is Maryland?"

"Maryland is one of the American Colonies—one of the best."

He summoned a ferocious scowl. "Then you must be a rebel!"

"Oh, no, sir," said she hastily. "I have never took sides. Only, I think Parliament is wrong—"

"Generally is. Beastly pot-house politicians, the lot of them," Colonel Fortescue smiled suddenly. "Pay no attention to what I say, Mistress Tryon. I am deucedly bored—and lonesome, dashed lonesome. Rode over from St. George's to see old Jerry. Wretched fellow hasn't a decent bottle of wine nor a wench worth bedding. Imagine it! Fine way to let down old comrade-in-arms. Gad, Ma'am, should have seen the two of us at Fontenoy! Just ensigns then, but *that was a day!*"

"Yes, sir," Katie said, still stunned with the realization that this splendid person had addressed her as "Ma'am." She plucked up courage. "—And your friend?"

"Major Jerry Allen is my oldest friend," he told her seriously. "Inconsolable for the present, poor fellow. Apple of his eye, only daughter, has just married; flown the parental nest. Jerry takes it mighty ill. Gad's my life, widowers take on worse than the rest, eh?"

"Yes, sir, I reckon they must."

Colonel Fortescue used his handkerchief to flick a minute speck of dust from his boot top. It was a very elegant gesture. "And how may I be of service to so lovely a lady?"

"Why, why—sir, I am right hungry and thirsty."

"Hungry? Thirsty? Shouldn't wonder. Dry work trudging along in the hot sun. Learned that in India. Well, swing up on Molly behind me. Have you to your destination in no time."

"Thank you, sir, but that's hardly possible."

"Eh? What's that? Hardly possible? And why not?" He looked at her down a rather large nose netted with tiny blue veins. "Why?"

447

"Because I haven't any place to go."

"No place to go? God's blood! Do you talk riddles?"

"Oh, no, sir," Katie replied as cheerfully as she could. "I—I'm on my way to St. George's. I hope to find employment there."

Colonel Fortescue stared, snorted, then quite deliberately unbuckled a rein and with it tethered his mare to a limb. Round-eyed, she watched him produce from his saddlebags a small paper package and a green bottle with a very long neck.

"Now then, Buttercup. Look like one, you know. Cheery, yellow hair; that sort of thing. Don't mind my calling you Buttercup?"

"Not when you tack a 'Ma'am' onto it," Katie managed to get out, utterly astounded at her temerity.

Colonel Fortescue caught his breath, reddened and started to say something. Instead, he grinned.

"Very well, Buttercup Ma'am. Fancy we might converse on your problems? Bad thing not to know where one is going. Like marching a regiment out of barracks without learning who you're going to fight, or where."

Colonel Fortescue produced a huge handkerchief, shook it vigorously and marched over to a level space. Precisely as a map he spread it beneath a cedar. On the square of fine cambric he placed his paper parcel and the bottle. Undone, the parcel was found to contain half of a frying chicken, some cold yams, three hard-boiled eggs and a piece of soggy-appearing fruitcake.

"When planning a campaign, Buttercup Ma'am, I find it wise to do so on a full stomach, provided there is food about. There is now. While you refresh yourself, I will tell you something of myself. When I have done, you may return the compliment—as far as you deem discreet."

Though the sun, soaring higher, beat down on the island with pitiless intensity, the temperature did not perceptibly increase in the shade of the giant cedar. Colonel Fortescue, clay pipe between fingers, eased his belt and sat with yellow shoulders resting against the tree. Thrust out before him, well varnished boots reflected patches of white clouds and green foliage.

Katie sat sidewise, trying to hide dust whitened feet under the hem of her dress. She tried not to make a pig of herself. But it was hard work.

"—And so," Colonel Fortescue remarked between puffs

on his pipe, "I said 'to hell with India!' No place for a white man. Stayed out there, though, 'til the Mounseers were licked. Smashed 'em at Wandewash, by Gad, but it took Plassey to do the trick for good and all." His ruddy features relaxed in a grin. "Got my share of the loot, too, for a wonder. It's all banked in London with two stick-sucking macaroni nephews of mine watching it like perfumed cats at a rat hole." The colonel wiggled his toe and considered it with interest. "Like to boot them both. Do 'em good. I say, Buttercup Ma'am, don't eat so damned fast—give you the bellyache."

Katie hurriedly put down the chicken leg and wiped her mouth on the hem of her skirt.

"Skirt to mouth existence, what?" Colonel Fortescue laughed 'til he turned purple and Katie wished she were ten feet under ground. Aware of her embarrassment, the colonel calmed, relit his pipe and continued.

"One day in Calcutta with native wallahs dropping right and left of the plague, I said to myself, 'Hugh, my lad, some fine day you are going to catch it, too. And what's the use?' I ask you, Buttercup Ma'am, what is the use of catching plague?"

"I shouldn't think there was none," Katie replied, returning as delicately as she might to the chicken leg. "Does it hurt much?"

"Confoundedly, Ma'am. So home I came. Made an offer on the Colonelcy of the 63rd infantry regiment. Plain stuff, line regiment, y'know, but I rather fancy their colors. Very dark green facings and green and white lace. Green flatters my complexion. Notice?"

"Oh, yes sir. I always did fancy red and green."

He broke into such peals of laughter that the mare started, cocking suspicious ears. "Green and red! Very witty! Dashed if it's not."

"And where is this regiment now?"

"Blessed if I know. Last I heard it was in Ireland. Sometime those moth-baits infesting the War Office may let me know if my offer was accepted."

"So you buy a regiment?"

Colonel Fortescue, chuckling, eased the silver buttons of his bright blue waistcoat. "Yes, and through the nose! Same way as commissions. Bad system. Too damned many *petits maîtres*, bastards, and scapegraces gotten rid of that way.

Dash it all, Army will go to blazes if they keep it up. Take my father, Ma'am. Served thirty-five years and took ten wounds. He died a major—poor as a church mouse. Didn't go to India like me. Yet any Countess Hotbottom can buy her bastard, who's never smelt powder outside a boudoir, a colonelcy!"

Katie, sighing with repletion, finished the last of some wine the Colonel had tilted into the cup of a hunting flask. "But why did you come to the Bermudas?"

"Look up old Jerry. Letters sounded so dashed low."

Here was an unsuspected angle, Katie thought. Imagine coming all the way out from England just to cheer up an old friend!

"Reasoned one might as well wait here to find out about the 63rd." Colonel Fortescue drew up his knees and clasped sinewy wrists about them. She saw that the backs of his hands were covered with great brown blotches. "Funny little place, the Bermudas. Odd people. Cut each other's throats for a shilling. Maybe they're just virile, not bad. Anything like the Americans?"

"Why, I don't know, sir."

"Eh, why not?" Colonel Fortescue demanded. "Said you were an American, didn't you?"

"Yes, sir." Katie began to plait some of the coarse native grass. "But I've never met any Bermudians."

"Eh? Met no Bermudians? Gad's life! Nothing else here, is there, but blacks and land crabs?"

"But it's true," Katie insisted. "I have only been in Bermuda since last night." Spurred by the wine and by Colonel Fortescue's frank interest, she found herself telling him everything—almost. He listened in silence, his mulberry-tinted features now tightening, now relaxing.

"So you ran away—a second time?" He was looking at her intently.

"Yes, I did."

"Why? Don't you know you can be branded for it?"

"Yes. But I couldn't go on, not like that. Me, I'm going to live—I'm going to get some place," Katie informed him serenely. She peered up through the branches at a ragged shred of blue. Not without pride she added, "Mr. David said so. I've learned myself to read and write."

Lost in thought, Colonel Fortescue lifted the bottle and

swallowed a prodigious gulp. Presently he said, "You are an uncommon gel—Ma'am," he added with a deliberate insistence.

Ma'am. Katie's chin trembled. She couldn't understand the colonel. Here she'd just told him everything—well, nearly everything—and he still called her "Ma'am"; made a point of it.

For a long while Colonel Fortescue seemed content to just sit under the cedar listening to a pair of catbirds tease each other in the shrubbery. Now and then they could hear a rider go *clip-clopping* by on the main road.

At last he said, "Need a roof over you, food in your stomach. I need companionship. Rented a great barn of a house near St. George's. Got more money than I know what to do with." He glared at her from slightly yellowish gray eyes and went, "Harrumph!" in his throat. "How'd you fancy—er—keeping house for me?"

Katie wasn't deceiving herself, but she liked Colonel Hugh Fortescue. Even the sound of his name tickled her. Besides, he seemed so lonely. Best of all, he was a colonel; a god in the world of corporals and sergeants. To cover her embarrassment she smoothed her skirt.

She heard him saying, "Suppose, Buttercup Ma'am, suppose we say you are my niece? Barring old Jerry, nobody on Bermuda knows anything about me or my family. Jerry won't talk."

When she remained silent, he began talking faster to cover his own uneasiness. "You can be my niece, though no Fortescue ever had your looks. All our women look like horses —nice horses," he added loyally.

She pretended to deliberate. Experience had taught it never paid to give a man a "yes" too readily. All the same she was so relieved she wanted to cry with joy.

"Won't ask much in return," he announced with a short little laugh. "Been years in the hot countries. Fought too many battles on the field of Venus to remain a very—ahem —ardent campaigner." He glared down his colorful nose at her, but didn't succeed in looking fierce. Only tired and lonely. "Well, what do you say, my dear?"

Katie's gray-green eyes swung steadily to meet his and the sun made a dull gold aureole of her hair. "Why, I reckon if you really want me to I will."

451

"Will you? Will you, really?" He caught one of her hands, pressed it hard. "Agreed then, my dear. Hope neither of us find cause to regret it."

With the best of intention Katie said demurely, "I'll do my best to please."

He flared. "Don't talk like that! Sound like a damned kitchen wench. You've breeding. Hands, ankles, the way you carry yourself show blood. Never forget it."

A shiver tickled Katie's shoulderblades. This might have been Mr. David talking. Mr. David—what had become of him? Why had Mr. Rob forbidden her to mention his name? She felt ever so worried about Mr. David.

Hugely delighted, Colonel Fortescue expanded, talked of plans, of matters she should know. She would be the daughter of a sister lost on a journey to India. Had lived in Maryland the past few years; that would explain her accent.

Having come to an end of the wine, he pitched the bottle away and, dusting his breeches, briskly got to his feet.

"Come along, Buttercup—no damme, I like Kitty better. We are going up to Jerry's to tidy up. Won't do to have my niece look like a wash woman's step-child."

It was an exciting business picking out a dress, a cloak, a bonnet, stays and some stockings. The shoes were a little tight, but she could get into them. Apparently Miss Allen had been favored, nay spoiled, by her father, one-armed and otherwise scarred.

"They're not the latest mode, Hugh," boomed Major Allen when Katie vanished with the black housekeeper. He had brightened at the mystery Katie presented. "But they're of good material. Cost enough. I presume the dress can be taken in to suit. You're a wicked, lucky dog," he chuckled. "Wish to God old Neptune would wash me ashore such a niece."

Colonel Fortescue nodded over his port. "Odd creature—amusing to have her around for a bit. Teach her a lot."

"Some of those tricks you learned out East?"

"Go to blazes."

"At your age," declared Major Jerry, "you're a bloody fool to do this. She would heat up a stone saint!"

"Maybe," Fortescue admitted and sat back, grinning. By God, this young American was a lovely piece—not insipid like most of the blondes he had known. Had her feet on the ground, too. He began wishing they were already back in St. George's. Steady. Wouldn't do to scare her. Spoil things. An ammunition wife like her wasn't to be found every day.

2 — GAUNT NEW HOUSE

AT the entrance to Mangrove Bay, Peter Ashton's barge overtook a whaling crew which, aided by two pinnaces was towing a sperm whale's lead-colored carcass. There were a number of trying factories near Sandys Narrows, Peter explained, head jerking to the rhythm of the oars. Most whales taken off the West End of Bermuda were killed on New Ledge Bank. Dozens of them appeared during May and June. As a consequence the more important whaling establishments were concentrated along the South Shore of Long Island. Eli's Harbour and the small twin harbours known as Port Royal seldom had less than three or four carcasses floating about awaiting their turn under flensing knives and blubber spades. Trying cauldrons were kept very busy.

In dull curiosity Rob eyed the great bloated carcass and saw barnacles and weed growing on long folds ridging its underside. A huge beast by comparison with the puny beings responsible for its fate. Overhead a cloud of hungry sea birds circled clamoring.

Once the barge swung around Chamberlain's Point the Virginian relaxed on dark blue cushions and watched Somerset Island appear in greater detail. In Mangrove Bay, a small, land-locked harbour, three sloops lay at anchor. They were all small, rakish craft reminiscent of the *Speedwell*. Two other vessels were tied up to wharfs jutting out from various points along the shore. Mangrove Bay's chip-littered water looked deep enough to accommodate any kind of trading vessel short of an Indiaman. On a sloping beach two sloops were under construction. The hot air resounded with the thumping of hammers and the rasping of many saws. One of the new vessels had just been laid down and had only a few ribs in position, but the hull of the other— she was of good size, say 250 tons—was better than two-thirds completed. Black workmen were swarming over her like ants on a jam pot.

Turning his head, Rob briefly watched other boats belonging to Peter toil in from the wreck of the *Desdemona*. They rode deep under cargoes of salvaged rigging, cargo, and ironwork. Ben, slumped on a mattress, lay in the foremost. Wincapaw, wretchedly uncertain of Miss Katie's fate, maintained a nervous chatter in the second boat. He guessed he must have been crazy last night. He was mighty sorry for it all.

Smoothly, Peter's barge entered the harbour, disclosing half a dozen large white buildings. Either they sprawled just above high tide, or clambered step-like up the bank from the water. Freshly tarred nets were looped along several beaches and many fishing boats encumbered the shore, suggesting marine monsters basking on a sand bar.

Peter waved a plump hand. "Yonder is Gaunt New House." He was indicating a large ocher-tinted structure climbing up from the water. Because the bank at that point was very steep, the house was constructed on three levels rather than built in as many storeys.

He used his fan to indicate a succession of properties: "Shoreleigh, that's the Harvey place over there. Beyond it is Bushy Park—belongs to the Fowles. One of the Gilberts owns Huntholm—that's the place farther back from the water. You can just see its roof."

But Rob kept his attention on Gaunt New House. Shaded by a pair of huge cedars, it was hemmed in on the right by a huge banana patch and many palmetto-roofed huts. To its left a long terrace stretched away. The Ashton home he soon perceived to be at once a residence and warehouse. In front of Gaunt New House an L-shaped dock built of limestone blocks jutted out into the clear azure of Mangrove Bay. A tall-sparred brig overshadowed this with her yards. The slave gang engaged in loading her stopped work to watch the blue and yellow pleasure barge pull in. Faithfully, bright shirts and bandannas were mirrored by the glassy surface.

On a series of board steps leading from the dock to a pair of cavernous doors waited a swarm of house servants dressed in varying shades of white. Even the brig's white deckhands interrupted their toil and lined her rail. All along the shore small groups of people were gathering. Quite a few of the onlookers were women shepherding small replicas of themselves.

"What is going on?" Rob queried. He didn't care a rap, but it was only polite to show interest.

"Curiosity. We don't often have Virginia cousins visiting us."

"—And arrive the way I did?"

Peter laughed until his stomach shook. "Makes you all the more romantic. Half the fillies in Somerset will be setting their caps at you." Then he remembered. "Beg pardon. I—er—have made your sad loss known about Somerset. Keep forgetting it myself, though, because you don't gloom."

"Easy—all!" A colored coxswain called from above the canopy. Smoothly, the barge coasted towards a series of tide-greened stone steps.

The rowers wiped sweat from broad foreheads and, turning, grinned at some Negresses who were flapping bright aprons and at a horde of excited pickaninnies who were jumping up and down. The men were itching to wave back but they didn't dare.

At the very end of the pier was waiting a buxom little girl in a wide-skirted dress of flowered callimanco. A slave boy wearing grimy linen breeches held a big green umbrella over the child's very dark head. She clutched a bunch of rather wilted nasturtiums in one hand and waved excitedly with the other.

"Hello! Hello, Cousin Rob!" she called.

"Susan, you may wave, but ladies do not scream." Another and bigger umbrella created shade over a tall, straight-backed woman whose jet hair was at odds with her aged features and fragile hands.

Hers, Rob felt, was the face of a person used to making decisions. Who could she be? Both Peter's parents, he had learned, were dead of a pestilence.

Peter waved amiably. "Hi, Sue! Here he is!"

"Welcome to Gaunt House! Welcome to Somerset, Cousin Robert!" the small girl piped and began clambering down the steps.

"Susan is irrepressible," Peter commented not without pride. "Watch out for her."

"Who is the old lady?"

"Aunt Lydia. She's not a real aunt, but she's as good as one. The Lord help you if she don't take a shine to you."

From his brig's quarterdeck, Captain Trott—Rob recognized him immediately—waved a wide straw hat.

Susan, rushing up, planted a moist kiss on his cheek. "My, but you're handsome, Cousin Robert!" In the same breath she asked, "Did you bring me a present?"

Aunt Lydia's onyx earrings expressed rigid disapproval. "Susan! That is not the proper way to greet a relation! You must not mind her, Mr. Ashton." Sharp but not unkindly black eyes took Rob's measure. "Because her governess is away and she has no lessons, Susan's manners are even more deplorable than usual."

"But, Cousin Robert, you *do* have something for me, don't you?" persisted the dauntless Susan.

Harrowed by the child's confident look, Rob remembered the ivory model. It might pass muster as a toy. He hesitated, then said, "Yes. I have brought you a little ship, but I'm afraid it got kind of battered in the wreck. I will fix it up in short order."

"Oh-h! Thank you!" Having ascertained this important item of information, Susan went scampering off up the wharf with her parasol bearer in hot pursuit.

"No good," Aunt Lydia observed crisply, "will come of such a child."

"Dinner is ready?" Peter addressed the black-haired old lady.

"Well, Peter, have you ever known a meal not to be on time? Dear, dear, you do make such a god of your belly!"

"It's your housekeeping encourages me in it."

"Nonsense," said Aunt Lydia, resettling an India shawl about thin shoulders. "And don't you go trying to get around me, either. I should have flogged you oftener when you were little."

Peter laughed, patted her hand. "Aunt Lydia, for her sins, has been condemned to raise three generations of Ashtons."

"—And a plaguy lot, too. Every last one of them," affirmed the old lady and big knuckled fingers smoothed her bombazine skirt. "Your father, Robert Ashton, was the wildest I ever did see. Fine figure of a boy, though, was Sinjin. Wager he raised merry hell around Norfolk. Eh?"

Rob smiled. "They still talk of the time he rode his horse right into a Baptist meeting because a fox went to ground under the pulpit."

A twinkle shone in the old lady's eye and Peter roared.

"Aunt Lyd came out from England with Grandpapa in— in— When was it?"

"Early in the Middle Ages," snapped the housekeeper. "I am going indoors. Rouse yourself, nigger." Aunt Lydia with a walking stick prodded her umbrella bearer into wakefulness. "Peter, take your guest in. His room is all ready. It's hot out here. I warrant Robert is ready for a basin of bombo and a meal of decent food. I know what kind of swill sailors eat aboard ship."

Obediently Peter continued along the wharf. He nodded at the brig lying to the wharf. "She's off for Halifax tomorrow with salt for curing codfish. They tell us the Blue Noses haven't adopted the embargo. Not yet at least."

Rob made no reply. The busy wharf, the smell of whale oil, the screaming terns, stirred unhappy memories. He wanted to be by himself awhile.

Peter, serious for a change, said, "Beside the *Active*, Hereward and I operate two other vessels. The *Adelphi*, she's down to Turk's loading salt, and then there's the *Ariadne*. Hereward left in her last week for the Canaries. We rendezvous there with ships homing from India and China. Quite a few Bermuda vessels go. Saves time." He winked. "Not to mention duty."

Still scanned by curious neighbors, Peter and his guest followed the salt-dusted wharf past a pen situated on the beach. In it perhaps a dozen great sea turtles lay like lumps of gray mud, awaiting their turn as an item of ship's stores. Often they were the only fresh meat a vessel carried.

Peter chose the left hand of two stairs climbing from the shore. As he passed, Rob got a glimpse of what would, in any other house, have been the cellar. Here it was a warehouse jammed to overflowing with merchandise. The bulk of it, though, seemed to be sacked salt and barreled whale oil. Judging by the persistent way chickens skirmished about the entrance, there must have been some grain in there, too.

Puffing gently, Peter led up a stair rising on the outside of the house. It was the Bermuda custom, he said, to build them so. To Rob's great surprise there was no veranda, even though the climate must be hot so much of the time.

Not even back home had he ever beheld such a swarm of house servants. Teeth gleaming, they bowed and curtsied and smothered giggles with no great success. Gaunt New House, though of moderate proportions, seemed overrun with them. There were, however, very few big boys and no grown men among the ragged staff whose pungent body odors permeated the room.

"We breed them fast as we can," boomed Peter, throwing open a shuttered mahogany door. "Need sailors, whalers, pilots, laborers in the shipyards. We make good money leasing them out."

The cousins entered the cool of a tightly shuttered room. Though the walls seemed free of damp, it smelled moldy. Along its walls was hung a row of portraits; most of the subjects were jolly, red-faced men trying to look impressive and women with dreamy eyes and fashionably drooping shoulders. For the most part the furniture was nondescript, though an occasional fine English piece stood out from among imitations done in cedar wood. Rob thought the tray ceiling was not so high as those in Virginia for a chandelier, dangling from a pulley, just cleared his head. What intrigued him most were a number of cedar knees resembling those used in ship construction. Here they served to lock the room corners beneath the roof plates.

Everywhere glowed potted plants—oranges, magnolias and gardenias. A cousin in South Carolina had forwarded the last. Far voyaging Ashtons, Peter explained, made it a practice to bring home such plants as attracted them. Vases crammed with roses cast a drowsy perfume into the air.

To a faint jingle of keys strung on an enormous brass loop, Aunt Lydia emerged from a room in which stood a dinner table. In her wake pottered a white-haired Negro wearing a livery of some sort. She stood, hands on her hips.

"La!" With one hand grasping the wrist of the other, she watched the approach of the cousins. "Does me good to lay eyes on a son of Sinjin's"—she always pronounced St. John that way—"and you do favor your father, Robert. Same sort of stubborn, be damned-to-you mouth and straight back, but you haven't his deviltry in your eyes. Your brother inherit that?"

Rob said he reckoned David had.

"I shall have to take you in hand, Robert. You look mighty peaked. Don't want you to grow into a blubber-tub like Peter, though."

Rob smiled. "I imagine in so charming a place it's hard to worry about anything."

"Don't you believe it. We have our share."

Peter smacked his lips and said, "Zeke, pass the bombo." When they touched glasses, he gave a friendly little nod. "Here's luck. No tide ever did run out forever."

3 — THE KING DAVID

"Two glasses of bombo are plenty on an empty stomach— three will knock your wig loose. Your room is this way." Aunt Lydia's straight figure marched off. The bunch of keys lashed above her right hip jingled. "You must not waste the water, Robert. We have no springs or rivers on the Bermudas, mind you, only the rain we catch on our roofs."

Peter lingered beside the punch bowl and refilled Rob's glass. He winked, tucked it behind a bowl of pineapples. "Aunt Lyd's a regular tyrant, ain't she?"

Waiting by the door of a bedroom stood two blacks. One was a small boy and the other was as strange a looking Negro as Rob had ever seen. The fellow's nose was high bridged, his lips rather thin, and his dark skin was of an unfamiliar coppery hue. Further distinguishing him were high cheekbones and black hair which was only wavy.

Said Aunt Lydia, "Sachem ain't much of a valet yet, but he is handy and willing. Been sick."

The curiosity Rob felt must have been obvious for Aunt Lydia uttered a cackling laugh.

"Needn't stare so. He *is* part Indian. The Massachusetts Colony shipped a parcel of Indian slaves here back in 1670 something. They were called Pekwats, Pequods or some outlandish name like that. Captured in King Philip's war— Well, Sachem, don't stand there mooning! Hump yourself! Unpack Mr. Rob's bag.

"Those Indians made bad slaves 'til the people here crossed them with niggers. Have to watch their tempers even yet." She indicated the round-eyed boy. "This one is called Lizard. He will run errands for you. Any time you want a glass of water or a window opened, just call him."

When Rob smiled at Lizard, the boy giggled, squirmed and dug at the floor with a broad toenail.

The bedroom proved light and airy and was a quarter occupied by a vast bed standing veiled in a mosquito netting. This remarkable contrivance was slung by a pulley from a hook let into the ceiling. Beneath the four-poster was a small trundle bed. Sachem, moving very quickly and quietly, was hanging clothes in a wardrobe which, by its massive brass binding, appeared to have come out of a ship. On the bureau stood a shaving mirror equipped with candle holders on either side. The candles were of real spermaceti.

From his window Rob got a view of the sea and of a series of small islands trailing off towards the horizon. Aunt Lydia told him they were called Watford, Gates, and Ireland Islands.

"Dinner in half an hour," Aunt Lydia announced. "Be on time. Guess you have brought an appetite with you. Our food ain't fancy, but I guess there will be enough until that silly embargo in America begins to starve us to death."

Rob had barely started in the direction of the washstand than Sachem glided over and poured the water for him. After that he helped the guest out of his coat and folded it across the bed.

"Where is my present?" demanded a small voice. Rob was puzzled until he noticed the cupboard door moving. A quick pounce produced Susan. She was red, but a determined look clung to her mouth. "I want my present."

"All right. But it isn't fixed up."

"I don't care. I want it now."

"Bring me that brown canvas bag," Rob told Lizard, hovering just outside the bedroom door.

Susan looked him straight in the eye. "You won't tell Auntie Lyd I was here?"

"Never a word, Susan."

"That's good. She says it ain't nice for girls to hide in a gentleman's bedroom."

From the depths of his bag he produced the model. Poor little *Grand Turk!* It seemed many lifetimes ago that Stephen Farish had opined that such was no fit name for a Christian vessel. It was strange to part with the model. Every line, every detail of her construction would remain forever etched into his memory. Yet, surprisingly, he experienced no regret at severing this link with the past.

Katie had been such a link. He was worried, badly worried over what could have become of her. He had missed the life keg straight away, but it was a long way to shore and there were sharks, plenty of them, among the reefs. Wincapaw had acted rather queer, but he hadn't been able to find the least evidence of foul play. Peter had promised that a search would be made.

When Susan first beheld the model with the stumps of her masts sprouting from the deck, her small face contracted, but it widened into a smile when she saw the lovely little figure-head and the tiny ivory cannon poking out of their ports.

"I warned you her rigging got carried away in the wreck, remember?"

"Oh, I love it! It's so pretty! It's awful pretty!" she cried, patting the bit of ivory. "Will you rig her soon, Cousin Rob?"

"First chance I get."

"What is she called?"

"Why——" Rob faltered. Maybe Farish was right. Because of the unmistakably Oriental figurehead, he had to think fast. "She's called the *King David*. See the crown?"

"That's a nice name. Oh, I just remembered. I have a Cousin David. Where is he? Is he coming to Bermuda, too?"

Cursing his own stupidity, Rob said, "No. He's in Boston."

"Doing what?"

"Time," Rob replied in a sudden flash of grim humor. Fortunately Susan was not curious.

"Tell me about him."

"Some other time," he said. "And now——"

But Susan had already gone racing down the corridor calling, "Peter! Peter! Look what Cousin Rob brought me!"

4 — HENRY OF SOMERSET

SUPPER was served late—around nine. Just Rob, Peter and the old housekeeper. Aunt Lydia did most of the talking, Peter most of the eating. Rob listened.

"Tell Zeke to hurry things," drawled the Bermudian. "Henry Tucker is likely to drive over this evening. Wants to meet Rob."

"Which Henry Tucker?" Aunt Lydia cocked a bright eye at Peter.

"Many of them?" Rob inquired.

"At this End the trees are full of Henry Tuckers. There's

one less than usual 'round right now. Colonel Henry Tucker of the Grove is away in America. He has taken—"

"—Never mind about that," Peter cut in quite sharply and, for a miracle, Aunt Lydia subsided.

"Well then, there is Henry, son of Colonel Henry. When he married Fanny Bruere, the Governor made him Colonial treasurer. He lives at the capital."

"London?"

"La, no! St. George's." Aunt Lydia complacently smoothed her dress of old-fashioned cut.

"Fancy he's not too happy there nowadays," remarked Peter, sipping his Malaga. "Not with his Pa and the Governor at swords' points over the embargo."

Again Rob roused himself from his indifference. "Any more Henry Tuckers?"

"Half a dozen more or less, but there's only one you need to remember." There was an undercurrent of gravity in Peter's light comment. "It is he I expect tonight. Unless I'm greatly mistaken, you will have considerable to do with him."

"Look out he don't skin you," warned the old lady and chuckled at Peter's angry look.

"He owns a fine property called Bridge House. It's near Somerset Bridge. Cousin Henry's a coming man—"

"—With taking ways," Aunt Lydia added.

Peter, seriously annoyed, heaved himself to his feet, spilling a snow storm of crumbs onto the carpet. "Come along. We can't talk with all that chitter-chatter—from the kitchen," he added in heavy sarcasm.

But out on a lawn to the right of the house the gabble of servants in the kitchens sounded even louder. Farther away a lonesome dog howled. Among the palmetto huts a rattle of pots and pans told of slaves finishing their evening meal. Otherwise the night was very still, very peaceful; voices aboard ships in the harbour could be readily distinguished. A boat put off from one and rowed over to another.

On a sort of terrace overlooking the harbour, a number of seats had been arranged beneath a clump of coconut palms; they had been planted by the builder of Gaunt New House, Peter said. Rob expressed surprise that so much of the vegetation appeared to be imported.

"When Somers landed in 1609 I judge he didn't find much more than cedars on the island," his cousin explained.

462

"Cedars, a lot of yucca and prickly pear. The biggest cedars have been cut. Over in Paget they say there are some damned handsome English gardens. Last year Nat Tucker sent up some oleander shoots from Charles Town. Colonel Henry put them in at the Grove and they've already blossomed twice. We'll go see them sometime—they're monstrous pretty."

While strolling along, Rob recognized a number of ships' figureheads mounted on the lawn: a lion, a crusader, and a very round breasted nymph. They had been recovered from vessels lost on the dreaded Northwest Rocks, Peter explained.

As usual two slaves were in attendance to each man. Laid out on a table were pipes and a box of what Peter called tabacos. He had gotten them from the Captaincy-General of Cuba by way of a wreck the year before. The name "Audace" was engraved on a huge pitcher of some wine drink. Rob chose a pipe and received it ready-stuffed. Lizard sprang forward carrying a glowing coal between the jaws of tongs.

Rattan creaked as Peter extended himself on a long chair, whereupon his "tiger," as the younger body servants were called, sank on his hams beside his master's feet. Lizard copied him. When some mosquitoes whined over from a walled garden not far away, the colored boys used whisks of horse hair to beat them away.

Peter said, "For Heaven's sake, Rob, undo that stock and slip off your coat. Lizard will fetch you some lemon oil. Rub it on your hands and face. Damned mosquitoes won't bother you then."

They had barely settled themselves than two figures loomed near, waited till bidden to approach. They were George Wincapaw and Peter Ashton's colored foreman. Eagerly Rob sat up.

When the foreman drew near, he pulled off a shapeless felt cap and dropped onto his knees.

"Well, Sambo?"

"Misto' Ashton, suh, ve done search' 'e sho' like you tol' us. Down by 'e Bridge rhud ve found a little keg. Mr. Vincapaw, he say it vuz off 'e *Desdemona*."

"You were sure about it, Wincapaw?"

Wincapaw knuckled his forehead quickly. "Aye, aye, sir. It was our keg, all right. Besides, we found Miss Katie's footprints and the place where she must have slept. I guess she's all right." The quartermaster's voice couldn't begin to express his relief.

"I still wonder why she'd run such a risk," Rob mused.

"Afraid of being taken up for a runaway, don't you think?" Peter suggested.

"Well, I'm glad she's safe. She's a damned fine wench. Oh, can you find Wincapaw a berth?"

"Easiest thing in the world," declared his cousin. "We can always use a good quartermaster." In the dark his tobacco glowed like a giant firefly. "Go down to the *Active* and tell Captain Trott I sent you. He'll bunk you somewhere. We'll talk wages tomorrow."

"Thank you, sir. Good night, sir." Pleased to escape the necessity of sleeping ashore, Wincapaw hurried off after Sambo.

From among the slave huts back of Gaunt New House came the faint *tap tap* of a drum, voices singing an unintelligible song.

"What do you want to do about that sick nigger of yours?" Peter inquired.

"He's not mine. He has run away from a slave contractor, but I don't intend to return him. Candless is a brute. Suppose you take him? When he's well, he's strong and a good deckhand."

Peter belched. "I'll give you the market price, £20—call it passage money. Give you credit, rather," he hurriedly amended.

For a time they smoked in silence listening to the peculiarly shrill *glee-glee! glee-glee!* of many tree frogs.

At length Peter inquired, "You figured your loss?"

"Yes, the tally is in my chest."

"That's fine. Tomorrow, we might go over it." He added to his tiger, "My handkerchief, boy. Fetch it." The handkerchief lay but a foot away. /

From inland came a noise of hoofs rapidly approaching and the peculiar ringing sound made by iron wheel tires.

Said Peter to his boy, "Run to the gate entrance and find out if it's anybody but Mr. Henry Tucker." The little darky vanished like a shot. "I expect we will have quite a few callers tonight. I tried to keep them off 'til you were rested," he explained, smothering another belch, "but they're all anxious for news. Own ships and all that."

"Suh, hit's Mr. Henry Tucker ob 'e Bridge House," panted the tiger. "An' Ah heerd mo' horses on 'e rhud."

Groaning softly, Peter got to his feet. "You are about to meet the leading Whig of the West End. Also, the most loyal of His Majesty's subjects. Cousin of ours by marriage."

"Your humble obedient servant, gentlemen." Walking across the coarse lawn appeared a long-nosed individual. He was leaning heavily on a stick and his jet eyes, Rob thought, were bold and dark as any Indian's. A Negro holding a hurricane lantern slouched along before him. Another followed, bearing a coat and a small hand bag.

5 — THE PARABLE

PETER actually walked fast to greet the caller. Once Rob had been introduced, Henry Tucker lowered himself into a chair with such an air of fatigue it seemed doubtful he could muster energy to rise again. He was really younger than he appeared for his wig was old, carelessly powdered and tied with a rather dingy yellow swallow-tail.

"And what might we be drinking, Peter?" he inquired, settling back to let his tiger fan him.

"Some of Aunt Lyd's Noyo punch."

"Good. My stomach has been none too steady these days." After the caller had lifted off his wig and had given it to a Negro waiting at his elbow, he wearily mopped his head. Dark hair on it had been clipped so close as to make him appear bald. Already he had scanned the Virginian from head to foot. "Is June in Norfolk as hot as this, Mr. Ashton?"

On occasion it was, Rob admitted. For all Peter's deference, he was damned if this narrow-headed, sharp-eyed fellow impressed him. His manner was just a shade too affable.

"I met your father once when he touched at Kingston, years ago. A smart trader—very. Always delivered his horses where they would bring a good price."

"Indeed?"

"Yes." The thin mouth narrowed, then relaxed. "Seems to me you favor him, Mr. Ashton."

"I would be flattered to think so, Mr. Tucker."

The lean figure leaned forward, clasping hands on the ivory knob of his stick. "You bring news from America?"

Peter came up with some wine. "Hold on a bit. Jemmy Burrough's gig is at the landing and Benjy Bascombe and Jimmy Fowle are coming over."

It would, Rob knew, require a terrific effort to talk politics and trade. He wouldn't have given Tucker much satisfaction if he hadn't been broke and wasn't willing to accept Peter's hospitality indefinitely. In order to get going again he reckoned he must try to learn the state of affairs in Bermuda.

If half of what that drunken swine Rudder had said about Bermudians and their business methods was true, he had better look alive. It would call for genius to come out on the long end of a deal. He really must learn what was going on. Salt, for instance, he knew, was selling for twenty-eight shillings a bushel in Norfolk, even higher in Philadelphia and New York. But these fellows didn't know it yet. Maybe —oh, what the hell was the use?

Two men wearing loose linen coats and trousers came tramping up behind their link boys. Small boats bumped and several sets of oars rattled down at the landing steps. Slaves came running out of Gaunt New House bringing rattan chairs. Under Zeke's direction many pitchers and bottles were brought out. Beneath a glowing fanlight Aunt Lydia's severe figure was supervising. A bright crack in an upstairs shutter suggested that Mistress Susan was eavesdropping.

A series of hearty greetings, gibes, and queries about the position of ships rang over the terrace. Perspiring mildly, Peter presented callers—George Lusher, Frank Morgan, John Harvey and a couple of Gilberts and Bascombes. In all their small talk there was a definite undercurrent of seriousness. Significant, too, was the way most of them, even the older men, deferred to Henry Tucker.

It was to him Rob addressed a question, "Is it true the Bermudas are hard pressed for food?"

Henry Tucker's sloping shoulders shrugged. "Some people are always hungry."

Said Benjamin Bascombe, "Nothing like begging the question, eh, Henry? Well, to tell the truth, Mr. Ashton, we ain't really hungry yet. But we will be, bloody soon, if Parliament and the Congress kill our American trade. I'm frightened to think of what's happened to the sloop I sent into New York."

"She will be all right," Rob told him. "The New Yorkers ain't strong on the embargo."

Bascombe brightened, swallowed a whole tumbler of sangaree. "Hear that, Jimmy?"

Fowle, a sturdy-looking man whose coarse black hair was clubbed with a white ribbon, spoke with bitterness in his tone. "You always were a fool for luck. Look at me, Mr. Ashton. My *Daphne* got took by a British cruiser off Annapolis last month. I'm out £2,000."

Henry Tucker nodded. "Every one of us has felt the pinch in one way or another. All our food comes from America and two-thirds of our trade. Except for a few mossbacks creeping about the Colonial Secretary's Office, England don't know Bermuda exists, and cares less. Me, I've two ships in the rice trade to Carolina and Trinidad. Where am I to send them if Congress claps this embargo on us?"

"Why not the West Indies?" Rob asked.

"No market. No prices there for limestone and salt. They've already more slaves there than they can feed." He gave a little barking laugh. "Don't you think the West Indies will feel the pinch worse than us, Mr. Ashton?"

Rob agreed. He said the Antilles couldn't get along without hard lumber, corn and livestock. There was no place they could get them but in the American Colonies.

Henry Tucker tapped his teeth with the head of his stick, looked up sharply. "Mr. Ashton, do you mind if I ask your opinion about a private matter? It concerns a neighbor, a young Bermudian. Here is what has happened. He is poor and weak and small for his age. His two bigger cousins each have property."

Tucker paused and slapped a mosquito from his cheek. "Because he was willed a little cottage, he is forced to live on the property of his Cousin John, but John won't give him anything to eat. The boy's Cousin Silas isn't so big and important as John, but he's more friendly. He buys what this boy carves out of wood and gives him food for it."

Other voices were still; the lantern lighted the dark, thin faces of Peter's neighbors.

Rob smiled. "Mr. Tucker, to my mind your young friend isn't so badly off. He's young and you say he has a roof over his head and enough to eat. A lot of people don't have half so much."

The Bermudian's close-cropped head inclined. "That is so, and he wasn't complaining. But here is what has happened just recently. His cousins have got to be on very bad terms;

467

in fact, they quarrel whenever they meet. Each wants the boy to side with him. Now if you were going to advise this young fellow, what would you say?"

Rob considered. "The boy hasn't other friends?"

"No. He'll go hungry if he sides against Silas, but if he rows with John, he will be driven from his cottage."

The Virginian considered. "I reckon he had better avoid picking sides—no matter what."

Henry Tucker broke into a cackling laugh and looked at the men about him. "There's your answer, boys."

Rob blinked, then grasped the gist of Henry Tucker's little story.

"You see, Mr. Ashton," Bascombe said, crossing the *t*'s and dotting the *i*'s, "we figure we'd make out better by cutting adrift from England. But how can we? The Bermudas measure only eighteen square miles with only five thousand white men and about as many blacks. The American Colonies lie six hundred miles away, so we can't expect help from them. Though we don't like the idea of it, the tea tax doesn't bother us much because we buy our tea direct at the Canary Islands rendezvous. And to us the coercive acts of Parliament weren't harmful until they stopped our trade with Boston." Bascombe shrugged perplexedly. "We're losing a lot of money here because nobody knows what laws have been made by whom. Only reason we have any vessels left is because most of our ships can show their heels to a Committee boat or a man-o'-war."

Here was familiar language. Rob smiled to himself.

"To tell the truth," Peter added, "we'd just as lief see Parliament ticked off; with us it's a plain case of trade or die. That's right, ain't it, Gilbert?"

The tallest man in the group nodded solemnly. "We don't raise hardly any food here on the islands."

"Why?" Rob asked. "Is the soil bad?"

Peter shook his head. "Our soil is rich enough, but farming is beneath us. Slaves would snitch everything from the gardens, anyhow." He chuckled. "I guess God never made niggers hungrier than the ones on Bermuda."

When Henry Tucker raised his voice silence fell. "It's just as Peter said. We *have* to build and sell vessels, carry trade and market our salt from Turk's Island; or we starve to death. The English, damn 'em, won't raise a finger to relieve us, though we have asked them several times."

"Why don't you tell Mr. Ashton about our petition to the Congress?" suggested a dumpy little man whose shirt lay open down to his navel. He spoke sharply to the Negro fanning him and the black quickened the beat of his fan.

The invalid hesitated. Obviously, he didn't like having his hand forced. "Well, it's this way. Last month, in May, some of us decided we knew which way the cat is going to jump. If the American Congress includes us in their embargo on the West Indies trade, we'll be sunk, permanently ruined." Henry Tucker spoke impressively. "So we called a meeting down in Paget's Tribe—one of our middle parishes," he explained. "We composed a petition to the Congress avowing friendliness and sympathy." As Tucker talked, Rob felt his black eyes boring into him. "We informed the Congress that, while unable to take active part in a rebellion, we will abstain from buying the British articles banned in America."

"—Such as tea?" Rob could not resist suggesting. Everyone laughed, but not heartily. Peter regarded his cousin in astonishment.

"We wrote that we would give American vessels every assistance. We offered to sell the Congress Bermuda-built sloops—they, ahem—would make excellent privateers."

Though Rob felt prone to observe that war prices would bring a pretty profit, he remained silent.

Henry Tucker leaned forward, looking at Rob through narrowed eyes. "We have even offered to pass on to the Congress information we pick up. We are eager to make life as hard for the bloody English as we dare. We have already begun, eh, boys?"

Several men nodded. "Yes, indeed, Mr. Tucker, we sure have."

The principal guest took a sip of the Noyo wine, delicately dried his lips on a handkerchief plucked from his cuff.

"Please proceed." Despite himself, Rob was interested.

"Well, sir, a delegation was appointed, headed by my estimable father-in-law, Colonel Tucker. It sailed for Philadelphia Tuesday last." Henry Tucker sighed, loosened his neck cloth. "We thought we had better send George Bascombe along. He's a smart enough lawyer to worry even the Yankees. Takes a Jew to skin a Bermudian, but a Yankee to skin a Jew—or so they say." Everybody laughed and had another drink.

"You can imagine we are keeping our fingers crossed and

are sending out no real cargoes 'til the delegation comes back next month with an answer from the Congress."

A hush descended. It was terminated by the little man in the loose shirt.

"—Always provided a bulldog don't catch our delegates—they'll get hanged as traitors if that happens!"

"I assume your sentiments represent those of all Bermuda. Is that correct?" Rob questioned.

"Well, not quite," James Fowle admitted. "But I'm damned if we don't represent the most important end of the islands. Those Tories hanging to old Bruere's petticuts don't own enough vessels to take notice of. Most of the smart folks live in the West End." He grinned. "A lot of us don't pay the King a shilling's worth of duty from one year's end to the next. The Governor tried sending a customs searcher this way, but he soon learned when to stay indoors. That's right, ain't it, Henry?"

Henry Tucker coughed behind a fragile hand. "I can hardly vouch for that, James. I stand for obedience to the law—er—whenever possible."

Peter Ashton snickered and more than one of the lounging Bermudians smiled to himself.

Fowle continued. "Yes, Mr. Ashton, we have old Bruere's hands tied. Last month we—er, some West Enders—pulled down the fort on Wreck Hill. The Governor hasn't dared send anybody to repair it."

Peter whispered behind his hand. "Since a detachment of the 9th left St. George's in '72, the Governor hasn't had any troops except a few old matrosses manning Castle Island. The fort up here was too old to be any good anyhow." He straightened. "John, tell my cousin what food prices are in St. George's."

"Hell, it's better he learnt what cornmeal for my niggers costs," Gilbert snapped. "Mr. Ashton, it's six shillings the bushel! Confounded blackamoors eat me out of house and home. If I can't keep my ships at sea, I'll go broke."

Mechanically, Rob made note of the price. Six shillings the bushel! In Norfolk you could load all the corn you wanted at a top of thirty cents the bushel. Other food staples were in proportion. The more he heard, the sicker he felt over losing the *Desdemona*. Peter's slaves, he knew, had unloaded some sacks of unwetted grain besides some salt pork and dried beans, but he had no idea exactly how many because

470

Peter seemed disinclined to quote figures. Maybe he could get together a little stake?

"Then the East End is Tory and the West End is pro-Congress?"

"You've got the size of it about!" Bascombe admitted, lighting a tabaco almost a foot long and as thick as his thumb. "Any more fights since Lexington?"

"Not that I've heard of," Rob told him. "They say a Yankee Army is blockading the British in Boston—from the land, of course. Reckon there will be some sort of a fight when Gage comes out."

"We shall soon hear," predicted the dumpy little man. "My *Mercury* is due back from New York any day."

For an hour and more Rob answered, as well as he could, an amazing range of questions. Were the Colonies planning united action? Were they making their embargo stick? What was being done about the Tories? How were the Provincials fixed for arms and munitions? The frequency with which the last question reoccurred gave Rob to think. Right now Peter's guests were looking mighty thoughtful and the atmosphere seemed a little strained.

Henry Tucker, frowning, changed the subject. "We hear that the Colonists up north are profoundly religious, Mr. Ashton. Is that true?"

"I reckon it's so, Mr. Tucker. My New England captain—the British put him in prison when they took my brigantine—used to say that on Sundays the dogs wouldn't eat their dinners except on the meeting-house steps."

Laughter which followed relieved the tension.

Peter shot his cousin a grateful look, then went over to the invalid and whispered something in his ear; Henry Tucker's head inclined rapidly several times.

As if by tacit understanding all but two of the guests began to say good night, strode off down the terrace, calling for link boys and grooms, or coxswains. Soon, only Henry Tucker, Peter and two others remained talking and drinking on the terrace.

6 — The Understrappers

Rob's cousin kept listening for something and when at last faint curses sounded at the wharf, he heaved a small sigh of relief.

On the terrace appeared a second group, rougher in dress. Many of them wore wide canvas breeches and long sheath knives swung over their buttocks.

"Well, may I be damned!" thought Rob recognizing a couple of men who had manned one of the wrecker whale boats.

By and large, this second delegation looked fierce, sunburned. They were liberally tattooed. Hard eyes peered out from beneath greasy strands of hair bound for the most part in eelskin or clamped together with strips of soft sheet lead.

To Peter's genial, "Dig in, boys," they helped themselves liberally, audibly to the refreshments. When they had had enough, they stood about smacking lips and ridding teeth of cold ham. Then, lighting pipes, the late arrivals swaggered over to sit uncomfortably on the edge of chairs deserted by the first group.

Henry Tucker coughed a little for attention. "Evening, lads. We were just talking about how hard it is on a man to lose a fine vessel like Mr. Robert Ashton's." Wooden-faced he turned to Peter. "Ask our cousin to tell the boys here how the wreck took place."

Though quite at sea, Rob told the whole story, omitting no detail.

A bandy-legged fellow on the edge of the group straightened up, listened very uneasily. His was a fat, heavy face marked by heavy brows. His little eyes were protuberant and bloodshot.

Peter laughed. "Don't look so worried, Gosling. We know you didn't do it. You were dead drunk—this time."

Everybody laughed at Gosling's uneasy grin.

"Yes, we all heard your wife giving you hell."

Chuckling, Peter came over to Rob. "When you got piled up, none of us could figure out whether it was Gosling or Hector Cazalles tied those lanterns to the cows."

"Lessen it was Dan'l Tucker," someone cackled, but Peter paid no attention.

"Yes, Rob, I was plenty worried because Gosling is a

friend of mine while you are my cousin. Makes it awkward —deuced awkward. But ha! ha! ha! it was Cazalles, damn his greasy britches. Must have been!"

Still Rob struggled for comprehension. He was finding it distinctly quaint that Peter, Henry Tucker and other leading inhabitants should be on such easy terms with men given to lighting false beacons. In deep perplexity he peered about and recognized a preponderance of predatory expressions. Later he learned that nearly every house on the West End was partially or wholly equipped with the gleanings of wrecks. Of course, most of the wrecks were genuine disasters, but there were still plenty of "accidents."

Henry Tucker, selecting another tabaco, managed to keep his face straight. "Dear me. So Cazalles has taken to lighting lanterns again? How very heartless. A typical Tory trick, I presume."

A Tory, eh? There, Rob felt, lay the hinge of this whole weird affair.

"Any of you notice some cows on Long Beach the night of the wreck?"

Silence.

"You did, didn't you, Will?" Peter looked steadily at the dumpy little man.

"Why, Peter, I didn't exactly. But I can find a couple of niggers who did. They'll swear to it."

"A nigger's word is no good in court. By the way, Will, I take it you care about that demand note being extended? Or are you ready to settle up?"

"Not till the *Mercury* gets back, Mr. Ashton."

"She is two weeks overdue already. Maybe you were looking for her when you saw Cazalles's cows."

"Yes, I was—I remember now. Cazalles come down to the beach about eight o'clock. Sure, him and that lame nigger of his."

Henry Tucker smiled, nodded and turned to a red-nosed fellow wearing a thin black beard. "How about you, Josiah?"

The other nodded gravely. "Why, yes, coming home from hauling fish traps, I saw them cows ever so plain. Just where was they?"

Peter spoke slowly, distinctly, "They were on Long Beach towards the right hand end." His red globe of a face shone on Rob. "How many lights did you see?"

"Why, I counted fifteen or sixteen," he said, but he was damned if he liked this business.

"Fifteen? That would be Cazalles's herd all right," Josiah agreed solemnly.

"You remember that? Fifteen cows," Henry Tucker prompted. "I am gratified to be given such a splendid opportunity to stamp out lawlessness. We cannot tolerate such goings-on in the West End." He cocked his narrow head at the dumpy man. "I heard Cazalles made a pretty piece of change on the wreck of the *Industry*. That right?"

"Sure he did, Mr. Tucker. Cazalles scoffed all her linen, all her instruments, seven thirty-twist cables, an' two of her pumps. God knows whatnot more."

Peter Ashton considered stars blinking white-hot through the palms. "The Admiralty court awarded him a share of her sale price, too. Around a thousand pounds, they say."

Henry Tucker cast Rob a wry, humorless smile. "In that case it appears you are another of the lucky Ashtons. Tomorrow you had better swear out a complaint before Nat Bell—he's J. P. for this end. A friend. Peter will talk to Cazalles."

Peter's belly began to shake with merriment. "I think Cazalles will be glad to settle out of c-court. Might even take some of his land to meet the bill. D'you know, Henry, my friend Dr. Chamberlain has had his eye on the right-hand end of Long Beach?"

Long after he had thrust his naked body between damp sheets Rob could hear the voices of his cousin and the guests droning on and on beneath the palms.

He was dropping off to sleep when the fragile sound of petticoats whispering along the corridor roused him. He heard them quite distinctly. It reminded him of Peggy. A door closed making a little rasping noise.

From this he deduced that Susan's governess had returned.

7 — Mistress Susan's Governess

EVEN after she had locked her bedroom door Andrea Grenville continued smiling. It had been a glorious night to be out of doors! For a provincial, young John Hinson had made a vastly gallant and handsome figure cantering alongside the curricle. La! The lad had turned some very pretty compliments, though they had held the ring of bookishness. Idly she pondered what might be afoot on the terrace. All the way back from Southampton she and Hinson had encountered horsemen following the main road to Mangrove Bay. They had been talking excitedly, the greater part of them, and only briefly acknowledged young Hinson's drawled greetings. A lot of mysterious traveling was being done, Andrea observed, since news of that silly skirmish up in Massachusetts had reached the islands.

Onto a table she dropped the armful of school books which had been her excuse for a trip to the Hinsons. A year ago she would have deemed it no excitement at all to sit in Mr. Ashton's old-fashioned blue and yellow curricle, but now it had been a treat, a monstrous pleasant diversion. She pushed back the hood of her green capucin.

Young Hinson's voice still lingered in her ears. "I vow, Mistress Grenville," he'd said, "your eyes show more beautiful tints than the iridescent sea off New Ledge Bank."

Intrigued by the compliment—the first in how long?—she shed her cape, then sought a mirror. Looking out at her was the same lively, rather long, but undeniably attractive face that she had inspected in Bristol. Only now the skin of it shone gold-brown instead of ivory-white. The scarlet mouth had retained its faintly reckless quirk while betraying a greater determination. A freckle or two had appeared on the bridge of her small aristocratic nose. The wide-set, long-lashed hazel eyes were sharper, more alert and less tired than those of the old Andrea, but humor still lurked in their depths.

Brifly she wondered what devilment Susan had devised during her absence. In Susan she recognized the small rebellious creature she herself once had been. Afraid of nothing, adept at every form of teasing, hardened as only a solitary girl among a family of brothers can be. She made a "face" at her reflection. "My dear, if you can force one jot of education into that tomboy's head, you deserve the Order of the Garter, no less!"

After lighting a second candle, Andrea undid and stepped out of her traveling costume. La! But it was hot. She pulled out the front of her dress and blew the damp cambric free of her breasts. Because several mosquitoes commenced to circle about her head, she hastily continued undressing.

Following a routine, she splashed water over her face and put some cologne under her arms. Next she reached for a saucer of salt. With it she scoured her teeth and gums. Years ago, some American had said that certain tribes of savages scrubbed their teeth in this fashion and so kept them years after they might have been expected to decay.

After seeing that the windows were closed—recently there had been a lot of swamp fever about—Andrea placed a candle on the night stand. Making sure her mosquito tent was secured all the way around, she lifted one side and slipped under it.

It certainly was smothering hot. Irritably, she pulled back the sheets and punched bolster and pillows into a towering parados of white linen. Still finding the heat insufferable, she pulled her nightgown up to her knees, then slipped it free of her shoulders and let it slide down into her lap. After fishing between the mattresses a moment, she located her journal. Dutifully, she wrote:

Tuesday, June 27th, 1775

Gaunt New House
Somerset I.

This Day a Vast excitement reigns over Gaunt New House. The long attended and ill-starr'd Cousin from the Virginia Colony arrives. When I consider that he is Brother to David Ashton I fall into a veritable Tizzy.

Andrea stopped writing, pushed out her lower lip and raised a stray lock from her forehead with a quick puff of breath. La! To think of sleeping under the same roof with David Ashton's own brother! What would Robert be like? Brows merged in speculation, she resumed her entry.

Mr. Peter Ashton tells us the blows his American Cousin has suffer'd at the Hand of Fortune have left him cold and reserv'd. It must be monstrous sad to lose a Wife in so cruel a Fashion. My heart bleeds for him.

For some moments she lingered, pencil poised, staring into space. David? Would Robert resemble him? Fervently she hoped he would not. Faintly the slow swash of combers over the reefs, the brittle noises made by the wind in coco palms reached her. She wetted the pencil tip with her tongue and wrote on:

Thanks to the offer of yellow curricle Journeyed this day to Mr. Hinson's in Southampton Parish; a vastly instructive journey and design'd, I suspect, to render the reception of Mr. Robert Ashton of a Family matter. It should be.

Did fear to cross the old Bridge over Sandys Narrows. Seems anxious to Collapse. One learns the worthy Members of the Assembly do naught but resist the Governor and wrangle amongst Themselves and so no Money is devoted to the Repair of it.

Was receiv'd most civilly by Mrs. Hinson, Surmise she designs to engage me as tutor to her two daughters. They seem meek Creatures, somewhat sickly of appearance and sly, I suspeckt. Prefer my lusty Susan. Was most gallantly attended by young Master Hinson. He vows his Father is a most confirm'd Whig. Rode home in the Moon's light. Fear it rous'd in me unlady-like cravings. Ah me!

Lost in thought, Andrea groped back through the journal. So much, so incredibly many things had happened since the *Charming Nymph* had left Lizard Light astern. To the last detail she could recall just how the Bermudas had looked when the storm-hammered brigantine went limping in to St. George's harbour. In her ears still rang William Cunningham's threats. He had been so merciless not one of the luckless, ailing wretches in his power dared to raise an outcry.

Smiling no longer, Andrea hunted her entry for that date,

Tuesday, February 7th, 1775

St. George's in the Bermudas, otherwise the Summer Isles.

Did contrive to approach a Native engag'd in bringing aboard Water and sea Turtles. Praise God there remain'd to me some few shillings and this bearded Fellow out of consideration for most of them, and a measure of Christian Kindness, did agree to Conceal me aboard his water Boat. The escape was cleverly contriv'd.

My Benefactor caus'd a Diversion by knocking over-board a coloured Boy who could not swim. His clamour and the bustel attendent upon his Rescue serv'd as a cover for my Evasion.

Reach'd the Shore safe with scarce six shillings remaining to my Name. Am most thankful at preserving this Journal and a small bundle of Effects. Thus am not yet altogether Destitute but am constrained to find Employment *at once!*

Wednesday, February 8th, 1775

St. George's, Bermuda Isles

Have convers'd with the Rector of St. Peter's Church. No doubt he is a Godly man, but also most untidy. He listen'd to my Misfortunes with Attention. Suspect his "Living" must be small since he offer'd no practickal Assistance. Has promised to read a Notice I have composed in Church on Sunday. Also, he will cause it to be forwarded the Length of these beautiful and curious Islands. Today it rains hard as I have never seen it in England. A damp Wind is blowing. God preserve the poor Wretches left aboard the *Charming Nymph.*

Sighing, Andrea inspected her original draught of the notice cards. "What affrontery, my chick, what vast affrontery!"

Mistress Andrea Grenville takes this Method of informing the Ladies and Gentlemen of Bermuda that she has had the Misfortune to be cast on the Island. She has been regularly taught in some of the first Academies in England and is well Inform'd in all the Arts.

If she is favoured with proper Encouragement she will continue in the Island as a Tutor for Youth and will engage to teach the following Branches in the most speedy and refined manner; viz, The English language gramatically, with Writing and Drawing, Arithmeticks, Spelling, Geography and French. Any commands addressed to her at St. Peter's Glebe House shall be attended to.

N. B. If she does not meet with proper Encouragement, she will pursue her Voyage to America.

St. George's   February 8th, 1775.

"She will pursue her voyage to America!" Andrea laughed so hard her bed shook.

Saturday, February 11th, 1775

Am reduc'd to the very Brink of Despair. Am apprehensive these Islanders have no such a craving for learning as poor Andrea for Food this night. My landlady is a churlish Widow who has but recently lost her husband at Sea. She eyes Me askance. She says I must Pay or depart on the Morrow. What then?

The answer, my poor Minx, is too obvious. Many of the young Bloods (They greatly overvalue their Dress and Address—not a bad pun for my present sorry Mood) would be prodigious pleased to improve upon the mulatto women with which they consort during their leisure Moments. Vastly shocked to hear of so many persons of colour and parti- (party?) colour bearing names so wellknown in the Community. If Andrea needs must yield to dread Necessity, she will use all her efforts to make a smart and admirable Whore, though God forbid such extremities arrive! I mind me of a saying of my Uncle George. "Every Gen'l must expect to lose a Skirmish now and then." Am still possess'd of an Obstinacy to learn what I can make of my life. All is not yet lost.

Tuesday, February 14th, 1775

Huzzah! Huzzah! By post Courier from the Western end of these Isles comes a letter. A Mr. Ashton— Strange Coincidence! He "rekwirs a Lady of gentil backgrownd to instruck my Sister." That is the very way he wrote. La! 'Tis obvious they need a school mistress at Gaunt New House. Off tomorrow by Boat to Somerset Bridge. Pray Mr. Ashton will not quizz me too close on my moral Convictions. Of late they have become so full of Holes as a lace Collar.

Her fingers flipped over two more pages.

Thursday, February 16th, 1775

Mangrove Bay, Somerset Isle, Bermuda

Installed this day at Gaunt New House. Am terrified lest I fail my advertis'd Skill. Mistress Susan Ashton is aged eight Years, a saucy, independent Snip. Like most of her Countrymen, she is suspicious and unloving of anything English. The formidable Harpy who conducts this Establishment regards me with a jaundic'd eye I fear. Mr. Peter Ashton, my employer is aged *circa* thirty years. A very jolly sort.

Later:

My suspicion is correckt! This family is close related to that of David Ashton! They know Little of him saving (as I already know) that he has Gambl'd away a considerable Fortune amidst the Follies of London. Have not mentioned Friendship with my adorable Fantom. Verily, his memory haunts me most inconsiderate. Can it be we have met scarce six times in all?

Great concern at Table today over a rumour that the American Colonies will Cease commercial Intercourse with the Bermudas. The Natives fear Starvation tho' their Governor Bruere whom all here loath and distrust protests that Governor Dunmore of Virginia has sworn a sufficiency of food will be shippt. This is quite beyond poor Me, but the Ashtons and their close Friends, the Tuckers, and the Gilberts and Harveys also are greatly exercis'd.

Friday, February 17th, 1775

Today first lessons in Arithmetick and Spelling. Mr. Peter could with advantage join his Sister in pursuance of the latter study. Says rather than waste time on a Horn book and Latin he ran away to sea in his Youth. His Arithmetick, however, is anything but faulty. Have never encounter'd a Person so swift and sure in mental reckoning.

Andrea closed the book and settled back. Drowsily she listened to the whine of many small black mosquitoes beating against the bed net. Reaching out through the muslin, she snuffed the candle, then on impulse slipped out of the smothering folds of her nightgown and lay quite still.

She slept.

8 — THE LASS OF RICHMOND HILL

LOUD hammering in the shipyards across Mangrove Bay aroused Rob from the abysmal slumber into which he had been sunk. Gradually he became aware of chatter in the slaves' quarters, of a chicken on its way to execution squawking in high desperation, of the distinctive rumbling of heavy kegs rolled over a stone floor. The noises conquered an unfamiliar impulse towards sloth.

He was parting the mosquito nettings when the door opened and Lizard thrust a black bullet head through the entrance.

"You avake, suh?"

"After a fashion."

"Breakfast, suh?" With an air of heavy responsibility the tiger peered under Rob's bed to see if the chamber pot had been used. He scuttled off, bare feet beating a brisk tattoo down the plain boards of the hall.

"Mornin', sir. I trust you slept well?" Sachem entered, bowed with a dignity somewhat damaged by the raggedness of his white linen coat.

In one hand he carried a pot of steaming water and Rob's razor in the other. Over his arm was a towel.

"Morning, Sachem."

"I can shave you in bed, Capt'n Ashton. Or, if you prefers, I can do it in this heah chair."

"I'll occupy a chair," Rob grinned. "Where I come from, only dead bodies are shaved lying down."

When the valet pushed out heavy wooden shutters, a torrent of sultry sunshine came leaping in. It yellowed the white-washed walls and projected bright patterns devised by waves on the bay. Cardinals were whistling among some nearby cedars and a bluebird, settling on a limb, peered in at Rob. It was queer to hear no mewing of harbour gulls. Apparently in Bermuda they were very few or non-existent.

Rob said, "Sachem, I reckon I'll shave myself after all. You can brush up my shoes, though."

"Shave yo'self, sir?" Sachem looked mystified, even worried. In port, none of the Ashtons ever lifted a finger. For a moment he doubted Rob's gentility.

Clad in a maroon and green dressing gown of Peter's and with feet comfortably tucked into red morocco slippers, Rob began breakfast on pawpaws sprinkled with lemon juice. In rapid succession appeared tansy pudding, ham, four eggs, buttered muffins and tea. Sachem would have brought in a small fried fish, but Rob balked.

"Do the people here eat as much as this every day?"

" 'Deed yes, sir. Mr. Peter would call this jus' a snack," the valet said. Then he added mournfully, "Don't get nothing so fine in the Quarters—just cornmeal mush and pork, pork and cornmeal mush. Fish and beans sometimes."

At twenty-eight most humans remain fairly resilient, so Rob, while tying a low black silk stock, commenced to whistle. He checked himself. From a new widower whistling might not appear seemly.

He considered his clothes. Stout serge and whipcord were heavy stuff for this climate. He reckoned he had better get some linens made and buy one of those broad-brimmed straw hats such as most Bermudians wore. Sachem reappeared, carrying the lightest of his blue serge coats. The buttons on its front and cuffs had been burnished until they shone like brazen beacons. Luckily some ruffles Peggy had starched and ironed 'way back in Norfolk remained fresh looking. He must do the Bermuda Ashtons credit. To make sure his stocking of white worsted was straight, he turned his leg.

Sachem sprang forward. "If you don't mind, sir."

"Good Lord," Rob said, "doesn't anybody do anything for themselves around here?"

"No, sir, not when they are the quality."

Ascertaining that Peter Ashton was aboard a ship in the harbour, he walked out to the wharf. The *Active* had sailed. During the early morning a bluff-bowed, chunkily built whaler had let go her anchor in Mangrove Bay. Because her water line showed inches below the surface, Rob reckoned she was homeward bound from a successful cruise. Her sails, moreover, were amber yellow with try smoke and her yellow-painted sides so slick with oil she rode amid an iridescent halo.

Rob waited for a humid breeze to swing her about. Vessels of this type did not commonly put in at Norfolk. Clustering about the whaler, many fruit and vegetable laden bumboats jostled each other and two water barges were pulling out from a point opposite. Slowly the whaler's name, done in bright blue, became visible—*Ruth W. Starbuck, Nantucket I.*

"In for water," somebody told him. "She's a Yankee, but a damned English-lover from Nantucket. Everybody is asking top prices."

Peter Ashton stood on the whaler's quarterdeck, his bright blue barge training astern. Glassware flashed. With him it was never too early nor too late for a drink.

Rob sighed and retraced his steps. Yielding to an urge to forget ships and everything concerning business, he strolled inland over a lawn of coarse, sun-bleached grass. For awhile he watched a Negro draw buckets from a well and carry them into a garden beyond a stone wall. An odor of moist earth beckoned him.

On his way over to it, he paused and looked back at Gaunt New House. Seen from this side the Ashton home was a rather simple, one-storeyed affair with many windows shuttered Bermudian-fashion. Single leafed and suspended from the window top, they were propped open at their lower edge. Tinted pale yellow, Gaunt New House boasted many trellises climbed by yellow and white roses. The low-pitched and whitewashed roof lent the structure a very restful aspect.

The roof, now that he noticed it, had also been fashioned of limestone. Gutters inclined gently towards a series of wooden conduits which guided rain caught on the roof into what must be some cisterns. These were two in number. Barely showing above ground, their roofs were cylindrical, designed to minimize the area struck by the sun at one time. Despite its swarms of servants, Rob decided, Gaunt New House by no means approached the elegant aspect of even a modest plantation along the Tidewater.

He passed a mounting block built to the left of a long, unpaved driveway which went winding off between alternate groups of cedars and clumps of Spanish bayonet. In the hot sunlight the leaves of the latter gleamed like the steel for which they were named.

At the entrance to the walled garden Rob hesitated, amazed and charmed by the profusion of flowers within: hollyhocks, columbine, larkspur, roses, and even English ivy. A pattern of walks, double diamond in shape, had been laid out as the approach to a latticed bower at the far end of the garden. The walls, he suspected, constituted a protection against such hurricanes as Wincapaw had said tore and screamed over the Islands during August and September.

He noted a moving patch of light blue. Someone was working behind the bower. Hoping it was Susan, he started along a path edged with bright yellow "everlasting." All at once a woman commenced to sing.

> "On Richmond Hill there lives a lass
> More bright than May day morn,
> Whose charms no other maids surpass
> O Rose without a thorn."

Rob stood frozen; haunted. Of all songs, why did it have to be that one? He was turning hurriedly back when a great electric-blue bird came hurtling from the top of a nearby tree. Screaming, it roared by his head and alighted among some morning glories on the bower's roof. Immediately a second macaw, a scarlet one, flew out of a cedar and, joining the first, besieged the bower with raucous abuse.

"Oh hush! I sing better than either of you—"

From behind the summerhouse stepped a young woman carrying an overflowing flower basket. Laughing, she snapped some shears at the birds, then turned. When she saw Rob, she stood quite still and her gaze fixed him so effectively he went scarlet. Neither of them spoke.

Andrea Grenville was thinking, He is like David—a little. Handsome, too, but in a different way. David's eyes were gray-blue and mocking; this man's sober brown. Yes, any resemblance began and ended about the nose and the strong white teeth. Her serene gaze moved from his head to the square silver buckles on his shoes. He was not so tall, slightly more than her own height, but considerably sturdier than the man she remembered.

Said he, "I beg your pardon."

"For what, Mr. Ashton?"

"How do you know my name?"

"All Somerset knows you came ashore yesterday."

"You are Susan's tutor?"

Andrea's laugh was surprisingly tremulous. "If I can be dignified with so august a title."

Rob was thinking he had never seen anyone quite like her. The straight way this girl carried herself, the fineness of her features and her poise seemed incongruous in an ordinary governess.

"You *are* Miss Grenville then?"

"Yes. I believe I met your brother in London."

Andrea, sensitive to nuances, was astounded to see his sunburnt features freeze, take on a wooden expression.

He said, "Oh, really?" Then, like a small boy caught in an embarrassing speech, he pointed to the macaws. "Can those birds talk?"

She couldn't help smiling at his lack of subtlety, but she liked it. "No. Mr. Ashton calls them Lord North and General Gage. The red one is General Gage."

"Why?"

"Oh, because they make a lot of noise and do nothing useful, I fancy." Confound it! What was there to talk about? For the first time in her life, Andrea found herself at complete loss. The easy, obvious subjects all seemed *tabu*. This pleasant looking young man had just lost his ship and his wife. It was also evident he had no inclination to talk about David. She couldn't help wondering why. David had always mentioned his brother with warm if careless affection.

"I venture it will rain this afternoon," she began lamely. "It's so close. Don't you think so?"

He answered almost shyly. "Yes, I think it is going to rain. Has it been dry?"

"Oh yes, very, very dry. The cisterns are so low Aunt Lydia is saving water. Susan is delighted. She now bathes once a week instead of twice."

Under the cool, friendly quality of her regard, Rob hated himself for getting so red and tongue-tied. He liked her brisk, precise speech with its rising inflection at the end of each sentence. He suspected that, alone of the household, she might be content to converse on something other than local gossip, trade or politics.

"I suppose this dry weather hasn't helped the garden any."

"No, but when it does rain here," Andrea replied, "the fishes swim right up out of the sea. They can't tell where the bay leaves off."

They both laughed nervously.

"I must catch Susan and start her lessons. I wonder," Andrea questioned, "can you help me about—about—" Oh damn! She couldn't think what to ask—how to insure seeing him again. She did so want to hear about Virginia and America.

"I can teach you Indian—Shawnee, that is," Rob told her at random. "I learned it from an old trapper."

"I am sure a knowledge of Shawnee will be very useful to Susan. Good morning." When she brushed by him an appealing quirk was curving the corners of her mouth.

9 — CLAIMS

ROB was still seated on a stone bench and undergoing the bright-eyed inspection of Lord North and General Gage when Peter's white-clad form came waddling down the garden.

"Greetings, Rob. I trust our chatter last night didn't keep you awake?"

"No. Slept better than I have in a long while. I enjoyed meeting your friends."

"Who did you like best?"

"I took a fancy to Daniel Bascombe, John Gilbert and James Fowle—or is his name Fowler?"

"Fowle." Cocking his head to one side, Peter grinned broadly. "And what did you think of Cousin Henry Tucker?"

"Why, I reckon I would think a lot about him," Rob drawled.

Peter laughed so hard that the macaws whirred off into the woods.

"'Think a lot about him.' Ho! Ho!" He quieted quickly and said, "If you'll bring your bill for damages to my office, we might go over it."

A small outbuilding near the land end of the wharf sheltered the offices of Ashton & Sons. Within it raged such helter-skelter disorder of ledgers, invoices and bills of lading Rob was prompted to wonder how anybody ever found anything.

In a hot semi-darkness Rob unfolded and placed on Peter's desk a single sheet of foolscap.

STATEMENT

Damages and Losses Suffered

To Value of *Desdemona*'s hull	3,500	Spanish dollars
To sails, rigging, hawsers, etc.	1,330	" "
To cargo damage	1,735	" "
	6,565	" "

Attached were copies of the schooner's Norfolk clearance papers, a customs manifest and an itemized list of damaged cargo.

Peter climbed onto a stool, puffed out plump cheeks and studied the statement. Presently he thrust forward an inkpot and goosequill.

"Will you sign this and date it?" When Rob had done so, his cousin gave him his seat but remained standing alongside. "Please write what I tell you.

" 'Statement of claim against Hector Cazalles, Merch't, residing in Chamberlain's Tribe in the Parish of Somerset.' "

In a firm hand Rob began to write. Certainly Cazalles had caused the wreck.

" 'I, Robert Butler Ashton, gent. of Norfolk in the Colonie of Va. herewith charge that on the night of June 26th this Hector Cazalles did, with Malice aforethought and in contravention to the Laws of the Bermudas, cause divers illuminations to be ignited and exhibited on the westward Coast of Somerset Island; viz., Long Beach. In consequence the *Desdemona,* schooner under charter to me, was diverted from her true course to her ultimate destruction and to the damage of her cargo.' "

"Where is the list of salvage?" Rob inquired.

"Lying about somewhere," Peter said, blowing on the foolscap. "It didn't come to much."

"Too bad; but you'd better deduct it from my claim."

"I will attend to it," Peter promised.

"Is that all?" Rob was eager to escape and when his cousin said "yes," he nodded and went out.

He had scarcely disappeared in the direction of the garden than Peter used a square of raw caoutchouc to erase Rob's penciled valuation of the *Desdemona.* 3,500 Spanish dollars became $5,500. The $1,330 claim against rigging rose to $2,110. When Peter set down his pen Rob's claim had soared from a mere $6,565 to 9,923 Spanish dollars.

The odd twenty-three dollars, Peter decided, would make a nice tip for the J. P.'s clerk.

10 — SETTLEMENT

DURING the next three days it rained in such earnest that for hours on end great slanting sheets of gray beat at the island and erased the horizon in a smoky vapor. Lashing wind and rain wreaked havoc in the flower gardens, filled row boats at their moorings and stung the harbour's surface into scaly patterns. But everyone in Gaunt New House wore a broad smile and the slaves often stopped, listened to the gurgling of water in the cisterns.

Aunt Lydia was positively jubilant.

This was for Rob, however, a difficult period. He took refuge in reading from cover to cover "Captain Cook's Voyage Around the World—A True and Authentick Account." He lingered in his room much of the time, sleeping and resolutely avoiding all thought on the past and, equally, on the future.

Peter, on the other hand, kept very busy. Every day, right after breakfast he would climb into a hooded one-horse chaise and drive off to an unannounced destination.

In the library, with its musty odor, a peculiar sense of calm prevailed; it was dispelled only by a febrile tapping of raindrops on the windowpanes. When Rob began whittling bone splinters into spars and rigging for the newly christened *King David*, Andrea lingered, quite as fascinated as Susan. To get the new top hamper in scale was no mean task.

"You are vastly patient," Andrea murmured one evening, her eyes charmed by the delicate fittings of the model's fore topmast. "And your hands seem so absurdly strong to do such fine work."

Rob flushed. "Maybe. But I don't reckon I can manage the rigging. Maybe you would help me?"

"I should be ever so pleased. You will have to tell me where the ropes belong, though."

Solemnly he shook his head. "Not 'ropes,' Mistress Grenville. Lines. Aboard a vessel there are cables, hawsers and lines."

"Oh, dear, how monstrous complicated." She stroked the little model. "She is really beautiful; such simple, exquisite lines would charm Sir Joshua. Dear pampered old Josh Reynolds; I wonder who sits for him these days?"

Something of the night's turbulence entered Rob's soul. An abysmal impatience with himself, with the world, a feverish disquiet which would not be stilled. An object, a branch most likely, struck one of the shutters a resounding blow. A ship in the harbour was dragging its anchors. A phrase of Farish's reoccurred. "Such a storm you couldn't hear yourself holler." Poor Farish.

"Following the sea," said he as he began putting away his tools, "is a dog's life."

The next morning Bermuda seemed a new place. The dusty gray-green of foliage had brightened to a brilliant emerald; the hot, dry aspect of the earth had vanished and on all the twigs sparkled lines of crystal clear drops.

"'E traps will be full over," predicted the fishermen slaves. Rested now for three days, they were delighted to see the water blue-green again. Sailors unclewed their sails in order to dry them.

Rob took to frequenting the walled garden. It was blissfully quiet in the summerhouse. There the distracting noises of waterfront and warehouse did not penetrate. By dint of many sunflower seeds and much patience, he enticed General Gage into becoming friendly. Lord North, however, still cocked a bright suspicious eye and backed away.

"Maybe it's an omen," Rob thought, "the way that red-coated bird makes up to me."

Sprawled on his stomach on a patch of lawn, he commenced a volume by one Juliet Grenville—of all names! He had not developed any real interest in her theme when his cousin hailed him. God in Heaven! Peter was actually trotting!

"Rob! Rob!"

Rob leaped up. "Eh? What's wrong? What's happened?"

Under one of his broad hats Peter was wearing a bright green bandanna. Sweat had darkened the underarms of his white jacket. Puffing, he drew near, a small canvas sack dangling over one shoulder.

"There, damn you!" He chortled and tossed the sack. Rob caught it, but it was so heavy it knocked the breath from his lungs, sent him staggering backwards.

"What's this?"

"Present from Hector Cazalles—rat him!"

Small tingles shot up through Rob's arms, across his shoulders and up into the back of his neck. The sack was bulging with coin.

"You mean to say Cazalles—?"

"Bloody Tory knew better than go—court." Scarlet features twisted into one huge grin, Peter pulled a paper from his loose, long-skirted coat. "There are your damages settled in full! Scared hell out of him. Listen to this piece of law." In jerky little sentences Peter began reading.

" 'Casting Away A Vessel. Whomsoever with intent—to bring a Vessel into danger—interferes with any Light, beacon, mark—or signal set for the purposes of—Navigation, or exhibits any False lights or signal is—guilty of a Felony and shall suffer imprisonment for a term of seven—Years with or without solitary confinement.' "

Peter scaled his hat onto the grass, mopped a streaming forehead. "When Henry and I promised Cazalles we'd see he got solitary confinement, he quit his back talk. He judged if ever we got him into jail we would see he didn't own a six-pence when he came out!"

Rob stood a moment, hefting the dirty, lumpy canvas bag. When the magnitude of what Peter had accomplished sank in, his eyes filled. He'd got hardened to abuse and sharping and deceit. He'd got so he could stand those things. But a great, a real kindness such as this—why, why, it was so damn' unexpected it hit him between wind and water.

"Peter, you—I— What can I say? Why—? Why should you? I don't understand."

Peter flung an arm about his shoulder, enveloped him in a gentle aura of Barbados rum. "Hang it, Rob, we are off the same vine, ain't we? There's not so many of us Ashtons but we must help each other over a stile." A look of shy understanding such as Anglo-Saxons occasionally exchange passed between them. Peter, looking embarrassed, advised, "You had better count it, eh? Cazalles ain't to be trusted."

They seated themselves and like two small boys tumbled the hoard onto a wide bench in the summerhouse. A moment they blinked fascinated by the glitter the sun drew from it.

Rob recognized Portuguese escudos, triple-milled moidores, pistoles, Spanish dollars and huge Ioannes V doubloons. He also turned over English Spade guineas, piatriens, and French Louis d'ors stamped with heavy Bourbon profiles.

"We'd better each count." Peter's eyes had grown luminous and he kept wetting his lips. In sorting and stacking coins, his fingers fairly flew. So swift were his calculations that he had done before Rob had got well under way.

As the total kept climbing, Rob began to look puzzled. "I don't understand this," said he. "My claim was for 6,565 Spanish dollars—less deductions against salvage."

A stubborn expression erased the genial lines from Peter's shiny pink face. "Henry and I got you five hundred dollars extra. Let's say the difference covers the rate of exchange. You'll notice there's some Bermuda currency here. It stands at a discount."

"Five hundred dollars worth of discount?"

"You better take my word for it, Rob. You don't understand these things yet."

Rob reckoned he understood well enough, but it would be churlish to argue any longer. Still, he didn't like not being exact. His instinct was all against it. "But what about that salvage?"

Peter clacked together two huge pieces of eight. Said he, surveying the treetops, "I wouldn't bother myself. Cazalles is a Tory, isn't he? There's no room for King's people at this end of the Island—at least, there won't be much longer."

Both words and intonation were familiar. It might have been Matthew Phipp talking, or Major Brush, or Neil Jameison.

The payment came, in all, to around seven thousand Spanish dollars! By God, he hadn't dared hope to handle so much in years. He felt a heap better, now that it would be possible to forward a sight draft to the *Desdemona*'s owner. He'd send the money by the very next ship. No. To hell with a draft! Hard money was mighty scarce in America. He reckoned Christian Southeby would be right tickled, provided he was still above ground.

Peter, too, was feeling complacent. The way Rob had quibbled over crediting Cazalles a mere $200 worth of salvage had tickled him no end. Did everybody in Virginia do business along such lines? He chuckled; if that was so, he'd emigrate in a hurry. Since Rob hadn't as yet grasped the Bermuda way of getting things done, there seemed no point in mentioning the whole sum actually paid by Cazalles. Um. His own profit in the transaction was unusually small. A mere $779 after splitting with Henry Tucker and setting aside the J. P.'s cut.

Henry had looked sour. But Peter hadn't cared because he knew Henry would make a good profit out of the forced sale of Cazalles's north pasture. Besides, there were such things as family loyalty.

He glanced at Rob who was wondering how he could ever prove his gratitude.

"Has the tailor finished your white ducks?"

"One pair. Why?"

"Henry Tucker is giving a party tonight—a sort of victory feast in your honor."

Rob hesitated. "I don't know— It's rather too soon after—"

It hurt him to see his cousin's expression fall. He guessed Peter was keenly disappointed so he added, "I will think it over."

"Pray do, Rob. I know how you feel, but—er—Henry Tucker has been helpful. Sets a damned fine table, too."

"So you really want my opinion?" Andrea said.

"I would greatly value it."

"Well, then, you had better attend Mr. Tucker's party."

"But what will people—"

"In these islands, no matter what you do or don't do, you will get talked about." Her softly melodious voice deepened. "I feel very sure—she—would rather you went. Going to a party will not make you miss her any the less."

11 — BRIDGE HOUSE

HENRY TUCKER's residence, being all dwelling and not part warehouse, was considerably more imposing than Gaunt New House. Of three stories, Bridge House was thick walled and roughly square in shape. It stood dominating a bridge over Sandys Narrows. Here, by a few feet, a narrow bright blue channel divorced Somerset Island from Long Island; largest of the Bermudian archipelago. Bridge House,

Peter remarked, had been built not many years earlier by Chief Justice John Tucker.

Apparently everyone of consequence and Whig convictions in the West End had been invited. While few coaches, curricles and chaises stood in the driveway, many riding horses switched mosquitoes under some trees. Behind a long carriage shed some slave coachmen gambled surreptitiously.

The gathering presented by no means as brilliant a picture as would a similar one in Virginia. There were fewer bright colors among the gentlemen's coats and waistcoats, their wigs often were yellowish and their stockings seldom of silk. The women's gowns, one and all, were hopelessly outmoded and their footgear suggested service rather than style. Yet all in all, the West Enders presented a cheerful, healthy and sunburned company. Fresh from the host's powdering rooms heads wearing natural hair shone white beneath crystal chandeliers.

On presenting Rob, Henry Tucker made quite a little speech. He touched upon Rob's Bermudian ancestry, and the fact that Bermuda and Virginia had for a long period belonged to the same chartered company.

"Our relations were so intimate with this great and flourishing colony that, in the last century, a parish to subsist a hundred people was set aside as a Virginia home for Bermudians. It is known to this day as the Bermuda Hundred."

He talked so long and so earnestly on this theme Rob wondered what he could be driving at.

Conversationally the island women appeared to better advantage than their men, who seemed shy and ill-at-ease to the point of surliness. For most of the ladies even this modest affair was a wonderful treat, an occasion of tremendous importance. No doubt for weeks to come it would form the chief topic of conversation. Nothing escaped their eyes. A new watch fob, a new piece of lace; who hovered too long over what girl and how did that plain little thing attract so many men? Lottie was supposed to be in an "interesting condition" but she certainly didn't look it, did she now? Dowagers in the background bridled when Rob was presented by the host, and more than one young lady giggled and surveyed him with a distinctly speculative glance. La! Such a handsome, upstanding young gentleman. And yet, so vastly sad and romantic looking.

It gave Rob an odd turn to be faced with reminiscences

about his father's youth. Queer that these people should have known and played with St. John Ashton before pretty, pert Molly Butler stormed in to disrupt his life.

"Never forget the time your Pa painted old Alex Lackey's chair with fish glue," sputtered a toothless old man who had been searching his wig for lice. "Stuff worked in—tore the bottom right out of old Alex's britches. Hi! Hi! Old Alex was the worst hated dominie ever taught in this island."

The drawing room of Bridge House was spacious and high ceilinged and boasted many mahogany sashed windows. He could judge how very thick the walls were from the depth of the window frames—eighteen inches at the very least. Separating this chamber from the dining room was a peculiar ornament consisting of a colossal fanlight backed with glass. A very intricate design had been executed in skillfully cut and joined wood. Henry Tucker looked mighty pleased when asked concerning it. His father, he explained, had ordered the builders to reproduce the design of a favorite piece of lace belonging to his mother.

On a handsome old sideboard in the dining room a row of silver bowls engraved with assorted ship names stood waiting. Slaves, delighted with a temporary importance, ladled out sangaree, sherry flip, rumbullion, claret punch and brandy sling. Between regiments of wine bottles mounds of oranges and lemons had raised a colorful breastwork. Just outside, two big bucks were strumming instruments they said were "banjohs." These consisted of violin strings drawn taut across the half of a bottle-neck gourd.

It was such a fine night, the guests began to escape the stale air in the drawing room. From the edge of a wide terrace they could see over Great Sound and pick out the lights of Somerset blinking in the distance.

Beaming, patently proud, Peter took his cousin in charge. He presented men, women and cups of brandy sling in such rapid succession that Rob began to take an interest. Noted a neat-turned ankle here, sparkling glance yonder. In the air was a blend of alcohol, pomatum, hair powder, perfume and perspiration. He found it peculiarly provocative.

Peter handed him still another brandy sling. "Want to go up to the library and watch the gaming?"

To Peter's surprise, his cousin nodded. Rob wondered why he had agreed. All his life he'd avoided gaming. Not on moral ground but because the risks entailed were, from a merchant's viewpoint, too illogical. A player, he felt, so often lay at the mercy of Chance. His money had always come too hard to be thrown away without his having anything to say about it. Besides, in that direction, David had taken care of the family's social obligations.

As he followed Peter upstairs his feet felt surprisingly light. His heart, too. All at once he began to wonder what being so damned serious all this time had got him? Hadn't he been careful, thrifty and hard working? What had it got him? Nothing! Not a single goddam thing! Gaily he clapped Peter on the shoulder. Damned if he wouldn't risk a whole pound!

When they made room for him at a long green table, the beating of his heart felt quick and loud as the sound of flushing partridge. An unfamiliar but delicious sense of recklessness seized him once bright-colored cards began sliding over the table towards him. For a fact, he hadn't felt so downright wicked since, on a dare, he'd shot General Forrester's white peacock arse-over-tip.

In no time at all he lost not one pound, but five. Sweating, he drank three brandy flips in a row and stayed. He reckoned it took time to get the hang of pharo.

"May be I had better throw my hand in," he said to Peter when he had lost another ten shillings.

His cousin would have none of it. "No, Robbie. Stay! Your luck's in. I tell you, it's in! Wouldn't do to back-out so quick."

Rob was dripping now, though like the rest of the players, he stripped down to his waistcoat of green duroy. So far he had been too happy to use his head. He would now. He drew several long breaths. Hanged if he was going to let a bunch of island hicks take a Virginian! Peter handed him a church warden pipe, ready lighted. After drawing several quick puffs, he felt better. It was eleven o'clock he noticed.

By three o'clock, four men lingered in the game. The rest had either slipped off their chairs in drunken stupor, or had got up, exposing empty pocket linings. Rob chewed smartly on a piece of bread and cold mutton while counting four stacks of gold coins. Peter's skill at figures was required to reckon exchanges. Though a man named Dill was the biggest winner, Rob hadn't done badly.

Methodically, Mr. Dill commenced counting coins into the

pouches of a money belt. "Come and play at my place sometime. You got card sense."

"Delighted, I'm sure," Rob mumbled and began fervently to wish Peter hadn't been so nippy about handing out those slings. There was a frightening lightness in his body and a queer buzzing at the back of his head.

"Five hundred and five Spanish," Peter beamed clapping him on the shoulder. "Nice work."

Imagine having cleared over a hundred pounds in under four hours! The realization plus fourteen brandy slings was too much. Rob went out like a light.

12 — THE MERCURY MAKES PORT

AROUND seven of a morning some days later, pilot boats working out of Mangrove Bay went racing for the open sea. Peter swore, was plunged into gloom because his crew had got away last. He judged he had better send his coxswain over to the slave boss to be dealt a smart two dozen with the rattan. Maybe the blooming spade would get over being so damned slack.

Rob, sleeping off an extra heavy wine and card bout at John Gilbert's, awoke with the dull reverberations of a cannon report in his ears. He sent Lizard down to find out what was going on, then with the help of Sachem, who had squatted outside his door since six o'clock, struggled into his clothes.

In Gaunt New House an excited undertone was sounding and from his window Rob saw rowboats of all descriptions go pulling out on the harbour. Hoofs sounded on the road, but when he got downstairs Rob found not a soul indoors. The newly-arrived vessel, a typical Bermuda sloop, was casting anchor off Harvey's pier. The beach between it and Peter's wharf was dotted with people, converging on Harvey's place like sand poured into a funnel.

"What's up?" "What's the news?" "Where's she from?"

Hovering on the fringes of the crowd Rob discovered Andrea Grenville. She was pink faced and hot and clutching the rebellious Susan by an arm.

"You shall not go into that crowd," she was informing her small, excited charge. "You will act like a lady and stay right here!"

496

Susan, still struggling, gave her a murderous look, but presently assumed such a meek and angelic expression that Andrea relaxed her grip. Quick as a spider, the child darted off amid the people.

Andrea, putting on a burst of speed which surprised and interested Rob, sprinted after her. But she had to give up and halted, making a droll little face. "Might as well try to catch rain in one's hands."

"I could do with a bit of rain." Rob had become aware of a pounding headache.

"No wonder. They say it's a job to drink any of the Gilberts under." There was, however, no hint of reproach in her tone. Her gaze had sought the newly-arrived vessel. Deck-hands were out on her yards furling the topsails. Further out on the emerald-tinted water smoke from the sloop's signal cannon still hung together, a dirty gray and white puff drifting towards the harbour's mouth.

"There's been a battle," a man shouted from the end of Harvey's wharf.

"A battle? Where, you dumblock?"

Everyone kept quiet for the answer.

"A big battle at a place called Charles Town. Near Boston!"

"Who won?" a dozen voices yelled at a skiff pulling ashore.

Turmoil ensued and it was some minutes before someone sang out, "They say the British whipped, but the Yankees killed a terrible lot of 'em!"

The sharp catching of Andrea's breath made Rob look at her. She stood round-eyed, nervously clasping her throat with one hand.

"I—I can't believe it. Why, the Provincials must have stood up to our troops."

"But the Yankees got whipped, didn't you hear?"

She looked at him, eyes narrowed, but she was seeing something beyond. "That is hardly the point. The Americans dared to stand up to our grenadiers. Think of that!"

"They were fools," Rob stated. He hated this intrusion of American news. "I reckon there will be a real war, now."

Andrea's gaze was on the sea and her fingertips pressed tightly against her palms. It was as if she were witnessing strange sights beyond the pale blue of the reefs.

In the skiff's stern a man cupped his hands and yelled, "Yankees have got Britishers cooped up in Boston! Colonies are rising!"

A bent old man sank suddenly onto a half hewn timber, buried his face in his hands.

A neighbor hurried over, put a hand on his shoulder. "Are you ill, Mr. Maltby?"

"—My ship," he croaked, raising blank eyes. "I cleared her for Philadelphia yesterday—carrying supplies for the fleet. The Americans will confiscate her, I know it! I know it!" Drearily, he commenced to snuffle. He was old. This ship was all there was left in his life.

More news began to circulate. The British loss had been appalling, over a thousand men in killed and wounded. What about the Yankees? Well, some said the Provincials had lost above four hundred, some said less. One item in especial sobered the crowd. John Bruere, the Governor's son, a lieutenant of the 14th foot, had been a casualty!

"Killed—or only wounded?"

"Killed leading troops against a place called Breed's Hill. He got shot all to pieces."

Lots of them remembered Jack Bruere, a young, laughing fellow with blue eyes and yellow hair. Many present had sons of his age. Andrea watched the realization become etched on the faces of the women. So the Governor's son had been killed! When the *Mercury*'s boat grated onto the sand, the crowd surged forward.

"A war has begun all right," the *Mercury*'s captain told them, stepping ashore. Everyone noticed he was wearing a cutlass in a sheath of brass and scuffed black leather. "Don't make no mistake about that! First I got chased halfway down the Delaware by a Pennsylvania Committee boat, then, by God, a damned British sloop of war tried to heave me to. Would of, too, if we hadn't had the heels of him."

People crowded around by five, ten, and dozens, so thick the captain elected to remain standing on the stern seat in his gig. It was lucky he was tall. Because his front teeth were lacking, he made a little sputtering noise when he talked.

"Hi, Cap'n Lightbourn. You hear 'bout your brother Steve's sloop?"

The master of the *Mercury* turned quickly, anxious in his turn. "No. What happened?"

"Bulldog stopped her off Long Island. Her leftenant pressed your cousin, Will Trott and Fred Perinchief."

A woman gasped in a stifled sort of way and rushed forward. "Took Fred? Why didn't someone tell me before? Oh, did they hurt him, Mister?"

"I don't know, Ma'am. All I heard was, being short-handed, the sloop lost both masts in a squall. She made into Newport under jury."

Around the outskirts of the crowd hovered a fringe of slaves, ring-eyed in curiosity. They looked mighty pleased when John Gilbert shouted, "Hi there, tell us what happened at Charles Town! Tell us again."

"Why," the captain said, striking an attitude and resting one hand on the wide brass guard of his cutlass, "one night last month—the seventeenth, I think—the Yankees fortified a hill outside of Boston and Gen'l Gage attacked."

"Send his regulars—or was it militia?"

"Regulars, but they whipped him twice." Captain Light-bourn grinned. Right now he was the most important man in Bermuda and he enjoyed the sensation. "I reckon the Yankees would have gone on whipping him 'til all the British was dead, only they run out of powder."

"Who run out of powder?"

"The Provincials, you numbskull," the captain replied irritably. "It was too bad."

Everybody began to talk. The young men full of bellicose chatter, the women talking worried or scared, or both. Merchants like Fowle, Richard Jennings, and Peter were frowning, trying to figure out what they had better do. Some of the shipowners with property already on the lap of the gods sat staring blankly into space, marked by their hopeless expressions.

Captain Lightbourn's greasy gray cuffs showed when he raised his hand. "Listen! That ain't all. Listen! I got more news. A paper in Philadelphia said Parliament—"

"To hell with Parliament!" "Hang North!" "Hooray for the Yankees!"

Peter Ashton climbed up onto an empty whale oil barrel. "Quiet, please! Quiet! What was it happened?" he yelled over the heads of the crowd. Right now he looked a different man, Andrea noticed. He didn't seem so fat. He looked big, anxious and determined. "What about Parliament?"

"You remember them fool laws the Parliament passed last April? About the American fisheries?"

"No!" someone shouted. "I was to sea then."

"Well, the King's ministers says ain't none of the Massachusetts people allowed to fish in the sea. Guess they claim the ocean belongs to the King."

A great clamor went up. Someone at Rob's side began to curse. "No fish to cure means no salt."

Another man growled, "The prices will go to hell!" The speaker glared desperately about. "What can we do if the salt market goes to the devil? Somebody tell me!"

Nobody answered. They were all listening to Captain Lightbourn.

"This same month the Royal Navy has been ordered to enforce the Fisheries law. They say the American Congress is so mad they ain't going to sell the English *and us* nothing more."

Peter's voice rose above a yelping clamor from the crowd. "Hold on there! That ain't certain yet. Now don't anybody get scared 'til Colonel Henry gets back from Philadelphia. He's mighty able and you know we have always been friendly with the Colonies."

Everybody began looking depressed and worried. To Rob's astonishment Andrea apparently had taken in nothing beyond the news of the battle, for she said:

"I vow, I would never have dreamt a rabble of farmers and mechanics could beat troops the French, the Spanish, and the Germans couldn't whip. What can it be?"

"What can what be?"

In a passionate gesture she faced him. "In what can those plain people believe so hard that they would face our Army?"

Rob, recalling Braddock's fate, the failure of Abercrombie at Ticonderoga and the skirmishes at Concord and Lexington, looked unimpressed. Andrea, standing there on the trampled sand, noticed this.

"You Americans, I fear, know little about the British army save some mistakes it has made in America." Andrea's head went back a proud inch or two. "Nevertheless, I assure you, Mr. Ashton, ours is the finest, the most capable army in Europe! In the end, it has never lost a war!" Her voice swelled, took on a ringing quality. "When the foreigners see red coats marching onto the battlefield, they are already half beaten. Yet, those simple farmers stayed to fight. You heard what the captain there said? The New Englanders drove back our soldiers not once, but twice!"

"Gage won the battlefield," John Gilbert reminded, coming from the throng.

"Reckon he did," Rob was astonished to hear his own voice say, "He bought a hill for a thousand men. Mr. Gilbert, I wonder if you know how many hills there are in America?"

"That's it!" Andrea's voice was vibrant. "That's the way to talk!"

Gilbert's large, good-natured face looked puzzled. "But, Ma'am, they tell me you are English. Why do you talk this way?"

"I *am* English! And prouder of it than anything else. It is because of that I hope those poor, untrained farmers will go on fighting."

As Andrea went on talking in a crisp cold voice, a puzzled expression crept over Gilbert's face.

"I do not suppose, sir, you are familiar with the London of today? Unfortunately I am—was, rather—and I will say that those who most should set an example are the worst. Smart society, so-called, is become a stinking cesspool of vice and scandal." Andrea continued as to herself, justifying hitherto unanalyzed thoughts. "If I talked 'til next week I could not make you see what the Court is like. It swarms with cynical self-seekers and seethes with corruption."

Her voice grew stronger, not louder. Half a dozen persons now were listening to the Ashtons' governess.

"Every bootblack in London knows that Paymaster General Dickie Rigby has stolen near half a million of public money. They know 'Bloody' Barrington takes bribes right and left—even boasts about it. What is done? Nothing!" Andrea's long eyes sparkled. "You must not misunderstand what I mean. At her core England is as sound as she ever was, but she has grown fat and soft with too many victories. Therefore, I pray the poor people in Boston will go on fighting!"

Peter came tramping along, alert, worried of expression and soaked with perspiration. Said he to his tiger, "Run down to the stables and tell Zacksee to ride over to Mr. Henry Tucker's in a hurry. I want him to come here. Tom and Cat-Eye can ride to Mr. Judkins's and Mr. Newsome's on the same message. Now git!" He looked about. "Where's my cousin? Let's hear what he has to say."

But Rob had disappeared.

Back in his room, Rob marched a nervous parade. He felt so wretchedly upset he sent Lizard down to the kitchen for a pitcher of negus. While he waited for the liquor, he commenced to work out trial hands at Macao. Tonight at Haydon House there would be another card party. The table stakes were to be the highest yet played for on Somerset Island.

13 — THE EAST END

FAMILIAR now with the scattered houses and comparatively scant population of the West End, Rob was intrigued by the compact appearance of St. George's Town. Presenting an irregular patchwork of white roofs and steeples glaring against a dull green background, the Colonial capital first sprawled along the shore of a large bright blue bay, then climbed a hill gently sloping away from it. In the harbour quite a few vessels were at anchor; a Dutch brigantine, round-bowed as any *mevrouw* in Haarlem; two Spanish schooners and a Swedish sloop. A trio of large armed merchantmen swung to their moorings off a small island that was completely walled. Over to starboard a slovenly French bark lay berthed at some distance from the rest of the vessels as if conscious of being unpopular.

During a trip paralleling the South Shore of the archipelago Rob was amazed by the number of little batteries and forts they sighted. The West End had very few defenses. On entering Castle Harbour Peter's pleasure yawl sailed right up under the guns of a really imposing fortress, but the yawl's mulatto skipper, quite unimpressed, spat in its direction.

Peter cocked an eye at a row of hoary battlements looming above the blue water. "Looks mighty impressive, don't it? But there's nobody there except a few old matrosses, garrison gunners, who ain't strong enough to load one of those 24 pounders."

Dotted by many islets and vari-colored reefs, patrolled by a host of snowy terns and long-tails, Castle Harbour and its ring of forts presented an eye-filling panorama on this mild, mid-summer's day.

Due to a light wind the trip from Gaunt New House had been slow. There was barely time for the cousins to change their linen at the Sea Horse Ordinary before they must start for the home of Sir Lovell Dandy, their host for the evening.

It came to be Rob's private conviction that, so far as Peter was concerned, this card party had been inspired by more than a love of gaming. Else why should he have been so confounded keen to accept the hospitality of so outspoken and fire-eating a Tory as Sir Lovell Dandy? His guess was that Peter was seeking an index to the Capital's reactions concerning Bunker's Hill.

Sir Lovell Dandy's residence had, for the sake of coolness, been constructed on the summit of the ridge rising behind St. George's Town. Like nearby Government House, it commanded a view of the sea on both sides of St. George's Isle. That Sir Lovell Dandy was a man of substance became immediately apparent. The gate posts of Pauncefoot Hall supported massive valves of wrought iron. These had been liberally gilded and so was an escutcheon supported above it by scroll work of wrought iron.

While they waited before doors of polished cedar, Peter muttered, "Watch out for Sir Lovell. He's damnably lucky and if he gets you down he won't stop kicking you." He winked. "Use your head, Rob. Remember you appear here as a sort of champion from the West End. Study his style of play before you plunge."

Rob reckoned this was good advice, but some time back he had adopted certain tactics; they had won—so far.

"Who else will be there?"

"Not many." Heels could be heard advancing within and Peter quickened his speech. "Try to get Sir Lovell and the rest to talk politics, but mind your own tongue! This ain't Somerset. Plenty of people are itching to carry tales about us Ashtons to old George Bruere."

Sir Lovell proved a thin, sharp-featured individual whose hair was so dark his jaws and cheeks shone blue as any Spaniard's. A deep cleft nicked the nobleman's chin and his eyes, though sleepy of expression, were of a restless blue-black. During their sail along the South Shore Peter had explained that Sir Lovell was living in Bermuda "for a reason." It had to do with a duel and a question of whether he had fired before the word. In any case, Peter averred, he was reputed to be St. George's most outstanding rake-hell. But for all of that, Sir Lovell was continually sought after and toadied to by families with eligible daughters. Titled bachelors were scarce as hen's teeth in Bermuda.

Pauncefoot Hall, Rob perceived, varied in many ways from any other residence he had entered in Bermuda, or for that matter in Virginia. Its architecture was uncompromisingly urban and English. Every piece of furniture was expensive and of unmistakably English origin. Portraits, prints and steel engravings, of which there were many, all concerned London. In the hall was hung a sensuous nude reclining in a particularly breath-taking attitude. It was the first painting of a full-figure Rob had ever beheld. Blushing, he gave the canvas a glance full of curiosity, but did not linger.

In brazen intensity Sir Lovell stared. Apparently he could not make up his mind. "Egad, Mr. Ashton, you seem blasé. My French tidbit is seldom so cavalierly dismissed."

After they had been served with sangaree in elegant silver goblets, the trio lit pipes, stood about talking until a knock sounded at the door and a butler in a green and white livery stalked by.

"Our fourth for dinner," drawled the host, "is a Colonel Fortescue. Know him?"

Peter said he did not but expressed interest.

"Not a bad sort, old Fortescue, but no *ton* to him. Not a bit. Egad! Other day I asked him whether he fancied La Belle Siddons. Know what the silly fellow replied? Ho! Ho! Ho! Vowed he wasn't familiar with such a vintage. Fancy!"

Rob, however, felt an instant liking for the stalwart, red-faced gentleman who presently appeared, looking very hot in a coat of bottle-green velvet.

"And how is your charming niece?" Sir Lovell inquired.

"Quite recovered from her sea journey, thank you."

"My service to her." Sir Lovell Dandy bowed, a smile flickering at his mouth corners.

Colonel Fortescue stared hard at him and spoke very deliberately. "Thank you, Sir Lovell. She will be vastly flattered."

"Mr. Ashton—my military neighbor."

"Servant, sir," Fortescue snapped. "Take it you are the Mr. Ashton whose gaming we have been hearing about? True you are a beginner?"

Rob nodded. "Yes, sir. I reckon I've been having some uncommon fine luck." But he knew his winning had resulted from more than just luck. The playing of cards had become a fascinating business. It stirred him most when stakes were high and instinct alone advised whether to call or to raise. Recently he had begun to find a measure of tolerance for David.

God in Heaven! When he recalled how he had slaved and had burnt midnight oil fighting to clear a hundred dollars in trade, he felt like laughing—or like kicking himself the length of the Bermudas. Why, night before last he had risen from Jack Dill's card table three thousand Spanish dollars richer than when he'd sat down a little earlier. He felt impatient for play to begin. Yes. He had been a fool, a bloody, stupid fool to go around worrying his heart out over the state of trade. To date he was over six thousand Spanish dollars to the good.

Sir Lovell led the way into a dining room resplendent with silver candelabra, pale green walls and a long table of delicately inlaid rosewood. It was set for four places.

"The others will be in later," he explained. "Only six of us all told. No use getting deafened."

As he sat there, Rob considered himself in a mirror across the room. His new white clothes were becoming, he felt, and the set of his lace stock not at all bad. Not too fancy, either.

Another thing pleased him. If he didn't come home too late, he would quite often find Andrea Grenville still up, reading by candle light. To the last detail she drank in his account of the play. Her clear features flushed and her long eyes would shine as if she might have been playing herself. Rob reckoned she must have once gamed heavily.

Lately he had rather taken to pitying Peter. The Bermudian had no real sporting sense; was only willing to risk ten pounds an evening. At times he openly envied Rob's amazing good fortune, almost resented it. But as a rule he was tickled clear through. Rob had already eased up on heavy drinking; when he got muzzy his card sense faltered.

From what Peter had indicated, tonight promised to see the highest stakes ever played for in the Bermudas. He was ready, by God! A money belt, heavy with gold coin, tugged at his waist; one thousand pounds—sterling. Soon he would add to it. He couldn't lose. Not with his brand of luck. He would go right on piling up the winnings. Tonight he was going to teach that blue-chinned snob a thing or two. He hadn't cottoned at all to Sir Lovell and would enjoy taking him down. Once a huge pigeon pot pie had been washed down with claret and the usual pastries and sillabubs had been served, Rob felt steadier. He was losing his awe of Sir Lovell's icy self-esteem.

Colonel Fortescue, while dexterously wielding a good toothpick, observed to Peter, "Damme, never fancied we bred such looks in my family. Niece takes to riding like an Amazon, veritable Amazon. Must present you."

Sir Lovell blew a crumb from the lace of his shirt front and tipped Rob an esoteric wink. He drawled, "I warrant the old boy's niece is handy at other forms of riding, too, eh what?" Fortunately, his was such a low voice that Colonel Fortescue, turning very red now with the port, did not hear him. Rob, surveying the veteran's granite block of a jaw, reckoned that this was lucky.

Sir Lovell and his guests had hardly repaired to a library in which a baize-covered table stood waiting, than the two other guests arrived. One was Colonel Andrus, a member of Governor Bruere's official family. He looked so lean, aquiline and acid of appearance he might have been nursed on pickles; he had an over-bred, nervous look about him. He acted, Rob reflected, as if he would bite your head off if you so much as looked cross-eyed at him.

The second man was an East Ender named Leonard Albuoy, a large, barrel-chested individual who reminded Rob of a story book pirate, so fierce were his swarthy face and bristling black mustache.

14 — VINGT-ET-UN

SIR LOVELL DANDY'S hands, astonishingly well muscled and supple, set the cards in the center of the table, pushed them into a precise rectangle.

"Well, gentleman, what shall it be? Pharo, Macao, vingt-et-un, or loo?"

Albuoy, still counting his chips, grunted, "Macao."

But otherwise the players favored either pharo—Rob's *forte*—or vingt-et-un, Colonel Andrus's preference.

"Suppose you cut?" Peter suggested. He had agreed to

bank, and to make change. He would not play; nor, for a miracle, would he drink much.

"If Andrus wins, it shall be vingt-et-un," Lovell said, tucking the lace of his sleeves into his cuffs. "If our Virginian friend cuts high, we shall play pharo."

Rob exposed the queen of hearts. But Andrus cut the ace of spades.

A pang of disquiet flushed Rob's cheeks. He didn't like getting beat by the ace of spades. It was an ill omen.

"Vingt-et-un, then. Table stakes, gentlemen?"

"Thousand pounds?" suggested Fortescue, settling square-lensed spectacles on his ruddy nose. "Friendly little game, what?"

Colonel Andrus snorted. "Three thousand pounds, I say."

Rob's elation wilted like a flower cut in the heat of the day. He could have killed Peter for the way he was grinning in the background. Three thousand pounds! Why, that was fifteen thousand Spanish dollars! Good God! Perspiration began beading the backs of his hands.

Mr. Albuoy shook his big head. "Not so fast, Colonel. We've got all night. Start slow and sprint to the finish, that's my motto."

Rob hurriedly said he thought Mr. Albuoy's idea was sensible, but Colonel Andrus's sharp yellowish features were taut with disgust.

Sir Lovell shrugged, rubbed his bluish chin. "Suppose we compromise on fifteen hundred as table stakes?" He turned to Fortescue. "Agreeable, Colonel?"

"Right," Colonel Fortescue mumbled from the depths of a bombo glass.

Rob felt sunk. Excepting Colonel Fortescue, these men knew too much for him. They weren't much like the jolly, hard-drinking merchants of the West End. These men were out for his scalp. They would take him all right. He reckoned he would stay until he got cleaned. With the cash he had left in Somerset, he would just about have enough to settle.

To steady himself he drank a deep gulp of negus, his favorite drink. The wine, water and sugar kindled a pleasant glow at the pit of his stomach, a glow which would die the next morning without leaving a taste of ashes in the mouth.

It soon grew hot in the gaming room and though Peter opened all the windows the players removed their waistcoats and stocks. Finally they rolled up sleeves and opened their shirts. Two wide white scars cut a swath through thick gray hair on Colonel Fortescue's chest.

"Tiger did it," he explained to Mr. Albuoy's question. "Thought the damned beast was dead. Wasn't. Savaged me. Taught me a lesson. Tiger takes a lot of killing."

From the start Rob fared badly, lost many close decisions. Time and again he would, by a single point, exceed the draw limit of twenty-one, or else the dealer would tie him and thereby win. He lost two hundred pounds to Andrus who, having discarded his wig, more than ever resembled a vulture. After only two hours Rob was out eight hundred pounds and still losing steadily. He had been a prize idiot to think he could go on winning! To get out of this would require all the salvage money! He would be flat broke again. How Peter must despise him!

Tree frogs in the garden piped their eternal *glee-glee, glee-glee;* far away, slaves were crooning a hymn. As the hours passed, the players grew curt. More and more gold coins appeared and were offered for Peter's appraisal. Arguments were settled by a pair of jeweler's scales. Fortescue pushed the spectacles high up on his forehead and left them there. Colonel Andrus, winning, grinned like a winter wolf. Mr. Albuoy, losing, glowered, called for new cards. Sir Lovell ordered fresh drinks and more fresh drinks. Rob writhed within himself. Peter began to look worried.

Rob bought a hundred pounds worth of chips, bluffed at the right time and stole a pot worth a thousand dollars.

Suddenly the cards became Rob's allies. So much so that Sir Lovell took an unflattering interest in the movements of the Virginian's hands, and Colonel Fortescue went gray along the cheekbones. Soon he called quits, eight hundred pounds in the hole.

"Not my night, and that's a fact," he declared, buttoning his waistcoat. "Pleasant evening. Obliged to you, gentlemen, Sir Lovell."

"Stay awhile longer," Andrus rapped. "We'll clip this cockerel's comb yet."

"Didn't come for that purpose," Fortescue announced in a level, subtly offensive tone. He looked the Governor's aide square in the eye and stood there, a sturdy, ruddy-faced figure holding his green coat over one arm. "Came to play a friendly game, understand?" It was plain he wouldn't give a pinch of ashes for Colonel Andrus, nor for a whole shipload like him.

He bowed to Sir Lovell again, thanked him for the dinner and then said to Peter, "Remember what I said; if you stay awhile this End bring your cousin around to Glen Duror. Kitty needs to meet young chaps. Right sort. Know where the house is?"

Peter said he did. Colonel Hugh Fortescue looked about the table, bowed stiffly, then swung, square-shouldered out of the room. They could hear the precise click of his varnished heels diminish along the red tile paving of the hall. To encourage coolness a servant began sprinkling it again with water.

"No manners, no sporting blood," Andrus observed, gulping a tumbler of brandy and water. "Mustn't expect it of a common-line officer, though."

"Colonel Andrus is out of the Guards," Sir Lovell explained with a thin smile. "And now, gentlemen, shall we resume play?"

"Right," grunted Mr. Albuoy. Apparently it was part of his game to speak as little as possible. His decisions he signaled with a beringed and none-too-clean forefinger. Alert and cautious, he was a hard man to take for much.

Around one o'clock Rob bought the deal. Immediately Sir Lovell and Andrus began a terrific piling up of bets. Five, seven hundred dollars on the turn of a card. Rob began winning by about the same margin he had previously lost. Peter sat easier on his stool and, grinning, made calculations in the small ivory-leafed notebook he carried. Sir Lovell and Andrus lost, and lost heavily; Mr. Albuoy stayed about even with the game.

At last, face gray and shiny with sweat, Andrus flung his hand onto the floor and got to his feet snarling, "The devil! I've had enough of this."

"Not my night either," Mr. Albuoy remarked. "Shall we call it a night, Sir Lovell?"

The host hesitated, glanced into Peter's book, then bit his lip as he nodded.

Sighing, Mr. Albuoy commenced counting out his chips. Peter guessed he was relieved to be out of this so cheap. Compared to the lacing the others had taken, he was as good as a winner. Mr. Albuoy raised his glass to Rob.

"Health, sir. You played well and I wouldn't have believed such a long run of luck was possible. Trust you will do me the honor of playing at my place when I get back from Surinam. Good night, all."

Sheer exhaustion robbed the winner of any sense of exultation. By the nervous tension of the last hour he was simply spent. He felt ten years older and his hands were shaking like those of a lover fresh from his mistress.

"It's going on four, Peter. Do you think—"

"Ah, so our fine Provincial friend intends to win and run?" Sir Lovell commented. "Notice, Colonel? Now that he's a winner, he don't fancy my hospitality."

Rob flushed and started to get mad, but Peter caught his eye. He had looked up at the way Sir Lovell had said "Provincial friend." Then Rob remembered.

"I only feared you might be tired, Sir Lovell. I would be flattered to enjoy a few more glasses."

Colonel Andrus looked down his thin beak of a nose and tried to look fierce, but he wasn't impressive. Only absurd and ill-bred.

"Well, I'm off directly. Never should have agreed to play with beastly Colonials in the first place. No manners. Fancy wanting to pull right out."

"I am ready to go on playing," Rob said evenly and walked to his chair. "Name your stakes and your game."

The colonel, however, merely pulled on a coat of red box cloth. "I'm not such a fool. He has some system, Lovell. I'm convinced of it. All Americans are sharp."

"Do you, by any chance, Colonel, imply that I have been cheating?" Despite his duty to Peter, Rob's figure magnified itself.

When he took two steps forward, Colonel Andrus shrugged, said coldly. "I will not go so far as to say that."

"You had better not," Rob remarked in a deadly voice.

Sir Lovell wanted to make trouble, but for some reason didn't quite dare to start anything. He motioned Rob to a chair.

"Don't mind Andrus. A chap can't lose a cool three thousand pounds and not feel it a bit. Least of all when the winner—ahem—er—is not even an Englishman." He refilled the glasses, held up his glass. "To His Majesty King George—and confusion to the American rebels! May they drown in their own blood."

"Amen!" Instantly Colonel Andrus raised his glass. He stared challengingly at Rob, but in a flash Peter called:

"To our noble King!" He drank, Rob with him.

The trap was so neatly avoided the disappointed look on Sir Lovell's face was a picture.

A rasping sound which might have been intended for a laugh issued from Colonel Andrus's throat.

"Mr. Ashton, you did not seem to relish the second half of our host's toast?"

"I didn't. I am a Virginian—and an American." For the first time it had come over him to consider himself one.

"Then you are a damned rebel!"

"No, Colonel, I'm a Whig." Rob was at pains to control himself, but he'd have given a lot to belt that sneer off Colonel Andrus's face.

"Bah! Don't equivocate."

"I am a loyal subject—" Rob meant it and Peter smiled. "As loyal as you, sir, but I fancy I hold certain rights."

Sir Lovell drawled, "In that case, Mr. Ashton, I hope you remain on Bermuda."

"Why?"

"Because the King's vengeance soon will fall with a heavy hand on the wretched, ungrateful traitors in America. Your insolent rabble will be hounded into the ground."

Colonel Andrus broke in, "If I had my way, by Gad, I'd make convicts of the women and hang every boy and man found under arms! I'd dragoon 'em till they squealed like stuck pigs! I'd burn Boston, I'd show those sniveling tradesmen not an ounce of mercy!"

"You might be able to do all that," Rob drawled, "but I reckon you will have to find better troops than General Gage has to do it."

"Better? Why, stab me, he has regulars, British regulars. Finest soldiers God ever made!"

"Maybe. But doesn't it seem they still aren't good enough? At Charles Town they ran twice. Add that to Lexington and there is three times your precious redcoats have cut and run!"

"Rob." Peter tried to intervene, but Colonel Andrus was on his feet, purple faced.

"Spoken like a true rebel! Worthy of the backbiting dogs who infest our American Colonies! Pah! Gad's my life, Sir Lovell, what else can the Ministry expect of the descendants of jailbirds, cut-purses and whores?"

Peter again threw himself into the breach. "Have you ever been to America?"

"No, but I know all about it. Beastly place," Colonel Andrus snapped. "Infested by red savages and rebels, wild beasts and a vile climate."

"If I had my way," Sir Lovell announced, "I would starve the beggars into submission. I would blockade every port, and if the King's ships were attacked, I would blow the rebel towns into brick bats."

"Leaving thousands of loyal and innocent subjects to starve and freeze?" Rob broke in. "Neither of you gentlemen know much about America. If you don't find out what is really what, you are going to lose a war."

"Lose? Bah!" Sir Lovell's fist came crashing down with such force a candle tumbled out of its holder and lay smoking among a bright litter of chips. "How can England lose? She has the greatest fleet on the seas, an army the French and Spaniards together couldn't whip. Come, come, do be rational. Take the wretched Colonials. They have no army, no navy, no powder even. We have everything. Why in Bermuda alone we have enough powder to blow half a dozen of your seaports into flinders!"

Quite deftly Peter put in, "And are the King's ships coming to take it there?"

"No," Andrus snapped, "not yet—but very soon, I fancy. I have advised the War Office we need a garrison in these beastly islands. Place hasn't been fit for a loyal subject since the 9th was ordered away—"

"Ah, it was a shame to see them go." Peter sighed. "Perhaps a battalion could be raised here in St. George's Town?"

Rob was inspired to say, "I heard something of a volunteer company recruiting at present."

"You are in error," Sir Lovell corrected. "There has been talk, but only talk. The local people are too close with the money to stand the expense. They will have to come to it though, if the West Enders keep on playing with the rebels."

Peter said, "You surprise me, Sir Lovell. Rebels at the West End?"

"Of course, but I expect they take it out in talk. They ain't troubling His Excellency over-much. Once they see what happens in America, they'll fold up quick enough."

"And plenty will happen, too!" Andrus promised. "What the American rebels need is the kind of handling Bloody

512

Jeffreys gave the Scots after Monmouth's Rebellion. Traitors must be treated for what they are. Hammer 'em, harry 'em, hang 'em! Beastly Provincials don't respond to kindness."

Following Peter's lead, Rob got to his feet again. "Do many gentlemen in England feel as you do?"

"Hundreds and thousands of them, I am proud to say!"

Rob thought, "Matt Phipp knew what he was talking of."

Sir Lovell, belching over some ham and pickles a white servant had brought in, glanced at Peter. "I say, Ashton, how much do I owe altogether?"

"Three thousand pounds."

"Bermuda?"

"Three thousand pounds sterling," Peter corrected smoothly, "or four thousand five hundred pounds Bermuda. By-the-bye, we are lodging at the Sign of the Sea Horse."

"Very well, I will send it to you in the morning."

Peter looked fixedly at Colonel Andrus. "My cousin expects eighteen hundred pounds sterling. If you wish, it can be paid at the Sea Horse, or at the Colonial Treasurer's office."

15 — COLONEL FORTESCUE'S NIECE

KATHERINE TRYON had never suspected life could contain so many delightful surprises. Every day, new and fascinating vistas became unclosed to her wondering gray-green eyes. To be mistress of such a magnificent—in her eyes—residence as Glen Duror was in itself dazzling. That she was in fact mistress in it, as well as of it, she was too practical ever to forget. Her every deed, her every thought, her every speech was dedicated to pleasing Hugh Fortescue.

What sheer rapture it was to climb into a bed boasting snowy white sheets! Imagine lying on a real mattress instead of on a bag of corn shucks. The business of lolling in bed until seven was in itself an undreamed of luxury. Imagine having all the pins she wanted—and soap! And a mirror with no flaws.

In the matter of clothes her cup of contentment brimmed. For a whole week after her arrival in St. George's the colonel strolled the town with her, selecting materials from the scanty stocks of the town merchants. Only once had there been any disagreement. Sternly, the colonel vetoed a dashing green and cerise changeable taffeta for which she yearned.

A sempstress was engaged and it was from Miss Harrington of the busy hands and busier tongue that Katie picked up many a useful item of information. She learned a great deal, too, about the people of the East End: for instance, who was making money, and who wasn't; which of the shopkeepers could be trusted; who owned a mulatto mistress and who didn't.

Yards and yards of satins, velvets, druggets, callimancoes, lutestrings and muslins passed through Glen Duror's back door and were delivered to a stuffy little room in which Miss Harrington cut and stitched. In other boxes arrived widebrimmed beaver hats, calashes, be-ribboned chips and leghorns. Also there were dainty mobcaps for house wear and bonnets for ordinary occasions.

Selection of her slippers afforded Katie particular delight. For her, shoes had always held a strange, almost sensual fascination. Never in her life had she owned more than a single pair at a time—clumsy, cowhide affairs stitched by country cobblers.

"You will need that pair of slippers," Colonel Fortescue said, indicating a pair of black satin ones, mighty pert because of scarlet heels and black rosettes.

He even bought for her a pair of high-heeled French pumps. They were sinfully expensive, Katie thought, but she was charmed with their fragility, even though they were just a little small and her ankles wobbled about to start with. Over her protests, Colonel Fortescue went on buying until she was genuinely dismayed, but the shopkeepers undulated in all directions.

"La! Uncle Hugh"—she had so practiced the term it slipped out with convincing naturalness—"you have bought enough for a harem."

"A bare beginning, my dear Kitty—" He had clung to calling her so. "That scarlet cloak with the puffed and ruffled sleeves will favor you."

It was only in setting Glen Duror to rights that Katie felt sure of herself. Inside of a week, she terminated that servile grafting from which every bachelor establishment suffers.

"'Pon my word, Kitty, you astonish me! You are capable. Very. Two pound' six off the green grocer's account. Fifteen shillings off the butcher's! Ho! Ho! Never campaigned with such a commissary officer before." He swept Katie into his arms. For all his sixty odd years, he was surprisingly strong. "Have a surprise for you tomorrow."

"Hugh, oh, really?" She dropped the "Uncle" in private. "You oughtn't to have done. You have done so much, too much, already."

"You must allow me this one last extravagance, my sweet."

He considered her, healthy, strong, and radiant in her gown of white and Lincoln green. Her hair she was wearing curled in the prevailing fashion, but without powder. Fortescue had not heeded the friseur's plea for any.

"What? Exchange gold for silver? Damn you for a poor businessman, Mounseer!"

Katie learned his personal tastes, even to trivial details. Hugh, for instance, preferred Virginian Sweet tobacco to the more popular Aronoko; he liked his morning basin of tea served lukewarm, and certain vintages with certain meats. Spices he adored, all except ginger, which he abominated. A little starch must be ironed into his ruffles, but not too much.

Her long and intimate experience with the colored race rendered her particularly adept in the direction of his cook, the serving maids and the butler. Everything in the house was kept neat without being fussy.

The colonel approved. "A chap could eat his dinner under the sideboard and shave in front of any window in the house," he declared.

No fool, Hugh Fortescue moved with discretion in launching his "niece." He began inviting male friends in to dinner. Mostly stodgy old fellows, they did not ask many leading questions. He took high delight in their praise of his Kitty's Junoesque beauty. One and all made much of the same remark.

"Gad, Hugh, how could a line of plain mugs like yours breed such a beauty?"

Chuckling, he would invariably explain Kitty's looks as coming from his brother-in-law, a famous beau of Maryland. "One of the Merrymans." He had adopted the name from Katie who remembered having served—in more ways than one—a horse fancier by that name at the Spread Eagle. Once the colonel was given a bad moment by the master of a ship.

"Merryman? Merryman? Hmm. Know the name well. A Baltimore County family. Great sportsmen, ride their foxes and wenches clean into the ground."

If anyone deduced the truth about the ménage at Glen Duror, fondness for Colonel Fortescue kept them mum. Even in his cups Colonel Fortescue never bragged about this ammunition wife as he had about her predecessors. Although he never worked it out in so many words, he liked her too much. He admired her lack of affectation, her good-humored commonsense, liked the spunky way she occasionally backed up what she felt was so. He liked, too, her grateful acceptance of whatever he chose to bestow. She never once had tried to wheedle an odd sovereign from him.

Colonel Fortescue's promised surprise arrived next evening before supper. It proved to be a slim, light-colored slave girl from Demerara.

"Zuleem is yours," he told Katie when the mulatto tiptoed in and bobbed an awkward curtsy.

"Mine!" The idea that she would ever own a nigger was unthinkable. Imagine frowsy, blowsy Katie of the Spread Eagle, owning a nigger! "Oh, no, no!" she cried hastily. "I—I couldn't, Uncle. It's not my place—"

"Damn it, girl, take this! Deed of ownership signed, sealed and delivered."

Katie for a moment was too overcome to utter a word of thanks. She just stood gazing at Zuleem. Owning something alive, she felt, lent a wonderful sense of power. Last time she'd felt a bit like this was when she bought that little trunk in Norfolk—ages ago. She had expected to go to New York with the sergeant. Even as she ran over and flung herself into Fortescue's arms, she wondered what had become of the sergeant.

When Katie noticed the mulatto was trembling, she said, "You can trot out to the kitchen. I won't use you tonight. Melissa will feed you and tell you where to sleep."

"Oh, thank you, Mistress, and de good God He bless you." Zuleem was mighty relieved. She knew she was good looking and had been thinking that his fierce-faced Englishman was buying her for—well—for what men like him generally bought light-colored gals.

"Oh, Hugh, dear Hugh, how can I ever thank you?" Tears of honest gratitude were gathering in Katie's big eyes and her delight was so patent the colonel was pleased right down to the ground.

"Stay as you are. Never try putting on airs, Kitty. Pay no

heed to the high and mighty airs of London society. Empty-headed parrots, the pack of 'em. Ruined my nephews. Made milksops of 'em."

Katie was too excited to eat much supper. To think of her having a nigger for her very own! Zuleem must be worth easy a hundred and fifty pounds—even two hundred. She would bring more still when she got trained into a real lady's maid. From the way she curtsied, Katie reckoned the mulatto must already have had some training. She would make Zuleem into a first class lady's maid, indeed she would! She would teach the wench how to sew and mend, if she didn't know already. She would make Zuleem work hard enough to keep out of mischief. Nothing was worse for a nigger than to be sitting around with time to get sorry for herself.

It was a magnificent evening. A glow silvering the crest of Government House hill prophesied moonrise. A breeze, balmy and soft as satin, stirred some palmettoes just below the veranda. From the bay lapping at the foot of the property came the clean salt smell of the ocean.

After dessert the colonel ordered an extra bottle of port and, lifting his glass, considered Katie over it.

"To beauty and brains. Rare blend."

"La, sir, you are too flattering." Rising, she swept him a curtsy, gazed up with adoring eyes.

"Hands further out from the side," he corrected. "Bend your waist more. That's it. Now, look up at me. Stay so; want to remember you like that."

Later, he asked, "Miss Harrington finished your blue ball gown?"

"Why, yes."

"Come upstairs. Want to see how it looks on you."

Long since the servants had retired to a row of "quarters" at the rear of Glen Duror so, pausing only to lock the front door, Katie ran upstairs. She took the dress into her room and brushed it free of loose threads. She understood the rite of trying on each new gown.

As a rule the colonel would come into her room, settle onto a windowseat there and, puffing gently on his pipe, watch her remove the gown she had been wearing. In the process of shifting petticoats, he would see—well—what there was to see. He almost never made a remark. Somehow the expression in his eyes was different from that of most men.

She guessed he wasn't just looking at a nude girl, at least most of the time he wasn't, but on a statue chiseled in flesh instead of marble. She had as yet no realization of how really exquisite her body was. Later it would become immortalized by the brush of Gainsborough.

When he came in tonight, he blew out the candles she had lit. Said he, "Moonlight will do. Makes you more like Juno than ever."

Purposely, she protracted the removal of the clothes she had worn down to dinner. Eventually she stepped out of her ultimate petticoat and made excuses to traverse the room several times, proud and pillar-straight in supple youthfulness. The air on her bare limbs felt cool and fine and she had powdered her body just before dressing. Under the chill her breasts stiffened. The colonel sat as if mesmerized, his pipe gone cold. Not for a moment did his gaze waver from the dim luster of her body moving on long pale legs, from the smooth lengths of silken stocking and the knots of ribbons sustaining them.

The blue ball gown remained half in and half out of its box.

16 — NEWS OF THE 63RD

FROM her window Katie noticed a ship dropping anchor in the harbour. She was a black, fast-appearing brig and flew the blue ensign at her main gaff.

She and the colonel were only half through breakfast when someone began pounding on the front door.

"Rat the scoundrel! Can't a chap bolt his eggs in peace? Tell whoever it is to wait."

But the insistence of the caller's rapping set Katie's heart pounding queerly. Had she, somehow, been traced? She cast a questioning glance at Fortescue. "Suppose I go see what he wants?"

Colonel Fortescue irritably prodded into a nest of sausages. "Better. Bloody fool will break down the door, else."

The butler was admitting a seafaring man who, when he saw Katie, swept off his round leather hat and jerked a clumsy bow.

"Servant, Ma'am. Colonel Fortescue live here?"

"Yes." Katie sighed in overwhelming relief.

"I brought letters for him." Reaching into a breast pocket, the mariner produced a pair of envelopes. One of them was large and formidable with great lobs of scarlet sealing wax.

Katie said to the butler, "Show this gentleman into the library. Will you have some beer?"

"Aye, Ma'am. 'Tis warming walking out from town."

"Eh, what's that? Letters?" With napkin still tucked into his neckband, Colonel Fortescue appeared from the dining room so fast the skirt of his yellow calico banyan billowed.

"Aye, sir, from England and America," the man called, retreating in the butler's wake.

"Har-rumph! Dash it, Kitty, where have I left my spectacles?"

Immediately she said, "They're on the sideboard," and ran to fetch the steel-rimmed, square-lensed affairs Colonel Fortescue fancied he needed.

When she returned, he was fingering the larger envelope. "Hmm! News from the War Office; about the regiment I expect. High time."

"—And the other?"

"From a friend in Boston, I judge. Now, by God, I will get at the truth of Charles Town. Won't believe militia stood against the regulars. Never have. No age of miracles nowadays."

Katie could see he was torn with indecision over which envelope to inspect first. The one from the War Office was his choice. Slipping a broad thumbnail beneath its flap, he sent the wax seals flying. Anxious, well aware of what this meant to Hugh Fortescue, Katie studied his expression. His eyes narrowed, then widened and in a series of little jerks followed the written sentences.

All of a sudden he gave a great shout. "It's mine! They accepted my offer! By Gad, Kitty, the 63rd is mine!"

"Oh, darling, I am so very glad." Katie flung arms about his neck, kissed him a resounding smack. "You wanted it so much!"

He was too excited to notice what she said and pushed her away. "Damme, girl, leave me in peace. Must find out——" He read the letter again, then from behind it produced an elaborately engraved parchment marked by many impressive looking signatures and gay with several bits of ribbon. "His

Majesty's commission as Colonel of the 63rd!" he announced, beaming.

"Oh, Hugh, I'm so happy for you."

Katie would have said more but was aware that the man who had brought the letters was watching from the library door. Suddenly an awful possibility occurred and froze her very vitals. She began going hot and cold by turns.

"Where is your regiment?" she faltered. Of course these orders in his hand were for duty in some faraway place like India, Africa, or the West Indies! As fearfully as she'd used to watch Ma Skillings's switch, she watched him search the War Office letter.

"Hum. Let's see. Let's see. Lord Barrington says the 63rd sailed from Ireland last May to—gad's my life, why it's in Boston!" He pulled the napkin from his neck. "Means active duty. Good. Want to smell powder again before I get put on the shelf. Kitty, my purse please."

Into the messenger's calloused palm Fortescue dropped two golden sovereigns. The gap-toothed seaman smiled wide as a horse collar and mechanically protested it was too much.

"Not a word," Fortescue boomed, "not a word, my lad. You have brought me fine news. Go get drunk in honor of the gallant 63rd!"

Katie's heart was tapping her heels. Although America was not distant, war conditions prevailed there. Trying hard to conceal her anguish, Katie followed the colonel into his study.

White knee breeches poked through his dressing gown when he seated himself. He was smiling in a strange, fierce sort of way.

"Now, my dear, we shall hear what Frothingham has to say. Frothingham is leftenant-colonel in temporary command of my regiment. Gad, it's good to say 'my regiment'! Looked forward to it for years. Stout fellow, Frothingham. A bit too partial to Malaga, though. Drinking is all right in barracks, but not in field. 'Tend to him when I get there."

Katie sat very still in a corner and he began to read the second communication. Very well she knew that whereas some high rankers in the British Army took their mistresses campaigning, a majority of them did not. Of course, this meant farewell. She mourned in silence. Life at Glen Duror had been much too perfect to last very long. It had been more like a wonderfully realistic dream than actuality. Still, it had been a privilege to know so fine and considerate a gentleman as Colonel Fortescue. She owed him more than anyone save Mr. David. Oh dear. Why did this news have to come so soon? Drearily, she commenced to reckon her resources. Well, anyhow, she owned Zuleem and she reckoned the Colonel would let her keep most of the clothes. She had saved a little money and would make out somehow. She always had.

The colonel's smile had vanished. Settled deeper into his wide winged chair, he was reading intently over the tops of the precious spectacles. Katie's depression deepened. Anxious lines were creeping over Hugh Fortescue's claret-tinted features. He sat up, wrinkles creasing his forehead. All at once he exploded.

"Incredible! Can't be so! Howe deserves to be cashiered! Bloody idiot ordered three frontal attacks on entrenchments!" He put down the letter, stared blankly into the fireplace. "Where to find replacements? There's the problem."

For many minutes he sat lost in thought, but in the end looked up and said, "Must face it, Kitty. Seems impossible, but the rebels whipped us. Actually, though not technically. Charley says Provincials lost only four hundred and forty men; thirty of them prisoners." He passed a hand over his eyes, drew a deep breath. "Know our casualties? One thousand and fifty-four men killed and wounded! Damned fine showing, what? Didn't flinch, though. Mark that. Men came back a third time after the rebels shot them to hell twice."

Still clutching Lieutenant-Colonel Frothingham's report, Hugh Fortescue arose, his face harsher than Katie had ever seen it. Like a sentry on guard, he began to march back and forth, seeing things not in the room, talking fast.

"Two of my captains are wounded, one dead. Better off than the 52nd though. They have three captains dead. In the King's Own every man of its grenadier company was killed or wounded; except four. Welch Fusiliers' grenadiers came out with three men uninjured. Provincials must have shot like Jaegers. Listen to this report Burgoyne wrote and showed to Frothingham."

His hand was trembling so hard Katie wondered how he could read:

—"These people show a spirit and conduct against us they never showed against the French, and everybody had judged of them from their former appearance and behavior when joined with the King's forces in the last war which has led many into great mistakes. They are now spirited by a rage and enthusiasm as great as ever people were possessed of. We must proceed in earnest or give the business up. The loss we have sustained is greater than we can bear. Small armies can't afford such losses. The troops are sent out too late. The rebels were at least two months before hand with us. I wish this cursed place was burnt."

In awe Katie watched two tears slip from the corners of Colonel Fortescue's steely eyes.

"Oh, the disgrace! British regulars slaughtered by a rabble of farmers and mechanics." He pulled himself together, summoned a wry grin. "Just my luck. What? Buy a regiment and find damned thing shot to pieces. Means work, my dear. Hard work. It is difficult to restore a proper spirit after such slaughter." As if possessed of an awesome realization, he stared at her. "The fire at Boston must have been heavier than at Minden!"

"Yes, Hugh," Katie said mechanically. "What will you do?"

"Do? Sail first vessel I can, of course."

There it was. Katie clamped down hard on her nether lip, struggled to keep her chin from quivering.

"Must sail directly. But first I must see if I can enlist a few stout fellows here. Wish to God you were a man."

"But—but I'm not—" Katie faltered.

"Eh? Eh? Of course you're not, thank God!"

Misery overwhelmed her. "I—I shall hate t-to see you go. You've been so—so awful good to me. "I—I—oh!" She burst into tears.

"Eh? See me go? What's this? Stop that damn' sniffling! We both go to Boston. Should find suitable diggings, don't you think?"

"Both go? You really aim to take me with you? Oh, Hugh —I do love you!"

At the passionate way she flung herself into his arms he blinked, patted her yellow head much as he would a good retriever's. "Dammit, Kitty, no regiment can campaign without a commissary officer."

Two weeks later they set sail for Boston.

17 — TALK BY CANDLE LIGHT

ALTHOUGH Peter Ashton was impatient to return to the West End as soon as Colonel Andrus's debt was paid, Rob would not leave St. George's Town until he had banked his winnings. Determined to play safe, he purchased drafts on London, Philadelphia and New York. It was absurd to go drifting around Bermuda carrying twenty-five thousand Spanish dollars, the sum total of his gaming profits.

This attended to, he indulged in a buying spree. For himself, an elaborately engraved gold watch complete with stylish seals; also a set of gold sleeve links. Because he had inherited his father's jewelry, he had never bought any. He felt as excited as a small boy buying a jack-knife.

At a gunsmith's he purchased a case of French dueling pistols. They were handsome and warranted to carry true for a long distance—thirty paces. They also weighed much less than the cumbersome affairs he had kept aboard the *Desdemona*.

Attracted by truly sumptuous gold tooling on the cover of Sir William Jones's "Commentaries on Asiatic Poetry," he purchased the volume for Miss Grenville. With humor in his idea, he bought for Susan a tiny chaise which might be attached to one of those goats which trimmed the lawns of Gaunt New House. For Peter he purchased another pair of pistols. They were not quite so fine as his own, so conscience-stricken, he supplemented the gift with a cabinet of fine Spanish wines.

Aunt Lydia, he reckoned, would be tickled with an enormous mantilla of fine Azores lace.

He spent half a day over his purchases and was homeward bound when the gunsmith came running up.

"Muster Ashton," said he, "my nevoo, 'e came by a pretty bit o' jewelry out o' a wreck off Tortugas. I vere a vundering if maybe you'd look at it, sir? 'Andsome young nob like you must 'ave plenty o' sweet'earts?"

"I have no sweetheart, and be damned for your insolence!"

"Vell then, maybe you've a sister, sir?" Unabashed the gunsmith shoved forward a towering Spanish comb of polished tortoise shell. It was a mighty elaborate affair and boasted many golden curlicues and scrolls tipped unexpectedly with chunks of amber and pink coral.

"Real gold, Mr. Ashton, so 'elp me. See? Yon's the acid mark I 'ad it tested wiv. It's the werry pink o' style and fit for a marchioness. It's werry fine shell, sir. Only five quid."

"Bermuda?" Rob instantly inquired.

"Yes—er—" The gunsmith's face reddened. He'd intended to ask for sterling, but Mr. Ashton had surprised him. Let it go. This was clear profit since the comb had been salvaged from a vessel wrecked off St. David's Island.

Rob deliberated. For Miss Grenville's small bronze head the comb might be a trifle top heavy, but since he had five pounds in his pocket, he bought it.

The cousins thoroughly enjoyed the return trip to Somerset Island. Peter seemed very satisfied over the results of the evening at Sir Lovell's and he was absolutely delighted with Rob's gifts. He insisted on broaching his cabinet of wines off Burnt Point so, long before the yawl weathered Spanish Point, both he and Rob were tighter than billygoats.

Off-key, they warbled:

> "Sing and quaff,
>   Dance and laugh,
>   A fig for care and sorrow;
>   Kiss and drink,
>   But never think.
>   'Tis all the same tomorrow!"

By sundown, they lay snoring gently in the yawl's cabin. Peter's quartermaster, a tactful soul experienced in such matters, allowed their nap to continue until the yawl lay alongside Gaunt New House wharf.

When he was roused, Rob still felt an exhilaration, but Peter's eyes were red and heavy.

"Goin' have bit in m'room. Goo' ni'," he mumbled and swayed off along the wharf.

" 'Pon my word!" Aunt Lydia, severe of expression, met Rob at the head of the sea steps. "Robert Ashton, I declare, you have got yourself a skin-full! A pretty state to come home in! Shame!"

The culprit smiled a broad, appealing smile. "Reckon I have, Aunt Lydia. What's good for it?"

"Tck! Tck!" One of the old housekeeper's hands clamped

down on her other wrist. "Your Papa used to find vegetables and olive oil good soberers. I will try to find some." She repeated her deprecatory clucking, tried to look severe, but suddenly laughed right out. " 'Pon my word, Robert, it relieves me to see you like this! I was fearing you had not a drop of wild blood in you." She came closer and lowered her voice. Her jet eyes sparkled. "You trimmed that Sir Lovell?"

"Yes, Aunt Lyd. Horns, hide and tallow!"

"Good. Sir Lovell is a bad 'un. I was worried for you." -

Rob put an arm about her, playfully jingled the keys on her ring.

Simpering, she pushed him aside. "La! Now I know you are fuddled! Eh? What is this?"

"Small offering, O guiding genius and wise preceptress of the Ashton clan." Bowing low, Rob presented the lace. "With my humble service, Ma'am."

It was wonderful to see the old creature's features soften. "Why, why, Rob! You bad boy! You should not have wasted good money on me. It is—it is much too beautiful for a withered body like me."

"It ain't half beautiful enough, Aunt Lyd."

As she pressed the mantilla's soft lace to her leathery old chin, the old lady's eyes filled. "You are a rascal!" she sighed. "All the Ashtons are—some more and some less. You are trying to get around me—just like your Papa." Skirts furiously rustling, she almost ran to the door and called, "Miss Grenville! Miss Grenville, come and see what Robert has brought me. Wait, call that lazy slut Betsy. Robert is hungry."

"Mr. Robert is back?" The eagerness of Andrea's tone was lost on him, but Aunt Lyd turned her parrot's profile to watch her hurry in.

"Well, Miss Grenville, maybe you would just as soon set a place? Now, Robert, go soak your head in a bucket of water. You will feel better. Your eyes look like brandied cherries. Go on, boy, do as I say!"

Though Rob yearned to prolong the novelty of this expansive mood, he swayed off. When he got back, both Aunt Lydia and Andrea Grenville were waiting by the table, expectancy in their manner.

"I was just telling Miss Grenville about your beating Sir Lovell Dandy." The old housekeeper slapped a moth miller into dust.

"I am so glad!" Andrea declared, an unfamiliar metallic ring in her voice.

Rob stared. "You know him?"

"Yes, I knew Sir Lovell." Andrea's gaze sought the red and white table cloth, came to rest upon a blue crock full of rich yellow butter. "—Before he was expelled from the Cocoa Tree Club. He is a dangerous man."

For a moment the scarlet lips tightened and Rob glimpsed the hard, bright creature Andrea Grenville must once have been.

"You should have warned Robert!" Aunt Lyd reproved.

A brittle little laugh escaped her. "Sir Lovell may have reformed. His disgrace was fearful. His oldest friends cut him dead. To let the past bury the past is a good motto. And now, suppose you tell us how the play went?"

Eagerly, both women listened to an account, punctuated by mouthfuls of salad, bread and milk. When he came to Colonel Andrus's remarks concerning America, Rob raised an eyebrow at Andrea.

"What he said about people in England feeling as he did— is that right?"

She nodded. "Many people, too many, know nothing and care less about the American Colonies and what happens to them. Only thing interests them is indulging themselves. Believe me, I know."

More snatches of what Sir Lovell and Colonel Andrus had said returned. For the first time Rob began to believe they had meant what they said about hanging all Americans found under arms.

Aunt Lyd said quietly, "I am an English woman and getting to be an old one, so perhaps I talk sense. I say it is a crying shame our governing class won't move out of England. If they did, they would not talk such tottle in Parliament." The old woman's bright jet eyes became tense. "While we are being serious, Robert, let me say this. The Tories here are much more powerful than Peter or that cocksure Henry Tucker believe. If they had a real leader in St. George's Town, every last Whig would get driven out. Do not provoke them. The armed might of England is back of them. There! I have said my say, so will leave before you start arguing." In a vigorous gesture she captured the milk pitcher. "Good night to you."

When Andrea also gathered her skirts and started to rise, Rob caught her wrist. "Please, I want to talk."

"If you wish, Mr. Ashton, I will stay for a little." She flashed him a quizzical, faintly derisive look.

Relaxing, he plunged into eager speech. "How do you account for all this luck I have?"

"Is it so unusual?"

"It is. I never gambled 'til I came down here."

"What!"

"That's gospel." He couldn't help adding, "I have been studying the cards. I have won——" He broke off. The liquor was leading him to talk out of turn.

"You were saying?"

"Why—well, I reckon it's around twenty-five thousand Spanish dollars."

Andrea picked up a bread crumb and commenced rolling it into a ball. "I don't suppose you will believe me, but in one sitting I won fifteen thousand sterling—seventy-five thousand dollars—from 'Jemmy Twitcher,' nowadays known as Lord Sandwich."

In the candle light she saw Rob's eyes grow round. "Seventy-five thousand dollars!"

"More or less——"

"What—what happened to it?"

Andrea held up a hand, blew an imaginary object from its palm. "I lost it. Just as you will lose this money you have won. Your luck will fade."

"But it isn't all luck."

"Is it not?"

"No. As I told you, I have studied the cards," Rob insisted. "I have learned how to gauge my opponents."

"I thought I had, too," Andrea remarked dryly. "I lost everything. For that reason I am become a governess."

Rob looked his sympathy, but was not convinced. "Isn't it possible that my system might be better? When money can be made like this, a man is a bloody fool to work like a galley slave."

"Is he?" Gently Andrea's fingertips commenced to rub one another. Said she in a soft voice, "In all this world I have five pounds, Mr. Ashton, but I will wager—at two to one—that your luck has broken, that I can beat you at cribbage." When she looked across the table, wild little glints were dancing in her look. "Have you played the game?"

"Many times." He chuckled. "It was at cribbage I took Jack Dill over the jumps."

"All the better. Will you wait?"

"Yes, but look here, I wouldn't enjoy winning your money—"

"Wouldn't you? La, sir, what makes you so certain you will win it?"

Before he could stop her, her skirts went swishing off down the corridor. Because of the way she had put things, he reckoned he was obligated to play, but he would find a way of returning her money.

Shortly after midnight Andrea Grenville pulled her pegs out of the counting board and slipped one hundred and fifteen dollars into a pocket of black silk.

"You see?" From beneath the wide wing-like brows her eyes regarded him. Smiling sweetly, she began collecting the cards.

"Can't understand it," Rob grumbled. "I almost had you."

"'Almost' is as good as a mile, sir," she mocked. "I am right. You have reached the crest of your lucky wave. If you keep on, you will lose. And lose, and lose!"

In the white walled dining room it was very still, cool, too. Down on the beach a turtle in the pen made a flopping noise. The tree frogs kept up their monotonous piping.

"Wait!"

Andrea, in turning away, halted, looked back over her shoulder. Never had she looked handsomer and faint color showed in cheeks tanned by the sun a golden brown.

"Suppose we play just one more game?" He didn't want her to go. Besides, he reckoned he could beat her this time. He hated to get trimmed by a woman.

"Very well, if you wish—but not for money." Her tone was impish.

He shuffled the cards between brown fingers still showing many calluses. "Then for what?"

"Why, why—a forfeit. Whoever loses must pay the other a forfeit."

They played harder than before. The pegs, scarlet and white, drifted the length of the board, then started on the home stretch, neck and neck. Andrea's eyes sparkled and her lips parted a little.

Rob counted his hand first. "Out!" he almost shouted. "Forfeit!"

As Andrea arose, out along her cheekbones the glow deepened. "Well, sir, to what am I condemned?"

He got up, skirted the chair Aunt Lydia had left and, taking her in his arms, kissed her—very soundly.

"La!" she murmured gazing at him a trifle breathlessly. "The bucks of Whitehall could visit America to advantage."

"Please don't say that," he begged. "I hate the word—Whitehall! David used to talk about it."

Her iridescent mood vanished. "I think I understand. Good night, Rob."

"Good night—Andrea."

He stood quite still. "Rob," that's what she had called him. He must say something more.

Before he found his voice she was at the door. "You had me, cold. I still can't see how you lost that last hand."

"Can't you?" Soft laughter drifted back from the corridor.

18 — COLONEL TUCKER RETURNS

THEY were all eating dinner and, despite Andrea's admonitions, Susan was chattering like a young magpie when a wild thudding of hoofs came from the driveway. They all could hear flying pebbles rattle in the underbrush. When it was reined in, the horse snuffled, blowing the dust and sweat from its nostrils.

A voice called out, "Where's Mr. Ashton? Well, never mind—tell him he's to come straight away to the Grove. Colonel Henry is back!"

"It's Jim Fowle," Peter said. Reluctantly he pushed away his plate, pulled the napkin from his neck and arose. Already the rider's hoof beats were diminishing in the direction of the Gilberts' place. "Jim don't fancy moving fast any more than me. Come along, Rob."

Andrea half rose, eyes on Rob's. She started to say something but flushed and resumed her place.

After considerable bawling and shouting saddle horses were got ready. Peter all the while was stamping and swearing with impatience. Jim Fowle must have ridden on to

Harvey's because, as Zacksee ran up leading a pair of sturdy, unimaginative horses, excited cries rose in that direction.

In the distance someone had begun to blow on a conch shell. Three blasts, then two short ones. Making a doleful wailing, another conch answered the first.

Peter heaved himself up into the saddle and the beast grunted under his weight. Gathering the reins, he said, "What Colonel Henry Tucker has to tell us means make or break for us West Enders."

His cousin must be terribly anxious, Rob realized; few things could have induced him to ride at a gallop. But he was galloping now, his fat bottom slap-slapping hard against the saddle.

They met other riders traveling the road to Somerset Bridge: Joseph Gilbert, Richard Jennings, Thomas Dickinson and Sam Harvey. All of them, Rob knew, had signed that petition to the Congress in Philadelphia. They looked plenty worried—just as worried as Peter. Without looking much to the right or left, they plugged along towards the Grove, Colonel Henry Tucker's property in Southampton Parish.

"Guess the delegation came back on her," someone said, pointing.

Rob saw a small rakish sloop, lying in the lee of a row of reefs. Beyond her the stripped skeletons of two whales lay like wrecked ships on a sandy beach. They gave off a powerful stench but sea birds were quarreling loudly over shreds of meat adhering to the massive yellow-white bones. Further away still, and shadowed by heavy yellow-brown smoke from a try works, stood the Flemish Wreck House. It had, Jennings remarked, been built almost entirely from the timbers of a vessel lost among the boilers opposite.

In white, sneeze-provoking clouds dust rose. It powdered the faces and coats of the riders but none of them slowed down. Somewhere ahead a church bell commenced a slow, measured alarm.

All the time more carriages and riders turned in from side roads.

"What's the news?" one called. "We going in with the Colonies?"

The scene began to remind Rob of that day the Lexington fight news had reached Norfolk. Looking around, he recog-

nized grimly expectant expressions. By the time the caval-
cade from Mangrove Bay had reached a private road leading
into Colonel Tucker's property it numbered about thirty people. More West Enders were waiting, hot and impatient,
before Grove House. The property, Peter pointed out, lay
in a rich, fertile little valley well sheltered from hurricanes.

Immediately the cousins dismounted and led their animals
to a wall-less shed already crowded with horses. Slaves were
busy trying to keep the fly-tortured creatures from biting
and kicking each other. Subdued greetings arose.

"The boys brought back an answer?"

"I ain't heard. What about it, Harry?"

"Ain't heard neither."

"I have! The Congress is going to help us."

"If they do, it will cost us a pretty penny. Thum Yankees
are closer than the bark on a cedar."

They made way for Peter and Rob—after all, they were
Colonel Tucker's relations by marriage. It was fine to gain
the cool, dim interior of the house. Surrounded by prominent
Whigs, three members of the delegation were talking in
undertones. Many faces Rob found unfamiliar. There were
men who had traveled west from the middle parishes of
Warwick, Paget and Pembroke. One delegate, it appeared,
had gone cautiously to spread the news in St. George's
Town.

There was no denying that Colonel Henry Tucker was
both handsome and impressive of bearing. Taller by a head
than the average, his large, well-formed features and shrewd
but kindly gray eyes could easily be seen. The leader of the
West End faction, though all of sixty, stood arrow straight
and in his well cut coat of mulberry velvet made as distinguished a figure as Rob had ever seen.

Gravely, yet with cordiality, he acknowledged the introduction. "It affords me the greatest of pleasure to welcome
a Virginian to my home. Mrs. Tucker and I shall hope to see
more of you, Mr. Ashton."

The buzz of voices in the stable yard and before the house
was growing steadily louder.

Henry Tucker of Bridge House sidled forward. "Well,
Colonel, I guess about all who are coming are here. Are you
ready to tell them what the Congress said?"

Weary lines momentarily aged Colonel Tucker's countenance. He nodded and, after draining a half mug of beer, stepped out onto a long, low veranda.

"Hi, Colonel!" "Nice trip, Harry?" "How did you make out?" Respect combined with affection was in the greetings.

"It's uncommon fine to be home again," Colonel Tucker declared, shaking hands in all directions. "Is everybody checked and accounted for?" he asked. "Won't do to have eavesdroppers."

Sam Harvey told him, yes, all the niggers were down by the stables.

"Very well, then."

The buzzing of flies, the stamp and snort of the horses in the background became audible in an ensuing hush. It suggested that silence which precedes the reading of a verdict at an important trial.

Colonel Tucker told his listeners that the delegation's westward passage had been swift, had required only eleven days. On July 11th the delegation had presented its petition to the Congress. He had had several interviews with a Mr. Robert Morris and a Mr. Benjamin Franklin, men high in the affairs of the Colonies.

Speaking in low, carrying tones, Colonel Tucker went on to say that he had pictured to the Congressional committee Bermuda's difficult situation; her willingness to coöperate in a general embargo on trade with England and the West Indies.

"I told 'em," Colonel Tucker said, "we would agree to ship nothing that the Congress didn't approve. I also told 'em we would furnish the Colonies with salt, ships, and would help American vessels touching here."

A breathless voice put the query everyone was dreading. "Well, what did they say to that?"

Colonel Tucker hesitated, spread his hands. "They said they sure enough didn't want us to side with the Crown. At the same time, Mr. Franklin made it clear it was all right for us to stay, outwardly loyal subjects." Politician-like, he glanced about quickly, trying to gauge the general reaction.

"That's good." "That's smart." "True." The cries sounded devoid of sarcasm.

"Mr. Franklin promised the Congress will exempt us from the embargo—"

"Hurrah!" A great resounding shout of relief beat against the front of the house, made horses shy; from under the veranda a pair of dusty mongrels appeared and scuttled off, tails between their legs.

"By God, that's fine! Hurray for America!"

In the shade of the porch, Colonel Tucker mopped his face. "They said they would send us plenty to eat."

Again a shout rose to the treetops.

"—But—" The cheering died with suddenness.—"Before this happens, we have got to enter into an understanding."

It was plain Colonel Tucker now had to come to an unpleasant point. "Until such an agreement is reached, we will be included in the embargo."

Peter blinked. "What does that mean?"

"Mr. Robert Morris says we must provide the Congress with statistics about our imports and exports; that covers food and merchandise."

"What the hell business is it of theirs?" "Why should the damned Yankees want to know that?"

"Gentlemen, gentlemen!" Colonel Tucker raised patient hands. "Right now you had better learn that in the Congress Maryland, Virginia and the Carolinas have just as much say as Massachusetts, New Hampshire, and Rhode Island. Sam, now I'll answer your question. The Congress wants those figures so they can make sure none of you bright fellows will re-export supplies they send for us!" He smiled a little. "I suspect this bit of news is breaking some hearts right now." He was right, Rob saw. Many had been busy mentally computing returns from re-shipping contraband to St. Kitts, Jamaica and the Bahamas.

"When they asked for proof of our friendship, I promised we would go on shipping salt. They've got to have it. They know it, too. Then Mr. Franklin pointed out a loophole in the embargo."

"What loophole?" Richard Jennings wanted to know.

"The Colonies will pass the cargo of any ship bringing in arms and ammunition! Mr. Morris admitted the Provincial armies are devilish short."

A thoughtful silence settled on the crowd.

"There's the whole story," the Colonel concluded. "Exemption and food against salt, arms and statistics. Now, I guess we'd better all go home and think this over." He turned to Henry Tucker. "When can we have another meeting?"

"Today is Tuesday, July 25th," stated the parchment-complexioned master of Bridge House. "Is Thursday all right?"

"—At your place?"

Henry Tucker shook his head. He was a careful man. "No, it wouldn't do."

"Where then?"

"You can meet aboard the *Daphne*," suggested a man on the edge of the crowd. "She won't be sailing until Friday." He wore expensive blue serge and spoke with a Pennsylvanian accent. He was a sharp-nosed, wide-eyed chap with burnt powder grains speckling one side of his face. His expression was aggressive, but thoughtful, too, and his eyes were suggestive of infinite patience. His name, somebody said, was Mr. Peacock. He was a delegate from Philadelphia to the Continental Congress.

Henry of Bridge House looked his gratitude. "Thank you, Mr. Peacock. We will meet aboard the *Daphne* in Eli's Harbour."

The meeting broke up, resolved itself into small knots of neighbors headed in the same direction. By twos and threes they rode off below cedars towering over the driveway. Road dust, raised by hurrying hoofs, caught sunbeams and converted them into long, slanting shafts of gold.

The West Enders were anxious to get home. Digging up statistics would be a job, but they would have to, unless they preferred starving. Nobody believed Governor Bruere's promise that the Governor of Virginia would keep the Islands well fed.

Long ago Henry of Bridge House had learned from Rob that Lord Dunmore retained but weak threads of power Everybody knew how the patriots had driven him from Williamsburg, forcing that hot-headed Scot to govern as best he might from a man-of-war.

It warmed Rob's heart to hear Mr. Peacock talk in such homelike way. While they jogged towards Eli's Harbour, h asked questions. Among other things, he was told that th Congress had appointed General Washington to be Comman der-in-Chief over all the Provincial armies.

"You Virginians have reason to be proud," Mr. Peacoc declared.

When the main road forked towards Haydon's Bay, th congressional delegate drew rein. Said he, warmly shakin hands, "It has been fine to talk to a fellow American. W must meet again soon."

534

Thursday, July 27, 1775

Gaunt New House

Today vast Excitement over Intelligence brought by
Colnl H. Tucker. The American Congress seems dispos'd
to grant exactly nothing for nothing, which Dismays
our good Bermudians. (God knows why it should.)
Everywhere a tremendous chit-chat over Embargoes,
La! Did Andrea once in Bristol declare the word to have
a pleasing sound?

Most Resentment rises because of a Demand for Sta-
tisticks. This day behind lock'd doors St. George Tucker,
younger son of the Colnl enter'd into long consultation
with Mr. Peter A.

Cannot fatham Robert A. He seems indifferent to all
politicks though he is most certainly of a Democratickal
Disposition. Perchance he is playing a deep Game.

Was in the Summer House scanning my Arithmetick
book with desperation. Alas! The empty vauntings concerning my skill in that Science have undone me. Must
study in earnest if I am properly to instruct my Pupil.
Was attempting a Problem in fractions and finding
them fractious, (La! My first pun this Week.) when I
descried Robert A. standing at the entrance. Have not
blushed so since, petticoats turned up, I was flogged before the School for a theft of Mrs. Pettigrew's comfits.

On noting the Arithmeticker and divers sheets of Paper cover'd with unhappy Calculations, Robert A.
frowned. Had he discover'd me purloining his Purse, he
could not have appear'd more Alarm'd.

What's this, he inquired, and when I did confess my
Ineptitude at Reckoning, he burst into such vast Roars
of laughter, I was cover'd with confusion.

Pray tell me, Mistress Grenville,—plague take the
rascal, he will not again employ the tenderer Term—
can you compute the Interest of £6-7-3 at 5½ per-
centum?

Replied that, perchance, I might do so at the end of a

Week. Thought him Zany when he queried whether I understood the Nature of a Drawback.

Do you understand the operations of a Bill of Exchange?

I told him no, with Wonderment increasing.

Do you understand what is meant by receiving Goods on Consignment?

When, crimson, I again did confess my Ignorance, he looked pleas'd as if I had made him the Compliment of a New Surtout. Rat the fellow! He is beyond my understanding.

Tartly I told him I had never design'd to make a merchant of myself. Looking at me prodigious queer, he ask'd what most in life I preferr'd.

'Twas on my tongue to give him the light Answer, but I said, A little Musick, a little Dancing, and the Management of a child. To shape a young Mind as a gardener clips box Bush is vastly intriguing.

You dislike Ledgers?

Prodigiously, I declared and confess'd that I have added six to six and made fourteen of it.

He laughed and vowed I had learn't the manner of these Islanders.

Seating Himself beside me he made bold to seize my Hand. In anticipation of Advances more worth of reproof, I offer'd no objection. For many minutes he discours'd upon his past Life. Alack! Without meaning it, he near broke poor Andrea's Heart. He has toiled so hard and has come by so little from it. Among other matters he confided what had mischanc'd between him and David. A sorry affair. Fear the two will never become reconcil'd but shall devote my best efforts to encompass it.

R. intrudes upon my Thoughts most persistent. Must discourage him. Neither he nor poor Andrea have yet determined the true Course of their Lives. Yet his hand on mine did lend a sense of Peace. La! 'Tis months since I have plagued this Journal with Inner Reflections, yet cannot give over. R. is like David in Frankness, cleanliness and Health. His humours are slower yet surprising witty. He is shrewder than even Peter A. suspeckts. Am relieved he has given over heavy Drinking. Can it be the late toast of Tunbridge Wells has a good

Effeckt upon him? What R. intends with his gaming Money he will not vouchsafe. Greatly fear he will continue. Alas! How steep lies the downward Path in that direction.

Find Life in the Bermudas increasing tiresome. The Islanders are so wrapp'd up in their petty Affairs, and in general display such Selfish Spirit am loath to tarry here longer than is requir'd to earn a passage to America. Shall endeavour to lure my sweet R. into another Game of Forfeits. Another Time must lose more Subtly.

Friday, July 28th, 1775

Gaunt New House

Am all of a Tizzy and a-quake with Mirth. Tonight my sweet R. has made me a Compliment of a huge Spanish comb. It is a hideous Objeckt and worst of all in hair the colour of Mine. But it must have cost him Dear and the tho't of me was touching. Express'd the warmest gratitude and tho't poor Andrea looked prodigious sweet and fetching in her new blue Gown (purchas'd with a part of my Winnings) but he would no more than kiss my Hand. Oh, rat the Fellow!

R. has begun my instrucktion in Shawnee—an unearthly language quite compos'd of Grunts and Growls. He vows I do well at it. Can but conjure a view of Andrea all Paint and Feathers addressing the Savages of North America. Perhaps I shall become a Red Indian Queen! La! When I did inquire, R. declared Indian women wear but beads, a Kilt of tanned Hides and a silver nose-bob! Would a nose-bob become me? La! I fancy Jemmy Twitcher and some of his fellow rakehells would pay a pretty guinea to see me with one.

But enough of these idle Ramblings. Will sleep now if my sweet R. does not intrude himself upon my Drowsing Moments.

Because the sky clouded over and the atmosphere was like a sweaty hand on his brow, Rob opened the living room windows. He lingered there, watching distant flares of lightning and listening to thunder sullenly rumbling out to sea. Caught up on his sleep by now, he was increasingly restless, more like his old self.

It was amazing to discover how rapidly his concept of Peggy receded to the distant, respected area of his mother's memory. For one thing, he had recovered the habit of thinking in the singular.

Sprawled on a windowseat with a Betty lamp casting its yellow rays, he resumed his perusal of a year old copy of the "London Magazine." It contained an article by some naval officer, a Sir Somebody with a whole alphabet following his name like a string of kittens after a cat. His "Remarks on the Management of Heavy Ordinance" were sticky going.

A regret kept pecking at his mind. Why the devil hadn't he kissed Andrea that time he gave her the comb? He reckoned it was because he didn't want to risk getting her mad at him. She seemed to better every situation simply by being there and no two women were wound with the same key. Must have led quite a life in London. God in Heaven! Imagine winning seventy-five thousand dollars in a single night. Must have got kicked around somehow. There was such a depth of understanding in her humorous, hazel eyes and her viewpoint was as sharp, bright and gallant as a drawn sword. Why, in some things she talked and thought very like a man.

He was finding it damned dull just sitting around, but what to do? In any direction a fellow looked he sighted nothing but trouble and danger in the offing. He reckoned he didn't object to personal danger more than the next fellow, but he had always hated fighting. It was such a waste of good energy. He fixed vacant eyes on a painting of a vessel which purported to be the *Adelphi*.

Right now he reckoned he had about broken even with the game of life. Without his being able to do much about it, Fortune had handed him a series of body blows, but now she was stroking him behind the ears like a pet cat. Cards had poured wealth into his lap; also without his having much to say about it. Therefore—he had always been fond of weighing the pros and cons—he reasoned he stood about even.

What was the next play going to be?

He got to thinking about Sir Lovell who had been expelled from the Cocoa Tree for cheating in a duel; about snide Colonel Andrus who, because he'd bought a commission in the Horse Guards, reckoned God was a blood relation. When he thought of the way those two had talked about what ought to be done to the Colonies, he got warm under the collar. It wasn't nice to think what Virginia would be like if they got their way. Open ports bombarded, seacoast towns burnt, Whigs hanged right and left. If the Ministers got their way, what would happen to commerce? Rob reckoned it would die and, like Farish said, the East India people would take over America. Well, that wouldn't do. They'd bleed Tidewater whiter than the factors already had. For the first time in months he remembered George Leavitt and Sandys's foreclosing on Powhatan. Besides, was it right for a country like England already rich and powerful to—

Something went *tink!* against a windowpane above him. He turned more quickly than he would have a year ago. Because the Betty lamp's glare was in his eyes, it took him a few seconds to discern a figure standing just outside a fan-shaped area of lighted lawn.

"Who is that?" he demanded sharply.

"Peacock," replied a cautious voice. "Been waiting for a talk. Can you come out?"

Rob's breathing quickened. "Reckon so. What's up?"

Mr. Peacock, however, was already retreating across the lawn. Rob, feeling a bit foolish, climbed out through the window. What ailed the Philadelphian to come mousing about at this hour, and so secretly? Thunder was muttering louder than ever and brighter flashes of light cast motionless cedars and palms into silhouette.

On the sea steps Mr. Peacock stood waiting. Said he without a by-your-leave or anything, "We will go down to the beach."

Rob demurred, asked, "What do you want?"

"Just come along."

The Congressional delegate led along the shore to a log half buried on the beach and lying in the lee of some nets drying on a rack.

"Since I don't dare trust a Bermudian," Peacock began, "I—"

"You can trust my cousin," Rob interrupted sharply.

"No doubt, Mr. Ashton, no doubt. Please don't get angry. You see, my ships once traded with these Islands. I know the local people better than you—or ought to," Peacock added grimly.

"What do you want with me?"

"You are an American," the Pennsylvania owner replied simply, "so I hope you can be trusted. God knows, we have plenty of sneaks and spys in America."

"Well?" Rob was irritated by the other's delay in coming to the point.

"You stand in with the Bermudians, don't you? I hear you do."

"I suppose I do. Why?"

Through the cloud muffled moonlight Rob could see Mr. Peacock's eyes white in the dark of his lean, powder-stained features. "I am asking you to lend me a hand."

"Why should I? What is the Congress to me?"

In the dim light he could see Mr. Peacock sit straighter. "The Continental Congress is the mouthpiece of a people fighting for their rights, fighting to maintain their self-respect."

"—And trade," Rob supplemented.

"—And trade," the Philadelphian agreed with a bitter little laugh. He was considering Rob more carefully now. The Virginian's last observation had both surprised and pleased him, it seemed. "Well, Mr. Ashton, the United Provinces need help, every bit of help they can get. Probably you have not heard that Parliament is bent on hiring Russian troops, barbarous savages, to beat us into submission? If they fail in that, they are sure to buy troops from old George's German cousins. Mercenaries shipped to America! How would you like to see them let loose in Norfolk?"

In the gloom Rob's jaw tightened. "Why, that—that can't be so! The King wouldn't send foreigners to kill his own subjects."

"Wouldn't he? Wait and see. They say in London it is not worth wasting good English lives on a pack of mangy Provincial rebels." Mr. Peacock smiled a sardonic smile. "No after what happened at Bunker's Hill."

"But Russians! Germans! The King would never allow his Ministers—"

"No? Recruiting parties are being organized in Hesse-Cassel. In Hanover."

Here was something new, infinitely disturbing. Rob asked, "How do you know this is so?"

"I am not on the Pennsylvania Committee of Safety for nothing!" reminded Mr. Peacock impressively. "Let me go on. These mercenaries will be the worst scrapings of Europe's jails. Have you ever had anything to do with Germans?"

"Not much. Only the ones in your Province."

"Well, I have. I have fought beside them more than once. Let me tell you this. The best of them are naturally cruel; not hot cruel like a Spaniard. It's in their blood. And that is not all."

Mr. Peacock slapped a mosquito from his neck, looked about quickly because not far offshore a school of mullets chased by a shark were leaping, causing loud splashes.

"The British fleet in America is to be heavily reinforced. Unless America submits, the King's Ministers have threatened to bombard and burn every port along the Atlantic seacoast!"

Rob sighed. It was uncanny to hear Sir Lovell and Andrus repeated almost word for word. "That doesn't sound encouraging."

"But wait. There is worse still to come. We have been prohibited any foreign trade. That means the end of our French, Russian, and Swedish trade—not to mention commerce with the Dutch and in the Mediterranean."

Shoulders hunched forward, Mr. Peacock considered the play of lightning on the silvery gray and empty harbour. "Yes, Mr. Ashton, our point of view in America is radically different from that of a year ago. Lord North's stupid threats and the King's indifference to all our petitions have made the change. Do you know that a good many people are talking independence?"

Rob shook his head, said slowly, "They will never win it. Out here it's easy to see why."

"On the contrary, Mr. Ashton, we have a chance, a good chance," Mr. Peacock declared so earnestly he carried a measure of conviction. "For one thing, we feel we have the right on our side. In Pennsylvania many thousands of us would sooner die than become slaves to the India Company."

"That goes for Virginia, too, I reckon."

"You see how it is? We must fight because we can't do anything else."

Rob shifted on the log, caught up a handful of sand and absently poured it from one hand into the other.

Mr. Peacock went on talking. "I don't know if it has occurred to you that we have a strong ally in the Ministry. North and Germain and the rest are hopelessly ignorant of America and they won't listen. They won't learn. Best of all, they won't work! The only real interest of most of them is the feathering of their nests. The King is stubborn about dismissing them, so their dishonesty and stupidity will be worth many regiments to us. Such men should not be too hard to defeat."

Mr. Peacock peered along the shore, then at the barren reef of Ireland Island briefly revealed by lightning. "But to even begin to fight, we must have powder."

"Do you know there is powder on this island?" Rob queried suddenly.

"How much?" Mr. Peacock's voice was eager, sharply anxious.

"A lot of it."

"Are you sure? How do you know?"

"An officer of the Governor's family said so the other night. He was hopping mad, so I guess he didn't invent it."

"How much?"

"He didn't say. But from the way he spoke, it was a lot."

"Can you find out?"

"I reckon so. I might even find out where it's stored."

The Pennsylvanian's cleanly-chiseled head inclined twice. "I know where it should be. What I must learn is whether it is still there."

"Why are you so curious about this?"

"The Pennsylvania Committee wants that powder, has *got* to get it. And to seize it, I must have dependable help. I can't rely on Bermudians to do the job; they will argue and waste time until somebody catches on. Again, I am not sure how many of them would risk their hides in a raid. They know St. George's Town swarms with Tories. That is why I have come to you."

Rob deliberated. Now that he had money again, it would be sheer nonsense to get himself tossed into jail over a fool political gamble. Then Matt Phipp's words re-occurred so forcefully he could see the grubby interior of John Holt's press room.

"What you want isn't important any longer. No one can live a wholly private life these days. Whether we want it or not, we are becoming small parts of a new theory of government."

He ended by saying, "What do you want me to do?"

"Find out for sure which of these West Enders really want to help America. Most of them are only figuring to save their own skins—not that I blame them for it."

"I will do that," Rob said, but without enthusiasm.

"Very well." Mr. Peacock acted as if he had been expecting an acceptance all along. "Now listen, and *keep this to yourself!* Somewhere on her way here is a sloop out of Philadelphia; Robert Morris's *Lady Catherine*. George Ord may be a hard-a-weather captain, but he is also a fine navigator." Mr. Peacock's forefinger tapped Rob's knee. "Aboard the *Lady* are forty men—hand picked by the Pennsylvania Committee. We didn't dare send a larger craft for fear of her being noticed off Bermuda." Rob listened in growing curiosity. "Ord is coming to carry off the powder you mentioned. Colonel Tucker's son, St. George, told Peyton Randolph about it in Virginia. Randolph told Robert Morris."

The Pennsylvanian fell silent as if revolving something in his mind.

"When will this sloop appear?" Rob still poured sand from one hand to the other.

"Within a few days—three at the most. No sooner I hope, because I haven't made the progress I had expected," Mr. Peacock confessed. "You, of course, understand that the *Lady Catherine* must do her work and clear out promptly."

Mr. Peacock, now that he had committed himself, talked faster, alert hard eyes boring steadily into his companion's face. Rob received an impression that it would not be safe to toy with such a man.

"You and I must get everything ready for Ord. We must make certain the powder is still there and how heavily it is guarded. I entertain serious suspicions of several of the biggest-talking Whigs around here. If you can discover who can be trusted all the way, Mr. Ashton, you will have performed a great and inestimable service to America. It's your country, you know."

543

"I will do what I can. Tell me, how do you feel about Colonel Tucker?"

In the darkness Mr. Peacock hesitated, rubbing his powder-blued cheek. "Hanged if I understand just where he fits. I am sure of only one thing about him. He will hesitate a good while before he will do anything downright treasonable —such as stealing powder for use against the King. Colonel Tucker has fine ideals and a keen mind; therefore I don't envy him these days." He pulled out a snuff box and spilt a little on his thumbnail. "What's your opinion on this other Henry Tucker—the one living near Somerset Bridge?"

Rob grinned. "What is powder bringing in Philadelphia?"

"Around one and one half Spanish dollars a pound," came the instant reply. "Why?"

"At $1.50 a pound, you can rely on Henry Tucker. I was wondering why he's been scratching about so."

"I don't understand you."

"He has bought eight half barrels within the last ten days. He must have learned the Philadelphia price."

"Yes. I told him."

"There is your answer. With a profit like that to be cleared, he will never back down."

Mr. Peacock cleared his throat and spat, making a little black mark at their feet on the sand. "That is encouraging. The sort of thing I need to know. Oh, one thing; we are going to need eight or ten small boats because the *Lady* daren't stand in too close to St. George's Town. One slip would spoil everything."

Mr. Peacock's belt squeaked as he got to his feet. "Let you know as soon as I hear from our ship. Night." Jerking a nod, he started down the beach, square-toed shoes swishing over the sand.

21 — THE CAROLINIANS

ON the morning of August 12th a strange vessel appeared off Somerset. Since she was schooner rigged and big enough for a British cruiser, alarm in the West End was lively until the stranger backed her topsails and sent a boat ashore. To the vast relief of Peter, the Gilberts and the Harveys, the stranger proved to be the *Charles Town and Savannah Packet* out of South Carolina. John Turner was her master and said he would like to meet the Whig leaders of the vicinity.

Accordingly, at sundown there gathered on the beach a deputation headed by Henry Tucker of Bridge House. Explanation of the schooner's arrival was simple, and afforded a curious but plausible coincidence. Another son of Colonel Tucker was resident in Charles Town, South Carolina, Captain Turner declared, and had mentioned the King's powder to the Committee of Safety. Forthwith, the *Packet* had been dispatched in search of it. Thomas Tudor Tucker was a great fool, Turner complained bitterly, to have so seriously underestimated the difficulty of a coup.

Mr. Peacock sat in the background saying not a word. It was plain he was trying to figure how to take this unexpected intrusion.

Henry Tucker directed a shrewd glance at him. "Well, sir, and where is this precious vessel you have been telling us about? If she were here, the business could be done in a hurry."

"Hanged if I know," grunted the Philadelphian. "She is two days overdue."

Rob, present at Mr. Peacock's insistence, only listened and, watching the faces, noted uneasiness in the manner of one Joseph Jennings. He acted as committeeman from the Flatts, a village situated on the North Shore near the center of the archipelago. His curiosity concerning the number of men and cannons carried by the *Packet* Rob thought was a trifle persistent.

"Could you keep your ship lying off and on for a few days?" Henry Tucker wanted to know.

Turner, burned almost black by the sun, squirted tobacco juice onto the sand, hooked big thumbs into a belt supporting a brace of boarding pistols. "Why, seh, I reckon I could tarry maybe three days mo'. Then I must git for Cha'les Town or mah owners will keel-haul me. This hyer venture is putting them gentlemen out of pocket. Yes, seh, it sho'ly is." He hitched his belt higher. "Still, I hanker to singe that damn' governor's nose. When we was layin' in St. Geo'ge's last week, he sho'ly made life a nuisance. From the way he kep' watch on the *Packet,* I reckon he maybe smelled a nigger in our woodpile."

"You don't say so!" Peter cried, looking very disturbed.

"Yes, seh, I do say so! That revenoo boat of his was always triflin' 'round."

Henry Tucker's expression grew graver. Rob could tell he, too, didn't like this news.

Peter said, "You're sure you didn't hint around about the powder?"

Captain Turner grinned. "No, seh. Warn't no need. Every nigger in town knows it's stowed in a garden back o' the Governor's Mansion."

Joseph Jennings coughed, ran a finger around the inside of his stock. "Boys, I don't like the sound of Bruere's being so suspicious. If you stop and think it over, this is pretty risky business. If we was to get caught stealing the King's powder, it will mean the gallows. That's treason."

The dumpy little man who owned the *Mercury* picked up his hat. "Joe's right. Me, I'd ruther starve a while than hang."

Henry Tucker's tongue crept out to wet his lavender-hued lips. "Old George Bruere would surely love to get our tails in the door, and that's a fact."

Next day the whole situation changed. Late in the afternoon a large sloop lifted topsails above the aching blue of the horizon and as soon as she showed a green flag at her foretop and a red one at her main, Rob guessed her to be the *Lady Catherine*. At twilight the sloop's anchor had gone plunging onto the sand at the entrance to Mangrove Bay and Mr. Peacock had nearly ruined a horse in getting over from Eli's Harbour. He discovered Rob fishing at the end of the dock, apparently indolent.

"Thank God, she's got here!" The Philadelphian sighed, studying the sloop lying with rigging etched against the violet sky. "Soon as George Ord gets ashore, we'll have a talk, Mr. Ashton. Meantime, please ask your cousin to hoist the lantern signals; I want the *Packet* to stand in."

Something in the Committeeman's voice stirred Rob like a shrilling of fifes and the smart *rattle-tat* of drums. He started off, but Peacock said.

"Hold on a minute. Whom can we trust?"

Colonel Tucker, Rob told him. He considered Bermuda's desperate need his first duty.

"Fine." Peacock's head inclined sharply. "Who else?"

"Henry Tucker of the Bridge; his cousin Jimmy Tucker, Richard Jennings—"

"—Jennings?"

"Not Joseph. Richard. Joe went home after the meeting yesterday."

"A bit mealy-mouthed, isn't he?"

Rob shrugged. "I reckon so, but Cousin Peter and the rest swear he's to be trusted. He owns a lot of whale boats down at Flatts. They are counting on them. You see, the Flatts is half way to St. George's from here."

Mr. Peacock gnawed his lip, watched the *Lady Catherine* put over a boat. Clearly, the protesting whine of her davit tackles floated across the water.

"What about your cousin?"

Rob stiffened. "Sir, he is my cousin. Besides, he is lending valuable niggers to move the stuff."

22 — PLAN OF CAMPAIGN

WHEN the Whigs gathered in Peter's warehouse, the others from force of habit granted Henry of the Bridge a conversational right of way. Quite a number of men were present; more than Rob deemed wise considering the seriousness of the topic under discussion.

"Our only chance is to strike before Bruere hears of ships arriving at this end," declared Henry Tucker, more pasty-faced than ever. "We must make our try tomorrow night."

Heartily Mr. Peacock concurred, saying he thought the West End was crawling with informers.

Captain Ord tilted back in his chair, scratched a broad red nose. "How many men are we going to need?"

"Between sixty and seventy," was the prompt reply. "How many hands can you spare for the shore party?"

"Not over thirty," Ord replied, staring at Henry Tucker as if he were something he had never seen before. "Need the rest to navigate."

"And you?"

If it was a fair night, Captain Turner reckoned he could make out with five men.

A pair of rats began scuffling behind a pile of hides while Henry Tucker considered. "Well, I judge we can count on about six good men from here—and as many slaves as you want. Incidentally, I intend going along."

547

"Eh?" Peter looked amazed at the idea of Henry Tucker's risking his neck.

"Yes. I am familiar with Government House and its grounds. Also Tobacco Bay."

"Tobacco Bay?" Bascombe queried sharply. "I was thinking of Catherine's Point."

"Fewer houses face Tobacco Bay."

"What about boats?" Mr. Peacock wanted to know. "We have got to have quite a few."

"I don't mind risking my skin," someone grunted, "but whale boats costs money. I only got two. If I lose dem, my family vould go hungry."

Someone else said, "Mine is too old and slow."

Richard Jennings said, "Never mind. Joe has plenty of boats. We won't need any others. Besides, his place lies halfway to St. George's; he will save us a damned long row."

"Now here's what I figure," the chairman said and, leaning further forward, was dwarfed by his shadow. In the lantern light the white of his eyes looked lemon yellow. "We will cruise along the North Shore as far as Burnt Point. You judge that would be safe, Colonel?"

Colonel Tucker, who had come in late, said, "It should be."

"We can row Joe Jennings's boats from there to Tobacco Bay and make our try for the powder."

"What with the *Packet* touching last week, I'll bet that old bugger Bruere has posted watchmen," Gilbert predicted. "He would suspect his own mother."

"Anybody who gets in our way," Mr. Peacock said with meaning under the surface of his words, "will get hurt."

Colonel Tucker arose immediately. "There must be no violence! It is one thing to—er—take His Majesty's powder, but I will countenance no violence!"

"Of course not, Colonel. Of course not." Henry Tucker's reassurance was prompt, but Rob knew it wasn't worth a pinch of ashes.

IN the *Lady Catherine*'s stuffy stern cabin Captain Ord held forth over mugs of lukewarm ale. Though the night was suffocating despite occasional spatters of rain, he still wore his coat. Captain John Turner, however, had undone his shirt clean down to his belt, exposing a weird design tattooed across his chest. It had been done in the South Seas, he said with pride. Mr. Peacock had shed his coat, but endured a waistcoat above his blue and white checked shirt.

Outside the door the sloop's quartermaster stood guard, but·Captains Turner and Ord had taken further precautions. Both their vessels had springs rigged to their cables and could be off within a few moments. What guns they mounted had been double shotted and in the cook's galley a nest of coals glowed, ready to light a gunner's match. Aloft, lookouts remained constantly on the alert.

Mr. Peacock had learned of no men-of-war at St. George's but reported the three armed merchantmen Rob had noticed still there.

Captain Ord, rubbing his palm, snapped, "Mr. Peacock, I'm double-damned if I like the look of things. Ever try to get a straight answer to a plain question 'round here?"

Captain Turner, though apparently absorbed in trimming his fingernails with a sheath knife, looked up slowly. "Hell of a tune if we-uns was heave-to off St. George's and find a couple of batteries opening up on us."

Mr. Peacock turned to Captain Ord. "Everything depends, George, on how much the 'Mudians can expect to clear on the powder. I wish I could be sure the profits are high enough to keep them straight. As it is, I have quoted Henry Tucker a shilling a pound above the market." He chuckled. "I guess they will be disappointed when·they learn what their infernal powder will really bring in America."

"*If* it gets to America," Captain Turner growled. "I don't mind tellin' you, Mr. Peacock, I ain't trustin' these heah 'Mudians too far. I dassent. Not with the skimpy little crew I got aboa'd. Tudor Tucker, he oughtn't have let me sail so God-damned short-handed. It warn't right!"

Decisive was Ord's gesture in brushing aside various charts. He caught up a sharpened bullet.

"Cap'n Turner's right, Mr. Peacock, dead right. We must stand on our feet so far as we can. Look here." The two others leaned over the table. "Let's count noses and see the best we can do."

"They's fo'teen and myself aboa'd the *Packet*," Turner drawled and, in spilt beer, sketched the number across the table top.

"And I have forty-seven. Let's see, now, that gives a grand total of sixty-two hands."

"You forget me," was Peacock's dry reminder. "Not that I'm important."

The red of Ord's face glowed through a three day's beard as he looked over at the Committeeman. "Sorry, sir. What about Ashton—the Virginian one?"

Peacock fingered his chin. "He's all right, I judge."

" 'Judge' won't do, sir," Ord insisted. "He's got a lot of Bermuda relatives."

"You can count on him."

"All right, if you say so. Any Bermudians you dare trust all the way?"

"Colonel Henry," Mr. Peacock returned solemnly. "If he tells me he will do a thing, I bank on his doing it, come hell or high water."

Ord picked up a pipe, turned it sidewise to light it at a candle flame. "Wish to hell we could manage this by ourselves."

He was badly worried, was Captain George Ord. Mr. Franklin and Mr. Robert Morris had taken him and Mr. Peacock into their confidence. They had disclosed figures, appalling, eloquent of impending doom.

"Upon the success of this expedition," Mr. Franklin had reminded them in his low, impressive voice, "depends the existence of our troops. Not until many weeks have passed can we secure gunpowder from any other source. The army besieging Boston has not enough ammunition to fight a hard skirmish. Should the British learn this, as they well may, even our valorous enemy, General Gage, will make a sortie and crush our people."

All this kept running through George Ord's mind. It would be hell to lose Mr. Morris's fine vessel and still worse to find himself and his crew put in irons—those that would survive a surprise. The jail at St. George's was the very worst hell-hole on the North Atlantic. Everybody knew that. What chiefly bothered him was Mr. Peacock's covert uneasiness and his lack of confidence in the Islanders. If the Committeeman felt easy he would have shown it, but instead, he was chewing the stem of a clay pipe so hard he had just broken its mouthpiece.

Aloft another shower drummed on the decks, sluiced over the cabin deadlights. Ord wished he was a smarter man than he was. What to do? What to do!

If the 'Mudians let him down there was one thing he would do. Before he cut and ran, he'd pour a broadside they would remember into the houses along Mangrove Bay. While he wasn't used to commanding expeditions of this nature, he was handy in a running fight. Last year he had blazed away at an over-inquisitive Spanish *guarda costa* and had driven it home. It was good that the South Carolinians were such a handy lot and game for anything.

Aloud Ord suggested, "Suppose we keep most of the slaves aboard? They are handy sailors. Won't let them keep even a jack-knife. They would be more useful here than ashore; niggers scare easy if things get tight."

Turner's grin bared big tobacco-yellowed teeth. "An' we'd take the white 'Mudians along with us?"

"That's my notion. It would leave most of our crews free for shore operations."

"Suppose we try pulling off the raid all by ourselves?"

Mr. Peacock shook his head. "If we try to freeze them out, the people ashore will turn ugly. Can't blame them, either. They want the powder's price—"

"Well, Turner, what are you thinking about?"

"I was speculatin' on that Virginian. I talked with him two or three times and he acks mighty casual. Hanged if I can make up my mind 'bout him."

"Well," Ord said, "I've made up my mind. Anything goes wrong, he's the first one gets shot."

24 — THE SUMMERHOUSE

BECAUSE of a wandering shower, Rob and Andrea went into the summerhouse. Thanks to a moon behind the rain clouds, the evening remained surprisingly light.

Andrea was feeling that elation peculiar to a woman conscious that her newest dress is a success. Full skirted, white, and sprigged with tiny blue flowers, it was indeed becoming. Sleeves tastefully puffed and ruffled emphasized the slimness of her arms. Tonight she had done her hair in a mode long out of fashion in London, but decidedly new in Somerset. It was coiffed over her forehead in an orderly riot of curls and called for one negligent lock tumbling down onto a bare shoulder. A thin black velvet ribbon, perkily knotted, relieved the pallor of her throat. Even Peter Ashton stared, made ponderous compliments between audible spoonfuls of soup.

Rob suffered a silent pang of disappointment that she had not worn his comb. He was mollified, however, by her swift tact in explaining that fashion made a comb impossible with this arrangement. She had, of course, evolved the excuse beforehand. Wear coral in her copper-brown hair she would not —not with a white and blue dress!

Somewhat remorseful, she smiled up at him, but he was looking out at the rain and the way it stirred a group of huge white yucca blossoms. "Someday soon I will build up a knot at the back of my head and wear it."

"Someday——" he repeated. Something in his voice made her look at him.

No call for padding on those shoulders. La! Half the beaux of Almack's and White's would give their eye-teeth for legs like Rob's. He was wearing a new outfit. Critically, she appraised and approved his choice of fob and seals. Though unaffected and solid, they lent a new and pleasing air of dash. The lace on his shirtfront and cuffs was good, even tasteful. She was enjoying his gift of repartee. Again and again some dry comment stretched her stays with her laughing. In some ways he grew daily more reminiscent of his brother.

"Well, sir, are we to proceed with our Shawnee?" she demanded, and her petticoat—silk once more—gave a satisfactorily coquettish rustle as she sank onto the white marble bench.

He turned, thankful that the rain had stopped. Soon they could go walking and perhaps—well, he was damned if he wouldn't kiss her. He would, even if he got slapped for it.

"Why, if you want." He seated himself at the far end of the bench and, clasping hands about his knee, said, "Now repeat after me—'*Theyh-lonee Tomaugh-con veuse mengoag.*'"

In the half light her teeth glistened. "It sounds foolish, but

552

I suppose it must mean something to an Indian. Well, then, 'Theyh-lonee Tonag-won veuse man agog——' "

His quiet chuckles filled the summerhouse, startled a huge toad foraging on the bricked walk. "Man is agog every time he looks at you. But that's not right. You'll have to throw a plural in there. '*Veuse men-goag.*' "

"...'*Veuse men-goag,*' " Andrea repeated. Good, he had got over his disappointment over the comb. "What does that mean?"

"It means, 'Our ways have met.' "

"Obviously, but still it is a pretty sentiment." She repeated the phrase several times.

"And now," said he, "repeat this after me. *Ke-tela ga-ait-altam amaug.*"

She said studiously, "*Ke-tela ga-ait-atam.*" At the way Rob gasped and stared before breaking into gales of laughter, she went hot clean down to her waist. "Why, what have I said?"

Rob choked and pawed the air, couldn't talk.

"What did I say?"

"Oh Lord! My Lord!" Grinning, he wiped his eyes. "If I only thought you meant it——"

"*Meant what?* Rob Ashton, you tell me this minute what I said." Andrea was irritated. Generally it was she who did the private laughing.

"Oh, Andrea dear, I can't. I vow I can't. It—it—was too—well, er—forward."

"Oh tush! At St. James's I heard a-plenty that would make a sailor blush." She caught his hand, coaxed. "Please, Rob dear, tell me what I said? Please, as a special favor——"

When he still would not tell her, Andrea arose. "La, Mr. Ashton, I had no idea you were a wretched, backwoods prig! Take your damned Shawnee and——and teach it to the macaws!"

"Don't go." His fingers closed over her wrists and tightened when she tried to wrench them away. Finding the pain was not entirely unpleasant, she wrenched harder as, naturally, he tightened his grip.

"Really, Mr. Ashton, you would make an admirable bear trainer, but this is not——"

His look came at her through the darkness like a gleaming lance point. "Andrea! Don't go. Please! This—this is the last lesson I am likely ever to give you." He let go her hands and

553

she whirled away but halted in the moonlight at the summer-house door.

"Last les—?" Andrea's wide skirt billowed with the suddenness of her turning. "What did you say?"

"I am sailing for America—tomorrow."

"Oh, Rob, you rascal. This is a trick."

"No, I mean it." His voice had tightened.

"You really are serious?" Andrea stood very straight, stiff fingers spread and pressing her skirt.

"Yes."

She came back, placed hands on his arms, tilting her head a little to one side, peered up into the shadowy outline of his face. "How are you going back?"

"In the *Lady Catherine*."

"Oh!" She looked away. "I had so hoped you would stay longer. It—it has been so—so nice for me. I shall miss—" Suddenly the truth struck breath from her body. "You don't mean you are going on the ship that has come to steal the powder?"

"Yes." His voice sounded matter-of-fact.

"But why? Why must it be the *Lady Catherine?*"

He led the way to a bench and when they sat down he began to speak but kept his eyes on the distant harbour. A light glimmer shone from the *Lady's* stern. Captain Ord must be working out some detail. Words began to come—effortlessly at last.

"Andrea, I reckon you think I am pretty dull. Maybe I am." He held himself with a subtle dignity. "Maybe most merchants are dull, but did you ever notice that if there were no merchants, there would be no nations?"

"Why, why, yes," she said, a flash of humor in her look. "Without merchants *I* came to grief."

"Well, it stands to reason that without merchants to do her business, America can never amount to anything. You understand what I mean?"

Long eyes, lambent in the moonlight, clung to his. "I believe I do, Rob."

"With the British feeling the way they do, with Parliament passing the fool laws it has, we can't trade in English ships or with English money. All I can see is that the Colonies will have to find their own vessels, establish their own trade routes and find money to do it. Fortunes will be made by those who get started early, but they'll have to run risks no assurance underwriter would cover. If I can get back to America, I intend seeing what can be done. My people need salt, arms and gunpowder. Soldiers can't bring them those things."

Lips tightened in a curious half smile, Andrea regarded him in silence. It was as if, in a region back of formal thought, something was being decided; it disturbed her in an odd, indefinable way.

He was saying, "Perhaps you undertand why I reckon I'll go along with Captain Ord?"

"Oh, Rob, Rob! You mustn't! The Bermudians are so tricky, they may trap you down there."

"Mr. Peacock says the expedition is short-handed. He needs every man who can be trusted."

"But, Rob, can you be sure the Bermudians will do what they say? Most of them are so—so self-centered. You never did trust Henry Tucker."

"He can be trusted this time. He hates the Governor and he stands to make a hundred per cent profit if we do get the powder away."

"Oh, Rob! Don't—" Her voice broke. "Suppose anything happens—to you—"

"To me?"

She raised her face, but her eyes were tight closed. "I have no idea of what—would become of me."

As if they had gone there a thousand times, his arms slipped about her waist and lapped over because it was so slender. To Andrea the moment became iridescent. She could not move for the blood flooding her body. She felt a torrent of it successively scorching her neck, her breast and her thighs. When his lips met hers, the tide turned, flowed away, leaving her weak, trembling and frightened. The hardness of him, the masculine odors of tobacco and shaving soap, the eager pressure of his hands were exhilarating, maddening. She felt a subconscious realization that he was not inexperienced in making love.

"My dear! My dear!" he whispered. As he pressed his cheek to hers, she felt the delicious scrape of tiny bristles; swelling blood drowned her again. When languorously her head tilted, the moon cast a radiance over her face, revealing the passionate curve of her mouth and the wild flutter of an artery in her throat.

"I had meant to wait," Rob told her, "until this business at Tobacco Bay was over. It's no use to speak now; it isn't fair."

"Why, darling? Why isn't it fair?"

"Suppose the Tories rig an ambush?"

"That cannot happen—until tomorrow. Tonight is tonight."

One by one, lights on the *Lady Catherine* and the *Packet* blinked out. They rode in solitary possession of the harbour; owners, chary of such dangerous company, had shifted all other vessels to safer anchorages. The perfume of cedar sawed in the shipyards hung strong in the air. Andrea's head reposed on his shoulder and she had slipped an arm about his neck as he sat supporting her across his chest. Like that it was very easy to kiss.

"Oh, my dear, I do wish I might sail with you," she murmured. "But of course, I can't. To storm off at a moment's notice wouldn't be fair. I must find a substitute. I vow I shall miss my sweet little devil. No, I couldn't leave tomorrow."

"I wouldn't hear of your sailing in a powder ship," he declared seriously. "Suppose we fight an action? Besides, I doubt whether Captain Ord would consider taking a woman aboard. Next to rabbits and ministers, women are the world's worst luck aboard ship."

"You flatter my sex, sir." She sat up, smiling. "Speaking of parsons, you had better have one primed and ready. Oh darling, I will reach Philadelphia quick as ever the next ship clears from here."

He kissed her and, despite a hundred silly flirtations, Andrea again experienced an utterly new and delicious reaction.

He said regretfully, "I must go now—there is much to pack. As yet, Peter does not know I'm going. I don't intend telling him 'til it's almost time to go aboard."

"He will be monstrous sad to see you leave," she predicted. "Peter is devoted to you."

"Half of anything I have is his, any time he asks. I will never get over his kindness."

She put out a restraining hand. "Rob?"

"What is it, dearest?"

"What was that I said in Shawnee?"

He only laughed.

25 — AUGUST 14TH, 1775: AFTERNOON

THE afternoon was hot and, thanks to a great raft of cumulous clouds hovering low over the islands, so heavy with humidity that a man's linen became drenched if he so much as walked across the room. The wind had died completely, leaving a frog-pond calm on the ocean, and the tide ebbed lower than in many months. Despite a dense heat haze everyone could see the outer reefs showing above water. Dogs sought the thickest shrubbery they could find and lay panting among bluish shadows. Birds flew about with beaks parted, and the slaves dozed or fanned themselves whenever they could. In the shipyards no work was being done. The sun was too shattering to be tolerated. Usually around three o'clock it grew cooler.

With Sachem's help, Rob was packing a horsehide trunk bought in St. George's Town. Though dressed in the evangelical simplicity of a shirt and straw sandals, he remained bathed in a perspiration that trickled down his spine and along the backs of his legs.

For once Sachem spoke without being addressed. "Mr. Ashton, sir," he faltered, "could you take me with you?"

"Eh? Take you with me?"

"Yes sir, would you please buy me?" The valet was looking desperately, overwhelmingly hopeful. "I would work mighty hard for you."

Rob looking up, noticed that today Sachem's Indian characteristics were particularly predominant. Save for his wavy hair, he might easily have been one of those nondescript Indians who in the springtime appeared in Norfolk offering furs for sale.

Crooking a forefinger, Rob slid it along his brow, detached a string of sweat beads. "Why do you want to come with me so bad?"

"Inside of me I feel like I was in jail on this island, sir."

Rob's interest was aroused at last. "How is that? Thought you had never been off the Bermudas."

"That's right, sir," the valet admitted, folding away a pair of silk stockings. "But my Pa, he used to say where our folks came from there is whole rivers running fresh water. They ain't none here. He says in America there is mountains so big if you climbed them you could stand right close by God. Mr. Ashton, I don't know why, but I—I just got to see them. Ain't anything here but a few little hills—" He broke off. "I expect you reckon I'm addled, Mr. Ashton, sir, but I want to go to a big country where there ain't so many people." He added with desperation in his tone, "I just got to! Something keeps pulling at me and pulling at me."

Rob folded away a neckerchief. "What is your value?"

Sachem hesitated, looked miserable. He had been dreading this question. "Two hundred and fifty pounds, sir," he gulped. "Guess I ain't worth it." Then he added eagerly, "I've learned me to read and write a little—"

"You are a good valet, too," Rob remarked. In the Indian-Negro's jet eyes he recognized an expression which stirred his sympathy. He had seen such a look years ago in the eyes of a captive raccoon. The Aitcheson boys got mad when he asked them to let it go and they beat him up because he sneaked over at night and opened the cage.

"I will talk to Mr. Peter," Rob promised, "but I don't promise anything.—No, the navigating instruments go in the chest."

Peter proved agreeable to a transfer.

"Take him. I must have been soft in the head when I paid £250 for him. Sachem's no good at hard labor—none of his breed are. And he ain't heavy enough to handle an oar or throw a harpoon. Suppose you know most of our crossbreeds make elegant whalers?"

"All the same," Rob said, "I reckon I'll buy him."

They were signing the bill of sale when they sighted Henry of Somerset limping down the water steps towards the office. He was in a great hurry.

"Now what the blazes has gone wrong?" Peter exclaimed in a low voice.

Sallow features flushed, neck cloth awry, Henry of Somerset stamped in, dust-powdered and trembling in his fury.

"We're in the devil's own mess!"

"What's wrong?" the cousins demanded in unison.

"It's Joe Jennings! The bloody bastard!"

Rob's breath stuck in his throat. Mr. Peacock, it seemed, had been right about the gangling committeeman from the Flatts.

"What's he done?"

Tucker glared about as if he would attack any movement.

"What has he done? The crotch-blistered coward has ruined all my plans!"

"You mean he can't let us have the whalers tonight?"

"He can, but he won't! Blast his crooked soul to hell!" Henry Tucker was outraged as only a shifty man can be when, for once, he is the victim of trickery. Panting, he sank onto a meat cask. "My cousin Jim sailed down to Flatts this morning to give him last instructions." Narrow chest aheave, Henry Tucker cursed dreadfully. "But Jennings tells Jim he's sorry, he has changed his mind and doesn't want any part of the business. He even had the confounded gall to tell Jim he might get a reward from the Governor if he'd peach on me!"

Peter joined in a flow of really artistic profanity.

Rob looked at his watch and saw it was four o'clock. Aware that the expedition was scheduled to set out at eight, asked, "Well, Tucker, what is to be done about it?" Recalling Peacock's distrust of the islanders, he was seriously disturbed.

"Try to scratch up enough whalers 'round Somerset," Henry Tucker growled. "Doubt if it will be possible, though. People around here are too poor to go risking their boats."

Rob said, "If it will help matters, I'll agree to underwrite such losses."

"You will? You mean that?" Henry Tucker looked incredulous. "Why should you? Your loss might run into hundreds of pounds."

"Call it a gamble, Mr. Tucker."

"Then you really mean your offer?"

"Especially in business matters I mean what I say. It has been a failing with me."

"In that case we'd better be getting out and hump ourselves," Peter commented. "What about boat crews?"

"You and Bascombe will have to attend to that," Henry Tucker said, "and Colonel Henry and I will collect boats and see they get here on time."

It was a revelation to witness the precise workings of Henry Tucker's mind. Within half an hour he had listed the boat owners to be approached, had estimated the requisite number of seamen slaves, and had dispatched messengers around the harbour.

Rob asked half jokingly, "Do you want my promise in writing?"

Henry Tucker started to say "yes," but, suddenly conscious

of Peter's intent look, changed to, "It ain't necessary. Your word is good with us."

Brushing away a fly which was skating over his close-clipped scalp, Peter inquired, "How do you think the American captains are going to take this change?"

"I'll attend to that," Rob promised. It was invigorating, it boosted his self-respect to feel the sense of responsibility. "Let me get this straight. I presume the ships will take the whale boats in tow and stand down along the North Shore?"

"Yes, as far as Crawl Point," Henry Tucker replied. "The *Packet* first and the *Lady* following. If the night wind blows strong enough, we can follow the inner passage. Ships would not be so noticeable from shore then. As soon as it gets dark, the whale boats will pull for Tobacco Bay."

"I hope you'll let me take charge of one," Rob said.

"That can be managed." Henry Tucker closed his eyes, spoke as if he were consulting a mental map. "Around eleven, both vessels will move further east, but they had better not go any nearer St. George's than Burnt Point." He mopped his face briefly and asked Rob, "Well, sir, and why do you look at me like that?"

"I was just wondering," Rob confessed, "whether Joe Jennings might take it into his head to ride on into St. George's?"

"He is a cowardly dog, and after what he's done today I guess he would sell his sister to a Jew," the Bermudian stated, then added, "but he must live on these Islands with the Colonel and me. It all depends on how much he figures the Governor might pay him for peaching. In any case, it is one chance we must run. In another day's time the venture will be too risky. Someone is bound to inform Bruere of American ships having been here."

26 — AUGUST 14TH, 1775: EVENING

NOTHING in Andrea Grenville's training allowed her to betray more than a mild concern over the expedition's fate. She had even managed to make a few jokes when Sachem, deliriously happy, lugged Rob's chests down to a boat from the *Lady Catherine*.

She felt proud of having maintained her poise during Susan's tearful farewell, and vows always to cherish the little model and never, never to let anyone hurt it. She had sympathized with Aunt Lyd who, cast in much the same mould as herself, would not weep, only blew her nose fiercely as any battle trumpet.

"I will be lodged at Smith's City Tavern on Second Street in Philadelphia," he told her between hard, lingering kisses in the library. "Mr. Peacock says it is near to the river and yet in the center of town. I will be counting the hours until a messenger says your ship is in."

Smiling whimsically to see how crooked her writing was, she had just now finished writing the address on the back of her journal. She had not wept or broken down. Of that she was proud. No use sending him off with memories of red eyes and a snuffy nose. Nothing would be gained by harrowing his sensibilities. He would have enough to face before long. She had only clung to him with an intensity of passion she had never dreamed she could feel. In the end she had whispered, "You must go now, my dearest. The boat is waiting."

Now she looked out the window. On the harbour the American ships looked ridiculously small and impotent. Three cannons of the *Lady Catherine*'s starboard broadside and the schooner's two, briefly reflected the sunset's dying glare. A good offshore breeze was blowing. She cast one final look at the ships and saw them getting up anchors and setting jibs and topsails. In spite of herself their outlines began to blur.

Rob was going. Kindly, dependable Rob. Dependable, that was Rob. Hadn't he had the rare good sense to stop gambling in time? Hadn't he slowed down on his drinking once his first nervous anguish was dulled? She heaved a small sigh, turned resolutely away from the window. For Andrea Grenville no mawkish mooning, no watching the ships out of sight.

Nothing remained but to keep quiet and hope for the best. She wondered why she couldn't forget Joe Jennings's mean, pointed face? Would he dare to alarm the Tories? He'd think twice; the wrath of the Tuckers was no trifling matter. Abstractedly she tidied her bureau, in her mind an image of ships standing in to shore, a sudden murderous crash of cannons. She had heard the sound of guns; the Tower garrison were forever firing salutes. But she had never heard the terrifying crackle of smashing timbers nor the high thin screams of mortally wounded men.

She must—she *must* stop thinking in this vein! Suddenly

561

she clapped her hands. When a servant wench appeared, she said, "I want the bath and hot water—lots of it."

"But, Missy—Ah don' know—"

"It rained last night. Damn it, wench, do as I tell you!" The oath relieved Andrea's feelings no little and she was even amused at the way the Negress goggled.

Andrea stamped her foot. "Will you do as I say?"

"Oh, yas'm! Yas'm!"

Half an hour later Andrea, hair twisted on the top of her head, was seated in a bath shaped like a gigantic saucer. Water was up to her waist and around her stood a number of brass pots giving off the smell of hot metal. She soaped herself vigorously, resolutely began to sing:

> "Had she never loved sae kindly
> Had she never loved sae blindly
> Never met and never parted—"

She faltered but sang a second verse, earnestly scrubbed each toe and by dint of some contortions cleansed her shoulderblades. Still she did not feel any better. Suppose she prayed a little? Would the Lord be offended if one prayed sitting in a bath? Probably not. She had always reasoned that if a person really meant a prayer, the Lord didn't care a hoot where it was said. Plenty of the most fervent prayers ever uttered were voiced outside of church. Abruptly she dropped the soap onto the floor, bent her head and, joining hands, prayed that there might be no trap at St. George's Town.

When she had done, she felt better; laughed at herself. What a picture! The Christian maiden at her devotions!

27 — AUGUST 14TH, 1775: NIGHT

IT was, Rob realized, surprisingly pleasant to be aboard ship again. The *Lady Catherine*'s gentle rolling and the creaking of blocks and tackles played a familiar tune. Mangrove Bay and Gaunt New House now lay astern; they had passed Spanish Point. A dim veneer of clouds obscured the sky but later there should be quite a bit of moonlight. The only thing troubling Rob was Captain Ord's stiffness with him all along.

The master's aloofness abated somewhat when he had asked to engage passage. Perhaps that was Ord's natural manner.

He was setting foot to the quarterdeck ladder when Captain Ord checked him with a peremptory, "Ain't no one allowed on my quarterdeck but the after guard of this ship."

Rob nodded. "It is as you wish, of course. I only want to know in which boat I'm to go?"

"In good time you will be given orders."

Puzzled and troubled, Rob went to the rail and looked astern. Towing easily, and with a steersman in the stern of each, four big dirty white whale boats trailed after the *Lady Catherine*. Because she was smaller and less likely to attract attention, the *Packet* had set sail earlier. They could see the gleam of her mainsail nearly a mile ahead. She was towing three whale boats of smaller size.

Rob looked at Negro seamen squatting on the deck amidships. Peter's slaves were fine big fellows. To his relief the four or five white Bermudians aboard acted very calm. Once the *Lady* got close inshore Ord called one of them up to act as pilot. It was just as well for just ahead lay the Stags, a wicked scattering of reefs. Surprisingly soon Crawl Point loomed through the afterglow. They could see the *Packet* heaving-to off it. Already the Carolinian schooner's crew was pulling the whale boats up alongside.

Rob could visualize Henry Tucker of the Bridge, his thin face tight, directing the movements over there. Opportunist he might be, but there was no denying he was a capable man in a pinch; capable and, by no stretch of the imagination, timorous.

Very soon the *Lady Catherine* drew up to her consort and, with canvas slatting, came up into the wind.

Dressed in dark clothes, Peter Ashton came over to his cousin. His expression was somber and he looked angry. "What's eating Captain Ord? Fellow keeps looking at me as if he expects me to shove one of these," he tapped the butt of one of the pistols Rob had given him, "into his ribs."

"He is just nervous, I reckon," Rob ventured. "After all, we've a ticklish job ahead." His eyes probed the indistinct shoreline. Right here the coast was bold with an inlet slashing deep into its dark mass.

"Flatts is over yonder," Peter said. "That bugger Joe Jennings lives in the little house to the left. Hope to hell he hasn't got to Bruere—"

"Avast there!" came a sibilant order from the quarterdeck.

Swiftly the whale boats were brought alongside and then Rob got a jolt. More than half the blacks destined to act as rowers were ordered to stay on board and a corresponding number of white sailors took up their place. Captain Ord would remain aboard, but Mr. Peacock was for the shore party. Rob immediately sensed the reason for this sudden increase in the number of Provincials going ashore. He hoped Peter did not; Ord's maneuver was scarcely flattering to the Bermudians. It was rather dangerous, too, he thought, considering how utterly at the mercy of Henry Tucker they all were. Without Bermudian whale boats, without native pilots, without the help of slave labor and without volunteers, the Americans could have accomplished nothing.

The whalers shoved off without putting out oars. The breeze being favorable, a leg-of-mutton sail was raised in each boat. Under the propulsion of brown, often patched canvas the whalers slid quickly out from under the *Lady Catherine*'s towering yards.

The sea was silver-gray, like French paper, and the flotilla steering inshore formed little black blots on its surface. Along the shore only some pale sand beaches and a very few lights were visible. Rob, seated on a thwart, wondered what was going to happen. The next hour would tell a lot. Recently he had given up trying to find omens.

For about half an hour the whale boats cruised in silence. Everyone kept staring at the cedar-shrouded slopes above the water. Now and then a man would shift his position and a weapon would clink. Rob could see the coxswain in the boat alongside throwing his weight on the long steering oar; a blue and white striped jersey he wore showed up surprisingly clear. He was a fool to have worn such a thing. Astern, the schooner and the sloop cruised slowly back and forth, remained barely discernible.

Rob strained his eyes at the shore ahead, but could see no lights. For clearer vision he shoved aside the handle of a pickaxe destined for use later. Peter's heavy figure sat slouched in the stern of a whaler to port. He certainly must believe in the necessity of this expedition. He was risking a fortune, everything, to take part. Damned lucky the interests of Bermuda and America, for the present at least, ran in parallel grooves.

564

One of the black men whispered over the *hush-hush* of waves alongside, " 'At Burnt Point ovah yander, suh, 'n 'at's Vale Bone Beh off sta'boa'd."

The steersman, second mate of the *Lady Catherine* uttered a small sigh. "Abner," said he to the man beside him, "I do believe we are in luck. If this wind holds we ought to fetch the beach 'thout touching an oar. It would save us making any racket at all."

The other agreed, but kept sticking out his head, as if he were expecting to see some threatening object.

The flotilla was sailing along, bunched like a flock of wild ducks startled by a hostile sound. Henry of Somerset sat in the stern of the foremost talking to Captain Turner. Everyone could see his thin arm pointing ahead at a glimmer of white. This, Rob deduced, must be Tobacco Bay beach for, on some heights beyond it, battlements showed as a series of gray and black planes. From his study of charts Rob knew this for Fort St. Catherine. The guns in it commanded the beach. The Bermudians, too, were painfully aware of the fact and kept looking in that direction.

Soon the land commenced to cut off the wind and the boats slowed. A sailor started to pick up his oar but was ordered to desist. On a low-pitched command from Captain Turner all the boats formed in line abreast and steered for the beach. Every one of the raiders knew that if any ambush had been arranged, its fire must any instant now crash into their faces. If that happened, not many men could hope to get away. The stillness became incredible, only the lazy wash of wavelets on the beach, a stirring of cedar branches and a merry gurgle rising in the wakes of the seven whalers.

Rob got a curious impression that his boat lay motionless while the shore moved out to meet her. A few seconds before land inserted itself under the keel, the steersman in a hoarse undertone ordered the sail lowered. Jumping overboard, the crew laid hold of the gunwales and they all heaved the big whaler further up on shore. It was a good thing the tide was making, Peter muttered.

The crews gathered at once, blotted out the white sand with their numbers. Acid and quite calm, Henry Tucker strode along the line of stranded boats. He leaned rather heavily on a cane.

Rob said to his boat captain, "Aren't we taking along those pickaxes?"

The other gave him a grateful look. "Jerusha! Clean forgot about 'em." He trotted over to the next boat. "Don't forget them shovels."

Rob was greatly surprised when Henry Tucker came to him and said, "Come with me."

The advance party consisted of seven men; Henry Tucker, Richard Jennings, Dan and James Tucker, Captain Turner, and the first mate of the *Lady Catherine*.

Said Captain Turner, "I aim to take along two mo' of my men."

Henry Tucker's teeth clicked as he bit off an angry remark. "Very well, but come on. It is growing late." He set off up the beach at a rapid pace. Soon the advance party was bending beneath cedar branches. Henry Tucker beckoned his Cousin James. "Where is the house we must pass?"

"Just ahead. Won't be nobody up, though."

On the seaward slope of Retreat Hill the going grew difficult. On it trees grew very thickly and the underbrush was dense. The raw, earthy smell of freshly ploughed land struck their nostrils, then the house came into sight. It was a white cottage, small, square and with windows tightly shuttered.

Soon a wall loomed ahead but, as Henry Tucker had predicted it was neither high nor defended by the usual collection of broken glass set in its top. The whole party scaled it without delay.

"We must be very still now. Government House lies right over there," Henry Tucker warned.

The men were panting, glad momentarily to ease the drag of weapons at their belts. They stood peering anxiously in all directions.

"Where is the magazine?"

"To our left. Now, Captain, suppose you post a look-out among those bushes. Two more men had better cross to the other side of the magazine."

"Is there any guard over the magazine?" whispered the mate.

"That," the Bermudian replied with a touch of grim humor, "we shall presently find out."

THAT the Provincials intended to run no unnecessary risk was patent from the careful way they arranged a ring of their own men as look-outs. Henry Tucker insisted, however, that one post be watched by his cousin. It was on a walk leading directly to Government House. The hot and anxious party could glimpse the faint loom of its roof through the trees. Rob deemed it a rather insignificant edifice.

Thirty strong, men came up from the beach, handling their tools and weapons. They followed Henry Tucker towards what seemed to be a gate let into a rise in the ground. It was an eternal instant. Everybody braced himself for a hoarse, "Halt! Who goes there?" A twig snapping under Peter's heel set half the party swinging about. Rob saw in the stone façade a massive double grille of iron bars secured by a chain and padlock. Behind it was a door of sheet iron. The raiders came crowding up. Some of the slaves standing white-eyed in the background were so scared their teeth chattered.

"God in Heaven," Richard Jennings groaned. "How the blazes are we going to get into the damned thing?"

Henry Tucker beckoned one of his own slaves, a little runt of a Negro. "Stilicho, you see that ventilator up on top?" He pointed to the summit of a grassy mound behind the entrance.

"Yassuh."

"You and Justin take crowbars and scramble up there—pry the roof off the ventilator. You can slide down a rope. I hear the inner door can be unlocked from the inside."

"You sure about that?" the mate of the *Lady Catherine* asked. He was so nervous his voice shook.

"Haven't time to answer fool questions." Henry Tucker sank on a stone curb lining the little road up to the entrance. "You men use your crowbars to snap off that chain. Hurry— it's after eleven."

Everyone's heart faltered at the resounding *crack!* one of the ventilator's roof boards made when Henry Tucker's slave levered hard. Rob could see the two Negroes heaving and straining up there against the stars. Meanwhile, a crowbar twisted windlass-fashion through the chain was being turned. The pressure only resulted in a gradual bending of two of the grille bars. All at once the chain gave a sharp *tang!* and broke, raising a shower of sparks. In front of the magazine sounded muffled stampings, the clank of iron on iron and the whispering of the Negroes above. Stilicho had rigged a rope and now only his head and shoulders remained visible. It was a tight squeeze, but he could get through.

From within the vault sounded a metallic scraping, then the noise of kicking. Gradually the inner door swung open, freed a rush of damp, dank air. Two huge toads hopped frantically about, scuttling at last to safety.

"Hell!" grunted the mate. "Why don't the bloody-backs store their powder in a dry place! Must be plenty of it spoiled!"

"Quit talking and get your men going," snapped Henry Tucker.

To deaden sounds of barrels being rolled over stone flooring the raiders arranged a path of canvas strips, brought for the purpose out to the entrance. Rob marshaled slaves and seamen impartially into a line. Fortune again smiled. His Majesty's powder was, for the most part, packed in half-barrels. One such keg was just small enough for a single man to manage. Rob's duty was to keep the line moving to arrange for transportation of the larger barrels.

One after another the whites and Negroes vanished into the gaping blackness of the magazine, reappeared bent under a burden. It was like watching ants at work on a hill. A thin line flowed steadily down Retreat Hill, disappeared in the direction of Tobacco Bay.

As they tired the raiders made more noise, a lot of it. They would blunder into a low branch or stumble. Sometimes they fell and their keg would crash off into the dark, making a terrific racket. At such times everybody froze in his tracks, stayed deathly still, listened for all he was worth. They could hear dogs barking in St. George's on the far side of the hill. Behind Government House an amorous cat made the welkin ring.

It was such hard work rolling out the heavier, iron-bound barrels and manhandling them over the rocky ground, that nobody realized when two hours had passed. No matter what the raiders did, the big barrels gave off an alarmingly loud rumbling.

Peter, dusty and puffing like a grampus, looked about noted that the lookouts were over their first tension. Diffused

568

moonlight shone faintly on pistol barrels and on the cutlasses that some of them had drawn.

Henry Tucker put aside a bottle of medicine from which he had been dosing himself. He beckoned Rob. "Mr. Ashton, suppose you go take a look and see how much more the whalers can manage? We will have to clear out very soon."

Lugging a small keg, Rob started down the beach. He could see fine now. Deer shooting at home was often like this. He felt relieved on Peter's account; so far the Bermudians had made a fine showing.

He had passed through the pungent body aura of a big bare-footed Negro and was starting down the beach when some branches moved, *against* the wind, in a thicket beside the path. Without seeming to take alarm, he swung out of line as far as he might. Yes, by God, somebody was in there! All in one motion Rob dropped his keg, leaped at the thicket.

The fellow gave a frightened cry, jumped up and began to run along a path. He was foolish. Had he dodged into the underbrush, he must have escaped in the thick gloom of branches, but apparently the fellow reckoned he could pull away. It was no wonder. Inside the first ten yards they covered Rob knew he was a damned fast runner. But he must be silenced! If he got away, he would raise the town.

Rob put on a burst of speed, concentrated on driving his legs. He began to close in. The fellow flashed a look back over his shoulder. He was either a white man or a very light mulatto. When he saw Rob coming up, he put on a spurt himself, began to draw away down a path which now traversed a small clearing. In it corn grew waist high to either side. Damn! If it came to matching sprints, Rob could tell right off the other would get away.

Since the fellow was wearing a striped waistcoat he was probably a house servant. From Government House? Rob began to tire. The fellow was a scant thirty feet ahead, but he might as well have led by a mile. And he was running faster. Rob made his decision, halted, grabbed up one of the many loose stones which had been hampering them both. Bracing himself, he heaved with all his might. He was good at throwing.

The rock took the man in the striped waistcoat at the back of the head. He went bowling over and over through the young corn like a shot rabbit. Rob jumped on him with both feet, hoping to drive enough breath out of his lungs so he couldn't raise a yell. He dropped flat beside his motionless adversary's warm, sour-smelling form. He listened because ahead voices had sounded.

Someone said, "Where in hell did Sam get to?"

"Down to the shack," a voice replied. "Sam's been laying that yellow-haired kid of Coolson's."

Rob deliberated only an instant before jerking out a handkerchief. He crammed it into the servant's slack jaws hoping it wouldn't choke him. Next he took the fellow's belt for wrist lashings and sacrificed a bandanna as hobbles. Only with difficulty was he able to pull the unconscious man off among the dew-covered corn stalks.

Back on the path to Tobacco Bay the carriers were standing stock-still, waiting. Three or four men were running up from the beach with firearms ready.

"Get away?" Dan Tucker queried hoarsely. "Have to pull right out if he did."

"No—got him. Go on."

When Rob reached the shore he saw that both Provincial vessels were standing in almost dangerously close to the beach. In fact, they lay under backed topsails not two hundred yards out, their canvas lustrous in the moonlight. Whale boats were continually pulling out to and from them. The thump made by barrels hoisted up the *Lady*'s side sounded so loud it seemed a miracle no alarm had been raised. There was room, one of the Gilbert boys said, for about fifteen more small barrels—six big ones.

By three o'clock His Majesty's magazine stood all but empty; only eight or ten large barrels remained. Captain Turner wanted to take them, too, but Henry Tucker was peremptory.

"No. By sunup you must both be out of sight of land. It is half-past three now. Besides, the wind acts like it might fail."

Peter went around withdrawing the lookouts and they helped to roll the last of the big barrels down to the shore. Everybody except the guards was dog-tired, their hands raw with splinters and whitened by dust.

By four o'clock all the stolen powder was safely aboard ship; two-thirds of it in the *Lady Catherine*, one-third in the *Packet*. All beaming smiles, his stiffness vanished as dew under the sun, Captain Ord swung down a Jacob's ladder and got into the stern sheets of the whaler containing Henry Tucker.

570

He gave him a heavy bag of coins. Clapped him on the back and said loud enough for plenty of witnesses to hear, "Well, sir, here's your advance. One thousand Spanish dollars. The Congress will be delighted."

Henry Tucker called Peter over from another boat. He said, "Suppose you and Dan help me count this? Ord ain't trusted us so there's no use trusting him."

Mr. Peacock frowned. "You will find the amount correct, sir," said he sharply. "You will receive your balance within a month."

But Captain Ord wasn't upset; he offered his hand. "That was fine work, Mr. Tucker, smart, every bit of it. Wish you were an American."

The other looked up from the stack of coins dully a-gleam in the seat. "I'm damned glad I'm not." Presently when he and Peter had cast up the total, he said, "I will call it correct —even if some of the coins are thin. Now, get out of here as fast as you can. We'll go back up the shore, in the whale boats."

The sloop's yards were braced in a hurry but long before the *Lady Catherine* stood out for the northeast channel her crew could see the Bermudian flotilla scurrying up along the coast to the westward. It was a long way to Mangrove Bay and they knew they must put the whalers away before daylight.

To the deep concern of all aboard the *Lady Catherine*, dawn broke with Bermuda still uncomfortably high on the horizon. Rob could even distinguish the white roof of Government House. At intervals a sullen booming of alarm guns reached the sloop, and it did not help matters to feel the wind fading.

Captain Ord looked thoughtful, then very uneasy. Said he, "If a breeze rises from over the Bermudas, they can overtake us."

Part III

Boston

1 — The Prisoner's Ward

LIFE in Boston during the heat of early August was not pleasant. It was desperately hard on body and soul. The sixty five hundred civilians remaining in the beleaguered town were feeling the first real pangs of hunger. General Washington, arriving in Cambridge, took command and got so strict about intercourse with Boston that soon fresh vegetables, eggs, milk, and fresh meat became curiosities. Prices went up and up and up. And every day the military put new regulations in force. The two-thirds of the inhabitants who were Whigs naturally came off worse than the Tories and the Royal Forces.

Old people and the infirm commenced dying at a fearful rate. There were as many as twenty or thirty funerals a day. Infant mortality contributed its quota to the ghastly succession of obsequies which, beginning the day after the fight on Breed's Hill, kept up. Under a terrible spell of hot weather wounded men perished by the dozen. Finally the slow and melancholy clang of church bells became so oppressive that everyone was glad when General Gage ordered them silenced.

It was only natural that bitter and often deadly hatred developed between townsfolk and the military. Though thefts, rapes and mutinous conduct were severely dealt with, the Royal troops, bored and discouraged, would not mend their ways. And they hated digging entrenchments ordered by the Staff. Some privates even stole Major Musgrave's fat mare and sold her for beef in the market. Depressing, too, were daily auctions of property belonging to officers killed in the battle. Grotesquely enough, Major Williams's fine saddle bridle and other accouterments were knocked down beneath the Liberty Tree. The 18th, or Royal Irish, were notoriously slack and even when sentences of six and eight hundred lashes with a rattan cane were handed out, its morale got no better.

As for the Bostonians, it made them sick to look across the harbour at the islands out there; many of them were dotted with sheep and cattle.

But of all the population, none fared so badly as the wounded of both sides. Thanks to General Burgoyne's firm attitude, the handful of wounded Provincials captured on June sixteenth were given quarters in the top floor of the Stone Jail. Humanely enough, he intended them to enjoy the benefit of every breath of air. This, however, was as far as Gentleman Johnny's good intentions were carried. Unluckily for the prisoners, General William Howe selected for his provost-marshal a plausible rascal but recently arrived from New York. If he knew that William Cunningham was a notorious swindler and a scaw-banker of the worst sort, he did not let the knowledge influence his decision. Under orders from this amiable officer, the prison ward windows were nailed shut. Mr. Cunningham said otherwise his prisoners might exchange treasonable communication with friends on the outside.

Located, as it was, directly under a slate roof, the long ward room was from dawn to dusk more stifling than the hottest corner of hell. Death struck rapidly in all directions.

Unshaven, unwashed and naked save for filthy bandages, thirteen of the original thirty prisoners had survived by August 14th. They tossed on woolen blankets that were clotted with blood and sticky from pus leaking through their dressings.

A scanty supply of water was brought to the gaunt and feverish wretches but once a day—at six of the morning. In the fetid heat of the ward it grew hot within an hour. When one of the prisoners, goaded beyond endurance, smashed a pane of glass, Mr. Cunningham ordered him taken out and scourged, mangled thigh or no mangled thigh. At his victim's thin wails the provost-marshal laughed until his huge belly shook, or so the guards said. They hated him, but feared him even more.

Before the end of July the name of William Cunningham had become a synonym for the most bestial avarice, sodden drunkenness and revolting savagery. When, as happened on two occasions, no food reached the helpless wretches in twenty-four hours, Dr. Brown told Cunningham just what he thought of him.

"Damn your bloody eyes! Those poor devils haven't eaten a bite in two days! I won't stand for it."

Mr. Cunningham's answer was a guffaw of strident laughter. "To hell with the rebels! If they're hungry, let them eat the heads of the nails, and gnaw the blankets, and be damned!"

No wood was issued with which the scarecrows beneath the roof could cook their few and tasteless rations. Men in the last stages of weakness must chew and suck at hard strips of salted beef—or go hungry.

From the dispassion of a semi-coma, David Ashton watched neighboring cots emptied. Whether Reverend Dr. Andrew Eliot, the aged minister of the New North Church, would be admitted to the ward was entirely problematical. Time and again David would bite his lips in a helpless fury when over and over again a dying man vainly called for the minister. Those of the wounded who were earnest churchmen suffered spiritual as well as physical agony.

The son of a prisoner named Leach aroused the meanness of William Cunningham's nature to a new pitch. One day the child in bringing to the jail some supplies for his father was forced to wait for admittance outside Cunningham's quarters. When the youngster overheard Cunningham drinking "death and damnation to all rebels!" he solemnly raised a mug of milk and in shrill tones drank "success to the Yankees!" The provost was furious and, bubbling obscenities, kicked the boy out onto the street. He was never allowed to return.

How he had managed to endure it so long, David could not tell, but he reckoned maybe it was because he had lain in so heavy a stupor. Because of it he had remained oblivious to many of the early horrors. The smells got him worst of all. For weeks the leg of Lieutenant-Colonel Moses Parker, of Doolittle's regiment, had stunk like carrion long exposed to the sun, had rotted slowly away. Yesterday, Dr. Brown had at last been permitted to amputate. The young colonel now lay panting, his whisker-covered cheeks so sunken that even secondary bones stood out in sharp relief.

"Reckon only the cast-iron ones of us are left," he croaked during that last dim hour before the rising sun brought fresh torture. "You'll pull through. So will I."

For the rest of that morning David lay naked, but parched and feverish. He was trying to forget the savage sting of a thousand flies, the duller bite of swarming fleas. And to think that not over a hundred yards away such things existed as fresh air, clean sheets, cold water and a real bed! Only a hundred yards away! It was maddening to be so weak. One man who could walk would, every morning, pull down the other prisoners' single coverlets. At night he would listlessly pull them up again.

In spite of everything, David was feeling some better and the hole through his shoulder did not ache so unbearably as last week. What had kept him going were the calls of that curious, tender-hearted creature called Madelaine. She got in to see him approximately once in three days; Mr. Cunningham's drinking bouts made regular admittances of visitors an impossibility.

How Madelaine had learned of his capture and whereabouts David often wondered, but she would never confess even when he asked. It was almost the only thing she kept from him. He reckoned some Tory friend had given her the information and that she dared not speak for fear of involving him.

So, every time a footstep sounded in the hall, he tried to identify it above the delirious moans of a young Rhode Islander who was slowly dying of a gangrenous forearm.

Ever so distinctly he could recall the first time she appeared, shy, brown-eyed and pleasingly curved. He recognized her instantly, though he had had a particularly bad night and his shoulder hurt like syko if so much as a fly lit on its bandages. It was strange he knew her so readily. After all, he had been more than half bozzled when he'd met her, and it was still dark when he went off to join his company.

One of the finest things that had ever happened to him was the way she came running past the other cots crying, "Oh, David, *David darling!* What have they done to you?"

That, and the luminosity of her big, rather sad-looking eyes.

He must have looked awful because the Collins boy was only strong enough to give seven shaves a week.

"Hallo, Bright Eyes," he had wheezed. "You'll excuse my not making you a leg?"

"Oh, David, your poor shoulder!" He would always remember the way she dropped on her knees beside him. She smelt so wonderfully fresh and sweet; a breath of lavender. The way she pressed her cheek against his very thin one. For a long time they had said nothing at all. The rest of the prisoners stared at her in dull curiosity. After a little she straightened, wiped her eyes. While dusting her skirts of filthy straw, she smiled tremulously. Her lips looked dark-bright and shiny, like oxheart cherries.

"I couldn't forget you," she whispered. "I couldn't! All day long while the cannons banged over there, I—I cried."

"Why?" His eyes, sunken deep in their sockets looked up steadily into her face. It was as deliciously smooth as he had remembered it, and the upper lip *was* as short.

"I had a dreadful feeling that something was going to happen to you. I can't explain it, but I did." Through a persistent screen of flies she looked at his face and never saw the dirt resting in its creases, never noticed the foulness of his blanket. "I shall never forget—us—David."

He forced a crooked little smile, raised one of his uneven brows. "Worse luck for you, my dear. I am not much help to anybody—not even to me." It was one of his bad days. He had to lock his teeth to keep from shrieking when she jostled the bed even a little.

At last Madelaine looked about, saw the grimy yellow walls all veined with cracks and defaced with bawdy drawings and verses, the gritty floor and the row of stinking, fly infested chamber-pots that got emptied but once in forty-eight hours. When Lieutenant-Colonel Parker shifted his position she turned pale, pinched her nose at the ghastly gangrenous stench that arose.

She had brought along a small basket. In it was food, a fresh shirt and, thanks to a rare piece of foresight, a clean pillowcase. It was that which pleased David most. All his life he had hated rough material against his features. He concentrated on biting down screams when, firmly, she began to sponge his lean and grimy body. One of her sweetest smiles wheedled from a guard a pot of cool water. To every one of the thirteen haggard wretches she gave a drink. Many of them could only look their unutterable gratitude. Others lay with tears slipping over smudged, bite-marked cheeks.

The prisoners quivered at a resounding tread in the corridor. Even before a hoarse voice called, "Where's that rebel's slut?" they knew it was Mr. Cunningham.

He stuck his head in through the door, drunker than usual, his popping eyes bloodshot. His great frog's face was even more lumpy with the disease which would eventually drive him into insanity. Madelaine flinched at the sight of this fellow bloated with unhealthy fat into a gross shapelessness.

When the provost caught sight of her standing above the

Virginian's cot, he caught his breath. David's heart sank. Was that bloody swine going to forbid her coming again? But Mr. Cunningham only stared, mentally undressed her.

"Get the hell out of here, you! Let these pigs stew in their wallow. Visitor's time is up," the provost grunted and spat onto the floor before he turned away.

Stooping swiftly, she kissed David on the lips. "You don't mind?" she whispered.

He grinned the ghost of a whimsical smile. "What makes you think I might? The competition you get here? Thank you so much. You have given me—all of us—hope." He clung to her skirt with his good hand. She halted, appalled at the feebleness of his grip. He had not been like that in mid-June. For days she had worn bruises from the unconscious strength of his embraces. "How are you making out?" he asked.

"I am all right," she said so quickly he doubted it. "I am staying with Tory friends and I have the money—" she faltered—"you gave me, all of it. And I managed to sell the house in Cambridge. Unfortunately for a quarter of its value. I'll come—"

"Guards! Drag that bitch out of there!" Mr. Cunningham shouted thickly.

Madelaine's soft eyes flooded him in one last quick look. "I'll come back as soon as I can."

2 — The Reverend Dr. Eliot

MADELAINE had first appeared in late July, about five weeks after the battle which people were beginning to call "Bunker's Hill." From then on she appeared whenever William Cunningham's sadistic temper permitted visitors. Time and again she arrived before the Stone Jail only to be ordered away. No one would be admitted that day. At such times she tried to hold back her tears, but when she thought of David panting up there in the heat, so desperately needing a change of bandages and decent food, she couldn't see the street.

By the tenth of August she felt sure he was recovering, gaining ground. From one visit to the next she could see an improvement. The swelling was going down and there was less blood in the stream of pus which kept pouring out of the stab holes. Though the infantryman's bayonet had gone clean through his right shoulder, the blade had passed under the bone and there were no fractures. The steel, of course, had been thick with dust and dirt. It was a miracle he had not, like so many others been carried off by lockjaw. Only an extraordinarily tough constitution had pulled him through.

Often Madelaine wondered how David really felt concerning her. He had said such beautiful, tender things that night. She could recall every word he'd said about the green star. "We'll keep it up in the sky where we both can look at it. It will always be our own private star." And she had said, "Always." She knew he was grateful, desperately grateful, but she didn't want to trade on that. Today, the fourteenth of August, she had learned about something for sure. She hoped they would have a bit of seclusion.

He was sitting with his blanket drawn up on his lap and, despite dark shadows cast by his unshaven beard, his tired features lit at the sight of her.

"Salutations, O daughter of Æsculapius and preceptor of bounty-laden Hebe!"

She smiled at him, a warm fond smile. "I declare, if you can handle heavy words like that, you will be up and on your feet in another week!"

When she had rolled back the sleeve of her yellow cotton dress and was cutting away the clotted bandages, he said, "You can't guess, Bright Eyes, how I have been counting the hours this time. It—well, we have had a working model of hell going on around here." He glanced at the second bed down. The Rhode Island boy was gone, and there was another gap. As for Lieutenant-Colonel Parker, it was a miracle that such a bag of skin and bones could support even a spark of vitality. The skin had drawn back from his mouth exposing his teeth; his cheeks were so sunken the face suggested a living skeleton's. Flies crawled in and out of the parted lips.

Madelaine raised a questioning brow.

"All up with him," David muttered. He looked at her steadily. "If there was only some way to make you understand how much your coming has meant to this awful place. If only there was something I could do to prove my gratitude. Without you, I should not have had hope—anything."

"Don't forget you once gave me hope," she said, her deft fingers applying the bandages. "I needed help very badly then. And you were so—so very sweet."

It was late afternoon and the heat in the prisoners' ward had lessened enough to let the other prisoners doze off.

"Since I can't sit up to kiss you," David smiled, "I reckon you will just have to bend down again." He murmured as she straightened, "Kissing you is like feeling fresh blood run into my heart. It *would* be my luck right now to be a wretched, penniless dog of a prisoner!"

The scent of lavender strengthened when she sat up and, dropping her eyes, said, "Nevertheless, you can give me two things I want most of all." Demurely, she folded small white hands in her lap. Then she looked at him under long dark lashes. "You have already given me one of those things. A man I could love when I felt I couldn't love again."

He actually colored under the reddish bristles on his cheeks. "Oh, nonsense! Bright Eyes, you don't know me for the silly fellow I really am."

"Don't! Oh, don't say that, David. You are fine! You have ideals. I know. You are far above those fellows fighting simply for the sake of trade. You are a nobleman! I don't mean with a title! You came all the way from Virginia, risked everything to fight in a cause."

Slowly he shook his head. "No, for me it was just a fine adventure."

"You may think so. But I know better," she insisted.

"Well, granting that you are right concerning my sterling worth—and I assure you you are not—what is that other thing you spoke of?"

Quietly she slipped onto her knees, rested her head on the pillow beside his good shoulder. "Darling? You remember that night—before the battle?"

"Yes. It was one of the most beautiful things that has ever happened to me."

She gave his hand a little squeeze and her voice took on a breathless quality. "You—you were very sweet and considerate. David."

"Yes, dear?"

"My husband—and you—are the only ones I have ever—" Her voice faded.

"I believe you—entirely," David said. "Things just happened the way they did."

She remained as she was, slowly stroking his fingers. "I am very, very, glad you said that. You see—I—well, today I—have missed my time—again."

His head snapped over and he looked at her hard. "You think—?"

Her soft brown head nodded. "I am sure of it. Or I would not have spoken. Life is so hard—even for children with—with a name." She looked up at him, so pathetically anxious that David smiled back at her.

To his vast surprise, the idea of fathering a child seemed somehow inordinately pleasing. Instinctively he looked on the problem from an angle odd to anyone else. He was enough of a stock breeder to reason that any child of Madelaine's most likely would be strong, sturdy and handsome. Funny how careful some men were about breeding cattle, horses, game-cocks; any creature but themselves. Why, he'd seen people who would have drowned the mongrel pups of a favorite hound bitch marry into a strain they knew to be rotten with insanity.

Well, why not? He was mighty fond of Madelaine; fonder of her than of anyone he had ever known. She certainly had stood by him. It was queer, too, the sense of peace she lent him. If he got well, it would be rather amusing to play at *pater familias*. Strange, how different he and Rob were. There was Rob married and probably a father by now. Since last year he reckoned he had come to understand Rob a lot better. When he got back on his feet, he would try to make it up somehow. They had always had such fun as lads.

Suddenly, he was aware of Madelaine looking at him with an expression of fading hope. He took her hand and kissed it, then said, "If you will do me the great honor of becoming my wife, I will be the happiest man in Boston."

Madelaine made a little choking sound and slipped her arms about his neck. "I won't let you ever be sorry, darling." She began to talk faster and faster. "I will be a good wife. I won't rest until the British—my people—let you go. I have friends. I promise that you will be exchanged as soon as you're able to travel. General Gage doesn't want to be bothered with sick and wounded prisoners."

"And when, Ma'am," David asked, "may I have the pleasure of marrying you?"

"Whenever you wish."

"Why, in that case, my dear, it's the sooner the better!" He cast a sidewise glance at the scarcely breathing figure of Lieutenant-Colonel Parker. "If you will wait only a little while, the Reverend Dr. Eliot will be coming in. Perhaps I can persuade him to perform a double ceremony, as it were."

"Oh, don't say that," Madelaine begged. "Must it be like this?"

"Cunningham only lets the minister come because Parker's a colonel." The old reckless smile flitted over his features. "It may be our only chance for a long time, and time, in this instance, seems a trifle important, doesn't it, Bright Eyes?"

3 — PEACE

MADELAINE ASHTON'S unremitting efforts soon bore fruit, and General Howe issued special orders that the ward windows be un-nailed, that the poisonous condition of the prison ward be remedied. Now that Lieutenant-Colonel Moses Parker had been buried with the rest of his fellows on Copp's Hill the air was better anyhow. Only eight cripples were left. Early one morning a fatigue party came tramping in and used birch brooms with great vigor. They stirred up dense clouds of dust but the open windows were a great help. The wounded men were so cheered they turned their heads to watch.

"God, stinks like a bloody backhouse," grunted the sergeant in charge. "Wish old Cunningham would get stuck in here."

Privates with handkerchiefs dipped in orange juice tied over their noses used a garden rake to scrape together odds and ends of paper, pieces of broken chinaware, sections of plaster that had fallen. Shuddering, they shoveled up a heap of festering bandages. It was crawling with fat yellow maggots.

"Now then, lads, lift this poor devil onto the next cot and we'll change his bed."

Miracle of miracles! Eight clean mattresses were lugged in. Four privates bore down on the nearest cot and each awkwardly laid hold of a corner of its mattress. At a word, they lifted it, patient and all, from the corded frame. Once a fresh blanket had been stretched over the new mattress, the prisoner was, as gently as possible, lifted back onto his bed. The work detail was eager to prove that they hated having had to be so brutal. Their contempt and fear of Mr. Cunningham approximated that of the prisoners.

David was feeling more comfortable than at any time since the battle. Only yesterday Madelaine had come in to tell him that this was going to happen. As usual the change had been arranged by General Burgoyne; he was known to have a soft spot in his heart for the under dog.

"Well, my lad, now it's your turn," the sergeant rumbled, and waved forward four infantrymen stripped to their shirt sleeves. The handkerchiefs over their noses had slipped off. "Nah then, up with him."

The four soldiers lifted. But one of them hadn't got a good hold or else the frail cloth covering of David's old mattress gave way. Anyhow, the invalid fell heavily to the floor.

"Would land on my bad shoulder," David gasped when, hurriedly the men picked him up.

"Begging your pardon, sir, 'tweren't my fault," protested the private. "See? The 'ole blinking corner 'as tore out." He was a nice-looking boy with a fresh English-pink complexion. "I'll get you some apples tonight," he added, very anxious to convince David he hadn't done it on purpose.

White-lipped, David said, "Better not. Might get into trouble. Can you see if any blood has started?"

"No, sir. It's orl right."

David was relieved. He knew the wound had been pulled; he was sure he had felt a newly joined tissue tear. His shoulder hurt like fury but, lying on his fresh and much softer mattress, he felt there was no use complaining.

One of the fatigue detail returning to fetch a forgotten broom gave a sudden gasp when he faced David's bed. "My God! What's that?" Beneath the bed a wide, sticky-looking pool was forming.

They called Dr. Brown, but he could not check the hemorrhage.

David Ashton never learned that he was dying. He reckoned it was mighty fine just to lie still and rest. Loss of blood made him so drowsy he forgot that God-awful pain in his shoulder and drifted peacefully off to sleep—forever.

4 — THE HOUSE ON GARDEN COURT STREET

FROM the first, Katie Tryon had fallen in love with the neat little house Colonel Fortescue's adjutant had found for them on Garden Court Street. Its brick and slate construction charmed Katie. Their new residence was set back quite a way from the street and had a towering walnut to shade the front porch. In the rear yard was a chicken run, but its former tenants had long since vanished down the gullets of marauding soldiers. She liked, too, the chestnut trees shading the street and the severe cleanliness of her new home, and the way great morning glories smothered the back porch and the tool shed. There was even an enormous gray cat, Peter, which condescended to let them live with it. When fish was on the menu Peter became markedly affectionate.

The passage from Bermuda hadn't been an easy one. Though it should have been completed in around ten days, the voyage had consumed over three weeks.

To her Boston proved a disappointment. From the way she had heard people talk, she had pictured Boston as a great, crowded city. Instead she landed in a modest town that failed to cover all of the narrow peninsula on which it was built. When she saw those wide fields and the woods fringing the great expanse of Boston Harbour, the town seemed more insignificant than ever. Of course, some of the streets were cobbled, the mark of a real metropolis, and there were lots of inns and rich looking houses. After living in St. George's and Roanoke County, Boston seemed lively; especially in the morning when guard details were tramping to and from their posts. On the Common troops freshly arrived from England were forever drilling and cursing beneath the summer sun. Boston might once have been a rich, important port, but she didn't think it was a patch on Norfolk.

Here was an atmosphere very different from that which had prevailed in Bermuda. There were so many soldiers in scarlet coats with bright and varied facings. At the wharves a host of ships of all sizes and rigs lay idle, rotting and weatherbeaten. The people wore a sullen, beaten look. Katie wondered if anybody ever laughed out loud like they thought something was really funny.

She went to look at the Governor's Mansion. It had a golden grasshopper for a weathervane. Next, she looked up Faneuil Hall because James Otis had called it "the Cradle of Liberty." The British referred to the building as "a damned vipers' nest." Uninterested as she was in politics, she still didn't feel right about the way the soldiers treated some of the churches. They had tranformed one into a theater and had stabled the staff's horses in another. After listening so long to soft Virginian and Bermudian accents, the twanging of the Yankee speech at first amused, then irritated her.

On the voyage she had reckoned she would try to find Mr. David soon as she got to Boston. It wasn't right for him to be in jail. But now she wondered if she had better be in such a tearing hurry? In some ways a matured outlook had modified her previous worship. Suppose she did find him, what would Hugh think? How could she explain her interest in him? Hugh was beginning to look hard at men who admired her too much. She didn't want to do anything that would make Hugh unhappy. Come to think of it, Mr. David was so smart he probably had either talked his way out of jail or had escaped. Maybe she had better wait until she knew the ropes in Boston before asking any leading questions. It might embarrass Hugh's official position to have his niece looking up a jailed rebel. Yes, it seemed better, for the time being, to let well enough alone.

Her chief concern was finding food fit to put before Hugh Fortescue. Every time she thought on what she had to pay for a bunch of shriveled carrots or for a quart of peas, her frugal soul writhed. Once they got settled, Zuleem proved a great help. The colored people of Boston, like most of their race, were finding ways to "make out." They produced chickens from the most unexpected places. It was well the colonel had brought the bulk of his wines along from St. George's. He was frightfully tired these days and needed them. The day he returned from first inspecting his new regiment, he walked like a man of eighty 'and wouldn't even look 'at supper.

"God, Kitty! Wouldn't believe what happened to us over at Charles Town. Simply ghastly. Short a hundred and fifty men of strength. Where in blazes am I going to find them? Where am I? The replacements the transports brought last month were just a lot of ignorant, bog-trotting Irish. Fellows hate our very guts. Yes, my dear, it will mean damned hard work before the 63rd is fit to be called a regiment again. Gad! There is no snap to them! No spirit! Beggars act like they don't fancy fighting these confounded rebels—"

"—Not on salt meat and rum," Katie observed.

He stared, broke into a cackling laughter. "Said you were a natural born commissary. Hobbs, Hobbs!" He bellowed for his orderly. "My boots."

She was looking a different girl now that she had a maid to curl and set her hair and to keep her ruffles ironed. Her voice was softer and her slips in grammar came only when she got excited or very tired. On shipboard 'most everybody took her for what the colonel said she was—his niece. He had taught her to walk and to curtsy and to say, "It is the *ton,*" "I do protest" and "Oh, you naughty fellow!" She worked hard at her writing and had read all of "A History of Greece from the Earliest Period."

The soldier servant, entering, saluted. Without command he about-faced and bent over the colonel's right leg. Colonel Fortescue braced his left foot against Hobbs's buttocks and pushed. Hobbs pulled. The boot came off. Katie ran to fetch his slippers.

Though she tried to make Hugh rest, he would seldom go to bed until after midnight. He held frequent interviews with his captains, most of them promoted by deaths on the slope of Breed's Hill. One of them was just eighteen and the other was hardly older. On their faces, Katie thought, was written what they had seen on June sixteenth. Several of the others were raw replacements with the ink hardly dry on recently bought commissions. The lieutenants were either callow youths or grizzled "career" officers—slack and embittered at the injustice of their fate.

He was called to attend many of the abundant summary court-martials. Desertions from the 63rd became frequent and Colonel Fortescue's jolly red face grew thin during the court-martial of two officers of the 18th infantry. Their case set all the garrison agog with scandalous rumors.

Katie did her best, a good, clever best, to help the colonel forget all these things. But it was difficult for he only returned late at night, footsore but doggedly determined to mend the state of things. She guessed that never in all his army experience had Hugh Fortescue witnessed such an appalling loss of morale as was sweeping the beleaguered Royal Forces. It was incomprehensible, it dismayed his honest soul.

Almost every day new earthworks were thrown up by the Provincials, inexorably tightening the ring about the doubly blockaded port. That it was a dreadfully weak ring, Lord Howe either failed to learn or ignored. Nor did he seem to guess that the besiegers, now under Washington, a Virginia general, were reorganizing their whole military establishment.

Around the middle of August the weather took an unseasonably ill turn. In from the Grand Banks an east wind drove a series of fogs, cold, damp, and bone-chilling. It shrouded Boston in a dismal, irritating pall. The garrison grew still more apprehensive. Rumors were flying that the Americans, stimulated by the arrival of some Rifle Companies from the South, were preparing to make a boat attack under cover of the mist. The nerves of officers and men wore thin. The Staff worked itself ragged.

Colonel Fortescue was eating his supper when alarm guns began to roar in the direction of Boston Neck. A bell commenced to clang.

"There they are, by Gad!" he burst out. Face lighting, he clapped on his cocked hat and dashed off in his dressing gown. In vain Katie called from an upstairs window that she had his tunic ready.

It came on to rain at dark and the wind howled and tore about the little brick house on Garden Court Street like a hundred banshees. While, moodily, she finished her supper Katie strained her ears for the sound of cannons. Two or three times she thought she heard some reports, but it might have been thunder. Looking out, she saw two companies of grenadiers marching by in the rain. They had their heads bent and their firelocks reversed and tucked under their armpits so as to keep the priming dry. Disconsolately, drummer boys slogged along behind, drums slung over their shoulders. They looked awfully small and young to be up so late.

Turning from the window, she went upstairs and laid out dry clothes. Then she sought the kitchen to make sure Zuleem was keeping some broth hot. She read awhile, poked the fire up and set some port to mull on the hob. But still there was no sign of Hugh. Though she tried to stay awake, she finally fell asleep with a candle guttering beside her.

It wasn't until seven of the next morning that Colonel Fortescue came home, irritable and furious at the incapacity of his company commanders. When he came stumping in, water dripping from the skirts of his dressing gown trailed down the hall and into the library.

"Hate to do it, but there will have to be changes! Horton ain't fit to handle a squad, let alone a company. Silly ass lost his head, ordered the men to fire on one of our own patrol boats. Dash it all, Kitty, can't have that sort of thing!"

"Come to bed, darling, and rest." Katie slipped an arm through his, began shepherding him towards the staircase. "You are soaked to the skin and you look dead tired."

"Damme, let go my arm, girl." He gave her a weary smile, then shook his head. "Can't stop. Harrington, my last major, is down with a flux. Hitchcock hinted that the smallpox is loose in my grenadier company."

Katie shuddered. "Smallpox" was a word that would always give her the blue creevils. There was, she knew, a lot of it about. The epidemic was getting steadily worse. Hardly any hour of the day but you could see a funeral on its way to Copp's Hill burying ground.

Hands on hips, her sturdy form barred his progress to the dining room. "Hugh, you simply must change those clothes," said she.

"Damme, no!"

"Then drink this."

He yielded rather than argue. "I find you monstrous severe this morning, Miss."

He lingered just long enough to swallow some scalding tea and a bowl of biscuit and broth then, pulling on a greatcoat, he tramped off into the fog once more. Thick as any blanket, it was shrouding the narrow streets of Boston, it purled lazily above the shining cobblestones and obscured everything above the second floor of the houses. Even dandelions dotting his lawn looked cheerless, drowned.

Bom-m-m! Hollowly a report came rolling in from the harbour. He started, then relaxed. It was only a supply ship groping her way inshore. Feeling chilly, he quickened his stride down Hanover Street, nodding now and then to friends. All of them answered vaguely or merely inclined their heads. The continued fog was weighing on everyone's spirits.

"Was a fool ever to leave warm countries," reflected Hugh Fortescue. "Blood's thin. Hang such a climate!" He was shivering now. To forget about it, he began planning. "Ain't sensible sending all the best men to the flank companies.

Recruits need stiffening of the old hands. Yes, damme, I'll put some grenadiers back into the line companies."

Tramping along over the wet sidewalk, and coughing now and then, he wished Lord Howe would for awhile forget about his port, his cards and his little whore. While the Chief-of-Staff diddled with Mrs. Joshua Loring, Jr., the army was going to pot. That was what! The hospitals were a mess, a disgrace. By Gad, today he would get the 63rd's wounded moved into decent quarters or know the reason why. When he reached regimental headquarters, he was still cold.

Katie was mending a rip in the lace on the colonel's second best uniform. At the sound of a carriage, stopping at the curb, she glanced up. That in itself was noteworthy; what with fodder so scarce, carriages were very few. Her heart missed a beat. Two red-coated officers got out, helping a third; Fortescue. Then came a man in black who carried a leather case under one arm. She flew out to open the front door. Eyes very round, she called.

"Oh, Hugh, are you wounded?"

The colonel was walking all bent over to the right. From half way down the front walk she could hear his painful gasps for breath. "No. Just a damned bad pain in my side. Nothing—worry about. Silly business. Be all right tomorrow."

The two majors supporting him didn't seem to think so, though. They looked very grave.

"Thank you, gentlemen. My apologies— Hobbs—my niece can handle me now."

"Niece, eh?" One of the majors gave the yellow-haired girl in blue and white a look. She had once served him at the Spread Eagle and he had stayed late. But he said nothing and she thanked her lucky stars. Maybe he hadn't really recognized her. After all, he was so *very* courteous.

"Don't stand there like fools! Get him inside in a hurry," rasped the man in black. "Every instant in this perishing damp hurts him."

The doctor sighed, shook his head. "Lung fever and a very heavy case, I fear Miss Tryon. I daren't bleed your uncle again."

Wiping a bloodied scalpel on his handkerchief, he turned from the big four-poster on which Hugh Fortescue lay shifting, talking in gasping, disjointed sentences of Madagascar, of Madras and of a place called Cuddapah. Occasionally he would struggle up, roaring furious, unintelligible commands in a strange language. He was fighting on the left wing at Fontenoy once more. When the delirium took firmer hold, he called for Jerry—his old friend.

Sitting in a corner and scared half out of her wits, Katie remembered the morning she and the colonel had breakfasted and talked at the entrance to Jerry Allen's driveway. That seemed to have happened years ago; in another life.

The doctor turned down his sleeves and went over to a tray of food. Said he, "You had better fix me a cot up here. The fever is very bad—and mounting."

Around eleven o'clock that night Colonel Fortescue's delirium gave way to a stupor and Katie thought she'd go crazy sitting there listening to Hugh's pitiful efforts at catching his breath.

Zuleem got very busy at the precise stroke of midnight. She set thoroughwort tea to brewing and, stepping out into a lashing downpour, begged, borrowed or stole "A Sovereign Cordial" against corruptions of the air. Until two she lingered over the kitchen fire murmuring West Indian spells over a mixture she called "oil of swallows." When she took it upstairs, the army doctor cursed and drove her away. She wept bitterly, then went below stairs and made a figure of the doctor out of beeswax from Miss Katie's sewing basket. When she had shoved needles into various tender and private parts of the manikin, she felt better.

As for Katie, she sat beside the four-poster, staring at a colorful sampler stitched by a girl named Cora Sue Huntly. She had made the "S" backwards, and in one place her design blundered through the frame. What Katie was thinking about was beds. It ran through her mind that all the really important things in a person's life happened in bed. You got born there. You thought the strange, lonesome thoughts a sick person thinks, in bed. The most delicious raptures life could yield were tasted, in bed. Then, at long last, you left off where you began, in bed.

In the early morning Colonel Fortescue opened his eyes and saw Katie sitting beside him. She was looking at her folded hands. The nearness of her was restful, but he felt very, very tired. Just before he waked, he had been re-living some marches he had made. For the first time in years he had recalled Dettingen and the bullet that had torn through his hat, and the time his horse shied on a dike in Belgium. The damned brute had reared into a swamp; another horse came plunging down on top. Then there was that near thing at Minden. He had seen again a French grenadier in white and blue holding a musket right at his chest; had it not misfired, the trail would have ended then. Dozens of times Death had passed him by, but now he knew the Dark Angel was at hand. Why, or how, he was so sure he could not tell, but he knew it.

The trail he had left around the world was long and varied. It set out from Biddeford in Devonshire and wandered to London. From thence it reeled away to the Low Countries, to Germany, to France, to Africa, to India. Back and forth, around, in and out, he had spun the thread of his life. Now the thread was to be snipped in a foggy little town in America. Hugh Fortescue could not feel especially regretful about it. He had had a damned full life. Hadn't he had his share of battle and adventure and hardship? And his fair share of fun, too? Right now it was a comfort to realize that he had seldom passed up a present pleasure for the sake of one that might never materialize.

It wasn't uncomfortable just lying still. Even yet, Katie had not noticed that his eyes were open. Katie. And before her Rachel, and before her Chloë, and before her Mameena of the mirrored thumbs and before her Zuleika, warm, brown and so very adept in bed. He smiled when he thought of blonde little Gretel waiting for him under the big windmill's arms.

There were, of course, one or two things he wasn't glad to remember. The way he tricked old Mohmand Din into signing a treaty he had not read; and the time he laid with Trelancy's wife just because she had wanted him under a full moon. But on the whole, it hadn't been a bad life. He fancied he had done his share as a British officer. He had obeyed his superiors. He had served his King—loyally, unquestioningly. And by Gad, he had never flinched, not once!

What would happen to the 63rd? That was the only thing which really worried him. Harrington was a good paper-work man, but no hand at understanding what had prompted a private to do some damned fool thing. Maybe Frothingham would fill the bill until somebody else bought the colonelcy.

By Jove, the colonelcy. Ought to be mentioned in his will. Hmm. He hadn't drawn one since he could remember.

"Oh, Hugh, Honey! You are feeling better?"

"Capital, capital! Pray send for Hallam—regimental clark, billeted Mrs. Cartney—next street." To speak, it seemed he must relay what he wanted to say to a second person, who in turn passed the idea on to another man who spoke the words.

Katie gave him one long look, then crossed to the door and told Zuleem to wake the doctor.

She herself ran through the dawn over to Mrs. Cartney's, but when she got back, leading the sleepy clerk, the doctor said, "Please, will you go out for a walk?"

"But I don't want to go. Ain't there nothing I can do?"

"No. It is the colonel's wish." He added irrelevantly, "It is a beautiful morning."

Swept once more in the current of unfamiliar forces, Katie obediently fetched her walking cloak.

"Come back in half an hour. No later." The doctor pointed his last words.

Katie went out.

There were quite a few people in her house when she came back up the bricked walk. Many officers, one of them very splendid in gold and white and scarlet. The doctor came hurrying out on the porch. He took her by the arm.

"My dear, he has been asking for you."

The way the doctor spoke put stitches in Katie's heart and, as she set foot to the stairs and fairly flew up them, she saw people waiting in the hall below stare at her. There were more men in uniform talking in undertones in the upper hall. When she passed, they, too, stepped back and looked curious, but she took no notice of them.

In the bedroom stood two captains she had entertained at dinner earlier in the week, the doctor and a man in a Geneva gown, a minister. When he saw her running in, Fortescue's grayish face relaxed. He broke off from some instructions to one of the captains.

"My own sweet Kitty." He smiled from the depths of a huge feather pillow. "Kiss me, and listen."

When she had done so, she sank onto the side of the bed looking down into the face she had always admired, and had recently come to cherish.

"Kitty, plagued sawbones here says I must report to a ne
C.-in-C."

"Oh, no, no!"

"Sorry," Fortescue gasped, but looked quite cheerfu
"Orders."

One of the captains began to blow his nose, made a hon
ing noise.

The minister stepped forward. "My dear," said he, "let m
spare the patient strength. It is Colonel Fortescue's earne
wish that I join you to him in holy matrimony."

Had the roof come crashing down, Katie could not hav
been more supremely astounded. Married? *Married* to Col
nel Fortescue? To a real fine gentleman like him? Kat
Tryon a colonel's lady?

"Oh no!" she choked. "Not me. I couldn't. It wouldr
be right. I—I ain't fit."

"Bother!" the colonel wheezed. "Rubbish! Damned mi
erable return—for happiness you've given—old crock. Dor
like stick-sucking nephews. You—courage, breeding. Mal
something of your life. Dammit girl—give me your hand!"

He wasn't strong enough to move, so she reached over th
bed, and took his fingers. They were as cold as ice. The tw
captains came closer.

The minister drew a deep breath. "Dearly beloved," l
began very softly, "we are gathered here in the sight of Go
and this company to join together in holy matrimony th
man and this woman—"

5 — NEW NORTH CHURCH

IT was a particularly glorious August afternoon and the tree
after the days of rain and fog seemed revitalized. The house
looked fresh, and the streets had been so washed they wou'
look clean for a little while. Children, freed from confine
ment, ran shrieking about open lots. The Reverend D
Andrew Èliot stood in the vestibule of the New Nort
Church. He was feeling very sad. So many people wer
dying. Being a very old man, he had known some of ther
thirty years or more.

Boston, he felt, was becoming a horrible place. Coul
this wretched, blockaded port once have been a haven c

peace and contentment? A place where people followed the Bible's precept about loving one's neighbor as himself? He was so weary of repeating the burial service its words came to him in his sleep. The British had done a wise thing in stopping those tolling bells.

He expected quite a crowd would attend Colonel Fortescue's funeral. The army chaplain who had begged use of the church had described the deceased officer as newly arrived in Boston, but already deeply respected by all who had known him.

Though the Reverend Dr. Eliot's hearing was poor, he guessed the cortège was approaching because children in Clark Street stopped playing. Then he himself heard the slow, solemn beating of drums. The drummer boys had loosed the snares of them and the drums sounded hollow—as if their heads were wet.

"Well, there's another bloody lobster-back headed for hell," grunted a hard-faced man carrying a carpenter's chest.

Passersby, aware that this was no ordinary funeral, halted to stare down Clark Street. A column, white, scarlet and gold, was advancing slowly along it.

The Reverend Dr. Eliot warned an assistant who opened the church doors. Within this Congregational Church was no glittering altar, no candles, no stained glass; its chief ornament was a handsome pulpit. People remarked on how unusual it was for an English officer to be a Dissenter. The others were Episcopalian, almost to a man.

The dull thud-thudding of the drums grew closer. From his post at the entrance, the Minister could see many wide white chevrons on the sleeves of four drummer boys swinging in unison. Following them came a platoon of the 63rd regiment. He recognized them by their very dark green lapels. They were from the regiment's light infantry company; he knew them by their short-skirted tunics and their low caps. They marched at half step, heads bent, white-gaitered feet coming down precisely together. The privates carried their firelocks with butt foremost and the brass heels on them gave off dazzling flashes. Two high-ranking officers wearing crêpe brassards stalked along before a gun carriage which, dragged by four big artillery horses, bumped and lurched over the uneven cobbles. The clatter of its iron tires echoed between the houses and scared up successive flights of blue-gray pigeons from horse droppings in the street.

A Union Jack was draped over the casket and to it had been secured the dead officer's sword and cocked hat. The pallbearers walked alongside. One of them wore naval blue, another a marine officer's white lapels. After the casket an orderly led a charger draped in black; jack-boots, reversed, had been thrust into the stirrups. It was, the Reverend Dr. Eliot recognized, the same charger they had used for Major Abercromby and young Lieutenant Bruere. He knew the animal because of the long V-shaped white stocking on the creature's off front foot. Odd, he should have noticed such a trifling detail. He resettled his gown and tried not to be troubled by the scowls the onlookers were giving the cortège.

After the charger marched a body of officers, then a platoon of grenadiers whose black bearskins towered high above the idlers on the streetside. A closed carriage came into sight. That meant a woman. A daughter? A wife? No matter.

The drummers wheeled, two to either side of the church entrance, but the escort continued on until the gun carriage was opposite the door. When it halted the six pallbearers waited for a surcingle to be cast loose then they reached for the silver casket handles.

From the carriage Katie watched them carry the casket into the church. Then she saw the officers of the 63rd file in, powdered wigs shining like snowflakes on dark ground. The troops wheeled into line facing the New North Church, and grounded arms.

The hired hack rattled on until the church door yawned to the left.

Zuleem stopped sniffling, said, "We is here, Miss—Mrs. Fortescue."

Mrs. Fortescue! Katie still couldn't get it through her head what had happened, even though a lawyer of the town had read her the Colonel's new will. To her he had left the whole of his property except a settlement on old Jerry Allen. That meant, the lawyer said, that she was rich, very rich! Richer even than Mrs. Neil Jameison back in Norfolk. When Hugh said he had more money than he knew what to do with, he had spoken truly. Think of it! She now had £80,000 and a home in a place called South Molton! Funny. She had no idea of where in England South Molton might be. Mrs Fortescue? Involuntarily she glanced at her wedding ring. How bright it shone against her black skirt. Her skin wa

594

sort of gold-colored, too. She had lain in the sun a lot at Glen Duror.

Before she realized it she was occupying a pew, alone except for Zuleem. Mrs. Frothingham, the lieutenant-colonel's wife, had offered to keep her company, but the way she spoke made Katie glad to decline. She knew, too, what all these officers must be thinking. They were right, but it didn't matter. Not now. They'd never guess, though, how dreadfully she was going to miss the colonel.

The service was over and the minister asked if she wished to ride out to the burying ground. Instinctively she doubted the wisdom of it. Was it not right to leave her husband's body with fellow officers who had known and loved Hugh Fortescue longer than she? She knew she hadn't really loved him in a romantic way. But she had been wholly devoted to him, nonetheless. He had been so fine, so kind and so very generous. It was a shame about his dying. For all his age, Hugh had been such good fun.

Yes, she reckoned it was right to leave him now with his fellow soldiers. She told the Reverend Dr. Eliot so, and remained kneeling, weeping quietly, while the last footsteps had retreated down the center aisle, until the drums had recommenced their muffled beatings, until the gun carriage's tires once more commenced to ring and rasp over the cobbles. Slowly the military music faded in the distance.

She looked up, startled to hear more hoofs at the church door, more tires rasping.

"Come, Zuleem," she whispered. "I reckon we had better clear out."

They were just a little too late. In the vestibule she paused to let pass four men in threadbare civilian clothes. Between them they lugged a plain pine coffin. The minister addressed the rough-looking fellows by name. Thanked them.

"It is very Christian of you to help the friendless in this way," he said.

Then the Revered Doctor went down the steps to assist a veiled woman who, on foot, had followed a shabby wood cart in which the coffin had been carried. She, too, had but a single attendant, an old woman who clutched her arm. Madelaine Ashton, mechanically climbing the church steps, saw a pretty girl in black waiting to let her pass.

A look passed between them.

"Come, my dear," the older woman urged. "Dr. Eliot is waiting."

Katie gave the young woman, a widow by the look of her, a tremulous smile. "Your husband?"

Madelaine could only nod and went on into the peaceful gloom of the church.

As Katie stepped into the sunlight, she heard the Reverend Dr. Eliot's voice for a second time recite, "I am the resurrection and the life."

Part IV

Philadelphia

1 — IN THE DELAWARE

A FRIGATE chased the *Lady Catherine*. Cracking on sail after sail, the man-of-war pursued her right into the entrance of Delaware Bay. She even harried the sloop past Point Norris. But when a big earthwork mounting cannons loomed below the village of Salem, she slowed. Then, as a trio of row-galleys began pulling out from shore, she sullenly came about. Just for spite, her commander fired a broadside, and because his trajectory was very flat, everyone could see the cannonballs come skipping over the river, like stones scaled by a small boy. They sank, however, before they reached the *Lady Catherine*.

"I'm a hundred years older, by God!" Captain Ord sighed, surrendering the wheel to his quartermaster. He shook as if seized by an ague. Rob, too, was mighty relieved to see the brown and blue painted man-of-war standing out to sea. From the *Lady Catherine*'s people he had had accounts of the way prisoners were treated aboard His Majesty's ships and he had no desire for first-hand experience. Looking white about the mouth, Mr. Peacock came up from below and quietly ground out a gunner's match under his heel.

"What in 'tarnation you thinking of?" Ord roared. "You know it's against orders to go below with an open spark? Want to blow us all to hell?"

Mr. Peacock smiled a tight smile. "No. But that powder wasn't going to get back into British hands."

Rob stared, felt his mouth go dry. Good God! Why, the idiot had been ready to blow them all to hell!

Ever since they had parted from the *Packet* off the Bermudas, the voyage had been speedy, and everyone felt fine over having lifted so much powder. The officers and the crew never got tired of telling one another what they had done.

Every time the teller's part grew more heroic. One night Rob lost patience.

Said he, "You couldn't have done a blamed thing without whale boats and Henry Tucker's running things like he did. Just remember that when you get ashore."

Mr. Peacock nodded. "You're right, Ashton. I'll admit I didn't trust them any farther than I can heave a bull by the tail, but they did their share."

Keeping one eye on the approaching row-galleys, Captain Ord said, "You are aiming to fit out a ship, Mr. Peacock?"

"Soon's I can locate some cannons. I'm going to pay off something I owe the Britishers. They burnt my shipyard last spring."

Ord said, "Better go slow, sir. You try shooting up English vessels and you'll find yourself hanged for a pirate. They say the Congress won't grant letters of marque."

Mr. Peacock winked at Rob. "When the time comes, I'm quite ready to take my chances."

The nearest galley now cruised less than a hundred yards off to port. In time to the beating of a sort of tom-tom, her oarsmen's bodies swayed now back, now forward. At every stroke they were bending ten foot sweeps and tea-colored waves fell sharply away from under the gundelo's prow. A piece of field artillery, wheels and all, had been mounted in her bow. A gun crew in brown uniforms were clustered about it. The row-galleys were of good size, capable of holding sixty or seventy men and their sides were stout and pierced for musket loopholes.

Without waiting for orders, Captain Ord brought his sloop into the wind and let go an anchor. Evidently satisfied that they were not needed, two gundelos put back towards a little cove in the low rising river bank. Upstream, sprawled Salem, a neat appearing village of red-painted houses. The whole river bank and a forest of soft looking trees behind it was veiled in a blue-bronze haze.

It was ten—no, eleven days ago that they had dropped the Bermudas below the horizon. Today, therefore, must be the 25th. He was wondering how quickly Andrea could find passage, when the sight of that British man-of-war, going on with the tide, gave him a bad turn. What if Andrea's ship wasn't so fast or so lucky as the *Lady Catherine?* The hell of a mess if her ship got taken and sent into New York. Why in time hadn't he reckoned on such a possibility? How could he find her if that happened? As he stood there by the rail he reckoned he would wait a month then, if he got no word, he would start looking for her.

Again he wondered how the Bermudians and their whale boats had made out. If any one of them talked out of turn, everybody, from Colonel Tucker down, would be in the soup and would have to fight to avoid hanging. He would not sleep easy 'til he got definite word of what had happened.

Raggedly shipping her starboard oars, the leading gundelo came alongside. A well dressed fellow caught a rope ladder and swarmed up the side with remarkable agility. He wore a definite air of authority and his deeply pitted face was tense. Without acknowledging Captain Ord's salute, he ran over to Mr. Peacock and, looking him square in the eye asked, "Did you?"

"Yes, Mr. Duane," the other replied, offering his hand.

The newcomer beamed, flung ecstatic arms about Mr. Peacock's shoulders, then pumped his hands so hard it looked as if he wanted to wring the arms off.

"Splendid work, sir! You have no idea how relieved everyone will be." Then Mr. Duane rushed over and shook Ord's hand just as enthusiastically. "Capital work. Capital, Captain! How in the world did you manage?"

Mr. Peacock interrupted quickly, "That is a long story, sir, and the report must be made to Mr. Franklin and Mr. Morris."

The other smiled his apology. "Of course. Stupid of me to forget. Got carried away."

Of the conversation Rob heard only the beginning. He had become absorbed in the approach of a second gundelo. There seemed something familiar about a figure on the row-galley's steering transom. A suspicion formed, grew quickly.

He turned to Mr. Duane. "Sir, can you tell me who that fellow is? The short man?"

The Pennsylvanian answered carelessly. "He? Oh, he's a Yankee delegate to Congress. Massachusetts Committee sent him down to advise us on naval matters."

He was right. It was Stephen Farish yonder. He was mighty pleased, tickled no end at finding him again. What ages had passed since last he had seen Farish sailing off in the *Assistance* with David and Johnny Gilmorin.

"Well, Captain," he yelled, "you're a long way off your course!"

The New Englander goggled. "Well, I'm a son of a sea cook!"

He turned to the gundelo's captain and immediately the oars quickened their beat. Quick as a squirrel, Captain Farish scaled the *Lady Catherine*'s salt-streaked side, paused on the rail until he spied Rob.

"Jumping Jehosophat!" he exclaimed. "This is mighty fine! How are you, sir?"

"Right well," Rob gripped Farish's fist very hard. "And you?"

"Tolerable, sir, tolerable. I wrote down to Mr. Jameison and was plumb took aback when he said you had pulled out of Norfolk lock, stock, and barrel. Said you'd sailed for furrin parts. That correct?"

"It was," Rob admitted slowly. "Things got pretty bad for me. But I'm back."

Mr. Duane of the Pennsylvania Committee of Safety began to look restless.

"Mr. Peacock," said he. "I guess you had better move your cargo to Philadelphia as quickly as possible. Committee's orders."

Rob noticed how careful he was not to use the word "powder."

While his anchor was being raised Captain Ord conducted private speculations on where the powder would be re-shipped. But he wasn't over curious. He had done what he had set out to do and had earned a bonus besides. If he got sent on another cruise like this he would insist on mounting six or eight more guns. When he remembered how near that frigate had come to making a prize of him he felt sick. The Britishers were getting all-fired cranky about arms and ammunition nowadays.

Stephen Farish said he was minded to stay aboard. Once the *Lady Catherine* got under way again Captain Ord dipped his Union Jack to the fort. Promptly its flag returned the courtesy. Rob couldn't help laughing; it was so absurd to be saluted by the very flag that had been scaring the delirious daylights out of the sloop all morning.

When he remarked on this to Farish the New Englander rubbed his bald brown head and drawled, "A mort of folks in

America still claim we ain't real rebels. They allow we are just armed petitioners waiting for an answer."

"Come below," Rob suggested. "My valet will break out some prime Oporto. We should drink to this occasion."

Farish looked hard at Rob an instant. "Valet? Have been in furrin parts, ain't you?"

2 — ROB'S CABIN

A LANTERN burned late in Rob's cabin. Long since, he and Farish had laid aside coats and waistcoats. The remnants of a meal and a third bottle of port stood between them. Sachem had yawned and yawned until Rob bade him clear up and be off. But instead of going to bed the half-breed went on deck and lingered there, staring eagerly at this new land. Laws! It seemed to go on forever. And there *were* forests and rivers.

Rob lounged on his new trunk and the sea captain sat on a locker sucking at a peculiarly rank clay pipe. They could, when they chose to look, see the river's bank slipping steadily by.

"Well," Farish was concluding, "like I said, your brother got us jailed but he got us out. I'll say that for him and, now that I look back on it, I don't abominate him the way I did. I guess maybe I, well, I see what he was driving at."

Rob sighed, passed a hand over his eyes, then rubbed their lids. Now that he had money again he wasn't feeling so bitter. He wanted David to meet Andrea. He reckoned they would get on.

"You can find him easy enough," Farish assured. "Like I told you, he was took prisoner and if he's been exchanged I ain't heard of it. Most likely he's still in that pesky Stone Jail." He paused. "Most of your brother's cruises are out of my soundings, Mr. Ashton, but he's sound at bottom."

As the night advanced, the conversation became subdued, solemn. When Farish learned of what had happened to the *Grand Turk* he groaned, stared blankly out of the porthole. To think the brig had never even sailed once! Kind of unjust, after all that work and worry. The news came as a cruel disappointment; all along he had been itching to learn how near the wind the brig would go, how fast she was. He had had more than an idle curiosity.

So pretty little Mrs. Ashton had slipped her cable? He was spell set to hear of it. Hers had been such a rare fine business head.

It was a comfort to think of Solace safe in Watertown with a sound roof over her head. The children were going to church and school again—which was also good. He didn't hold with letting such matters slide.

He wondered how Mr. Ashton had made all that money, for, sure as preaching, he had money. His shoes, his clothes and the way he carried himself said so, even if he didn't.

Once Rob had finished talking, Farish relit his pipe and described how he had tackled the Massachusetts Committee about fitting out some cruisers. Once he had pointed out how British transports were, all unarmed, bringing supplies to the enemy, they got to work and fitted out the *Margaretta*. In quick succession she captured the *Diligent* and *Tattamagouche*, supply vessels. The stores they took pleased General Washington as much as the loss of them depressed the English cooped up in Boston.

"Seeing how things worked out on the Bay, the Pennsylvanians wanted to do the same, and I got sent down here to tell 'em how. Says I to Mr. Benjamin Franklin, 'If us fellers make the water unhealthy for the King's ships, his troops will just naturally starve. Why don't we build ships of our own, real men-of-war'?"

Rob sat up and, shaking his head, poured a glass of port. "We couldn't hope to fight the Royal Navy! They'd blow us out of the water."

"What makes you so sure? Just stop and cal'late a mite. For nigh on two hundred years we've been building the finest, fastest ships in this Kingdom." Farish's voice gathered volume and his wintry eyes flashed. "Our captains are every bit as smart as theirs and better at dodging a customer too tough to handle! With a bit of training I'll bet our boys can shoot a dummed sight straighter than the King's ships did at Bunker's. Shucks! For all the damage they did they might have been shooting dried peas."

"Did the Pennsylvanians listen?"

A shrug lifted Farish's shoulders. "Don't know. Like all the delegates they're skeered another Province will benefit by their work. That Virginia feller, Washington, asked them to start a navy some time back, but they ain't got 'round to it. Know what Washington did? He calls one of his army captains and says, 'Now, sir, I want you to take a passel of the troops of *my command* and march down to Beverly where you will find a schooner fitted out at the Continental Army's expense. I herewith order you to march across Buzzard's Bay and to attack any enemy force you come upon.' Neat, eh?"

Rob laughed. General Washington, he agreed, was pretty shrewd.

3 — PHILADELPHIA

ON arising Rob went straight up on deck. He found it fine to smell the land again, to see familiar types of houses and barns. Even the muddy current stirred warming memories. Above a bend in the river showed the steeples and roofs of a great city. Philadelphia with a population of almost 20,000 was the largest and richest city in British America. Mr. Peacock said it boasted several theaters and nobody knew how many taverns. British Naval officers liked Philadelphia best of all American ports; the girls there were jolly and some of them not above an unpremeditated cruise between the sheets.

To the sloop's masthead had been hoisted a private signal, a yellow flag with a blue St. Andrew's cross. No sooner had the *Lady Catherine* got under way again Captain Ord than a barge came pulling to intercept her. It brought orders for her to dock immediately. Rob found it significant that a gang of laborers were ready and waiting to unload. At the shore end of the pier lounged sentries from the City Troop. They looked as smart as regulars in their jack-boots, smart brown and white regimentals, and burnished helmets.

Captain Ord, Mr. Peacock and Mr. Duane hurriedly disembarked and joined a knot of serious-looking men in dark blue uniforms. To the opposite side of the wharf a small sloop was tied up with hatches open, crew ready and whips rigged. Even while the *Lady*'s hawsers were being made fast laborers began dropping onto her deck and took off the new arrival's hatches. Without delay they commenced to hoist out the powder and a low murmur went up when the sun shone on broad white arrows done on the keg ends—it was the Government mark. In rapid succession barrels were heaved on deck, weighed and checked by an officer in a dingy blue

603

and white tunic. A good half of the King's powder was sent rumbling and bumping over to the smaller vessel.

Rob was superintending Sachem's efforts to pack the last of his gear when Farish hunted him out. The New Englander was grinning, showing all the gaps in his teeth.

"You should hear what that Peacock feller has been telling the Committeemen about you. I cal'late he's a spryer story teller than Dan'l Dee-foe."

"Reckon he must be. Why all this hurry over trans-shipping?"

Farish looked grave, closed the door. "You'll not let on?"

"Never a word."

"Well then, the Ordinance Officer at Cambridge made return of thirty-six rounds a man but when the General checked up he found there weren't but eight! If the British take a mind to come out and fight, they can whip our troops all to hollow. May have done so already. There's rumors about that the siege is going to be lifted right away. Now you understand?"

"Yes. But in that case why don't they take all our load? Washington must need every speck of it."

"You ain't dealt with the Congress yet. A bunch of delegates are dead set to send an expedition against Canada. Maybe two. It's a pet idea of old Ben Franklin's. I ain't none too sure this much powder will do any good. Still, like we say to home, 'half a bed is better than none.' "

"On the other hand, there are also circumstances when half a bed is a damned sight more enjoyable than a whole one."

"Well, I vum!" Farish broke into a cackle.

"Meet me at the New City Tavern tonight and we'll celebrate. Bring along Ord if he can get away."

"What about Peacock?"

Rob said, "No. Let's have a sea-going bout."

"Good enough. But—" Farish still looked doubtful—"the City Tavern is a mighty expensive place."

4 — MECHANICS' HALL

MR. PEACOCK and Captain Ord had already departed when Rob followed Farish on deck, but they were in time to see the powder sloop cast off. Could it slip past that frigate lurking between Cape Henlopen and Cape May? Suddenly it came to him that this might be Mr. Franklin's real reason for holding back so much of the cargo.

On the wharf he paused, looked about. It was at once familiar and depressing to see so many dismantled ships. There were even more in sight than in Norfolk. Paradoxically, a shipyard across the river was going full blast. When Rob remarked on it and on the size of two vessels being laid down, the mariner winked and looked wise.

That same morning word was brought that Mr. Franklin wished a few words with Mr. Ashton. Would he be good enough to call? Captain Farish might stop by also. It was with some trepidation that Rob accepted, and around three of the afternoon set off.

The streets of Philadelphia were, most of them, sixty feet wide and had real sidewalks for pedestrians. Municipal pumps stood at frequent intervals and the brick pavement was clean swept. On entering Second Street, Rob found he could see nearly half a mile along it.

Farish, striding along, identified various buildings. This was an experimental prison called a "bettering house." The inmates were homeless folk and insolvent strangers who became stranded in the city. Here they were provided with work and kept until they had earned enough to carry them onwards. The plainness of the buildings, it appeared, was due to the powerful influence of the Quakers. The Society of Friends fancied no decorative fol-de-rols. On the other side of town, Farish explained, was a handsome brick hospital and barracks large enough to accommodate seven or eight thousand troops—more than the whole garrison of Boston. There were many churches—Episcopal, Lutheran, Quaker Meeting Houses, and even a Roman Chapel. Rob, cutting a real swath in his best claret velvet suit, listened interestedly.

Market Street astonished him. It was a hundred feet wide!

Along it streamed flocks of sheep and geese, produce wagons, carts and wains.

Outside Mechanics' Hall, Farish halted, squinting up at its ivy-hung walls of red brick.

"Better take a good look," the New Englander advised, head cocked to one side. "History is being made in there; some good, some bad." His big voice thickened. "But this Congress will not disband until Parliament guarantees our rights."

Rob insisted on halting long enough at the Three Crowns Tavern to get his hair powdered. After that he stood Farish to a glass of flip. He felt nervous. The prospect of talking with so celebrated a man as Benjamin Franklin seemed appalling. Anxiously, Rob inspected himself in a mirror. He had lost weight, all right, and the lines of his face had deepened, but his clothes were of conservative good quality and his hair properly albemarled. In his new lace stock and linen shirt he was damned if he didn't look like a nervous bridegroom. He was glad of this opportunity, anyhow, and he hoped he would make a favorable impression. Recently a plan had been taking shape in his mind; it was an idea which would call for the consent and backing of an influential man.

Farish, too, had spruced up. His black cocked hat was shining and his brass buttons free of dust.

"Let's go," he urged. "Ain't nothing to get skeered over."

Mr. Franklin was working in a dark banyan and a Turkey red turban, the day being too hot for a wig. Beside him stood an austere, severely aristocratic gentleman in black and white. Mr. Peacock came forward from the background, presented Rob. Farish they had met before.

Rob, taking Mr. Franklin's hand, felt his fears vanish. Whatever he tried to say he reckoned would be taken in the right way. What a depth of humanity and humor lurked in the septuagenarian's gray eyes. His head was big and its forehead was so lofty it swept up like the dome of a building. Gold-rimmed spectacles with square lenses had been pushed above the old man's brows. A trace of sensuousness marked the set of Mr. Franklin's mouth, but it served rather to mellow, than to weaken, his serene, surprisingly alert expression.

Smiling, he waved Rob to a chair, set down the quill with which he had been writing and said, "Mr. Peacock has been telling Mr. Morris and me about the assistance you afforded him in the matter of the Bermuda powder."

"Really, sir, I—" Rob colored like a boy praised before classmates.

"Pray don't attempt to deny it. Our agent tells me you offered surety for some whale boats this expedition had to have?"

"It was not required," Rob reminded. "At least, I haven't been told so."

Mr. Franklin leaned forward and, without taking his eyes from Rob, began to toy with a curious device which looked like a gun lock but resembled none Rob had ever beheld. Mr. Franklin's rich, strangely magnetic voice went on.

"Mr. Peacock's report further states that you participated in the—er—removal; and by apprehending an onlooker, possibly saved the whole expedition from disaster. For that, Mr. Ashton, pray accept the thanks of this Committee."

Rob did the best he could about belittling his efforts. He played up the work of Colonel Henry, of Henry Tucker, Peter and the rest. It was only fair. He did this through no particular access of modesty but because it was right to confess that his interest in the raid to start with, at least, had been haphazard; an escape from boredom and inactivity.

Mr. Franklin pulled down his spectacles, shot Mr. Morris a fleeting glance. "Our friends in Bermuda will not regret their part. I am sure the Congress will prove—in a practical sense—how sensible it is of their genuine good will." The old man's manner was entirely grave, but a faint twinkle danced at the backs of his eyes. It conveyed knowledge that Franklin very well understood the true motives of the West Enders.

Morris smiled pallidly. "Indeed, Mr. Ashton, this powder could not have arrived at a more propitious moment. Perhaps some day you will do me the honor of dining with me?"

Rob shook hands all around and prepared to leave, but Mr. Franklin looked over the tops of his spectacles. "A moment more of your time, my dear Mr. Ashton. I have come to believe that abstract praise is stimulating, but not nourishing. Is there perhaps some concrete matter in which I might, to your advantage, use my inconsiderable influence?"

Rob's heart lifted. "Why, yes, sir. I would like mighty well to come across eight 12-pound cannon, six swivels and powder and shot enough for them."

Mr. Morris wheeled, definitely startled. "God bless my soul! Well, sir, and what can you be wanting with cannon?"

"I fear that is not the point," Franklin interposed. "The point is that Mr. Ashton wants them. From the exactitude of his request one might infer that he knows what he is about." A fold of the turban flapped when he inclined his head. "Rest assured, Mr. Ashton, that I shall do my best. Pray where can one communicate with you?"

Rob told him; then, perspiring heavily into his stock, went out. Mr. Morris's voice, sharp and petulant, followed him.

"But hang it, Ben, it's illegal, downright illegal to sell cannons to private individuals, and you know it!"

"Tut, tut," came the memorable voice. "If we wait for lawyers to pass on our decisions, we shall find about our necks something less pleasing than linen."

5 — WATERFRONT

DURING the next week Rob devoted his time to combing shipyards and little estuaries along the pleasant banks of the Delaware. He wanted only one type of vessel and about her he had definite ideas. She must be fairly new, very fast, roomy in her hold, and big enough to mount eight guns. She must have a good-sized forecastle to accommodate the big crew a privateer called for. Copper sheathing, too.

Time and again a sloop or a brig came reasonably near filling his requirements, but always there was something wrong and Rob wouldn't have her. Even when the owners cut their asking price to shreds, the solid young Virginian would not listen and went rowing off in his chartered barge. He offered so good a price, three hundred Spanish dollars per ton, that men came from 'way down river, from over in Jersey, from the Upper Chesapeake inviting him to their yards.

Despite his preoccupation, he twice a day cocked an eye on the Customs House flagstaff. It showed signals describing the impending arrival and presumed nationality of incoming vessels. By greasing the palm of a retired sea captain in charge of the signal halyards, he arranged for a special signal flag, half red and half yellow, to be shown as soon as a vessel clearing from Bermuda made port.

He was growing so confounded anxious over Andrea's continued non-appearance it was good he had something to occupy him. After supper was the worst time. It was then his imagination really got under way. Ten days now and never a word, let alone sight of her. Suppose a sloop-of-war gave chase to Andrea's vessel? Suppose, as so often happened, the man-of-war fired a shot into the chase?

At such times he resolutely stopped thinking and went out to look up Farish or George Ord. They, too, were keeping an eye out for a vessel for him. Usually he had little trouble in steering them into a nearby ordinary and standing them to a new drink he was growing fond of. It was called a julep, the Irish barman said, and had been invented in France. Crushed mint leaves, ice, dash of sugar, and cognac. Because it was now late summer, ice made these drinks rather expensive. However the pungent scent of mint and the skim of frost on the outside of a silver tumbler, added to the resultant sense of reassurance, made a julep not such a bad investment, Rob reckoned.

Whenever Farish could get away from manifold sessions with the committee Congress had appointed to study the question of a navy, he would join Rob in rowing about the harbour. Every few days there would be new vessels to look at. By the dozen, ships were being confiscated by Provincial Committees of Safety for violations of the Association.

Rob got to know a great deal about Philadelphia. He even went down as far as Gloucester where Benjamin Franklin's latest wrinkle, *vaisseaux de frise*, would be sunk. These would narrow a channel and force passing ships into the range of land batteries. These defenses were, in effect, great frames spiked together and weighted with stones. Uprights, rising to within a few feet of the surface, would certainly foul the keel of a vessel attempting to pass over them.

The price of almost every commodity was rising so fast Rob itched to get going again. He made friends with various merchants, located a small but substantial warehouse with a sound wharf, and studied current prices. Plenty of warehouses were empty, their Tory owners fled or in prison. For a starter he bought in a fine lot of dressed leather at the public auction of some contraband goods. Cloth of every kind was selling at a price to warm a merchant's heart. Retailers were paying $15 a barrel for July flour and the price of powder had risen to $2.50 a pound. Most serious of all was the shortage of woolen goods—shortages which even the busy looms of the Dutch at Germantown were unable to affect.

At night Philadelphia's streets were no less lively than by daylight. Everywhere swarmed delegates to the second Continental Congress. They had, most of them, brought along wives, children and servants. At the same bar Rob often recognized the soft drawl of a Carolinian, the rapid fire accents of New Yorkers, and the nasal twang of a New Englander. As a rule the delegates got on famously. Every night the cockpit at Mine's Alley was jammed, and the brothels did a roaring trade. Every inn, tavern and ordinary was turning away guests by the dozen.

Rob found it easier nowadays to engage a stranger in conversation. In this fashion he picked up news to his advantage.

In Robert Morris's elegant great mansion he dined alone with his host off china that matched, and he ate with silver service bearing a single monogram. When he thought of Henry Tucker's and Peter Ashton's tableware, he couldn't resist a reminiscent grin.

The Philadelphian proved acutely interested in a description of business conditions prevailing in the Bermudas.

Like a corporate ghost a white butler—the first Robert had seen in the Provinces—directed the courses of the meal.

In the wavering glow of many candles the old aristocrat's parchment-hued features took on a gilded aspect. He lifted his wine glass and, staring into clear yellow sauterne observed, "Once the British reinforce their fleet, our unarmed merchantmen will not be able to dodge about any longer You can be sure of that. At the same time, if our trade to the French West Indies and with the Dutch in Curaçao falters, our effort is doomed since it is from them we get the bulk of our arms and all of our hard money! I presume you know how utterly valueless Provincial paper is becoming?"

Rob said he knew.

Mr. Morris's reflection was perfectly reproduced in the highly polished mahogany of the dining table, even the gesture with which he offered an enameled snuff box.

"Has it occurred to you, Mr. Ashton, that we merchant carry a heavy responsibility? When serious fighting begins, i will be on us that Congress and the Continental armies wi lean."

The banker rested both elbows on the table and hunche

forward a little. The lace at his cuffs seemed like jets of foamy water running out of his sleeve.

"For us, Mr. Ashton, there will be small glory, though our lives and fortunes will be in a greater jeopardy than those of fire-eaters and of young bloods strutting about in regimentals." Mr. Morris stared absently at lace window-curtains veiling the vitreous black of his windowpanes. "I wonder why we do it?"

Rob felt mighty flattered to have one of the richest men in America talking to him like this. There wasn't a hint of condescension in Mr. Morris's manner—not a trace.

He said, "Maybe it's because we love trading. If I'm left no choice I don't mind fighting, but I take no pleasure in destroying property and killing people. It's a bad business with no decent returns."

For coffee they retired to a little library where they talked until a clock on the hall stairs chimed eleven. When Rob got up, he had learned at which ports in Guadeloupe and Martinique you could find prime wines, clothes and weapons. Also where, in the Spanish West Indies, you could expect to get the best prices for hard lumber, salt food and livestock.

Rob wandered down a succession of clean broad streets on his way back to Smith's City Tavern.

At the porter's lodge he inquired for news of a Bermuda vessel.

There was none and the red-nosed fellow grinned. "I declare, sir, a fellow would think you was expecting treasure."

6 — THE SPEEDWELL

NEXT morning at breakfast Rob picked up his host's copy of the "Pennsylvania Gazette" and idly ran through it. He perused the usual advertisements for runaway slaves and bound boys, the rewards offered for deserters from this or that regiment. A woman with "a young breast of milk" begged possible clients to inquire of the printer. The Pennsylvania Committee published a warning that no man must use gunpowder on "bird, beast or mark." The ship *Peggy*, Captain Charles Kirby, had been taken prize by H.M.S. *Viper*. Jaws

611

working briskly on a roll, Rob turned the page, noted the smudgy reproduction of a ship and read:

> Brig *Speedwell* to be sold at publick Vendue
> by order of Penna. Comm. Safety. 300 T.
> burthen, now lying in the River at Gloucester.
> Very fast. Bermuda-built of cedar.

Speedwell? Rob fumbled an instant then as soon as he remembered, grabbed his hat and rushed out. Like a bull of Bashan he charged into Farish's quarters at the Bunch of Grapes and routed him out.

"Come along!" he cried. "I must have your opinion."

When they recognized Stephen Farish, a quartet of slovenly militiamen deserted their card game and started buttoning their tunics. To Rob's immense satisfaction, the brig was that same *Speedwell* which had overhauled the *Desdemona*. Though not quite so trim as he remembered her, the brig was, nonetheless, a handsome piece of work. Her owner, a Bermudian Tory had lost her for smuggling contraband. Rob reckoned he knew a little how the poor fellow must be feeling.

That she was indeed carefully put together, Rob soon decided. Being of cedar and therefore worm-proof, the *Speedwell* required no sheathing, either or lead or of more expensive copper. The weight thus saved should help her footing, Farish argued. There were so many ships idle only two other bidders put in an appearance, and the auctioneer was all for postponing his vendue until Farish stalked over and said a few words in his ear. Strangely enough, he changed his mind then.

From truck to keelson, from stem to stern Rob examined the prize. Then he went over every bit of the planking he could get at; studied the masts and yards for cracks; had the sails set down and the cables brought on deck. He sniffed at the bilges and found them sweet. The pumps were adequate and worked well when he tested them. He couldn't believe his offer of $18,000 would be snapped up by the vendue agent.

"Mr. Ashton, you were over-hasty," Farish reproved. "With a little haggling you might have got her for $17,000 or maybe $16,500."

Rob said, "What's the difference? The cash goes to the Committee and they will buy supplies for the army with it."

Farish chuckled. "You ain't such a dumblock, Mr. Ashton, even if you are a Virginian."

Rob grinned and cocked an eye at the rigging, freshly tarred and bright in the sunlight. "What do you mean?"

"Next month you'll be importing supplies that Congress needs, and get it all back."

"Do you think those bulwarks are solid enough to stand shot?" was Rob's innocent query.

Farish laughed and slapped his thigh. "You're pretty smart, by Godfreys. Eh? Oh yes, they're solid enough, but I'd support the deck beams below. In a heavy sea, gun carriages can throw a lot of weight about."

A weight lifted from Rob's heart. It was easy to visualize the *Speedwell* mounting eight guns and carrying half a dozen swivels on her rails. Provided he could find a good sized crew of the right sort, it would take a big man-of-war to make him heave-to. But the problem of manning his brig gave him little concern. Privateering had not yet begun and hundreds of ablebodied merchant seamen were hungrily tramping the streets.

On the way back upstream his imagination caught fire. He reckoned he would have a light yellow streak painted along the *Speedwell*'s black side. He would order constructed a magazine which would be fire-proof—no matter what happened. Of course, he would have to enlarge the forecastle at the expense of the forehold; with four men to a cannon it required quite a few men to fight even eight guns.

Though Rob hadn't said a word of what he was planning, Farish marked his enthusiasm.

"Don't run on too fast," he advised. "Like I told you, the Congress ain't ready to issue letters of marque."

Rob looked into Farish's bright blue eyes. "When did I say anything about taking prizes?"

"Nary a word, but I guessed you were figuring on it."

"Not for awhile. Right now I only want guns so's I can drive off anybody who tries meddling with my trading. Seems a man has to fight these days for the right to carry a cargo of goods."

"I'd say it took a smart feller like you a good while to figger that out," was Farish's dry comment.

"I reckon it did, Stephen, but from now on—God help anyone who gets in my way!"

When he got back to town, he went to his bankers, arranged for the $18,000 in drafts on New York and London. His deposits there were good as gold, Mr. Menken assured him, but it would be wise to conserve his Philadelphia deposit against open warfare with the Mother Country.

On his way to Smith's City Tavern Rob began stopping off at various inns and boarding houses. He invited everybody with whom he had been friendly to a gaming and drinking party. He had found his ship, so tonight, he promised them, would be a celebration. It would be the liveliest Smith's City Tavern had ever housed.

He felt so damned happy he wanted to beat somebody up. By the Lord Harry, he was going to get tight, tight as a lord! Tomorrow he would get after Mr. Franklin. Buoyantly, he hurried back to his lodgings.

7 — CELEBRATIONS

THAT his guests were not slow in putting in an appearance Rob learned while wiping his razor. He could hear first arrivals tramping in downstairs, also the voice of the landlord welcoming them in a hearty tone.

"How-de-do, Mr. Brewer! A good evening to you, Mr. Buchanan. Pleasure, Captain Thornburr. And, Mr. Gutkneich, how is your health this fine evening? Gentlemen, what's your pleasure?"

Rob was sousing his face into the wash basin when someone knocked.

Scrubbing hard, he called, "Come in." The door opened, but his eyes being full of soap, he made no effort to turn.

"You are forgetting the back of your neck," a soft voice pointed out. Rob spun about as if a bayonet had jabbed him.

She waited smiling, radiant in a lincoln-green traveling cloak. The hood of it was thrown back from her hair; by the lamp light it looked more like bronze than ever.

Andrea began to laugh. "Oh Rob! If you only knew how funny you look!" She began to giggle and the giggles grew into laughter, somewhat nervous laughter, which broke down Rob's paralysis of astonishment.

Dripping soap and naked to the waist, he rushed at her, arms outstretched. His arms closed about her and she strained against his chest hard, hard; even when the wet on his body soaked through her dress. He held her at arms' length, laughing to see soap on her chin. He kissed her again—and again.

Standing straight, arms limp at her side, Andrea could only look at him. She could smell the soap on his face, but mostly she was aware of his peculiarly exciting aura of masculinity.

Hurriedly he wiped his face and hands, then shut the door. His back was broad and brown looking, and a trickle of soapy water was following the length of his spine. She began to laugh.

"Go ahead. You'll see me like this a good many times."

"I know, Rob, but you will never look so funny."

His arms went around her again, lifted her clear of the floor with a grip that made her ribs ache.

"Oh, darling, darling! You have been so long getting here."

"You might have looked for me," said she pretending to pout.

"Why, I did! I—they never—" Then he remembered. In his excitement over the *Speedwell,* he hadn't once looked at the Customs House flagstaff!.

At length Andrea suggested in a small voice, "Hadn't you better put me down? All this soapy water is ruining my gown and—oh sweeting, I do want to look nice."

He sobered at a sudden thought. "Good Lord! I clean forgot. Peter and the rest, they got back all right?"

The hazel eyes grew steady. "I vow it was a very near thing, but they got the boats hidden, and scattered in time. Governor Bruere nearly went wild; all that next morning he rode about St. George's like a mad man. He ordered some armed merchantmen to pursue, but the captains either told him to go to blazes or took so much time getting off it was no use."

"Has anyone talked?"

"Not when I left. The Governor offered a free pardon and £100 to whomever would turn King's evidence. La! Peter and the rest were frightened for a while— Oh, while I remember, he gave me this just before I sailed." She pulled out an envelope. It contained a draft on London for £1,000.

"A wedding present to us. There are some other things in my green sea chest. Colonel Tucker, Susan and the rest you know, they were all very pleasant—"

Suddenly he grabbed up a banyan and rushed to the head of the stairs roaring for Smith. He closed the door, but she heard them talking.

By straining her ears she heard the host ask, "—And where shall I put the lady's things?" Rob's answer was only a confused murmur. Then Smith's voice boomed, "Yes, sir, directly, sir! You may rely on me, Mr. Ashton. I'm tactful—have to be to get on."

When Stephen Farish appeared, the porter directed him to Mr. Ashton's room.

"Come in, man! Come in!"

Farish guessed Mr. Ashton must be lit up like a Roman church already, but when he stepped in, he found Rob sitting at a table set with supper dishes. Opposite him was a young woman, handsome in a stately sort of way—he could tell that by the way she carried her head. Her body was well rigged and her eyes were something special. Right now she was talking and laughing so hard she had hardly touched her food.

The New Englander rubbed his eyes. Godfreys, he was thinking, Miss Grenville was a lot more lively than he had been led to believe. A good thing it was, too. Robert Ashton needed a lively, laughing wife, not a serious, quiet one like—

Rob made quite a ceremony of his introduction. He could tell Andrea took right away to the brown-faced, chunky little Yankee, in spite of his critical, piercing eyes and bald head.

After Rob and Farish had drunk a toast, Andrea proposed the *Speedwell*. It was a pleasant meal in the big bedroom with the cheerful yellow paper and curtains of blue and white gingham.

At last Rob said, "Suppose you go below and ask the gentlemen not to get drunk for awhile."

Farish nodded. "What excuse will I give 'em?"

Andrea flushed down to her bodice, said, "Why, I believe a minister, a friend of Mr. Ashton's is calling in half an hour."

"Eh?"

"You'll honor me a lot by standing as best man?" Rob asked simply.

"Jumping Jehosophat! You don't mean you're going to get spliced?"

"Within an hour at the very latest."

"But the banns? The papers?"

"Published and ready going on three weeks. Now get down below, will you?"

"Lord A'mighty," Farish muttered, clattering downstairs. "And the wind used to change while he made up his mind!"

In a charmed haze Andrea unpacked and took out a dress of ivory satin Aunt Lydia had sewed with her own capable hands. It was all so deliciously headlong, so romantic, so incredible—and yet so very real.

In Mr. Smith's best private dining room, hurriedly aired and decorated with flowers robbed from the tavern garden, Mr. Peacock, George Ord and Stephen Farish watched the marriage of Andrea Gray Grenville and Robert Butler Ashton. They all kissed the bride and beat Rob's shoulders until they were sore. Farish blew his nose very hard.

Later when the bride and groom appeared at the head of broad stairs leading to a great coffee room on the ground floor, such a cheer went up that the watch turned out.

The rafters rang to toasts, more pointed than tactful, the inevitable suggestions concerning proper size of a family. Eyes shining, Andrea went among the laughing, cheering merchants, mariners and delegates. Two of them hoisted her to their shoulders and carried her about the room. She had to bend her head to avoid the beams and the mugs hung to them. Andrea loved it all. The crude genuineness of the compliments, the lack of affectation. She could see these men thought a lot of Rob, really wanted to see him happy.

8 — SHAWNEE

THE clock of St. Paul's Church had just announced three and Rob was drifting off into a pleasurable haze when Andrea raised her head and blew into his ear.

"Stop it." Sleepily he smacked her bottom, unguarded at the moment by more than a bedsheet.

"Stop it yourself, you bully. I only wanted to ask a question."

"Good God, Madam, something more? I thought we'd settled everything." He saw her profile as she looked out of the window.

"Yes. Can you see a big star out there? It gives off such a lovely greenish light."

"Want me to fetch it for you?"

"No. It's so beautiful where it is."

"All right, but you can have it any time you want it—it's your star. Good night, dearest."

She said, "Don't go to sleep. Rob?" She tweaked a couple of hairs on his chest.

"In Heaven's name, what is it now?"

"Remember—back in Bermuda—?"

"Yes, a lot of things."

"The summerhouse—?"

"I seem to remember a summerhouse."

"Don't be irritating, Robert. You know what I'm talking about?"

"If I get really waked up, I'll spank you. You may not realize it, Mrs. A., but I have work to do tomorrow."

She chuckled ever so gently. "Do you recall an accomplishment of yours? Shawnee?"

He grinned in the semi-darkness and the bed creaked when he rolled over onto his stomach and stared at the dark flood her hair made on the pillow.

"Now that we are married—we are married, aren't we?"

"Feels like it, somehow."

"Well, then, what was it I said that time, that made you laugh?"

He laughed until a glass on their night stand jingled.

"Rob Ashton, if you don't tell me this minute, I'll—"

By an effort he quieted, slipped an arm under the cool smoothness of her shoulders and put his lips close to her ear.

"Honey, what I told you to say was, 'We two have met. Will you talk with me?' But you didn't say that. You said, *Ke-tela ga-ait-atam?* It means, 'Will you sleep with me?' "

"Did I?" Andrea Ashton sighed. "Well, then I'll give you an answer. It's—never a wink, you rascal!"

Though the green star had slipped out of sight around the window frame, Andrea still lay with fingers locked behind her head.

It was something to have things settled—to have the aimless years ended. Yes, something had been settled—for both of them. They had Rob's ship, they had each other, and they had faith. The years might bring hardships, but there would be no faltering on either part. The fires of the last two years had welded them too firmly together for that.

Andrea Ashton slept.